© Nikki Goodeve Photography

About the Author

Born in Kent and now living in East Sussex with his wife Judy, Nigel Dyer has lived and worked in the UK and Europe. He ran his own consultancy specialising in marketing for the financial services, legal and IT sectors, has published several books on creative marketing and was a regular contributor of articles for the financial services press. He has a degree from the Open University. Nigel was privileged to be made a Freeman of the City of London in the nineties. He is a passionate owner and restorer of classic cars and a dedicated Francophile

Wigs, Lies and Alibis

Nigel Dyer

Wigs, Lies and Alibis

Olympia Publishers
London

www.olympiapublishers.com
OLYMPIA PAPERBACK EDITION

Copyright © Nigel Dyer 2023

The right of Nigel Dyer to be identified as author of
this work has been asserted in accordance with sections 77 and 78 of the
Copyright, Designs and Patents Act 1988.

All Rights Reserved

No reproduction, copy or transmission of this publication
may be made without written permission.
No paragraph of this publication may be reproduced,
copied or transmitted save with the written permission of the publisher, or in
accordance with the provisions
of the Copyright Act 1956 (as amended).

Any person who commits any unauthorised act in relation to
this publication may be liable to criminal
prosecution and civil claims for damage.

A CIP catalogue record for this title is
available from the British Library.

ISBN: 978-1-80439-691-9

This is a work of fiction.
Names, characters, places, organisations and incidents originate from the writer's
imagination. Any resemblance to actual persons, living or dead, is purely
coincidental.

First Published in 2023

Olympia Publishers
Tallis House
2 Tallis Street
London
EC4Y 0AB

Printed in Great Britain

Dedication

This book is dedicated to my wife and best friend, Judy.

Acknowledgements

Thanks to my wife, Judy, for her help and patience with me and the book. Thank you also to the many friends and colleagues who have chipped in with advice and guidance. And to those whose names and memorable elements of their characteristics I have used in creating many of the book's personalities, I hope you forgive me for taking your names in vain!

Prologue, February 2014

Hello, I'm Stanislaw George Pchelski, normally answering to "George" (Stan is a bit old fashioned these days and I've hated it since childhood, anyway), currently a resident in Her Majesty's High Security Prison Upper Heywood in Oxfordshire, convicted criminal number 10500102.

I was convicted of company fraud and sent down in 2009 for a full sentence of five years; out in three with "remission", for what the public refer to as good behaviour. In the cold light of day, of which there have been many in this bloody prison, I viewed myself as an opportunist thief rather than a hardened criminal, although judge and jury clearly had a different opinion.

My record, undoubtedly, shows my date of birth as 19 June 1964; my next of kin as my younger sister, Marion Naismith of East Cooden, East Sussex, and although they are not allowed to ask these days, my religion is C of E, just for the record, something my father insisted upon despite coming from a Polish Catholic background, being intensely proud of his adopted English citizenship. This was spurred on by my grandfather, who escaped the wrath of the Nazi occupation of his homeland for the green and pleasant fields of England, taking up arms with the RAF, as they say, for his adopted country.

I stand one metre seventy-five in my stockinged feet and weigh seventy-nine kilos, and that's a lot less weight than when I went inside (anyway, that's five foot nine and around twelve and a half stone in old money). The food isn't as bad as you'd think, but there's no grazing between meals, so my suit, when they finally let me out of here, will hang off me like a sack of spuds. No distinguishing marks or tattoos. Blond hair cut short but not army style, and blood group A Rhesus negative completes the picture.

Copious photographs will, for sure, be on file: frontal, left and right profile etc., etc. all holding my inmate number clearly (certainly not photos you'd use for a passport application). And of course, a set of my smudgy fingerprints.

Somewhere in the system in a file (probably), in a computer system with the police at CRO (definitely) and on the infernal internet would be the reason I'm in this bloody place until, all being well, thirty days from now, 3 March 2014.

Why am I not in a cushy billet in Ford Open Prison in sunny West Sussex? After all, mine was a white-collar crime. Yes, I was, for nearly three years, in Ford, and it is a relatively friendly place, providing you are well-behaved and don't get into any mischief, with plenty of sport and vocational courses, and indeed, freedom of movement within the hundreds of acres and a largely 'professional clientele' of insurance fraudsters, bankers who have abused their positions of trust, money launderers, hackers, and quite a few naughty civil servants amongst a myriad of others.

And then there's the do-gooders — some civilians who lecture and arrange courses to make us, inmates and recidivists alike, want to be good citizens when we leave — equipped with certificates to help us get meaningful jobs as ex-cons and not be a burden on society, or indeed recidivists.

I'd read somewhere, in one of the many books I'd read in Ford, that a guy leaving prison after ten years or so would have lost track of the change in technology — not just tablets and iPhones and Android this and that but the technological improvements and developments of forensics, communication, banking and data-base management, even GPS. Even those who had the wherewithal to get illicit phones still had a minimal insight as to the technological changes in the big world outside the walls. I was, I should say am, computer literate, which helped my ability and provided the opportunity to defraud my employers, at the time. So I kept up with every course that was available all to, as the prison visitors put it, 'help us find a better place in society on release'.

I'd taken a course in plumbing and comms technology, as well as electrical installation and even carpentry and gardening. I learned a lot from a guy in Ford open prison about credit-card fraud and identity theft. When you're inside, and there's not much on the TV, it's amazing what encyclopaedic information is available, and other inmates are more than happy to share their experiences, and dare I say it, skill sets. Of course, we're not allowed computers or mobile phones inside prison, in theory anyway, but the two days a week in the prison library allowed me, broadly, to keep au-fait with computer and software development in computerising the book-lending facility for the prisoners and sometimes even helping the guards.

Half the homeowners, let alone the so-called insurance experts, in the UK would be shocked if it ever got out about the number of ex-cons working on their precious mortgaged homes as electricians, plumbers, builders etc.

However, and there is always a "but…". Six weeks before my release after three years, trouble came along and I was in the thick of it — wrong place; wrong time. Not my fault, but the screws always say "everyone says that" — in the toilets, a scuffle, and for reasons I can't explain I ended up with a home-made knife, a shiv they call it in here, in my hands and an obnoxious, arrogant guy, Mike Wright, holding his arm with blood coursing down to the floor. No, it wasn't me, but somehow I'd rubbed up someone the wrong way, as had Wright, but this time, I was to be the fall guy. My fingerprints, so no contest. Wright, sensibly, refused to make a complaint so, after a minimal enquiry by the Governor's office, I was transferred 'for my own safety and that of others'. The result? Two years extra on my sentence and a move to this place — high security HMP Upper Heywood.

And Upper Heywood is a whole new can of worms. Violence, drugs, alcohol and sexual depravity is abundant. I made a good friend here, Terry, rough and ready but he saved my bacon several times — once a violent attack, again in the toilets, a favourite place for violence, and once a near miss sexual encounter that still sends shivers down my spine, and inevitably I'm told, an altercation in the canteen where I, apparently, sat in the wrong place. They don't like "posh" sorts in here and white collar crime almost defines you, de facto, alongside reading what is perceived as high-brow books and newspapers and a desire to play a very low profile.

I shared a cell with Terry Beddall, or rather, he allowed me to take the upper bunk in his cell for the best part of two years. Tel, as his friends called him, is a big man, around six foot tall and broad with it. A man not to cross, yet, surprisingly, happy as Larry settling down with a book on the History of Art. A bit of an anachronism. He'd been a sergeant in the Logistics Corps and had committed a slight, his word, infraction of the rules regarding shipping of whisky to the officer's mess in Wiesbaden, Germany, where he had been caught in the hold of a Hercules transport plane, drunk as a lord, with some five crates short on the manifest. Although it hadn't been a solo enterprise, he took the can as an NCO. A few nights in the brig, a bit of gratuitous violence from the MPs, a dishonourable discharge and the start of his life of crime.

He was, hopefully not still is, a career burglar and Peter man, or safe breaker, but not too clever with the detail. He'd been caught twice and this was his second term in prison for theft from commercial premises, attracting a ten-year stretch — out in seven if all goes well, and that'll be in November this year.

He taught me a lot about prison life, what to avoid and when to turn the other cheek and I'd like to think that our conversations, after lights out, will make him think twice before repeating the pretty obvious mistakes which he told me had led the police to him like a magnet.

***

I was convicted of what is loosely called white collar crime — of fraud — inside an insurance company, a significant Lloyd's Syndicate — Beech Underwriting, specialising in high-net-worth clients. They employed me in a position of trust, as they described it at the trial, and had been reticent about prosecuting due to their reputation and commercial standing. The City of London fraud squad persuaded them to stand up and be counted and take the possible PR flak to discourage others. However, Beech went for a lesser charge and proceeded on the amount they had unearthed as 'missing'. It was still a serious amount of cash.

I'd been creaming off a good bit of cash for five years or so, more or less since joining the company, most from the claims reserves of those same HNW clients (that's putting claims estimates on hold whilst details are sorted out — sometimes taking a year or two to resolve). Their systems were, even in those days, archaic, with more money than sense and paper-based audit processes that were more pre-war than even legacy systems. Their advertising always stated that they would settle claims with no quibble, as their clients were straight as a die and their staff equally inscrutable. Oh really! Their naïvety stood out like a sore thumb and the temptation was there. Yet there are still insurance companies today that hold the same mantra.

Everything was going really nicely for me, bought some classic cars, here in the UK and some hidden away in the ubiquitous French barns in France, and a couple of properties over there too. Three or four I had garaged around London so I could enjoy using them — for love and a bit of an investment — and I'd opened some accounts here and in France, salting away the ill-gotten proceeds, allowing me to execute my Plan B to retire "gracefully". And then, on a flaming June day in 2005, I met Charlotte…

Chapter 1

I met her in a famous chocolatier in Piccadilly, London. I can't remember the name. She was directly in front of me, being served with geranium-flavoured chocolates. I'd gone in there solely for a posh box of chocs for my little sister's birthday.

A smartly uniformed assistant was offering us a tray of sample chocolates with exotic flavours, from violet to chilli and lime. This seriously glamorous lady in front of me turned and caught my eye with a smile that made my pulse race, even to this day, although that sort of memory is common in prison!

I drank her in from head to toe. Gorgeous. Tall, statuesque, without an ounce of fat on her, early to mid twenties at a guess and dressed to kill in a black sheath dress, or at least that's what I think you call it, legs to die for and spike heels; immaculate hair, a brunette, perfect make-up and sufficient cleavage to dream about, all wrapped in a perfume the smell of which I'll never forget — Armani Diamonds, as I later found out.

She ate the sample and immediately pulled a face.

'That's Chilli and Lime, madam,' the shop assistant said, hoping, I suspect, for some positive feedback but patently unnerved by my fellow shopper's reaction.

'Not for me,' she said, grimacing. 'How about you?' She turned to me.

I'm sure I spluttered, partly thinking smutty thoughts about this dream of a female. I managed to reply, 'Nor me. I prefer the ordinary stuff. Chilli and Lime? Not my cup of tea at all, sorry.'

'Me too. Uggh! I need a drink after that and not tea!' Again, she raised a quizzical eyebrow, as if tempting me. And I needed no tempting, I was one hundred percent willing and able.

'There's a nice wine bar a couple of hundred yards down the way. Care to share a bottle of something with me?'

'Fine,' she replied after a slight pause. 'Let's go.'

The shop assistant turned away to answer the telephone whilst my stunning lady awaited, with her hand out, her purchase. For a brief moment,

I saw blind fury in her face. She swept the counter with a glance and swung, almost in a synchronised movement, her handbag to demolish a display of fancy chocolates onto the floor. Smiling at the crestfallen assistant, she mouthed an insincere apology, reached for the package and receipt and we left the shop. We walked out together, she linking her arm in mine. I'd completely forgotten my sister's present, but that would wait. She referred to the incident as her *"petite vengeance"*, giving me the clue to her beautiful soft French inclination in her voice, as we walked, commenting that the days seemed to be gone when the customer or client mattered most. And referring to the shop assistant, 'that stupid girl will have learned a lesson today.' I saw then, and in hindsight, can recall many other times when she 'lost it'. She demanded attention one hundred percent and woe betide anyone who denied her that pleasure.

Anyway, I was glad I was smartly dressed in an Armani suit and a white crisp button-down collar cotton shirt and what the Americans call loafers. I had the impression that jeans and a polo shirt would not have cut the mustard with this lady. It was one of those days in summer where you hope that someone you know would notice you walking down the street with a gorgeous bit of upper class totty on your arm. From her polished accent, just a faint hint of the continent, and clearly her dress, designer label handbag, immaculate hair and general demeanour, she was just that.

'My name's Charlotte Bertin, Charlie to my friends. What's yours?'

I think I stammered, 'Just plain George.'

'Well, plain George, what shall we have to drink?'

Taking a window seat at a round table made for two in the wine bar a few yards along Piccadilly, drinks ordered — a nice Chardonnay, ice cold with condensation on the glass — we laughed about the chocolates.

And on the second bottle, she opened up with a potted version of her life story — married to a French property developer, CEO of Bertin et David, for five years, who'd gone off with his blonde German accountant ten years younger than him. No children, fortunately, she said wryly. One older brother, Philippe, a professional politician, one of Nicolas Sarkozy's lieutenants in the UMP party until he had blotted his copy book with an expenses issue, so he'd changed direction, as she called it, to start-up an internet company, financed with family money, and had done very well out of it. Dot.com companies were an area, I knew, the French had some catching up to do and so on. Little did she know what I was up to! She'd had a classy Swiss and English 'finishing' education, hence only a slight French inflexion in her voice if you were listening for it, all from a wealthy family named Foubert, a name that went back one thousand years or so, living in luxury in the middle of France. Months later, I had wondered, as time went by, why she constantly seemed to be flitting off to France. In all honesty, I assumed she was having an affair or two. No problem for me until I realised that I was totally hooked.

We had spent only a few minutes on my background. Not much to tell really, I suppose. Grammar school education, no university stuff, just drifted into insurance as a cradle-to-grave occupation, as was the in thing in those days, married, divorced, no kids. Usual stuff. I was more interested in her, more interested if she was to be lying naked next to me, somewhere and soon.

She really lit up the cocktail bar with her smile. I was, to excuse the pun, drinking her in all the time. Anyway, one drink leads to another and another and we were off on a whirlwind affair that lasted, on and off, for three years or so, with endless parties, a voracious appetite for sex, good clubs and restaurants and plenty of retail therapy, as she described it.

One day, in a restaurant for an extended lunch, I'd asked her if she had a job or career, because she certainly didn't work any sort of normal business hours, if at all. She must have been early to mid-twenties at that time. She smiled at my question, and with a typical wave of her hand, dismissed it. Her response was really dismissive, as I recall; she has, or had, a part share in a fashion boutique.

I can remember her actual words… 'It's where I get most of my clothes, although you, Georgie boy, seem to prefer me naked!' That was the end of the conversation. I'd looked around to see if anyone heard her remark. Then I realised the comment had been an invitation. So, there had been other things to do!

She had this smart flat in The King's Road, Chelsea. A two-bedroom duplex thing, beautifully decorated and furnished with a gigantic bed in the master bedroom. Quite frankly, they should have re-named it the Mistress bedroom; it was all decorated in black and gold, with sexy pictures and a mirrored ceiling. The neon lights from the road offered sufficient illumination and she never drew the blinds. She liked to dominate and was pretty physically strong and usually got her own way in bed, anyway. And there always seemed to be bottles of champagne in her drinks fridge and dirty glasses in the kitchen and dishwasher. It was, for me, a new lifestyle. Exciting, exhausting and bloody expensive.

All this meant serious money. Income I didn't really have. So that need became the catalyst for the slippery slope — patently, the decent salary and company perks were insufficient. Fortunately for me, mine was not a company that rigidly enforced 'normal office hours'.

With Charlie, or rather for Charlie, the ante had to be racked up and quick. Yes, my motives were largely governed by something regularly stirring south of my waistline, but that's the way it was. In hindsight, it was stupid because slow change, gradually increasing my skimming and re-cycling the company funds, was unlikely to be noticed but sudden step-change always attracts attention.

I tried not to be too greedy, but Charlotte's appetite for the good life was expensive — Wimbledon, Goodwood, Ascot. She liked the champagne lifestyle, all day every day.

'Get some champagne, Georgie, darling.' She had abbreviated my name almost from day one, and had that delightful habit of squeezing my arm when she said my name. 'Today, let's have Mumm — it's such a nice champagne.'

It was a standard request — the only difference was the brand chosen and it rarely rested with one bottle.

Beech Underwriting was a generous employer, certainly for their senior staff, anyway, and providing I could produce receipts, were happy that people like me were entertaining the right sort of people at the right sort of events, in the foolhardy belief that those same people could be their clients this year or next. And then there were the inevitable corporate hospitality days. Smart events, inevitably chosen by the Chairman's wife, Lady Lucy Beech — Chelsea flower show, Henley Regatta, Open Golf at Sandwich, Royal Birkdale or Gleneagles. I took Charlie with me to many of these functions and she had most of the Directors almost begging to bring her another glass of champagne or strawberries or whatever. A real hit. I should have realised then that these guys had more disposable income and whopping great expense accounts than I could dream about, which was exactly what Charlotte loved.

With all this entertaining, receipts were necessary but easy to obtain, but some things had to be paid in cash and just couldn't be attributed to client entertainment. I needed a decent car, not a pretentious Aston Martin but not a Ford either. Over the years, I'd had the usual BMW and Mercedes company car offering — nice but didn't stand out in a crowd sort of thing. I needed something different but affordable. I opted out of the company car scheme and instead received a helpful boost to my salary and bought a 1969 Mercedes 500SL Pagoda in a colour they called "moss green". A bit of a gas guzzler, but what the hell. I checked it over with my Grandpa P; it was one of my serious interests from teen-age that he'd taught me. It had been owned by an army major injured in the Falklands conflict and hence unable to maintain it, so a good price and a head turner, and after some restoration work with Grandpa P, certainly good enough to get the car-jockeys at hotels and restaurants to want to open the door for her and park the bloody thing. All status stuff.

Ironically, prices for these old Mercs went through the roof as the recession bit and I was facing a substantial profit were I to sell it on.

Then, after three years or so of the good life, the hammer blow. Charlotte was drifting away, there was no denying it. She was increasingly 'I'm busy that day Georgie, perhaps another day' or, as happened several times, 'I'm off for the day with the gang from school.' Suddenly it was all over. 'Bye Georgie. I'm off to New York for a few weeks' — a text message was all I received. I should have seen it coming. I'd learned a lot about her over those years of our relationship, so I shouldn't really have been surprised. Devious bitch, I'd thought, with more than a tinge of jealousy. A few weeks later, I saw a picture on the internet, on one of those news feed channels, of a society wedding in the Big Apple with all these prats dressed up with American cowboy hats. Looked like one of those long distance lens paparazzi photos. I wouldn't have recognised her but for the caption giving her French surname of Bertin, Charlotte Waller as she now is. Angry with her? Yes. Let down? Definitely, yes. Jealous? Absolutely.

At work, a few days, literally, after the fateful text message came the second hammer blow. A new management team at Beech Underwriting, resulting from the imminent retirement of the founder and chairman and a goodly part of the board. New experience in the business of spotting anomalies in accounting procedures, led by one of those guys you come across in business, every now and then, who have an innate ability to spot a bum steer of a figure or result in pages and pages of accounts.

Andrew Templeman, complete with red braces and a moustache, lovely man, one hundred percent business oriented (much later, I read in the FT that he'd been made CEO and was taking the company into public ownership).

Andrew buttonholed me in the corridor, catching me off-guard.

'There's a problem, George, old chap. It's been worrying me.' He called all the blokes in the company 'old chap'. He went off on a tirade of financial speak whilst I stood there, quietly panicking whilst my mind was racing.

'Yes, umm. There's a black hole in your area of claims reserving. Our computer systems have been somewhat archaic and I have had a team from an IT consultancy working on it for some time. They are a bit scathing about its simplicity. We seem to be, umm, correction, are paying out significantly more than we should be. 5.34% to be precise. That means that we're short of nearly, umm, two hundred and fifty-eight thousand pounds, and on the basis of the past five years, significantly more.'

I was stunned, reeling from this seemingly impromptu conversation with colleagues wandering past and saying 'hello' as they went and oddly wondering why a man as clever as this seemed to preface everything with 'umm'. Reserving is, simply put, an estimate, emphasis on the word estimate, of what a claim might cost, often sometime in the future, even years ahead. Then monies are paid out to whoever/whenever. Easy to fix, some insurance companies have gone under because of under-reserving in the interests of share price or profit or fraud. Just so, I thought, as my brain was racing.

'I have no option but to, umm, suspend you, pending investigation. This is the consensus of the new board. You will leave, umm, the office today and consider yourself on formal gardening leave. Umm. Please take your personal possessions and await an official communication from HR. Of course, George, old chap, you will retain, umm, all your normal senior management benefits, salary, expense account etc. whilst we try to clear this, shall we call it a, umm, discrepancy.' His voice was placid, heartless; I don't know exactly, but with those words my world caved in.

It was unusual to be addressed in this way in the corridor but that informality was easier than the formal minuted process — all typical of the gentlemanly approach of the company and Lloyd's as a whole.

I had no option than to agree as graciously as I could muster whilst spluttering my puzzlement — no excuses just concern that there was a gross error somewhere. I had been half expecting something, inevitably, after my spending spree on Charlotte, but would have preferred to escape at my own speed — famous last words.

'I'm sure there'll be a rational explanation, Andrew. I'll do anything to assist.'

My mind was racing. Had I put in the appropriate stops in the limited coding inserted in the so called system to wipe part of the record? Andrew's estimates were way off beam, far too low, but I certainly wasn't going to correct him.

A month later, I'd spent time carefully checking all my accounts, both here and in France to make what remained believable, should an investigation get that far. The bulk was well hidden under a pseudonym of Alan George Turner at an address in Clerkenwell, SE London, and some under another identity of Peter G Appleton, basically a sophisticated mailbox address masquerading as a smart apartment block. The rest at several addresses in France, including the majority of my collection of classic cars, some ten vehicles, mainly in tip-top condition which, over there, don't need the same off-the-road registration palaver as in the UK so are virtually untraceable.

I'd created a second identity some years ago, more out of interest than any particular reason. In reading Frederick Forsyth's novel *The Day of the Jackal*, I idly thought to follow the pages, instructions almost, that he laid out and see if it could be done or whether it was an author's imagination running riot. To cut a long story short, it worked and I had my new identity of Alan George Turner after some poor mite who had died in the late 1960's as a new born infant living just long enough to be named and buried. Because computers were in their very infancy — the UK Government only started digitising its records in early 1973 — it was not difficult to obtain a new passport, credit cards — again in their infancy — and even a driving licence, but for that I had to retake the test — a nerve racking experience. And bank accounts were as easy as pie to open new accounts in those days. Much later, I found a perfect reason for a second identity and kept all the accounts and documents bang up to date. I duplicated the process, again just for the fun of it, so I was George Pchelski aka Peter George Appleton, born in York, and Alan George Turner, born in Boston, Lincolnshire. It seemed very sensible to keep the name George, just in case someone called your name in the street or wherever. Patently, no one would call out the name Alan. And I had thought, any official listing would place the name Turner under the initial A rather than G for George. A bit more difficult for anyone else to find the appropriate death certificate.

All very useful in hiding accounts and assets and movements through passport controls.

After six weeks, I heard from the company's HR manager that there was a possibility, only a possibility, of prosecution. They were taking advice on the matter, but meanwhile, all the company's property must be returned. A company chauffeur would come the next day if I'd be so kind as to have everything ready: files, lap-top, business phone and so on. Kathy Calman (known universally as Kathy Calamity), the HR manager, assured me with pretended sympathy that the company's reputation was paramount and I was not to worry. Gentlemen to the end.

Rather than the company chauffeur, the very next day the City of London Police fraud squad arrived at my apartment just off Shaftesbury Avenue. Well, in truth it was a pretty ordinary one-bedroom flat in a slightly unfashionable road off Shaftesbury Avenue. Anyway, they just banged on my door, having gained access from street level probably from the concierge, or really the lady who cleaned the common areas, but it's nice to pretend. But I did wonder whether they would smash it down if I hadn't answered quickly enough. The rest is history.

***

No, I'm not bitter. Bit ashamed that I'd let down the family and my Grandpa P. Fortunately he wasn't there one hundred percent due to the ravages of age, so maybe the bad news passed him by — hope so. Yes, I was guilty, and really, my time inside works out at a pretty tidy tax free sum per annum if the amount I 'obtained' by fraud is divided by the number of years — even allowing for the destruction of my little UK based empire, as 'one is not allowed to profit from crime, Mr Pchelski. Everything you own will be sold to recoup the losses incurred by your employer,' as "Your Honour" the judge put it.

I'll be fifty or thereabouts when I get out, assuming nothing spoils that plan. My little sister has promised to collect me from the gate on the 3rd March at ten a.m. Marion is a loving, and fortunately, forgiving sister who turns up every Thursday afternoon at three p.m. for a thirty-minute visitor slot. A long drive for thirty minutes, but that shows the sort of person she is. Yes, I get nagged a lot but deserve it, I'm sure, and it's worth it to have a visitor.

Her husband, Bob, although he preferred Robert, an accountant always immaculately dressed even when mowing the lawn, is not so forgiving and tolerates me on the basis of blood is thicker than water. No doubt, when I go to stay with them immediately after my release, I'll be lectured and questioned ad nauseam.

We have no parents, now. They died in a nasty crash when we were in our teens and we were looked after by Grandpa P, as we called him. An old man now, with moments only of lucidity, he still speaks with a Polish accent even after seventy-odd years in the UK after his demob from the Polish Free forces of WW2 in 1946 — hence my Polish unpronounceable but memorable surname. He ran a successful motor dealership for fifty years after the war and taught me everything I know about engines and created that love of classic cars. He had no time for modern electronics and satnav and all the gadgets. That's the lot of my family — I do have an ex-wife who discarded the Polish name after our divorce, as it was not "uber cool". Last I heard, she was floating about the Mediterranean with an array of toy boys, living off the divorce settlement, no doubt — a significant amount at that. Girlfriends? Me? Well, a few over the years but nothing permanent, nobody in particular, but I'm no celibate. I had thought that Charlotte might be the one for me, but that wasn't to be.

Chapter 2

27th February 2014, a few days early from my expected date of release, I was to be set free for no other reason than prisons always, apparently, prefer to get their clients, as the Governor called us, out on a preferred day — in this case, Thursday. Nice for me, but a bloody nuisance for my sister, as I was only told the night before and she wasn't going to be visiting just before my release. Their little game, I suppose.

I was woken early by Tel. For a big man, he was almost tearful. All sorts of conversations about the future for him and for me had occurred after lights out the night before. I thanked him for helping me when times had been, literally, rough, and strangely, he reciprocated by saying how he had learned to think things through better and to try harder not to make careless mistakes.

I told him that if he wanted to meet me, I'd be at Bills Café in Green Street, Cambridge, on the first Thursday after his release, on the 14th November at eleven a.m. That'd be US Thanksgiving day — the thought made me smile. If he wasn't there, I would return the following Thursday and so on for a month.

I can recall almost word for word the brief conversation with a wry smile.

'I could phone you, George. I'll grab a phone when I get out. Yeah, yeah, it'll be a burner. The lads told me all about them.'

'No, its better that there's no record anywhere, even on a throwaway phone. You know how the Fuzz follow the futures of old lags like us. Just meet me there if you want to. I've a bit of money, so I might be able to help you, a start anyway.'

'But why Cambridge?'

'Ever been to Cambridge, Tel?'

'Nah — couldn't even get into grammar school.' He looked up and smiled.

'Seriously, Terry. Because no one knows you or me there. You can get a train or a bus and pay cash, always.'

Just then, and timely, before we had an emotional scene, I thought, the door clanged open automatically and the chief screw, Mr Condon, entered. His nickname is fairly obvious — change the last 'n' for a 'm'!

'Come on, Polish, time to be on your way. Say your good-byes, give him a kiss, and let's be having you.'

'Fine, Mr Condon. Just for once, could you call me by my proper name?'

'Fuck you, Polish! I can't be bothered to remember your stupid fancy-sounding surname. It's Polish, as far as I'm concerned. C'mon, I haven't got all day.'

'Cheers, Terry. Good luck and don't forget Bill.' I thought that was enigmatic enough for both Terry and Condom.

'Cheers to you, to George Pchelski, and thanks again.'

***

I left prison exactly on time, clutching my paper sack with my belongings, in my ill-fitting, badly creased suit — I'd lost quite a bit of weight — and shoes, five years old, that squeaked, and £42 that remained from earnings from my part-time work in the prison library. The sound of the armoured gates ringing in my ears to rub it in accompanied the booming voice of the Assistant Governor.

'See you soon, George. You'll be back; they all come back sooner or later, you know.'

A shrug sufficed. No point in creating antagonism by bickering or swearing. Just a shrug.

Marion was waiting, as promised, despite the date being changed, in her silver Lexus Hybrid something-or-other model, just at the limit of the parking area, as if she wanted me to walk those thirty paces or so.

'George, I heard what that man said. "See you soon, George, that's what he said".' She sounded really worried.

'Just a gibe, sis. They say that to everyone.' I dismissed the comment with another shrug and got into the car, putting my sad little package on the back seat.

'You really won't be going back inside that horrible place, will you? It'd be more than flesh and blood could bear. Bob keeps saying "you can choose your friends but not your family". Please be patient with him when you see him. Let him have his say. The kids won't be at home for a week or so — Easter break from uni, so for now it'll just be the three of us.'

'No, Marion, I'm not going back in there, I promise. One mistake is plenty. A few days with you and Bob, and then buy a car, find a little flat maybe have a holiday in the sun and then start thinking of the future.'

She slammed the door, stuck the thing into Drive and looked at me. 'Trouble with you, George, is that you swear black is white a mite too often. And George, put your seat belt on; you don't want to be breaking the law straight away, now, do you?'

The engine in these hybrids is so quiet that I swear I heard her chuckle.

Nice detached house in a cul-de-sac with the inevitable immaculate lawn and electric gates. It felt strange as the gates shut behind the car, bit like prison. Three days in East Cooden was enough. I had to apologise umpteen times and offer constructive thoughts on how I was going to live now I had no income and no savings. I told them that there was little chance of any career in my specialist field with my track record and I was thinking of living in France and pursuing my second love, that of classic cars, Europe being a big market for collectables. To be fair to Bob, he did offer me a loan to tide me over, which I accepted graciously on the basis it avoided unnecessary questions.

With Bob's almost laughable £500 in my pocket — if only he knew — I decided to leave on the next day's first cheap day rail ticket to London from Bexhill. That last night was to be the last of the inquisition.

Marion asked over dinner, 'Did you have any other visitors to that awful place?' It seemed like a non-sequitur. I looked up and knew that she knew.

'Well, yes. A pal from the old days, just catching up. Nice, really, that he bothered. Oh, and then there was an old girl friend of mine from years back, nosing around. God knows why. Perhaps she thought it would be fascinating going inside a prison to see the sad old lags. Charlotte's her name. She's married to some big-wig now, in the US of A, fancy wedding and all. Must have been visiting the UK, I suppose. So I suppose, as an old lag, I'm the coffee table talk at her soirees.' It was an odd subject to bring up.

'I did wonder, George. She called me, or at least I presume it was her. She'd got the number from the concierge at the old London flat. I told her about the visiting hours and rules. She didn't sound over keen. Said she had a couple of questions for you. I thought she'd just drop you a line. Actually, now I think about it, she never did give me her name.'

'Sounds like Charlotte,' was all I could think to say. Again, I was intrigued.

Once I was alone, I could recall that day quite vividly. One day, a good few weeks before my release, after Marion had gone that Thursday, I got a visit from the warder in charge of A wing.

'You're a lucky lad, Polish. You've got another visitor today. Look lively, she's a tasty dish, far too good for the likes of you.'

I followed him along the corridor for the second time that afternoon. He was moaning that it wasn't in the rules, but the Deputy Governor had agreed. 'She must have given him a blow-job or something, Polish. He doesn't allow breach of the visitor's rules normally. How come a sweet thing like that wants to see you?'

'Wouldn't know, sir. You haven't told me who it is.' It was always best to call them "sir"; it seemed to work when it came to favours. I knew it couldn't be Marion returning, because in anyone's wildest dreams the adjectives "tasty" and "sweet thing" wouldn't really apply. Laura Ashley green. Yup, that's my sister.

And there was Charlotte! Looking magnificent, bronzed, showing off a stunning hairdo and impeccably dressed in a green shimmery suit that set off the tan perfectly, although, from past experience, the 'no cleavage look' was a somewhat demure change. Terry was at another table with his sister, a regular-as-clockwork, Thursday-afternoon-at-four-p.m. visitor. He looked across his sister's shoulder with an almost imperceptible nod of approval. The screws on duty looked like they were about to have wet-dreams.

'Hello, Charlie. What brings you here?' I never fail to be intrigued by this woman. She disappears from my life and then pops up again and the blood starts coursing through my veins, although I know whatever it is she wants, it'll be short-lived.

'I just was passing, Georgie, and wanted to talk to you. To say sorry for our breaking up a while back…' One of the screws looked up at the "Georgie" name and raised a smirk.

I interrupted, trying to keep my voice down to a whisper. 'A while back, a while back? It was, what, nearly six years ago when you buggered off to the US of A.'

'Was it really as long ago as that? Sorry again, George. Lot of water under the bridge and all that. My husband got a title, so I'm now Lady Charlotte. What d'you think about that, eh?'

I shrugged. What else could I do?

'But God, Georgie what a place…' She wrinkled her nose as she cast an eye around the small tables and the people sitting there. 'I really came to find out when you are to be released and if we could meet up then — somewhere more private. I've got a proposition for you or, rather, I think I have.'

'Been bruised by you before, Charlotte. Not sure I want to go down that route again. In fact, I am sure. I don't wish to go down that route again. And that's final. And what's with the change of hair? I liked the brunette look.'

'I must have upset you to call me Charlotte. Anyway, let me finish, Georgie.' She always had used the 'Georgie' when she wanted something and plain George when she was in control. She continued, 'I know a thing or two, you may not know, about how you came to be in here and thought you would be interested in knowing who, the why and the when. And maybe, what you could do to even the score against certain people. And I changed my hair colour, it's a wig, to show off my tan — like it, do you? It's been a couple of years now — and anyway I don't want to be recognised here of all places. So, I'll probably change it back. Who knows?'

I gave her the once over again and nodded approval, trying to get her back to the subject she's raised. Yes, I admit, that one sentence of hers had created the interest and would sit in my head for the next few weeks. When I'd calmed down, we chatted for a good ten minutes about prison life; were there any real villains; what the food was like and no alcohol; how could I cope and so on. I pointed out my cell mate across the room and told her that he was a real villain and was inside for burglary and safe-breaking. I have to admit I said it for effect to score a point.

'My! He's a big man and good looking in a craggy way. What's his name? And who's the girl with him? His wife?'

'God, you haven't changed, Charlie.' It was difficult to be annoyed with her for long. 'Charlie, you're like a bitch on heat. His name is Terry Beddall and he's a good guy to have as a friend. And before you ask, he'll be out and free in November, all being well. You'll have to curb your appetite until then. And that's his sister. She visits religiously every

Thursday afternoon at four p.m., getting the bus from London to Oxford and then another bus out here. That's dedication.'

'You're being a bit mean, Georgie. Didn't seem to stop you, did it? What was it, now? Sex al fresco, bit of domination — you liked that, I seem to recall, or was it the sexy stripping in public? Whatever.'

After another ten minutes, the warder called 'Time' for the session. Charlotte was the last to leave with a casual, 'Maybe we'll meet in April, George. I'll call you.'

Chapter 3

A month or so later, at the beginning of May, I got a call on my new mobile, a SIM-only contract on a second-hand phone. Best, I had thought, to keep costs down, to save nagging from Robert about the use of his loan.

Charlotte wanted to meet. I was still fascinated by her remarks at visiting time a couple of months ago, so went along for the ride, so as to speak.

She suggested a river-side pub, The Stopham Bridge, near Pulborough in West Sussex. Good food, apparently, and quiet mid-week. The next Thursday, at noon, I headed for sunny Sussex by the sea. I drove my new old car, a Rover 75 estate, considerably past its prime, but does what it's supposed to do and cost just over a grand after some bickering with the dealer. I turned up in a new Armani suit with an open neck button-down collar white shirt to show I wasn't poverty stricken, despite her raised eyebrows at my car.

'You've changed, Georgie,' she opened after we'd got some drinks. 'No champagne today, darling, it wouldn't be appropriate here. I do think a low profile is in order, don't you?' Low profile and Charlie just didn't stack up. I raised an eyebrow and thought "touché".

'Charlotte, or should I call you "Madam" or "The Honourable" or something after your big society wedding? Of course, I've changed, dahling! So would you after five years in a cell.' I put on a faux posh accent, probably to goad her. I was irritated. I'd driven from Essex, where I had a small house, a smallholding I suppose you'd call it, I'd bought years before as an investment using my other identity, Alan G Turner, and purportedly rented it from the owner, complete with a formal rental agreement and rent book should anyone enquire. More to satisfy my curiosity than anything else, I asked, 'Let's get to the point shall we? You said some strange things when you visited me. Spill the beans, and anyhow, how did you get my number? My sister again, was it? She's just trying to get me to settle down with a nice lady. Certainly wouldn't be you!'

'Don't be silly, darling Georgie. I'm just the same old Charlie. And yes, it was your sister, or rather her son, Harry. Nice young man, at Newcastle University, apparently. I told him I was a good friend from the past and wanted to meet you to try again. I think he believed it.'

I shook my head. This woman, tasty though she still is, is a born liar. I let it pass.

'Anyway,' she continued, 'my husband, or nearly ex-husband, is a real bastard. That's one of the reasons for this out of the way place. The divorce is going through, but slowly. I've got to be so careful. Tony would use anything to put me down in the courts when it comes to buying me off. The more smut about me, the cheaper it is for him.' She looked around, somewhat theatrically, to see if anyone was listening. 'Anyhow, it is Lady Charlotte, nowadays. Did you spot the hateful man getting his peerage?'

'Uh huh!' I had had some feedback from the old firm people, but didn't want to go there with her. I glanced round too, and seeing nothing untoward, repeated my earlier comment. 'Let's cut to the chase.'

'Well you might have a little more sympathy but anyway… Tony was instrumental in your being sent down. I don't know the ins and outs of it but he did sit on the board of your company, still does for that matter, and delighted in telling me time and again "your boyfriend won't be drinking champagne for an awful long time". That's you, George.'

'Tony who?' I played it very off-hand.

'Tony Waller. Surely you remember him? You introduced me to him at the Goodwood Festival of something or other. That's where it started. Anyway, you are right. He is now Lord Groombridge, so I'm Lady Groombridge, for the moment anyway.'

'Good God! Waller — couldn't stand the man. I suppose they give titles away to any Tom, Dick or Harry these days. I didn't realise, didn't make the association, but then it was in the USA and I saw the crummy photos of everyone dressed up like latter-day cowboys, so why would I? But then I don't take Hello or OK magazine. We were largely limited to the Sun or Mirror or one of the other Red-tops and certainly society magazines or face-book or whatever aren't available inside.'

'No, Georgie, he bought the title. Thirty thousand pounds, it cost him, towards the Conservative or Liberal Democrats party's funds I guess. And worth every penny, he says.'

'Anyway, your point is?' I shrugged with indifference, wondering why I was there, a hundred or so miles from my real home.

'The point is that Tony got you sent down and appropriated your collection of classic cars, including that beautiful old Mercedes, at a knock down price. He's part owner and director of a company, auctioning classic cars in Duxford, and he fixed the auction by having all your cars withdrawn from sale at the last minute and buying them seriously cheaply afterwards. He tells me all this in detail, George, and relishes every minute. The Mercedes he bought for seven and a half grand.'

'What? That car was worth around twenty-five grand and upwards! And the TC and the Morgan and the 1962 E-type? Those as well?' I was amazed rather than angry. She nodded.

'All of them. He said he'd got them as a job lot. And then he destroyed them all, cut them up for scrap and drove a JCB over the E-type, just like in the *Italian Job* film, or so he said, or should I say, shouted through hysterical laughter you could hear above the sound of the digger things engine. Money no object. All except the Merc, which he polishes himself every week whilst singing "I Got You Babe"! He keeps repeating "revenge is sweet" and laughs in a false sort of way. I hope you're angry, Georgie. What was it, that Mercedes? I know it was old but lovely.'

'1969 500SL Pagoda in light green metallic, moss green colour typical of the decade. Remember the shape? Iconic. Fabulous.' I had to stop thinking about it. It just made my blood boil. 'But why tell me all this, Charlie? It's history. Nothing I can do about it. No, I'm not angry, more puzzled. Sounds like he was jealous of you playing the field and I was just one victim he could get at easily.'

'You seemed to like it, our little romance, George. Didn't notice you fighting me off.' She leaned forward, showing her cleavage in the short shimmering black dress beneath her opened jacket with a tantalising view of a frothy lacy bra. Mouth-watering memories, but this time brain over-rode heart, or loins as it had been. 'Like what you see, darling? Could be yours again, you know.'

'No, Charlotte! Once was enough. And you've changed your hair again. Must say I prefer it to the bar-maid blonde look.' That was unnecessary, I knew, but I just needed to score a point. She pouted. 'I still don't understand…'

'I thought a bit of revenge would do Tony good, and you could be the man for it. It would suit my book, I confess. The divorce settlement and so on and you would get a reward, so as to speak, for your time inside. The company weren't going to prosecute before he changed the opinion of the board. Remember that?'

'Of course I do. That's a silly question. I'm not sure what you have in mind and I'm equally sure I don't want to get involved. I remember that childish incident in the chocolatiers in London when you took your revenge.' Staring straight at her, avoiding looking at the tantalising cleavage.

She just shrugged. 'You know me, Georgie. I just can't tolerate fools.'

'Well, from the very fact we are here, I guess your version of revenge this time is a mite more serious. But tell me, I'm intrigued — that word again, Charlie. It always comes up when you express your devious little mind and use your body to make the point.' I waved my hand towards the obvious.

'Tony had some business interests in New York and Southern California, all to do with old cars. It was exciting and to start with he was, well, different. Big society wedding, first class travel anywhere and upgrades in restaurants and hotels but little else. Pretty free with his fists when he was crossed or drunk or both, but cleverly rarely anything that showed. Then he would grovel and take me down Rodeo Drive or wherever and spend money like water. Real Jekyll and Hyde, I think it's called. I met this guy, an American golf pro, yes I know it sounds corny, but he wanted me for me. Not the society wife bit or the fancy finishing school accent and manners. Just me. Jerry wanted me to divorce Tony, and when Tony found out, he had both his legs broken by his cronies in the car trade. Jerry apparently would never walk properly again, certainly never play golf to any standard anyway; not fair for a man of thirty-nine, good-looking guy too.'

I nearly interjected that it would have been surprising if Charlotte had picked an ugly bastard, but thought better of it.

She continued with what sounded like a well-rehearsed script. 'And I was beaten up by the same guys a few days later. The police put it down to a mugging on the streets of Santa Monica. Bastards took my best handbag too. Does that explain why I want some revenge, George? What do you think?'

At the time, I didn't query how the police knew it was the same people; it just didn't register. I was quite used to her lies and half-truths that my sub-conscious must have discounted what she was saying and I have to admit a tantalising view up her skirt as she crossed her legs mid-sentence didn't help my concentration. 'C'mon Charlotte. Sounds like you need a heavy mob, not a white collar guy like me. Not worth the risk for you, I'd have thought. Take whatever you can from the divorce and put it down to experience.' I could see where she was coming from and it did sound like Waller needed a good going over, if she could be believed, but really good liars always work in something true to make their lies more plausible. So how true was this little vignette?

She gabbled on, with her idea of a revenge plan. I was only half listening; my mind was on other things. I let her ramble on, deliberately not showing any spark of interest. She looked peeved that I was not paying total attention and nudged my elbow to make her point. 'Listen to me! He's away every year in Courchevel, skiing and fornicating. Always the same time — Christmas and two weeks of January. And in the Suffolk house, during weekdays, there's a lovely housekeeper, a German lady, Monika, but she takes the same time off every year to go to her family in Hamburg.' She turned on that sexy look that I recall from our first meeting in the chocolatiers. Enough to melt any heart.

'Get someone to burgle his house, you must know someone like that. It's worth three million and the contents are insured for two million. I saw the insurance policy once. And cancel the insurance beforehand. That'd put the wind up him. And there's always loads of cash in the house in an old safe. All sorts of currencies. That'd hurt him too. I'd be surprised if he declares it for income tax. His solicitors handle all the insurance stuff through a firm in Ipswich and a Lloyd's broker, Mantels, I think they're called. They'll be in the phone book. He's always buying and selling things and cars so they sort it all out after he rings them with the details.'

I shook my head. 'Life isn't like that, Charlie. I'm an old lag — who's going to listen to me? Mine was a fair cop, as they say, and I've paid the price. I'm not going back inside. Capiche? Your insurance angle would do no more than be a minor inconvenience to your husband. Just a couple of phone calls and the problem would disappear for him. He's done it before and probably will do it again. It really does, or should I say did, happen all the time when someone disaffected thought it'd be clever trick. He's well-connected, so for him no big deal. Think again if you want to get your revenge. Your so-called plan is sadly inadequate, my dear. Not worth a can of beans. If you need revenge, start again and don't call me.' I threw in that

35

last remark to emphasise the point but had to admit, to myself of course, the idea of him having to argue with insurance companies and loss adjusters with their usual intransigence did give me a warm feeling, but...

She carried on as if she hadn't heard a word I'd said. 'Maybe you could get your old Mercedes back, too. He'd never be able to prosecute because you could show that he'd got it through fraud or whatever it's called.' She watched me carefully. I leaned back and if body language is any sort of science she knew then that I wasn't going to play. 'I thought, well, if you can't help, isn't there someone you knew inside prison who would like a nice little earner?' She reached across and brushed the back of my hand. 'I need a good thief...'

'That's an oxymoron, my dear.'

'Well, I know you stole a load of money from your insurance company. Tony told me and I went to the court that day. You wouldn't have recognised me. I was on the balcony and I had to wear a wig and sunglasses.'

I was ahead of her. 'So that's why you wanted to know about Terry... In case I didn't want to play...' Again, I shook my head, but this time in disbelief.

'Terry? Terry who?' She looked up at me with an innocent expression.

'You are a devious little minx, Charlotte. No mistake. You know as well as I do who I mean, and NO, emphatically NO. Terry is not the guy for you. And anyway, since when did you take up golf unless it was drinking champagne in a club house somewhere?' I looked for a reaction; there was none. 'I think I've heard enough, Charlotte. I don't want to know. This conversation didn't happen. OK? I'm going now and get on with my life.' I wanted her to know that she had gone too far.

'Sorry, George. I only mentioned it as I thought you'd like to get your own back. Nobody gets hurt or anything. Just a bit of harmless revenge...'

'No! Revenge is rarely harmless. Enough. I'm out of here. I've got better fish to fry. And I hope your relationship with this golf chap works out better than ours did.' I know I sounded almost saintly, quite hypocritical, really. I would like to nail this bastard who'd ripped me off but I wouldn't trust Charlotte with the milk money. I'd had an inkling of what was going on with Tony bloody Waller rocking the boat, from a chum in the company who visited, contrary to "company rules", whilst I was on gardening leave, even before the supercilious Ms bloody Calman had arrived with her shallow HR platitudes.

'Devious, not a man to trust,' he'd said, but I'd never made the connection with Charlotte. Trust? That in itself was farcical, bearing in mind my activities.

'It's a long story about Jerry, so I won't bore you with it. Wouldn't you like some fun in the car before you go? I forgot my knickers this morning and it's a big car, over there?' She looked at me coyly, if ever Charlie could really be coy, and smoothed the dress down those enviable thighs and pointed at a newish Range-Rover with darkened windows in the shadows of a huge conifer.

'No, again, Charlie. My brains are not in my pants any more. Find another mug.' And with that I got up and walked across to my dilapidated Rover.

As I drove away up the A29 towards London, I mused on her conversation. I was puzzled why she wanted to tell me her daft, naïve, idea for revenge, as she called it. Surely she would know that it was a foolhardy idea with zero chance of success. Whatever else she was, she wasn't stupid. Maybe it was just frustration on her part after the so-called abuse from her husband. She must have known I wouldn't tell the police. Well, I would have been laughed at. Low-key was my objective with the boys in blue. I knew from my colleagues inside that once an old-lag, your name often came up with anything vaguely similar to the cause of your incarceration. Computer records just flagged up all likely suspects. I suppose I was a bit flattered but there was a warning flag fluttering around in my head as I negotiated the M25 interchange. I needed to place a word or two of caution in Terry's mind when, or if, I next saw him. It was never a coincidence that she had recalled his name. She never had seemed to be a person who mentioned names without a purpose. I parked the thoughts and headed towards the Dartford Tunnel and the M11. My mind turned to her insistence on revenge. I'd seen those examples of revenge before, albeit pretty minor events. If she found a mug, and with her obvious attributes, that wouldn't be difficult to attract a red-blooded male with aspirations, it would re-focus the law's interest in me. I needed to ensure cast-iron alibis and distance myself.

Chapter 4

I had a lot of thinking to do about my future, new plans and personal issues to resolve. The glorious summer of 2014 helped a lot. Two weeks in Brittany, beaches and rural places we used to visit as kids with Grandpa P, helped. During the war, he'd walked from Poland via Vienna and Marseilles to Brittany to get a fishing boat across to the UK to fight for a free Poland. So, he loved Brittany, and we holidayed there regularly and had quite a lot of friends in the community who had admired his feat of getting from Poland to the UK, and we benefitted as kids from those connections.

That summer, I had a great time, on my own mostly, and an interesting time exploring some of the remote areas in the centre of the region. Had a few beers here and there and spent a bit of time and money on a pretty English woman of forty or so, who was on her beam-ends for money. She was lying on the beach at Carnac with a tiny bikini which got my blood racing, and with a few drinks and a nice dinner, 'hey presto', a week-end of fun and frolics. Name? Marie or Madeleine something like that.

Later in the summer, with Marion's help, I found a small, but comfortable, flat in South East London (Lewisham to some, and to social climbers, it was Greenwich) and it even had a parking place, although gratuitous vandalism was the price to pay for parking any decent car there. Nevertheless, parking places were like gold dust around there. Bob was pleased to see I was involving Marion and had stood guarantor for the deposit and first few months' rent and told me to buy a reasonable suit for interviews and the like.

Unbeknown to Marion and Bob, sorry Robert (he preferred to be called that) I had bought, or rather my alter ego, A G Turner, had bought the place in Essex twenty years before, a smallholding with a cottage sort of house and barns, all untraceable to George Pchelski and a brilliant place to get away from everything. I told my sister about looking to rent a place because I wanted to pursue my interest in classic cars as a career and needed a barn-like facility. I never had any visitors there; not even the milkman called and any mail could be picked up at the next village, which had a rudimentary post-office.

In September, I met up with my old pal, Ian, in the wilds of Dungeness, Kent. Ian Stead, widely known as Issy for reasons lost in time, had been a junior claims clerk with me and a few others in our first job with an insurance company and saw an opportunity to divert some funds by linking up with a dodgy loss-adjuster and a garage repair outfit. It worked well, for him, until someone at the company's bank had dinner with its major client in the area — our employer, the insurance company's claims director — and two and two made five. You can imagine the conversation: 'How could a lowly claims clerk have such a big income etc., etc.', Issy was dismissed after he had disclosed how the scam worked and the names of those involved. As a somewhat naïve twenty-odd year old, I stood up for him when they first started talking of prosecution, and was told that it would be better for all concerned if I left to pursue my career elsewhere. I suppose that's where it all started when it had seemed so easy for Issy, so why not follow suit? Crikey, almost like déjà vu! Issy has had a repair workshop and garage for over twenty years with his cousin. He's a bit like James Garner in The Great Escape — a scrounger. He could find anything, make anything, anywhere — electrical, mechanical, wireless, CCTV - everything and one hundred percent discreet. I suspect he's off the police radar now, but sensibly, he remains very careful and he's choosy about the work he takes on.

I'd long been musing about what next in my life, so I gave him an outline of my 'Plan E' (E for escape drudgery) with a list of things I would need, alongside things he would have to construct and alter. I promised a car and throw-away mobile, as he was always on the poor side of comfortably off. He liked the idea, thought my demands were feasible and do-able in the timeframes allowed and liked the promised pay check enough to take him to his family in Australia, all whilst emphasising he wanted it to be risk-free as far as he could control things. No contact with anyone else involved was his rule.

His parting shot: 'In three months or so — should be possible. Anything I can do to help, George. Least I can do for you for standing up for me all those years ago and only sorry I didn't visit you inside, but that would have put me back in focus to the boys in blue.' Least I could do was to shake his hand and agree.

Chapter 5

Eleven a.m., Thursday 27 November: Bill's café in Cambridge. Sitting outside in a watery winter sun; coffee and a round of toast with their fabulous jam. Close to idyllic. Waiting to see if Terry would turn up. Lots of promises made in prison are a bit shallow so my expectation level was not at its highest.

I'd brought along a throw-away mobile for him, were he to turn up, removing any future needs for meetings. You never know how clever the authorities would be in making two and two equal five with two old lags who'd shared the same cell meeting up after release — it would certainly get the tongues wagging.

Just five minutes past the hour, Terry arrived, looking much different than I'd expected. Smart suit and tie, neat hair cut — quite unexpected. He could have been any of the dozens of business men in and around the cafe. I was in jeans and a sweatshirt, no logos or patterns, and loafers. Quite innocuous, I hoped.

We spoke about everything and nothing whilst the waitress brought more coffee. Terry explained that the smart clothes were a gift from his sister; 'a new start' she'd said and he'd got a posh girlfriend down in London. I was surprised, bearing in mind he'd only been released a couple of weeks before, but there you go. I was still foot loose and fancy free and enjoying it, too.

I had told TB that I would try to help him for old times' sake, but he was inquisitive about my plan for the future and wanted to get involved. I wasn't ready to tell all. Instead, I asked him about his last weeks inside. He passed it off as 'more of the same' but was a bit put out that there had been no one to meet him outside the gates.

'Had to get a bleedin' bus to Oxford and then to London, unlike you,' he complained. 'But I've got this bit of crumpet now. Friend of my sister's. Lovely stuff — blonde, I've always liked blondes, fab tits and legs up to her arm-pits and she and my sister told me to smarten up. Hence the clobber. Name's Angela. Well, Ange, that's what I call her, anyway. She bought me this posh phone and yes, it's a throwaway one. She taught me how to use it, camera, messaging and all sorts. Even found my way here with it, George. Might marry her someday, if she'll have me or shack up with her any road.'

I'd smiled and made some positive comments, can't remember what, now. I wanted to get back on track. There were things, I told him, in train but also things that I would need him to accomplish if the plan were to be a success. I needed a team from his army days. The sort of blokes he used to talk about, ad nauseam, disciplined and organised. He listened and nodded.

'I know a few mates like that. I'll make the calls. Most of them were involved in my little problem at RAF Brize Norton when the whisky went walk-about. Couldn't have done that little scam on my own. They owe me for taking the can. Hey, George, mate, can we get some more coffee — that strong stuff something I really missed inside. Can't get enough of it now.'

The waitress was hovering so I asked for two cups of double espresso for Tel and an Americano, black, for me.

'That's fine, Terry. They've got to be prepared to take orders or it won't work. It is illegal, but no violence at all. On a lighter note, it should be lucrative too. I won't list things for you. It's unsafe to have anything in writing. Find me these guys and you and I will meet somewhere quiet up North. I'll need them for two weeks or so in early January sort of time. They'll need to be able to drive, have a current passport, same goes for you, and no record preventing them from European travel. Short haircuts. You and I will talk over the phone.'

The waitress arrived with the coffee so the conversation turned to the weather and other insanely British subjects until she moved away. Tel quaffed both cups in quick succession, muttering between gulps that it was the best he had tasted. I raised an eyebrow, thinking that his taste buds hadn't got a prayer. He commented that he was catching up on lost time so always drank coffee quickly.

I gave him the throwaway mobile. 'Only for use on this plan, Terry, that's important. No phoning the girlfriend, OK? It's got plenty of pre-paid call time. Everyone involved will have the same. It is the difference between doing this properly and being caught. Capiche?'

Tel nodded and mumbled, 'Understood, mate. I've got this Samsung thing for private calls.' He pulled it from his trouser pocket. I was concerned that he would use it, taking photos and the like and told him so. No social media stuff or Googling had to be the order of the day. He still didn't understand the traceability of this sort of stuff any more than I did. I just knew it would and could happen.

I continued, 'When you've found your lads and got their agreement, I want their measurements: height, chest, inside leg, waist, all the stuff to make sure a uniform fits properly. Oh, and head size for a cap. Some kiosk type photos, that's all. But no names. Sorry to keep on about it. Everyone will be away from their homes for two to three weeks. All expenses paid, so as to speak, and a nice pay off if all goes to plan. Use the story of a contract up north in construction and logistics. That should fit with their history, then. The idea, Terry, is that they don't know me and I don't know them. Each part of the organisation works independently. Less risk that way. Use this burner mobile phone to send the information I've outlined. Understand?'

Terry nodded, again. 'Can't you tell me what and when?'

'No, Terry. Until the next phase is locked down. No more information. But let me tell you that the courses you did on antique restoration and the history of art will stand you in good stead.' He looked at me quizzically. 'Here's something to be going on with.' I handed him a carrier-bag from Waterstone's Book shop, which he eagerly opened. 'And no booze on the job, that's going to be one of the rules. OK?'

Again, Terry nodded. 'What's with the book? Miller's Guide to Antiques.' He looked puzzled as he riffled through the pages.

'Thought you'd like to brush up on your reading, mate. You always had your head in books like that. There's something else in there too. Five hundred quid to be going on with. Leave it in there until you're somewhere quiet.'

'Oh, OK! Thanks. What about vehicles? Location and targets?'

'All in good time, Tel. Do you want in? There is risk involved, of course. It's no booze, no smoking in cars or anywhere, and always wearing latex gloves. What I'm saying, Tel, is that that is my way and then the chances of you or any of your team ending up inside for a long stretch is minimalised. I spent a long time in Upper Heywood listening and most of the chats between the guys was about carelessness being the root cause of being nicked.' Giving him a mini-lecture, with Terry's undivided attention, to reinforce the ground rules was important, including the use of false names so there's no chance of being overheard and identified and absolutely no violence, explaining in words of one syllable that violence would mean more attention from the boys in blue and longer sentences if caught. Then, smiling, I asked 'So, what's your answer?'

'Understood, George. You are bloody right. And I do appreciate the lecture. I listened to you, you know, over those months inside and I know you are right. I'll get on to it as soon as I get back to the smoke. And thanks for the dosh. Don't like my sister paying for everything. She's not very well off.'

'Good. I've spent a lot of time planning this exercise. Let's make sure it works well.'

We promised to touch base by phone as soon as there is news to tell. Leaving separately, I paid the bill and went off in the other direction. Just a handshake and part three of my plan was starting to be in place.

Chapter 6

George met with Tel, again, in York in mid-December, when the influx of tourists for the ubiquitous Christmas market in the ancient Shambles part of the city made them inconspicuous from any prying eyes. Terry had set up a team of eight ex-army guys who were willing to join in and obey the rules and seemed to have the skill sets required. Explaining the idea and the roles a bit more kept Terry interested without giving away the detail. He had the information for uniforms for Issy to obtain and some blurry photographs for the fake identification documents he would be preparing. He gave Terry four thousand pounds to keep their interest whilst they waited for a start date and to rent, quite legitimately by two of the team, two white Ford Focus cars from different rental agencies at airports and for Tel to rent one for himself — must be white. He gave Terry a set of typed lists for equipment he would have to find and the address of the warehouse. All paper to be totally destroyed.

Just a couple of weeks later, in the last days of December, George called Terry. 'Terry, all the components of the plan are in place, now. Get your team up to the factory unit by late afternoon on Friday 2nd, after dark. You've got the co-ordinates. Yes, I know they'll be miffed about New Year and so on, but it has to be now. Not everyone to arrive at once. Discreet is the word, just in case anyone sees unusual vehicles on a remote country road. That'd be bad news. You and your team just have to wait for the signal to start as we agreed. You've got your lists and they must all be destroyed before you leave for the base. Understood?' He listened for the agreement before ending the call.

George had been impressed with the detail and enthusiasm of Ian Stead in his phase of the operation. He had gone way beyond the possibilities that had been outlined, managing to get aerial photographs to assist in the overall plan.

George had rented a disused vegetable processing factory, one of quite a few in the area, using Issy's pseudonym, Mr Ian White, for cash, no questions asked. It was really isolated, about five miles from the target, and as a bonus, all the vehicles required could be parked inside with no light showing, away from any prying eyes. After Issy had thoroughly surveyed the area, George met him at the factory to talk through the detail. Later, he'd assembled all the equipment that had been identified as necessary over his long months planning and analysing in prison, plus other items reflecting changes in technology that Issy had pinpointed. Because it was winter and that neck of the woods was known for cold winds from the east, he had purchased three propane-powered space heaters, each purchased innocently from trade suppliers in different parts of the country. They had discussed the issue of really bad weather and a contingency plan, knowing that there had only been five occasions in the previous fifty years where there had been what the media called a Dickensian Christmas, and only thirty-eight times when a scattering of snow had laid in the same period. A good gamble, Issy had thought, and a week's delay feasible albeit difficult if the weather was seriously bad.

Issy had 'wrapped' a Volvo coach that he'd purchased for cash at an auction in Doncaster, which was altered to George's peculiar specification — a rear door and ramps — but externally it still looked like an ordinary coach, much like the one used in the *Italian Job* film. It was due to be removed to a location that was totally out of sight after its adaptation and dressing in the livery of a real classic car auction firm in Duxford, showing graphics of slightly out of focus super-cars, complete with GB plates and a Union Jack flag. It seemed appropriate to use that name, as it was a real firm, bearing in mind the bastard Tony Waller's involvement if Charlotte was to be believed. They had stolen two removal lorries from a bankrupt removal firm's yard in Hampshire, all decked out in a pre-printed vinyl skin, rather than paint, to enable rapid removal by using a warm air gun like a hairdryer. He was in the process of dressing up the four white Ford Focus in Suffolk police livery, all rented legitimately. Wrapping was not a methodology that had even occurred to George and it enabled each vehicle to bear fictitious names and logos. God alone knows where he got the plastic sheets printed. He'd mounted a roof bar on each bearing the traditional 'blues and twos' flashing lights with which most people are familiar on police vehicles, and each car had a vinyl panel on the roof displaying the car number of the Suffolk constabulary, in case they were seen from a helicopter doing random surveillance. Three long wheel base transits and a couple of school buses had also been 'liberated' by Issy and his cousin and locked away in the factory unit. All the vehicles could be returned to their normal state in no more than thirty minutes.

The electronic and communication requirements were all in place, linked by blue-tooth connection, to both of them, not that George had any remote idea how it would work, but relied on Issy's assurances that it would be invaluable.

Terry had been enthused by the logistics put in place by George's Mr White. 'Mate,' he'd said on the telephone, 'I gotta tell you, whoever this Mr White is, he's bloody marvellous. Now I understand why you lectured me about the devil is in the detail, detail, detail.'

He had gone on and on about the police uniforms, vehicles and in particular the coaches being a good choice and George had explained that with schools still on Christmas break they had been readily available, yet seeing one on the road in the holidays raised no suspicions and they weren't guarded or secure in their depot. The police cars similarly were basically Ford Focus 5 doors and looked like real police cars with Suffolk Police colours, stripes and county crest and even the flashing lights wired up to a simple toggle switch. All the vehicles had cloned number-plates which would be removed after leaving the area. Issy had spent hours on the internet identifying white Ford Focus cars for sale in local papers, magazines, to copy the numbers. Private sales probably meant that the sale vehicles were taxed and insured and had valid MOT tests, which would mean that the automatic number plate recognition cameras in all police cars and static cameras would show the vehicles to be valid, and providing the driver was not being a complete arsehole, they would not be stopped. He'd got the twenty thermos flasks and sandwiches kept in an electric cool box without exposing anyone to the risk as to why someone wanted twenty of this type and twenty of that. Every detail that would make this a successful plan. That, George had said, was what Mr White was good at.

He'd even left sleeping bags, a small equipped fridge and black plastic bins for all rubbish, even soap, spare toilet paper and boxes of blue latex disposable gloves. As George had told Terry, 'It has to be. It's important! Not a fag-end or those latex gloves anywhere. Remember the forensic people can read fingerprints from the inside of those gloves — or so the Americans would have us believe. So be extra careful.' He'd added, 'Mr White will attend to disposal and cleaning up afterwards, but don't make it any more difficult for him than absolutely necessary.'

Chapter 7

'It's Sunday night, Terry. All the components of the plan are in place now. It will be tomorrow night the 5th. You and your team just have to wait for the signal to start, as we agreed. You've got your lists and you must destroy them all before you leave there. Sorry to nag, but it's important. Understood?' He listened, again, for the agreement before ending the call.

At eight o'clock the next evening, George started to panic. No answer from Terry's phone. It just flipped over to messages. Twenty minutes later, he called back, 'What's up? You sounded a bit panicky.'

'Where the hell have you been? You're not answering your phone?'

'Just went out for some fresh air, George. Nothing to worry about. Took a little drive to get used to the lie of the land. The GPS system ain't that good. No problemo. Didn't see a living soul and there's zilch mobile reception out there in places.'

'OK, OK! Sorry, it's just that everything happens tonight. Get ready. Sorry again, but there's been a lot of planning in this, it mustn't go wrong. I'll call again around eleven. Make sure you're there and keep off the bloody phone.' He rang off.

His next call was to Issy, who interrupted him before he could start. 'Where's Terry been, George? He's been out of the factory for nearly three hours since darkness fell.'

George muttered that he'd said he'd been out for a drive, but by the sound of his voice he wasn't comfortable, but Issy eased his mind with a comment about 'yeah sounds sensible stuff.' He related the next stage of the plan and timing to Issy and rang off.

Chapter 8

PC James Edwards awoke with the telephone shrilling. He glanced at the electronic alarm display as his brain connected with the reason for his rude awakening — one thirty a.m., Monday January 5. Much as he was obliged to be on duty at any hour, the basic lot of a rural policeman, it was rare to be called out in the small hours. It was one of the reasons he had applied for, and got, the position. A quiet life with his wife, Alyson, for the rest of his career. Being forty-six, with his wife having recovered from a serious illness, they'd re-evaluated their lives and decided that a peaceful existence was preferable to the rat race of city life. Messing up the sergeant's exams in Birmingham a few years ago had been the last straw, a sort of an omen.

There was something nice about cruising the area during the day, seeing the farmers and villagers — cup of tea here and a polite 'hello' there and only occasional petty crime to solve. An idyllic life. It really was unusual to be woken in the middle of the night — only half a dozen or so times in the four and a bit years since they had moved to Stradbroke.

'Hello, Police,' he mumbled, sitting now on the side of the bed.

'Jim — it's Pete from the fire station. One of my units has just radioed in from a fire in a barn at old Haisell's place at Fressingfield.'

'That drunken — no, I shouldn't say that — that Haisell has had a fire amongst his ramshackle array of falling down buildings? For crying out loud, Pete…'

'Less of the acid, old son. I'm calling you first before getting on to Brigade HQ. If you listen to me instead of going off half-cocked…'

'Sorry, mate. OK, I'm awake now…' It was unnecessary to do more than mumble the apology — they knew each other well enough.

'Fire number one happened about half a mile from Haisell's — at Barns Farm, the Mickerson place — you know it?'

'Course I know him — it, I mean. So, there've been two fires. Shit! OK, you were right to call. Thanks, Pete.'

'Yup! Two fires with what looks like the same cause too. Of course we'll have to check them out, but my guys say smell of petrol and gunpowder — like fireworks — around the seat of the fire.'

Edwards was wide awake now, clutching the telephone between his ear and shoulder whilst hurriedly pulling on his uniform. 'Suspicious, you reckon then? Not kids?'

'Nah — even kids don't do this sort of thing, at night in winter, anyway. Feels suspicious to me, but that's your field. Maybe old Haisell has torched the place for the insurance money and done a neighbour too. Wouldn't put it past the old bastard. Anyway, Fred's over there now. Mickerson reckons he saw a car, not a local by all accounts, coming down the lane during the day with a bloke in an anorak and baseball hat. Sounds odd, so thought you ought to know.'

'Thanks, Pete, sorry I was short with you. Put it down to age. I'll get over there straight away. I'll switch to the car radio if you get any more news.'

Alyson had awoken at the sound and movement in the room. Edwards calmed her. 'Just a routine small fire thing. Got to go and look. That was Fireman Pete.' They both smiled at the reference to their friend — Jim had been called 'Policeman Jim' on their first meeting — so it was natural to carry on the silliness. He continued, 'If I don't go then the next thing'll happen is bloody Ipswich HQ will be calling me asking for reports.' He kissed her and carried the rest of his clothes downstairs.

Before leaving the police house, he called his HQ. 'Got a funny one here. Someone with a grudge or just plain mad. Call you when I find out more.' He relayed the details, much as the fire brigade had told him, and rang off to a chorus of, 'Good luck' from the duty officer at HQ.

He drove off quietly through the village. In the open countryside, he shifted up into fifth gear and cruised at a comfortable sixty mph, happy in the knowledge that few other people would be mad enough to be travelling at this time of night. The flashing blue light on the fire engine lit up the night sky for miles around. All in all, about thirty minutes since the call — not a bad response time, he thought. Not four hundred metres from the farm gate, his radio phone bleeped. He picked up the receiver, not sure who would be calling him.

'Jim? Another fire. This time at James's farm. This is looking silly. D'you want any help?'

He responded, 'No, let me get there first — it's only a few minutes away. I'll call you.' He ended the call and immediately tapped out a series

49

of numbers for Pete at the Fire Station. 'Pete?' Without waiting for any niceties, just an acknowledgement, he continued, 'Another one for you, Pete. I'm going over there now. Direct your people to James's Farm — about half a mile from Mickerson's place, at Metfield. ASAP — OK?'

At James's Farm, some ten minutes later, an irate farmer in a wax jacket and green Wellington boots, with his hair all awry, was spraying water from an inadequate hose with inadequate water pressure onto an active fire that threatened — even to Edwards' inexperienced eye — to destroy a sizeable wooden barn.

'How goes it, Ted?' Edwards posed the banal question to be cut short by the irate farmer.

'How goes it? How goes it? What sort of a stupid question is that? This is fucking arson — that's what this is. Thought that's what you buggers were supposed to be doing — stopping things like this. Don't you worry, I'll be raising it at the next police committee. S'pose you've just got out of your warm comfy bed.' Farmer Ted James never failed to remind all and sundry that he sat on the police committee for the region, often being quite tiresome in bringing friends' and neighbours' issues to the committee in a mistaken idea of public interest.

Edwards responded, careful to bite his tongue — he knew Ted James of old, 'Listen, Ted, the fire brigade will be here soon. They've been attending a fire up the road at the Mickerson place and another before that. So, we're doing all we can. Did you see anything suspicious during the last day or so? Have you got any disaffected employees — workers you've dismissed or whatever?'

'No, no, nothing like that. Well, there was a white car — a Ford Focus, I think. Well, light coloured anyway. Yes, a Focus hatchback thing, come to think on it, although I'm not really into cars; these days, most of them look the same. You don't get many strange cars this way in winter. Not that don't belong around here, anyway. But then, it's a free country and I've got my work to do. About three this afternoon, down Brown's Lane on t'other side of the village. I've some grazing over that way and was mending the gate that some pillock had broken — probably some youngsters out bonking in the cold night air, I expect. Didn't think twice about it — noticed the number though, or most of it any ways.'

Edwards latched on to this straight away. Perhaps this was going to be an easy one, he thought. Strange car, registration number, trace, arrest, bingo — PC Edwards in everyone's good books. 'What number, Ted?'

'ZJO were the three letters and it was a newish 13 plate. Didn't get the numbers though. Still you police wallahs should be able to trace it if what I see on the TV is anything to go by.'

'2013 registration. Are you sure about the letters?'

'Course I'm sure. Wife's initials, before we got married, like. Think about it. Zoe Jane James, but her name was Owens then, see? Damn car was covered in mud — could hardly see it was white; might have been a light creamy colour. Didn't see the driver. I expect it was one of those townies coming up here to buy up a couple of farms for their weekend homes. Bloody people. Though maybe not. They don't usually drive Fords, they're usually in shiny 4x4 Chelsea tractors… D'you reckon it was them that torched my barn?' His tone was far more conciliatory than before. Now he was seeing some possibility of action.

'Don't know. Really don't know. You all right there for a moment? I just want to call in the information to HQ — maybe they can trace the car. Judging by that flashing blue light coming down the lane, here's Fireman Pete's boys — soon have that under control now.' He walked quickly through the mud to his four-wheel drive Land Rover Defender and reached for the radio microphone.

'Duty Officer.'

'That's not bad — must be a quiet night answering after only two rings. That you, Neil?'

'Yeah. Jim?'

'Good to hear you, mate. Look, can you check a registration number for me with the DVLA licensing centre, pronto? I know I could do it, but I'm a mite busy with three irate farmers. Think it's a Ford Focus. Think it's white or a light colour, 2013 or thereabouts. Last three letters are ZJO. Zulu, Juliet, Oscar. Got that? See what you can turn up. This is the third fire I've been to tonight. This one at James's farm at Metfield. He reckons he might have seen a car with those letters on the number plate. Think the fire'll be under control soon. See if there's any info from DVLA. Call you back, as I'll be away from the vehicle for some time.'

During the course of the next hour or so, Edwards asked searching questions of the other two tired and very irritable farmers. No extra knowledge came his way — except for confirmation that a light coloured car had been seen in the lanes around the farms during the day. At nearly four o'clock, he climbed, wearily, into his bed. The fire brigade had coped admirably, saving the three properties from total destruction and promising to investigate the cause of the fires in the cold light of day — each fire was, for them, a minor incident, common enough in the height of summer or even during a dry autumn, but in January, pretty unusual. They reckoned the responsibility lay with the police and their reports would be available during the day.

Chapter 9

Stephanie was in bed with David when the doorbell rang with its awful musical chime. David stirred with a jerk and prodded Steph, as he insisted in calling her, who, after a few drinks, could sleep through anything.

'Who the fuck is that?' He glanced at the luminous display of the alarm clock. 'Two fucking a.m. on a Monday night in the middle of winter,' he said vehemently. 'What the hell's going on!' He groped in the dark for his jeans and pants by the side of the bed where they'd fallen as she'd stripped him. His shirt was around there somewhere, but he needed to get out of bed to find it. As he cast around, he found her sexy thong and smiled to himself at the speed with which she had ripped it off when they were desperate to get completely naked some three or four hours earlier.

'I don't know, do I?' she replied dozily, desperate for sleep.

'Well it can't be your fucking husband can it, you dozy cow!' He nudged her viciously in the ribs. 'He's got a fucking key, hasn't he?'

'I wish you wouldn't say 'fucking' to everything, darling. I don't mind when we're in bed, you know, but you're always saying it. Now, leave me alone, I wanna go to sleep.' She rolled over and closed her eyes.

David reached over and shook her. 'Listen, Steph, the door-bell rang and it certainly isn't carol singers in fucking January is it? I can see flashing blue lights through the windows at the front. It's two in the morn…'

His comment was interrupted by the bell ringing again with, this time, a sharp bang on the woodwork of the front door and the letter box opening against its spring. A voice echoed through the still and quiet house. 'Anyone there? This is the police. Come on, open up!' Then there was a repeated banging on the front door, as if to emphasise the message and give it urgency.

'Hell's teeth, Steph. Get dressed or put on a dressing gown or something and find out what's happening. Didn't you hear? It's the bloody police! What the…'

'Shut up, for Christ's sake. I'm trying to think straight.' Stephanie, now wide awake, pulled herself out of bed and stumbled across the room to rescue her dressing gown hanging behind the door. Half in panic, and half as a natural reaction, David threw himself out of the bed and hastily put on his clothes, blinking in the light as Steph flicked the switch.

'Maybe it's got something to do with your old man. Perhaps he's had an accident or something.' David blurted out the possibilities whilst crawling across the room to the wardrobe.

'Don't be so fucking daft. There I'll use your own language. It's the only one you seem to understand. Just hide up here. Crawl in the wardrobe if it makes you feel better. But for God's sake, keep quiet!'

As she went down stairs to the front door, scratching her head in semi-wakefulness, he stood, out of line of sight, at the head of the stairway, listening intently, fingers fumbling with the buttons on his shirt.

She reached the bottom of the stairs, calling, 'All right. All right. I'm coming!' as the banging noise started again. Her call seemed to do the trick. The noise stopped as suddenly as it had started. With flashing blue light, like a stroboscope, flickering through the glass panel to the side of the front door, she stretched for the light switch that would illuminate the porch, outside and the hall where the burglar alarm control panel was situated. She looked fuzzily at the panel and then hesitantly keyed in the right numbers. Right first time, more by habit than skill. She waited for the bleep and opened the door. The cold January night air hit her, her breath condensing as she spoke. With puzzlement in her voice she asked, 'Yes, Officer? What's going on? I'm…' She was cut off in mid-sentence.

'Madam, sorry to disturb you. It's Mrs Stephanie Davis, yes?' He glanced at his clip board to verify the information as she nodded. 'Nothing to worry about. Is there anyone else in the house?'

She could feel the gorge rising in her throat. 'Nothing to worry about! Nothing to worry about! Do you know what time it is?' she screeched.

He held up his hands to quieten her and continued, 'Sorry, madam, let's start again. I need to know whether you're alone in the house. Is your husband at home?'

She nodded her head, puzzled. 'No. No, I'm alone. My husband's, er, away on business.'

The policeman nodded, ticked a box on a clip board and carried on, 'Please get dressed quickly. And I mean quickly, madam. There may be a problem in the village, and for safety's sake, we want to get all the residents out of harm's way. Do you understand?'

'What sort of harm? What's it all about...' Stephanie grasped the urgency but couldn't track in her mind what could possibly cause such a problem. Knowing that David was upstairs didn't help her thinking processes, especially as she had now lied to the police.

Again, the policeman stopped her in mid-flow, noticing the puzzlement on her face. 'Look, madam, I'm not supposed to tell you so don't you go mentioning it to my guv'nor, the sergeant, or I'll be in dead trouble. There's a problem down at Rose Cottage...'

She in turn, interrupted. 'What, the Arab people? Christ, not a bomb, is it?'

The policeman, eyebrows raised momentarily, calmly said, 'Please get dressed, madam. We haven't got much time and we have to clear the whole village. And you're here alone?' He'd been told to double check.

She hesitated. Despite having been awakened so roughly from such a deep sleep, her brain worked quickly. It wasn't the first time she'd had to react fast — a couple of times she'd nearly been caught out with a couple of her men friends and had to lie convincingly. She turned round and glanced up the stairs — no sign of David. 'No, no, officer. My husband is away on business so I'm alone here.' She prayed that David wouldn't show his face to give the lie to her statement.

'C'mon, madam. I'll get into real bother if I don't get you dressed up warm and cosy and into the coach,' he pleaded with her. 'This explosive device may go up at any moment. For God's sake, hurry.' By now, he had edged into the hall. She turned and ran up the stairs, two at a time, to the bedroom, conscious all the time of David, probably hiding by now, and the policeman waiting at the bottom of the stairs, petrified that he'd follow up the stairs.

'David, David! For Christ's sake, where are you?' she whispered, frightened because of the risk of discovery as well as the possibility of the bomb.

'Over here!' he called under his breath. He had to repeat himself before Stephanie heard his call from the en-suite bathroom. She pulled on some jeans and a sweater. It was bloody cold despite the central heating in the well-insulated modern house. With the front door wide open, the winter's night air had permeated everywhere. She found her sensible walking boots and a blue waxed jacket from its hanger, whilst whispering loudly, 'David, there's a bomb about to go off, you know from those bloody Arabs I told you about. The police are evacuating everyone from the village. Christ, it must be bad!' As soon as she had said it she realised her mistake. David poked his head out of the swing doors to the en-suite and looked visibly pale. She hoped he hadn't heard the bit about it being really serious, so carried on to cover her mistake, 'You'll have to stay here. Get out of the back door after I've gone. The garden roller is parked by the fence as usual so it'll be easy for you to scale the fence and straight down the lane you'll probably be all right — that's away from the cottage where they live.'

He picked up on it immediately. 'What do you mean 'probably', and 'it must be serious'? For crying out loud, I'm coming with you.' His whisper became dangerously loud.

'Shhh, listen to me. You can't, you just can't! I've lied to the police and it's more than my reputation is worth. I'm not going to let this put my marriage on the rocks. You have to understand that. You'll be all right. I've told the policeman that I'm on my own. You must see that you can't be seen now. God knows what I'd do if my husband found about us.' She continued unabated, whispering, 'Look, I've got to go! I'll make it up to you, David, when it's all over. All the sex you can handle, any way you want it. OK? Even stuff I don't like.' She looked at him for a reaction.

He smiled, thinking Christmas was coming around again. This with the sound of heavy footsteps on the stairs and a voice, 'Come on, madam. Come on, please!'

'I'm coming. I'm coming!' She looked pleadingly at David still framed in the doorway, blew him a kiss and ran down stairs, hoping he would not follow. She flicked the switch to make sure the alarm was off and smiled at the thought as she did so, slammed the door, and with the policeman escorting her, she climbed into the coach waiting at the end of the cul-de-sac.

With headlights illuminating another coach and lots of cars, she could see people milling around the village green. There were a few of her immediate neighbours huddled together on the cold yellow school bus, dressed in a variety of hastily thrown together clothes. Two policemen stood at the door, ticking names off a list. Her policeman had gone, presumably to waken some other resident.

'Where's your husband, love?' policeman No.1 asked, after she had pointed to the name Davis on the list on his clipboard.

'Oh, Henry is away for the week,' she replied, almost automatically, looking at the people on the coach, which was almost full. She sat down. Three more couples were bundled in: the publican and his wife, Eric and Kylie; Phil and Diane — he the managing director of a computer software company and his partner, a fabrics buyer for one of the London stores. Their live-in nanny, Maria, sat behind, looking very bewildered, clutching their newborn baby in a shawl. Simon and Clare, from the end of the Close. The management consultant, Simon, sat on the other side at the front, muttering about the inadequacy of policing but no one was listening. That Mrs Legon, the housekeeper for that pompous Churchman Baker, sat near the back, clutching her handbag across her stomach, but he wasn't there, on her coach anyway. The wife of the local MP, Anthony Wellard, Minister for Work and Pensions, looked up as she passed and smiled in that supercilious way that politicians' wives have perfected, almost laughable as her hair was partly covered in a scarf, not quite disguising the hair rollers. There were some others at the back of the vehicle she recognised but didn't really know personally.

The second policeman stood at the front of the bus and caught their attention. 'Please keep calm, ladies, gentlemen, children — and babies!' He smiled. 'We'll have you back to your warm beds as soon as it is safe. My colleague will come round the coach in a moment to collect any mobile telephones, laptops, tablets or other radio equipment. You can place them in the polythene bags provided and write your name on the label. We mustn't have any radio signals in the vicinity. You'll get a full briefing when we are in a place of safety. Coffee and the like will be provided. Please don't worry!' He swung into the driver's seat and gunned the engine. The doors closed with a 'shussh'. He drove off carefully.

As he turned the corner, she glanced up at the front bedroom, not sure if it was a trick of the reflected light from a street lamp or whether David's face was framed in the window.

***

David had been watching as the tail lights of the coach disappeared, noticing signs of activity all around the village green. Several police cars were parked about a stone's throw away, with blue lights illuminating the village green. He took time dressing properly whilst trying to think what was best to do. He cursed Stephanie. She'd been a bloody good bit on the side for months now. Bloody good in bed and readily available, as her husband was frequently overseas for long periods of time. But this bloody caper was a bit rich — putting her reputation in front of his safety. 'Cow!' escaped his lips as he stared out of the window.

His car was parked on the outskirts of the village, in an entrance to a field behind a substantial hedge. Not hidden, but certainly out of sight, a regular hiding place over the months. He lived fifty or so miles away, and like Steph's husband, Henry, was not due home to his wife and family for another few days yet. His job gave him the freedom to be away for days on end.

Henry Davis was a business consultant to the off-shore oil industry and very comfortable on it, too, whereas David was only a sales manager for an electronics company, earning reasonably but not to the standards of Stephanie and Henry. They had a house he'd dreamt of, with a huge garden backing on to fields and fabulous bathrooms with mirrored ceilings and whirlpool baths with showers bigger than his whole bathroom. Didn't he just know how fabulous. His three-bed semi would have fitted into the ground floor. He'd met Steph, looking radiant, at a discotheque in Ibiza the previous summer. She'd gone there for some sun with a girl-friend; he'd gone with his nagging wife, Sandra.

Stephanie's girl-friend had scored with the hotel manager. David's wife, Sandra, had gone to bed early with her regular excuse of a stomach cramp, an excuse she always turned on when he was having a good time. Reluctant to follow immediately to their pokey hotel room overlooking the hotel service area, David muttered he'd follow shortly after a beer or two. Stephanie, as he now knew her, was in the bar alone, so it seemed natural to talk to her.

She'd been dressed to kill in a white mini dress contrasting with her bronzed face and shoulders. The dress shone in the ultraviolet lighting, fashionable in those days in night clubs and bars. As it was his last night, he sidled up and politely asked if she would mind him sitting on the adjacent bar stool. No problem there. Several drinks, and a few dances later they strolled off for a walk along the beach. There had been a mutual understanding of the intention — she had been ever more attentive as the evening had worn on. Dancing with her, he recalled, was almost a sexual experience in its own right. Her body had slid over his, pressing her hips against his in a grinding motion whilst she kissed him. In the dark, in the lee of a rock outcrop, they had sex — one of the more memorable of his conquests.

He'd thought it would be a one night stand and was amazed when she had suggested meeting back in England. He'd accepted with alacrity; after all, she was bloody good at sex, with an appetite for it, too. It had gone from there — meetings here and there over the months and a regular visit to her home when Henry was away, parking in the field and scaling the rear fence. She even had the wit to disarm the security light that normally floodlit the rear garden. Providing he was away before first light, there had never been a problem.

He knew it wouldn't be difficult to get to his car, but if the police were running any road blocks at the three entrance roads to the village, as seemed likely, he could well stopped and questioned. That form of publicity he couldn't afford any more than Stephanie. He was supposed to be in Bristol. Laying low in his car for a few hours on a viciously cold night might not be an enviable way of spending what remained of the night, but better than the possible alternatives.

There were lights coming on all over the village and the sound of car and heavier vehicle engines. He sat on the bed and tried to think of a solution. A bomb, she had said — was it really a danger that far away from this Rose Cottage, or was being caught 'in flagrante delicto', with all that had in store, the real problem? Rose Cottage, he knew from what Steph had had time to say before she left with the policeman, was at the other end of the village, but on the other hand, he'd seen on TV newsreels the damage caused by IRA bombs in the City of London in the 1990s, let alone the 7/7 attacks in London. He sat there, head in his hands, not sure what to do.

After a while, he crept downstairs, carefully feeling his way in the dark, conscious, all the time, he mustn't switch on a light — although that wouldn't stop him boiling the kettle. A cup of strong black coffee would clear his head. He felt his way to the cupboard and found the coffee jar. He needed to sober up. Those last two glasses of Henry's brandy had been too much. The shock had restored his thinking processes, but he still felt physically jaded.

Barely a minute had gone by when he heard the sound of breaking glass and the front door opening. He almost cried out, 'Steph, is that you?' but he couldn't fathom why she would break the glass. It told him to be cautious — probably years of extramarital relationships with husbands arriving home at inappropriate times, he reflected. He smiled to himself at the thought of the near misses he had had in his time, peering around the door frame of the kitchen, ready, if necessary, to slip out of the back door which was always left unlocked when he was 'visiting'. He was, after all, familiar with this escape route — another lesson from the past.

The lights went on triggered by the switch cluster just inside the hall. Two male voices echoed through the empty house.

'Christ,' the expression just escaped from his lips almost as a hiss — the noise, he was sure, would be heard by the men. Carefully, incredibly slowly, it seemed, he opened the back door and slipped outside. A fraction of a minute later, the kitchen light went on. Framed in the light, in that fraction of a second before David withdrew into the shadows, were two policemen.

He could hear odd words of their conversation but only odd words until one called to the other, as he disappeared from the kitchen, 'Brown, you start upstairs. I'll do the drawing room and lounge. Looks like there's some nice stuff here. Hey, what's that?' David's heart sank. It was the electric kettle switching itself off, automatically. A pause; he could feel the sweat dripping down his back, followed by the same man's voice adding, 'Ah, don't worry about it, Mr Green, it's only the bleedin' kettle.' He'd chuckled at the forced 'Mr'.

David felt icy cold despite the sweating, expecting one of them to realise that even the oldest electric kettle doesn't take that long to boil.

He pulled himself closer to the outside wall hoping there would be no further reaction from the police, grateful that his coat was a dark colour and warm to boot and even more grateful that she had put a dud bulb in the security light or he would be bathed in 500 watts of white light right now.

'What the hell was going on?' he asked himself, hearing the distinctive noise of a heavy diesel engined vehicle, which sounded like it was in dire need of a service, coming into the close. By moving silently to the side of the house, he could just see along the side, through the slats in the ranch style fencing, a green removal lorry stopping outside. From his vantage point, he could just distinguish part of the name on the side the neatly pruned hedges — 'GREENF'. He regained his position by the back door and glanced in — nothing. Was it time to climb the fence and run? He hesitated.

Within a minute or two, all the lights went off almost as suddenly as they had gone on. He had difficulty with his vision because of the dearth of light to the rear of the property and his eye's familiarity with the intensity of light over the previous few minutes.

He edged, again, over to the side. The furniture van was still there. He was very uneasy, suspecting that this was an elaborately staged burglary and he was right in amongst it. With bent policemen, what chance had he got?

'What's your game, you little shit? Gotcha! Did you think we didn't work out that someone had been using the bleedin' kettle? What are you, some sort of rat-bag tea-leaf nicking things that don't belong to yer?' Without waiting for a reply, he looked at his mate and laughed.

David nearly jumped out of his skin. He felt the hand on his collar. It sent prickles up his spine. Spinning round, he faced his antagonist, 'Er, officer, er…'

His captor roared with laughter, joining his colleague. 'Hear that, Mr Brown? He reckons we're the filth!

'Fuckin' idiot. Should have gone to Specsavers!' They both laughed. 'Too much TV, that's what I say. Wouldn't recognise a real copper unless they was in fuckin' police station! Probably stands to attention at pedestrian crossings.'

David figured it out in that second. He swung at his assailant, trying to break free of his grasp, but he was faced with a bigger and more agile opponent.

'Answer my question you little fucker!' said the bigger man.

David's bravado was returning. 'Fuck off yourself and let me go.'

The 'policeman' changed his grip. David found himself being lifted, bodily, from the ground. The man he had identified as Brown reached across his partner for David's wallet. This, David thought, was his opportunity to run. Chances are, he reasoned, he knew the lanes of this village better than these two. He struggled free but only for a fleeting second. Brown got hold of him. David lashed out. Brown hit him heavily and he felt himself falling backwards out of control and in a weird sort of slow motion. His head hit the metal frame of the patio doors. He felt a warm wet feeling at his collar before drifting into a sort of unconsciousness. He knew the man was rifling his pockets but could do nothing about it. He could hear a man's voice saying, 'Leave 'im. He'll be all right — just banged his 'ead. Check his pockets for any ID and take his wallet and any keys and his mobile and destroy it; take the SIM card too.'

He came round sometime later — an hour or two, or maybe only a few minutes perhaps — it was still dark. He didn't know. Trying to focus on his wrist to see his watch was impossible — his eyes couldn't make out anything. 'It's because it's dark', his brain reasoned through the haze. He knew it was bad — his mind was fuzzy but there was a peace flooding through him. He remembered something — the name 'Brown' and the word 'Greenf'. He couldn't remember why there was an 'F' on the end of the word. He made a superhuman effort to move but found it impossible.

For no reason that his brain could possibly fathom, he wrote, clumsily and in his own blood, the words, that seemed so important, on the glass of the doors. He tried, again, to pull himself up but couldn't make it. His eyes closed and he passed into oblivion.

Chapter 10

The coach pulled to a halt inside the fenced-off enclosure of the sand-pit, alongside another similar single-decker school bus.

'As some of you will have realised, this is Thorndon Sand Pit. We consider this the safest place in the circumstances. We won't keep you here longer than is absolutely necessary. I expect you'd appreciate your beds.' Smiling, the policeman continued, 'I've got to leave you for a short while. Please stay on the coach for your own safety and no smoking. Thank you. Oh, is Mr Whitaker on this coach?'

The 'policeman' acknowledged the raised hand of the publican of the village pub, The William and Mary. 'Mr Whitaker, I'd like you to take charge for the time being whilst I'm away. Perhaps you'd come to the front so I can brief you.'

Eric Whitaker moved forward and they stepped off the coach. He gave Whitaker a walkie-talkie radio with a flashing red light and instructions on how to use it when the green light flashed. He finished the briefing with, 'You understand, sir, that it is dangerous up there. The frequency on this walkie-talkie radio is secure. Electronic interference from mobile phones and so forth can trigger other electronic gadgets — just like on aircraft and hospitals. That's why we've taken the phones etc, and of course will return them ASAP. GCHQ are monitoring all calls in the region and it would be an offence if anyone were to try to use an iPad, phone or whatever, I trust you will remind everyone of that. Coffee, tea, sandwiches and blankets are there at the rear. On no account must anyone leave the coach. This business can get very messy and we need the help of a senior member of the community in cases such as this and…'

Whitaker rose to the bait, 'Of course, officer. As a publican, I'm used to keeping people in order. You go about your duty. No problems here.' He waved to his wife, Kylie, sitting half-way down the length of the coach — all dressed up like a dog's dinner with make-up and showing her cleavage like it had gone out of style, despite it being the early hours of the morning, as one of the other residents had been heard to whisper to a neighbour.

On the other coach, similar conversations were being held with rapid acceptance by the person chosen to 'lead'; just as the boss had predicted. The three men in their smart 'police' uniforms had learned their scripts well. The village had been effectively cordoned off with 'police cars' and police tape. The sand-pit gate had been secured with a fresh padlock and heavy duty chain and the bag of mobiles and tablets, wrapped in kitchen foil, had been thrown into the bushes, well away from their owners just in case one rang, remote though that would be at that time of the night.

Chapter 11

'One hour and fifteen minutes. We're about seven minutes behind schedule. Get your arses into gear, gentlemen. We've got a job to do. Load those removal lorries now and quick. And pick anything else that looks interesting. All jewellery and silver goes into the bag, not your pockets. Most will be traceable. Don't forget to cut all the land-lines at every house. Understand?' Terry addressed the team as they returned to the village centre from the sand-pit. George's briefing on a strict time-table had impressed him.

Having read the brief from Mr White, Terry knew which three houses held the most promise. He started with the MP Anthony Wellard's place and disabled the alarm, which his wife had enabled before leaving the house with the 'policeman'. He focussed on the pictures and antique furniture whilst looking for any safe. With his basic knowledge of antiques and art gained over courses he'd attended over the past few years, he was able to identify interesting items, and with his helmet-mounted camera and mobile, waited for confirmation that the items were worth flagging for the removal team. Each item then bore a yellow ticket. Paintings, he knew, by John Trickett were worthy of note, probably two or three thousand for the group and some nice high value antiques — an escritoire and card table and a set of ten Georgian chairs in the dining room, but the table was rubbish — veneered chipboard at best.

The electronic kit provided by Mr White was proving invaluable on unusual items, with George advising him as soon as the video link went through. He gazed around the dining room and spotted the Tabriz carpet, around twelve feet by nine, and as he did so, he received the affirmative from George to flag it up for removal. His feet sensed the unevenness in the floor as he rolled it up and there was the safe.

Three minutes later, he had the door open and found a file of papers bearing the House of Commons insignia. No time to investigate, he placed them in his back-pack, along with a pile of bank notes Sterling and euros and some nice looking jewellery.

Next house was a large place with green shutters called Porten House, after a nineteenth century industrialist. It was a large Victorian mansion with seven bedrooms lavishly furnished with high ceilings, and ghastly flock wallpaper. This was one house in particular George had told him would have cash, and plenty of it. The guy who lives there, George had said, uses money rather than bank drafts for most things. He scouted the exterior for the alarm contacts, and strangely, found a rear door ajar. Must have been in haste when the evacuation took place, he thought.

He couldn't find the safe at first, but after combing the ground floor more objectively, he found it inside a cupboard in a large cloakroom, all set into the wall. An old Chubb, probably fifty years old and as heavy as lead, but easy to open; probably more use in case of a fire, he mused. Inside, a few loose notes, barely a hundred pounds worth in various currencies. He stuffed what was there into his bag, along with some linen bags and boxes containing gold jewellery. He smiled at George's comment in his ear-piece: 'nice one, strange there's so little cash though' and spotted a Georgian mahogany pedestal partner's desk and matching bookcase — all flagged up on approval from George. Some of the books looked interesting — leather bound might be first editions; might be worth something, so again flagged. Upstairs, a wardrobe of designer label gowns and dresses and he was tempted to take one for Ange, his posh girlfriend in London. One particular Dolce & Gabbana dress looked just right, so, without focussing the camera, he pulled it from its hanger and stuffed it inside his jacket. He moved on, conscious of the time and the timetable that George had drummed into them.

The Canon's house had been identified specifically by Mr White. Somehow, he had gained access to it when selling an aerial photograph of the property, arranged several weeks before Christmas. Terry knew what to flag from a list given to him and immediately burnt.

'Nothing in writing Tel, nothing,' George had said and although it was difficult, Terry understood more and more that this was the way to go about it. A long case clock by Richardson, about 1760, according to the name plate on the dial, worth about ten thousand pound, and a large regency dining table, William IV, another ten grand — all flagged up. The safe, a Chatwood Milner from the 1920s, was a piece of cake, standing in the study 'good as gold', thought Terry. Inside, some cash and jewellery and papers. He discarded the usual stuff of wills, deeds and insurance, but a small brown sealed envelope attracted his attention. He slit the end and removed the contents. Inside, a series of photographs spilled on the floor.

'Oh ho! What have we got here?' he murmured almost to himself. 'Dirty bastard! Well, Mr Canon Baker, into little boys are you? You'll pay for that, you hypocritical religious freak.' He slipped the photographs into the envelope and put it in his inside pocket, not quite sure of the what, the how or the when, but sure he would find some way of making the Canon pay. The other papers he returned to the safe and slammed the door shut, cut the phone cable, closed the front door and re-joined the team.

'No point in advertising which houses are the targets,' as George had said.

It was time to join the rest of the group, the 'policemen', who'd had to strip the less opulent houses of anything noteworthy and fill the furniture lorries with goodies and some household items, beds, bedding, a fridge or two again, according to a verbal list given to them by Terry as a result of the conversations with George.

Terry checked that phase four was complete and sent the group to collect all the flagged items and then back to the disused factory with the next set of instructions: to put the valuables in the transit vans and pack the back of those trucks with the household items as if it were someone moving house, should anyone do a preliminary search.

Ten minutes later, as he scanned the village to ensure everything and everybody was clear, Terry heard the familiar sound of a heavy diesel engine as he prepared to leave the village green. George had warned him of a vehicle approaching and the approximate timing. He stood back in the shadow of a large tree and waited and watched.

George expertly reversed the adapted coach through the wide five-barred gates to Porten House. But not to the front door, but to the right, along a long drive to another double gate and then a large, modern construction barn-like building several hundred metres from the house and out of line of sight.

'Right, Issy. Bolt cutters. There, on the front seat.' Issy had been clearing up the factory unit, waiting for the signal from George to move to the next phase. They cut through the padlock and chain securing the gate and similarly on the barn building double doors.

Whilst the alarm light was on, nothing happened as they swung the doors open. Issy commented, 'Wow! That I didn't expect. Why is the alarm not activated?'

George shrugged. 'Sometimes laziness, sometimes faults. I don't know. Maybe it's been disabled at the house by Tel. I thought he was told to reconnect everything.'

'But what would we have done if it had started shrieking like a banshee?'

'I don't think it's a central station alarm. The police have given up on those years ago because of budget cuts and so on. Come to think on it, it wouldn't matter, no one near to listen.' George shrugged again.

Issy looked at George, puzzled. Everything he knew about George said that he did think of details.

'Move on, Issy. Time is not on our side.' By the light of their torches to add to the interior's deliberately dim lights and with the low hum of a huge air conditioning unit the only sound, Issy whistled quietly at this display of wealth. The walls, covered from ground to eaves with metal garage and car marques advertising signs; shelves with colourful vintage oil cans and old petrol pumps with their fabric hoses hanging grotesquely from their sides, shouting names that had disappeared seventy or more years ago. As their eyes became more accustomed to the ambient light, ten classic cars, most underneath cotton covers with their manufacturers' logos. A Bugatti, two Ferraris, a 1925 Rolls 20/25 cabriolet and a couple of 1930's full blown Bentleys, a Porsche 356C, an E-type, a pre-war Bugatti and a pagoda top Mercedes-Benz.

George continued, peering into the corners of the huge expanse, 'This is what I've come for, Issy. This is where the real money is. About three million, I reckon, but we can only take two. It's the Porsche 356C and the Ferrari 275GTB/4 1966, judging by the badge on the cover. I happen to know the Porsche has some decent provenance and the Ferrari likewise.' Pointing to the green Mercedes, George shook his head, 'That's a car I want to destroy. For personal reasons, believe me, Issy, I need to… A sledge hammer will do it, and a bag of sugar in the tank — best Tate & Lyles specially brought for the occasion. And up there, hanging on the wall, those number plates.' He laughed, in an ironic way, 'They're the plates from my old cars that were sold when I was sent down. Bastard.'

'But why, George? I thought you loved these old cars,' Ian Stead looked puzzled.

'I know classic cars, Issy. Grew up with them. Just look at that Bugatti type 57 Gangloff-Stelvio over there, the black one in the corner, without a cover. Only ninety or so made, and each one different. Gangloff was the coach builder par excellence and each model is named after something or other in the Alps — hence Stelvio. Straight eight engine, usually 3.2 litres.'

He opened the bonnet catches and lit the engine bay. 'Shit, it's a fake, a repro. It's got some bloody awful American straight eight engine — wouldn't fool anyone — and the chassis has been altered. Even though it's been botched, there's one thing I must do...' He looked around, took a squeezy bottle of brake fluid from a shelf mounted on the wall with loads of cleaning materials and special engine oils, and wrote on the bonnet 'fake' The brake fluid immediately started eating at the cellulose paint work. 'I hate fakes, especially when they're owned by people like this bastard who can afford the real thing. It's a long story, mate. No time now. Sad we can't take them all, but there is reason in my madness. Get the two of them loaded and off you go. Drop me off where we agreed to pick up my car. And I'll see you in a few days. We both need to establish plausible alibis.'

Issy loaded the two cars with help from George and drove the converted coach out into the open, stopping briefly to secure the doors and the gates with new padlocks and chains. Terry remained in the shadow as they drove off, knowing he had things to do.

Chapter 12

Jim Edwards returned home exhausted. He'd never been any good if his sleep was interrupted. It seemed only a minute or so since his head had hit the pillow but the alarm clock brutally told him it was already seven thirty a.m., not even daylight.

Alyson, his wife, shaking him, 'Jim, darling. Wake up. Sounds like something big happened during the night…'

'Yeah, yeah, I know,' he muttered as he brought his disoriented brain to bear on the words from his wife. 'Fires — got to sort them out. But it'll wait 'til nine or so. Need more sleep.' Every muscle and nerve in his body told him to roll over and get some rest, but his hearing was becoming acute — almost hearing the alarm in his wife's voice. She was a pretty stable individual, not taken to overreacting, yet her tone of voice conveyed something more serious than some weirdo with a grudge and a box of matches running amok amongst some local yokel farmers.

'What are you talking about?' He brought himself up on one elbow to concentrate in the half light on his wife's face, fighting the uneven struggle between sleep and urgency.

'Phone call, about five minutes ago. You've to call back your sergeant in ten minutes. I said you were in the bath. There's been a big burglary and what looks like a murder down the road at Eye St Mary, sometime during the night…'

He literally jumped out of bed. 'Bastards! Ten to one those fires were a diversion…'

'What? What do you mean?' Alyson sat on the edge of the bed, looking enquiringly at her husband as he pulled on his socks.

'Sorry, dear — think about it. I get called away in the middle of the night to the easternmost point on my manor whilst something big is pulled off in the westernmost part. And where are we? Answer — quite near the village of Eye St Mary. Is the Pope Catholic?'

Less than five minutes later with two pieces of toast and a cup of strong coffee, he was on the phone to HQ. And after a succinct briefing from the duty officer, he realised the seriousness of the situation.

'You'd better get yourself down to Eye St Mary. And P.D.Q! Detective Chief Inspector Philippe LeFanu is over there now. Looks like a big 'un — especially with this suspected murder. 'Bout the fires — I'll send one of the lads over and let you know…'

'Maybe there's a connection, sarge. Can't put my finger on it — might just be a coincidence, but it's just too pat. I can't remember when a criminal actually arranged to have the police off his back. Looks funny. Did you get a make on that car number I called in about last night. I spoke to Neil Adsett. Did he leave me a message?'

'Sort of…'

'Sorry, guv. What d'you mean sort of?'

'DVLA say several cars, seven to be exact, with registration ZJO, Ford and in a light colour or white. They're being checked out and eliminated. Could be your bloke got it wrong or, bearing in mind this multiple theft and possible murder, it could be a false plates job.'

'Well false registration number makes some sense. I believe old Ted James about the number he saw. Perhaps there is a link with this Eye St Mary thing. The idea is plausible. I'll get over there straight away. Got to keep the boss happy!' He rang off, gulped the last of his coffee and ran to his car, clutching his portable electric razor in his left hand. Seven minutes was all it took — a short cut involving driving through two private farm estates helped him — he raced up the eastern access road to the village, seeing two police cars at the entrance to the sand pit.

He stopped and asked the PC on duty for the DCI. He just pointed up the road towards the centre of the village. 'Village Hall is the incident centre. Blokes setting it up as we speak. Up there, mate — looks nasty, though! This is where they held the hostages. Just searching for clues here. Two coaches that had been nicked and three plastic bin liners full of mobile phones and other stuff. That's all we've got here — that and a load of irate locals and churned up mud that'll really get up my old lady's nose when she has to clean up my uniform. And take care with the Frenchie, LeFanu, he's in a right mood and he's bloody sharp.'

Edwards waved and revved up the engine. The conversation was going nowhere. He screeched to a halt on the edge of the village green amongst several other cars and a police Transit van. He pushed forwards in the crowd of fellow police officers surrounding the man he had heard of but had never met. Detective Chief Inspector Philippe LeFanu, aged late forties, maybe early fifties, was an imposing man of maybe six foot, immaculately dressed with a sheepskin coat tossed casually around his shoulders, one of those people that always looked smart even if they were digging the garden. Speaking of which, even his Wellington boots looked designer label and expensive. A single man, his wife had left him years before, no one knew why, and they had no kids. One of the team added that he had had to pick him up from his house one time for a meeting. Nice detached place, but nothing remarkable. Aggravatingly good looking, slim with a receding hairline, already greying at the temples, and aquiline features, giving a clue to all as to his Gallic ancestry. Rumour had it that he'd been recruited direct from University straight into CID to be fast-tracked, with a bright future ahead and a Frenchie at that, but he'd obviously done well in his early career to reach DCI status, but if the rumours were true, he had blotted his copy book with an arrest about some dockside drug smuggling, causing embarrassment to his then bosses. A bit outspoken and being seen as a foreigner, at that. Result? He'd been sent to deepest Suffolk from the Met. Usually a point of no return.

Most of the police team were in Wellington boots. Jim looked down at his own shoes, covered in mud and dirty water as he tried to circumvent the puddles in the tired asphalt of the miniscule car park. LeFanu detected his discomfort and smiled, knowingly.

'DCI LeFanu?' he asked, having come, almost unconsciously, to attention in front of the man. 'PC Jim Edwards, sir. Just come in from Stradbroke as requested. This is my patch.'

'Where've you been, Edwards? There was a call out for you an hour or so ago. I would have thought you locals would have been first on the spot.'

'Sir, I was following up on a series of small farm fires…'

LeFanu cut him off in mid-sentence. 'If I were you, Edwards, I'd get my *cul*, of course, in English, em, arse into gear. Stop pissing around with silly little local squabbles resulting in a tin pot fire or two and get to grips with the real problems of policing. This is a major robbery — one of the biggest on record in the county and what looks like a murder to boot. If you want to stick to being a local bobby then I'll have you transferred to the Isle of Skye or somewhere — where your talents will be vested in parking fines and directing tourist traffic and you'll learn to wear appropriate clothing in the winter.' He pointed mockingly to the unfortunate's shoes.

Edwards gulped. Not that he would have minded the Isle of Skye right now, he thought. 'Sir, I must insist... That was a very unfair remark...' It was a brave move. He blurted it out without thinking — instantly regretting it.

LeFanu held up his hand to stop Edwards in mid track as a uniformed sergeant approached. 'Frank — start the house-to-house. It's Tuesday morning and the shit is about to hit the fan. I want lists. Lists of what's been nicked, even allowing for the blatant exaggeration that often happens with burglaries; who lives where — who's away. And everything there is to know about this Arab character and his wife the villagers are talking about. And photographs, lots of photographs. Then I want interviews with all the residents — anything and everything, no matter how small, and displayed on these boards for all to see.' And looking at his team, he announced, 'We're looking for connections, ladies and gentlemen. Get to it.'

Sergeant Frank Shaw, a career officer, at the wrong end of his career and resentful of having been passed over for promotion despite passing his inspector's examinations two years before, barked instructions to his team who were standing around two of the police vehicles. Seconds later, they were moving away, spreading out around the village, one of them giving him an 'up yours' gesture behind his back.

'Right, Edwards — tell me why you think I'm being unfair.'

Jim was amazed. The nervousness brought on his stutter that he had tried with some success to master over the years. 'Er...er. I have some information that I think is relevant.' He stood there, freezing in the cold wind that whistled over the fenland, deciding to take a flier — guessing that his assumption was correct.

'Sir — we reckon, that is the Fire Brigade and me, that we had a serial fire raiser last night. He, presuming it was a 'he', did a series of fires as far away from here as is possible — on my patch. I think it was a diversion to make sure that there was no one around here, police I mean, who could be called. From what they tell me, the timing was down to a T. The person was seen during the day and we think the car he used looks like it had false plates — HQ are checking with Swansea. We have a brief description — wouldn't be enough for an identification parade but...'

LeFanu interrupted him again. 'Thank you. Jim, isn't it? OK, Jim, perhaps I was unfair — heat of the moment and all that. My apologies, that is useful information. Make sure the duty sergeant has the information for the incident room. Now I'd like you to assist him — Frank, Sergeant Shaw, on the house-to-house. Presumably you know these people, or some of them. I want to know all there is to know about this Middle-Eastern chap. What's his name? Oh and find that DS Jones for me, pronto.' He looked around him for a response.

Edwards interrupted, 'Faruk, sir. Iqbal and Shaida Faruk. Only Arab people in the area, as far as I know. I had to talk to him once or twice — minor stuff. Driving a vehicle with a broken rear light, a beat-up oldish Citroën. Had to warn his missus once that the car should be registered at her home address, here and not the previous one, in London, somewhere. Sort of thing that happens all the time, guv. I can give the lads a description — best as I can remember. Oh, and the house — Rose Cottage, that is, had been empty for about six months and was rented out to this Arab chappie about October time. The agents are...' He paused whilst trying to think. '...Mickleson and Latham, over in Eccles. I remember because of the agent's board outside.'

'Right. Thank you. Incidentally, may not be an Arab — these days best to say Middle-Eastern until we know better. Anyway, see if this Faruk character is anywhere to be found. I reckon not, myself, but you never know. And get someone to talk to the estate agents, too, please. If my guess is right, Faruk is in it up to his neck. There must have been some planning in the locale for this to work, judging by the two conversations I've had with residents. And Edwards, good that you stood up for yourself. I'm never in the best of moods at this stage of an investigation. Oh, and one last thing — do people dream up a false registration number or clone it? Look into it, will you?'

Edwards was stunned. This was basically an apology from the man himself. He mumbled an, 'Of course, sir. I will look into it. Right away. Thanks, guv. Sorry, I mean, sir.' as he moved away, catching a brief glimpse of a smile on the chief inspector's face.

He followed the chief inspector through the double doors to the village hall, a converted World War Two Nissen hut with the corrugated iron structure, painted green outside and a nasty pale blue inside, with chintzy curtains at the tiny windows, noticing his boss shaking his head in disbelief. This was to be the incident room coupled with a mobile incident trailer housing all the sophisticated telecommunications links with HQ and Europol and Interpol, which would arrive in around thirty minutes.

Meanwhile, a truck with desks and equipment was disgorging its load. A British Telecom van was rigging up new lines through a window from an adjacent telegraph pole. It was the first time in Jim's career that he had seen, let alone been involved in, such a mammoth operation — there was action everywhere, with police and civilian staff scurrying about setting up equipment.

The house-to-house inquiry took a large part of the day. All the information available was logged onto the newly installed computers to look for common ground. Several of the houses were empty, the residents away somewhere and others that Edwards identified as second homes, equally empty, including the large house on the outskirts, Porten House, the home of a Lord Groombridge, according to Jim Edwards. Photographs appeared as if by magic and were affixed to a large scale map of the village and its environs. Macabre pictures of the dead man, lying on the patio of one of the nicer modern houses, and the scene of that particular incident were stuck onto a separate easel. Before noon, the walls were decorated with printed lists of information for cross-referencing, with LeFanu pacing up and down, scratching his chin whilst he was patently deep in thought.

'Canon Baker says that a bit of cash was taken, some jewellery that belonged to his mother and some valuable furniture — it's listed on Board A — but nothing else. His housekeeper looked a bit doubtful when she heard him tell us. Sounds like it might be an insurance thing. Mrs Wellard, the MP's wife, gave us a going over but seemed more worried that her freezer had been nicked, alongside some State papers which, inevitably, are vital to National Security, she says. Could give us some grief that one. Porten House is the only other one that stands out and there are some obvious things missing from various houses — pictures, furniture but they could be from IKEA for all we know, until we get some ID.' Sergeant Shaw had designated this task to WPC Ford, who had made comprehensive lists to help with the questions from the detectives.

'Excuse me, sir. Porten House, Lord Groombridge is always away at this time of year, and his housekeeper goes to Germany — family thing, too.' Edwards looked across at the DCI and received a nod in return as he clicked his fingers at Sergeant Shaw to add the information on the white boards and then settled in the little ante-room designated for him.

Shaw then scribbled on the white board. 'Aerial photographs in four of the houses that we have had access to. They look recent and all in the same or similar frames.' He said to Detective Sergeant Jones, 'Apparently, this guy, quite smartly dressed and with a southern accent, was flogging these aerial pictures about a month ago. Cheap as chips. Suggested them as Christmas presents, that sort of thing.' And with a smirk on his face, he added, 'The boss is looking for you — not best pleased either that his bag man isn't dancing attendance, Detective Sergeant Jones.'

Ignoring the gibe, DS Jones, LeFanu's deputy turned. 'Log it, Frank, alongside the note you've just made. Might be relevant. Could be casing the village. If it is, it's really quite clever. Fits with what we know about this team. Any idea of the people who did the aerial bit?' A shrug from Shaw answered his question but irritated Jones. 'Well, couldn't you bloody well find out?'

'Don't come the acid with me, DS Jones,' he snarled at Chris. ' You're the bloody detective.' Jones again ignored the gibe. Shaw was known for it, starting when he had been passed over for promotion the third time. Many of the team were wary of him.

A call came in for Edwards from Ipswich. 'Jimbo, this one was a cinch. My guess is someone copied the number rather than made it up. That's if it's the same one. It's always possible that that farmer bloke got the letters wrong. He said the car was covered in mud. My hunch is that we've made a connection. The only ZJO registration number unaccounted for belongs to a white Ford Focus for sale by a private punter in Eastbourne, Sussex. Been advertised online for a while, and hasn't left the drive of his bungalow for five weeks. Winter is a bad selling time, apparently. According to our traffic guys, this type of cloning is getting more and more common especially with road tax and insurance getting pricier and the change from registration numbers that identified origin by county or whatever.'

'Hmm. Got it. Owe you one, mate.' Edwards was convinced that they had found something significant but was not sure how to use the information. 'S'pose there's nothing more on the anorak with the baseball hat?'

'No, mate! The three farmers all reckon that it was a bloke, but after that the only thing that stacks up is the anorak and hat. No height, colouring or anything. My guess is they'll be more use if we get to drawing a picture of a suspect or even an identity parade.'

'Hey, thanks again. Look I've got to go. I'll call you if anything turns up. Appreciate it.' Edwards rang off. No sooner had he put the receiver down than Sergeant Shaw called him across. 'Jim, here's the lists of residents. Check them through. Seems like three were away from home last night and still are and another five houses are second homes, so unused this time of year. It's that time of year. Know anything about any of them?' Jim scanned the list. The three missing families were prominent in the village. He didn't like to add that he'd already passed on this same information. No one liked to cross Sergeant Shaw.

'Know two of them but the other — no. Ask the neighbours, I guess. I have only one listed as a property to check but not until Wednesday — tomorrow. Our only titled resident, Lord Groombridge, snotty individual but there you go, always tells us when he's away and expects us to guard his place, Porten House.' Pretty posh place, PC Edwards commented, although he had never been admitted beyond the kitchen and hallway on the ground floor. 'Never hear from his wife, though. She doesn't appear there very often, apparently, but there is a housekeeper lady, Mrs Braun, a German lady — always makes me a cup of tea… But the other residents — nothing that I recall.'

'Fine. Oh, and Jim, that damn woman, the MP's wife, is raising Cain. Having words with the powers that be at HQ — give me some more grief, no doubt, with the DCI. Said that her most valuable stuff had been taken. Not good enough — you know, all the usual. Her husband will be on his way back here after some debate on the Schengen Agreement in the House.'

'The what?'

'You know, Jim, this zone in Europe where people can cross borders without needing passports and the like. Read about it in the newspapers.'

'Oh yeah. I read about it, now you mention it. All this immigration stuff.'

'Yes, well it seems his safe has been breached and papers all over the place — Government papers usually kept in the safe. She doesn't know if any are missing. Make a personal visit, will you? Fact-finding, you know the routine. Keep her happy. Maybe this is bigger than we think — eh?'

Edwards asked, 'Do you think the burglaries were a front for that then, sarge?'

LeFanu interrupted their conversation. Neither man had seen or heard him come up behind them. 'Don't think anything, Edwards — have to know. I'll get on to Special Branch about the papers. Could be a reason for this whole charade but I doubt it. More likely a bonus for the thieves. And it won't be long before the bloody press descend upon us and start their own guessing game. I want a group meeting for briefing in one hour. Please arrange it, Sergeant Shaw.' He stalked off to a screened-off area of the village hall more usually used as a tiny committee room. It was being equipped with two telephones, computer equipment and a coffee machine, already bubbling away on a canteen table that served as a desk.

He called over his shoulder to the sergeant positioned outside the office, 'Sergeant, get Mr Jones and send him to me quickly,' adding a perfunctory, 'please,' as an afterthought.

No more than three or four minutes later, his number two, Detective Sergeant Jones arrived, looking flustered. In his late twenties and singularly unfit, he always wore a suit and tie but was one of those people who would never look neat around the neck no matter what. LeFanu sighed and tried not to look peeved that Jones had had to be found, but supporting his immediate staff, didn't want to criticise too openly. 'OK, Chris, we need to sum this thing up.' He reached for a marker pen and approached a series of easels, on which wipe-off boards were mounted. 'Fact one — multiple well-planned burglaries. Fact two — traded on fear of the presence of this Faruk character. Make a note to bring him in next.' He noticed the look on Jones's face. 'And don't tell me he's done a runner?'

'Yup. Got it in one, sir. His wife's gone too, by all accounts. No car, no forwarding address and the place, Rose Cottage, had been rented, furnished. Got someone on to the letting agent, but no information yet. And no prints yet — looks like the place had been wiped clean. We know about the car, apparently been in a couple of scrapes in the last couple of weeks. Got a registered address in East London — surprise, surprise! I'll lay money that it's not a private residence. I expect the bloody thing'll turn up torched or in an airport car park in a couple of weeks, happily rusting away.'

'Not really. Surprising, I mean. East London, there's a huge Middle-Eastern population there — Bethnal Green and eastwards. My guess, too, is that the address doesn't exist or it's an accommodation address. God knows why there's not a more exhaustive check for genuine addresses when a car is registered. Anyway, I reckon that they were part of it. I can see the hysteria now. Bomb scare; media hype; Middle-Eastern terrorists in village.'

'I suppose that'll explain the mobile phones in the bin-liners, eh, guv?'

'Yes, you're probably right. Mustn't use them in hospitals or on garage forecourts or on aircraft — we're all conditioned to that. Hardly surprising that you have to hand them in where there's a bomb-scare. Most of us don't understand the why, but follow the rules. No, I reckon the terrorist factor is just a diversion, bit of bigotry mixed with xenophobia does the trick. What we need to know is: was that the only role for our friend? Anyway, probably explains the lack of warrant cards too. Not one of the villagers asked to see the bit of card to prove they were genuine — but that's probably what we'd like to believe people would do. Dark, cold, middle of winter, small hours of the morning, flashing blue lights, police cars, police uniforms and fear — would you ask to see the warrant card, and even if you did, would you know if it's genuine? Enough. Move on. Call Sergeant Shaw again, will you, Chris, and see if that local bobby, Edwards, is around.' It gave him a breathing space to pour a coffee and scribble some notes adjacent to his broad headings on the boards.

'He'll be here in about five minutes, sir. Apparently he's setting up a meeting of the crew at your request?' Chris said it in an inquiring way. Sergeant Shaw had not known what the meeting was about.

'Yes, yes. I asked him to arrange a meeting so that everyone knew our stance with the media. In fact, I'm amazed that they're not here already — the media I mean. Try to maintain the road blocks at the entrances to the village. Call it a crime scene, and we have to allow SOCO to finish their investigations. And get it logged onto the HOLMES database — it looks like it'll qualify as a large major enquiry. And essential visitors only. OK, let's get on. Anyway, the third part — who is the man who was murdered, if it was murder, which it certainly seems to have been? Do you agree?'

Jones nodded. 'On balance, I'd say murder — possibly accident but remote...'

'Any clues? Was he part of the gang?' He scribbled busily as he interrupted the detective sergeant in mid flow.

'The woman who reported it — Mrs Stephanie something or other.' He pulled his notebook from his pocket and flipped over the pages. 'Stephanie Davis. Tasty bit of goods.' LeFanu glanced up at him and shrugged his head. 'Sorry, sir. She was shocked finding the body when she walked back from the sand pit in the early hours. She was on her own. Husband's away on business. Says she's never seen him before. Got some photos that we'll show round the village soon. And one of the lads has come up with a car. A white Vauxhall Astra, about two years old, I reckon, with the window smashed in and the number plates missing. It's in a field about two hundred and fifty metres out from the village on the south side, near the hostage place. Checking the VIN with DVLA for registered owner.'

'OK. What's the connection?' He glanced at his colleague, noticing the shrug of his shoulders, 'Well, check it out. Could be one of their cars — perhaps broken down. Maybe stolen and abandoned. Doubt it myself. Don't like coincidences. Could be anybody's, I suppose. Now, let's see. Next piece of information is the coaches. Where was their depot; any CCTV? Stolen to order, I dare say, but I want some history. Right, who is not in residence? I've asked Edwards to pick that one up. Find out how he's getting on with that. And I want a list of the skill sets this gang needed — you know safes, locks, some muscle men, drivers… oh, and someone to handle the alarms. Is this some sort of inside job? Ask the Met for a list of likely suspects, too.'

'Why, sir?'

'Had you ever heard of the village of Eye St Mary? Well, barely — hardly the headline village in the local news, is it? In the last eight years or so, I had never heard of it, in work terms, anyway. And we're relatively local. No. Now why choose this village — barely a hamlet? Sure, it's a rich village and only a few miles from the town of Eye, with its Saxon church and disused US airforce base. But this tiny village? Some notables but plenty of other locations with much easier access than this. Perhaps it's the very remoteness. I don't know. Not all have three or four seriously rich people, alongside a lord, an MP and a pillar of the church as residents. There has to be some sort of connection. Get on to the anti-terrorist branch at Scotland Yard and get a trace on this Faruk and his wife — Shaida, wasn't it? With a name like that, it sounds like a fix. If you wanted to worry local residents, then stick a guy and his wife with typical Middle-Eastern or Asian names, the sort we read about every week in the media, and you're half way there.'

'Already done, sir. That's why I was late. Drew a blank with the obvious lists of terrorists, jihadists and people under the microscope. They're checking now. Could be it's a job to get funds or whatever. Incidentally, the London address is a fake.' He glanced at the message on his mobile phone screen. 'It's a café next door to the police station in Tower Hamlets usually frequented by our boys, inevitably. How's that for a cheek?'

'Yes, indeed. No, to answer the other point. Something tells me that these guys were using the Middle-Eastern connection as a diversion. I had a similar issue a few years ago in the Met; cost me dearly, that error of judgement. Can't dismiss it though. Well done for second guessing me, Chris.'

'Sir. I'd like to concentrate on locations with our local bobby, Edwards.' He looked up at his boss, who nodded at the question.

'Concentrate on where they came from. They had a lot of vehicles by all accounts. Maybe some stolen a long time before — some like the coaches, probably more recently. We know about those coaches from Bury St Edmunds bus depot, even had the address on the side of them. But where did the other vehicles come from? Where did they keep them? Must have been, what, a ten to fifteen-odd mile radius, maximum, if that. Needle in a haystack, I dare say. But Edwards knows the area pretty well. And get the locals to interview the coach operators from Bury and get reports nationwide on all stolen vans and trucks.' LeFanu looked distracted. Tapping his teeth with the marker pen. 'And Chris, get them to start with the west — away from the area of the fires last night.'

'Fires? What fires?'

'Edwards thinks he was called away from the police house in the small hours to attend a series of arson attacks, as a guarantee that he wouldn't be in the vicinity of this little lot.' He gesticulated towards the village from the tiny window. 'OK, so, start with the west. Could be a double bluff, but you have to start somewhere. They'll be away from wherever by now. What is it, best part of fifteen or sixteen hours on? Suppose you've put people on the Channel and North Sea ports. Not that we know what to look for, but something might come up. Though, to be honest, this looks well planned; I can't believe that they're going to be that stupid.'

'All ports and airports on extra vigilance for forty-eight hours — that's the maximum they'll do without specifics.'

'I know, Jones. Can't blame them. But you're right, they must have had a base around here. My guess is fifteen minutes driving time. On country roads? What's that? Three to five miles at night. But could be more. Would they risk driving police vehicles much more than that? But to be fair, who's going to stop a police car in the small hours and our own people have been distracted by these fires? When the chief constable hears that, he's going to go wild. I want to know how they got those cars, and where are they now? And quick — before he asks me the question.' The conversation continued, trying to come up with a rationale for the why, the how and the motives.

They were interrupted by the sergeant politely knocking on the door. 'Your meeting. Everyone's here, sir. Sorry to interrupt you.'

'Yes, one moment, Sergeant.' He closed his conversation with Detective Sergeant Jones and moved to the main hall. 'Ladies and gentlemen. A little hush please.' The emphasis was on the word "please". 'It's the wrong side of Tuesday and we're all tired. My main concern is the media. I'm surprised, frankly, that they're not here already. They're going to love this — incompetence of the police; local MP burgled — State papers missing; man dead, looking like murder; then the terrorist question. PC Edwards is our man on the spot. Most of you know him. Edwards, put your hand up. Right. We have no comment, I repeat, no comment. Does everyone understand? I will give a news conference this evening from Ipswich. Meanwhile, for the foreseeable future, I want road blocks to try to keep them away. We have a presence here and need to keep the public away whilst we conduct this investigation.' He looked around the group for acknowledgement, most still shivering and still in their anoraks and winter coats, as the heating in the Nissen hut was pretty ineffectual.

'And,' he continued, 'it's a big scene of crime and we don't want all and sundry trampling over the place. There are only three things we know — one, a large scale burglary, two, a bomb threat, and three, an unknown man has died on the site of the burglary. We don't know who or how — could even be an accident. Until we know more, everyone else will have to wait. Do I make myself clear?'

A hub-bub of assent from the thirty or so officers on duty followed him as he left the main hall.

Chapter 13

Terry's phone rang. 'Yes, boss?' Beddall, whenever there were others around referred to George as "boss" and tried to get his team to use their pseudonyms to avoid any accidental use of names that could be traced.

'I've been trying for twenty minutes to get you. Who've you been calling? I told you, business only on this phone. I hope its not that bloody girlfriend of yours...' George sounded angry.

'Sorry, boss. Couple of wrong numbers... and I'm not used to this mobile phone lark.'

'And where were you last night after the job? I tried to get you but no response.' George waited for a response.

'Sorry, boss. Didn't hear the phone. Went around the village to make sure everything was locked up tight. Then I got lost getting back. Crap reception up here. Even the bloody satnav was playing up.'

'Enough! Now, listen carefully. Is there anyone missing from your team?'

'What? No. What d'you mean?'

'The police have found a body in the village. Outside one of the houses that your guys hit and a car abandoned in a field near the sand-pit. What's the connection? Did you see anything on your rounds?'

'No, mate. I did look around. Perhaps he wasn't there. Honest, don't know, mate. Nothing to do with us. We did find a car, a Vauxhall, in a field in the way, so we stripped its number plates and smashed the window to move it forward a few yards out of the way. No, before you say it, boss, the alarm was a piece of cake. Anyway, how d'you find out about the police?'

'Never you mind, Tel. Inside track, that's all you need to know. Just keep your eyes and ears open. I don't like coincidences any more than our friendly policemen. I want to know if there's anything out of the ordinary. And finding bodies means that the police will up the ante on looking for us. I told you absolutely no violence.'

'Well, I did have to have words with a couple of the blokes who were being a bit arsey about taking orders. I'll keep an eye on them. Let you know if anything comes up. If I find they had anything to do with it, I'll bloody do them over.'

'Whatever. And Terry, keep off the phone.' With that, he rang off, still worrying about the way the police would rack up their response. Burglary was one thing, but a body and a theft was another. And the body would take precedence.

His next call was to Issy. 'Get rid of the ZJO plates, quickly. They've got a make on it.'

'Ahead of you there, George,' Issy replied. 'I'll monitor what goes on in our base-camp and let you know. I know you know Terry well, but I think he's lying. Just so as you know. Anyhow, I'm ready to do a quick and dirty clean up, if you know what I mean, if they move faster than we thought in tracing the base. I'll move the removal vans out first and park them up.'

'Knew you would, Issy. Thanks. Keep an eye on the team. I hear what you say about Terry. Something's taking his eye off the ball. And he reckons there's a couple of problem guys there. Hope he isn't into protecting them unnecessarily. Over and out.' George didn't understand some of the technology that Issy had put in place, but he trusted him, and in the end, was only interested in the results. Sometimes, he thought to himself, it would be better to be face to face.

***

'Now, you two, you've been a bit bolshie since we got back here. What gives?'

'Nothing, mate. Just an argument between the two of us. Nowt to do with you, Beddall. Just fuck off and leave us alone.' Green was the loudmouth of the two and always had been a handful, even in the army days when, as Corporal Dungay, he'd been in the brig on a couple of occasions and been stripped of his rank for punching a lieutenant investigating some petty theft.

Terry was angry. He'd been entrusted to set up the team and thought he'd chosen good guys from the old days. 'What about this bloke the fuzz have found on a patio behind the house you cleared, then?'

'Dunno what yer talking about.' Green faced up to Terry. 'Going to ring the police and report us, eh? You fucking idiot. You wouldn't even get close to the phone.'

'You're the fuckin' idiots. A dead man and the police will up the ante in trying to find us. And that means heat wherever we go.'

Brown butted in. 'Didn't know he was dead, honest. Thought he'd fallen over and banged his head. So, don't come the acid with us, see? That's all there was to it. So we left him and carried on with our work.'

'Dungay, you're bloody stupid, probably killing the golden goose, you arsehole, and as for you, Michael Goodfellow, you're about as clever as a dog turd and you've got a stupid name to go with it. I'll sort this out later, you stupid bastards. We've got other things to worry about right now,' was all Beddall could think to say, his brain mulling over the issue of the police involvement. He'd be guilty by association if it was murder rather than accident. It put a new angle on his future.

Issy, eaves-dropping electronically, relayed the conversation to George with the comment, "two to keep an eye on, George. And TB could give you a problem too." George agreed instantly. He'd seen Terry lose his temper before in prison.

Chapter 14

'Now, Chris what do we know and what can we guess at?'

'Simple one first, sir. Coach operators reckon they were nicked around eleven p.m. Security is low key this time of year, what with school holidays and the like. Locals interviewed the security guard — night watchman by all accounts — who looks clean — mainly there to discourage vandals and to open the gates for the drivers on school runs. Fell asleep, he says. Bit of a dead end there. More interesting, though, is two furniture removal trucks stolen from a bankrupt firm in Overton, Hampshire, about a week ago. Again, got the local people to do a check. Could be local knowledge, but with the internet these days, info like that is easy to come by. Would fit, wouldn't it, guv? Lots of stuff to move and the most innocent of things to see on a road is a furniture lorry at any time of day or night. Apart from that, loads of Ford Transits and the like — all colours all ages — all been nicked in the last ten days. Might be a connection, but could be just normal thieving anywhere in the UK, especially this time of year.'

'Interesting. Could be what we're looking for. Make an all points alert UK-wide — we want sightings of those trucks. What about the stuff that was nicked?'

'Lists being drawn up, sir. Paintings, furniture, clocks, carpets — oriental stuff — and antique books — first editions, they say, but I wouldn't know. Plenty of jewellery and cash, of course, and strangely fridges, freezers, microwaves, TVs, curtains, carpets and bed-linen. Weird or what?'

'Maybe, Jones, maybe. Soft furnishings I can understand. Using them to protect the valuables, perhaps, but white goods and the other stuff? I agree, unusual. Keep on to it.'

'Just one more thing, sir. We've got the estate agent from Eccles coming in later to talk about the Rose Cottage letting to Faruk. Meanwhile, I wanted to look into the Porten House thing, where Edwards was asked to keep an eye out, you may recall. It's a big house and a rich man by all accounts. Anyway, I've put a team on checking around the village up to a mile or so for remote buildings and suspicious vehicle movements.'

'I'll join you in a few minutes. Get a car round, will you?'

They stood outside the side entrance to Porten House, shivering, despite LeFanu's sheepskin and Jones in his quilted jacket, complete with 'North Face' logo. The wind was from the east, as it usually was at that time of year, bringing with it flurries of snow.

'Lovely house, sir. Must be, what, seven or eight bedrooms and umpteen bathrooms. Nice open-fronted three-car garage, nothing in it but… and I can see a beautiful Victorian greenhouse through that gap in the hedge.'

'Mmmm. Just so.' LeFanu was thinking and this almost automatic acknowledgement of Jones's comment was typical. There were no signs of forced entry. The rear door to a utility area and boot room was wide open and the alarm was off. Standing by the Jacuzzi, they were both startled by the sudden outburst of noise as the pump suddenly started circulating the water under the cover. The cover lifted a fraction, which caught their eye.

'What the hell is that? LeFanu looked puzzled as his mind connected the dots — Jacuzzi, hot water, jets, automatic timer.

Jones glanced back at his boss. 'They do that sort of thing. My brother has one in his garden. Not quite as grand as this one, but still. Never seen the cover lift like that, though.'

'Open it, Jones. Looks like those plastic clips free it up.' He pointed to the straps that secured the top.

'Nope, guv, they're locked down — need a key thing, I think. Jeez, there's an almighty pong, too.' Jones reeled.

'Break it open, then.' Jones tried pulling and twisting but no go. 'Kick it or find a tool. That smell is nasty and…'

As he did so, Jones's right foot severed the plastic clips and the lid rose further, relieved of its restraints. 'My God!' Jones managed to say before doubling over, retching. Floating face down was a distended body, naked but for a brief pair of blue swimming trunks, grossly distorted and bright pink in colour, and in some places a revolting green and the smell…

'Who the hell is that?'

'I think, sir, it could well be this Groombridge chap. After all, it's his house. The owner of this place. I saw a picture once in the local rag, not of his backside I mean, but it could almost be anyone… it's hard to tell. He's blown up like a bloody balloon. Maybe if we turned him over?'

'Are you sure you're not making a quantum leap, Jones? Location, homeowner and body combined into a result? According to Edwards, he's usually in Switzerland or France or somewhere this time of year.' Jones looked peeved at the remark. 'Switch the machine off, Jones, and make a note of the exact time, too. Forensics will want to know that to estimate the time of death.'

Jones scouted around and found the master switch and cut off the power. The bubbling ceased, leaving an eerie silence. DS Jones was calling the operations centre in the village for back up and the SOCO team to get the forensic people out there. His call was received by a civilian clerk, who passed the message to Sergeant Shaw.

'The boss has found another body up at Porten House, in the Jacuzzi of all bloody places. We've to get a SOCO team up there pronto, and to get forensics, Dr Renata, and say it's very urgent, guv,' the clerk said quietly. 'You may want to get involved, as it seems it wasn't a very thorough search, Sergeant Jones says.'

'Bollocks to Detective Sergeant Jones,' Shaw mouthed, careful not to allow anyone to hear. He took three of the team outside and wanted to know how come they had missed the obvious when searching for access to Porten House, knowing that he would be facing criticism from LeFanu when he returned.

The somewhat diminutive Dr Renata Howe arrived at Porten House after twenty minutes, all suited in baggy white Tyvek overalls, boots and a mask, with her assistant, armed with several cameras, who immediately took photos of every angle available. The body was still floating grotesquely, and despite the overall smell of chlorine, the atmosphere was all pervading and choking.

'We've got to get him out of the water onto this plastic sheet, and quickly, if I've any chance of establishing cause of death and the time.' She was on the verge of gagging but managed to control it.

'Right, three of you get in there and take it easy with that thing. With all that heat, presumably it will be almost impossible to estimate the time of death, Doctor?' Jones motioned to three uniformed police.

She smiled, as only forensic people can when exposed to such gruesome sights and the inevitable urgency from the investigators. 'No, hang on a minute; leave the body. It's going to be difficult. This is not the first time, nor probably the last that a body has been found in a hot tub. I've not seen one myself, but in 2013, I think it was, Whitney Houston was found in her bath which was incredibly hot — she'd been there for some time, many hours, and there was a high degree of skin slippage. It's called the Nikolsky sign, if you want to know. This one has been there, I would say at this stage, considerably longer than two days. Text book says that around thirty-six hours after death, neck, abdomen, shoulders and head would start to form a discoloured green, followed by bloating. Here, gentlemen, is that effect. We start by taking water temperature and water samples and of course, the exact time.'

'DS Jones has that information, don't you, Jones? Taken from the display at the front of the machine at the moment we discovered the body.' Jones, who was in the process of emptying his stomach for the second time into an adjacent rose-bed, waved an arm in the affirmative.

'Well, we should drain the water. There's a plug thing bottom right, then you three get out of the way and let the medicos do the moving.' She pointed at the underneath of the hot-tub. 'I want the filters bagged and checked together with a sample of the water — after this length of time, bodily fluids seep out, let alone blood.'

Both LeFanu and Jones looked away, with LeFanu commenting, almost under his breath and audible only to DS Jones, 'Does everyone have to be so graphic. Give me an old-fashioned shooting or stabbing anytime.'

Dr Renata, eye-brows raised at his remark, continued to her team, 'And have the thermostat checked for accuracy. Might be an idea to get a representative from Jacuzzi to explain how the things work. There's a phone number on that label above the radio console, bottom left. Find out who checked and balanced the chemicals and when. That would give you some pegs in the ground regarding dates.'

LeFanu nodded to Jones, who acknowledged the request. 'Doc? Is this natural causes or sudden and suspicious?' LeFanu was showing his impatience, his mind trying to connect the incidents in the village.

'I don't know. Give me some breathing space and I'll see if there's anything to point us in the right direction. Despite the discolouration, there is evidence of some bruising on the shoulders and neck consistent with forcible holding — perhaps under water. It'll take a proper examination to establish anything else. Drowning is a possibility, but this one may be complicated. Finger prints are impossible after this length of time, but somewhat academic if we have an ID. Unconscious from a blow to the head and then being forcibly held underwater. All are possibilities. But you will have to wait for the PM. And there's a lesion which could be a chain of some description — like a Saint Christopher medallion, maybe being wrenched from his neck.'

'Right and thank you. My first thought, Doctor, is, or rather from Google,' he tapped his mobile phone to indicate the information he had found, 'is that people do die of heart failure if the temperature is too high or they have a weak heart, and there have been instances of drowning, but the top was locked down. Although, I suppose, that may even be possible. People do lock them down to prevent kids and others using them. Perhaps someone locked it down without knowing about the body?'

'Are you trying to do my job, Detective Chief Inspector?' There was a distinct note of sarcasm in Doctor Renata's voice.

'No, no, sorry. Almost musing out loud, that's all. No, I'm beginning to think it is another murder. Too many 'could be' and 'might be' questions.' She could see that he was assembling all the available information as he spoke.

'People who believe that a death like this hides the time and location to any killing have probably watched too many police thrillers on TV. Not so. It just makes it more difficult to be precise, but the body and internal fluids, even stomach contents, are effectively cooked after long exposure to temperatures in water of 37.2 degrees Celsius, as the thermostat seemed to have been registering. I would guess that he has been in here two to three days. But don't hold me too it. There is, of course, still the possibility of a simple drowning, but we'll know more after the post mortem. Patience, Detective Chief Inspector!'

LeFanu himself gagged, the bile rising in his throat at the thought. 'Thanks, so maybe Friday or Saturday onwards, Doctor. That means, possibly, no probably, two murders and a convoluted wholesale burglary. Who the blazes is behind this? Right, Jones, meeting of all those not keeping the crime sites safe back in the control room in fifteen minutes. No excuses.'

And to the forensic pathologist, 'Doctor, please let me know if there are any obvious signs of violence or whatever as soon as possible, even if it is a guesstimate. Jones will be there at the post-mortem, won't you, Jones? Good experience, eh? I need to know something, anything, before the balloon goes up with the media. They're circling already after Monday's events and this could be a very high profile death and we don't need to be pilloried in every red rag top in the country and maybe even wider.'

LeFanu scratched his right ear — a habit of a life-time when he was seriously puzzled. '*Merde*, I just don't get it,' he mumbled, half to himself. 'Theft I can understand, usually, but the death of the guy on the terrace back there and then this. C'mon, Jones, back to the drawing board and I'll contact HQ for some more assistance. We need to be doing door-to-door. If this was a day or so different in timing then maybe someone saw something or someone. And I don't understand why the uniform boys didn't spot the rear door was open.'

'At the time, sir, it was just a matter of ringing the bell and waiting. The guys just didn't know which house had been done.'

'Hmmm!' LeFanu was not amused by this oversight.

They ducked under the police tape that surrounded the Jacuzzi and the land between it and the house and yet more, securing the whole premises, signed out with the constable on guard and returned to their cars. Jones had a word with the uniformed people to ensure the house was secure without touching the doors before the scene of crime people had investigated. A two-minute drive brought them to the Nissen hut control centre, where a group of police and civilian help were standing outside in the cold; some smoking; some eating burgers — an enterprising vendor had, somehow or other breached the police cordon around the village and turned up outside the adjacent pub and was doing a roaring trade.

'Sir, excuse me.' One of the uniformed constables, interrupted Jones's train of thought. 'Constable Judy Bell, sir.' A pretty young thing who had recently joined the squad and DS Jones knew had aspirations to get into CID. 'If there's a body in this Jacuzzi and someone either killed the victim there or put him there after killing him, they would be rather wet, wouldn't they? Wet towels, clothing or something?'

'Good stuff, Constable. Yes, they would, and if they're wet there'd be towels or robes or clothing which may be dry now but could be dirty or soiled and could help forensics with DNA. Get yourself up there now and check. But be careful, it is a crime scene until further notice and maybe two, what with the theft and then this death. Is that OK with you, sir?' LeFanu nodded and Judy Bell walked off.

'Incidentally, Jones, what the hell is that burger van doing here? This whole village should have been sealed off.'

'Already given him his marching orders, sir. Apparently stores his van in the winter months in one of the village farm's barns. Bit enterprising and the lads and lasses needed some sustenance, short term. Thought we could ask the publican if he could lay on some grub and coffee. I don't expect he's doing a roaring trade at the moment.'

'Mmmm. Do it. Later, we'll go over to the pub and see if there's any local gossip.'

Jones smiled at the thought of a warm table inside the old converted cottages that were The William and Mary pub and the latent promise of a beer and maybe some hot food. 'Sir, one neighbour told our guys that Lord Groombridge's housekeeper was away whilst he was off skiing in Switzerland, France or wherever. He goes every year at this time and she goes to her family, they think. She only works Wednesday through Friday, unless he has visitors, so she won't have been here since Friday, ten days ago. Maybe she does the Jacuzzi chemical balancing thing? I sent a text to my brother and he says the chemicals need to be done every few days; more if it is in regular use. Perhaps he came back earlier than expected? We've tried her cottage in the next village but no answer, so the trip to Germany seems to stack up.'

'Are we safe in assuming it is this Groombridge fellow? If so, anyone else than the housekeeper available to confirm identity? Close relatives, family? Wife, maybe? We need definite ID. Find an address in Germany if you must, but find a contact, pronto. And get a download from DVLA and the Passport Office for a photo ID. Won't be good quality photographs, if past experience is anything to go by, but it'll help.' LeFanu was reluctant to assume murder until confirmation or other evidence was found.

'Yes, sir, we'll get the date of birth from the driving licence number anyway. Might help, as you say. Passport office is usually much slower in responding to our requests than the driving licence people, anyway, especially this time of year. And there is a wife in London, apparently. Not got contact details yet, just a feed from a lady in the village, and there's two adult kids in the USA. Again, waiting for some examination of a few papers and a laptop in the house with a seriously encrypted password, so no immediate access to address book functions. No mobile phones, though. Not much paper around, but still looking. No address book or anything — seems like a big clear out. No mail either. Looking into it. Having difficulty with the safe. Got an expert coming in from Ipswich HQ. The whole place is quite spooky, actually. No photos or paintings of real people, which I would have expected. But and it's a big but…, a stack of empty picture frames. Many of them look to be silver. Odd or what?' LeFanu nodded.

'And,' continued Jones, 'just got a call from the doc, sir. Cause of death: blunt force trauma causing massive cranial haematoma, whatever that is, to the back of the head, followed by drowning. There's water in the lungs etc. Probably held under water to make sure of the job, so as to speak.'

'In layman's terms, Jones, a haematoma is damage to a blood vessel, vein or whatever in the brain, causing leakage of blood. Must have been a hefty blow. That probably also answers the question of the bruising that the doc pointed out. Time of death?'

'Just coming to that part. She estimates thirty-six to seventy-two hours prior to our discovery. But she favours Saturday. He'd eaten poached salmon, potato and carrot and some sort of chocolate pudding. The toxicology screen indicates no recent drugs, but alcohol, probably white wine of some sort. Could be champagne. How the hell do they know that? The bubbles wouldn't show would they?'

LeFanu shrugged. 'On the basis of stomach contents,' Jones continued unabated, 'and the bloating of the body and temperature, this is their best estimate. More tests to do. She has modelled a mark on the back of his head. It looks about eighty millimetres in diameter and there's a pattern at the base of the mark consistent with the base of a heavy bottle. It's weird. How do they know that, sir?'

'They've got databases that we've never heard of, Chris. Wonder where he ate his last meal; no signs in the fridge, presumably, of leftovers or whatever?' Jones shook his head. 'Glad they have these sources of information, too. Did she say whether there is any possibility that it could be self-inflicted — say by slipping and banging his head?'

'Well, there are various seats and shelves and corners under water, but she was pretty firm about the bottle theory. D'you reckon they get free samples of bottles to check them out — good if it was champagne — all that free booze…?'

'Get real, Chris.' LeFanu shook his head in frustration.

'Sorry, sir. Mouth running away with brain. Anyway, I've seen the downloaded DVLA licence photo and it certainly looks like it's this Groombridge fellow. Passport stuff, as you predicted, will take longer and won't really add much to the equation — they model the DVLA photo licence on the passport picture.'

'Yes, yes. Finished?' Philippe LeFanu was quick to absorb information and process its relevance and needed to move his thoughts on. Without waiting for anything more than a nod from DS Jones, he continued, 'Where's that young lady, I forget her name, looking for towels and the like?' His mind was flipping from scenario to scenario.

'PC Bell. Judy Bell. She says only towels in a gigantic airing cupboard. All neatly folded and colour co-ordinated, apparently. There is a wet room adjacent to the garden door, but it is absolutely bare. I've asked for the drain to be lifted.' Jones checked his note-book again. 'And sir, no clothes. I mean, if he entered the Jacuzzi of his own accord, he'd have left a pile of clothes somewhere. You wouldn't hang them up and go out in the middle of winter. It's odd.'

'Odd is an understatement. Well done. Good thinking. Don't know much about Jacuzzis, but the guy is naked or nearly so. It's January. I agree, wouldn't you take a robe or a towel with you and hang it up somewhere?'

Jones nodded. LeFanu shrugged and suggested he got someone to ask the suppliers about chemicals and timing. DS Jones continued, 'My brother got some free dressing gowns from Jacuzzi with their logo embroidered on them when he bought his. You'd expect guys like Groombridge to have that sort of thing too, wouldn't you? And WPC Bell says that there's nothing like that anywhere. Maybe they took everything away with them. Because it is bloody funny behaviour in January not to have warm dry stuff to change into. Maybe we should ask his missus, if we could find her.' LeFanu acknowledged the comment with a nod whilst he was clearly thinking about other matters.

His phone rang, interrupting his mental flow. 'Not drowning per se. Blunt head trauma followed by submersion, probably being forced under water whilst unconscious or semi-conscious but incapable. Weapon? Definitely a bottle, Chief Inspector, and without exhaustive testing, it looks like a champagne bottle. That would have caused the injury, judging by the shape of the indentation. There's an odd mark at the base which seems to be the bottle casting as you see on better champagnes. From the shape, we think it is Veuve Cliquot. Not one hundred percent, but close to being definite. A pretty heavy blow by a strong person with an element of surprise would be our surmise.'

'Hold on, Doc!' And turning to DS Jones, he relayed the gist of the doctor's comments.

'And go back to the house and look for food scraps, maybe in a freezer if not the fridge, dirty plates etc., and in particular, champagne glasses and champagne bottles — empty and full. Sorry, but search the dustbins and recycling bins, whatever. Get the uniformed guys to help.'

He smiled at the thought of uniform's reaction to having to root through the dustbins. 'Sorry, Doctor. Sent them out to search. Maybe we'll strike lucky.'

'One last thing, Chief Inspector. Underneath the body, we found a model car — kid's toy, die-cast. A green Mercedes 500SL Pagoda convertible, it says on the bottom. 'Made in China' inevitably. 1/43 scale. Whilst that's odd in itself, it looks new, but has been painted badly — not original. Maybe there's a message?'

'Interesting! Doesn't sound like the sort of house that has kids around. Everything seems to have its place, according to DS Jones here. Tidy to a fault, verging on OCD. I'll think on it. Send me some pictures, will you?' Oh, hold on, again, Doc!'

Calling to Jones, he added, 'And see if there are any kids toys around. Pronto!' And then, 'Sorry, Doctor. Sending Sergeant Jones and his team there. Maybe he'll find something that'll give us a lead. There's an increasing amount of odd bits to this story.'

LeFanu's mobile rang fifteen minutes later whilst he was marking up the action boards with Sergeant Shaw. 'Jones, sir... No empty champagne bottles or opened bottles. Checked with the neighbours; they said the bins were all emptied on Monday morning as usual, even though it was a bank holiday weekend. First dustbin and recycling collection of the New Year. Looks like the housekeeper put them out in advance. If it's anything like my bin men that time of year, it's all erratic as to when they empty them, and we're just unlucky in that Monday was the day. But I did look in the dishwasher like they did in an episode of New Tricks — I like that programme because... '

He was stopped in mid-sentence by LeFanu, who, from his voice was losing patience. 'Yes, Jones, we all know of your love of TV police thrillers. Saints preserve us from film and television buffs. Was there anything in the bloody dishwasher?'

'No, sir, well, one champagne glass, clean as a whistle. The machine had done a full cycle. But that makes a set of five champagne glasses, called flutes apparently, but you'd know that, sir, wouldn't you? Anyway, probably one missing to make six, but an odd one might have been broken anytime in the past, I suppose. Apart from the one glass, absolutely empty, not even plates and cutlery, which we expected to find because the doc said he'd eaten recently. I mean before he died. Oh, and no sign of any children, toys or the usual kids' stuff. I did check the shredder. Few bits of stuff in there, so I've bagged it for forensics — looks like photo paper. Anyway, one lady, a cleaning lady at a nearby neighbours, said there had been a blonde woman out the back with a black beret sort of hat. That'd be Sunday. There's a rear gate onto a field and then the road. She says there was a small blue car, with a tail-gate, she thinks, full of black plastic bin liners. It passed her on the road near the bus-stop lay-by about ten minutes later. She can't swear that it was the same vehicle but believes so. She says, as it slowed for traffic, it had a label 'DIESEL ONLY' on the petrol tank flap thingy.' He added the parenthesis with his hands. 'Anyway, that'd make it about three p.m. Sunday the 6th, she reckons. And sir, I've laid into the lads for not spotting this rear access door to Porten House and marking it on the plan. Sorry. They couldn't access the house from the front door so left it at that. Sorry.'

'O-kay,' LeFanu said with scepticism, sounding through both syllables. 'Presumably no registration number or any more detail?'

Jones's response told it all.

'Well, store it on the action board for the house-to-house when you get back... Maybe someone else will have seen her. Anyway, it's probably a hire car. These rental companies usually make it obvious about the fuel to use by marking the flap. But maybe a blue hatchback; maybe a hire car... it's too vague to investigate at the moment.'

'Before you go, sir. A thought. Why only one glass and why glass? My brother never allows glass anywhere near his hot-tub. Always plastic. And anyway, a tidy sort of bloke to put his glass in the dishwasher and switch it on for just one glass and then go to the hot-tub.'

'Maybe, maybe, Jones. Our doctor friend thinks he drank more than one glass; maybe the whole bottle? But my thinking too. This whole thing is odd. It's all too clinical. Everything clean and tidy and no loose ends. It does smack of a third party killing him and then cleaning up after himself or herself, if the bin-bag story can be believed. Look around for inconsistencies. There's different MOs here; Porten House differs from the

Manse and so on. So, there is a murderer on the loose. They've been very clever and everything about the thefts and the other death is very well thought through. It's unusual. There's got to be a connection. I just don't believe in coincidence. Maybe they've been too clever or maybe trying, with some success, I might add, if I'm right, to deliberately confuse us.'

'There are loads of champagne bottles in a drinks cupboard thingy, more a room than a cupboard. About twenty bottles of this Veuve stuff with a yellowy orange label the doc was talking about. I'll bring one back, shall I, for forensics? Perhaps it's a batch that can be traced?'

'Good idea, Jones. That's seriously good champagne, probably bought from a wine merchant rather than a supermarket. Maybe a trail there? We'll make a detective of you yet.' LeFanu was not noted for his humour, particularly at an early stage of an investigation, but every now and then he made an attempt. Something about his French origins and humour not translating across the Channel he always maintained. 'There are two ways of looking at this. All the signs are of a clever, somewhat convoluted attempt to muddy the waters. A clumsy try to make it look like accidental death or whatever, and then a real clean up. It's so clumsy, it doesn't fit with the careful and well-executed plan to rob the whole village. The first death might have been the anomaly. We need to look at these things individually and then together. There is a management theory called Ockham's Razor, Jones, which does usually apply in crime investigation. It basically states that the simple answer is probably the right answer. But in this case, it is like someone else responsible for this convoluted mess has read the same book. So it is more like a reverse of the principle. We just have to find the simple raison d'être by discarding all the blind alleys that they're very unhelpfully providing.'

'Yes, I think I understand, but surely, sir, most amateurs who commit a crime do so using methods they read or saw in paper-back crime novels or TV detective stories. Where else would they get their ideas from?'

'Yes, yes, we all like *Midsomer Murders* on television, Jones, and yes, we all know the sergeant there has the misfortune to bear the same name as yours, but there the similarity ends. Let's get back to the matter in hand. Could there be a link with the thieves but not the theft? Why did they choose Porten House?'

'They didn't, though, did they, sir? They chose the majority of the village. All those with occupants within three or four hundred metres and a couple of the second homes. There's some serious money and influence in this village from a relatively small number of expensive big houses. It was just the central core and Porten House that seems to have had the big thefts. They ignored some houses and even the pub.'

'Yes, yes. But think widely. Could they disguise the real purpose of the thefts and maybe the murder and maybe the more valuable stuff in Porten House or the Manse or the bloody MP's house…' He paused, assessing his comments. 'Yes, maybe that's it. All the other houses are a blind to the real purpose. I'll need to think that through more clearly. But there are a myriad of 'maybe statements' in what I've just said. What if person A wanted to get rid of person B, our body, and got wind of the burglaries and saw it as an opportunity and maybe a way of passing the blame onto the thieves. Maybe Person A figured out, or thought, that the Jacuzzi murder would distort the prediction of the actual time of death, allowing them to be well away and armed with alibis. Though, you may well have a point, Jones. If you had inside knowledge of the whereabouts of the housekeeper, with her annual German visit, our victim would be unlikely to be found until the German lady returned, except in exceptional circumstances like the thefts and our subsequent arrival on the scene. So, deliberate timing messed up by the thefts?'

LeFanu paused, summing up the issues. 'Mmmm, good point. Without the thefts, he would have been unlikely to have been found for anything up to a week or so. Indeed, did the thefts occur after he had been killed and maybe the thieves didn't hear or smell or see what we saw? Walked right past the Jacuzzi, maybe? Doesn't bear thinking about. So, who has motive? How many people crossed swords with this Groombridge character? How many would take that to extremes and like to see him dead? Sounds like you've got some checking up to do. Put someone bright onto it. And don't forget Debretts for the Lord and Lady bit and those two offspring in the USA. Presumably the elder of them would inherit the title and suchlike. Motive? Lots to do, eh, DS Jones? Get back here as soon as possible. And find the bloody wife before the media do.'

Calling to Jones as he walked away, LeFanu asked, 'How did he get there anyway? You pointed out the open fronted garage and there were no cars there?'

'Maybe in the blue hatchback, sir.'

Again, he shrugged and added, 'And where did he get his fancy lunch?

Chapter 15

The next morning, Wednesday the 7th, Jones's team didn't take long to establish background, most being readily available online, and a call to the Institute of Directors in Pall Mall, London gave them a whole string of Directorships past and present with connections to Lord Groombridge and under his previous name, Anthony Waller. The detail Jones's people had established was complicated and thorough.

In DCI LeFanu's tiny office, Jones summarised, 'Director of Paddick Classic Car Auctions PLC, non-executive director of ASATS, a clothing company based in London, Director of Beech Underwriting, a Lloyd's syndicate turned PLC — insurance stuff for the rich and famous, by all accounts, and a half dozen other directorships here and in the US of A and Switzerland.' LeFanu wrote down the company names and gave a 'thumbs-up' to DS Jones.

'Hasn't got an inherited family pile or historic mansion sort of thing but very comfortably off,' Jones continued. 'Rumour has it that he got his lordship thing by donating a ton of money to the Liberal Democrat party in 2010. Porten House is listed as his main house. Married first to a Melissa Grey, old family money. She died in a skiing accident in Courchevel fifteen years ago. Nothing fishy, by all accounts, except apparently the same place he visits every year. Maybe that's strange; maybe not. Currently married to Lady Groombridge. Her? Old money again, sir. Family name of Foubert, French origins, goes back to William the Conqueror. Apparently, according to a source I know at Tatler magazine, the marriage is solid as a rock. Both parties were known to play the field, but nothing recent. Could be a motive, perhaps. Bump off the husband could be beneficial to the wife. Life assurance, maybe? Family with plenty of money — old money, they call it. She lives in London, Chelsea, inevitably, not a regular visitor to this neck of the woods, and in Montargis, France, the French family chateau. I believe that's where she is at the moment, says my contact. So, no idea where that is but you're the Frenchman, sir.'

'Umm. A hundred kilometres or so south of Paris, Jones. Pretty place, too, lots of canals. Get Europol to do some searching. Any children?'

'Not from that marriage, as we knew. Two from the first, based in the States; one in New York and one in San Francisco — neither married or with kids, we believe. Got the Americans doing some checking on their movements. Could be a motive — inheritance or even the title. Anyway, should hear in a day or so.'

'Discreetly, Jones, discreetly. We don't even know one hundred percent if it's murder. And we are assuming it is Groombridge, as I said before. Agreed, on the balance of probability, but we must be careful. Talk to the company secretaries of those organisations where he's involved. They don't need to know he's dead, so just the 'helping us with our enquiries' approach for the time being. Find out the roles, popularity, background stuff. That may be another source of motive. Get all that information on the wipe-off boards. It's easier to glance at it than reading a screen. Find out about inheritance rules. We, certainly I, don't know how that works. And then we need more on the first death. Has he been identified yet? Oh, whilst you're about it, ask if anyone at the Duxford car auction place could identify Groombridge. It isn't that far away. But be subtle. Seems like the wife either doesn't know or care about her husband's whereabouts. Where the bloody hell is she?' He scratched his right ear in puzzlement.

'The auction house is actually in Duxford, not that it matters much regarding distance. In answer to your first question, no, sir. But we've got the registered user of the Vauxhall Astra with the broken window from the vehicle identification number and spoken to the company that owns it. It's an electronics company based in Milton Keynes and the registered user is a David Grant, one of their sales managers, who should be in Bristol but they're unable to contact him. Maybe that's our man? Seeking more information about him and his employers have promised to scan a photograph from their HR records after the usual arguments about data protection and human rights. Should be here soon. Secondly, I'll ask at the auction house. As you say, it isn't too far from here, so maybe there'll be someone.'

'We'll wait on that ID, but it's another strange event. It's bloody miles from Bristol. Why here? Anything on the scrawled message on the patio door glass?' Jones shaking his head gave LeFanu the answer. 'How goes the search west of the village?'

'Negative, sir. I've extended the range to five miles, with Edwards' help and some uniformed guys from the next patch.'

'There are too many questions unanswered. It's uncanny. I want answers. I think a trip to the local pub is in order. I've always found that it's the centre of gossip in small communities and we need to put some background to our thinking and the key characters involved. Ready?'

Jones nodded and they walked across the village green towards the pub, little more than a cottage in a row of half a dozen cottages in various stages of disrepair. A couple of trestle tables, with ashtrays desperately needing emptying, each with a stained and torn umbrella, stood outside on the muddy grass.

They introduced themselves to Tim Whitaker, the landlord, a florid-faced individual of around fifty, wearing jeans and a sweatshirt bearing the Greene King brewer's logo. He explained that there were only the two of them at this time of year, he and his wife, Kylie, who waved from behind the bar at the sound of her name. Whitaker had been the landlord for twenty years, but as the village lost a lot of permanent residents, largely agricultural workers being replaced by second-homers, the business had reduced so that it could only now support the two of them. He had a micro-brewery in one of the adjoining cottages that enabled them to make ends meet, and they sold a few crates to people in surrounding villages and towns. He was a garrulous know-all type, as LeFanu had suspected, supported by Edwards' observations earlier in the week.

'What can I do for you, Chief Inspector?' After ordering a beer for Jones and a dubious glass of Bordeaux for himself and a couple of the ubiquitous beefburgers and chips with a mucky squeezy bottle of Heinz tomato ketchup plonked in the middle of the table, LeFanu started on his agenda. 'Tell me about the Faruk couple, Mr Whitaker.'

'Ikky, that's a nickname for Iqbal Faruk, was a regular for a couple of months and drank like a fish. Often we had a chin-wag over the bar. Sometimes his wife, Shaida, came in as well for her Henri Winterman's panatellas...' He looked at DS Jones, who wore a puzzled look. 'They're long thin cigars, Sergeant. And yes, it is unusual for a woman to smoke them, and more unusual for a lady of that religion. But the customer's always right. We have to buy them in specially. In fact...' He looked up and called Kylie over, telling her to cancel an order with the catering suppliers for any more stocks.

Kylie, LeFanu thought, was around thirty and probably had always been a barmaid, judging by her blousy appearance, with Jones making it obvious that he admired her cleavage, forcing LeFanu to nudge him unseen under the table. Noticing the look and reaction, Whitaker announced that Kylie was his second wife, having been the bar manager until his first wife had departed for pastures new.

Kylie, leaning provocatively on the adjacent bar, commented that she had always thought that Shaida wasn't her real name because Ikky had called her Amira. 'That's "princess" in Syrian, I looked it up. She dressed like a Muslim with the hijab some of the time, but I saw her in a Bury St Edmunds coffee shop once in jeans and a spaghetti strapped top showing most of her tits. Sorry.'

LeFanu smiled. It was just the sort of information he sought. 'Smoking? I thought that wasn't allowed in Muslim thinking.'

'Well, she did, and irrespective of any religious rules or the weather, stood outside and puffed her way through a couple of packets a week. Funny couple. I quite liked them. Anyway, must get on.'

'A moment, please. Both of you, tell me about Lord Groombridge and his wife.'

Tim Whitaker looked at his wife and shrugged. 'Not much to tell, really. He bombed around the village in his fancy car like he owned the place, far too fast too, but never came in here. Arrogant bastard...'

Kylie interrupted, 'Last time I saw him was when he raced through the village in that fancy car of his just as I was locking up shop — about ten thirty-ish. I'd gone outside to padlock the hatch to the cellars, Tim had crashed out in bed long before that and I...'

Jones stopped her in mid-sentence. 'When was that? Can you recall? It is important.'

'Friday. Yes, I'm sure it was Friday. Last Friday. We'd had quite a bit of business on the 1st and things had dropped off, which is why we closed early on the Friday.'

Jones acknowledged the comment, saying it was useful to know when exactly Groombridge had arrived home, bearing in mind what had followed. 'No sighting of the car on Saturday, for example?' She shook her head and her husband likewise. Then he asked about Lady Groombridge.

Kylie was quick to answer. 'That bitch. Wife? Well, I think I saw her twice in five years. She came in here with a couple of her friends —

glamorous types. Got the feeling they wanted to mix with the rough people. Had the cheek to ask if my tits were real. Gave them a kick, I suppose.' She shrugged, seeing Jones staring at her cleavage, and added that she was fed up with the car transporters that delivered fancy cars covered in weather proof covers with posh logos at all hours of the day and night, blocking the narrow access roads into the village and messing up the verges. 'And he, Groombridge, well, the taxi firms did well in delivering and collecting all sorts of trollops to his house. Mind you, we did well from the endless suppliers and tradesmen delivering things and mending…' She stopped when she saw Jones looking puzzled. 'You know, painters, window cleaners and the like and those car people stopping here for a drink, so maybe we shouldn't complain.' She glanced at her husband who shrugged.

'Mrs Davis? Stephanie. Anything about her?' LeFanu tried to bring the conversation back to his subject.

'The whole village, I should think, knew she had a bit on the side and regular, at that. Do these people really think that a car parked in a field on the outskirts of a small village overnight won't be noticed? Stupid cow.' Both she and Tim had very little positive to say about the other residents and second homers. The MP popped in for a couple of drinks now and then — Tim reckoned he had told his wife, miserable woman that she is, that he was out canvassing amongst his electorate. They covered the other residents but nothing untoward was known.

'A last thing, if we may.' DS Jones looked at them both. 'The 'so-called' police on Monday night. Any thoughts?'

Kylie started. 'Their hair was too long. Like you see on the old TV police thrillers. The more I looked at them, well, I had my doubts, but my husband thought they were the real McCoy, didn't you, darling?'

'There you go, twenty-twenty hindsight again.' He looked across at her.

'Thanks. If there are any more questions, perhaps you would help?' LeFanu, not wanting to get involved in a squabble, paid the bill and they got up to leave.

Jones had one more question. 'The cigars. Anyone else smoke them? Did Mrs Faruk smoke them on her own outside?'

Both Kylie and Tim nodded. The moment was defused.

'Perhaps one of my team could ask you to supply some food and drinks to the team over at the village hall — non-alcoholic, I'm afraid.' Tim gave

LeFanu a thumbs-up sign.

LeFanu, outside in the cold air, told DS Jones to empty one of the ashtrays into an evidence bag. He added that they had not learned much, but it all helped, and the Faruks were probably 'actors' for the specific reason of diversion and long gone, but it would be worth checking but not to give it priority. Chris Jones wondered out loud why Groombridge hadn't been in to see Kylie, bearing in mind his liking of bimbos. LeFanu nodded in agreement and suggested he didn't use words like that.

Chapter 16

George finally got through to Terry.

'This is urgent, Tel. Plan C, now! Get the long wheel base Transits packed and out of there by tomorrow morning and staggered departure as planned. All the crap at the back and adjacent to the side door to the load bay. Good for a quick inspection, anyway. Cars too — get them ready to go. Strip them of their livery. Mr White will be there to clean up tomorrow after you've all gone. Go! And Terry get off the bloody phone. I told you before it's not for personal use. Good job I got hold of you, at last. The fuzz are speeding up their thinking. I'll talk to you later.' He didn't tell Terry about the second body the police had discovered. It had sounded like they were all running around like headless chickens. He finished his call by adding, 'You ring me in one hour forty-five minutes. Understand?' George was annoyed. He'd tried several times and each time left messages but no returned call from Terry. Ian White was on standby to move the lorries with his cousin, who'd assisted in driving to the factory but knew no more than it was a little 'cash no questions deal'.

The unloading and re-packing the long wheel base Ford Transit vans took time. Each looked like it was a house move, with cardboard boxes, mattresses, white goods, bedding, ladders, tools and equipment — all clearly on display, were anyone to raise the tail-gates. Behind those household items lay the real gems of paintings, antique furniture and Persian carpets — all the items that Terry had flagged. The removal lorries were being packed with black plastic bin-bags with the stripped off vinyl sheets bearing the livery of the cars. Each nearly ready to go at a moment's notice.

Wearing latex gloves, they cleaned up around the cooking area and toilet, bagging up the remnants of their stay and discarding their gloves in a separate bag with their police uniforms before donning more clean blue gloves and their own clothes.

Chapter 17

'The answers to some of our enquiries are starting to come in, sir. I don't expect much more now until later today. Got some of the guys to do some chasing then.' Sergeant Shaw clutched a sheaf of papers.

Philippe LeFanu told him to update the boards and talk him through the answers as he did so. 'But Sergeant, call DS Jones and the other team leaders in first, otherwise you'll be repeating yourself and wasting precious time.'

Sergeant Shaw mouthed an obscenity, careful not to allow LeFanu to see his face, muttering about being a servant. Five minutes later, with the group assembled in the small office area, spilling out into the main hall, Shaw started his update.

'Sir, in no particular order, we have the following…' He looked around for approval. 'The dead man is David Grant, the sales manager from an electronics firm, who should have been in Bristol. The DVLA driving licence picture was not good enough, but their scanned personnel file confirmed it. No ideas why he was in Suffolk rather than Bristol. His employers are looking into it. So, still on our lists of possible bad guys.' He looked around for a reaction and received none.

'Well, the rental agency from Eccles, Mickleson & Latham, were asked to take a short term rental agreement for a guy and his family, who turned out to be Faruk and wife. He was on a short-term work contract in Ipswich, they were told, and as winter is a difficult time to rent out properties in this neck of the woods, they got agreement from the property owner to go for it. Needless to say, the firm in Ipswich denies all knowledge and Mr & Mrs Faruk have disappeared off the face of the earth. His rental reference is from a hoax address in Ashford, Kent. I guess the agents were pleased to get a cash-in-advance deal. A dead end. No reason at this stage, I think, to doubt the agency.' He paused for breath and comment.

'Who is the owner of the property, sergeant? With all their apparent planning, it seems strange that they were reliant on the chance of a vacant property where, exactly where, they wanted it. Collusion, maybe?'

'Lord Groombridge, sir. Well, one of his companies into property management anyway. We obviously can't ask him now that he's the jacuzzi dead body, can we?' He looked around for a snigger but only saw deadpan faces. 'Anyway, apparently he's got quite a few small properties around East Anglia and the Fens — none of any particular value. The agents reckon worth around two hundred and fifty K in total and all with second charges from the banks. We've checked them all to make sure none of the others is being used by the gang.'

'Thank you, Sergeant. And thank the team, please,' LeFanu responded. 'Still strange that they found that place — Rose Cottage — bloody convenient. Bear that in mind, please.' He looked across to Shaw and gave him the sign to continue.

'OK! Next, the interviews with the residents achieved little apart from moaning and groaning, except, that is, for the little item about the aerial photographs. We've established from a sticker on the back, that it was a small firm at Swaffham, an old war-time aerodrome, that does these sort of pictures. Apparently, a Mr Ian White of Ipswich arranged it through them and collected the pictures in mid-December. Age about fifty, medium build, brown hair, smartly dressed, wallet full of cash. Address in Ipswich. That's all we know. Got someone checking the name and address, probably a false one but we'll try. Couldn't believe we'd be that lucky as a man called I. White lives there. Checking as we speak, sir, but he's the best part of ninety. Cash on the nail deal, no paper-work sort of stuff. We believe it was this man who was casing the houses for the thefts. Apparently, he asked to use the toilet in at least five houses on the same afternoon.'

LeFanu interrupted, 'Don't spend too much time on that. If other matters are anything to go on, that'll be another dead end. Better to try to ID this Mr White from the pilot or whoever at Swaffham. Maybe they've got CCTV?'

'No CCTV, but I hear what you say, sir.' Shaw looked again at his notes. 'Then there's a guy at the car auction company, a Mr Guy Scott, a director and the company secretary, who knew the victim. Says the wife, Charlotte, is French and comes from some place called…' he glanced at his notes, 'Montargis. And she's normally in France, rather than in their flat in Chelsea at this time of year, and her husband is skiing, apparently. Her name before her marriage was Bertin and at the time of the marriage her husband-to-be was just plain old Anthony Waller. Think I've got that right.

He, Scott, that is, attended his wedding reception party here a few years back and has got some photos, as you'd expect. He's coming over tomorrow morning to Ipswich hopefully to do an informal identification of the body in the Jacuzzi. Well not "in the Jacuzzi", you know what I mean…'

'We know about Montargis. Get on with it, Sergeant. What do you mean "hopefully"?'

Shaw bristled at the criticism. 'Well, he doesn't seem terribly keen — weak stomach for that sort of thing, he says. I did quiz him but…'

'C'mon, Sergeant. These people have homes to go to.' DS Jones was frustrated by Shaw's casual approach.

'Hang on a minute, Sergeant Jones.' Shaw was dedicated to detail but had never been a good communicator and often caused frustration at the amount of time it took him to get to the crux of any matter. Every criticism bit deep and fuelled his disillusionment with today's police methods and made him count the days until his retirement in 2017.

Jones bristled. 'Detective Sergeant, please, if you're going to take that tone with me, Sergeant Shaw…'

LeFanu stood, clearly frustrated. 'Enough! Hear it from me, gentlemen. Get on with it and stop petty squabbling. Why would Scott volunteer and then play the weak stomach routine? I'll call the *Quai D'Orsay*…' Seeing the look on Shaw's face, he continued, '…that's the French police in Paris, to find her or at the very worst to contact her to get her to contact us, and quickly. And get that man Scott to come here too.'

Shaw, pleased that the pressure had been taken off him, continued reading from his notes. 'Both of the victim's parents are dead, some years ago, apparently, so no hope of formal ID there. Got that from LinkedIn, sir.' He looked up, hoping for some praise, which was not forthcoming. 'It was about the time he got his peerage thing. Probably used his inheritance or something, as he effectively bought the bloody title for thirty grand. Anyway, they died of…'

LeFanu interrupted, 'Unless it is likely to influence this case, I think that'll be *information inutile*, as the French say. Useless information, in other words. Mark it up and carry on, quickly, please.'

Shaw frowned and glanced again at his notes, ticking them off with a pencil as he went. 'That's about it for the moment, sir. We're awaiting confirmation from the US about his two children, adults really, Richard and Naomi, resident there for some time but nothing untoward as far as we know. Also, we've started an enquiry with Swansea vehicle licensing about all Ford Focus 2011 to 2013 models in light paint colours that have been sold, bought privately or rented in the last three months. Thought the so-called police cars could have had a lick of paint or something. That's it.'

'Bright thinking about the Ford cars, Mr Shaw.' LeFanu smiled; he knew that a little bit of praise worked wonders with police jobsworths like Shaw. Two of the team glared at Shaw, who always liked to be in the limelight, but rarely was with senior officers, expecting, however, sycophancy from his junior ranks. 'Have we got a wife or family for this David Grant fellow? Seems to me that we've closed down, or potentially closed down, some avenues which doesn't really help us, or me, when it comes to the press conference this evening. Is that what the bad guys want, or are they sufficiently clever to have orchestrated all these blind alleys? Where is, or are, the errors? There has to be one or more. There always is. Tomorrow, at eight a.m., ladies and gentlemen, we start all over. I've asked HQ for some more civilian bodies to help and the publican is bringing over some food and stuff.' There was a desultory cheer. LeFanu picked up his coat and left the building, heading for his car.

Chapter 18

'Issy? It's George. You heard all that? A second body in a Jacuzzi. How did that happen? Who the hell is it? We're going to have serious heat now. The Faruk people — away and safe? Issy, it's like there is another parallel plan to ours. Don't know who or what, but if we were nabbed by the boys in blue, it'll be the devil of a job to explain.'

'Yes, mate. Couldn't agree more. We need to back off and fast. Don't know who the second body is, unless it's this Lord fellow. They're not saying anyway, or if they are, they were out of range of the microphones. Bit weird the Jacuzzi bit. I can't believe it's anything to do with our team but then there's the first body — David someone or other. Have to wait and see. Means the boys in blue will rack up the activity, so we'll have to be ready. No problem re. our Middle-Eastern chums. Car's at the bottom of a chalk-pit in Kent and they're on their way to a holiday in Sharm-el-Sheikh. I took them to Gatwick myself. All legit, under their real names. They did a good job making sure the local fuzz were not intruding on the village on Monday night. A local saw them, but it was an old biddy with only half her marbles, apparently, so no great shakes even if she were to report a suspicious car. She rapped on the window and told them to 'bugger off'. They pretended to be putting their clothes on — you can guess the rest.' Issy was laughing at the picture he'd conjured up.

'OK. That's really funny… I'll tell them to finish the process of loading and start the disappearing act. You'll have time to clean up and then you get out of there fast on Thursday late afternoon.'

Chapter 19

'Jones.' He answered the telephone begrudgingly. It was ten o'clock on a Wednesday night.

'Chris, it's Philippe. Not interrupting anything?' He paused. 'OK to talk?'

Chris Jones muttered an OK, whilst he wouldn't admit that his girlfriend, Cathy, was slouched on the sofa next to him in a state of undress, slurping white wine.

'Sorry to bother you, but I've been thinking…'

'Thought you would be, sir. What's up?'

'The press conference went well. Couple of off the wall questions about the MP's stuff being missing — national security issues — almost like they'd been given a feed of information. Probably the wife of the MP. Usual stuff in response — proceeding down several avenues. Unusual crime with complications. Yes, there's been a death but cannot release information until next of kin have been contacted. Anyway, got me thinking. We are making connections, but the modus operandi are totally different. How's this? Burglary motive is obvious — rich pickings and maybe Government papers — need time to sort that out. Clever way of moving everyone out of the centre of the village. I read the house-to-house reports carefully. Aerial photos could have been the way to give them detailed plans and layouts, and by all accounts, they let the photograph salesman into their houses to use their toilets. For God's sake, how many times does anyone need the toilet in the course of a morning? That's rhetorical, Chris. This David guy is either one of them and quarrelled or had an accident, but that doesn't explain the writing on the patio door or his car having the number plates removed. My guess is he was wrong place, wrong time, if being with his lady love, as the publican told us, is the wrong place! Maybe he's a burglar on his own. Doubt it myself, but we need to check. Need to talk to his work colleagues over at Milton Keynes. So, it ends up as a serious burglary. And then there's Anthony Groombridge — that is so different. Deliberately clumsy, toy cars, empty wine glass, clean towels, no photos etc., etc., so what were we supposed to discover? What was, or is, the message that the bad guys are trying to let us discover? What was the motive? Money or inheritance or revenge or jealousy or what? We need to separate the two things — burglary with, perhaps an accidental death and a murder, not necessarily by the same person or persons but not to be ignored either. I think we should have two teams and a link man between them. Organise it tomorrow, perhaps? What d'you think?'

'I think you are right, sir. Like you, I've been mulling it over. The autopsy on David Grant is more like accidental death. Could be a fall or being pushed. Apparently, there is bruising on both arms and no ID, keys, phone or anything but there were samples from the carpets and signs of recent sexual activity and the remnants of a lot of booze, consumed no more than ten hours before. I've a man visiting the Milton Keynes HQ of his firm tomorrow morning and David Grant's wife is coming over to make the formal identification at Ipswich morgue. I think we need to talk to this Mrs Davis woman too. She isn't telling the whole story, but my gut feel is that David Grant's death is a side show and he's nothing to do with the main stream. Maybe he was shagging this Davis woman, quite tasty by all accounts. Sorry, I have said that before, I think.' He had noticed the raised eyebrow of his boss at the remark before. 'And was caught with his trousers down. Maybe he was in the wrong place at the wrong time, as you said, and the bad guys caught him and roughed him up a bit — pushed, shoved, who knows. Yes, sir, I know, a lot more 'maybes'. And another thing that came in late — the inheritance thing is not a motive. Not that sort of peerage, apparently. Don't quite understand, but will know more tomorrow.'

'Chris, there are still too many questions unanswered. We need to find their base. That's got to be a priority. Oh, and I've spoken to the French police. They're going to contact Lady Groombridge this evening, if she's at this place we were told about. Apparently, it's a chateau. Bit of money there. Should hear tomorrow. One question for you to mull over… If it had been snowing, wind, like normal for January, fierce and from the east, etc. etc. how would they have managed to pull this little lot off, sorry for the grammar! Could they have delayed things; did they have a contingency plan? There were a huge number of logistics involved and a foot or two of snow would have scuppered the whole thing. We've been lucky in one sense that it is relatively mild for the time of year, but no one could have second guessed that. That's it. Thanks, Chris. Sorry to disturb you.

Goodnight.'

Chris Jones snapped off his phone and sighed, his brain racing nineteen to the dozen. A lot of thinking and not a lot of sleep, tonight, he murmured, just as well as his girlfriend being fast asleep, probably with boredom.

Chapter 20

Eight thirty a.m., Thursday, PC Jim Edwards button-holed DS Jones as soon as he got out of his car. 'I've got a bug on my car, sir.'

Jones looked at him strangely, 'As an opening gambit, Edwards, that is likely to get you a transfer somewhere remote, pretty quickly. Explain.'

'I cleaned my car first thing this morning. In the half light, first day for ages without rain, and found this bit of plastic stuck under the rear bumper. I didn't touch it, I mean, remove it, but have a look.' He pointed to his car.

Jones bent down and saw the little black box. Taking plastic evidence bags from his pocket and carefully not touching it with bare hands, he pulled it from the bumper and dropped it into a bag. 'Well done, Edwards, firstly for keeping your car clean at this hour of the day and this time of year and secondly for finding this. You're right, it's a tracking device — a bug, as you call it. Why? We need to tell the boss. This could be important.'

Edwards was positively beaming and with renewed confidence. 'I reckon, sir, that they, the bad guys, wanted to know my whereabouts on Monday night.'

'Quite probably. Let's make the others aware of it, shall we? Well done.'

DS Jones found LeFanu just before the meeting started and showed him the plastic bag containing the black box. They shared Edwards' opinion about the why. DCI LeFanu shared his concern that this find confirmed his belief that the thefts were professionally orchestrated.

Promptly, at nine a.m. that Thursday morning, the group under Jones met Edwards's team, who reported that a Mrs Agnes Pearce had stopped one of his police cars and spoken to the WPC driver about a suspicious car.

'An old Citroën, we reckon, because she described the two arrow heads of the logo on the front, parked outside her house on the Monday evening, late, around mid-night. She'd been taking her dog for a walk and seen two people canoodling, as she put it. A man and a woman, with the woman in the driving seat. She kept an eye on them and they raced off at about two a.m. In the opposite direction than they were pointing — away from the village. I'm paraphrasing, sir. She's an old lady but seems to be compos mentis. She did say there was a lot of late night goods traffic that night going through that road. And there's a load of cigar butts in the road, which annoyed her because she does look after her house and garden, even the verge outside.'

'Crikey, she's a late night bird. Why didn't she report it?' Jones said, 'If only people would report odd behaviour, it'd make our life so much easier.'

'Apparently quite common, sir. Lots of lovers meetings sort of thing, but strange it was on that junction, the B2013. It's a main access into the village about a mile out, but not a busy road at any time. And were it not for those fires and if I'd been called out in the night, I probably would have used that route. The fires meant I used the farm tracks.'

'You think it was something to do with it?'

'Yes, sir. I think they were spotting. If the fires hadn't got me out then I could have been going down that road had something else happened. The heavy traffic is really unusual, even at harvesting time. The road's just not up to it and these guys seemed to have had a lot of vehicles'   .

'Makes sense, Edwards. Worth a speculation. Put someone onto exploring the detail with Mrs Pearce — car type, colour etc. etc. Sounds like it could have been these Faruk people and the smoking things fits with what we know from the publican. And you say they had a beat-up Citroën, yes?' Edwards nodded. 'So, let's concentrate on the segment of the countryside that connects with that road. I'll tell the boss. Feels like they could have been some sort of look-out. We did a DNA test on the cigar ends from the pub ashtray, but nothing came up in criminal records.'

Refreshed by a night's sleep and having the press conference out of the way without too much hassle and criticism, LeFanu had re-focussed on the issues and the motivation of his team. They all gathered in the main hall, clutching their Styrofoam cups of coffee, waiting to hear the tasks set for the day whilst the wind and rain whistled past the old building.

He shared the information about PC Edwards's tracking device with the group and said, 'Listen up. If they were smart enough to bug Edwards's car, what else could they have done?' The question posed by LeFanu stopped his team in their tracks. 'I want you to do a bit of dreaming,' he said. 'This group was well organised. They had a purpose. We don't know the full reasons yet, but let's suppose that the death of David Grant was an accident — hitting him to silence him, perhaps came across him unexpectedly. That is the one piece of this jigsaw that I can't rationalise and that may be putting us off the scent. The second death or murder may or may not be connected, but it is connected by definition of being at the same, or roughly the same time, and being in, more or less, the same location.'

The detective chief inspector showed his frustration by pointing at the wipe-off boards. 'A lot of information, but little or no progress.' He continued, not wishing to lose the momentum. 'This is a very high-profile case. We're under the microscope and it's a miracle that the media has been kept at bay with two unexplained and violent deaths and some high profile people baying for our blood.' He looked around the team for acknowledgement of the issues facing them, and continued again. 'We're going round in circles. These people are, or have been, pretty clever. Leading us into cul-de-sacs, blind alleys and making things very tedious. So, ladies and gentlemen.' LeFanu changed tack and asked, 'What would you have done if you were this guy?'

Bringing all his man management skills to bear and trying to create some enthusiasm, LeFanu was trying to get an edge — knowing that much of police work was chance — finding that loophole the villains had overlooked and the coincidence that gave the game away. 'OK! Use the wipe-off board and each of you write one idea that could be a critical success factor for the bad guys. No talking or criticism, in the true spirit of brainstorming — that's for later.'

He handed the marker pen to Sergeant Shaw. Frank was hesitant; new ideas were not his bag. He liked this man, LeFanu, for getting things done, although he found the orders he issued should have been structured and given to junior staff, but he was at a loss with this kind of business analysis exercise. He shrugged his shoulders and passed the pen on to a diminutive WPC standing next to him. LeFanu frowned at the reaction from Shaw. She walked forward, purposefully, and wrote, equally deliberately.

'Get the stuff out of the country.' LeFanu raised an eyebrow, smiled and gestured for the pen to be passed on. Another WPC walked forward, not so self-assured, and started writing. Shaw looked on angrily, concerned that he was so devoid of ideas. She wrote in silence, 'Bug the police headquarters.'

DCI LeFanu was startled. His face told it all. 'Stop! Ladies and gentlemen, stop.' It was quite definitely a command. 'Let's all go outside for a breath of fresh air. We'll reconvene this meeting later.' He walked to the board and wrote quickly and neatly, in capital letters, 'NOT A WORD.'

Half a minute or so later, he called his group together, standing stamping their feet on the tarmac apron in front of the hall, shivering in the damp air on the village green. 'WPC…' he peered at her badge. 'WPC Ford. Come to the front please.' She moved forward. 'Please explain yourself.'

'Well, sir.' Blushing a deep crimson, she started, overwhelmed by the attention she was getting. 'If they could bug Jim, I mean PC Edwards's, car to find out what he was doing, I thought they could bug the village hall here, before we came along, to find out our thinking. It was almost certain we'd be using it. It's the most logical place to base our enquiries. It wouldn't be difficult. Sorry, sir, but that was just an off-the-wall idea. I…'

'Off the wall? Nonsense! That's what good detective work's all about.' He turned to Sergeant Shaw, who was scowling at the rear of the circle. 'Sergeant. Get on the phone and get someone to check out that village hall for surveillance bugs.' As the sergeant walked back towards the hall, he bellowed, 'No, Sergeant, not the 'phone inside. Use your brains, man!' Many in the group sniggered as he got his come-uppance. Shaw gritted his teeth, knowing he hadn't any options.

Shaw muttered under his breath, 'She might have a body to die for but she's still a WPC.'

One of his colleagues, in ear-shot, commented, 'Yes, guv, and she does things for the police uniform that the designers hadn't intended.' Shaw had no option than to smile and nodded, slightly embarrassed that he had been overheard.

With his crew standing shivering on the grass outside the hut, LeFanu knew he had to engender some activity to keep the spark going. 'Right, some action and some thinking. First, I want a team to do another house-to-house, starting first thing tomorrow, and find out if there is any commonality. Someone visiting, whatever. We've got a tenuous link with this man selling aerial photos but not proven. Maybe, like Jim says, someone offering to do decorating or whatever.'

Jones interrupted, 'There was a film with Sean Connery that did that…'

'Yes, yes, DS Jones. Back to today, please. We're three days in and not seeing much progress. Then, I want another team to ask around the neighbourhood here of any vehicles that are remembered — particularly vans. Edwards, you better take charge of that one, as you know the area and the people hereabouts. And I want everyone to keep those thoughts in the forefront of your minds until tomorrow and any new ideas that you think of. Start now and we'll meet again later — outside, like now until we know what, if anything, Sergeant Shaw's people have found. Thank you, one and all.' He walked off to the car park adjoining the hut to find his car and driver to make some "secure", as he saw it, phone calls whilst Shaw was sorting out the possibilities of microphones in the Nissen hut.

Shaw's people did their job well and quickly, restoring some degree of credibility for him. Several of them looked dirty from clambering in the roof trusses. A close search of the building revealed two small electronic bugs secured behind the beams and a tiny camera. LeFanu had insisted, by using sign language, that they were to be left, and returned to his car telephone to call DS Jones.

An hour later, they gathered outside again, clutching the inevitable coffees. LeFanu called for quiet. 'OK ladies and gentlemen, today is going to be one of your more difficult days.' They looked at him, suspiciously, as he continued. 'This place is bugged, sound and vision, although the vision bit is pretty restricted. Note the tense of my remark. It is bugged. We must all go in there like nothing has happened, knowing that our villain is probably listening in to everything we've said and will say. You must continue your conversations and investigations but not give anything away. Someone, somewhere, probably not that far away, is listening in and could easily detect that we're on to him. At this minute in time, I believe we have an advantage. Just remember that an absence of information will be as much of a giveaway. Right, particular thanks go to WPC Ford.'

There was a desultory round of applause — not because the thanks weren't genuine, but because the weather did little to raise spirits and most were thinking how to handle the situation inside the building.

He turned to WPC Ford, an attractive, stunningly built woman in her late twenties. 'Susan, I really appreciate your thoughts yesterday. It will not go unnoticed nor unrewarded.'

She blushed and addressed LeFanu, a little embarrassed. 'Actually, sir, it's Susie, sorry.' She was glad that she'd had the courage to put her idle thought to the group the previous afternoon. It had been touch and go, at the time.

He marched in, and gazing at the ceiling braces in the main hall where the surveillance bugs were situated, announced, 'Right, ladies and gentlemen, you've had your break. Not saying it wasn't deserved, but now back to the grindstone. House-to-house is called for. Sorry one and all. I know it's miserable out there, cold and now it's raining. I want to know how they cased the village. Someone, somewhere has visited this place in the last few months and I want to know who it was; when it was; why and how. Report back — let's say…' He paused, glancing again at the bug and then at his watch. 'Report back at eleven a.m. sharp.' Several of the group looked at him a little strangely before realising why he was repeating his instructions.

'Another thing, ladies and gentlemen. We won't get much real policing done in here, sitting nice and warm, with those damn computers. I want a detailed list of everything that's been stolen — alongside the name and address of the owners. Listed on boards, please and that's every damn thing that's missing, no matter how small.' He gesticulated, once more at the surveillance devices, which were indicated by orange stickers, smiled and walked out of the hall, followed by Sergeant Jones. He left behind him the hub-bub of comments referring to him as a hard-hearted bastard. Exactly what he wanted his unseen listener to hear.

Outside, it really was raining hard. They ran to his Vauxhall Insignia Estate car and sat, damp, in the rear seats whilst the windows steamed up before the air conditioning could take effect.

'*Merde*! Chris, who and where is this turd who is listening in to my every thought? I was starting to think we had a leak amongst us, so I suppose it's a comfort that this bastard has just been boxing clever. So, everyone who's been in residence in this village and the immediate surroundings for less than three months — no, call it six — I want to know their names and backgrounds, and pronto. And any guests too. Even families at Christmas or whatever. Most of that will come from the previous interviews, but make sure it's thorough. The postman, milkman, whoever — try the Manse and that dragon of an MP's wife and include anyone in a footprint of five miles around the village to start with. This is really pissing me off.'

Jones nodded and added, 'The technical boys have told us about the potential of the gadgets discovered even though they're not the latest available, stating that it was possible to have a relay station that may be no larger than a fag packet, providing it was hidden a couple of metres from the ground. Old kit, been the rounds and virtually untraceable — made in their millions; made in China, inevitably. Battery duration about a month, depending on the condition, temperature and location. That opens up many options, sir.' Jones was concerned about wasting the team's efforts if it really was a fool's errand.

'Instinct tells me to leave it. Concentrate on the fact that he's sitting somewhere listening directly to every fucking thing that's been going on in that hall. If we draw a blank, then we'll have to think again. This guy's bloody clever. He's got almost every angle covered. He must have left something. We need his base. It must be near here. Any progress? If he's any sense, and I think he has, he'll be away from there pretty quickly.'

'We've got a lead as to the likely direction of whatever sort of base they may have, or had. Edwards's team picked it up from a member of the public who thinks she saw something suspicious. A parked car in an unusual way — won't bore you with the details, sir, but it makes sense with those fires on Monday night that Edwards raced off to sort out. It's a hundred and eighty degrees taking the village as a centre to where this woman saw this car. Fits with what we'd guessed.' Jones snapped shut his official black note book and got out of the car. He raised his eyebrows as the chief's car roared off into the murk. This was only marginally better than groping in the dark, he thought.

Fifteen minutes later, he rang the DCI's mobile. 'The French police have come up trumps, sir. Probably you calling them to speed them up, I suspect.'

'I will make a detective of you yet, Jones.'

'Anyway, sir. They're flying Lady Groombridge into Norwich airport from Orly. Cheap and cheerful on a KLM flight; that should appeal to her, I think! We'll have to pick up the tab, I expect, but it seemed important enough to agree and otherwise we would have had to go to France. She should be landing in a couple of hours. They're an hour ahead of us — of course, sorry, you'd know that. I've sent that WPC Ford to pick her up and bring her directly to Ipswich HQ. Hope that's OK? And before that, we've got this Guy Scott character coming in to the village HQ. I told him to come here rather than Ipswich — thought it might be a better use of our time. You remember, sir, the guy with the weak stomach, but he's got some photos to show us and he's not that keen to view the body in the morgue.'

LeFanu nodded, *'Bien sûr*. Sorry, I mean that'll be fine.' He was starting to think in French. He closed the call and returned to his paperwork.

***

'Issy?' George said, and without waiting for acknowledgement, 'Did you pick that up? They said a Mrs Pearce saw our Arab friends parked... Any problem?'

'Nah. Told you before. Their car is long gone and there are plenty of people who could give a description if the police asked, and then what have they got? The pair are well away. Just points them roughly in our direction.'

'There's something strained in the buzz of conversations in that village hall. Maybe they know about the microphones? It feels like our information is about to dry up. Can they trace any of the kit?'

'George, my old mate. Course not. Did you think I'd let you down like that? It was inevitable that they'd find it — could have been a cleaning lady or anything. Lasted quite well, I thought. Well, it's still operating but you noticed that the conversations are a bit stilted — me too. Not the same banter and swearing... not sure. Maybe he's a seriously clever bastard, this LeFanu character.'

'Yeah, well. It was a bit of a surprise. I could kill that WPC. But still, if you're sure. Sounds like LeFanu is using his brains a bit; maybe that's why he's a DCI. Still don't know the identity of the victim in the Jacuzzi. Some guy from Duxford is going to do an identity check soon, I think. Don't know what cooks re. the wife if it is this Lord fellow. They're onto the French police regarding her. Should find out soon. Did you listen to the local news yesterday? He told the press absolutely nothing of interest. Quite clever. We'll have to watch him. Cheers, mate.'

'Cheers, George, and don't worry so much. We've still got an edge. Couldn't pick up much from the meeting room inside the hut — it's partitioned off and has storage above — couldn't get in there with a mic. Maybe they've been talking about whoever it is. Can't tell.' Issy shut down his phone. He had work to do to remove all traces at the factory as soon as was feasible and that needed some thinking.

Chapter 21

Mr Guy Scott arrived at the village hall in a red Ferrari Dino, complaining of the pot-holes in the road and the officious nature of the police. As Philippe LeFanu observed later, all that revving of the obviously powerful engine was all for show and it had been a pity that there wasn't a foot or so of snow to find out whether he really could drive the flashy vehicle when the sun wasn't shining.

A WPC rapped on the door of LeFanu's cubicle. 'This guy from the car auction place is here, sir. Wants to talk to you.'

'Well, has he identified our Lord chap at Ipswich? If so, what does he want?' LeFanu sounded irritated with the interruption.

'Well, no, sir. He says that when it comes down to it, he hasn't the stomach for it. Apologised profusely. Says that it has to be down to Groombridge's wife or his kids. But he does want to speak to you, I don't know what about. Shall I show him in?'

'Yes, yes. Get on with it. I haven't got time for chit-chat.'

Guy Scott, the auction house director, was shown in to the tiny office that served as LeFanu's centre of operations. Two chairs and a small desk loaded with computer screens and a coffee machine. He handed over his business card identifying himself as director and company secretary. LeFanu looked up impatiently, thinking that this guy was still in selling car mode, dressed in his shiny suit and loud tie, let alone his precocious car. LeFanu, unreasonably, instinctively took a dislike to his visitor.

'Coffee, Mr Scott? I can't offer many creature comforts here, but that's the way of it in a serious murder enquiry. Time is of the essence.'

'Thank you, no. I am in a bit of a rush myself. Tony's death, we are assuming it is Tony Groombridge?' He looked up for confirmation and LeFanu gave a non-committal shrug. 'Anyway, we can't get hold of him by phone or anything, so it has created a wagon load of work for us back in Duxford. I'm so sorry that I couldn't help with an identification but...'

'I do understand, Mr Scott. It is always difficult for those with a weak stomach.' He couldn't resist the barb. 'We are pursuing finding his wife.

But I must stress that until we have a formal identification we cannot confirm it is Lord Groombridge. Well, I understand you wanted to speak to me. How may I help?' LeFanu was frustrated by the interruption, but equally interested in why a busy business man should want to travel from the middle of Cambridgeshire to talk in this little village rather than getting on the phone.

'Well, Detective Chief Inspector, first I thought these photos, albeit about five or six years old, may help. Course, they got married in the US, so this was like a post wedding reception for UK friends, not the actual wedding.' He handed over a small pack of photographs of wedding guests in familiar surroundings to LeFanu, as the reception had been in the garden of Porten House. DS Jones had crowded into the office at LeFanu's request and immediately recognised the formal gardens to the front of the house and an array of expensive cars in the background.

'Please point out who is who, Mr Scott.' Jones was looking for familiar faces in the group shots.

'They're not very good, as photos go. Mobile phone cameras always seem to be a bit shaky, I'm afraid, certainly were then, anyway. I wrote the names and contact details that I could remember on the reverse, Mr Jones, after printing them off. Charlotte, sorry, his wife, is the one wearing the large black sun hat. She always complains about the sun and her complexion. The others? Well, largely her friends, but I wouldn't know them by name unless they were in the news. No reason to, I suppose. Tony took a dim view of the need for another party. But there is another thing. We've, that's the team at the firm, read all the newspaper reports and the TV news and no mention of his, Lord Groombridge's, I mean, extensive collection of classic cars. Were they stolen too?'

'What cars? We haven't found any, have we, sir?' Jones interrupted, puzzled.

'A large building, like a barn, modern purpose built, of course, air conditioned and so on, about three hundred metres from the house, through a substantial gate, I seem to recall. Been there a couple of times to wax lyrical about his collection. Almost stroking the cars, I have to admit. Must be a dozen or so, seriously valuable cars in there. It is, I mean was, his hobby; actually more than a hobby, more what he did and he is, was, seriously wealthy. Naturally, we knew about most of the cars — that's our business.'

LeFanu saw that it was pointless to stress, again, that Groombridge had not yet been formally identified.

'If you have ten minutes, Mr Scott, would you accompany DS Jones to the house and point this out.' And turning to Jones, 'We have no keys, so better take someone with you in case this barn needs to be opened, and someone with alarm experience, too.' And returning to Scott again, 'Thank you, Mr Scott. We do appreciate your coming over at short notice, but we are having difficulty in locating his housekeeper, and his wife, the Lady Charlotte, for that matter.' LeFanu excused himself from the pointless discussion.

Jones and Scott drove up to Porten House, followed by another car with three others with tools and equipment. Jones had turned down the opportunity, as Scott put it, to drive in the Ferrari and had proffered the front seat of his Mondeo. Jones asked Scott about the relationship between Lady Charlotte and her husband. Scott said he hadn't seen Charlotte for a year or so but thought that the marriage was solid as a rock. But he observed that, without being a fly on the wall, who really knows.

Jones pursued this line. 'We've had difficulty in locating her in the UK, sir. Obviously not here, nor at the London flat. We got that address from one of the other companies, of which he is a director. We've appealed to the French police and they have located her, and she should be flying in to Norwich sometime soon today.'

'She always did spend a lot of time in France, at an old family home, like a mini-chateau, I believe, near Montargis, down near Auxerre, I think. We wouldn't have an address for that, but her surname was Bertin before marrying Tony, Sergeant. I think I mentioned that to someone earlier. That may be her maiden name or from an earlier marriage in France, I understand. Maybe French records will help with the actual address or, indeed, Charlotte herself?'

Jones drove to the heavy metal gates way up an un-metalled drive by the side of the house. There was a large padlock that looked brand new, which provided little resistance to the policeman with the bolt cutters.

Scott looked around. 'So far so good, Sergeant. Perhaps these thieves didn't know about the collection.'

'Don't count on it, sir. It has been known for thieves to replace padlocks to slow down enquiries. Nevertheless, let's get on.' Jones shivered in the cold January air. He'd left his fleece-lined jacket at the Nissen hut

HQ in his haste. The barn loomed up past some trees, quite out of sight of the house and very secluded.

The doors to the barn were Impressive and again closed shut with a seriously substantial padlock and an alarm winking gently.

'Shit,' Jones muttered. 'Sorry, but this may take some time, sir.' His men cut the padlock and swung the doors open, accompanied by a stony silence.

'That's odd. Why no alarm? It's not a silent central station job. We checked all alarms for the village two days ago. Looks like this one is active but… OK, let's go in.'

Guy Scott looked at the shambles as the lights flickered into life. There, in the front, was the green Mercedes with a smashed windscreen and headlights and several other cars, barely recognisable in their damaged state.

Scott exploded. 'Holy cow! Who could have done this? He loved these cars. Pride and joy stuff, especially that Merc. Look, on the remains of the bonnet there's the cleaning kit he used every week, as he told me months ago, yet everything else is slashed, dented, paint stripper, broken glass. It's a write off, near as dammit, as are the others. There's, what, two million in insurance claims here.' He walked around, examining the vehicles, and stroked each one like they were family.

Jones's face showed that he had no idea of the value in this barn and that the figure of two million pounds put all the other thefts into context. 'Motive, sir? Any ideas of the why, assuming, of course, that Lord Groombridge himself didn't cause this damage.

'No way would Tony do this. It would be like cutting his own wrists. Someone he's pissed off big-time, I suppose. It's nothing to do with us — as an auction house, I mean.' Scott looked around, shaking his head in disbelief.

'Even thieves don't waste time causing damage like this, as a rule. They're more interested in stealing what they want and running. Interesting, though.' Jones paused as a bell rang somewhere in his brain. 'When we found Groombridge's body, we found a die-cast model of a green Mercedes. I don't know much about old cars like these.' And pointing to the damaged car, 'What model of Mercedes is this?'

'A 1960s Mercedes Pagoda top 500SL, late sixties, but the plates are missing so I can't be sure. But about then, I'd have to check. He does all his insurance stuff through his solicitors, Strube and Barberis. They're our lawyers, too. And an insurance broker somewhere, but their name escapes me for the present. I'll check and maybe they can assist with the portfolio of cars. There's two missing, I think — see, over there, a space and another over there where there is a slight oil stain. Maybe he sold them, whatever they were. The insurance people should be able to help. But a model car? That's strange. His children are adults living in the USA, long past kid's toys, and no grand-children that I know of.'

Jones found out a lot about the victim and his family in the next ten minutes and established that he was a difficult man to work with, noted for his temper and intolerance — information that supported comments from work colleagues at the other companies with which he was involved. Apparently, a good looking man in his early to mid-forties, rather fancying himself as a ladies' man. Very pedantic in his dress — always smart without being adventurous. No, no, to jeans and a T-shirt, as Guy Scott put it. Jones had to warn Guy Scott not to talk about what they had seen, wanting to keep the details away from the media. Scott agreed, and on return to the village hall, roared off in his Ferrari with a flag of Scotland on the number-plate.

'Got a lead, I think, sir' he blurted out as he rushed into LeFanu's office immediately on return to the Nissen hut HQ.

LeFanu raised his hand to command silence and gesticulated towards the telephone he held in his right hand and up to the ceiling where the bugs had been marked and mouthed, 'HQ.'

Jones raised his hands as an apology and retreated. A minute or two later, his boss left his office and sought out Jones. 'C'mon, coffee and a stroll in the freezing air. It'll sharpen up my wits.'

Jones explained the connection with the cars and the possibility of two being stolen but the rest being trashed.

'But what's the lead? OK, you've traced the errant wife and found a new motive for murder — or at least one that we had not identified. It seems that we've just more questions? Correct me please.'

'Sorry, guv. The model car under the body is the same I think, exactly, even to the colour, albeit poorly painted, as the real Mercedes that's been trashed. By all accounts, it was Groombridge's pride and joy. The motive for murder has to be linked to that car, as the die cast model was put in the Jacuzzi for a purpose… Whatever that may be.'

'Or to lead us a merry dance, Jones. Or to direct us to someone else.

They're playing us, whoever he or they are, like a professional angler. It could be the reverse of Ockham's Razor.' LeFanu looked frustrated, knowing, as he did, that there was a lot of pressure coming from the assistant chief constable's office in Ipswich for results. 'I get a funny feeling that Mr Scott wasn't here solely to help us. Was he genuinely surprised to find the damage or was it a fishing expedition?'

'Fishing? Possibly. I don't really know. I still can't rationalise that he wants to come here, and then chickens out at identifying the cadaver and then claims he's so busy. I think we should keep him on our radar, and the company, too. I think the thefts are linked. I am more and more convinced that our first victim, David what's-his-name, could have been an accident or certainly not pre-meditated anyway, but this other victim? That smacks of murder, through and through. Then we have the motive of the cars and maybe, just maybe, he, Groombridge, that is, caught them at it.' Jones looked at LeFanu for a reaction. 'Scott made a big thing about these cars being Groombridge's pride and joy. Loved them like a child; couldn't bear to see them damaged in any way, etc., etc. Maybe it isn't him, maybe he is still in this ski resort place — we do need to establish that...'

'I hear what you say, Chris, although we have zero grounds to even think it is anyone but Groombridge until we have some ID. But I agree with most of what you say, but these guys... If it was the same people who killed who we assume is Anthony Groombridge — let us assume that for the time being — why strip him and create this elaborate subterfuge of the champagne bottle, wine glass, no photographs? Certainly not the aerial pics, or papers, a safe that appears to be locked tight. Why was the back door of the house wide open, and why was the alarm inoperative on the barn with millions of value stacked in there? And then there's this die-cast model car badly painted in green. Too many questions, still. And we can ask Madame when we see her about her husband's whereabouts and the ski place address and ask the French gendarmerie to check for us. For them, it's a phone call or two.'

'But what is this Ockham's Razor thing? You mentioned it before, but I still haven't got a handle on it.'

'Jones, it's management speak, basically. Ockham's Razor simply expounds that the simplest solution is usually right. A simple example, with which you will be familiar in your avid TV police thriller watching if nowhere else, is the last person to see a victim is frequently the perpetrator.

So we go looking for the obvious and it isn't there. OK?'

'Right, sir. Now, I think I understand. So these people are confusing the issue to make it difficult for us to spot the real reasons for the crime or crimes by giving us loads of potentially simple options.' He said it with some obvious doubt.

'Right, DS Jones. Spot on. We assume that the thefts and murders are connected, and indeed, the death of Mr David Grant, whilst the whole thing may be much more convoluted. Meanwhile, we go haring off, that's the English expression, I believe, looking for obvious motives and making simple connections because it is the obvious choice. Or maybe, it is just coincidence. These guys, or this guy, is clever if he is second guessing us like that. The bugs in the control centre gave him, or them, an enormous advantage over us.' LeFanu scratched his ear, again. 'And Jones, please don't ask why its called Ockham's Razor. I've no idea. Look it up.'

'Right, sir. Anyway, we've got a phone number, from Guy Scott, of the people, lawyers by all accounts, who arrange the insurance for the fleet of old cars. Shaw is chasing for a schedule by email, as we speak, from the insurance broker they use. And they've talked to Mrs Davis. Clever, they dropped a hint that David's wife, Mrs Grant, should be on her way to the village and would probably want to see her. That did it. She cracked, and yes, David Grant was a lover and turned up regular as clockwork when the husband was away. Parked his car in a field and legged it over the back fence, hence the flattened grass in the field beyond. He must have been a regular. She even disconnected the security light and placed an old garden roller next to the fence — smart thinking. Usual stuff, pleaded for us not to tell her husband. Then she started on about being a victim — jewellery and money stolen — so she hadn't been thinking straight when she denied all knowledge of the poor sod who died. She had told the bad guys that she was alone and the boyfriend had had to get out later. Well, that's the current thinking. But we can only assume it was the thieves who found him there and Bob's your uncle, so as to speak.'

'I never fail to be amazed by the English language, Jones. Who is Bob?' Jones shrugged. He wasn't sure how to respond until he saw his boss smiling. 'No doubt there are some strange expressions in French, Jones. Good work. Now, continue…'

'He could have slipped, I suppose. Maybe banged his head, but that wouldn't explain the bruises on his arms and the writing of the name on the glass. God knows what "Greenf" means. On balance, sir, I think he was shoved and then banged his head. So maybe aggravated assault or manslaughter rather than premeditated murder. And she's just a stupid bitch probably bored with life in a remote village.'

'Agreed on all counts. A caution to Mrs Davis for wasting police time is about the long and short of it. Let uniform branch handle the disciplining. It'll all come out at the inquest on Mr Grant and maybe she'll have problems enough at home to keep her on the straight and narrow. Leave it to you, Jones. Let's move on.'

No more than ten minutes later, Jim Edwards knocked on the door and whispered into DS Jones's ear about the unkempt individual who waited a few paces away. Jones nodded and shut the door, leaving them outside whilst he had a few words with his boss.

LeFanu nearly blew a fuse when PC Edwards wheeled in the rather dejected, scruffy man into the office, which had been cleared of the surveillance devices.

'This is Ramsbottom, sir. He's got something to say and he'll only talk to the boss. Sorry, sir, but... Anyway, he's the local gamekeeper — or rather he keeps the game he catches, if you get my drift...' He looked about him to see if anyone had caught the gist of his joke. Jones and LeFanu both raised their eyebrows and shook their heads.

DS Jones started in 'Get on with it, Edwards. We've an investigation to run.'

LeFanu added, 'I'm not interested in his career in poaching. That's your problem. Why is he here?' It was as if Ramsbottom wasn't in the room.

'I don't care if you are the guv'nor. I've been dragged here to help you... well, just effing watch it, see?'

Edwards, in trying to redeem himself, glared at Ramsbottom, adding, 'Help us now and I might forget the poaching, the results of which are on your kitchen table right now.'

'Edwards, why is he here? Please get on with it.'

'He thinks he saw something a few days ago at an empty factory warehouse unit, about seven miles from here. We picked him up on our extended search, sir.' He unfolded an Ordnance Survey map and pointed to the location.

LeFanu, looking at Ramsbottom, recognised that a direct conversation was likely to be quicker. 'What did you see, Mr...' looking at his note book, 'eh, Ramsbottom.'

'Sheepsarse, that's what people call me,' he responded with a leer.

'Oh, do get on with it. I haven't got all day.'

'Well, guv'nor, there was this bloke leaning on the gate, like. We chatted for a bit. I offered him a smoke and a rabbit, too, but he wasn't having any. Took all I could do to get his name. Unfriendly, like. I told him my name, you know, the Sheepsarse bit. Usually gets a laugh… What was it now?' He scratched his head. 'Oh, it'll come back to me in a mo. He said he was in charge of the factory place for some firm down south. Funny, though I never seed anything. Well, there was a big truck thing with windows like a coach, and a white or whitish car. Dunno what make or anything. But that's all, and I work that area…' He looked at PC Edwards. 'Well, you know, it's, like, my patch.' The others in the room were getting frustrated, but all knew it would take time.

'Anyway, I heard this generator thing, but there weren't no lights, no other cars, nuffing. Thought it was a chopper or plane or something so I asks him.'

'So why didn't you report it?' Jones snapped at him, sharing LeFanu's obvious frustration. And to his boss, Jones commented 'Perhaps that's where they stored the coaches they nicked from Bury St Edmunds.' LeFanu shrugged.

'Listen 'ere. There's no need for that tone of voice with me. I'm trying to help. Is there a reward or anything? I didn't report it 'cos I didn't see nuffing and I'm no grass. Anyway, he said I might get a little job there, sweeping up and things.'

'More like you'd have some explaining to do,' interjected Edwards.

'I ain't a grass but a cup of cha and a fag would help my memory. I did see a coach thing, in blue it was, through a chink in the window when I was cleaning up.' He looked up at LeFanu.

Edwards interjected, 'More like you were looking to see if there was anything you could nick.'

Ramsbottom ignored the comment and turned to LeFanu. 'Ain't you got one of them artist fellows. I've seen them on the telly. I could describe him a bit.' Edwards, on a nod from Jones, arranged the tea and a packet of cigarettes from a colleague.

They wouldn't allow Ramsbottom to light up the cigarette, but he managed to pocket the packet offered. 'Ian. That was his name. Told you a cup of cha would do the trick.'

'Second name? C'mon, Mr Ramsbottom, think.' DS Jones tried a more friendly tone.

'A colour it was. Now… White, that's it.' Both DCI LeFanu and Jones exchanged a knowing glance at the name.

The conversation had taken nearly fifteen minutes, as LeFanu pointed out angrily, after they put Ramsbottom at a table with the police artist, without a great deal of expectation of a meaningful result.

LeFanu thumped his desk in frustration. 'We could have had all that information in three minutes, gentlemen. And that time would have been better spent. Third time the name Ian White has come up. Got to be an alias, but feels like he's an important member of this team.'

Calming down, they quickly talked through this result and identified the location and access roads on the map.

'Get a team out there now, Sergeant Shaw. Armed response as well. And wait for the back-up. These guys might be armed and certainly dangerous. This might be the break we're looking for. Approach the place silently. No blues and twos or sirens. We want to catch them napping. They won't be expecting us.'

Chapter 22

'Issy! Did you hear that chatter?' George was looking for reassurance. 'Not LeFanu this time, but it sounds like he had an interview and part of it is being relayed around the room.'

'Yes, mate. They got most of the gear but missed one. Not good reception but that's because I hid it well. They'll find it soon — still double checking apparently — but the police team are back at their desks.'

'Did you hear that one of them is called "Sheepsarse"? God, what is the world coming to…'

'Actually, George, I have to confess something. When I was at Factory B, a bloke came up and starting chatting. Name was Ramsbottom but said everyone called him 'Sheepsarse'. I gave him a tenner to sweep up the concreted drive in and said to do it every Thursday afternoon and I'd leave him a tenner in an envelope behind the drain-pipe. I was testing out the generators and pinching a few bits for the main base. But I did say my name — big mistake, I know. Didn't think any harm done, as it wasn't the main base. There's two cameras and microphones there as back up. Should give us an hour or two breathing space.'

'Wish you'd told me, Issy. But good thinking. When they arrive at Factory B, as you call it, we'll know to get our skates on. No harm done as you say — in fact might be a pretty shrewd blind. See you.' With that, George shut his phone and laughed. He'd tried to think of anything that would buy time as the inevitable police activity increased, before a failure to find anything would mean that their investigations would be wound down because of costs — but all that had been before bodies started turning up. That'd mean longer term heavy duty turning over every stone and blade of grass. Issy had up-staged him with creating another diversion. And him saying his name had been a mistake, but thank the Lord that it was a pretty common or garden name.

'Smart stuff,' he thought, almost out loud.

Chapter 23

LeFanu and Jones drove at breakneck speed from Eye St Mary to the Ipswich HQ to await Lady Charlotte Groombridge. Their driver was expert — it was his job and he'd been well trained to drive fast, use his lights to forewarn difficult traffic and accelerate away when opportunity presented itself. They were both seething at the timing, wanting to join the search for the depot or factory unit that the thieves had been using, but recognising the importance of formal identification of their murder victim. Even more frustration set in when an hour and a half later, after a flight delay from France following the inevitable Air Traffic Control work to rule in France and a fast drive the forty-six miles or so from Norwich airport, WPC Ford knocked, and hearing the OK, entered DCI LeFanu's office on the third floor of the Ipswich HQ with Lady Charlotte Groombridge. With her coat draped over her shoulders, she looked stunning, in a pale pink suit with a short pencil skirt and a crisp white silk blouse, showing the hazy outline of a lacy, low-fronted bra, all looking immaculate despite the undoubted cramped conditions of her flight. Stiletto heels that were high enough to get a look of admiration from WPC Ford and dark stockings completed the outfit, alongside a Dolce & Gabbana hand-bag, prominently displaying the iconic D&G logo, and a sufficiency of gold jewellery to demonstrate her background. Ford introduced Detective Chief Inspector Phillippe LeFanu as the senior investigating officer and Detective Sergeant Jones as his deputy. WPC Ford offered her a chair and then, at a sign from LeFanu, sat near the door.

'Lady Groombridge, madame. Please excuse the surroundings...' He gesticulated to the bland interior of the office. Chairs with vinyl seats that didn't match and a carpet of dubious vintage, with a range of metal filing cabinets against the wall. 'I'm only able to offer you some fairly average coffee...' He pointed to the harmless little machine on a small table near the door. 'Can I interest you?'

She shook her head. 'It's bad enough being in this miserable part of England in the pouring rain, let alone having to drink indifferent coffee in this office that looks like it was furnished by a charity shop — and that, on a bad day. And this is your headquarters. *Zut-alors!* Anyway, no matter.'

Their conversation started in French. A courtesy from DCI LeFanu, in an effort to put her at ease. He apologised for the basic flight but she shrugged and made an aside that the cabin crew had spoiled her above and beyond what was necessary. He carried on, explaining why he, a Frenchman, was in such a position in the British police, having come to the UK at the age of ten when his English mother split from her French husband.

After a difficult silence of maybe ten or fifteen seconds, Charlotte raised her eyebrows and asked, 'Does that mean you have forgotten all the French ways?' Again, she looked around her disparagingly.

DCI LeFanu was completely thrown by this remark and stuttered, 'Eh, hardly, madame. I was ten years of age and really consider myself English through and through, although I do visit my family in France regularly so I am not entirely devoid of knowledge.' He was clearly narked by this twist in the conversation from that which he had carefully planned beforehand.

'Enough of this, madame. My sergeant is looking a little confused. May we continue in English?' She shrugged again and smiled, a very disarming smile. He continued, 'We're here to ask you some questions about your husband. Naturally, we offer our condolences; we do believe that the victim is your husband. We would have preferred to speak to you straight away but circumstances would not allow, but I believe the French authorities broke the sad news to you. I would like to record our conversation, if you have no objections.'

'Why so? I thought this was about identifying my late husband.'

'Madame, we believe this is about a murder and that makes things more complicated than you might think. At this stage of an investigation, there is so much information to distil that it is easier to refer to a tape than have to bother you again. You will, of course, have a copy of the tape, should you wish.' He looked at her.

Again, she shrugged. 'Please call me Charlotte. I've never really got used to these English pompous titles.'

They established that she had been married and become Charlotte Waller in 2009, and in 2012, Lady Groombridge, when Anthony received his peerage and should be known now as Charlotte, Lady Groombridge, as his widow. Jones scribbled madly in his black note book, glancing at

LeFanu with a twitch of his eyebrows. LeFanu acknowledged the subtle sign and moved on. 'And before your marriage, Madame Charlotte?

'I was married before, to Charles Bertin, a *homme d'affaires*, as we call it in France. A businessman.' She glanced across at DS Jones, before continuing, 'He was in property. He left me, I mean we divorced in 2005, monsieur. Are you married, Chief Inspector?'

'I don't think that is relevant, madame. But yes, I was and unfortunately the relationship foundered. She thought I was really married to the job. Probably quite true; it is often a policeman's lot. However, I must ask you, as a matter of course, and we do ask everyone remotely connected to any crime the same question, we need to know where you were at the time the crimes were committed, to eliminate you from future and further enquiries. When was the last time you saw your husband? Where were you at the estimated time of the murder of your husband, which would be the 1st to the 5th of January?'

'*Pas de problem*. In France, *cher* Chief Inspector, celebrating the New Year, which, as you know, is not solely the 31st December and back to work, as it is here. I always go to my family for Saint Sylvestre. Can't do with the skiing and apres-ski with tepid, indifferent red wine they call *gluwein* in Courchevel, unlike my husband, who revelled in it. He goes to Courchevel every year at this time without fail. Has done for years, even before I knew him. Usually goes about the 20th of December, so that was around the last time I saw poor Tony,' She smiled. LeFanu reflected that she was doing a lot of shrugging and smiling. He was seeking some sadness or remorse or something removed from the off-hand approach she was showing.

'Is there anyone there who could tell us when he arrived and when he left?'

'Not really, monsieur. Ours was not that sort of marriage. We didn't check up on one another. Of course, in an emergency I would text a message to his mobile. He lived on that. There is a concierge, a building manager, but I don't have their number. Perhaps they will know more. The address is, what is it?' She gazed at the ceiling with some disgust at the nicotine coloured paint, which obviously hadn't been re-painted since the indoor smoking ban, whilst thinking. 'Yes, No.7, Rue des Alpes. Perhaps the local gendarmerie can help?'

'No mobile phone was found, madame. Do you know where it is? Perhaps the number?'

'Er, no. It would normally be in his pocket. Perhaps the thieves took it? The number is...' She checked the address book on her mobile phone and read it out. '07185 943768.' She looked so innocent, so naïve.

'Thieves, madame? Why do you think there were thieves?' Again, she shrugged.

'OK, we'll check through channels. Any enemies that you could think of?'

'*Oui, bien sûr!* He was a jealous man, and ironically, so were the fathers, brothers and husbands of every bimbo this side of the Alps, I should think. And some business people that he'd, how do you say it, umm, "shafted", that's the word. No one by name, I'm afraid. Fortunately, he kept his business life isolated from me.'

'Thank you for your frankness. Who, madame, could vouch for your being in France at the time? We have to ask, you understand.'

'*Bien sûr.* My mother and younger brother, Philippe, and our housekeeper, and oh, various people on the estate. I probably went out shopping around that time, but it wasn't for a long time. The sales you know! I do like le shopping.'

'Did you meet anyone or is there someone to substantiate your whereabouts? It is normal practice in matters like these to establish everyone's whereabouts, madame.'

'Really? Perhaps I should be indignant about your asking for an alibi, but I do understand.' She paused, smiled weakly and looked LeFanu straight in the eye before continuing. 'No, shopping is for me alone. Of course, I have a handful of receipts and credit card slips somewhere which, I suppose, would explain where I was and at what time. Maybe the shop people, Galeries Lafayette, Printemps and some others, would remember me. Oh, now I come to think of it there was a nice security man, Dominic, his badge said, at the exit of Agent Provocateur, the sexy lingerie shop...' She looked at LeFanu and winked. 'Yes, he stopped me, as there was one of those silly electronic tags on a rather nice revealing brassiere I had purchased. All sorted out amicably, I assure you, DCI LeFanu.'

She stared provocatively. 'Perhaps, Chief Inspector, you would like a trip to Paris to do the rounds of the nicer shops? But please, remember I am a victim here. My husband, well...' She turned away, with tears welling.

LeFanu hastily changed the direction of his questions. 'No matter. We would like to know, exactly, the last time you saw your husband alive. We need to track his movements. We tried to locate your children when we couldn't locate you. They have been informed of their father's untimely death by the US immigration people. You may wish to contact them soon.'

Charlotte recovered quickly. '*Mon Dieu*, Chief Inspector. They are not my children. No love lost there. Money grabbing pair. You, Mr LeFanu, if you have any adult children, will know what I mean.' LeFanu looked at her and added with a shake of the head, 'None, madame.'

She continued, as he wanted her to do. 'They treat their father as a money making machine and me like some sort of member of his harem. I don't know what will happen when they get their inheritance. The title stops with Tony's death. He bought it, effectively, from funding your Liberal Democrats pitch in 2010 elections — cheap way to get recognition, I suppose, that's my Tony!' She spoke scathingly. 'I get to keep my title, more or less, for my life-time or until marrying again and those horrid children remain 'the honourable' for their life time. It's called a life peerage, I believe, in the funny English way of it. But all these sorts of things take time, and it's too soon to start asking questions of the lawyers. Then I'll have to think again. Oh, the last time I saw Tony was at a party at Gordon Ramsey's Claridges on the 20th December. He left from London to fly to France the next day. I had a fearful hangover, I recall.'

'Thank you. Surely he will have left you well provided for?'

'Oh yes. I'll have the Chelsea flat for as long as I want and a generous allowance and maybe some capital from the estate — I've no idea what, but the lawyers will be gathering with his will to be read and probate to be secured, which I understand takes forever in this country — and France, for that matter. I understand that trust funds and wills are notorious for being turned over from their original good intentions. Sorry, I mean over-turned. I'll have to wait and see. I am not close to my step-children, Chief Inspector, and they are not close to me. Whether they try to deal me a bad hand of cards, time will tell. But it does sound like you are searching for a motive.'

'Not at all, we have to explore every angle and money is often a key driver in these sorts of events. Was there any life assurance?'

'I believe so, but what and how much I haven't a clue. He was very meticulous, but the detail? Not really my concern, or wasn't my concern until now. He handled all that sort of thing and rarely, if ever, consulted me. Somewhere, there'll be the name and address of his lawyers. Whilst the wheels of progress move on inexorably, I will probably spend more time with my French family whilst the dust settles and the lawyers do what they are good at. Sorry about all the mixing of metaphors.' A moment later, she reached for a tissue in her bag and theatrically, LeFanu thought, wiped her eyes. Remorse or theatre? She was good, the detective thought.

'You don't sound that sad or am I reading the signs wrongly?'

'No, no. I am sad, although you may not see that in my face.' Again she smiled. 'We had a good, albeit short marriage. He played away a bit — so what's new? I have to say, I hated the house in Suffolk — cold, drafty and in the middle of nowhere, with the nearest shopping back to London really. But we had some good times, too. One thing, I am surprised that he returned from Courchevel so early. Perhaps the snow wasn't good, they call it champagne snow, apparently — not good for skiing but good for drinking or perhaps that's a volte-face. Or maybe the apres-ski was equally bad?' She smirked.

'Indeed. Did your husband have any lady friends in England who would have visited him in Suffolk?' LeFanu and Jones looked closely for a reaction.

'Oh, Tony had lots of lady friends, as you call them; others may call them by a variety of unpleasant names. Here, there, anywhere. I think the English call it profligate. So, yes, to answer your question, probably one of many.' It wasn't a look of resignation, it was just a matter of fact look that she gave.

'A blonde about thirty to thirty-five, we believe?'

'Oh, not that I recall but probably — what do they say, "gentlemen prefer blondes!" Why would I know about his dalliances? Not exactly the topic of fireside chat with one's partner, is it?' She laughed and tossed her head. 'Seriously, have you asked Monika, the housekeeper, she may have a better idea of visitors to the house?'

LeFanu ignored her question. 'Why no photos, madame? There were very few, if any, signs of your presence in the house.'

'I really don't know, monsieur. Certainly, I had my share of being in society magazines and avoid all the social media completely. They're only one step from YouTube as they say. But what you say is strange. There are, usually, a couple of framed pictures in the entrance hall and in the salon. Perhaps Monika tidied them away.' And with a smirk, she added, 'Maybe it was to not make his lady friends jealous. The photos were in quite valuable frames, I seem to remember. Perhaps Monika…?' Seeing DS

Jones shake his head, she continued, 'No? Well, she always goes away to Hamburg at this time of year, bless her. The house is empty, so no need for her to be there. She'll be back soon. Sorry, but I have no idea of her address in Germany. Her surname is Braun, but that is probably no help at all.' She smiled, again at her little joke. 'A *petit blague*, Chief Inspector, as you realise, being a Frenchman.' And glancing at DS Jones with a captivating smile, 'A little joke, dear man. For your notebook, it is Braun, as in electric razors and such like, although no connection with that industrial empire. But translates to a common name 'Brown' and there are millions of them in Germany like in the UK. Another little joke, dear Sergeant.'

Chris Jones reddened at the remark and squirmed a little in his seat as she stared at him. 'Yes, we are still awaiting her return from Germany, madam. We're told by a neighbour that she is normally away for a week.' He looked enquiringly at Charlotte, with only a shrug as a reaction.

With a cue from Philippe LeFanu, he decided to move the conversation on. 'In your absence, a colleague from one of his associated businesses, Paddick Car Auctions, agreed to perform an informal identity of your husband's body. A necessity, I'm sure you would agree in the circumstances of being unable to trace your whereabouts.' A nod from Charlotte was sufficient.

'Ah, *oui*. That'd be Guy, I expect. He did send me a text message. Perhaps that is why you do not think I am being emotional?'

DS Jones scribbled a note which LeFanu could see. 'Scott never gave us a contact number!' LeFanu nodded.

'However, as the next of kin you must formally identify him. I'm sorry but that is the way the law is here. We have no one else to formally identify him. In the end, Mr Scott was unable, for health reasons he says, to give us a preliminary identification to enable us to proceed with our investigation and in your absence we have had to make some assumptions, but yours is the legal process. I will arrange that for you. WPC Ford, whom you've met, will accompany you down the road a little way to the hospital at Heath Road.' LeFanu was studying her, carefully, deciding to force the issue and to see her reaction.

'Oh my God, I can't stand that sort of thing. Closed coffins always. But if I must, then I must. Let us make it quick then. I would like to have the funeral as soon as possible.' And almost as an afterthought, she continued, 'I prefer to remember people as they were. Even my dear husband. Perhaps you think I am being callous, is that the right word?' She accented the word heavily in French.

'The same word in French as in English, madame, albeit different pronunciation. And no, I think it an understandable reaction. I think that we will be able to release his body very soon, assuming your confirmation.' She smiled graciously. A different sort of smile that he had detected before — more in relief, he pondered. Continuing, he opened a new line of questioning, 'On another subject, US Immigration and Homeland Security told us that you had been involved in a fracas in New York a year or so back. Please tell me about it.'

'Just a mugging. They took my handbag — a Coco Chanel. Very expensive too. I was annoyed about that but if you stray off the right streets in New York that's what can happen. I was distracted.' Both men acknowledged the famous brand name and WPC Susie Ford, sitting quietly, nodded in appreciation.

'And what about your golf coach, Jerry Gold. What happened there?' She was visibly shaken by the question but recovered equally quickly.

'Oh, he was set upon a week or so before, I think, I can't remember exactly — the police put it down to a gang. Maybe even the same lot, as it was quite near to where I was set upon. Broke his leg, or at least a serious injury. It's unlikely that he'll ever play golf again, certainly not professionally. Very sad. I feel quite upset really. Nice man.' She smiled weakly, dabbing her eyes with a fine handkerchief rescued from her handbag 'Oh my... Do you think there is a connection with my husband's death and my accident?' LeFanu scribbled a note.

'Doubtful, madame. We have to explore every avenue. Do you play golf?'

'No. Not really. I had a go. Didn't like the dress code much, or the weather, on occasions. A few lessons to try but I was 'lacking ball control', as Jerry put it. He thought that was very funny, I recall.'

LeFanu ignored the levity, 'And your late husband?'

'No, no. He couldn't stand the game. Too slow and you get stuck with people you don't like for hours on end. Leastways, that's what he said.'

'Why New York, madam?' DS Jones picked up the conversation.

'Shopping and the theatre, mainly. California is for movies and little culture, I find, and anyway, Tony was always shooting off here and there on his business deals. Great place for old cars apparently, and I was lonely.

I have some good friends in the Big Apple. But I do fail to see what this has to do with Tony's death.'

'Sorry, we have to explore every avenue. It is building a picture for us, that's all. Another question, Charlotte. What about champagne, did your husband prefer any particular brand?'

'Another strange question… But yes. Veuve Cliquot yellow label. He ordered it from Berry Birch in St James for both the house in Suffolk and the flat in Chelsea. He has an account there. He loved the stuff. Me, I prefer Mumm. He rarely drank anything else — alcoholic, I mean. Perish the thought on a plane flight if they didn't have Veuve Cliquot. He would throw a strop and drink water instead. Why do you ask?' She looked a little perplexed.

'He was hit on the head and we believe that a champagne bottle was the murder weapon whilst he was in the Jacuzzi.'

'The Jacuzzi?' she shrieked. 'What the hell? He died in the Jacuzzi?' Her concern turned to uncontrollable laughter. 'Sorry. He loved the Jacuzzi and he loved champagne and I believe he loved naked girls in there with him, although I've never seen it. It creates a bizarre but very funny vignette, don't you think? Perhaps you need to find a strong young girl with a motive or her husband, father, brother or boyfriend.' She shook her head in disbelief.

'Well, whilst I appreciate your comments, who was it who did the chemical balancing stuff, and why no robes and towels?'

'No idea. I expect it was Monika. I hate the thing. Unhygenic, especially after it had been used for his sex games. Sorry — his big boy's toy and no expense spared. However, I do remember an array of fancy dressing gowns in the wet-room on the rare occasions I went in there. Uggh!' She smiled.

'Describe him to us, if you will, madame, sorry, Charlotte.' She smiled as LeFanu was trying to bring the conversation back to facts that would help him understand the murder situation.

'Well, he is, was, forty-three years of age, born on January 3rd 1971, typical Capricornian. Just had his forty-third birthday. Always had a big party in Courchevel with his 'friends'. And before you ask, birthdays are not big with us, sorry, weren't big with us. Slim, fit, hardly surprising after all his sexual encounters.' She hesitated and glanced at the two detectives but saw no reaction. 'About one metre seventy-eight. Translated to just under six foot, for your sergeant's sake.' She smiled at DS Jones again, pausing before continuing, 'A very meticulous man, verging on obsessive compulsive — you only have to look at his colour co-ordinated wardrobe to understand that. Everything in its place.' DS Jones acknowledged the remark with a nod. 'He went to university studying chemical engineering and joined the Army soon after leaving uni. He was a captain in the ordnance branch, whatever that means or entails. The RAOC, it's called, or was. He left the Army after two years in Afghanistan and went into business buying and selling old cars, or today's classics, as he called them. And has done rather well at it. Oh, and he got his peerage from the Liberal Democrats in 2010, at minimal cost. As he put it, "best investment I've ever made". Most of that stuff is from reading the obituary draft for the Times newspaper, alongside a fuzzy photo of him in Army uniform twenty or so years ago. Really bizarre reading and having to approve his obituary. They prepare them years in advance for famous, notorious and titled people and update them regularly. I'm not sure which category he fits into.' She smiled and her eyes sparkled. 'Last time they contacted him for an update was a year or so back. We laughed about it then, I recall. But he rarely talked of his past. Maybe it was Afghanistan. I don't know.' There were tears in her eyes which, in the circumstances, LeFanu took to be genuine.

'A private man in one sense, then. But what about his cars? By all accounts he had many.'

'I don't really know much apart from they are… were, I suppose… his pride and joy. He could bore for Europe on the subject. He had a business involvement with the auction company near Cambridge. You have met Mr Scott. Anyway, I can't remember the actual place, but it's a couple of junctions down the motorway from the City of Cambridge, and he bought a few and sold a few here and largely in the USA and Switzerland. I last saw them in the summer. He rarely drove them, apart from around the grounds. Me, I like a big car that does what I want. GPS, aircon and power. Old cars are tedious, boring and usually uncomfortable, although they can be worth a fortune, so I understand.'

Sergeant Jones tried to move things along. 'A last question or two, if I may… Do you know the alarm code for the house and the car building and the safe?'

She shrugged. '*Non, cher serjeant*. I know the numbers for the London flat because I use it a lot, but I'm not good with all these security numbers,

Sergeant Jones, and anyway, on the rare occasions that I go to the Suffolk house, I am usually welcomed there by my husband or dear Monika. I usually go there with my friends just for a change of scene.'

'Who would that be, madame?' LeFanu interrupted.

'Oh, the gang — Fi and Ronnie largely.'

DS Jones made a note. 'And the safe?'

'Well that is, sorry was, his very private domain. There should be stacks of cash in there, or there always has been on the rare occasions I have seen it open. His was a cash business, or so I understand. In loads of foreign currencies too. He usually put my jewellery in there when we were away for Christmas or in the safe in Chelsea. I'd be very distraught if that had gone missing. Will I have to visit the house now?' She looked troubled by her own question.

LeFanu picked up the conversation, amazed that she seemed more upset about her jewellery than her husband's demise. 'We will need your fingerprints to eliminate you from the investigation. If you would be so kind, WPC Ford will arrange that momentarily.' Charlotte shrugged. LeFanu continued, 'At the moment, the house and grounds are a crime scene, but in due course, you may wish to visit. Your clothes, perhaps, and personal possessions? The lawyers will advise you, I'm sure. Do you have a mobile number, in case there are any other details to sort out? We may need to look at the flat in Chelsea and maybe the villa in the Alps.' She nodded and then shrugged. 'I would like to attend the funeral, madame. We would be discrete, of course.' He looked at her for a reaction.

'Of course, Monsieur LeFanu, as you wish. It will be a memorial service rather than a funeral. I have seen TV thrillers, both here and in France, and there is always a sinister police figure hiding in the bushes. This time it will be in town I have decided. Fewer bushes!' She giggled at her humour, which had taken LeFanu and Jones off guard whilst Susie Ford was desperately trying to suppress a giggle herself, as she was sitting facing her two bosses.

'Sorry, messieurs. There are times when a little humour can lower the stress, I find.' A coy reaction, but the irony was not wasted on the two detectives. 'The lawyers will be sorting that out soon, I understand. I called them after the gendarmes had contacted me. I have the number somewhere if you need it.' Lefanu nodded. 'I expect,' she continued, 'it'll be a week or so and it will be a simple affair. What else would a loyal and loving wife do than arrange it all?' For the first time, they could see a touch of sadness in her body language and facial expression. She was able, they both thought, to change her approach to questions very rapidly, making it difficult to assess a true reaction.

'I understand, madame, from a directive from our chief constable that, assuming your identification is positive, our people will authorise the release of your husband's body in a few days. Again, my condolences.' He made the point, in his way of speaking, that the instruction from above had been an unnecessary nuisance.

'Yes, of course, Chief Inspector, Here is my card with all the relevant numbers and addresses. And I am sorry if your boss, if that is who he is, put you under any pressure. Tony was very friendly with some of the senior people in the Home Office. I did speak to one of them, a John Mullin. I suspect he, or they, passed the message on.' Without waiting for a reply, she continued, 'I would like to finish with the funeral arrangements as soon as possible. Not a good thing to delay. And will of course, make sure you know the time and date. I will stay in the London flat for a few days to sort out the arrangements. You may call me there if you have any further questions.' She looked relieved that the interview was over, but LeFanu was starting to doubt his own interpretation of her reactions.

'Yes, madame, we will call you. Incidentally, did you take British citizenship when you married Mr Waller?'

'*Non!* I am proud to be French and there didn't seem to be any advantage. Living here most of the time, anyway, I have never found the need. And you, Chief Inspector, are you French or English?' Again that smile, this time slightly quizzical.

'No, madame. I am a British citizen, but then that was a decision by my mother when I was only ten or so… Again, thank you for your candour. Because of the nature of this case, madam, you must let us know if you are thinking of leaving the country.'

She raised an eyebrow as she stood to leave. 'Just in case, you know?'

He continued, 'WPC Ford will arrange for a car to take you to London, after your identification, unless you wish to stay in the locale — an hotel perhaps?'

LeFanu relaxed as she left the room, accompanied by WPC Ford. 'Chris? What is she hiding? The body language doesn't fit the words. She's a clever lady. And I've heard of power-dressing, but never seen it in action.

I bet every item of clothing and accessories were chosen with meticulous care, probably whilst keeping the gendarmes waiting on the doorstep, if there is such a thing as a doorstep in her chateau.

'And here we are in plain old suits.' Philippe LeFanu looked at him with a smile, raising his eyebrows. 'Sorry, sir, not old…' Jones winced as he looked down at his shoes, which were still covered in mud from the village. 'Don't know yet, sir. But wow, yes, that is body language with a difference. Just the way she walks. A very beautiful, sexy lady. And those shoes… my girlfriends call them FMS. Shoes to die for.'

'What the blazes is FMS? No, don't tell me, I can imagine. Chris, put your tongue away, its hanging out!' Jones coloured with embarrassment and LeFanu continued. 'Forget that. Now, what have we learned from that little bit of theatre, apart from the fact that she is clearly a manipulative woman who uses her body and body language to full advantage? Perhaps there is more to the Guy/Charlotte relationship than meets the eye. I'd like a profile on him — financial, personal and connections.'

'Agreed.' Jones said enthusiastically, recovering quickly from his embarrassment. 'She switches from being an upper-class French woman with a brilliant command of the English language to being an English lady with a fascinating French accent. During the course of that interview, the word meticulous has come up at least three times. That smacks of her planning and manipulation.' LeFanu nodded, taking in this aside from DS Jones. 'My take is to look into this golf coach chap and their relationship, for starters. Everyone is saying the marriage was solid, but the admissions by her and the rumours don't follow. And she's too easy on the financial arrangements. She's a spender — just look at her clothes, those shoes and the expensive handbags found in Porten House, and that's only a fraction, I'd guess. Need to look at the other properties, maybe? Certainly get the gendarmes to check out at Courchevel — why did he leave there earlier than usual? Check the bank statements and credit card companies. That'd be my first guess. And whether there is any significant life assurance. Could be a motive there. And then we need this Monika character, and soon. And I think we need to check Lady Groombridge's alibi. Sounds vague to me. Don't know how exacting the French police would be on things like that.' He looked at LeFanu for his thoughts.

'I really don't know, Jones. As I said, I left France at age ten and only visit five or six times a year to see my sister and father. We have to trust to a certain extent and I can only rely on my father's comments, when we've discussed futures and career paths etc., that the French police tend towards the pedantic.'

'Well, sir, were it not for that, I'd say we have the magical formula: motive, opportunity and means.'

'Plenty of ands, ifs and buts in the conversations we've just had, Jones. But you are spot on. Get to it. Ask the gendarmes to check out the alibi with the family, again. They're more likely to get an honest answer than if the British police try. And get someone to check the Inland Revenue people — perhaps they have an address for this Monika lady in Germany, presuming she pays tax here. Her little cottage is locked up tight at the last count, you said, and she keeps herself to herself, according to her neighbours. But in this whole matter, there's some relationships that I don't understand. I'm beginning to smell a link but can't see it. I want everyone we know who has been linked into these events listed, and all their movements wherever and whenever since mid-December to the present date. Planes, boats and trains and don't forget French tolls and even the Dartford tunnel link.'

'One thing, sir. You noticed my raised eyebrow I think.' LeFanu nodded. 'She's literally just been told of her husband's death, yet knows that her title changes if she's widowed. And we're not even a hundred percent sure it is her husband. Strange priorities, don't you think?'

'Maybe, maybe. Perhaps she knew that from somewhere in the past. It could be the society set speak that kind of language. I was more interested in this Guy Scott character having her phone number. That irritates me. I will have another word with him in due course about wasting police time. Incidentally, a rhetorical question maybe, but why are the Duxford auction company so busy if we haven't even confirmed Groombridge's death? Surely that follows later, particularly as he was part owner and so on? It's like they already knew — but that is a quantum leap and assuming that they are not worried and concerned about the future of their business. Perhaps they're up to something else. Looking in to the real ownership and the books would be useful. There's a team of forensic accountants somewhere in the damn building. Let's have a profile of this motor trader, too. I just don't trust that Mr Scott. Weak stomach and all that. Pah! Meanwhile, let's have the formal identification sorted and then we can get on with solving two deaths, let alone a complex burglary.'

'Agreed, sir, absolutely. Maybe this auction house is a clearing house, as they say. Maybe we should get the fraud squad involved, and/or HMRC.'

'Maybe indeed, but we must not take our eye off the ball, to use one of your famous sporting metaphors. Look, get onto Sergeant Shaw and find out about this place that idiot Ramsbottom identified.'

'I still can't get that image of the Lady Charlotte strutting out of here with WPC Ford. That was like models strut, straight out of a fashion show. Do you think she walks like that all of the time?' Jones was visibly licking his lips.

'Enough, DS Jones. Put your tongue away, stop dreaming and let's get on with the job.'

Chapter 24

'Tel. They're edging towards you. They could be there in an hour. Get your boys out now. And you follow tout suite. Scram now and call me when you're fifty miles or so away. No one takes the same route. The furniture lorries should have gone and the transits next. All go to the drop-off points we agreed and pick up the drivers. Get out now and that gives Mr White an hour or so to do some tidying. Good luck.'

'Yeah, yeah, the furniture trucks are on their way. Transits soon, next five minutes or so. How do you know this stuff, George? I know they're racking up the ante. Two bodies and so on but…' Terry sounded worried. 'Is it all going tits up? It's all gone so well and then this…'

'Listen! I haven't time to explain. A few minutes ago, they got a lead on your location. They've got to make that lead fit with the exact place and then plan a raid and probably another hour to assemble back-up from Ipswich. Just get ready now!' George closed the phone to stop any more discussion and immediately rang Issy.

'It's OK, George, I'm nearly there. Ten minutes max. Moment TB's gone, I'm in there mopping up. I picked up on the same conversation you did and they've found my little hidden mic — such is life. Sorry, again, but that old poacher bloke caught me unawares. I thought he was as pissed as a newt. I'll have a sweep in the factory and be gone. The Volvo coach dropped a bit of oil there when I stored it before you took the cars. Anyway, I'll destroy the phone when I'm on my way. You've got my normal number but don't use it unless you have to. Next stop, Melbourne and the family. Looking forward to it.'

'Good on you, Issy. Neat trick about a Plan B factory. Do what you can. If push comes to shove, just scram. And enjoy Australia. Quite fancy it myself, but I don't qualify — prison record and all that.'

***

As darkness approached at the end of the afternoon, arriving at the factory they'd identified, the team under Sergeant Shaw's leadership found it empty and pretty clean, apart from two industrial warm air dryers, a propane space heater that was still warm, an empty fridge with the door open and water from melted ice on the floor, some carpets, stepladders and a heap of chairs. The floor had been pressure washed, and was still wet in places, as had the concrete apron in front of the doors. A new padlock on the gate and on the main doors hadn't stopped them vaulting over the metal five-barred gate and peering in the windows. There was an element of doubt that they could be approaching someone innocent's property, until they rounded the corner of the building.

Around that corner, lethargically sweeping a path, was Ramsbottom, evoking an angry question. PC Edwards was furious. 'What the hell are you doing here, Ramsbottom?' Shaw looked at him in amazement.

'Sweeping up, like what I told your people. Bloke left me some dosh so I got to do what I promised. No one here now, any road. Can't do no harm. Anyway, you never said I couldn't do some work here.' Ramsbottom looked over the locked gates as the police cars blocked the road.

'I'll deal with you later, Ramsbottom. Get away from here now and don't come back or I'll personally roast you with your pheasants or whatever.' PC Edwards was angry, knowing that he'd come in for a bollocking from DS Jones, let alone Sergeant Shaw and a ribbing from the others. The padlocks were cut in seconds with huge bolt cutters.

Jim Edwards looked across at his sergeant. 'This looks like a dead loss anyway, guv. Place is dirty, apart from the floor, but it's old dust and apart from the new padlocks on the doors and gates nothing to see. Some stuff left and I reckon it could be the things nicked from the village that they didn't want in the end.'

'We'll have a forensics team up here anyway, Edwards.' And gesticulating to the figure of Ramsbottom standing in the road, dragging on his fag, 'And make sure that man's life is difficult. We were prepared to turn a blind eye to his poaching and the like because he'd helped us, but this is ridiculous and it'll give him something to think about.' Sergeant Shaw smiled as he turned away.

Shaw was the first in the building, having put on the blue plastic shoes and cover-alls whilst the banter was going on. 'Same old electronics here, same as back at the village hall.' Shaw looked into the rafters and spotted the microphones straight away.

An hour later, DS Jones joined them. Outside, Shaw walked quickly to DS Jones to tell him his findings. 'Not as cleverly hidden as the village hall ones, though.' He looked to Chris Jones for a positive reaction but received none.

'Maybe it's another blind, but we have to double check.' Jones gazed about him, eyes clouded with doubt.

Jones sat in his car, away from the crowd of SOCO people who were crawling over the abandoned pea processing factory unit. Their body language told him that it was a total waste of time. Even the concrete apron in front of the double doors had been swept by Ramsbottom, leaving no sign of tyre tracks, footprints or even discarded fag ends. He called Chief Inspector LeFanu with the news.

'Tell the lads to spread out a bit,' he said to Jones. 'This could be a blind, but my guess is this is a diversion. An early warning to them to get out fast. Extend that guess into a possibility. They are, or were, holed up not far from here. Get Edwards on the case; maybe there are other factories like this.'

'Another example of Ockham's thingy at work, sir?'

'Just so, just so.'

'I'll brief the team and leave it to Sergeant Shaw to organise things here and around the location. If there is one factory, there'll be others. They passed their sell by date when the price of peas dropped…'

'Yes, yes, Chris. Got the drift. Let's move on. The electronic bugs should have been removed by now at the village hall. There's not much future in being based there. Just leave a small team to wrap up the loose ends and we'll pull back to Ipswich. I've to see the ACC about resources and to bring him up to date with our latest find — or not, as you've just pointed out so succinctly.' LeFanu was really frustrated by the lack of success and was prepared to show it. 'Let's hope he can be positive. *Mon Dieu*, someone has to know something.'

PC Edwards was left with an Ordnance Survey 1:25000 scale map spread on the bonnet of his Land Rover, drawing rings round sites of old and disused factories and processing units, farms and large barn structures, any of which could be the target.

***

'Terry, get moving now. Whatever is left, Mr White will remove. They are no more than three or four miles from you. Scram! It could take them an hour or maybe half a day, but it's getting too close for comfort. Talk to you later and see you over there.'

As he closed the call, Terry looked, wild-eyed, around the warehouse. Starting to feel uneasy and knowing that the forensic people could turn a fag-end into an identity parade in short order, he cast his eyes around, looking for any signs of disturbance. The team were ready to go, so he bundled a few plastic sacks into the boot of each car and told them to go to the next phase — each taking a different route and dumping the sacks, where they'd be lost forever. Similarly, the Transit vans were stripped of their livery and the number plates changed yet again.

Terry's car pulled out onto the road, heading south, as Issy's car came into view. Issy used a broom to sweep tyre tracks from the concrete road to the main doors and a high pressure hose to clean the obvious parts of the interior, stuffing bin liners into the back of his car. He jet washed the floor of the factory and removed all the remaining signs of occupancy, including his microphones and cameras. His car was full of black plastic bin-liners, with the only remaining piece of equipment being the generator. Even when, or even if, the police turned up there, little signs existed that it had been used recently, apart from being a little cleaner than would be expected. He put an old, rusty, five-lever padlock on the main doors and on the entrance gates and left for Heathrow Airport, stopping only at three industrial estates to dump the black bags, randomly, in their skips.

It had taken him nearly forty-five minutes to clear all the obvious stuff and he reflected using ex-army types had been a brilliant idea. They were all used to living out of kit-bags and not making much mess.

Issy had watched as Terry's car left the factory, heading north. He was impressed that Terry's driving was slow and measured, not the panicky reaction he expected from watching the video feed from the factory unit over the last hour or so.

Chapter 25

Friday morning, just before nine a.m., and George, now using the ID of Alan G. Turner, complete with his second passport and driving licence and a minimal disguise of a poor fitting toupee (always memorable to the exclusion of other distinguishing features), a few days growth of beard, greying quite naturally, and the inevitable glasses bought from Poundshop and matching his ophthalmic prescription of two times normal sight, drove the converted coach with the two cars on board through the controls at Newhaven. He knew from past experience that there was less bureaucracy and checking fuss there, providing they could get a good look at the cargo then everything went smoothly. He had duplicated export documents with the correct numbers — easy with a little bit of computer dexterity and a good quality printer — certainly good enough for the staff at the port. Coupled with the livery on the coach, it was easy; he'd done it before on a test run with a little MG that was safely tucked up in the barn in Brittany. Just over four hours later, he was in France, heading west for the bridge at Le Havre and Brittany.

On the Thursday evening, to say that Terry Beddall had been scared would be an understatement. As he had driven, deliberately north, from the factory at a steady and unexciting pace, a convoy of police vehicles passed him. Eyes on the road ahead, nevertheless, it started a feeling of panic. Gone had his devil-may-care attitude. Scared was not usual as a reaction, but he knew he had changed in the last few years, what with Ange now in his life (or would be when this caper was over), and George teaching him, as that was how he saw it, even his sister pleading with him to calm down and not go 'inside' yet again.

He had the pictures he had stolen from Canon Baker burning a hole in his jacket pocket. He had to do something with them for the sake of his brother, Rod, but that had to be it. The straight and narrow next. Then, there was the bundle of papers with the House of Commons crest in the same pocket. Those he was tempted to dump, but where? Those sort of things had an un-erring habit of turning up again, as he had read in the newspapers many times.

He had turned left onto the A14 to travel westwards and then the dear old M1 to go south, alongside thousands of other vehicles. M25 westbound or anticlockwise — he could never get his head round that expression — Heathrow was the sign to remember.

George had explained to Terry this next part of his plan, the riskiest part, was crossing the Channel. Each vehicle was to use a different route and meet in Paris before finding out, from him, after a telephone call to George, where the final destination would be. George had told him it was still a better option than having the gang visiting their normal haunts in the UK and getting rat-arsed and maybe boasting a bit. His passport was in order, although it was due to expire in three months. He'd got a new one a year or so before being arrested. The car was a legitimate long term car rental and he had swapped the plates back in a rest stop on the A31 before reaching Portsmouth. There had been a lot of police on duty around the ferry terminal, but that was becoming a norm with all the immigration issues and terrorism. They didn't seem to be terribly interested in car traffic.

A midnight ferry from Portsmouth and a quiet, and luckily calm, sea journey to Ouisterham in Normandy with a cabin and a half-hearted sleep, courtesy of Brittany Ferries, put him on the road to Paris not long after seven a.m. French time on Friday morning. He had changed clothes in the miniscule cabin and was ready to throw away the old jeans and sweatshirt and shoes, 'just in case', as George had said. He didn't know which route George would take, nor where the end destination would be.

He reached the underground car-park at Porte Maillot, just off the peripherique. He'd been worried about driving in France, but the GPS system in the hire car worked perfectly — plug in the address and follow the aggravating woman's voice guidance. He had slowly got used to driving on the wrong side of the road after a couple of near-misses, but the road from Caen was easy after getting onto the D613, it said, through Lisieux and follow the signs for Paris.

The traffic had been light in the early morning since leaving the ferry terminal at Ouisterham/Caen. Closer to Paris, inevitably, the traffic built up around the access to the peripherique; still easier than the M25 at ten a.m. on a Friday, he thought. A moment's panic as he distinguished between 'Ouest' and 'Est'. Several junctions further on, he saw the distinctive tower block of the huge Concorde Lafayette hotel, built over a multi-storey underground car-park complex. A bit of derring-do to cross the major roundabout in front of rapidly moving and horn-sounding traffic and he had been rolling down the ramp to the parking area. Carefully avoiding the security cameras — the position of which George had identified for them all — he drove down to Niveau-3, three floors below ground level and parked. The rendezvous with the others was scheduled to be in three hours — time to get a coffee and have a wander about. He strolled up the Avenue Des Grandes Armees towards the Champs Elysees.

Three hours to waste — he had an English newspaper, yesterday's, that he had bought on the ferry. At every street corner, there seemed to be a newspaper stand, with boards outside covered with lurid stories. He hardly knew a word of French, but the stories were universal — Francoise Hollande, the seriously unpopular President of France, with his fancy bit on a Lambretta scooter, terrorist threats from the usual bunch of thugs, he thought, and celebrities in dresses that left little to the imagination, or some bishop or other pictured with little boys. This Paris Match seemed to be the equivalent of the News of the World, as it used to be. To try to read a French newspaper was, to him, an impossibility, but anyway, in a place like this there were so many foreigners that it hardly seemed to matter. But he bought a copy of Paris Match — it was the germ of an idea.

Returning to the hotel, around two hours later, he went to his car via the stairs — the lift entrances, he knew, were covered by cameras. He had some thinking to do.

At a quarter past one, the first of the Ford Focus cars with their legitimate registration numbers drove into the car-park — so far, no problems. He waved casually to the two occupants, Black and Rose, as they meticulously locked their car and moved towards the stairs — all carefully marked on their maps. He would meet them later — in Cafe Leffe on the ground floor. Car two and three were late, but nothing to worry about — many things could have held them up. That containing Green and Brown was next. He saw them arrive and they saw him — an unnecessary flash of the headlights by the driver seemed to light up half the dimly lit car-parking area.

'Fucking idiot,' Terry muttered. 'Don't they have half a brain between them?' He beckoned to them to come across to his car.

'What's up, Beddall — sorry, Mr Grey or whatever,' Green said belligerently.

'Change of plans. And less of the acid, eh? Put your bags in the boot of this car. We need to drop one more car. Don't ask me why. The boss says so —, and contrary to your opinion, he knows best.'

They both shrugged. 'Couldn't give a shit, mate. You can drive. I've had enough of this bastard country anyway.' The two moved away and unloaded their luggage into the back of Terry's car. He, ever anxious that the third car should arrive, got out to help, glancing over his shoulder every time he saw lights approaching. He moved across to their car and slid into the back seat.

'Hey, what d'you think you're playing at?' Brown asked.

'Just get in. We're going to drive down another level and leave the car there — out of sight and out of mind. OK? Stop bickering and do as you're told, will you? And keep your driving gloves on. Capiche?' Green shrugged again, glancing briefly at his partner, Brown. Engaging first gear, he pulled out of the parking bay.

'Careful, you idiot. You're going the wrong way. We don't want to advertise our presence.' Terry rapped him on the shoulders to emphasise the point. Green reversed up easily, aggravated by Terry's remark, and carefully negotiated the ramp down to the lower floor.

'Over there — between that dusty Toyota Landcruiser and the wall. I want to have words with you two.' He pointed over Brown's shoulder to a place in the half shadow.

Ten minutes later, he emerged and using the stairs went to the Café Leffe. Both Dungay and Goodfellow had not been difficult to control in the confines of their car, both full of mouth so much that they did not expect what happened. And Goodfellow became a gibbering wreck when he saw Dungay's neck being wrenched by Terry from the back seat of the car. He was distressed about using violence, but knew what had been done had to be done. Terry wiped the car with some sanitised cloths he had bought in Portsmouth ferry terminal, and with some difficulty, put both bodies in the boot of the car, covered by the hatchback shelf, emptied their pockets, including passports, tickets and ID, two bracelets that looked valuable, and covered the bodies with some black plastic and left.

While he had been busy, the third car had arrived and at the café Black and Rose were drinking coffee and reading newspapers.

'Hello, mate. Where's the others?'

'Don't know. I'm getting a bit worried. They're well overdue now. I think you guys had better move on, soon.'

Black asked him, 'What's that on your sleeve, mate? Looks like blood.'

Terry thought quickly. 'Stopped to help someone that fell down the stairs — an old biddy with her grandson, by the looks of it.. That's why I've been some time. And me not speaking a word of French. I'd better go and sort it. There's a toilet over the way there.' He disappeared quickly, sure that his face had given something away. Sure enough, there was blood on his sleeve — he'd missed it earlier. Fortunately, his jacket was dark blue and the wet patch from sponging the blood wasn't too obvious and his shirt and jeans were unmarked.

'OK! Mr Black and Mr Rose.' He smiled at the continuing use of their pseudonyms. 'Just give it another ten minutes. I've got a couple of things to do here, so I'll hang about for those two.'

Rose replied, 'Don't give a shit whether they turn up or not — pair of shits, they are. Can't believe how much they've changed since we was in the RLC together. Yeah, all right, mate. You go an' do your business — hope she's nice! Good as gold.' Terry wasn't in the mood to argue, grinned and went to order another strong coffee.

Ten minutes later, he returned to the table, having gone to his car briefly, and quietly said, 'I've got you all, or rather the boss has, air-tickets to Barcelona, one way, from Charles de Gaulle Airport with Air France. You've got about four hours before take-off. And stay in Spain for a minimum of a month, if you've got any sense at all. Shouldn't be difficult for you guys to find a bar, night club and a bit of crumpet to keep you amused. Then fly back if you want to, but not together. So scoot! It's a cheap flight, but there's also an envelope for each of you with your pay-off. Two thousand quid each, in euros, as agreed. Your passport numbers have been registered with the airline, as they have to be, and you must leave the cars in the long term parking with the original number plates and destroy the false plates. Boss says that's important, so do it! Eventually, they'll be returned to their rightful owners, but not until the fuzz have gone over them with a fine-tooth comb. Just don't park anywhere near each other, OK? Wipe them down, guys, and no fag-ends or sweet wrappers. Check again before you leave them and all keys in a bin. No, not the same bin, Idiot. And the boss says thanks.'

'One thing, Tel, why drive these bloody cars all the way over here and then dump them? Don't get it. Not arguing, just curious.'

'Mr Black, sorry, but, the boss reckoned that getting you across the channel gives you freedom to travel anywhere in Europe without passports. Stay in the UK and there's always the risk that the fuzz might pick up anyone of you for any reason - speeding, getting pissed or whatever. Makes sense to me.'

They nodded in agreement and were quick to finish their snacks and get going. One asked about Dungay and Goodfellow, again. Terry replied that he would wait for them with their tickets and envelopes and no doubt they'd get a later plane if they hadn't arrived soon, which seemed to close the conversation. A passing comment of 'Good luck' and handshakes all round and he was left alone in the café.

He found a quiet corner and rang George to tell him that one team wouldn't make it to Spain. 'It's that pair that I reckon did that bloke in, mate. They ain't arrived. I reckon they've done a runner or they've been picked up. One of the lads told me they'd got a gold bracelet or two supposed to be in one of the houses — what d'you reckon?'

'As you said, mate. Give them another couple of hours and then carry on. There's not much else you can do.' Terry, anxious to play the part, started to ask questions. George cut the conversation short. 'Listen, mate! Don't worry about it. Maybe they've been picked up for speeding or just fucked off, maybe they stole some cash and thought enough was enough, especially as you gave them a hard time at the factory unit. There's nothing you can do apart from waiting an hour or two. Got to go. Catch up with you, Saturday, with the Transit vans. Call me again later, if something comes up about those two. Call me from a café in a small town to the west called Ploermel. Café is called Les Quatre Soldats — the four soldiers. Plenty of parking there in the square. OK?' He gave Terry the coordinates for the satnav systems and rang off.

A second call, this time from a kiosk phone in a Parisian street, to the offices of Paris Match, connected him to the English-speaking section and a Madame Francoise Querhault-Remy, whose name was printed in the edition he had bought. Fortunately, she spoke good English. He asked if they were interested in a story about a senior English Church official as a paedophile. Several questions followed, with Terry being very cagey about the details. She suggested a meeting which Terry declined, promising to call again after he had thought it through. He had no intention of meeting, but couldn't see any other way of making any money out of the story. She suggested a price depending on the quality and told him that he'd have to trust them or meet them — the choice was his. He rang off, trying to figure it out. He was determined to sell out the churchman — there was too much hypocrisy in the church. One of the reasons he hated anything to do with the church.

He returned to the hotel complex to wait a little longer before proceeding to the exit roads from Paris. While having a coffee, he thought about the Paris Match deal. A few thousand euros and a lot of risk, but George would see him all right money-wise; so why create more grief? And anyway, he had the nice dress for Ange.

He walked across the concourse to a tabac. George had told him before that tobacconists sold stamps and envelopes. 'Envelope, *s'il vous plait* and un stamp.' He gesticulated in the air for a large envelope, and fortunately, the word being similar in both languages and a simple pointing to the corner of the envelope demonstrated his need for a stamp.

'Oh, *timbre. Oui.*'

He responded to the man serving, 'That's the word, ain't it?'

The tobacconist sighed and passed over the envelope and stamp and took the proffered ten euro note from Terry's gloved hand.

He wrote the envelope to Francoise Remy carefully with his left hand to disguise the writing — difficult still wearing his gloves. Anxious not to arouse suspicion from others in the café, he simply stuffed the photographs inside and sealed it with a wetted finger dipped in his beer.

'George'd be proud of me,' he thought. 'It's like I've been watching too many cop thrillers.' He smiled. Another twenty minutes and he'd have to be on his way. Another walk up to the Champs Elysees and a yellow post box in amongst the throngs of tourists and the deed would be done. And then a longish drive to Brittany and the next stage.

Chapter 26

On Monday morning, after a weekend of playing catch up on paperwork, DS Jones button-holed his boss on the way from the car-park. 'We've had an email from the insurance people with a listing of all the cars in Groombridge's classic collection and a couple of day-to-day vehicles, if you can call 'every day' a newish Range-Rover and a very nice and expensive, by the sound of it, 2014 Bentley Continental GT convertible in Imperial Blue. Interestingly, there's a list of acquisition dates and four of them were bought on the same day. He sold a couple a month or so before and there are several unaccounted for. Three of the missing had been owned by a George Pchelski about five or six years ago, as is, I mean was, the green Mercedes.'

'Talk to that chap Guy Scott again and see if that is usual behaviour for him or others who collect these cars. Find this Pchelski character too. We need to talk to him. DVLA should give us an address. And then my bet is that Mrs, I mean Lady Groombridge, has the Range-Rover, but where is the Bentley? Circulate the number and see if it gets picked up by ANPR. Same goes for the Range-Rover. And why haven't we heard from the French or her? Chase it, please.'

'Already notified the registration numbers, sir. The traffic cops will programme them in, then it's just a wait and see, unless you want it put on the news.'

Lefanu shook his head. 'Not at the moment. I don't want to fuel enquiries from the media at present. If there's no success from official channels then maybe.'

'One thing, sir. I bought a classic car magazine. Idle curiosity, really. From the sales invoices, I had been surprised that these old cars seemed so cheap. Thought I might buy one. The mag says for similar cars, a value around five to ten times what Groombridge paid for them. OK, I could be wrong, but each car was more or less undervalued by a huge amount. What d'you think?'

'Maybe. Anyway, good. Well thought through. Maybe this auction house is a key, but not relevant at the moment to our enquiries. Second thoughts, leave Scott. Park it for the time being, excuse the pun, Jones.' He smiled, knowing that he was not known for his humour. 'My question about this Groombridge is: how did he get home? It's a bloody remote location and no car on the drive or in the garage, as you pointed out. Could he have used one of the classics? Maybe one of those that's missing, but then where is it now? Did you check local taxis? Although, there's no sign of credit cards or wallet, let alone receipts.'

'Not a local taxi certainly. Could be a long distance firm, I suppose, but finding them would be like a needle in a haystack. Airport job, someone he knew, which airport — definitely a long job to even try. I'd like to keep on to this car auction house if you don't mind, sir. I've a feeling that they are linked with the thefts and the damage.' LeFanu acknowledged the request with a nod.

'We need to talk again to that charming wife of his, and quickly.'

An hour and a half later, Chris Jones button-holed his boss in the corridor. 'Long shot, guv, but I tried the Bentley dealership in London that was named on the insurance listing and although they played hard to get — usual Data Protection stuff — they told me the Bentley is in for accident damage repair. Not an insurance job, apparently. They got a call on last Wednesday morning to pick the car up at the Chelsea address of the Groombridge flat. Looks like it hit an immovable object, like a concrete bollard, apparently. They don't know anything else — terribly discrete people, you can almost see it: "No, sir, we don't ask our clients etc. etc., we just help them when they require our assistance." They left a courtesy car, normal practice so they say. It's a Range Rover Evoque. We've got the number, and according to the Met, it's parked in a legal parking zone near the flat and hasn't moved and is branded "Park Lane Bentley Courtesy Car". Pays to advertise? S'pose that's what you get with a seriously expensive car like that.'

LeFanu responded with a nod, his mind elsewhere. 'More enigmas, Chris. More questions with endless possibilities of answers. This villain is leading us by the nose. We've got to break out of the circle and start investigating the crime, not just waiting for the next cryptic clue. My boss is taking a lot of criticism from his superiors and the media about the seeming inaction. And it seems that the journalists are asking the right questions. We find something out and hey presto, they ask about it. Maybe a leak, I don't know. Bear it in mind, please. Anyway, when the ACC gets criticism, it isn't long before it arrives in my lap. One minute we're on reduced resources because of no results or leads, and the next he's loaning people to help. It is difficult to keep a cohesive plan going, but there it is. At the moment, it's more assistance, more boots on the ground. The ACC has agreed more people, reluctantly, I might add. And Chris, HQ say we have to divide our efforts. We're to have some assistance from the Met in the shape of a lady detective inspector, a...' He referred to his notes. 'A Ms Samantha Miles. Yes, and before you say it, she is known as Smiles to her close cronies, but hates it, so her Met boss told me. Best get it out of your system before she arrives and tell the guys and gals with a sense of humour not to go there! We'll have access to specialists at Scotland Yard as and when needed, but she'll be alone on secondment, so lend her that bright WPC, Susie something or other, for continuity. And no petty squabbling. I know Sam Miles out-ranks you, but she has considerable experience in murder investigations and this has all the ear-marks of being pretty high profile and staying that way, internally anyway.'

Immediately, he noticed, as expected, that DS Jones was peeved and sought to remedy the negative body language. 'You take the existing team and concentrate on the thefts and the death of David Grant.' Noticing the forlorn expression on DS Jones' face, he continued, 'The assistant chief constable has locked himself onto our progress, no doubt realising that it'll only be days before the media start criticising again. His comment, Chris, is results do not equal no results plus excuses. The fact that we're all working our butts off, as you would say, is academic. OK? DI Miles will be staying at a B&B from Monday through Friday for a few weeks. So I'm counting on you to make sure she's looked after. OK, find this base of theirs; that's a number one priority.'

Jones, rather disappointed, muttered a 'Certainly, sir' and returned to his car to pursue Shaw and Edwards in their search.

***

ACC Moore stopped Philippe LeFanu in the corridor about the staffing issues. In the privacy of his office a minute or two later, he showed LeFanu DI Miles's staff file with the comment that she seemed reasonably qualified but he didn't approve of women in senior positions — far too many TV shows featuring glamorous girlie cops giving ordinary females ambitions above their status, as he had put it. LeFanu heard, with a little amazement and a raised eyebrow in disbelief his boss's view on misogyny, but useful information about senior attitudes for any future discussions.

Three days later, a meeting was set up by the assistant chief constable to introduce DI Samantha Miles to the team. She was in her mid-thirties and dressed formally but smartly, gaining visual approval from the male members of the team and some admiring glances from the females too.

ACC Moore made it plain that the decision had come from the highest level and the secondment was temporary, initially two months, to add some expertise in a confusing and complicated crime where results were currently not forthcoming but needed quickly, and that this resource was not to be wasted. He had made the remark pointedly to LeFanu. Philippe noted that he had avoided all reference to Ms Miles's skill set, which he had already seen in her file.

She then had spent some fifteen minutes establishing her credibility with LeFanu's team after Moore had donned his cap and disappeared from the room with the inevitable remark about "more important things to do…".

Chapter 27

On the Tuesday 13th January, good as her word, Charlotte put in place the cremation arrangements, a private function, and notified Detective Chief Inspector LeFanu's office of the time and date of the memorial service. It was to be in London, Chelsea, rather than Suffolk, at the Chelsea Old Church in Cheyne Walk, near the Albert Bridge, at noon on the 16th, with canapes and champagne at the Draycott Hotel afterwards.

Jones, seeing the note for LeFanu, commented that the Groombridges couldn't possibly have made do with sandwiches, and no doubt the Hotel chosen had been chosen with care. More like a party than a wake, he was heard to murmur. He recalled the conversation earlier with Charlotte about it being a simple affair and reminded his boss to take some sandwiches! LeFanu was more pragmatic, thinking of the difficulty in parking in Chelsea at any time of day or night and that it would mean a whole day away from his desk.

'What they give me to eat and drink, Jones, is academic. I'm there to watch and listen. And my driver will be sitting in the car for bloody hours. And I have to say, it will be an odd feeling, potentially standing next to a murderer, whoever that might be.'

On the due date, he attended the memorial service, somewhat envious of his driver, left eating a sandwich and listening to the radio, whilst he stood "suited and booted", as the English say, in a Gucci charcoal grey suit with white shirt and the inevitable black tie. The service was, in essence, like most Anglican funerals. Celebrating the life of… rather than the more mournful Catholic approach. LeFanu was more interested in the attendees. Charlotte had greeted him at the church and offered him the typed list of guests, as she called the attendees, which had caused LeFanu to raise an eyebrow.

Her friends, by the look of them, were dressed to kill — more akin to Ascot than funereal; certainly the colour black was not dominant. At the wake, or party would be a more appropriate word, he spoke to Guy Scott, reluctantly, knowing that serious conversations with him were well overdue. Later, he had been introduced somewhat sarcastically by Charlotte to Lord Groombridge's son, Richard, who had arrived from the USA specifically for the memorial service rather than the cremation.

'Detective Chief Inspector LeFanu, this is my step-son, the Honourable Richard Waller-Groombridge, a high-end realtor, as he calls himself, who has come all the way from America for this little party.' She managed to put stress on the words 'all' and 'party' to good effect, gaining a sneer from Richard.

'Bitch,' he muttered as she turned away.

'Why so, sir? LeFanu asked.

'She's a tart. Always getting her own way. Lies like a trooper, or whatever the feminine version is. And her gang of school friends are not much different. When I was eighteen, three of them accosted me — my step-mother, well, she wasn't that then, looked on to what was tantamount to gang rape. All she did was clap her hands and take some photos. Even as a randy youth, it was not funny; not nice, more spiteful. Mind you, my father was not much better, with his endless bimbo relationships. Perhaps they deserved each other. And as for that so-called car dealer, Scott, well, I think he organised the little ménage à trois or whatever — some sort of tribute to his partner, my father. Anyway, are you the man investigating his death?'

'Indeed, I am. We have some progress, but not enough to identify the perpetrator. It is very complex.'

'Uh-huh. I think he had it coming to him. He pissed off so many people in his life and not just because of his love of girls — business people too. You must have many suspects, I guess. Home in the US, I still use my original surname of Waller to avoid being button-holed by irate business people. Naomi, my sister, is lucky in having a married name. You will detect, Mr LeFanu, that there is little love lost in our so-called family. I am not bitter, the old sod gave me a good education and a financial start in life, but I am only really here as a courtesy rather than desire to mend bridges with that cow. And my sister feels strongly too, hence why she is not here.'

LeFanu was amazed at the outburst. 'Have you been in the UK recently?'

'Ah-ha! Does that question indicate that I could be a suspect?' Seeing the look on his face, he carried on, 'No, I hate my step-mother and loathed my father, loved my birth-mother, using the expression that the Yanks eschew, but since her death, father and that cow have never entered my thoughts. No, I haven't been to the UK for about two years. Maybe I could prove that, maybe not. I'd be looking at his gambling, Detective. Some nasty people in that line of business — I know I have had one or two of them trace me and pester me, more like harassment, about Father. If I was looking for a motive, it would be connected with that.'

LeFanu looked at him in amazement at the comments. 'Excuse me for asking, sir, but what you have just said is definitely at odds with the eulogy you delivered not an hour ago.'

'Get real, Detective. I wasn't at the crematorium — was told about it only a day or two before and some of us have to work for a living, unlike that bitch. Eulogies are expected and get reported or talked about, especially for one of Her Majesty's Peers of the Realm. My comments are more private, although I don't really care who hears them one-on-one. Here is my card, should you need to speak to me again. I must touch base with one or two people that I have seen. Goodbye.'

LeFanu was stunned by the abruptness of his departure. He edged over to the gaggle of dressy females hovering around Charlotte. Two were blonde, and one red-head and one brunette. He wanted to look full face at the blondes — just in case. He was haunted by the regular appearance of a blonde in the case. Wishing he had a camera, he just needed to be able to recall a face. Seeking to leave, he spoke to Charlotte, and in passing, asked about her friends. 'Oh, that's Veronica, Fiona and Catherine and Sally — she's the one in the all-revealing purple strapless number. Catherine lives in South Africa, so has made a special effort to come to London. Lovely girl. They're part of the old school gang in Oxford and some of them from our fun days in Switzerland — where we first met at the so-called finishing school. We meet up pretty regularly. They're here for moral support. You've met my step-son, so you will know what I mean.'

'Indeed, madame. An unusual relationship, I imagine.' He shook her hand and offered condolences and prepared to leave. Three girls were crossing the foyer, just ahead of him, arm in arm. Something jarred in his mind but he couldn't put his finger on it. He shook his head and left.

Chapter 28

The Transit vans, packed to the gunnels with household goods on show should anyone open the loading doors, made their way across the Channel without mishap by way of three different ferry routes: Newhaven-Dieppe, Portsmouth-Caen and Plymouth-Roscoff, arriving in France ready to be driven to a destination that George had agreed with Terry. Terry had taken a call from each as they landed in France and had given them the co-ordinates of the café in Ploermel. He needed each van to arrive at different times to escort them to the unit George had rented not far away. As each had a different driving distance, the timing was perfect.

The converted coach containing the two seriously valuable classic cars — the Ferrari and the Porsche — had been parked in one of the barns at Ker-Boulard, a dilapidated farm house and barns a few miles from Ploermel that he had rented for the winter. George had stripped off the wrapping applied by Issy and it had reverted to its original blue paintwork and livery advertising a coach travel company, windows still blacked out, striving to be reasonably innocuous. The two cars were easily off-loaded and covered in tarpaulins.

George, under his Turner identity, had rented for three months only for just two hundred and fifty euros cash, a virtually derelict building about ten kilometres south of the café. Terry led one van to the yard opposite a disused sawmill in Roc St Andre, a small village that had been by-passed by the main road and was virtually a hamlet with hardly any traffic. Not like he had remembered it from his childhood, before the dual carriageway by-pass had been built. Each van was off-loaded into a shed building out of sight of any passing traffic and then, paying off the drivers, he sent them back to the ferry terminal to return to the UK, where they would leave each vehicle in the long term parking at the terminal with their original number plates and cleaned down inside. They knew they would be found eventually hence, Terry lecturing them, using George's own words, about prints and fag ends, sweet wrappers and DNA.

When all three were on their way again, Terry Beddall called George's mobile to confirm and stood there, shivering in the cold wind, to wait. George was close by in the now-empty converted coach, and the two of them man-handled the valuable goods into the empty interior, using the ramps at the rear. Terry was to follow the coach in his car to the Brittany base of Ker-Boulard, a small farm with copious out-buildings on the outskirts of Locmine, a small town known for its abattoirs and the many British who lived in the area.

'Tomorrow, or at worst in a few days, Tel, we will have our pay-off. I'm waiting for a call from a contact, a Swiss guy who wants the cars and the stuff. He should arrive by plane at a local airfield and give things the once over. The plan is he sends a couple of drivers and a furniture lorry and they take everything away, including this bloody coach and the classic cars. Job done. OK?'

Chapter 29

'Sergeant Shaw, I know it's difficult,' said LeFanu. 'But I've a new brief from above, and I mean above. We have to find this bloody base, and quickly. We can't afford the resources to drive around in concentric circles. We've got a couple of extras coming, civilian help. Put a person on the phone to the agents and spiral out from one mile to twenty miles.'

Shaw added, 'DS Jones, we've spoken to estate agents, or rather Edwards has, in the area about a mile or two out from the factory we found and in that line of business. We've asked what's for short-term lease that could take a dozen or so vehicles. Only one possibility and that's been empty for three years. Nothing untoward. We've looked at twenty or more units which could be possibilities. Nothing. They must be long gone, and apart from forensics and a few clues, past history of this gang says that they're pretty thorough. We'll keep trying, if that's what the guv wants, but...'

'One thing that puzzles me is padlocks.' PC Edwards had overheard the conversation and looked up as DS Jones was about to return to his car. 'Nearly everywhere we go, guv, there seem to be new padlocks. That factory unit that seems to be a blind alley — new padlocks on all gates and doors; the field where they parked the coaches with the residents — new substantial padlocks, and you said that the Porten House gates and barn place where the cars are kept had new padlocks, too. Maybe we need to look for places that don't have new padlocks — part of their double bluff, maybe? Why would you fit new padlocks on a derelict building? With your agreement, I'm going to look at that one building that's been empty for three years, which looks like no one has been there for those three years.'

LeFanu, mulling over the information and almost thinking out loud, 'Good thinking, Edwards. Get to it. We'll give this exercise one more week and then I'll go to the top to scotch any further investigation on this front. After that amount of time, the forensics we might find will be useless anyway. Sergeant Shaw, I suggest you carry on until further notice. I know it's a bugger of a job, but there it is.'

Two hours later, and it looked like Edwards had solved the puzzle. Some three miles away, there was a forlorn-looking building set back off the road and the gates and full height double doors were secured with old, rusty padlocks. Climbing the gate, he saw a pile of old pallets and assembled them into a make-shift ladder to peer through a dirty window about seven feet off the ground. Inside, he could see some bits of machinery which just looked out of place. He called in his 'find' and asked for a forensics team.

Results of a quick but reasonably thorough examination that afternoon confirmed that the building had been used by the thieves but scrubbed clean of identifying marks of occupation. One small rubbish bag remained, almost hidden behind a second-hand but newish generator, containing the box for a cheap surveillance camera matching the make and model they had found in the village and the other factory unit, some rags and a pile of new industrial plastic sacks, marked builders' merchants Travis Perkins. Even the floor had been swept clean, removing all traces of tyre tracks.

Edwards was thanked by Sergeant Shaw, who had predicted that the exercise would be a waste of time and had made sure everyone knew his opinion. LeFanu confirmed that he had not been holding out much hope for a careless fag end or identifying item, but the job had to be done. It had been expected, as the gang seemed to cover their tracks literally and metaphorically and they had had plenty of time to do that. Shaw was briefed to ask the obvious questions of the agent for the owners, but it really was a case of closing that particular avenue.

But headlines in the Ipswich local rag that evening stated, "Base for murderers and thieves located" and the by-line "slow off the mark police finally found their needle in the haystack". LeFanu was almost waiting for his phone to ring, expecting the ACC to blast him. He knew they had a leak but who?

Chapter 30

George took a phone call from his buyer, Felix Andervert, and arranged to meet him on the 15th at the little airport, more of an aerodrome really, of Meucon at the edge of a forest, just outside the boundaries of Vannes, an old city in southern Brittany that George knew well from childhood family picnics. Next day, they set out in Terry's car to meet him.

Felix was a tall, imposing, Swiss forty-something, Terry thought, dressed like a businessman and immaculate, despite a two hour flight across France in a small uncomfortable plane from the airport at Mulhouse, near the Swiss border, which served that area.

Terry commented to George, as the Swiss strode across from the plane, 'I could make a Swiss wristwatch look happier than him.' George laughed and told him to be quiet. They returned to Ker-Boulard with him to check the contents and the two cars. He was not impressed with Terry's Ford Focus and kept brushing imaginary flecks of dust from his suit.

At the barns, George threw open the doors to show the two cars — Andervert couldn't help but stroke the Rosso red bonnet of the Ferrari.

'George, I know this car. It was sold at Monterey seven or eight years ago. It belonged to a famous American musician, I forget his name. No, now I remember, it was Isaac Hayes.'

Terry looked at George and mouthed, 'Who?' George shrugged; music wasn't his thing.

Felix noticed and added in English, with barely a discernible accent, 'He wrote the music theme from Shaft, amongst many other favourites of mine. Wonderful music. I want this car for my collection. And that Porsche 356C, I have to have it too. There are some reasons which I don't wish to explore, before you ask. It will match the other one I have — same colour and age — well, it will when you get the parts you promised and the restoration is finished. Make the price sensible and you have a sale.' He raised an eyebrow.

'Patience, my friend and one thing at a time,' responded George. Terry was just standing back, waiting to be asked for help or a coffee or anything.

'Just take a look at the other stuff we've brought for you. It must be an all-in job, Felix, but I'm sure that most of it will be saleable in Switzerland or Germany. We just need to agree the price and the arrangements. *Oui*?'

'Maybe, maybe, but if you have brought me much things more suitable for a brocante, sorry, garage sale well…'

They looked at the antiques which George and Terry had laid out neatly and Andervert nodded in approval.

'Good, very good. I will take all this, but not the freezers and televisions. You will have to dispose of them yourself. I will pay one million seven hundred and fifty thousand euros. Some now…' He patted his briefcase. 'And the remainder when my drivers collect this and the two cars — should be in two or three days from now. Agreed?'

'C'mon Felix, you know that is too cheap. You make it two million and we're flying. And I'll get the parts for your other Porsche for nothing.' He smiled.

He frowned, but knew this was a one-off sale. 'OK! You did get the exact cars I wanted, so it's a deal. Take me back to the plane in that dreadful little car of yours, well, the Ford, rather than that heap of sheet Clio of yours.' Foreigners never seemed to be able to pronounce "shit", but George got the message. 'Perhaps you can afford a better one now. *Oui*?' He handed over the brief case with half a million euros in used five hundred euro denominations. 'Take care of using these notes, George; a lot of people don't like them and a lot of people remember those passing them.'

They returned to the plane and Felix took off with a promise to do business in the future.

On the way back to Ker-Boulard, they stopped off for a celebration drink and a huge sigh of relief from Terry. 'What are we going to do with those fridges and step ladders and televisions. We can't sell them, can we?'

'No chance, Tel, we'll have to destroy them or dump them carefully. We've a couple of days to worry about that. We need to remove any serial numbers and so on — a blow torch should achieve that quite easily. I can understand why he doesn't want that stuff, but it was vital to disguise the trucks coming over here. He's a wealthy and very, very private man who lives in a tax haven in the boundaries of Switzerland and any truck arriving there would be odd if it was full of second-hand fridges and the like. You should see his collection of cars and old aircraft. It's in an underground hangar — absolutely huge, aircon, the works. He showed me once, but only the privileged few, believe me.'

'I do, George, I do. Just as long as his money is good, eh?' George nodded.

Chapter 31

'Have you seen this, sir? It's a headline on Google from Paris Match.' WPC Susie Ford showed him the printed sheets. 'I can't read the French much, sir, but it is talking of our Canon Baker and has some pretty disgusting photos with little boys. Thought you'd be able to help, because of you being French and all.'

LeFanu grabbed the papers, and whilst reading, translated out loud for the group a summary of the story. 'They'd been sent to Paris Match anonymously. Some photos that feature Canon Baker show him in… well, to simplify, show him as a paedophile.'

WPC Judy Bell, who was in earshot, whispered an aside to her colleague, but her stage whisper was overheard. 'Nothing new in that now, is there?'

'Enough, WPC Bell. Go up to this man's house and bring him in. Take someone with you. Arrest him, if necessary for his own safety. If he's not there, find him, and quick. We don't need the media all over this like a rash. It'll be trial by media again. I will speak to Paris Match immediately.' With that, he returned to his tiny office, with Detective Sergeant Jones close behind.

'My sister, Jones, is a journalist with Paris Match and whilst this isn't her by-line, she'll maybe be able to find out how they got hold of the story.' He grabbed the phone and punched in the number of his sister's mobile. Jones excused himself to go and sort out the problem with the Canon, which had all the earmarks of a media frenzy.

***

Vivienne Dubois answered her mobile with a terse, '*Oui*' and then an immediate softening when she realised it was her brother. 'Oh, it is you *mon frère. Ça va?*'

'*Ça va, ça va. Oui*, who else calling from this number?' With a French father and an English mother, he had followed his mother to England when their parent's marriage had broken up, whilst Vivienne had remained in her beloved Paris with her father. Years later, their father had died from a stroke on holiday in Thailand. Vivienne had already married and had been independent at the time. They'd become closer in adulthood, particularly after Vivienne's acrimonious divorce, and frequently phoned each other, speaking in French and English with equal ability.

'Phillippe, you should really take out a subscription to this magazine. It always seems to feature strange English men with very strange habits.' She burst into laughter at her little joke play on words. 'This, *abbe*, how do you say it? A bishop who plays with little boys. Not nice, *n'est-ce pas*?'

'*Ma cherie*, pretty poor joke. English church people do not wear "habits". But a good try in a foreign language. Anyway, Vivienne, that is what I wanted to talk to you about. In English, it's not a bishop but a canon. I can't say very much, as it involves a current investigation. I need to know how, when and why your magazine received the information and the pictures.'

'I thought you might call when you saw the story. He, this pig, lives close to you, I think.' She made it sound like "peeg", which brought a smile to LeFanu's face. She continued, 'I asked the lady, Madame Francoise Querhault-Remy, one of our journalists, and she said it was strange. An Englishman with no French at all, apart from the "*merci*" and "*bonjour*" that the English say so badly, called from a telephone point in the street in the centre of Paris, just before we put the magazine to finish — how do you say it? On Friday. The envelope came Monday. Anyway, he wanted to know if we were interested in a story. She asked to meet to talk about money and he said he'd think about it, but at the time, all he wanted was an address and a name. Bizarre, *oui*?'

'*Oui, d'accord*. Bizarre. And we say put the paper to bed, just to improve your English. In the post, you say? Was there an envelope, a note or anything?'

'*Attend, Philippe Pas de lettre. Peut-être un envelop. Mais, dans la poubelle, immediatement*. Sorry. There was no reason to keep it. A French *timbre*, posted in Paris on Friday. Ah yes, *je comprend*! The finger-prints. *Pardon*. Oops! Sorry we speak in the English.'

'Not 'the English', just English. You must polish up your language skills, *ma cherie*. Anyway, I must go, Vivienne. Ask Madame Querhault-Remy to keep the photographs safe and not touch them any more. We might need them. And before you ask, there will be no juicy follow-up story for you, sorry. So, please ask your colleagues to play it low-key. It's a nasty business and this seems to be only one part of it. *Au revoir.*' After a couple of brief exchanges between brother and sister, he rang off.

LeFanu called from his office. 'Find Detective Sergeant Jones immediately and get him here.'

A few minutes later, Chris Jones rushed into the room, clutching a huge mug of coffee. 'Sorry, sir. Hope I'm not holding things up. Getting the Canon business sorted and... well, I'll fill you in in a moment. How did you get on with your sister?'

LeFanu repeated the gist of his conversation and then asked the questions that had been popping up since his call to his sister. 'Why France? It seems that all roads lead over there. Are the bad guys there? Have they got a hideaway? Who sent the photographs? Were they from the robbery?'

'We just don't know. It must be too much of a coincidence to consider it to be anyone else but someone in this gang of bad guys. And I'm sorry to intrude on your thoughts, but there is some more bad news sir. It's why I was late. The people I sent up to the Manse to secure Canon Baker on a just-in-case basis, as you instructed... well, to put no finer point on it... he's topped himself.'

'What?' Whilst LeFanu hadn't been concentrating, still thinking of the issues surrounding the Paris Match article and the French connection, the words from DS Jones filtered through and Jones had his undivided attention, describing the scenario of the locked study door at the Manse and the housekeeper in tears, not being able to get the canon to answer her.

Jones recited the conversation he had had with his people, 'She had thought, apparently, that he'd had a heart attack or something when our people arrived. They broke the lock and forced the door. Not easy; it's a substantial house and solid oak doors, as you'd expect from a Manse owned by the church. Anyway, they found him there — literally hanging from a rope attached to a chandelier and a chair knocked over beneath. He had left a note, a one-liner seemingly, saying "sorry" and signed by Baker. She had said that he had several telephone calls, which had become very loud, and then had gone to the garage for something, before he had shut himself in his study about an hour before we'd arrived.'

'My God! People are dying in every direction, and there doesn't seem to be a real connection. I have little sympathy for the canon himself, but his sins seem to have caught up with him. But what a way to go and the aftermath… Hope you have a WPC helping the housekeeper lady and contacting all those that need to be contacted.' LeFanu was shaking his head. 'And Chris, part of the aftermath, in a selfish way, will be managing the paparazzi. They, too, read Paris Match. Lock down the village again. If this is a suicide, and it looks like your assumption is correct, it has little to do with our enquiries and I would prefer not to have another body too closely associated with our investigations. It will slow down our team. See to it, please. If we manage it correctly, via Ipswich and the ACC or someone high up, maybe it will divert some attention away from our investigation. And ask the housekeeper to confirm what was missing in the thefts — maybe she'll have a different take on it now. Might sound callous, but we need to know how Paris Match got their information. The two events may be quite divorced. And now, I need to talk to the assistant chief constable right away. This might well take some managing. Then we'll need to talk again. Give me ten minutes, please.'

'Wilco, sir. All done regarding the village security, sir. Already turned away seven journalists. Like bloody locusts, they are. The housekeeper, Mrs Legon, confirms almost exactly what was stolen, except for anything that was in his safe. She had never seen him with the safe door open. And of course, there's that aerial photograph on his desk. Starts to make the connection, do you think?'

'You are probably right, Jones, but we mustn't make too many assumptions. Evidence is what we need. Evidence and direct connections. So many questions, Chris. If they went to France, they must have used the ferries or the tunnel. They would have needed trucks, cars or whatever. We need the vehicle photos and records from all the companies that cross the channel between 6th to 10th January. All English registered vehicles. There'll be hundreds, if not thousands, to plough through. All ports from Harwich to Plymouth. The Assistant Chief Constable will probably offer yet more clerical resources, so we'll get a team from HQ to help. I want you to think about how to narrow down the field. Get a couple of the lads to help, meanwhile. Maybe that bright girl, Susie something or other. She's sensitive and thinks out of the box.'

'Wow! See what you mean. Instant reaction is to cut out the branded articulated trucks, like Eddie Stobarts, and concentrate on panel vans and Ford cars. They seem to be favourite. I'll think some more, but we'll need

DVLA links to check ownership. Real people, not just computer links.'

LeFanu nodded. 'That's why we've got some civilian help from HQ.'

'Must be hundreds, if not thousands, of British registered cars lying around France at any given time. The French police will have better things to do than check on the validity of registration numbers unless there's just cause. My brother says Limoges airport car park has more old Volvo Estates English registered than probably exist in the UK. And if we're dealing with cloned numbers, it's going to be a nightmare.'

'Chris, that's why you're a detective.' Philippe LeFanu gave him a wry smile. 'You can limit searching for the time being by assuming we're looking for Ford cars and Transits. That's worth a bit of a gamble. It may be an error, but it's a good starting point from what we know already. Maybe they went on the ferries or tunnel or whatever. However, it is more important to know where they went, rather than the method of crossing the channel — that, after all, is a given. But I'd also like to know where those furniture trucks are. Leave me for the moment. This'll be a difficult call to the boss.'

***

LeFanu knocked at the ACC's door and smiled inwardly at the pompous sign — ACC Andrew Q Moore, MA and a string of other degrees and qualifications taking up two lines on the sign. No one seemed to know what the 'Q' stood for, but many rumours and sneers abounded. Assistant Chief Constable Moore was not best pleased by LeFanu's phone call and interrupted another meeting to talk face-to-face. Philippe LeFanu stood more or less to attention in front of his boss as he ranted about the little progress.

'And now, ' ACC Moore continued, 'you present me with another high profile death — this bloody Canon fellow. It's not good enough, LeFanu. I read your file and was not impressed with your track record. How you ever got to DCI I find hard to understand. Buck up, or else I'll find another lead.'

LeFanu, rather frustrated, interjected, 'Sir, that's unfair. If you have read my file, you know why I was transferred here. It was…'

'Enough, LeFanu. I'm not here to argue finer points with you.'

'Sir, regarding the death of the canon, notwithstanding the coincidence of the location, we believe it is a suicide and justified, by the look of it.

Surely it is only obliquely connected, sir? Maybe it will serve to disorient the journalists, coupled with the Paris Match article?'

ACC Moore seemed to accept the changed issue. 'Maybe so, maybe so. I will seek advice on that score. Has there been a leak internally, or…'

'I think,' responded the DCI, 'I think that the article published in France is the catalyst, but my senior team are being especially careful about release of information.'

'Enough said for the time being, Chief Inspector. But we need some tying up of these loose ends and some bloody results.' LeFanu nodded and left the office, thinking that the hierarchy had forgotten everything about detective work in favour of their reputations.

Chapter 32

Two days later, after a phone call from Andervert's younger brother, a large refrigerated truck arrived from Switzerland, complete with the livery of a wholesale butchers in Berne. They loaded the truck with the antiques and valuables and placed large boxes of frozen meat, obtained from an abattoir in Locmine, to disguise the load. The cars were driven onto the coach again and the two drivers handed over two large brief-cases of euros and departed.

George and Terry shook hands. 'Deal done, my friend. Peace and a quiet life for me, Tel.'

'Me too, George. And thank you. In the next few days, I'm going to Paris to meet up with Ange. I am going to ask her to marry me and go to live in Spain. Maybe a little bar or something. Keep my share of the money for the moment. Just give me some play dough for the time being.' George nodded and counted out six thousand euros, telling him that there was another hundred and fifty thousand when he was ready.

'That's sensible, Terry. Don't want to carry that kind of money around Europe, let alone back to the UK. And remember what our Swiss friend said about spending five hundred euro notes — they are unusual and noticeable. I'll get it to you whenever... Now, let's get rid of these bloody fridges, microwaves and TVs and what have you.'

They took several of the machines to the local dechetterie, having cut the cables and removed the doors. 'Then we'll do the same with a similar rubbish dump somewhere else. We can't destroy some of these things, so we'll show the disposal people that we care by permanently disabling them and removing, or making illegible, maker's names and the ID plates. The French like that sort of thing.'

Terry nodded. 'Makes sense.'

A day later, they had disposed of the items, had a massive bonfire of the stuff that would burn and closed up Ker-Boulard for the last time. Terry was to be off in the morning for Paris and George to his bolt-hole on the coast.

Chapter 33

'DI Miles, I know the ACC has suggested, not quite ordered, that we divide our labours with you and your team, concentrating on the Groombridge side of things, and DS Jones's team following up everything to do with the thefts and the first death — David Grant. But as time goes on, it is not that simple to divide our team quite so specifically.'

She acknowledged the comment with a nod and clearly wanted to talk to the DCI.

'What's bothering you? Anything I can help with?'

'No, no, sir. I agree about the investigations, though. It is not right to divide labour when these issues seem, at the very least, interconnected. It's just that something's nagging at me and I think it's important. It's to do with Groombridge. I've read all the relevant files and notes and screen reports. I was wondering, why Groombridge?' DI Miles looked across at Lefanu, who returned the gaze, puzzled.

She continued, 'I live in Westerham in Kent and there is a place called Groombridge relatively near, so on Sunday we, my husband, Peter, and I, went there for lunch. Old manor house, not quite a castle but going that way.'

'And?' LeFanu was distracted with a complex report to the police commissioner on levels of staffing and results. Replying to criticism, really.

Smiles continued, 'Well, the ancient family name is 'Waller'. Presumably why our Mr Waller chose Groombridge as his title. We met this chap, a local, in the Crown Inn in the village and he told us the history. All about Henry V at Agincourt in 1415. Apparently, Waller junior captured a French noble — Duc d'Orleans — and got knighted by Henry Five for his troubles…'

LeFanu looked up with a smile on his face. 'So, is this another nail in the coffin of Anglo-French relations? You've got Trafalgar and Waterloo and now it's Azincourt — that is the correct name, incidentally.'

'No, no. Sorry! Almost thinking out loud. I just got to thinking on Sunday and did some checking. The Wallers came over with William the Conqueror — slightly different spelling in those days — and were staunch

Catholics, as you'd expect. Then the family had its successes like Azincourt and then, later on, one of the Wallers became a general in the Army and number two to Cromwell, Oliver, that is.'

'Do get to the point. History is interesting, but I don't need a lecture right now.'

She shifted from one side to another. 'Well,' she continued, without batting an eye-lid at his comment, 'whilst our Groombridge is only a remote part of the family, the Wallers were Catholic then became Protestant. The local church, built by the family, is Protestant. Everything is Protestant except one anomaly that I could find...' She paused. LeFanu again looked up. 'From the file and the autopsy report, Lord Groombridge had been circumcised. Now it did, does, happen that some non-Jewish males are circumcised because of health reasons or whatever, but it got me thinking. I contacted the Harley Street doctor for the family; I called Lady Charlotte for his name and so on.' Reacting to his raised eyebrow, she continued, 'No, I didn't tell her about my hunch. Lo and behold, Anthony Waller had not been circumcised — certainly not in the first thirty years of his life, any road, and certainly not to the intimate knowledge of Lady C, I'll be bound! So, I got to thinking which male in this crime or series of crimes do we know with a Jewish name and probably, possibly, therefore, circumcision at his Bar-Mitzvah or whatever it's called.' She paused for effect.

LeFanu shrugged and suddenly snapped his fingers. 'Certainly the funeral or memorial service or whatever was at the Anglican church in Chelsea. So, following your thought process, I think...? Maybe the golf pro. Jerry. Jerry Goldfinger, or something like that, wasn't it?'

'Nearly so, sir, Jerry Gold. USA Homeland Security say that the family abbreviated its name a generation ago. It had been Goldstein. I asked for an up to date photo. It's just come in — quite remarkable resemblance to Groombridge/Waller. Same height, give or take a centimetre. Same build, same hair colour, albeit Gold's was shorter and eyes much the same. And he could have been wearing a Star of David medallion thingy — many Jewish men do, I'm told. That might explain the mark on his neck that Dr Renata mentioned in her report looking like a chain of some sort was wrenched from his neck, and a wrist watch mark on the right wrist — a bit unusual maybe. Probably a valuable watch, but who knows. Maybe I'm clutching at straws, sir, but there's something that my hunch tells me we've missed.' She looked for a reaction.

LeFanu riffled through the pile of papers on his desk and then scanned the notes on his laptop. 'Good detective work, Sam. Now, somewhere here we have the photo of the UK wedding party — albeit from a few years ago. That man, Guy Scott from the auction house in Cambridge, sorry Duxford, brought them.' He looked up at DI Miles, still standing in front of his desk with a smile before she could correct him. 'Compare the picture of this Jerry Gold to the photo of Lord Groombridge and see what gives. If you're right, and I hope, in a way, that you're not, it looks like your secondment to this unit, Sam, will be extended, sorry! We may have to start talking at length to the Americans.' He looked straight at her and tilted his head in acknowledgement. 'Get to it, DI Miles, and solve this bloody murder. Now, please see if you can find someone to locate DS Chris Jones for me and both of you join me, please.' He smiled as he leaned back in his chair and stared at the ceiling mulling over Samantha Miles's hunch. She had been a good choice by the ACC.

Some twenty minutes later, DS Chris Jones knocked and entered DCI LeFanu's small office with DI Miles. He was pacing up and down, a sure indication that he was juggling with pieces of information that had yet to settle down into a pattern. He started off by confirming that the two teams must keep each other informed about any developments in the light of the intertwining of the crimes. 'However, both of you, something is bothering me and I can't get to the bottom of it. It's to do with my sister.'

'Family matter, sir? Miss Dubois, or is it Mrs Dubois, seemed to have been very helpful.' He looked at his boss, not knowing whether to intrude on personal issues and puzzled that the DI was included in the conversation.

A moment's pause before LeFanu clapped his hands. 'That's it! Well done, Jones.' Without seeking a reaction, he continued, 'Dubois is the issue. French women's names change on marriage, just like English, except they usually, or more often than not, take their maiden name before the husband's. So Vivienne would be LeFanu-Dubois, but I remember now, she thought that sounded pompous in a journalistic career, so just became Dubois.'

DS Jones nodded, still puzzled by this diversion but loath to proceed down this path of LeFanu's family business.

'Don't you see, Chris? Think of Madame Charlotte's fatuous comments earlier about me having an intimate knowledge of the French way of life, and couple that with her first husband — a Monsieur Bertin —

why wasn't she Charlotte Foubert-Bertin before her second marriage to Groombridge or Waller? I don't know whether she decided to follow the same path as Vivienne and discard the maiden name, but she's a society lady and hyphenated names, especially from ancient, well-respected families, would count for something, if the stuff you can read in the society pages of the newspapers are anything to go by.'

DI Miles interrupted, 'Got it, sir. A question, though. What is the name on her French passport? And I suppose, can she have two? And again, just thinking out loud, what is the duration of a French passport?' She looked across at LeFanu who, again, was gazing at the ceiling in contemplation.

'Oh yes. Ten years, the same as the UK. Don't know about the cancellation of one passport on marriage. I've got dual nationality and therefore two passports. Worth asking my sister. That'd be the easy route. And maybe this two passport avenue is to explore further.'

***

'We finally managed to get a locksmith to open Groombridge's safe, sir. Some mechanical part had been bent, apparently, and even though it's an old safe, it was difficult. Anyway, there were some documents, including Groombridge's passport, no fingerprints at all, before you ask. Wiped clean. Why would anyone wipe a passport?' LeFanu said nothing, just raising an eyebrow. 'There was a will dated October last year, written by Strube & Barberis, solicitors of Lowestoft, a whole raft of DVLA car log books and accompanying car documents, and interestingly, two life assurance policies, taken out about three years ago, for three million apiece. Curiously, though, there's one on each of them for the same amount. My mate, in that sort of business, tells me that she'll get the bundle and if they had both died, the kids would get two lots. It's got a fancy name, but that's what it does, so Lady C is going to be seriously rich. Oh, and we found some bank statements so have spoken to HSBC, his main bank, apparently. Basically, he was in deep doo-doo. Owed a fortune to the bank and a few other institutions, overdraft bigger than all our salaries put together by the look of it. All three properties he owned are mortgaged up to the hilt, so little equity there, I guess. And those rental properties similarly so, albeit held in a company name one hundred percent owned by him. Oh, and from some bank statements, several large payments, over the last six months, to

Crockfords…'

'Who?' LeFanu was writing down the amounts as Jones reeled them off.

'It's a posh, members-only gambling club in London's West End, sir. Looks like he's also thousands in debt to a casino in Las Vegas. I spoke to them, Crockford's, I mean. They were a bit cagey but their comment was that they never forget a debt and they exchange information with other casinos and the like world-wide. A serial gambler will be black-listed if they default. Not that that'd be relevant in this case, as he's dead, and gambling debts not being enforceable against family members in this country, legally anyway.'

LeFanu nodded. 'So he is a big loser too, or at least it looks that way. Maybe he wins in cash but pays his debts by cheque? Don't know how these things work, Jones. Check it out. But it fits with something his son said at the funeral thing about gambling debts. Interesting. Maybe we have some sort of motive here.'

'No money in the safe, though. Just title deeds and some paper bands for currency — sort of thing the banks wrap up bundles of cash into. There's Swiss francs, euros, US dollars — all empty wrappers. Presumably, the thieves took the cash. And some receipts for cars purchased that don't seem to match the insurance schedule. Maybe there's a reason for that. I'll talk to Mr Scott again. The papers were in a bit of a mess, though. Didn't really fit with the tidiness of everything else, but that's possibly the bad guys riffling through for valuables, stock certificates or whatever.'

'Watch that man, Scott, Chris. I'm not at all confident that we're getting the whole truth from him, or the involvement of his classic car auction company, or whatever they're called. Tape any meeting. And Chris, get someone to look into the will. I'm interested in any differences between this seemingly current version and any earlier document. I need to update the ACC. Another one of his scapegoat things. Don't repeat that, please.'

***

LeFanu went straight to ACC Moore's office and was admitted immediately. Obviously they are taking this seriously, he thought.

'It's been nearly two weeks and apart from that odd suicide, all you have to tell me is that this victim, the Jacuzzi murder as the media call it, is not the person we thought it was. This is an egg on the face thing. We released the body on best authority and now… This will go higher up the line of command, you realise that?'

LeFanu nodded, thinking that the decision to release the body for cremation had come from that same source "higher up the chain of command" but the blame would come back down the line, inevitably. 'I would like to say, sir, that we are only querying the identity of the victim at this stage. More checking to do without the benefit of the cadaver, of course.' ACC Moore coloured at the implication of LeFanu's comment. Philippe continued. 'We are checking all airports in and out of France to establish this American, Jerry Gold's, movements.'

'Bring in that bloody woman who identified her husband when it is clear it wasn't him, and find out why. Throw the book at her, arrest her or something. We need that information before the media accuse of incompetence.'

''Agreed, sir. But I must leave it until we have some verification, otherwise it will be, as you say, egg on face twice. She's a French citizen and we know that they can be vey protective of their own, and I should know!' Moore waved his hand as dismissal. The interview was over. LeFanu thought that his bosses would have some explaining to do.

DS Jones was waiting for him two floors up in the HQ building, propping up the door frame of his office with yet another mug of coffee.

'Thought you might need this, sir.' LeFanu nodded his thanks. 'Sir, a Stanislav George Pchelski was the registered keeper of the Mercedes 500SL, PKP166G, re-registered as ALG111, until seven years ago, alongside three other cars. All sold at auction to, guess who, Anthony Waller, now Lord Groombridge. The missing Porsche had been owned by a film celeb from Los Angeles, I forget his name, but it is on the file, and the Ferrari, equally from across the pond, was owned by someone called Isaac Hayes. All the provenance is there, and of course, they are all left hookers.'

'Left, what?'

'Sorry, left hand drive…'

'You certainly are into this petrolhead game, aren't you…'

Jones smiled. 'And we've got Pchelski's address, but he moved years ago. Landlady gave us his sister's address, near Bexhill, in Sussex. We're onto it, sir. I'm arranging for a woman police constable from Eastbourne

Nick to interview her today. She's been briefed.'

'Good work. I don't expect she'll give us much, but there may be a link somewhere. It would pay to speak to this Polish guy about how Groombridge got hold of those cars.'

'Indeed, sir. But I think he's English, not Polish.'

***

Marion Naismith was very nervous when the WPC knocked on her door. She was reassured, straightaway, that no harm had come to her family, an understandable reaction.

Her first question when asked about Stanislav George Pchelski was, 'Oh my God! He's not hurt or anything?' Seeing the shake of the head by the police constable, she continued, 'He's my brother. He's not in trouble again, is he? He promised me he would stay out of prison.' After a few minutes, the whole story of George's criminal record poured out.

'Not at all, madam. We want to talk to him about some cars, old cars, he owned a few years back. We can't seem to get a handle on his current whereabouts. That's all there is to it.'

'Well, he had a pretty green thing — a convertible, quite posh, I think. Don't know what happened to it after, you know, the prison thing. Had some others, too. Grandpa P taught him a lot and I think that's where the love for old cars was born. Come to think of it, I think it was a Mercedes.' Seeing the police woman writing busily and looking up at the mention of a green Mercedes, she continued, 'Anyway, I have a mobile number for him and the address of the flat he rents, but he told me, us, I should say, that he was thinking of moving to France pretty soon.' She found the number and scribbled the details on a notelet pad on a coffee table by the phone, adding that he travels around a bit nowadays, never seeming to stay in one place. 'Don't really know why he keeps a flat in London.'

'What does he do for a living, then? I imagine it must be difficult for him now, after prison,' the WPC asked sensitively.

'I don't really know. We gave him some money to tide him over to get adjusted. I think he does work on classic cars for a few garages, sort of restoration stuff. I don't understand, really. And he finds obscure parts all over the place, mainly Europe, but once or twice the USA, I believe, although he doesn't talk about it much. It was his first love, ever since he was a child. Our grandfather, Grandpa P, owned a garage franchise for many years.'

'What did he, I mean your brother, do before…?'

'He was quite senior in an insurance company. Can't remember what it was called. He was there for years.'

'Any other family, madam?'

'No. I don't think so. Even though he's my older brother, he has always been close mouthed. I think he would have told me if he had married again. He had a girlfriend for a while, but no one current that I know of. He was married, but divorced years ago and no children. I'm the closest he's got, apart from Grandpa P, who's over ninety now, and he lives in a flat near Boston in Lincolnshire, one of those supervised places. I would ask you not to bother him.'

'Of course, I understand. Were we to need to talk to him, we will contact you first. But why Boston?'

'The Polish air force people seemed to gravitate to East Anglia during the war and I suppose he just stayed there. He loved France, probably because they helped him escape to England after he walked from Warsaw in 1940. We used to go back to Brittany for holidays nearly every year after my parents died. He loved the people and they loved him. Of course, age prevents him going, nowadays, but he always gets me to buy Christmas cards for him to send.'

Interrupting her, gently, from her reminiscing, the police constable focussed the conversation on the questions she had listed from DS Jones's instructions. 'Madam, thank you. Do you have the ex-wife's contact details?'

Marion shook her head. 'It was a long time ago and the whole thing was a trifle acrimonious'

'And did you ever meet the girlfriend? A blonde or brunette?'

'No. I wouldn't know what she looked like. When George talked about her, it was all in the past. All over a long time ago, by all accounts. I think the prison thing put the lid on relationships like her. I spoke to her once and she called me another time and spoke to one of my sons, instead, to get George's mobile number.'

'I don't suppose you have her number or name, address something?'

'Er, no. Let me think. Her name was quite posh-sounding. Charlotte, that was it. Sounded a mite foreign, but these days it's impossible to tell. Don't know the surname or anything else. He was going out with her for ages. That's an old fashioned expression, isn't it?' She smiled.

'That could be useful, thank you. You've been very helpful. We'll call if there are any other questions. In the meantime, perhaps if he calls you or visits, could you ask him to call me, at Eastbourne, or the chief inspector. No problem, it's just to tie up some loose ends.' She handed over a card with her number and wrote DCI LeFanu's office number and the contact numbers of Ipswich police HQ on the reverse. Outside in her car, she rang Detective Sergeant Jones and relayed the information from Mrs Naismith, and because it was worrying her, asked DS Jones why an ex-girlfriend would be calling George Pchelski some years after they had parted company.

Jones's reaction to the ex-girlfriend's name was simply a shout of 'YES!' He pulled up the record for Pchelski from CRO and almost ran to LeFanu's room with his laptop.

There was only one answer from DCI LeFanu. 'Find him, but be sensitive. Lot of 'might be' statements here. Just because he's an old lag doesn't mean anything relating to this issue. Could be a coincidence — innocent until proven etc. Might be worth finding out who his mates were in prison. Might be a connection, but tread carefully. Might be a link with the devious Lady Charlotte. There are plenty Charlottes in the world, but this is starting, again, to look like coincidences. Let's talk to her again.'

'Wilco! I'll tell Smiles about this development, just to keep her in the picture, so as to speak. And I thought a transcript of the court case might be useful, too. I've ordered it up.'

'Watch it with the "Smiles" comments, Jones.' Jones nodded, anxious to find the connections.

Fifteen minutes later, DS Jones rushed back to see the DCI. 'Sir. Bingo! Pchelski's employer was Beech Underwriting. Basically, a case of wholesale fraud. That's the same firm that Lord Groombridge is, I mean was, a director of — sorry for the bad grammar. All his, Pchelski's, possessions were sequestered by the court on conviction, including a small collection of cars. Maybe, at last, we're making some links?'

'Thanks, Chris.' LeFanu almost grinned. 'Find Pchelski, pronto! Looks like you and Inspector Miles will be working together hand-in-glove after all. Just a hunch, Chris, but find out who was insuring the house and those bloody cars. Bet they stick together and they're all insured with his Beech Underwriting pals. Look for the connection. Maybe in the documents in his safe?'

Jones nodded.

Chapter 34

Only a few hours later, Jones rushed into see his boss. 'You wanted a connection, sir. Here it is. News from the French police. A British national, name of Terence Alexander Beddall, has died under a train in the station of Lyon. That was Thursday the 15th. A CRO check — just routine — and hey presto! The interesting thing is that Beddall was in Upper Heywood nick for a long stretch for burglary, second time inside. Good man with safes apparently. And sir, guess what! His cellmate for two years or so, up to last spring, was a certain Stanislav George Pchelski, inside for big-time insurance company fraud. Name ring any bells, sir? Rhetorical question, really.'

'Yes, yes, of course. The guy who owned the cars that Groombridge bought. But why was Beddall in Lyon? Nice city and all that, but hardly the metropolis of France…'

'No, sir, it's in Paris'

'Ah! You mean the Gare de Lyon — the big railway terminus for the South of France. Is it murder or an accident?'

'Yes, sorry. It does say the railway — the SNCF. No further knowledge at this point — they are investigating but there are some odd points, apparently, which is why they contacted the UK.'

'Keep me informed, Chris. Some of our coincidences are sorting themselves out at last. Where is this Pchelski character? As we agreed, bring him in to help with our enquiries, rather than being heavy-handed,' LeFanu mused, gazing out of the dirty window at the car park below. 'But why was he in Upper Heywood? That's not a white-collar location.'

'No idea, sir. I've called for a download of the files and the visitor's log for both him and Beddall.'

***

'So, what do we know of Beddall's death? *Merde*… We needed to talk to Pchelski. There has to have been a link.'

'It seems, sir, from what the French police have now told me, that he was poisoned with strychnine. Rat poison is the only legitimate use I've ever heard of. There was the Lambeth murderer in the 19th century, who killed loads of prostitutes here and in the USA and Canada — painful and fairly quick death, apparently. It was in a course I did at the police college Hendon.'

'Quite so, Jones. Quite so. In France, until recently anyway, it was possible to buy strychnine-based rat poison in garden centres and DIY supermarkets the length and breadth of France without any form of identity. Scary stuff, eh? It will be almost impossible to trace, if my assumption is correct. I have to say, I wouldn't even care to guess how much of the stuff would kill a man — a spoonful or a glass full. If it was rat poison, then how would you know? But if he was hit by the train, as seems to be the case, maybe there was just enough poison to give him extreme pain so he ran for it — unfortunately in the wrong direction.'

'Sir, the investigation into Beddall's death shows some pretty good CCTV footage with him seated at a table in a station bar, underneath a flash restaurant called the Train Bleu.' LeFanu acknowledged the comment with a nod of his head. 'He was with a rather tasty-looking blonde woman in her mid-thirties in a red coat and a black wide brimmed hat, wearing the inevitable sunglasses and carrying a large handbag. Only a fleeting glimpse of her face, which is partially obscured by her hand. We've downloaded a copy and I'm having it digitally enhanced. Apparently, he had several cups of coffee and gave her a shopping bag. She pulled out a dress and then screwed it up and put it back into the carrier bag. All this from a waiter who was waiting for the money. Also, he, the waiter, that is, said the girl or companion disappeared a few minutes before the incident whilst still in his line of sight. They seemed to shake hands or touch and then she stood up and went.'

LeFanu looked puzzled. 'Stating the obvious, Jones, but if it was murder, then she will be a suspect for the gendarmes, and if there was another root cause, then she's an important witness. And if it was deliberate pre-meditated murder, then she had to be there before to study the ground; check the camera angles, even choosing the right seat. But when? No one will be willing to check CCTV over the last week or so. But sad to say, my money is on murder. '

'No mobile phone but a wallet with credit cards and a fair bit of Sterling and high value used euro notes in an envelope, nearly four thousand pounds worth, passport and driving licence — all in the name of Terry Beddall, address in London. Lives with his sister, we've established. Also a set of Ford car keys with Enterprise car rentals on the fob, with a UK phone number. And a diamond engagement ring in a box in his trouser pocket with a receipt for cash, euros, that morning from a jeweller just off the Champs Elysees. Apparently, he up-ended the table, smashing the cups etc. and stumbled across the concourse doubled up, seemingly in acute pain, and trips across the railway line — too late, he is hit by an oncoming TGV train from Lyon. Gendarmes rush over. Place is sealed off etc. DOA at the hospital. Gendarmes have taken statements from others on the concourse and the staff in the bar and they've taken away the cups and saucers for analysis. Interestingly, there was an H&M bag on the floor underneath their table, containing a screwed up D&G dress, European size twelve. Expensive, the gendarmes said. Not the sort of thing you'd buy in H&M, apparently. And he was smartly dressed in a BOSS suit with a blue shirt and yellow tie. Expensive shoes, too. Could be something to do with the engagement ring, maybe?'

LeFanu raised an eyebrow. 'Hmmm. Maybe is the right word! However, they always say poison is a woman's game. Maybe she added it to his coffee. Pretty horrible way to die, by the sound of it. Maybe the dress tells us something. Certainly the size of the lady and maybe height. Is it traceable? Get one of your young female team to do some ringing the dress retailers. Dolce & Gabbana is expensive, but how common, I've no idea. We need to identify the blonde... that's the second or third time I've said that. Coincidence, or am I clutching at straws, Jones?'

'Well there are plenty of blondes around, but we have drawn a blank at the blonde in Eye St Mary and as you said — what are the links? Didn't we comment on the expensive dresses in the wardrobes at Porten House, or is that a quantum leap? It would be good to eliminate a few of our suspects sometime soon. How do you fall in front of a train? Weird.'

DCI LeFanu acknowledged the thought with a frown. 'Point taken. Let's talk to his sister PDQ; perhaps she's aware of his associates and whereabouts, and by then we'll have seen the file, too. And the train thing, Jones: we, in the UK, have raised platforms; the rest of the world, almost, have platforms level with the track and steps up into the trains.'

***

A car picked up Beddall's sister from her home and drove her to Ipswich Police HQ. She had agreed to the meeting after a visit from the local police in Clapham, who asked for her assistance after broaching the bad news about Terry. Aged around mid-thirties with mousy brown hair, the passing of time had not been kind, but she had clearly dressed in her "Sunday-best" but was noticeably emotional when she arrived. Out of courtesy, and sympathy, LeFanu and DS Jones met her in the car-park and escorted her inside to a conference room on the first floor, confirming that the driver would take her back down the motorway to London whenever she wished.

'We were sorry to bring you the bad news about your brother, Ms Beddall. I hope you now feel able to answer some questions so we can get to the bottom of this dreadful event.' Chief Inspector LeFanu had an ability to get the best from people who had been victims, or closely linked to victims, by showing an empathy rather than just sympathy.

'Please, call me Sharon, everyone does. I live in Clapham, on my own, or rather when Terry was inside I was on my own. I suppose I'm on my own again, now.' She sighed. 'Our brother, Rod, died, tragically about twenty-five years ago, 3rd June it was.' She sat down, smoothed her skirt, and smiled a little wan smile. 'And that was the end for our parents. They just gave up and both died within a year. Terry shared with me after that, and shared the expense. I haven't got much money. Anyway, I thought the police lady said it was an accident. Terry, I mean.'

'Well, Sharon, it was an accident, as far as we can tell, but we are trying to establish why Terry was there and who he was with at the time.'

Trying to relax her, DS Jones offered her some tea, and smiling, started gently on his question matrix. 'How did you get to the prison every week for nearly seven years — regular as clockwork, according to the visitor's log?' Jones wanted to know how she could take at least a half-day holiday every week. 'Do you have a job, Sharon?'

'Well, I do work seven days a week as a home help to an old lady who lives nearby in Clapham, and she understands. I mean, understood. But money is tight, which is why the lifts I got the last few months of Terry being inside were such a Godsend.' Tears welled up in the eyes.

'How did that come about, Sharon?'

'A nice lady gave me a lift back into Oxford for the bus, oh, I don't know, about six months before Terry was released and then picked me up and dropped me off every Thursday, loads of times, and a few occasions right into London. We became good friends and she visited me several times at the house in Clapham around the time that Terry was released and Terry, well, he was head over heels for her. They became an item not long after.' Sharon was trying to hold back the tears.

'Sorry to keep asking questions, but we do need to get to the bottom of this. How did you meet her?' Jones was doing his best to keep Sharon calm.

'Well, she was standing by the gate having a fag, I think, when I came out of the visitor's centre seeing Tel, one Thursday afternoon. It was near the bus stop and she offered me a lift. Angela is her name. She's been visiting someone — her brother or cousin or something in B wing which has a separate visitor's centre.'

'No, it doesn't.' Jones apologised for snapping as soon as he saw the surprise in her face.

Sharon looked puzzled and then defensive, 'Really? Oh, well, she said it did. Maybe I got it wrong. Again. Funny, that, now you talk about it. Anyway, we got talking and became friends. Come to think about it, now, I think she said her cousin's, brother's, whichever it was, name was Tony, but she never spoke about him. When I asked, she dismissed his being inside as stupid mistake on his part.'

LeFanu looked up, puzzled, and excused himself, telling a WPC in the corridor to search all with the name Antony, Anthony, Tony in Upper Heywood prison at that time and include staff as well as prisoners.

Jones continued. There was something here his intuition told him and he didn't want to wait for LeFanu to return. 'Sharon, did Terry meet her often over the last few months?'

'Yeah! Quite a bit and text messages! So many every day. I didn't know he could do text after, well you know, being in prison all that time with no mobile and these smart phones nowadays, but he managed. In fact, I don't know where he got the money to buy such an expensive phone. He wasn't exactly flush with money, although he did give me a little from his earnings in prison. Very welcome it was, too. Then when he went up north, he had a job — electrician or something — for a couple of weeks or so, he said. He did that in the Army for a while before switching to the logistics people. Anyway, after he went up north, everything seemed to stop with Angela. It just dropped off the map. He was devastated and rang me every day to see if she had called. She didn't even call me. So much for friendship, I suppose.' Sharon couldn't stop the tears as she spoke. LeFanu, who had discreetly returned to the interview room, signalled for a break and the constable on duty went in search of fresh tea and sandwiches for them.

She started talking again after a few minutes, 'Unusual surname, though. We used to laugh about it. "Darling", that was her name. You know, he would say, "Hello, Angela Darling, darling" — that sort of thing. Silly, really, what you remember.'

'So, where did she come from?'

'London, somewhere, I think. But she said she had relatives or family near Banbury or somewhere beginning with B. She did tell me, but I forget. Sorry.'

'No matter, Sharon. No photos, I suppose?'

Sharon shook her head. 'I think maybe Terry had some on his phone. He'd become quite a dab hand with it. I expect you need the number? It's 07867 444670 pay-as-you-go, and I think it was with Vodafone, but I can't be sure. He used to look at his photos on screen regularly.'

LeFanu returned to the table. 'Thank you, Sharon, we'll put a trace on the phone number. Unfortunately, we haven't managed to locate the mobile. Anyway, can you describe her to me, Sharon? We think she has been involved in a nasty crime, so we're trying to trace her.'

'Oh Lord! You don't think she had anything to do with my Terry's death, do you? Oh my God, what have I done?'

'No, no. Sorry, Sharon, I put that badly. A description would help, though.'

'She's about thirty something, more or less my age, but I've had to work every day and I know it shows.' She fingered the fringe of her hair. 'Blonde, tall, good shape, about a size twelve. Terry liked her boobs and long legs. Not posh, but not common either and swore a lot. Always smartly dressed, a bit sexy but not too obvious. Always wore those really high heels. Can't cope with them myself.'

LeFanu raised his eyebrows almost automatically. 'The blonde again?' he muttered almost inaudibly, except for Jones, who had almost anticipated the reaction.

'What sort of car did she drive?' DS Jones continued.

'A silver one.' Sharon obviously didn't know precisely but Jones pressed her.

'Saloon car or hatchback or what?'

'I'm not into cars, but a hatchback I think. It was quite nice. Newish, I think. Could have been a Ford but I'm not sure. Had satnav and bleeper things when you went backwards. Now I think of it, there was one funny thing.' Jones perked up, raising an eyebrow in cynical anticipation. She continued. 'One day, she had a wedding ring on, just a plain gold band, no engagement ring or anything. I was worried that Tel was getting involved with a married woman so I mentioned it. She said that she wore it to stop being pestered. Said that blokes left her alone if they thought there was a husband somewhere. Never wore it again, though. Odd that.' Sharon paused.

'What did she do for a living, Sharon? Do you remember anything about it?' LeFanu asked whilst Jones excused himself for a few minutes.

'Oh, yes. She went on about it when we were in the car. She ran a fashion boutique in Bicester Village. You know the one that has lots of fancy shops selling designer label stuff. Can't afford it myself, but I did go there a couple of years ago with a friend and realised it wasn't for me. Full of Chinese clearing out the bargains, but not in my price range. Nice, though. It was called… Oh, what was it? Yes, I remember, "Love It to Bits". Nice name. I suppose that's why she always had such lovely clothes. You could tell, you know.' She sat back, expecting the next question when DS Jones returned clutching a file.

He flicked through the pages of reports and translations from the gendarmes and some photo extracts from the station CCTV. 'Would you mind, Sharon, just looking at these photos we've had sent over from Paris. I know it might be, no, will be distressing, as Terry is in one or two, but we do need to identify the lady. Do you know her?'

Her reaction answered the question. Clearly distressed, she murmured, 'Well, yes. I'm almost sure that's Angela. It's not a full frontal but she does look awfully familiar, from what I can see. Is that a French railway station? What's she doing there?'

DS Jones responded, 'Yes Sharon, it's the Gare de Lyon. The station for the south of France, and we really don't know why your brother was there, or this Angela lady. But we do appreciate the information, and again, sorry if we have worried you unnecessarily.'

LeFanu also expressed his thanks, and again, his condolences to Sharon about Terry's untimely death in Paris, suspecting the conversation wouldn't get any fresh information and arranged for a car to return her to her home.

'Jones, that was inspired. Get CRO to check all the A Darlings in the UK and northern France, although I have my doubts that that line of enquiry will bear fruit. See if there's anyone around Banbury or Bicester with that surname. Surely no one would choose a false name that was so memorable — it sounds like we're being fed a deliberate foggy issue of a false name. I'm getting more suspicious of this lady. Remember the blonde driving off in the village around the time we think the guy was murdered? Odds on it's the same one. A blue car that time, albeit. Check the prison CCTV; maybe they have something if she was visiting or even in their car-park, as Sharon says. Maybe the car number. The visitor's book. Anything! Why no mobile? Sharon says he lived on it. Maybe this woman took it. And look into this boutique thing. I've made a note of what she said. Remember the dress in Paris? Maybe they're agents, or whatever they call it, for D&G. I don't hold out much hope, but we've got to check.' He handed over the note about the "Love It to Bits" boutique. At a nod from Jones, he continued, 'All roads seem to be leading to France. I think a trip to Paris is called for, tomorrow. I'll clear it with HQ. Get your passport out; we'll be there lunch time tomorrow.'

Chapter 35

Next morning, both men boarded the five past nine Eurostar train from St Pancras International to Gare du Nord, Paris. 'First of all, sir. Got a call from the lads. The boutique thing doesn't work out for us. They've never heard of a woman called Angela, let alone Angela Darling. There's four girls there and not one is a blonde, apparently, and there's never been a blonde employee, *quelle surprise*! And no, D&G is a rather specialist designer label, shops-only stuff, above their price ranges. Beddall's file makes interesting reading though, sir. May I draw your attention to his first run-in. Page three.' He turned the laptop around for LeFanu to see.

LeFanu tracked through the electronic document, skipping to the summary first and then to page three. He looked up with a smile, 'Like your attempt at the French language, Chris. Didn't really expect that the shop would be of much help. They, if it is a "they", are clever, and that would have been too simple. Good old Ockham, eh? Of course, we could wonder how she chose that particular shop. Perhaps she's been a customer in the past?'

'Thought of that. There are just too many people of all nationalities going through that Bicester Village place. Red herring, I'm afraid. And Pchelski only had two visitors, according to the log, whilst inside at Upper Heywood nick and Ford Open Prison. His sister, regular as clockwork, and a colleague from work, and he's been checked out as OK — retired now and living in Cheltenham. Bit sad, really. Years inside, and only two people turn up to visit.'

LeFanu shrugged and returned to the screen. '*Mon Dieu*! His brother Rodney hanged himself after being abused by a priest and Beddall took it out on the cleric and was sent to a young offenders' institution for that. I really shouldn't say this, but he should have a medal.'

'Yes, sir. I understand, but now make the connection with the "unfortunate" demise of Canon Baker in Eye St Mary and the article in that edition of Paris Match that your sister sent you, and we have some answers.' DS Jones raised his fingers to emphasise the quotation marks around the word "unfortunate".

'I'm ahead of you, Chris.' LeFanu confided. 'If those lurid photographs were stolen from Eye St Mary, or even if they were some sort of blackmail material, it could easily be enough to send Baker over the edge. I doubt whether the Anglican church officialdom will comment either way.'

'It does fit with the anger that Beddall had as a youth, as you can see from the transcripts, and that probably dictated his career path in crime. But Baker wasn't the name of the church bloke who was beaten badly by Terry Beddall.'

'No matter. Sounds like Baker was of the same mould, which would be enough, I suspect, for Beddall to exact some revenge, although we are making two and two equal five. All this is fine, Sergeant, but we need to move on. Having explanations like this do not help catch the real villains. They explain rather than solve. And will be lost in files somewhere, no doubt. Such is the real world. It does, however achieve one thing; Baker isn't a suspicious death — suicide, as we thought. I will inform the ACC accordingly.' He passed the laptop back to Jones.

'We put a trace on that mobile phone. It's been dead and untraceable since the accident at the station. Probably the battery and SIM card have been destroyed. Vodafone are giving us a list of calls made and received since it was bought. Most of them appear to be from throwaways, so no trace of the callers. However, we're onto it.' LeFanu acknowledged the comment without changing his stare through the window of the train as it approached Frethun in the Pas-de-Calais.

'The other thing, sir.' He interrupted LeFanu's train of thought. 'There is no trace of an Angela Darling going through any point of entry to Europe, let alone France, within the previous ten days, or exiting back, for that matter. In fact, there is only one Angela Darling listed in the UK. So, it is likely that whoever it is has another name. But it's being checked out.'

LeFanu muttered a, 'Thanks' without moving his gaze, deep in thought.

Approaching Paris Gare du Nord, DS Jones's mobile buzzed with a text message. He excused himself and read it. His eye-brows raised at the message content, attracting the attention of his boss. Jones passed the mobile to him to read for himself.

'Two more bodies, Chris? Who, where and when? And is it anything to do with us? Who the hell are these two?'

'I'll call to get more detail when we get off the train, as the reception here in the Paris suburbs is poor, to say the least. As you saw from the message, it is two Brits, been dead for a few days from broken necks and found in the car park of a large hotel in Paris in the boot of a British Ford Focus with false registration details, but obviously a hire car from the UK. Smelling a bit ripe, apparently, which is why they investigated the car.'

'Hmm. Beggar's belief. Call HQ as soon as possible. I've got a bad feeling about this. Everyone around this case seems to be destined to become a corpse. So far we aren't having stabbings and gun-shots, not yet anyway, but it is still bloody violent…' He scratched his right ear-lobe.

***

Despite the rain, rushing across the pavement outside the railway station to a bar for coffee and a much deserved, in LeFanu's mind, baguette allowed Jones to make his call back to Ipswich from the comfort of a table that didn't move and enabled him to take notes. It was a long call and it was obvious that LeFanu was itching to find out more.

'Pretty horrible story, sir,' DS Jones started, after closing his phone. 'Two guys found in the boot of the car three floors below ground after a pretty horrid smell, by all accounts, was reported by a motorist parking down there. No ID or paperwork, but obviously a British car. As we knew, false plates, but as luck would have it, the real plates were under the carpet in the spare wheel well in the boot. The local police were quite cute and called the rental company in the UK. In this case, it was Hertz and got the name of the person renting it. A Mr Neil Dungay of Billericay. The other guy we haven't identified yet apparently. Now, sir, we know a lot about Mr Dungay. Been up before the beak in Colchester several times for GBH and cautioned three times for drunk and disorderly. The interesting thing is his Army record. Demoted from corporal for what amounts to theft. Guess what? Beddall was in the same regiment, Royal Logistics Corps and they were both in the brig together, albeit Beddall ended up at Her Majesty's pleasure and Dungay just got chucked out of the army. Bet we find one or two of his oppos were there too. Getting a fingerprints analysis and DNA reference to help. All UK armed forces have their DNA registered on recruitment, for obvious reasons, so it should be easy to check with the Army people.'

'At last we're finding some solid links, Chris. Thank the guys and girls for their work. This "oppo", as you call him — a colleague from the past? Perhaps they had a leader in the Army who is behind all this? It's the sort of thing that happens. Another quantum leap, Chris… Lord G had an army background. Officer stuff, I remember. Someone with brains uses the team spirit of the ordinary ranks. It has been known. See if there is any connection — maybe same unit or whatever, but it is a leap of faith at this stage. Worth checking out with Sam Miles, perhaps, whilst we're enjoying all Paris has to offer with the local gendarmes.' With both hands, he put the word "enjoying" in quotation marks. 'And ask the guys to double check army records. If this guy, Dungay, was a dishonourable discharge or whatever, maybe there was a specific incident and others involved. Let's go and meet the local police and see what they've got to say.'

***

In a freezing cold wind from the east, they took a taxi to the Quai d'Orsay. The driver, recognising his passengers as English, took them in a roundabout way through the tunnel at the Pont d'Alma to show them, in a macabre sort of fashion, 'Zis is where your Princess Diana died,' much to the annoyance of LeFanu, who acknowledged the fact and told him, in voluble French, a direct route would have been preferable.

They were to meet the colonel in charge of the investigation and his colleagues, who were concerned with the death of Beddall and greeted them with steaming hot French coffee and croissants and a friendly approach when they realised that LeFanu was French.

'We thought you might have a French connection, but you are a Frenchman.' Delivered with a beaming smile, he continued. 'Monsieur, this is a copy of Monsieur Beddall's electronic rail ticket from St Brieuc in Brittany to Paris Montparnasse. *Arrivée* nine twenty-five a.m. TGV takes about two hours thirty minutes.' The gendarme gave Jones a digital print-out.

DS Jones took the ticket print out and smiled at the officer, recognising his rank from the elaborate uniform and feeling underdressed in his jeans, sweatshirt and slightly crumpled raincoat. '*Merci, monsieur.* So where was he from, say, nine thirty until twelve fifty, even allowing, say, an hour for the shopping trip for the engagement ring, according to the receipt, and thirty minutes to get to Gare de Lyon when the CCTV picked him up?' One of the gendarmes looked non-plussed, shrugged and frowned at Jones's French accent.

And to the detective chief inspector, Jones added, 'No one has a clue at the moment, sir. Police are checking CCTV. Local police are checking the car parking at St Brieuc for a Ford, British registered, and any other UK registered cars. My hunch is that we seem to have come across loads of Focus cars in this scenario, so maybe. Well, it's just a maybe… God knows how long it'll take the French wooden-tops.'

'Sergeant, try to keep it friendly. We need their help. It's bad enough for me, being a Frenchman in England, having to live down Waterloo and Trafalgar, let alone Azincourt, as Sam Miles pointed out, without annoying the local boys too much. And they do speak English better than you speak French!' He smiled an acknowledgement to the gendarme, who shrugged as only the French can.

***

An hour or so later, sitting in a pavement café on the left bank of the Seine, Jones's mobile rang and after a few minutes and some '*oui, merci and au revoir, monsieur*' said in the most appalling French accent, enough for LeFanu to grimace, Jones snapped the cover back and smiled. 'That was the colonel's side-kick. Bingo! They've found it. Pretty high-end hire car — got all the gizmos. They've opened it up without the keys and without the alarm going off. Smart, eh? They'd make good car thieves, that lot! Nothing inside — a bundle of papers in an envelope in the boot. Apart from that, clean as a whistle. An electronic bug found under the rear valence and a gas oil, diesel, receipt from a place called Baud. Know it, sir?'

'Why? Who was tracking him? This blonde woman maybe? Same device as before, I wonder. And yes, I do know of Baud. It's a small nothingness market town in the middle of rural Brittany. Why there?'

'Gendarmes will circulate a picture of him in a thirty kms radius of St Brieuc. They're suggesting concentration in the South. Why south? Why thirty kms? '

LeFanu pondered a moment and then, 'Of course, he could have got the TGV from several stations in Brittany. My guess is that St Brieuc would be the most convenient or nearest. Big town shows up on a map. No guarantees, but a good starting point for a search. Why buy diesel in Baud? Search goes south, at first, at any rate.'

'And sir, a café proprietor at a Bar Marianaude in the centre in this Baud place says they think they recognise Beddall from the photo on French TV, TF1, and says, if it is him, he's been a regular for a while with another English guy. Apparently, he parked in a restricted area for disabled people so drew some attention from the locals. You know the Brits, taking the mickey about French parking regulations. A white smallish car is all he could remember. One of them went across the road to the Maison de la Presse. The newsagents, apparently, but of course, you'd know that, sir.' He referred to his notes, 'No real description that we could recognise. 1 metre 70, maybe 1 metre 80 tall, middle aged, not fat, not thin, brown hair, quite long. Loads of them speak English in that neck of the woods, apparently. Lots of ex-pats there — even a local cricket team, would you believe. So could be anyone — a resident, a tourist or a bad-guy.'

'Never understood cricket, Jones. Weird sport. Who the hell do they play in deepest darkest Brittany? Rhetorical question, before you go off hunting, Detective Sergeant.' He laughed as he said it. 'But seriously Chris… Is this yet another red herring to take us off the scent? I'm starting to doubt my own senses and intuition. Maybe this blonde woman is behind it all. But what the hell is the motive or motives? Any fool can dump a car in a remote location and leave some pretty obvious clues. But why a tracking device?'

'Don't think so, sir. It can't be a red herring for Beddall's murder. And he had to come from somewhere. Why not Brittany? And his parking ticket time links with the departure of the train. But is this woman behind it all? The brains maybe. We haven't anyone else, so, as she keeps cropping up, it could well be. And certainly Beddall's track record is not a planner, more someone who takes orders.'

'Jones, the report of the interview with Pchelski's sister talked of Brittany as a place she and her brother used to visit regularly. Is that another coincidence or…?'

'Well, I wouldn't have thought she is involved…'

'I'm inclined to agree, but I am a great believer of that mantra of policing: doubt everyone and question everything.'

'But it's a big place and thousands of Brits go there on holiday. Been myself as a kid.'

'Mmmmm!' Jones could see that his boss had other thoughts in his mind. 'Chris, if we've got access to his car, we might find out where he's been.'

'Don't follow, sir.' Chris Jones looked puzzled.

'Satnav, or GPS, as the French call it. It is complicated to delete previous addresses from the system. I know I got completely confused by mine when I had to take a huge detour getting to HQ one day — an RTA, complete with air ambulance blocking the road. I tried to delete the route and it took a long time to figure it out. If the Enterprise car rental people fitted satnav in that hire car, or it was there from manufacture, then the chances are that our villains might not have deleted the previous entries. I'd expect, for example, to find that Beddall had keyed in the address of the railway station. He wouldn't be likely to know exactly where it was, would he?'

Jones interrupted the flow of LeFanu's conversation, 'And he wasn't expecting to die, so he wouldn't have cleared the memory anyway. Brilliant thinking, sir.'

Philippe LeFanu acknowledged the compliment with a smile. Jones continued, 'It was a plug and play device, apparently. But having been in the nick for some years, he probably wasn't very familiar with the sort of back-office part of the satnav system. Sorry for interrupting, sir.'

'No, no. Spot on. I hadn't thought that through. But you're right. Anyway, maybe it'll tell us where he was prior to getting the train. Maybe we can back-track his movements? On my car, there's a "get me home" button. It automatically gives a route to your start point. That would be interesting, wouldn't it? Oh, GPS in France doesn't use post-codes like the UK. It works on latitude and longitude co-ordinates, so it is very precise. Got to be worth asking our French police friends to look. Get onto it, will you? They'll probably need the keys, so it'll take some time to get them from Paris to St Brieuc.'

'And maybe it has Bluetooth telecoms, which means all his mobile phone calls are logged too.'

'That's something I didn't think of, Chris. That could be very useful, even if they're using throwaway phones. Good thinking, you'll make inspector yet!' He smiled. 'Maybe we're finding the loopholes in their elaborate plans to fool us, because, to me, that's what it's been looking like.'

DS Jones called the colonel's office and spoke to the second in command, a Dominique Fleizmann, and explained their thinking, largely in English. He passed on his mobile number and was told the gendarmes in St Brieuc would call him direct.

Chapter 36

'The Breton gendarmes have come back to us. There's a message on my phone and a three-page fax waiting for us at our hotel. The GPS has been removed and they've analysed all the addresses. Some were from a previous hirer, apparently floating around southwest England, so we've discarded them. Very interesting stuff, they tell me. Got an address in a town called Ploermel, somewhere called Roc St Andre, they had to spell that one out for me, and another that just has those co-ordinates, they're checking that out. And a hotel in Paris — The Concorde Lafayette; that's where those two bodies turned up. Coincidence or what? Oh, the post-code of a factory unit in Suffolk was listed, and I've sent that info back to Ipswich in case it's another location we don't know about. Oh, and also the Porten House address. And the home address you talked about is his sister's place. Loads of others — in York, Banbury etc., but just pubs and cafes. Full info on the fax. You were dead to rights, sir.' Jones looked pleased.

'Well, that ties him in with the thefts and maybe the Jacuzzi murder, but we mustn't forget that there could have been another driver at any time. He might be the killer, but who wanted him dead?' He paused. 'And Jones, nothing at all to link with this blonde woman?'

'Nope. He wasn't using hands-free Bluetooth in the car, so the phone thing will be a bit more difficult and needs some help from Vodafone. Maybe we'll pick up phone numbers he was calling or texting, but my guess is that they're not that stupid to have hung onto a hot phone. They're going to impound the car and are doing fingerprints and the usuals. The bug is quite new and has a sticker still attached — RadioShack, Edgware Road, London. And our guys have checked the serial number; it was a cash sale — one of many. Made in China and virtually untraceable. Not the same as those in the village hall or the factories and completely different from the one found on PC Edwards's car. And of course, it has to have a receiver — some gadget for reading the location information. Doesn't work with a mobile phone app, apparently. I think that it's not connected, or directly connected. Excuse the pun.' He looked up and saw LeFanu weighing up his comment.

'Carry on, Chris. I don't necessarily agree but…' He paused. 'Wait a minute, though. Check out all the locations on that GPS.'

'Already being done by our team, in conjunction with the local gendarmes, sir. Place called Ker-Boulard was rented by an Englishman, a Monsieur Ian White. Cash-strapped French farmer, apparently — no questions; cash in hand stuff. Another address was a café and shop in the middle of town, according to Google Earth, and yet another a semi-derelict building in this Roc St Andre place. Gendarmes found a local who said he had seen some vehicular traffic but no people. Interesting as well is a private house in St Gildas de something or other. A cottage near the sea owned by a Brit from Suffolk as a second home.'

'Nothing left around or discards, I guess?'

Chris Jones shrugged. 'No such luck, sir. Anyway, they didn't need the keys for the car, so they're onto it. Take back what I said about the French wooden tops, although they're still using fax. That went out with the ark. HQ says it's the first time in a year or more that they've received a fax, but apparently still pretty normal usage from France, and there's the copy waiting for us at the hotel — sometimes it's better to read, eh sir?' LeFanu nodded, mind racing. 'Another thing, sir. The French police have identified a Citroën Picasso parked for a short time next to Beddall's car. Driver took some time to change a tyre on the driver's side. Then got in and drove away. No ID from the cameras — probably a white male, but that's it. Oh, and front number plate obscured. They say they may be able to pick its rear plate number from other cameras, but not to be too confident, or words to that effect.'

'Indeed! Keep me in the picture, so as to speak. Could be the placer of the electronic tracker or a genuine local.' LeFanu looked at his detective sergeant, and scratched his right ear, 'But Chris, this blonde is bugging me. There's something I'm missing, we're missing. Start to think of all the women in this case. Where were they at the crucial times?'

'Charlotte's alibi stacks up, apart from a few hours — not enough time to get to England and back, if we believe the alibi she's got. The gendarmes have reported that it seems legit. We've still got the issue of the dual passport to resolve. Angela is still an unknown. She pops up, if it's the same woman, several times, including the Paris murder. She's my favourite, so as to speak. Clever, whoever she is, how she chose that table in the bar on the concourse with only her back to the CCTV. Obviously planned, well, I think so anyway; even when she got up from the table, we've only got a fleeting view of her face and rear views in a red coat and the back of her head, or rather her large black hat, as she walked away.'

LeFanu's mind was racing. Not sure of why or what it meant, but he had a vague feeling that he had hit upon something important. 'Mmmm! Still not enough. And Mrs Stephanie Davis, the lady with the paramour, is a non-runner, as is the non-existent Monika and Beddall's sister. O-Kay, think, as well, of all the males we've come across and see if there could be any other connections.'

Jones added, 'I'm still not comfortable with the daughter who didn't turn up for the funeral thing and also this American golf pro. Stony silence about him, notwithstanding Smiles's assumption about him being the victim in the Jacuzzi...'

'If you had met and spoken with the son you would not be so surprised. No love lost there at all — not one iota.' LeFanu suddenly clicked his fingers. His mind had been concentrating on the events on the station concourse. 'Eureka! Check the CCTV in and around the ladies' rest rooms. I want to see everyone who entered and left. If you are right and she chose that table carefully, then maybe she chose it for other reasons too — escape and proximity to somewhere she could change her appearance. You know, Jones, you commented about the way she walked, Lady Charlotte, that is, when she was here for an interview. Positively drooling, I seem to remember.'

'Yes, true. I was, like every other red-blooded male,' he replied hesitantly, face reddening from the neck up.

'Well, we have a woman walking away from the camera at the café. Perhaps the CCTV will pick up something similar — movement of the head or hips. It's called kinesthetics, apparently, or so DI Miles tells me, and the walk of a model down a cat-walk is called sashaying. Whole new language, but it might give us a lead from the feeds from other CCTV around the station and exits.'

'Maybe better to have a female searching as well?'

'Just so, just so. The French will be able to help. You know, Jones, you have just reminded me of the funeral. I couldn't put my finger on it at the time, but Lady C and her friends all walk the same way. It is sashaying; it is the right word. Perhaps they are taught to walk that way at these finishing schools. Ask around the lasses.'

Chapter 37

There were twenty relevant CCTV cameras on the concourse, and with a three hour time window agreed, it was a long job to concentrate on the seemingly thousands of women walking to and fro. No sign of a blonde woman in a red coat — several were close, which took a lot of time to investigate and cross reference. DS Jones took an overview role, with two female gendarmes, and inspected the video of the hue and cry that had started resulting from Beddall's death under the train. From the ladies' cloakroom adjacent to the steps down to the platforms from Le Train Bleu restaurant, what appeared to be a young, long-haired brunette in a cream coloured coat, blue jeans, white trainers and a dark blue French beret, clutching a white carrier bag with a Galeries Lafayette department store logo, caught Jones's attention. He had the tape replayed at slow speed. There was something about the way she walked and moved her head. The comment from DCI LeFanu about sashaying bugged him. He scratched his head and called the DCI to come to the viewing room in the security offices. It had taken three hours of staring at screens and he needed to be sure.

LeFanu was there in five minutes, and with a clearer head, listened to Jones's explanation. 'Just look at the walk, sir. It's just like you said. I've seen that before, but it could be on the television or in a film or just a girl in the street. I thought a second opinion would be worthwhile. I hope I haven't wasted your time.'

'*Excusez-moi, monsieur l'inspecteur. Vous parlez francais?*' one of the lady gendarme screen operators asked of LeFanu. 'I only have a little English. *Je m'appelle* Mimi Le Blanc.'

'*Oui, naturellement. Je suis Francais.*' They spoke at a speed that was completely wasted on Jones's school-boy mastery of the language. After a few minutes, LeFanu turned to him and said, 'Mimi here,' he smiled at the lady, 'thinks we should change the colour of the coat and digitally remove the hat and maybe even change the hair colour to blonde so we would be looking at like for like. I've no idea how, but obviously here we have an expert.' With Jones nodding furiously, he turned to the gendarme Mimi and smiled. '*D'accord, mademoiselle.*'

No more than two minutes later, she had reconstructed the lady using similar shades for colouring as the still frame from the café CCTV. It was a good match and both DCI LeFanu and DS Jones spontaneously applauded her work.

'Now we can try to track this lady across the concourse and outside maybe. Brilliant.'

'What she's just done is way beyond my understanding. That was pretty amazing and it must be state of the art technology. Thinking of our wedding photos from Guy Scott, our guys simply said they could have been manipulated. Maybe we should ask your friends, that colonel chap, Jean-Paul David at the Quai d…'

'Quai d'Orsay, Chris. Good idea; if they've got the technology, maybe they can help. Have you got the pictures?'

'No, they're back at base in the file. Couldn't bring everything. We could get them couriered over, or maybe a digital copy? But going back to the CCTV stuff. The thing that attracted me, so as to speak, was the way that woman walked. Like we said, there is something distinctive about it. Can't put my finger on it but there's something…'

'You're absolutely right, DS Jones. You are a detective. I've seen that walk before too. And I think it's our Lady Charlotte, or pretty close, anyway. There were two blondes at the funeral service — one at least, I believe, a school friend of Lady C. I'd like to know more about them.'

'Really, sir?' Jones couldn't resist the gibe. LeFanu was not amused but acknowledged that his choice of words were asking for a comment. 'Just think of that time in the office when you stood there with your tongue hanging out. Think of the stiletto heels and the smile? I doubt whether we could prove it. The DPP would laugh us out of court if we brought someone to book solely on the way they walked. Public prosecutions need more tangible evidence. But it could be a good assumption to start looking in that direction and re-start our enquiries with fresh enthusiasm, don't you think?'

'Absolument, *mon brave*!'

'*Bien sûr, bien sûr*, indeed, DS Jones.' He raised his eyebrows at the schoolboy French and inevitable appalling accent, and turning to the gendarme, Mimi, he asked if there was any notable technology that members of the public could use to doctor a photograph.

She told him that it was easy to do but if a really professional, almost indistinguishable effect was required, it was a specialist task, limited to people with high-tech kit and expertise.

He asked in French, 'What do you mean by "almost indistinguishable"? Can you look at a photograph and tell whether it has been changed?'

'Eef it is digitale, monsieur. Then *oui, plus facile.*'

LeFanu beamed. And to Jones, he gave a thumbs up sign. 'We're getting there. Jones. Definitely getting there. Do you remember Charlotte telling us what her brother did for a living? High-tech internet, dot.com companies. Another coincidence? Maybe, or the beginning of a crack that may become a chasm.'

'A whole new set of questions, now, sir. A whole lot of new thinking. For example, if, and it's a big if, at this stage, Charlotte's brother manipulated those photos, then he's in this up to his neck, and then we can't trust her alibi either.'

'First things first, Chris. Let's get those wedding party photos examined; maybe they've been doctored. And this lady, Mimi, seems to be the person to do it. I'll clear it with the French people'

Jones interrupted. 'You mean photoshopped, sir?'

'Whatever. You know what I mean.' He went on to describe Samantha Miles's hunch. 'Only one person has identified Groombridge and that's his wife — understandably — but what if this is an elaborate con? What if the dead man is someone else? Maybe this Gold character. Maybe Lady bloody Charlotte is pulling the wool, as you say, and has deliberately mis-identified the cadaver, knowing it would be cremated and therefore impossible to prove one way or the other. But why? We need that Monika lady and pronto. How did that car dealer, Scott, get those photos? And a bit of conjecture here, what if Groombridge wasn't murdered? You said that he was in debt up to his eyeballs. Is that a motive? Lord Lucan disappeared heavily in debt and guilty of a murder, but how much more Machiavellian to find a substitute. If we're right, the chief constable is going to be red faced, having given permission for early release of the body for cremation. Anyway, Jones, can anyone do this photoshop stuff? I mean could I, or you, with a modicum of technical computer knowledge, do it? That's my question, rather than looking for experts. The whole thing has got me thinking… Get onto it, please.'

'I'll find out from the techies. Should be no more than a phone call or two. It feels right, what you say and DI Miles's theory, but where will we get any substantial proof? Maybe we start with your not-so-favourite man, Guy Scott. His profile has come through on my phone. Age forty-two, born in the UK. Started working for Caffyns luxury car division in London, married and divorced, no children. Moved to the USA for a few years. California, of course, the place to buy rust-free old cars, apparently, and buying and selling there before moving back to Cambridge area, where he bought the business and expanded it. Maybe some probing questions and veiled threats about a business investigation outlining our suspicions — no, call it findings about the values of these bloody cars they auction.'

'Just so, just so, Detective Sergeant.' LeFanu had that look of mulling over the implications of Jones's comments. After a half a minute or so, he continued, 'This could be a fit-the-facts hypothesis, an induced hypothesis, it could be called, so we must be careful, but what it does is, we start looking for clues under different stones and most of those stones now seem to be in the UK. The clever people in training call it "already listening". It means you, all of us, have difficulty looking away from the obvious, much as you have just done. Well done. Three gold stars! We need a team meeting and I'm not sure what extra value we can add by staying in France much longer. Home tomorrow.'

LeFanu decided that they would have dinner at Le Train Bleu at the Gare de Lyon and walk the scene of the crime on the train concourse below. Nothing better, he had exclaimed, to understand the full lie of the land and have one of the best dinners in Paris, and it was to be his treat. Two bottles of a good Bordeaux wine and a handsome *gigot d'agneau,* carved at the table after they had spent thirty minutes or so exploring the concourse layout, served to give them ideas.

'Chris, get that D&G dress back from the French police and let's try it on Charlotte — not literally, of course, Chris, before you start having dreams. If it is hers, it gives a direct link to Beddall, and why did the girl screw it up and throw it back at him in that café directly below us? Any self-respecting person would not bite the hand that gave them a dress like that, even if it was not brand new. Perhaps she recognised it, knew who it belonged to — sorry, bad grammar. So who?'

'A rich bitch, size twelve.'

'Good answer, although a bit misogynistic, I think!'

'And sir, if you always wear a hat, it could be to disguise what's underneath. I know some people who have had the misfortune to have chemotherapy who do just that. We think that wigs are involved. A large hat covers a wig.'

'Indeed. And a carrier bag from a posh department store could carry alternative clothes and a wig.'

'This Jerry Gold supposition is playing on my mind…'

'Mine too. Ever since I spoke to the ACC about it. Expand, Chris. Throw your ideas on the table.'

'If, and it's a big if, it was a substitute for Lord G, we have all sorts of motives — the gambling, huge debts and so on for needing to do a Lord Lucan and run. Charlotte said they were like duplicates. If it were him, we should trace his movements into the UK, starting with the USA. Where did he fly from and where to?'

'Excellent. I knew those two bottles of Bordeaux would loosen the little grey cells, as Hercule Poirot says, and there was a book, I recall, by Agatha Christie called *The Mystery of the Blue Train,* and here we are. Get onto it tomorrow. And yes, before you comment, I do watch the odd bit of TV crime thrillers!'

Chapter 38

They returned by Eurostar, first class, with a compartment to themselves with papers and laptops spread around, alongside some real French coffee. DS Jones's phone rang as they left the environs of Paris and reception improved. He looked shocked and LeFanu waited impatiently for the call to finish.

'Beddall's car just blew up, sir. They were moving the car onto a transporter with some device they use if they haven't got the keys, and up she went. No one badly injured, damage to the truck, but bugger all left of the car. Papers with the House of Commons logo all over the car-park and some peripheral damage to other parked cars. Lucky that was all it did. Needless to say, they've got the equivalent of the bomb squad investigating.'

'*Merde*!' LeFanu always fell back on the French language when under stress. He'd explained many times that his mother, whilst English born, usually spoke in French when she was under strain. 'Nasty but bloody clever rigging a booby-trap like that. Lucky they removed the GPS device, Anything else, apart from what they reported and finger-prints? Who's behind this? It is clever. Maybe that Citroën Picasso in the car park the gendarmes mentioned. Destroy the evidence, enabling us to track movements, but maybe we are ahead of their game thanks to the "wooden tops", as you called them. It looks like if Beddall had survived the Paris incident, then he would have died in his car at St Brieuc. Belts and braces stuff — they, whoever they are, needed him dead. Why? And if we'd had the keys and started the car by conventional means, then "boom". Whoever it is is nasty and acts with complete disregard for others' safety. Not just a thief and not just a murderer. But you're right, thank God no one was seriously hurt. Up to now, all these incidents have been without weapons — no guns nor knives, thank God — but a bomb, that's a totally new MO. The gendarmes and probably the anti-terror people are going to be especially active after that. And that could be good news for us.'

'Sir, who do we know with any experience of explosives that is connected with this case? Lord bloody Groombridge. Do you recall, sir, Groombridge's CV/obituary that Lady Charlotte trotted out for us — Afghanistan and all that? But that would mean that Lord G ain't dead!'

LeFanu nodded and added, 'And a gang of bad guys from the Logistics Corps who have probably all been on a course or two, much as you have been on weapons training. No, I think that's a quantum leap at this stage. Good thinking, though.' He scratched his ear for the umpteenth time that day. 'Mmm,' he was heard to mutter as he left the carriage to find more coffee.

Through the tunnel and into Kent, and Jones's phone rang again. 'The gendarmes have called, saying that the device on Beddall's car had a timer and was linked to the number of times the driver's door was opened. The explosion could have happened anywhere, anytime. They can't determine the duration of the timer or number of times the door lock was operated before it went up. It could mean that the device was installed anywhere, including the UK.'

'*Merde*!' He paced up and down, obviously weighing up what had just been said. Jones looked on, puzzled. 'Two things, Jones. Have HQ and DI Miles got anywhere with tracking Mr Jerry Gold? That's now a number one priority. And secondly, what is the motive for killing Beddall? Can only be he knew too much, but about whom? The woman, Angela, or the killer, and maybe mastermind, of the whole bloody thing.'

Jones responded, saying, 'There's another with an obscure motive and that's this Guy Scott fellow. I know you've always doubted him and I tend to share that view. I'd raise the ante on him straight away, Not for a murder, necessarily, but involvement, I'd put my pension on it. But we must be careful it doesn't take our eye off the real issues. He may just be a man with an eye for the main chance — making money.' LeFanu nodded, still mulling over the events of the last forty-eight hours or so and called his driver to meet them at St Pancras International station.

Chapter 39

At two p.m., they arrived back at the office, having spent the complete journey on the phone, checking this and that and telling the team the progress and dimensions of the information gleaned. LeFanu asked a civilian clerk to locate DI Miles.

Jones was about to leave when she arrived. 'She's waiting outside to speak with you, I believe. Shall I stay on?' LeFanu nodded.

Samantha Miles entered the office, looking stunning in a grey pin-striped suit and high heels, and sat opposite the DCI.

'Well, sir, DS Jones, you seem to have collected some more bodies on your continental visit.'

'Indeed and good afternoon to you too.' He outlined the developments in France and the questions they mulled over on the train. 'Well, Sam, what about this golf pro fellow? Has he left the USA recently? Get someone on your team to check his movements with Homeland Security, but go gently and with UK border force here. You know how sensitive they are about us accusing their nationals. We have no evidence against him. We would just like to close avenues of enquiry — that sort of stuff.' Miles nodded and scribbled in her official black note-book before grabbing her mobile phone to relay the instructions.

Jones added, 'One more thing, sir. We have Monika's address in Germany, Hamburg, from the German Embassy in London. Fortunately their English was better than my schoolboy German. They have made contact with her family, who are puzzled that she did not turn up this year as she always does, at exactly the same time, for nearly ten years. They have tried to telephone her, but no answer. Last they heard was the 3rd January, when she said she was coming two days later than planned by Lufthansa, as usual, from Norwich to Hamburg. She usually travels on New Year's Day because the flights are cheaper, apparently. They, the family, assumed it was her employer needed her there for the celebrations or something.'

'I'm uneasy about this, Jones. Very uneasy. Think what I said before, only one person has identified Groombridge. If this Monika lady had been in situ, she would, undoubtedly, have been able to give us a preliminary ID. Conversely, had she been at the house, then she could be in some danger. Seems like everyone who could help isn't available. Let's hope there's some other explanation.'

'I'll get a couple of the WPCs to visit her home — it's only a mile from the village, I understand. She used to cycle over every day she was on duty. And we don't want to upset her if she's just ill or something.'

'Agreed. Thanks to the both of you.' LeFanu swivelled his chair to face the window as they left the office and mused about the implications, were they to be true, of a substitute body.

An hour later, Jones knocked on LeFanu's door with an ashen face, accompanied by DI Miles. 'We've, or rather the locals have, forced an entry into Monika Braun's cottage. The two WPCs noticed an awful smell when opening the letterbox to attract attention, as there was no answer to the doorbell. They called it in. A neighbour said that she hadn't seen her for a couple of weeks. They effected an entry through the rear door and she was found lying dead on her bed. Curtains drawn, central heating on full blast too. Twenty-four degrees centigrade. SOCO are there now and forensics first opinion suggests it looks like deliberate suffocation. Feels like she knew her attacker. One of her shoes was by the front door and the other by her bed, yet the place is immaculate. They're looking at the external location too — Locard's principle stuff. More to follow. An airline ticket for a Lufthansa flight on the 3rd January was in her handbag, much as we thought, and a bag packed ready for the off, so as to speak. The travel agency in Peterborough she used told us that she called on the 29th December to amend the flight and they couriered the new tickets over on the 30th December to Porten House. All was in order, then.'

LeFanu stood up so quickly that his chair fell over. '*Merde, merde, merde.* For Christ's sake! Whatever next? There's too many bodies. Let's hope this poor woman is the last of it. Get someone at HQ to contact the German authorities and also ask Dr Renata to give us an urgent appraisal of the when and the how.'

'There's another thing, sir.' Samantha Miles started, 'I've spoken to a contact from the past in Washington DC Homeland Security, and despite the difference in working hours, they've reacted more or less immediately — it was less than an hour ago that I asked.'

LeFanu and Jones both simultaneously made the same comment,

'Bloody quick!'.

She continued, 'The only record they have of our golf pro, Mr Gold, travelling outside the USA is a return trip to Paris Charles de Gaulle. Outbound by Delta Airlines, flight number DL1016, from New York on the 27th December and returning to the US via Canada, Montreal on the 6th January by Air Canada, flight number AC871, arrival 18.55 local time. One suitcase only, but it was cabin baggage only on the outbound from the USA — unusual for a long international flight, but not unheard of. No hotel bookings can be traced in France, at this stage anyway, and no flashy golf matches in the vicinity. He re-entered the US by Greyhound bus from the Casino in Montreal — used to be the French Expo 67 pavilion, apparently, and innovatively called the Casino de Montreal.' She looked at LeFanu for a smile but was waved on. 'And has an enormous bus station underneath — a twenty-four/seven facility. He returned at three a.m. on the free bus on autoroute fifteen, via St Bernard de Lacolle in Canada, to Champlain, NY. It's a tiny border crossing with minimal fuss, apparently. Bloody weird way to return to the motherland. We checked and there were plenty of alternative flights from Paris at that time and availability too. More to follow, apparently.'

As soon as DI Miles had delivered her news, Jones added, 'And on another subject, we're still waiting for an answer regarding the photo business from the techies.' LeFanu nodded.

'Before you go, sir,' continued Miles. 'There's something funny about this case. Drawing on my experience of twenty or so serious murder inquiries, I started to think about parallels whilst in that horrid little B&B. Bad guy wants to kill Groombridge, for whatever reason. Maybe makes a mistake and kills the wrong guy. Creates a snowstorm of other activities to disguise his purpose. Kills others around him — maybe because he is known or careless or both. If he was really good, professional, if you like, he wouldn't need to. So I think he is an amateur. Good at organising, maybe good at thieving and disposal, but not thinking of the day-to-day. Could even be Groombridge and the snowstorm is Gold.'

DI Miles and DS Jones could see LeFanu was assessing the information and posing himself mental questions, but with little enthusiasm for the suggestion. They left the room quietly.

Chapter 40

An hour or so later, LeFanu called for Chris Jones and Sam Miles. 'OK, you two, try this... If we're right in our guessing, then we either have Groombridge impersonating Mr Gold to get into the USA or wherever, or Gold impersonating Groombridge for whatever reason. And I can't think of a logical reason. Maybe our body wasn't Groombridge, but was it Gold? The circumcision that Dr Renata mentions in her report is odd, just doesn't fit with what we know about our lord fellow, but odd is the right word. It could mean nothing at all — maybe just a sexual preference — but unusual to have it performed on a mature adult. Not enough for a decision and too many coincidences. Think of Gold; did Lord or Lady Groombridge happen upon a doppelganger in Gold? If so, was a plan hatched thereafter to get him to the UK? Either way, we need to trace either of them. Too bloody late to check DNA, as the body was cremated, so we're to rely on the autopsy report. Maybe this Charlotte is the clever one — no wonder, perhaps, that she insisted on an early release of the body of her dearly beloved. Speak to Dr Renata again, Jones, you know her. See if there are any DNA samples or anything. Perhaps anything skeletal that she noted. Gold was purported to have been injured in the fracas that Charlotte mentioned. And DI Miles, please look into how Gold could have got into the UK from France in that period between arriving and leaving France. Particularly the weekend of the 3rd and 4th of January. Could be a false passport or impersonating someone else. All names we have go into the checking process.'

'Sir,' Samantha Miles interjected. 'I appreciate this is a roundabout way of saying things, but please hear me out...' She told them both about her hobby of doing cryptic crossword puzzles and sometimes how she knew it is the right answer but couldn't figure it out from the cryptic clue. Noting the questioning look on both their faces, she continued, 'Assume that it is Gold in the Jacuzzi, then other things potentially fall into place; assume it is Groombridge in the water, then it sounds plausible that Gold was involved — explaining his brief trip to Europe. Which one then goes on to fit the little boxes on the puzzle itself?'

Both DS Jones and DCI LeFanu nodded, and again, got up to leave. She spotted the look of doubt in both their faces and added, 'I know, before you say it, I'm reacting to coincidences and conjecture, but it must seem against logic to say that Gold was in Europe at the same time as the murder of whoever it may have been. And bearing in mind the relationship with Lady Charlotte, why did they not meet, or why did Charlotte not say so if they did? We do need US Homeland Security to try to trace either of them in the USA; Canadian immigration to check after that plane arrived in Montreal; the French to check on departures, CCTV etc. and we need another searching interview with the Lady Charlotte. Wish we could ask Gold's family, but not for the time being, at least. The Yanks would throw a wobbly if we started questioning their precious citizens.'

LeFanu pondered what had been said for a couple of minutes before speaking. 'True to your last point. But I think it is unlikely we'll get any quick results from our friends across the pond. You do have a valid point in the analysis. We need two streams of thought, as you say, and both kept separate for the time being. Get to it! Set up another interview with Lady C and another with that Mr Guy Scott. Maybe there's a serious motive buried in there. Meanwhile, we've lost sight of the bloody thieves. And the only good news is that we'll probably get reinforcements and the bad news is a load of criticism and unholy media attention. Mind you, we've been lucky. The attention span of the media is short and directly linked to the salaciousness of the crime. Here, they simply know, or think they do, that a noble lord has been murdered. Anyway, I thought the US authorities did fingerprint checks on all immigration, even their own people.'

DI Miles bristled at the apparent criticism. 'I did check about the fingerprint checks, sir, and it does tend to be random. With the bigger airline hubs, it's rigorous, but the smaller entry points less so, and at night, at a bus station in the USA, there could be sloppiness. The US authorities wouldn't admit that, but the Canadians were more open, although that's their unofficial version.'

'Of course, Sam, it wasn't meant as a criticism. You wouldn't expect anything else from the US authorities, or ours for that matter. So, let's continue with one of our assumptions and consider that Gold has another reason for an indirect entry back into the USA, legitimate or otherwise. Were he a murderer or involved in the murder of the Jacuzzi victim, then why draw attention to himself by a complicated re-entry? Conversely, Gold or someone else died and Groombridge assumed Gold's name, papers etc. and entered the US as Mr. Gold. Why? I accept that entry via Montreal could be easier than, say, any of the main hubs. But could he, just as easily, disappear without the complications of a murder?' He paused and scratched his ear. 'Ah, except for the insurance angle. Hadn't thought that through.'

'Indeed, sir. And we're talking of a considerable amount of money, several millions at a guess, going to Charlotte,' Chris Jones interrupted. 'Life assurance, value of the contents stolen, the cars, and presumably, the sale of the properties depending on his will, although there are some thumping great mortgages on the properties. We do need to keep tabs on that lady.'

'As you say, Jones, indeed! Taking those assumptions, she must be in it up to her pretty little neck, either way. Without lecturing you both, "follow the money" is a good tenet. A thought, though… if our guess, and it is a guess, that Groombridge has "disappeared" by substitution of a body, the now-deceased Mr Gold, and we know His Lordship is an inveterate gambler, by all accounts, yes?' Both DS Jones and DI Miles nodded and LeFanu continued with his thoughts, pacing up and down. 'Let us assume, for a minute then, that he went to this casino from Montreal airport and then by bus to the USA. You said that his flight from France to Montreal arrived at seven p.m. local time, and allowing for delay and baggage collection, customs etc. and the trip from Pierre Trudeau airport, he had to waste some time before his bus trip to the USA. And if so, what did he do? A hotel, restaurant, or did he go into the casino?'

He looked up for a reaction before continuing with his theory. 'Always with a bunch of "ifs"… Maybe our Lord Groombridge is a creature of habit with the casino as a magnet — and they have twenty-four/seven restaurants and so on. If so, will he be on their CCTV? Worth checking it out under both Groombridge and Gold's names. These casino people have to be pretty thorough. And last of all, where did he go next? It was early morning, from what you've said, Jones. He'd need a car or a bus or train or something. Check with the bus and train people and the hire car people in that town. Can't be many of them, even in the mighty US of A. Where does it go to? Maybe they have CCTV, like in many UK public transport methods. And Jones, ask your friends at that Crockfords place if they can help with a contact name at Montreal. Lots of jobs for you. Pass them out to the team and get on with it, please.'

'I'm onto it. And sir, I'm also looking into the Courchevel end. Was Groombridge there over the last few weeks? If so, how did he get there and how did he get back to the UK? Was he alone? Maybe there's a cleaner or building manager who can help. I've got that Susie Ford, good girl too, looking into it for me. Incidentally, or maybe not so incidental, Dr Renata is still miffed that she was pushed into a decision on the autopsy by instructions from above to release the body, and that's one favour we won't get again, she said. I assured her that it was not of our making but…'

'I hear what you say. Bloody strange to have had that instruction so soon after the autopsy — the powers-that-be have their own agenda. Anyway, Chris, on the other matters, excellent, excellent.'

Chapter 41

George had picked up on the news on BFM, the twenty-four/seven French news channel, the dreadful announcement about Terry Beddall being hit by a train in a French railway station. George's French was good, without being totally fluent, so he'd watched the repeat news twenty or thirty minutes later. And still shocked, he started thinking of the implications. He knew why Terry had been in Paris — he'd been besotted by her for months and had been texting her like a love-sick teenager, with George having to arrange massive top-ups for his phone. He'd announced to George, and half the customers in a bar in Brittany, over a few drinks, his intention of wanting to marry Angela and was going to buy an engagement ring before meeting her in Paris. Fortunately, in mid-winter, George had mused, most of the customers were locals and ignored the British visitors. There was no news about the circumstances of his death, apart from the incident with the TGV train. He thought that the next few days' broadcasts, newspapers and internet news may have more to say. He could only guess it had been a dreadful accident without any rhyme or reason.

Ouest France, the local regional newspaper, carried the news of an explosion in St Brieuc at the railway station car park. A British car, a Ford. Suspicion of terrorism etc., etc. It did seem, to George, that everything that could be attributed to terrorism by the French raised their international profile. It still made his blood run cold, as he knew Terry had left for Paris via the St Brieuc TGV.

His mind wandered, considering the actions the French police would be likely to take and then the natural involvement of the UK police. Then they would find Tel's prison record and it would only be a hop, skip and a jump before they made a connection with him. He had long been thinking of going to Poland to look into the family history and this seemed to present a perfect opportunity. He concluded that a thorough clean-up of Ker-Boulard and departing was now an urgent necessity.

He determined to ring his sister once there, knowing that Scotland Yard, or whoever in the British police, would contact her as his registered next of kin in official records. He pondered flying to Berlin under his assumed name. If the police checked, they wouldn't find that he had travelled to France, as he had used his second identity. He decided to return to the UK by a tortuous route and then fly under the Pchelski name to Germany and then, because there were no border controls in mainland Europe, the Schengen effect, he could be anywhere. So, if they checked, they'd find him in Berlin renting a car under Pchelski name, all quite legitimate and miles from the base in Brittany.

There was no further news about the cause of Terry's accident, apart from the fact that the police in France were looking for a blonde woman, aged about thirty-five, seen on CCTV leaving the café bar where he had been sitting. George knew that Angela was a blonde, and from his conversations with Tel, he was supposed to be meeting her that day to try to get her to say "yes" to marrying him.

George had cleaned up everything so, should the gendarmes trace Terry's whereabouts prior to the Paris incident, no clues would be found. He decided on a bus, as it would leave no record of his travel, checked the bus timetables and arranged to go to Vannes the next day.

Dropped off at the huge exhibition centre a mile or so south of the ancient town, he caught the free park and ride bus to the centre and then walked to the railway station, conscious all the time about leaving a trail that could be exposed easily. From Vannes, he took a train to Nantes airport, a couple of hours away, careful to buy his flight ticket with cash, and then an Air France flight to Gatwick, alongside a load of ex-pats. Changing his passport and carefully hiding the nom-de-plume version in the lining of his suitcase, he flew from Stanstead, having used the Gatwick Express to London and then the airport express to the Essex airport. A three-hour journey to Berlin's Schonefeld airport, a thirty-minute train ride from the centre of the city at Alexander Platz station, he stayed overnight at an IBIS hotel, and the next morning he rented a Volkswagen Golf to drive to Warsaw.

From the airport in Warsaw, he called his sister on the mobile number she would recognise and established that the British police, the Inspector LeFanu, whose voice he had heard many times over the Bluetooth audio link, wanted to speak to him. Marion gave him the number that the WPC had given her, and instead of berating him, she was calm in repeating the WPC's comments that the police simply wanted to talk to him about his old cars.

George told her that he was trying to trace Grandpa P's family in Warsaw at the Archives of Modern Records. He told her he was interested in the period before Grandpa P left Warsaw in 1940 to start his mammoth walk to Brittany via Vienna to freedom, which was true, although his researching the family tree part was an exaggeration. From the TV programmes he had seen in prison, tracing the families of Polish exiles from the 1940s was going to be a sorry task with predictable results.

Checking into the Novotel Warsawa Centrum, a quick taxi ride from Warsaw Chopin Airport, he called the detective chief inspector from his room on the eleventh floor.

'Detective Chief Inspector, I understand from my sister, Marion Naismith, your people want to talk to me about my cars, as was. And your name and number was given to her by a WPC that called on her. This is the first opportunity I have had to call.' He'd decided that he would play totally innocent about Terry's death and would express surprise were it raised by LeFanu.

'Indeed, Mr Pchelski. I wonder whether we could meet with my sergeant, who is investigating a serious group of thefts in which one of your cars you used to own was severely damaged. A green Mercedes convertible, I can't lay my fingers on the registration number at the moment.'

'I'm in Poland at the moment, Mr LeFanu, looking into my family's past. "Who do you think you are" stuff. My grandfather escaped the Nazis and came to England in 1940. I called my sister and she relayed your people's message, hence my call. If it's about my cars, as was, then it all should be a matter of record with DVLA. It was years ago, after all. I should be back in the UK in a week, or maybe two. Perhaps then, or can I help you over the telephone?'

'Maybe so. A few questions for the time being, then. First, of course, would you like me to call you back? These mobile calls cost a lot, I think.'

'No need. Vodafone charge me three pound a day irrespective, more or less, of volume or time of calls. Fire away.'

'Nothing to do with the cars for the moment, but you know of a Mr Terry Beddall?' George knew this question would arise but was caught on the hop at the suddenness.

'Terry? Of course, Chief Inspector. You obviously know a lot about me and my time inside and the whys and wherefores of that. Terry was a good cell-mate in that awful place and saved me from a couple of unpleasant incidents with the regulars. Good bloke. Must be free by now, if my memory recalls…' He paused, seeking feedback and warning of the next question.

'I'm sorry to have to tell you that he died in a tragic accident in Paris on the 15th January, that was a Thursday.' LeFanu himself paused, listening for a reaction. He found second guessing reactions over the telephone more difficult than face-to-face meetings.

George was ready for this bombshell. 'What? How, where, what happened?'

'I can't tell you much except what was in the news. He was hit by a train in a main terminus station in Paris. Died more or less immediately. Sorry to be the bearer of bad news.'

'My God! A train? How strange. Wonder what he was doing in Paris. As far as I remember, he had only been abroad to the typical Spanish places for sun, sand, sea and sex. Can't imagine him in Paris. Actually, thinking on it, I'd like to go to his funeral. Will that be in the UK? He looked after me and I expect that sister of his will be distraught. He told me they lost their other brother, tragically, a good few years back. You wouldn't understand, Mr LeFanu, hopefully anyway, that inside Her Majesty's Prisons, you build a relationship with others, in particular your cell mates, and in the hours after lights out, you talk about anything and everything. In my case, I don't doubt that I talked of my love of classic cars, and at one time, owned a few, and he ranted on about antiques. But back to your questions. I don't get the connection between my cars and Terry's death?'

'There may be no connection at all — maybe coincidence — although, Mr Pchelski, I don't like coincidences. But to answer your question, I don't know about the funeral arrangements. You'd probably be best talking to his sister. I can't give you her number. Data protection and all that, you understand.' Without waiting for a comment, he continued, 'We believe that he was involved in a major theft in Suffolk a few weeks back, which culminated in a murder. Some antiques, valuables and a couple of seriously valuable classic cars were stolen and many more damaged. One of those cars was owned by you, according to DVLA, the Mercedes I mentioned earlier. They had come into the possession of a Lord Groombridge, alongside three others that you had owned, which seemed to have disappeared from the DVLA database.'

'Ah-ha! Now I think I see where you're coming from. The judge, DCI LeFanu, as recompense for my sins, confiscated all I owned, including my small collection of classic cars, the green Mercedes, a pre-war Morgan, a 1962 E-type and a 1947 beautiful little MGTC. Maybe this lord character bought them at auction or whatever. I wouldn't have a clue about any that are missing — could be many reasons for that. It was years ago. Maybe they were scrapped or cannibalised or simply sold abroad. Does happen, though sad in its way. Of course, I would have talked of them, I'm sure, but then they were taken away. Last I saw of them was a few days or so before I was arrested. They could have been scrapped, for all I know. I did love that Merc though. I bought it with my grandfather. It meant something to me.'

'You mention auctions. Any reason?'

'No. It's just the way that collections of cars are sold, or leastways was. I've just got a beat-up Rover nowadays and a few dreams. I work on classic cars for some friends and clients around the country and that's about as close as I can get.'

'Did you know of Lord Groombridge, Mr Pchelski?'

'No. No I don't think so, unless I've read about him somewhere. And no, I don't read the gossip columns. No, definitely not.'

'He used to be a Director of Beech Underwriting, your employer before your arrest.'

George wanted to sound annoyed. 'Yes, I do remember my employer of ten years, DCI LeFanu. It'd be hard not to, bearing in mind the circumstances, about which, no doubt, you know all. There was no Groombridge, that I recall, on the board at that time. I'm getting impatient about what you want to know. Can I ask you to stop pussyfooting around and get to the point?'

'What was it? Ummm. Tony Waller, that was his name before he received his peerage. That ring any bells?'

'Good Lord! Sorry. Gosh, Tony Waller.' George tried to buy some time. Of course, he had made the connection with Charlotte but she had never mentioned her husband under the peer's name — it was always Tony this or Tony that. He hadn't associated her with him, miserable bastard that he was, when he'd heard of the marriage in America, it was only much later. 'He was a nasty bit of work in the office. Always wanting favours for his cronies, claims that were borderline or plainly not admissible, that sort of thing. We just reacted to instructions that came down from the chairman, a no arguments "do it" instruction. He might have done a tour round the offices once or twice, and there were the inevitable corporate hospitality events, but that's it. I did some presentations to the board over the years but nothing sticks out.'

George was again trying to buy some thinking time. He remembered the visit to the prison by Charlotte which the police could probably establish from the visitor's book and then make another connection to him. He decided to give them the lead which should trivialise the information if they tripped over it. 'One thing I should mention, now you've made the connection for me, I did have an affair with a lady whom Waller married subsequently. A Charlotte Bertin, but it was all over years ago when she got married in the USA, and became Mrs Waller, I seem to remember. Thought she must be mad marrying that rich bastard, but there you go. She kept in intermittent contact after that, but only chit-chat. I always thought that I was coffee table talk at her soirees or whatever. You know the sort of stuff: "I know a prisoner" sort of thing. When you know someone well you hardly ever say "I say, what is your surname today?" Do you? But why would he buy my cars, that's what puzzles me. Unless they were cheap, I suppose. He always was a wheeler dealer, as they say. Distress sale, they call it, don't they?'

'Just so, just so. But maybe you have answered your own question. Something to do with his wife? He, too, is dead, Mr Pchelski and it is being treated as murder, so you will understand the tenor of my questions.'

George replied, 'God! Two deaths? Are they connected? No wonder you're rooting around for information. She did say, ages ago, that there was a divorce pending and that he could be a violent sort of chap, but I've heard no more than that. Sorry I can't be of much help. I'm just trying to make ends meet and enjoy my interrupted life. I was guilty as charged, but I've served my time and learned my lesson. I suppose I should add, without casting any blame, that Charlotte had an expensive lifestyle which made me greedy to oblige. My fault, didn't know when to say "no".'

'What did she do for a living, so as to speak, whilst you were slaving away in an office?'

'Had a half share or some percentage of the business anyway, in a boutique in the King's Road. Fashion, I think. Never seemed to interrupt her schedule from enjoying herself at my expense — well, you know what

I mean.'

LeFanu paused before asking the next question. He was finding too many coincidences and wanted to be sure that he was not building things together too simply. 'As a last question, perhaps… How long have you been out of the country?'

'Just under three days this time. I visited some pals and came to Poland via Berlin for a few days and then needed to locate some parts for a couple of old Porsche 356 from Stuttgart for a dealer in Sussex, quite near my sister's, as it happens. That's the sort of thing I do nowadays, travelling all over the place, sourcing rare parts for rare cars. I'm fairly cheap against these professional restorers and can usually work pretty quickly. Italy today, Germany tomorrow and the US of A the day after. It keeps me out of mischief.' George immediately thought that he had gone too far.

'Yes, well, I would hope it would!' LeFanu showed by his voice he was not amused by George's flippancy. 'And yes, your sister told us. Thank you. Incidentally, do you speak Polish or Italian or German for that matter? Must be difficult.'

'Well, yes. I could swear in Polish before age three. I'm a bit rusty since my grandfather retired, but it's all coming back. Most of these car people have a smattering of English, fortunately. And I'm reasonable at French, and strangely, there is a link. We spent holidays with Grandpa P in France most years. But again, I expect my sister told you that.' He knew that Marion would not have been subtle and would answer any question posed and then some.

'Indeed. Thank you again. I would wish to talk to you again. Please arrange to come back to the UK, sooner rather than later, and let me know your travel arrangements. I'll let you get on and thank you for calling.'

George countered with a, 'No problem. I'll call you,' remark and closed the call.

LeFanu called for DI Miles and DS Jones to review the conversation with Pchelski. 'I believe him, or at least what he's told me, but at the same time I'm doubtful. He's well prepared, like he already knew about Beddall. Odd. And I'm not getting one hundred percent of what he knows.'

Sam Miles interrupted, 'He could have picked it up from the TV news, almost anywhere in Europe.'

'True. It's just a feeling I have that we've got another example of truths mixed with half-truths and damned lies. This guy is clever, no doubt about it. He gave me some information that he knows, if we want to, we can find out. Like his relationship with Charlotte. And he said she's told him that there was a divorce pending. That's news to us, but could be a motive, perhaps. He travels all over Europe, quite legitimately it seems. He speaks French reasonably. All circumstantial, I admit. But it leaves me on edge. His mobile number needs to be checked for communications from whoever over the last two months or so. Chris, get someone on to the mobile phone companies tout suite.'

'Do you think he's our guy? The brains, maybe?' DS Jones asked.

'I just don't know, Chris. Check out his time in the prison — both Ford and Upper Heywood. See who he was mixing with; what he could have learned. On another tack, if one of you is going visiting, or talking to prisons, we never found that Angela Darling woman on the prison CCTV or her brother, cousin, Tony or whatever, for that matter. She doesn't appear on any visitor's log either. Maybe some chats with the staff might give us a lead. I should think that Charlotte, in all her glory, arriving at a prison would be a subject for a lot of chit-chat. I am sure she's a key player in all this. I'm inclined to think she might be the brains, but where's the motive? All we have so far is money and even divorce usually translates into money — and she had plenty of that anyway. Damn, I should have asked him more about her. I'll do that this evening. We have his number now.'

Jones stood up to go and remembered two points that had been resolved from earlier conversations with his two colleagues. 'Couple of points before I go. Crockfords are having a few words with some US colleagues regarding Lord G's habits. They think, like the rest of the world, that he's dead, but let's see what they come up with.' Both LeFanu and Miles nodded. 'And Champlain as a point of entry into the USA is fairly low key. For example, it's three hours driving time from Albany, three and a half hours or so by bus or by train. But to New York, you can double those times. We are checking the car hire firms, as that seems the most likely because the bus and train people don't need ID. The CCTV facilities are not that brilliant — even Homeland Security admit that.'

LeFanu acknowledged the comments and Jones left the room with his black notebook full of actions. DI Miles asked LeFanu what he had in mind next.

'A large wipe off board and a collection of coloured pens, Sam. And in this instance, a map with coloured pins so I can track everyone's movements and if any are missing, it gives you guys something to do.' He had a twinkle in his eye as he said it. 'That's what I need, alongside a good bottle of Bordeaux and some peace and quiet. It's the advantage of being single again. I rule my own roost. Hang on a minute, something has just registered. He said that Groombridge, Waller as was, was a nasty bit of work and always trying to do deals that were not quite straight — fiddling insurance claims and the like.'

'Strange remark coming from him, by all accounts, except he got caught fiddling the books and Groombridge didn't. '

'Just so, Sam, just so. Let me ramble a bit.' It was his way of showing her how he liked to work. 'Now, if our lord fellow was always persuading, Pchelski's words, the board to bend the rules, you can bet that when Pchelski's assets and cars were sequestered by the Courts, Beech Underwriting would have had some say where they went for disposal. Bingo — Paddick Classic Car Auctions picked them up for a song. I'd lay money on that. We might be starting to see some motive here. It's big money, according to Chris Jones.'

'Sir, it doesn't explain the damage or the missing cars, though.'

'Maybe, maybe. If Groombridge is, sorry was, a scum-bag, as Pchelski suggests, then it could be a way of converting cars into cash — an old fashioned insurance fraud, like Lord Brockett a few years back, but they caught him and he enjoyed Her Majesty's Pleasure for a few years. Question is, of course, who did it and how and when?'

Chapter 42

His phone vibrated with an SMS message.

'Georgie, your friend, Terry, has had a heart attack or something in Paris, Gare de Lyon and is dead. Sorry. Can we meet? Do miss you. Kiss, Kiss.'

Georgie panicked as he read the message and replied, 'Keep away from me, Charlotte. You're bad news.' He pressed send then removed the SIM card from the phone and the battery. The damage was done. There was no point in destroying the phone, but he needed some thinking time without any interruptions. The police would have his number from his sister or from his call to LeFanu and could, probably would, arrange a search of all calls made and received. So, if they were inclined, they would know he had had a message from Charlotte and that he had replied and probably exactly what was said. He just felt he needed breathing space and some strong coffee.

Putting on a warm jacket despite the sunshine and sitting in a bar on the plaza outside the hotel, he tried to analyse if he had accidentally laid any trails that the clever DCI LeFanu could follow. She, Charlotte, had unnerved him, again. She had a habit of doing that over the years. She knew too much about him, including the phone number. The issue of the wholesale damage to the cars had an uncanny ring to them, redolent of his conversation with her in the Pulborough pub. No doubt LeFanu would find out from her about their conversations on that score, even though he had been dismissive of her so-called plan at the time. LeFanu had mentioned, almost in passing, the theft of the cars and the damage at Porten House. Perhaps, George thought, he would now ascribe that to another of Groombridge's scams, like he had orchestrated as Tony Waller.

Of course he knew about Charlotte's new name after the marriage. He'd hoped to have put her off the scent at the time and equally hoped that she had not gone after Terry to achieve her objectives against her womanising husband. If only Issy was around to talk to.

Everything fitted with some of Terry's disappearances at the factory and the dilatory way he answered his phone when George had called. Or was it this Angela woman? Who was she, and could she have got involved? Had Charlotte got her to inveigle Terry into the mad-cap scheme to get revenge, and had it all gone wrong? It was as if there were two or more agendas operating and he only knew of one.

He googled Lord Groombridge from his tablet. There was not much information, except he'd been murdered in Suffolk at his family home. Married to… Director of… and other information akin to an obituary. George felt he needed information about the things LeFanu had alluded to but had no one to ask. Was she seriously dangerous, or just the old Charlotte being devious, and with no husband, looking for a bit of nookie, as she used to call it, with a bit of rough — him. His thoughts took him both ways with no clear direction. He reassembled his phone and it immediately rang out its musical chime, and almost without thinking to look at the caller ID, he raised it to his ear. It was not a number from his contact list.

'Hello George. It's DCI LeFanu, again. Sorry to bother you so soon. Hope I'm not interrupting anything… I've tried you a couple of times.'

He sounded so polite, so unassuming, that George was un-nerved and stuttered, 'No, no, just taking coffee in the winter sunshine. Phone was on the blink for a while, rubbish reception, so I moved to a table around the corner of the building. What can I do for you?'

'A question that's nagging me, George. You don't mind me calling you George? To be honest, the Polish surname takes a bit of getting used to.'

'No, no. I'm used to it. Carry on.'

'Do you know of a lady, a blonde aged about thirty-five, called Angela Darling?'

'Wow, that's a name to conjure with. I bet everyone calls her "a darling". Lovely. No, when can I meet her? Sorry, Inspector I'm being frivolous. Put it down to the sunshine and caffeine.' He had bought some time to think of a riposte a little more serious. 'No, I've never met the lady. I'd certainly remember.'

'George, it is serious. You haven't answered the question. Do you know of a lady called Angela Darling?' He put the stress on the word "know".

By now he had had time to think. 'No to that question too. Who is she? Ah, I bet that's the woman you told me about before on the station.' As soon as he had said it, he knew he'd made a big mistake. He listened for a reaction.

'George, I've never said there was a woman involved. Just that it was an accident. Perhaps the caffeine has addled your brain? Come on, George, out with it.'

George had two options, his brain was telling him. Close the call and run, change into his other identity and go, or answer a little of the truth and hope it would suffice. He chose the latter. 'Yes, I heard of it on an international news channel before you told me about Terry. The French police are anxious to interview a blonde lady etc., etc. Because I'm an old lag, I try to avoid any contact with anything bad. It's a good policy but then you get caught out in a lie, like this. I'll be honest, Terry had a girlfriend. He was absolutely besotted with her. Her name was Ange, that's what he called her, no surname, just Ange. He rang me ages ago, after his release, and told me that he wanted to marry her and was going a hundred percent straight from then on. That's all I know, I swear.'

'Which news channel and where were you at the time? George, I need an honest answer now or I will arrange for you to be apprehended in Poland and brought back here in chains!'

George knew he meant it, just from the tone of his voice. He'd heard enough when they were listening in at the police temporary HQ in the village hall. 'France, Chief Inspector, France. I heard it on the twenty-four/seven news channel BFM. I always watch that in Europe, if I can. They were pretty dramatic, typical media, and they talked of an unknown young blonde woman seen leaving the scene moments before Terry met his death and the police want to interview her — that sort of thing. That is all I know. And before you ask, I haven't been near Paris for years — too expensive for my pocket these days.' George was filling in time trying to plot the next question.

LeFanu opened, 'If you picked up that information from BFM, George, undoubtedly, you will also have heard of the explosion in St Brieuc. We believe that that was Beddall's hire car that went up — fortunately with no injury.' He paused, seeking a reaction.

'Yes, sure, I read about the explosion in Ouest-France. Terry's car? Why on earth? But who was involved? No idea. The paper reckoned it was terrorism. But if it was Terry, how, when and why? Sounds like someone was trying to kill him, or put the frighteners on, maybe. What about Paris? Is it a, what do you call it, a suspicious death? Maybe they tried and failed in Brittany and had another go in Paris or vice versa.'

'Just so, just so, George. That may be a quantum leap. Now perhaps you realise why this is being taken so seriously. And what did you mean when you said "from now on Terry was going straight?" There is an inference there that he was up to no good immediately before. And next time, Mr Pchelski, when asked a question by a police officer, of any nationality, kindly give an honest answer or you will find yourself in deep trouble.'

'OK. Understood, and sorry. I think it is my bad choice of words. Maybe Terry just was showing the influence of a good woman and so on.'

'Ummm. Doesn't it strike you, George, as a most unusual coincidence that Mr Beddall's car was in St Brieuc and various other addresses in Brittany, seemingly in the company of a fifty-year-old, or so, English man and you are, or were, in Brittany at the same time and you are in your fifties? Best of friends, by your own admission, yet you don't meet up?'

'Yes you are right, Chief Inspector. Two plus two does equal five. Your assumptions are spot on, but only as far as being mates. Terry did come and stay with me for a few days and we did go out, as you do in France, for a few bevvies — why not? He took off for Paris in his car. But that's as far as it goes. I might be a good friend, but I'm not his brother, as the saying goes. I assumed that he was driving back through Paris en route, as they say, for the UK. Why St Brieuc?'

LeFanu took a flier. 'Border Security has no records of your going to France or returning to the UK, for that matter, George. Certainly this side of Christmas. Think, George! I want some details — dates, times and locations.' He knew that he could be wrong about George's movements and was prepared to apologise if necessary. He'd found that sometimes taking a risk with a question paid dividends.

'I don't know. St Brieuc? A logical station for TGV to Paris, I suppose. Perhaps he thought the train was an easier option. And explosives — well, I wouldn't touch them with a barge pole, indeed wouldn't know how to. Definitive! And before you ask, I did not see anyone fiddling with his car whilst it was parked at my place — absolutely not. Just a boring little Ford. And as far as France is concerned, it's not my fault if Border Force were asleep at the time. Used the ferry, Newhaven-Dieppe, both ways, went there about the middle of December. There's not much work for me at that time of year in the UK.'

'Thank you. Please check the dates and copies of the tickets and when

Mr Beddall arrived. And I'm glad you make that point about the car he was driving. We also found a tracking device under the rear bumper, so whoever it was knew exactly where Beddall would be at any given time. That fact alone takes you off that particular hook, as you knew where he was. The bomb maker remains a mystery, but the technicians are investigating, as you would expect.'

'Are you saying that the bomb was on the car when he visited me; when we went off into town for drinks? Shit!' He waited for an acknowledgement from LeFanu.

'No, we can't say that. It could be or the bomb could have been installed whilst the car was parked, or anywhere really. It's hardly the busiest car park in France. But the bug — that had been there for some time. So, whoever it is knows your locations as well. Be warned. Were it me, I would double check my car every time I used it. These guys, whoever they are, are not simpletons when it comes to IEDs. Think, George! Without being melodramatic, your life might be in danger. We call this an Osman warning. It is recognising people concerned with an incident who may be at serious risk. So we need names and places, and as a survivor, so far, you may have that information. I leave it at that, George, but think carefully.'

'What you say is seriously frightening. You probably want to know my address in France. I rented a small house. You know, I'm sure, DCI LeFanu, the rental situation in France is different than the UK and there are minimum rental periods. So I signed up for three years revolving rent; three months' notice. But it's cheap. It's in a village Grandpa P used to take us every year, so there is sentimental reason. Wish I could buy it, but not for the foreseeable future. Got it from an English guy who advertised in Private Eye magazine. Property market is dead as a dodo in France, so he's looking for an income and hoping for a recovery in the market. I do have an option to buy clause, but that's just a dream. Top of the cliffs a few hundred metres away, couple of bars and restaurants and the inevitable boulangerie.'

He gave LeFanu the address at St Gildas de Rhuys in Brittany, co-ordinates and land-line telephone number and told him that he had a French car, an old Renault Clio, that he used for local journeys. George was trying to show the DCI that he was an open book.

'Ummm! Any other addresses we should know about in France or in the UK, George? Maybe any locations that Terry Beddall might have visited?'

'No. That's me done. Can't speak for Tel, obviously. I just can't believe that someone wanted to kill him with a car bomb, let alone pushing him under a train thing. I'm stunned.'

LeFanu decided not to elaborate on Beddall's death, letting the media do its usual trick of exaggeration and blaming the railway administration infrastructure companies, as they did in the UK. 'Right. Move on. Angela Darling, who is she?'

'Right, assuming that Ange is Angela Darling, she is, or was, a girlfriend of Terry Beddall. They were very close. Understand they were introduced by his sister. He called her Ange, as I said before. He only got together with her after he left the nick. And yes, he called me once or twice looking for a job. Couldn't help. Hard enough to make ends meet. My sister's husband had to give me a sub.'

'Would it surprise you to know that he was meeting her in Paris and we believe that she is the mystery woman?' LeFanu regretted that he was not able to face George Pchelski. He knew he always established the truth quicker by studying his opponent. There was another pause from the Polish end.

'No. I mean, yes. I had no idea. Yes, I've just told you he was hellbent on going to Paris, but I didn't know he was meeting anyone; thought it might have been for the flesh-pots. I've never met her, nor even seen pictures. It was all in that time after I'd been let out and recently. Speak to his sister, I'd suggest.'

'Did Beddall ever quiz you about these cars when he called you?'

'No. He wasn't a car junkie like me. Cars are cars would be his answer every time I started drooling about TV programmes in the nick.'

'So when he called you,' LeFanu knew he was winning, as often it was the little asides that gave the game away — and this was George's second faux pas, 'which number telephone did he use, George? His phone is missing and we need to analyse all calls to find the lady.'

'Oh! I can't remember. My sister gave me an old phone and I got a SIM card, pre-paid thing, when they released me. Couldn't afford anything fancy and they were all too complicated for me — certainly if my brother-in-law's Android thing was anything to go by. You miss a couple of generations of phone improvements inside prison and it takes some catching up.'

'Answer the question. Enough of this swanning around, giving me this hard luck story. If you don't really remember the number then give me the network provider, George. That much you will be able to remember, won't you?'

'I'm almost sure he said it was Phones4U, but I really can't remember the number.' George sounded resigned. 'And I didn't log Terry's number either, only a few months ago I wouldn't even have known how to find a phone log. I can now — have to, with my job.'

'Thank you. Now, George, is there anything else remotely relevant that you want to tell me before I have to drag it out of you in Ipswich or court?'

'I don't know what's relevant to you. The only thing I can think of is that Charlotte Waller, whatever she calls herself, did call me, or rather sent a text message and told me about Terry — but I already knew. I told her to get lost, or words to that effect. And she did visit me in prison not long before they let me out. No reason particularly, a bit of coffee table talk, I suspect. "I visited a prison yesterday" sort of stuff, except she claimed that she'd had a falling out with her husband. Bit of booze, bit of jealousy and he turned violent. Some guy she knew, something to do with golf I think, was beaten up, broken legs and so on. Mind you, it could have been a scuffle and Charlotte's sense of the dramatic made it broken legs etc. Can't add to that. Oh, she did say in the text message that Terry had had a heart attack. I'd thought he was pretty fit, but there you go. Heart attack? That didn't come over in the news, did it?'

Using the poison story was useful now to jolt George. 'He was poisoned, George, that is no exaggeration. Not pushed under a train, as the news tells everyone. Nasty stuff, too, and very painful and not quick. Then he staggered under an oncoming train. There would have been no recovery prospects from the poison, so maybe his death was a mercy, too, apart from the trauma for the train driver.'

'That is terrible. Fucking hell. So you're telling me it was this Angela woman? I'd kill her myself for that... I don't really mean that, Chief Inspector. Shit'

'What was that?'

'Just spilled my coffee. Hang on!'

LeFanu could hear the mutterings and then George saying, presumably to a waiter, *'To samo proze'*.

'Sorry, Chief Inspector, cleaning up the mess and asking the waiter for another flat-white coffee.'

'Fine. I should hope such action is not on your agenda, George. And I'm not saying it was this Angela, or anyone else for that matter. You are making assumptions. Anything else to add, now you know that?'

Without trying to buy time because of the shocking news, George blurted out, 'Yes, damn right. She was meeting him in Paris on the day he died. He spoke to me and told me that a good few days ago. And the old phone number was 07756 457863. Sorry about that. I thought you guys would zero in on me and give me grief because of my history. The SIM card was destroyed immediately after I picked up the news of his death.'

George was both sad about Terry and angry with this Angela woman. If he could have told LeFanu anything to get her caught, he would have. But most of what he knew was guesswork — it fitted why Terry was always on the phone and why his SIM card facility constantly needed topping up. The phone number he had given the detective was the disposable phone that he had only used to talk to Terry in the past few weeks having destroyed its predecessor when the vans and cars were on their way in France. He couldn't be angry with Terry for obvious reasons, but kept remembering the number of times he had said 'business only' on this phone.

'It would have been a slow and painful death, George. Strychnine. I really would think that the train hitting him was a blessing.'

'He didn't deserve that, Mr LeFanu. No one does.' George acknowledged the replacement coffee with a nod to the waiter and took a long sip of the scalding strong coffee.

'Just so, just so. We have not released that information to anyone else, so please do not repeat it. Knowledge like that might help us to catch the culprit.' LeFanu had taken the risk of releasing the poison information to find out if a leak occurred. Whilst he had no control over the French investigation or the leaky French media, he did have an understanding with the authorities that restricting detailed information about the death of Beddall might assist in the longer term.

George simply acknowledged the comment with a brief 'Uh huh!'

'I was hoping you would be honest with me. Now, I must insist that you are back in the UK, at Ipswich, in seventy-two hours. I will send a car to pick you up if there is any difficulty.'

'OK, Chief Inspector. You win. I'll postpone my searching for car bits and for ancestors.'

'Good and then you can talk to me about Porsche 356 cars.' He rang off. Pchelski's phone was being monitored, so any reaction to his comment would be interesting, although he was partly convinced that George wasn't that stupid.

A third conversation originated by LeFanu took place a couple of hours later. 'George, sorry, it's me again, DCI LeFanu.'

'Uh huh. What now? Do you want to buy a Porsche? I'll give you the number of a bloke in the UK but it'll cost, big time. There aren't many of them left outside private collections.'

'No, not at the moment. As I said before, conversations about Porsches will wait until you are back here. There are all sorts of questions about that.' He paused, trying to build up the pressure and putting George on edge. 'No, I wanted to talk about Charlotte.'

'Listen, Chief Inspector, that's ancient history. I've moved on and she certainly will have done. A couple of contacts for old times sake and that's it. Ultimately, there is only one person Charlotte cared about and that is Charlotte. I was but a few moments in her life!'

'Very poetic, George. Very. OK, What I wanted to know is did she ever meet Terry Beddall?'

There was a silence. Then George commented, 'I told you she visited me in prison. Well, even that was strange, now you mention it. I'd had a visit from my sister, as usual, that day. She always came on a Thursday. You could set your watch by her. Bless. I'd just been returned to the cell block when the screw came and got me because I had another visitor. It was Charlotte, and he told me she had special permission from the deputy governor or someone high up because you're only allowed one visitor session per time. Anyway, Terry was in the room on another table, across the way, because his sister was there, too; she came about an hour after my sister's time. I remember him giving me the look, across the room, of "who's that tasty bit of stuff?" and her asking who he was. They didn't meet to my knowledge, but maybe some other time. I don't know. Naturally, he quizzed me about her back in the cell after lights out. It was like he was having a wet dream about her, if you know what I mean.' George didn't wait for a reply but carried on, reminding himself and telling LeFanu as his recall added detail. 'I remember, she asked about the lady with Terry, thinking it was his wife, so I told her it was his sister who visited as regular as clockwork, just like my sister, I suppose. Why all this stuff about Charlotte?'

'Just trying, George, to put all the people, including you, who had any connection, no matter how remote, into the picture — where they were, when and where. Boring stuff, but necessary to eliminate from enquiries. Did you ever go to her shop in Chelsea?'

'Good Lord, no! High-end girlie fashion, I imagine — don't like shopping anyway. Charlotte knew how to dress to kill. Oops, shouldn't have said that. Figure of speech only, Detective. I used to drool when she turned up. I'm sure others did too.'

'Just so. My sergeant is one!' This gained a relaxed laugh from George.

'Tell him to take care. She's a dangerous and expensive piece of baggage. Better to dream, eh?'

'Incidentally…'

George responded with a nervous laugh. 'Nothing from you, sir, is incidental.'

'Well, maybe, but we're trying to iron out all sorts of things. Could Charlotte have contacted Terry B after his release?'

'Crikey. That is a serious leap. He had to get a bus and a train after release to get to his sister's place. He told me that. And I think that's where he met this Ange lady. She is, or maybe was, a friend of his sister. But I can't see how he would have made contact. Chance, maybe?'

LeFanu ignored the comment and continued, 'Do you know how they met? The sister and his Angela Darling?'

'Yes. Terry spoke of it whilst we were both inside. He was worried that his sister hadn't got much money and coming to Upper Heywood every week was draining her pocket and then this lady offered her a lift every week. For Sharon, it was a no brainer. This lady was visiting some relative or other in the prison so it was no skin off her nose, either. Then they became friends. Mutual understanding, in the same boat, I suppose. But you can get all this from his sister. Why me?'

'No reason. I may need to talk to you again before you get here. Things are hotting up.'

'Good, I suppose. Certainly good if it gets that bitch her just desserts for Terry, well, that was unforgiveable.'

LeFanu closed the call and switched off the recording, leaning back in his chair to re-assess what he had learned. After a minute or two, he reached for his dirty coffee cup to seek a refill.

Chapter 43

Back at Ipswich, having the number George had given him, LeFanu had the phone records analysed. One number stood out. There was no way of knowing who was at the other end of the calls in and out, but it gave a number to check. Second stage analysis showed several numbers from that disposable phone; a few to George's number and a lot to another disposable. There were photos too, the technician told him, that had been added to text messages. It would take time to get those downloaded via the service provider.

He relayed the conversation to both Miles and Jones by playing back the recording he had made. They discussed the nuances of Pchelski's answers, made more difficult because it was not face-to-face.

Sam Miles then opened up with, 'I think he's guessing that Charlotte and Angela Darling are one and the same, taking things a bit further than we thought, although not a million miles away. But that doesn't stack up with the D&G dress thing. And another thing, if my memory serves, Pchelski's sister, Marion something or other, told us that her brother was thinking of settling in France, as his career, understandably, was in tatters in the UK. But that conversation between her and her brother was immediately after his release and therefore well before the thefts, murders etc. had occurred. So, Pchelski being on Beddall's satnav is understandable for him to visit an old "friend", if that's what old lags call each other.'

LeFanu, looking puzzled, butted in, 'Could still link. If someone offered you a screwed-up dress that was yours, what would you do?'

'But why would he offer Charlotte a dress that he'd presumably nicked from Charlotte's bedroom wardrobe? I need to ask her, I'll call her now that we've got the bloody dress back from France. Anyway, back to Pchelski; he's obviously very angry at the Beddall murder and might make a slip or two because of that anger. I think he knows more than he's telling. It's always said that if you get people angry enough, they find it hard not to tell the truth.'

'Agreed. That's why I told him about the poisoning. Basically, you would have to have lived in France, or know someone very well who had, to know about the availability of strychnine in rat poison being readily available in a garden centre or the like. Keep thinking of France and who we know there with an old chateau probably with some of those unpleasant creatures running amok. It is bugging me. I know, strolling around a DIY superstore or a garden centre, you could easily chance upon the stuff on the shelf, but why would you notice such a thing? Someone would have had to tell you. Come back to that. Anyway, back to George. I don't believe that Pchelski will trip up by using the phone we know about, unless it is to lead us up the garden path. He'll just buy another phone. His movements when he gets back to the UK will be interesting, though, and I want him tailed discreetly. I still don't believe he is a murderer. He was genuinely upset about Beddall. But I do agree with you, Miles, that he knows more than he is telling. What about you, Jones? Anything to add?'

'Well, thanks for using my name in the drooling over Charlotte part. I think we need to ask Charlotte how and when she knew Beddall, and make it face-to-face and record the interview so we can study it later. And just a thought, could the Lady C have been waiting outside the prison gates every Thursday for months to take Beddall's sister to London or wherever? Doesn't sound like her. Once yes, two or three times, maybe but for months? No. What would be the point?' He looked across at DI Miles and gulped before carrying on, 'With a body and attitude like hers, she could have picked him up anytime to suit. Sorry, that does sound super sexist, but I am trying to make a serious point.' DI Miles smiled an acknowledgement of a point well made.

LeFanu put up his finger to call for quiet when he picked up his phone and pressed speed-dial and audio. 'Dr Renata. Just a quick question. You remember our Lord G death. Were there any skeletal issues? Broken legs sort of thing?'

'No, Chief Inspector, definitively not. Without even referring to the files, bit overweight but other than that fit as a flea. You're not having much luck with this case. Ever growing list of cadavers, it seems to me. Incidentally, and a shortish answer, please. You went to the funeral, what is a Jewish funeral like?'

'No, it was Anglican, a memorial service only. The cremation was a few days or so earlier and was a private thing — even the son didn't attend. Nothing out of the ordinary, the service I mean. Why?'

'He was Jewish, I'm convinced of it. It's one of the reasons I didn't quibble about signing off the cadaver so quickly. They always want an early burial, even within twenty-four hours of death, if at all possible. How odd! Well, something else for you to think on. Anything else? I am rather tied up.'

'No thanks, Dr Renata. That's it.' He pressed end and replaced his phone on his desk and turning to his two colleagues,

'Could she have made an error? It is odd.' LeFanu turned to his colleagues with a puzzled look on his face. 'I did think that releasing the body that quickly was really strange but assumed it was orders from above, as Lady C told us.' Both Samantha Miles and Chris Jones burst out laughing at the pun and had to explain it to Philippe LeFanu, who acknowledged his faux-pas and joined in the laughter.

'Back to the serious business, please. You heard. Pchelski tells us about a pending divorce, yet Charlotte does the "I love my husband" bit. Pchelski tells us that the golf pro has two broken legs. Dr Renata carried out the post mortem on the Jacuzzi body — no broken legs, historically or otherwise. Pchelski tells us this is what Charlotte told him. Either, or even both, of them is a liar. Or we're back to it not being Gold but maybe it is Groombridge. One option to consider is that the victim is a third person, maybe Jewish, and Groombridge simply used someone's passport, or a fake, to escape his creditors and any prosecution for involvement in wholesale fraud, and of course murder. Any or either of these scenarios stack up to a certain extent. But I do like your point, Jones. Pretty basic way of putting it, but a good point. If it wasn't Charlotte waiting at the prison gates like Lili Marlene, who the hell was it? Is this the nebulous blonde — possibly known as Angela Darling? And on balance, Charlotte, Lady bloody Groombridge, told someone about Sharon Beddall's regular visits, habits. Although, proving that is almost impossible without the other person.'

Both DS Jones and Samantha Miles nodded, but Miles weighed in with her thoughts, 'I hear what you say, sir. Gold might have lent his passport to his doppelganger for forty pieces of silver, so as to speak, to aid Lord G escape the long arm of the law, let alone the loan sharks. But he's recorded as returning to the USA, so a one way ticket for Lord G into the USA would open up an enquiry as soon as the computer spewed out a mis-match. If the former, then where the hell is he now and how would he get back home to the USA? Lost/stolen passport is a possible excuse, and then the American embassy for a duplicate, but no such info from the Americans. I favour the earlier theory.'

LeFanu, scratching his ear, as was his habit, replied, 'I tend to agree, but we will be faced with questions as to the 'why' of our theory, so it is best to eliminate other possibilities. Nothing we're saying would stand up with the DPP. Those prosecutors are pedantic in the extreme. And your analysis is good, Sam. Take it one stage further, though. If Gold came here, on whose passport? Lord Groombridge would be an obvious name, but it could be a false passport or someone else's document. Border Force are pretty good, but stressed mistakes can happen at busy times. Therefore, did Groombridge leave France directly for Canada on some passport or other, after leaving, under strange circumstances, Courchevel?'

Chris Jones, almost bubbling over with enthusiasm for this approach, added, 'Two things occur to me. One, who killed the man in the Jacuzzi? Gold or someone else connected with the thefts — maybe a Mr Big, Ms Big or Beddall. The second point, I think, is that we have Lord G re-entering the UK from Paris. If it were Gold using Lord G's passport, wouldn't someone on that flight recall something or whatever about him? By all accounts, Lord G was an arrogant man and I can't see him on an Easyjet-type cheap flight, can you?' He looked at DI Miles with a grin, both just looked at him as he had said the blindingly obvious. 'And there's the third point, now I come to think about it. Groombridge's passport in the safe, wiped clean. That in itself is odd, but doesn't that tell us that either it is Groombridge or it's meant to look like it was Groombridge in the Jacuzzi. And therefore, who put the bloody thing in the safe? And who had the access code, apart from Groombridge himself?'

'So, if someone arrived using Groombridge's passport, they are either still in the UK or had another document to leave the country, or they are as dead as a dodo.'

'I like the point. Me, Chris, I'd go for the lying option. Another point, without wanting to cloud the issue further… We are assuming the information given to us by Pchelski is true. It maybe that to his belief it is what Lady C said, but is it a lie by her in the first place?' DI Miles replied.

LeFanu nodded and added, 'If Lady C had more than one passport, then maybe so has our villain, or perhaps she brought a passport into the UK for someone to use to leave. Although, thinking out loud, Border Security should pick up the discrepancy unless it's a valid UK passport. Circles again lady and gentleman, circles.'

Sam Miles had been typing furiously on her laptop whilst LeFanu was talking. 'This chateau has loads of outbuildings and surely would have a team of gardeners, judging by the Google Earth view of the place and its grounds. And gardeners could mean familiarity with pesticides. Methinks we should ask Madam about it.'

LeFanu and Jones both nodded, and by pointing at Sam, placed the responsibility firmly on her shoulders to investigate.

'Before I go and get on with those items, you recall, sir, your request to map everyone's movements…' LeFanu nodded. 'Well, an early inconsistency is Mr Pchelski. According to UK Border Force, there is no record since early December of him leaving the UK and returning. So, how come he was in France? OK, so Border Force are not infallible, nor are the ferry operators but it does beg a question…' Both Jones and LeFanu nodded. And Jones added the point about the possibility of dual passports.

Chapter 44

Analysis of Terry Beddall's phone activity showed photos of two cars. Magazine photos of a Porsche 356C and a Ferrari 275GTb/4. But strangely, bearing in mind George's comments, not a solitary photo of the love of Terry's life, Angela Darling, or any other woman for that matter. LeFanu and Miles both thought this particularly odd and the detective chief inspector related an earlier conversation with Charlotte about avoiding publicity like the plague after her marriage and the lack of photos in Porten House. 'But maybe there's another phone. Who knows?'

Jones explained his theory about the cars. 'Someone, maybe this Angela woman, sent the photos to Beddall to tell him to identify those two cars and not damage them like all the others because they were to be nicked. Pchelski told us that Beddall wasn't a petrolhead, so he would have needed some guidance. Can't fit in the logic of the green Mercedes or the model of the car in the Jacuzzi. So he goes to the barn place where the cars are stored, fixes the alarm — he's got a track record for that sort of thing — and smashes up everything he sees except, for the Porsche and Ferrari. Breaks open the safe — again he had a track record for safe-breaking — and then nicks the dress... How does that sound? Added to which, there were no Porsche or Ferraris in the garage, barn thing, that fit the description — so, who took them? That's a car transporter solution, not just driving the things away, isn't it?'

'Brilliant, Jones, except for the fact that we can't prove a damn thing. The publican's wife talked of car transporter vehicles in the area... But every potential witness is dead. It does hang together as a theory, though. Miles, opinions?'

She looked up from her laptop. 'Sorry, I was reading some of the notes of the thefts, and in particular, the cars and the wonderfully helpful Guy Scott. Listen...' She read out the reaction of Scott and Jones when they entered the premises and discovered the damaged cars, not knowing at that time that two were missing. 'The Bugatti Gangloff-Stelvio, whatever that looks like, had the word "Fake" etched into the bodywork with, I understand, brake fluid. You'd have to be pretty cute to know that kind of detail, and that doesn't stack up with Beddall — or what we believe is his knowledge. According to my husband, Peter, some of these replicas are as good, if not better than the original. And brake fluid has changed over the years, apparently, to not be as corrosive as the old stuff that just eats into the type of paint they used then, called cellulose, as against modern paints which are called 2-pack. Wow, I've just exhausted my total knowledge of cars and paint.' She smiled.

'Well, if all that is true in this case, then Beddall, to continue with DS Jones's argument, would have had to have been told which and what to do. That ties in with the photos that the techies have recovered — effectively, they are instructions. Presumably, and in the absence of any other information, the instructions to damage and destroy were verbal, alongside any involvement in the thefts. Now, somewhere else in these notes, Charlotte says she only likes all mod-cons in cars and they bore her, or words to that effect. That doesn't necessarily rule her out. Maybe she really is a born liar, certainly at best economical with the truth. Something else to explore in the next interview with Her Ladyship?'

'Agreed, both of you. We still have no proof. Let me give you another scenario. The man we know here with the expertise is Pchelski. He could have done the damage; could have stolen the cars; could have sent Beddall two pictures to show off. Just as plausible. I'm building up some questions for this guy, who is a self-confessed devotee of old cars. Perhaps he would be angry enough to damage a replica, especially when there is some history between him and Groombridge. Before you say it, he says he had no idea who had bought his cars. That's another tale that might or might not be true. His visitor at the prison — the now retired employee — would he have known that Pchelskis car, or cars, were insured through Beech Underwriting and therefore their value?'

Jones looked puzzled. 'The other expert, so as to speak, is Guy Scott and his cronies at the auction house. Another thought, just to confuse the issue, I'm afraid, is when were the cars stolen/damaged? Could have been before Christmas for all we know and not connected to the village thefts or the murders.'

'Indeed, Jones, but maybe his surprise, when you two discovered the damaged cars, is as false as some of the things he's said? Maybe 'discovering' the thefts and damage with you, Jones, wearing a policeman's hat, has given him cast iron evidence for a bona-fide insurance claim? Maybe he was a bit anxious at the time to drive up here, as you said at the time. And you are right, we are connecting the two issues of burglary/theft and murder. And I don't know whether that is the right positioning. *Merde*!'

'If it was any or either of them, Sergeant, that sent the pictures to Beddall's phone, and it's a different number than that his sister gave us, then would he have the knowledge to download pictures or delete them? God, they seem to have umpteen phones these guys. Am I unusual? We know that prisoners tend to miss out on a generation or two of technological innovation — and phones are a good example of that. His sister said, in the interview transcript, that she was surprised at his ability to operate a newish mobile phone. Sounds like someone may have helped him. But we are always hearing of mobiles being smuggled into prisons, so it could be that an inmate gains experience that way. Maybe someone deleted pictures of the girl from his phone. Which would explain why he had no photos of his greatest love on his phone, but according to his sister, he had taken lots of pics of her. But I'm reliably informed there are electronic gadgets that can permanently delete stuff from the innards of a phone or computer. Perhaps she doesn't want to be identified! What a surprise.' Sam Miles crossed her arms in a demonstration of satisfaction.

'Stop. You are both making too many leaps of faith. I agree what you both say is plausible, but unfortunately basically unprovable until, or unless, we uncover more information. I need more coffee and something to eat.' He got up and left the office with his colleagues, LeFanu to leave the building for his favourite coffee shop, Caffe Nero in town, and Miles and Jones to eat in the staff cafeteria.

Chapter 45

Sam Miles had called Charlotte Groombridge on her mobile to ensure she would be at the Chelsea flat so they could conduct a second interview and get a feel for the London home of the Groombridges.

The apartment, on the first and second floors, with fabulous views, was in a seriously expensive area of Chelsea, Flood Street. Rosetti Gardens Mansion had been built for Lord Radnor in the late nineteenth century, and lately converted into luxury apartments worth, according to Zoopla's search engine, around three million pounds apiece. They had to ask at the porter's lodge for a call to be put through to the Groombridge residence, as the porter called it. LeFanu hated this style of pre-announcement; as he put it, 'It gives them warning. I prefer the surprise tactic, but that is how the other half live, I suspect.'

The door opened miraculously as they approached it. The housekeeper, obviously forewarned, looked imperiously at the two of them. 'Yes?' she asked.

'We have come to see Lady Charlotte Groombridge, as I suspect you know already.' Samantha smiled as she said it. As they were escorted in, Samantha asked, sotto voce, 'Do tell me, what is that exquisite perfume that Lady Charlotte wears?' again with a soft smile.

'Armani Diamonds,' was the terse reply. Samantha nodded in appreciation.

Lady C entered the room, the drawing room as the lady housekeeper who had answered the door referred to it, immaculate make-up and hair, and dressed to kill in a sheath-like dress, cut well above the knee, in shimmering gold with a low front, amazingly high stiletto heels, which raised an obvious eyebrow for Sam Miles and a smile from LeFanu. As she entered the room, Philippe LeFanu was reminded of DS Jones comments about the walk of a model. Phillipe instantly recognised the background music as Mendelssohn's Violin Concerto in E Minor. A beautiful melancholic piece, he reflected, but the cynic in him thought the music had been stage managed for their benefit.

She gestured towards a sofa, patently an expensive piece. 'Do sit down. I don't believe I have met you, Mademoiselle…'

Sam produced her warrant card as LeFanu told Charlotte Sam Miles's title and field of expertise. As always, he was looking for a reaction.

'Scotland Yard. Wow! Things have escalated a bit from the rural police force involvement.' Again, her smile seemed captivating or shallow if you were used to it.

LeFanu launched into his list of questions that had been bugging him. 'Madam, you didn't tell us about George Pchelski.'

'Georgie? Well, the rude response would be that you didn't ask about him. However, what do you want to know? I had an affair with him ages ago. He's a lovely man. It all finished when I married Tony in the US. I've had quite a few boyfriends in my time, Detective Chief Inspector; I'm not a nun, you know. And not long after that, Georgie went to prison. Game, set and match, as they say at Wimbledon, I believe.' She sat back with her arms crossed, which inevitably accentuated her cleavage, much to DI Samantha Miles's amusement.

'Did I say something funny, Ms Miles?'

Samantha Miles was quick and cutting. 'Actually, madam, it is Mrs, but I would prefer the Detective Inspector title, if you don't mind. It focusses everyone on the reason we are here.' Patently, LeFanu thought this is two women who would spar for points. So he let Sam take the lead role whilst he listened and watched with interest for reactions.

'Have you ever been in George Pchelski's green Mercedes convertible?'

'Mrs, sorry, Detective Inspector Miles, I'm not a car person, as I told your boss here. He is your boss, is he?' Without waiting for any response she continued, 'Powerful big cars with aircon, GPS and electric everything are my forte. Not yours, perhaps?' Fifteen-love, thought LeFanu. Charlotte carried on, unperturbed, 'Yes, I have travelled in that car, years ago, now. But you know that already don't you? My memory is that it was nice in the summer in town with the hood down but fairly nasty in bad weather and on a fast road. I didn't realise we were here to do assessments of cars — á la Top Gear, as they say.' LeFanu realised that the conversation was going to continue with point scoring, so intervened to take the temperature down a degree or two.

Charlotte's body language changed as LeFanu brought the

conversation round to a creative level, adding some pseudo deference to her. 'Tell us about George, Lady Groombridge.'

'Yes of course. Let me see...' She turned towards him, obviously preferring talking to men, which could be a weapon for LeFanu in the future to push her into losing her temper, which often let some real truths emerge from the froth of lies and half-truths.

'George had a real passion for his cars and was seriously miffed when Tony bought them.'

'How did he know who had purchased them? He was in prison after the judge ordered the disposal of his assets.'

'That must be a rhetorical question, as I haven't a clue. Perhaps officialdom told him. That's why you two are detectives, isn't it?' Clearly she was riled by the conversation, but it looked like her upbringing forced a polite but acid response.

Glancing at Sam Miles with a slight frown suppressed an outburst from her. 'Do you think, madam, that "miffed" is the right word? Could he have been angry rather than miffed?'

'I suppose so, dear Chief Inspector. I wouldn't know. Come between a man and his big boys toys and anything can happen. I have spoken to him only a couple of times since and that only for old times' sake.' She crossed her legs provocatively, changed her seating position again and effectively side-lined DI Miles from the conversation.

Not to be out-done, Samantha Miles interjected, 'You sent a text message to him two days ago. Is that what you mean by speaking to him?' Whilst it was said in an aggressive tone, she smiled as she delivered the message.

'I'm sorry, Detective Inspector Miles, we seem to have got off to a bad start.' Charlotte turned, quite deliberately to face Sam. 'I am under a lot of strain, so please forgive me.' Short of fluttering her eye-lids, this was verging on the theatrical, LeFanu thought, recalling the theatre of the previous interview. 'George was, is, I suppose I mean, fanatical about his cars. A bit like my late husband. I'll never understand it; cleaning the blessed things, putting specifically designed covers on them to keep them warm, just stopping short of talking to them but rarely using them.' Again, the supercilious smile and as if it suddenly dawned on her. 'Oh, God! I see where you are coming from. Do you really think George, lovely calm Georgie, could have murdered my husband, in revenge or something?'

'Strange word "revenge", don't you think? Your husband appears to have bought the cars quite legitimately.'

'To be absolutely honest with you, Detective Inspector, I think George may have had a run in with my husband at the insurance company. Tony was a senior director there, you know. And George was a fair way down the food chain. Great English expression, *n'est-ce pas*? Maybe that's where it started.'

Disregarding the comment, Philippe zeroed in on the earlier observation by Charlotte. 'More to the point, Lady Charlotte, do you think he could have killed your husband? It, obviously from your comment just now, had occurred to you?'

'Yes, it had crossed my mind. Anger is a strange thing. Sitting here thinking about it all, over the past weeks. The funeral services and all the letters of condolence do make me wonder who could have done such a dreadful thing. We may not have been the closest marriage in the world, but I did love my husband, despite all his failings.'

Then, pulling the conversation back from the rambling quasi-emotional comments from Charlotte, LeFanu pressed, 'And the text message, madam?'

'He told me about his pal inside the prison, Terry. I can't recall his last name, in fact I don't think I ever knew it… And I read in the French newspaper about his death in Paris. I get the French papers in London regularly. I sent George a text message in case he had missed the news because he travels a lot.'

'So the newspaper said a Terry Beddall had died in Paris and you assumed it was George Pchelski's friend? Of all the Terrys in the world? Strange case of two plus two equals five, don't you think? Did you know Terry was in France, or George, for that matter?' He studied her carefully for a reaction, expecting her to shilly-shally around to buy some time.

After a gap of what seemed ages, she looked up. 'Chief Inspector, I had a brief affair, if you can call it that, with Terry. I don't make a note of the surnames, but the newspaper report rang a bell. That's all — no mystery. With him, more of a one-night stand, as you English call it. He was fucking good too, if you'll forgive the expression, but afterwards conversation was extremely limited and very one-sided. It didn't last long before I became bored. And anyway, he was besotted with another lady, a blonde, so I was just a shag, a posh fuck — almost the opposite of my piece of rough, I suppose. Maybe something for him to brag about. Certainly, I told my friends and we laughed about it. Anyway, he told me he was going away to take a holiday with this blonde lady in France, so I suppose I did make the quantum leap you refer to. Nothing sinister, I assure you.'

'I may come back to that issue. Referring now to Mr Pchelski, you seem to know a lot about him, bearing in mind he is a long lost boyfriend. Actually, how many times have you seen him or spoken or even text messaged him since the break-up six years or so ago?'

'I don't know. Six years is an age. Probably three or four times. There's no harm in it, is there? We parted on good terms after a whirlwind affair. A lot of fun and laughs. I did meet him after his release to see if I could help in any way. Quite frankly, I would have let him have me again, in the biblical sense, DI Miles, of course. Come to think of it, I may have mentioned about Tony getting his cars. Sorry, slipped my mind.' She tossed her head as if that explained her apology.

'Have you been out of the UK since we last spoke?' LeFanu was back on his mental list of questions, convinced that she knew more than she was telling.

'Yes, I confess, Mr LeFanu, despite your instructions *au contraire*, I did disappear for two or three days to see my mother. She's not well.' Again the toss of her head and the nervous, he thought, brushing of a stray strand of hair from her forehead. Past experience made him suspicious of sudden illnesses in the family of interviewees under pressure. She continued, '*Merde*, am I a suspect, too?'

He ignored the excuse. 'May we see your passport?'

She visibly blanched under the perfectly applied make-up. 'Er, *oui*. Of course. I'll get it now.' She stood up. 'You will take tea, of course?'

'No, madam, we do not have the luxury of time,' responded DI Miles, rather abruptly and without seeking reference from her boss.

'So be it.' Charlotte flashed back and left the room in search of the document.

'Sam, I've seen that walk before. What do you reckon? You've seen the CCTV from the French railway station. Could it be the same one? Think about it. She becomes very French and seductive when she chooses.'

Samantha Miles nodded in agreement, but before she had a chance to respond, Charlotte returned with her red EU passport in the name of Lady Groombridge and handed it to the DI, whose hand was outstretched, restoring her commanding position.

DI Miles riffled through it, noting the international stamps, and placed it in her handbag. 'Not a British citizen then?' Charlotte shook her head and was about to respond when Miles continued, 'We will return it soon, madam. Just a few checks to make, and after all, you did agree with the DCI, here, not to leave the country, didn't you? So it won't be important will it?' That was an "advantage Smiles" point, LeFanu thought.

He followed through, 'And the other passport, Madam? The French-issued document before you married Mr Waller, Lord Groombridge?'

She looked crestfallen. 'Ah yes, of course, I'd forgotten that one. It must be around somewhere. Might even still be valid. I'll have to look for it. It may be in France. God, I haven't thought about that for simply ages. I could ask my brother to search for it. Would that help?' LeFanu nodded. He knew it was a long shot; he hadn't checked with the French authorities about the existence of a second current passport, but his sister, Vivienne, had told him that it was possible, particularly in France where celebrities were concerned.

Samantha Miles, not to be outdone by the stance taken by Charlotte, used LeFanu's approach of rapid changing of the subject of questions for a last question. 'Who is Ronnie? Is he another of your conquests, madam? We'd like to know more.'

'Oh dear, Detective Inspector, you really do need to brush up on your detective work. Ronnie is a female. You know, the short form of endearment for Veronica. One of my best friends. Surely you have friends whom you call by a short form of their name, don't you?'

Samantha was suitably embarrassed and knew she had reddened at the onslaught. 'Thank you, madam. At this stage of our investigation, it was just another name in a long list of names. Now we know it is the person, sorry, the lady, my DCI met at the memorial service.' LeFanu thought she had recovered well from the veiled insult.

'Tell us about her and your other friends.'

'Well, Ronnie, sorry Veronica van Outen, was at school with me. A Dutch girl by birth, but like many of us, more international as we grew up. Lucky to have had wealthy parents with foresight, wouldn't you agree?' And without waiting for a response, 'Fiona, or Fi as we call her, was also at the school in Basle, Switzerland, for a while. Lovely girl, although not quite as privileged as we were. Catherine McKay was a diplomat's daughter, similarly privileged, but that is the how of it at these schools. Anything else? I really am a trifle busy at the moment.'

'One last point, Lady Groombridge. We'd like to look over the apartment, in particular your late husband's wardrobe, and yours too. It's just to fill in the gaps in our thinking, nothing sinister, I assure you.' LeFanu liked the way Sam had regained control.

She shrugged, as she had done many times in the previous interview. It was as if she was expecting something of the sort. She knew there was little she could do to stop the low-key search, short of demanding a search warrant, which would put her in a particularly bad light, and led the way up to the first floor of the enormous duplex flat. DI Miles opened the wardrobes and made an aside, deliberately loud enough for Charlotte to hear, about the fabulous designer label display, particularly Dolce & Gabbana, which she said was her all-time favourite, reminding her of a shop she'd visited recently in Bicester. There was no reaction from Charlotte apart from the ubiquitous shrug. Miles almost gasped as she took in the array of clothes, every designer label she'd ever seen. Twenty or more pairs of jeans, all beautifully folded and co-ordinated by subtle changes of colour. Charlotte admitted that it was an inherited trait from her husband which the *femme de ménage* (the housekeeper) kept up, tidying all the cast-off clothing in her dressing room. Miles's eagle eye spotted an expensive pair of jeans screwed up on top of a clothes basket, Robert Cavalli, seriously expensive at about twelve hundred euros a pair, she thought, from the logo on the rear pocket that she could see. But the thing that caught her eye on the jeans was a small smear of green against the glitzy design.

'Sorry,' Charlotte said. 'The housekeeper isn't up to date with the cleaning because of all this fuss about Tony.' She reached to snatch the jeans away from Samantha, but was not quick enough.

'We'll take these, Lady Groombridge. I will, of course, give you a receipt.' Charlotte could do little but nod, although the colour seemed to have drained from her face despite her immaculate make-up. 'Whilst on the subject, may I show you this?' DI Miles produced the crumpled dress.

'Well, it looks like one of mine, from a couple of years back but... I really don't know, but...' And gesticulating to the wardrobe full of dresses, she shrugged. 'But really, just look at the state of it. Do I look like a person who would own something like that? Did you get it from a charity shop or something?' She looked at DI Miles with a piteous smile.

Groombridge's wardrobe in a separate dressing room was interesting in that there were patently three suits missing from a colour co-ordinated display of thirty or so. The colours clashed rather than gradually changing. Shirts, all by a Hawes & Curtis of Jermyn Street, similarly displayed, where there appeared to be six missing from their rack. She took some photographs adequately displaying the colour difference and focussing on the labels.

'My husband likes their shirts and never wears anything else. Button down collars and short sleeves he always says are for the hoi-polloi.' Miles just stared back as if nothing had been said, noting the use of the present tense in Charlotte's remark.

LeFanu thanked Lady Groombridge graciously as they reached the hall, leaving the music still playing in the background on its umpteenth repeat, saying quite forcibly, 'That'll do for now, Charlotte, Lady Groombridge.' Samantha Miles smiled and held out her hand.

Charlotte recovered her composure quickly, and as a parting shot, said, 'Tell me, my dear, do they call you Smiles behind your back?' That was game set and match to Charlotte, judging by the black look from Samantha.

'Please don't forget about the other passport, now will you, madam? We can't have it being used and you being arrested at any port of entry or exit. Now that would be embarrassing for you, wouldn't it?' Miles grabbed back a little of the score. It was going to be an interesting journey back to Ipswich, he guessed.

'Well spotted, Samantha,' he remarked as she drove north for the Edgware Road and he examined the pair of jeans that she had "confiscated" inside an evidence bag.

'Bitch, that's all I can say! I'd like to see her being torn apart in prison. Do you know how much these jeans cost? Well, probably no. But they cost around twelve hundred euros a pair — I saw exactly that pair in a magazine at the dentists' — and she just screwed them up and chucked them in the dirty linen basket. Close to Utopia, having that much wealth, I suppose. My God, I felt so scruffy in there. Never again!'

LeFanu laughed. 'Don't worry about it. You look absolutely fine. That's the way the rich live, I suppose, though it's hard to imagine Charlotte, Lady Groombridge, picking up a paint brush, let alone painting in those fancy jeans. As to Utopia, I think that family is more like dystopia'

'Maybe, sir, but it depends on what she was painting! What if the green paint matches the green on the toy car?'

'It's a long shot, but get it analysed by the lab toute-suite. If it was the paint you suspect, then it places her well and truly on the scene and at the right time. But if so, then if she suspects that we're onto something, she could well be a flight risk. However, we will wait and see, but don't you think it's a mite too obvious to keep those jeans in full view knowing we were coming?'

Miles nodded. 'Take your point, sir. I'll set up a low-profile surveillance team, just in case. We've enough justification of suspicion of involvement to warrant it. But you're right about the way the other half live. That apartment was the size of a private airfield and looked like it had been decorated by an escapee from Hollywood.'

'Mmmm. Do that. The surveillance part, I mean.' His mind was already on other things.

Chapter 46

The green paint wasn't a match for that on the car, much to Samantha Miles's annoyance. LeFanu told her not to beat herself up about the mistake; that it might possibly have unnerved Lady C's arrogance. Miles had the expensive jeans properly laundered and packaged and made an appointment to return them to Charlotte Groombridge in London, knowing that she was going to have to eat some humble pie.

Lady Groombridge accepted her apology with a smirk on her face. ' I was fond of those jeans. You know maybe that once in a while one gets the perfect fit. And you've made a perfect job of cleaning them — quite a vocation?' She looked at Sam Miles with a false smile. 'It was careless of me to spill the paint, but hardly an issue for me, anyway. I could have told you, even shown you the tiny tin of green enamel, if you had but asked, and even shown to you the beautiful Venetian vase with a tiny chip — careless of me, before you say so, to damage such a precious artefact. Anyway, all of that would have saved you such a lot of time, which you perhaps could have spent trying to solve my husband's murder. Still, never mind.' Miles was furious but could not show it.

'One question for you, if I may… Just to show, I hope, that I am actually human…' Samantha smiled, almost through gritted teeth.

Charlotte looked up, cautiously. 'Yes? What now?'

'Your home in Montargis. I looked on Google Earth the other day. It is huge and obviously pretty old. Fantastic. How old is it?'

'Really, Detective Inspector, I have better things to think about, but if you must know, to satisfy your curiosity, it, or rather the land, was gifted to my family by the Sun King, Louis, in 1703 in return for some trivial favour or other by my ancestors. It is a cold damp building with enormous up-keep, labyrinthine underground tunnels which seem to bring in the damp. Give me Chelsea any day.'

'Bet there's lots of creepy-crawlies and things then.'

'Oh, for God's sake! Yes, yes, rats, mice, even some snakes. What would you expect? You are obviously a townie.'

'Absolutely.' Miles smiled and gave a mock shudder at the thought of the spiders and other vermin. 'But my husband,' she continued, 'had a family house which he inherited in a small village in Kent. Only three hundred or so years old, wooden beams etc., and spiders and mice aplenty. Can't get rid of the field mice who emigrate inside in the autumn. Always looking for a miracle cure, I suppose... Or I'm stuck with them!' She paused, smiling her best effort at a genuine smile, looking at Charlotte.

'Well, we use rat poison in France — or rather, the gardeners do. Horrid stuff and smells — yuk! Strangely, DI Mills,' Samantha decided not to correct her about her surname, looking up inquisitively. 'I had to bring some over to the school I attended, as they had the same problem in old buildings and just couldn't get rid of them — but that was years ago. Haven't seen any since, but then I don't do *les pepinieres*, garden centres as you call them, or supermarkets. Anyway, enough of this. I do have things to do.'

'Thank you for your time, madam, and again, apologies about the jeans. I do hope you find we have had them cleaned to your satisfaction and I am glad we have had this little incidental conversation to clear the air from previous encounters.' Graciously, Charlotte accepted the comments and even showed Sam to the door herself.

Sam Miles sat in her car and made a recording of her conversation and observations. She smiled to herself as she calmed down, driving north on the M11 in her Ford Mondeo Estate car. She called LeFanu and explained that she had had to eat crow about the paint but wondered what exactly Charlotte had been painting with a small tin of green enamel. Lefanu had commented that he couldn't imagine she would know how or where to buy the bloody stuff, let alone use it, which had brought another smile to Sam's face as she raced up the motorway. She then recounted the conversation about rat poison, evincing a "well done" response from LeFanu. To Sam, there was a satisfaction that her apology meeting had maybe borne some other fruit. It made some sense to the issue of how well known strychnine and its use could be.

After they'd closed the call, the DCI mulled over the original conversation he and Sam Miles had had with Lady C in her apartment. It was peculiar that she had not mentioned she'd been painting or commented that she was, say, a budding artist or whatever. Surely, she would have said why the paint. Normally anyone in that situation would say — oh yes I was painting my "xxx" and spilled a drop or two. Silly me. He considered the options, which included the notion that the soiled jeans were deliberately on view to him and Sam Miles to create a diversion.

He called Sam Miles on her car phone. 'Sam. Is it a coincidence that she was using green paint? It sounds like Ockham's Razor again. The simple solution is the right one. Maybe she wants to be involved. Needs to be in the limelight, knowing full well that she has an elaborate "get out of jail free" card with alibis that are unassailable, but meanwhile she is centre stage. Sort of infamy. If we are right, then she has succeeded in wasting time and perhaps we're missing the real issues. I am confused.'

Sam Miles replied that she was having similar thoughts, commenting that she seemed to take a childish pleasure in proving her wrong about the paint on the jeans — almost like a revenge for daring to criticise or…

LeFanu agreed, stating that delay and confusion never did solve murders. They decided to shelve the paint issue.

Chapter 47

Next morning, LeFanu, Miles and Jones met promptly at eight a.m., each clutching a cup of Starbucks coffee as they entered the building. 'My thoughts are this, both of you. I'm getting pressure for results from above; pressure from the Met to return you, DI Miles; pressure from everyone, it seems. We know we're stumbling, hoping to pick up on something to give us direction, and we know whoever is behind this is either bloody clever or lucky. So, DI Miles, I want all the files, interview notes and tapes, background and the movement map to be passed to a team led by acting DC Susie Ford. Three or four people should do it. I want them to try to find what we've missed, coincidences, locations whatever. There's always something, and we don't have the time to analyse every word that's been spoken and don't want to, either. We want... no, need them to point out anything we've missed or where we've failed to make connections. We will not be too sensitive if it looks like we are being criticised — stress that point to them, please. Fresh minds whilst we've got our hands full with other tasks. We're too close to it. And put that new guy, DC Dodd, in there too — he speaks French and understands a little of the French mentality, and maybe WPC Bell. Final choice up to you two. These villains often make mistakes and we need to be damned sure we've not missed the obvious. Give them three days maximum. No interim debates or discussions with us. Just conclusions. And every, and I mean every, meeting, from now on, will be recorded so that they or others can listen without having to ask questions. They, the questions, will obviously follow. OK?' He looked at both of them. Both nodded enthusiastically, commenting almost together that fresh thinking was needed, as they had felt that everyone was going around in circles. 'And thanks for the coffees, Jones. My turn next time.'

The meeting was over quickly, and still clutching their take-away Starbucks cups, they went to their respective desks.

***

DS Jones arrived at LeFanu's office thirty minutes later, clutching some papers. 'Slightly strange answers from the people in Courchevel, sir. Groombridge went there more or less as normal before Christmas but left on the 1st January, presumably to return to the UK. As he did not have a car, a taxi took him to Moutiers. We've tracked the taxi — unusual, as it was on New Year's Day and therefore memorable in that hedonistic place — straight to the railway station, where there is a direct connection to Paris from Courchevel, about twelve miles or so, all told, to the station, that is. It was unusual, according to the concierge of the ski lodge where he has his ski lodge cum duplex apartment, for him to return to the UK so early. First time in years, he said, and on New Year's Day too. And apparently he just blamed business commitments.'

'Umm. Possible, I suppose. But unusual behaviour patterns are always interesting, especially when the end result is murder.'

'Anyway, everyone knows him there, sort of big English "Milord" stuff. He had a haircut on Wednesday the 31st December…'

'Oh, for God's sake, Jones.'

'No, bear with me, sir. It was a short haircut, almost a crew cut, apparently. All the people there thought it was hilarious, largely because he is an arrogant man and hates change of any sort. Hence my word "strange". I was just thinking that a certain Mr Gold had a short haircut too.'

'True, Jones, true. Maybe there is a connection there. Go on…' LeFanu was himself putting two and two together.

'The concierge, fortunately for me, speaks good English, as there are a lot of Brits there in the season. He checked out Lord Groombridge's lodge for me, as he arranges cleaning and maintenance for all the owners, and noticed there were three suits missing. Sounds like he had a duplicate wardrobe there, as we saw, in the Suffolk house, in terms of clothing and so on. He doesn't usually bring more than a small overnight bag with him. This time he purchased a proper suitcase from a local store, a blue plastic sort of thing — nothing flash. All, as you say, sir, out of his usual behaviour pattern.'

'Just so, just so.' Jones knew that this answer was buying a little thinking time for his boss.

After a pause of a few seconds, DS Jones continued. 'No record of a train ticket purchase, but that wouldn't be unusual. We may be able to trace a credit card payment, but that'll take time. He flew to the UK, by KLM, to

Norwich airport; seems like they're the only people who do a direct flight from Paris Charles de Gaulle on the 2nd January, arriving at six thirty p.m. Presumably, then by car to Eye St Mary although no car seen or parked at the house, as we know.'

'Well done, Jones. Enter the details on the map. I need to know where everyone is at any given moment of time. Although, knowing what we do about the Groombridge family, I can't see him using cheap one-class flights willingly. Bizarre.'

'Bloody strange marriage, that. He's in Paris, a hundred kilometres or so from Montargis where his wife is and they don't meet up. Maybe a steward or stewardess will remember him. Can't be many peers of the realm on cheap flights.' LeFanu nodded and Jones wrote a note in his black book.

'Hang on a minute…' Jones raised his hands in an apologetic gesture. 'Wait. We know when Lord G left Courchevel, and the date we think Gold, or whoever, left France for Montreal? There's a gap. Damn, damn, I should have spotted it before. That could be when the bomb was planted on Beddall's car — if not, what was he doing wasting days in Paris? And seemingly on his own. Odd!'

'Jones, that is very good thinking. It fits the facts, but there could be a dozen other reasons. We think…' And he put the emphasis on the word "think". 'We think that Lord G is our phantom bomb maker, but we simply don't know. And I'm not sure whether it is worth pursuing. Let the French work on it. Maybe a rental agency in Paris with Citroën Picasso cars — although that is a quantum leap, I admit. If we knew it was Lord G, what would it add to our knowledge base? If we knew what he was doing in that time lapse, it might help, and I guess it's only Charlotte who can tell us that.'

'Maybe they did. Maybe they did, meet up, I mean. Not really for us to judge regarding their relationship — pure speculation. Now, if you said handing over or swapping passports or something like that, then that would be relevant and some. But you remember she said she goes shopping in the sales or whatever in Paris. Maybe they met up then. All the more reason for substantiating bloody Lady Charlotte's alibis and those that gave them and what is the whole truth and nothing but the truth from that lady. Someone I knew, stupidly, lent their credit card and PIN number to a friend and they went on a shopping spree. If that happened, it would make like an alibi but one that would be difficult to break, wouldn't it?'

'As you say, sir, just so! I looked up the sales in France, thinking of taking the girlfriend for a weekend in Paris, and they don't operate like the UK. No wall to wall sales in the shops. They have to start mid-January or thereabouts. Maybe by law, I don't know.'

'I believe that's true, but for women like that shopping is a way of life, I suspect, and the word "sale" is an excuse for another lunch or whatever. Speaking of women, where is Smiles?' It was the first time he had used her nickname.

'I think she's investigating some of the loose ends, hoping to find a fresh approach where we are stymied. She's got Sergeant Shaw looking at other visitors to the prison on those Thursdays — maybe a description of the woman or car type, whatever. Got to be done, but I wouldn't place a bet on a result.'

'Good. I agree with the possible outcome but... From what you say, the roles have changed a bit now that the two major events of the thefts and the murder are inexorably linked. You two getting on all right? No squabbling?'

'No, it's cool. She's good. Thinks outside her box and doesn't talk down to the troops, or me, for that matter. Get a feeling she's learning from everything we say and do.'

LeFanu glanced up and nodded, almost saying that's why she's here and an inspector. 'Think we need a three-way meeting. Sort it for tomorrow morning, will you, Chris? Early, too.'

LeFanu had arranged for bacon sandwiches and seemingly unlimited coffee to be laid on in the conference room on the third floor for the meeting with his colleagues. His now famous map with pins and coloured lines was mounted on an easel, showing the movements of some of the people identified in the investigation so far. For him, it was a key tool, better than a laptop screen as you could stand back from it. DS Jones and Samantha Miles arrived promptly at eight forty-five a.m. as had been arranged. He was in the process of entering the known movements of George Pchelski. Leaving the UK by air from Stanstead on the 17th of January, bound for Berlin. Next place identified was Warsaw, when he had called him on his mobile, with, apparently, a stopover in Berlin somewhere down the line but no detail.

A surprise "guest" turned up five minutes later: the assistant chief constable. ACC Moore was an imposing figure, mid-forties, known throughout the force as arrogant, with the ear of the chief constable, politically correct in everything and destined for higher things. He shook hands with each of the team and then sat erect in the uncomfortable plastic chair in his uniform, covered in medal ribbons, with his hat, covered in scrambled egg, as Jones liked to call it, carefully placed on the conference table, away from the Styrofoam coffee cups and his laptop beside it. He started what seemed to be a prepared speech regarding the investigation to date, including the enormous amount of man hours spent for little or no concrete answers. He was clearly in command of the facts and reminded the team several times of his and his superiors' disappointment.

'I am here, to determine whether a change of senior staff might engender some results, rather than more theories with little or no grounding in reality. And/or…' he added, scanning their faces, 'a reduction in the head count.' His comments created an instant bristling amongst all three of the investigating team, but a glance sufficed, from Philippe LeFanu, to his two detective colleagues to suppress any vocal objections.

ACC Moore sat back with his arms folded, refusing coffee offered by Inspector Miles. 'I want results. I'm sitting in on this meeting to assess where you are and what next. We have five, possibly six, murders, one alleged suicide, potentially a large, well-planned theft, some international enquiries which are giving my boss some pressure diplomatically, as well as media wanting someone's blood. At the moment, we're having a honeymoon from the news media, but it won't last. Fortunately, they haven't made the same connections you have between the Paris murders, the German lady and Groombridge. I want to listen to where you are planning to go from here and not a revamp of history. Resources are precious. Do I make myself clear?'

All three nodded. There seemed little point in arguing with the obvious.

ACC Moore pointed to DCI LeFanu, indicating he should proceed.

'Right, DI Miles, you have been tying up some loose ends. What have you and your team established that we didn't know already?' He added the last part of the sentence to make sure the other two recognized the message from HQ senior management.

She stood to speak but a gesture to remain seated was enough. 'Well, sir, I thought that the French were almost anal about administration but Charlotte, Lady Groombridge, has at least three French passports that we know about. All three appear to be valid and current. One as Lady Charlotte

Groombridge — fine, that one is in our possession; one as Madame C Bertin — her divorce was only in 2008, well within the currency of a French passport; one in the name of Foubert-Bertin. As you concluded, it had to have been a possibility with the way the French do things, without going into the reasons which are complicated, tedious and will not achieve any progress. Incidentally, the Waller passport was surrendered when she applied for the Lady G version. Meanwhile, I have had the transit lists checked by the UK Border Force people in all three names. I have to admit we had not had an automatic search instigated under F for Foubert, as part of a surname, up to now that is. So I now have some more information for your map, sir.' LeFanu rose and stood ready to add the new information to the crudely drawn sheet.

'Well, under the name Foubert… That's Charlotte's maiden name and the French add it to the married name, sir.' She turned and faced ACC Moore.

He interrupted, 'I've read all the reports and am well aware of the characters so far exposed. Please carry on without deference to me. Until I ask you a question, it is as if I am not here. OK?' Strangely, he beamed.

'Charlotte came to the UK, via the Dieppe to Newhaven ferry, I forget the exact date but I've got it somewhere in the file. She travelled in a French registered hire-car. A Citroën C4, rented from Europcar in Paris in the name of Bertin — still used on her driving licence. We believe she had someone with her but it appears that he, or she, had crossed the channel as a foot passenger. We cannot identify him or her except by hearsay of a Border Force operative at the time and some cloudy CCTV at Dieppe terminal. At nine thirty p.m., it was pitch black and pissing with rain, excuse my language, and a busy boat. We could arrange, if necessary, to check every passenger in every car, but before giving time to more work, I took a raincheck and thought a straight question to Madam Charlotte might give us the answer less painfully.' LeFanu nodded and she continued, 'She returned, alone, i.e. no passengers in the car, via Newhaven to Dieppe two days later, getting the nine a.m. boat, arriving in France at two p.m. their time. The car was logged back on Europcar's main computer after four days being handed back at their Montargis depot. Mileage was just shy of seven hundred and fifty kilometres, which means that she didn't go far in the UK. Paris to Dieppe is around two hundred kilometres; multiply by two for the return journey and add a hundred or so to her French house, leaves only around two hundred and fifty klicks from Newhaven. Say sixty-five miles each way. Drawing a ring around Newhaven means Gatwick, maybe Croydon to the north, Chichester to the west and somewhere between Hastings to Folkestone to the east. Interestingly, there's the Channel tunnel rail link at Ashford, Gatwick of course, and main line rail links to London. Why, is the question? Maybe it is just an innocent trip. Move on, eh?'

LeFanu had put two new lines on his map with annotations as to time and people involved and nodded pensively. 'Just so. So much for staying in the country. So much for her alibi, then. So much, as we said before, for the people who gave her an alibi. Shame they're French citizens or we could haul them in here tout suite. Do we have any ideas as to whether they have any more significant part in this than lying about Charlotte's whereabouts? I get a feeling about her that she is a free spirit and moves when and where she pleases. If her passport in the Foubert-Bertin name is legitimate, then we can do no more than interview her, and her alibi grantees, if there is such a word.'

'Agreed, sir. The next piece of information I have was gleaned by WPC Ford late last night. After your trip to Paris, she sent the photographs that Guy Scott gave us to that lady gendarme, Mimi LeBlanc, for a high-tech check as to whether they had been doctored.' Looking at Moore, again, she blushed, 'Sorry that's history again.' He nodded and made some notes on his laptop. Continuing, Miles added, 'The photos of Groombridge had been photoshopped using a very sophisticated technique requiring very high resolution kit, better than we had access to in the UK at short notice, anyway. One person we have not investigated, sir, is Charlotte's brother in France. He gave her an alibi and has a dubious record in politics in France, culminating in his leaving Sarkozy's UMP party and setting up a "dot-com" company employing very high tech equipment, largely in the film and media markets. No facts, but an uncanny coincidence. As an aside, sir, I do think we should consider getting a permanent transfer for WPC Ford to CID. She's very bright and does not take information solely on face-value.' Miles had thought a plug for this lady well-justified, and even more so as the ACC was listening in and she had provided a useful new string to their enquiries. LeFanu plainly agreed by a nod and a scribbled note.

Again, she continued, 'We needed those photographs to identify Groombridge as our victim, as we cannot arrange DNA testing as he was cremated, shall I say, somewhat prematurely.'

'Yes, yes. We know about that. Unfortunate use of bureaucratic pressure and all that.' Moore was clearly uncomfortable.

'The photos show a clear resemblance, facially, and in comparison to photos supplied by the American authorities, to our second really interesting person, Mr Gold. He's the US citizen who currently seems to be off US Homeland Security's radar, having never left the USA before, and has a spotless record, apart from apparently being the subject of a violent attack about four years ago. But we have no medical evidence of injuries.' She folded her notes and sat down.

LeFanu smiled and turned his attention to DS Jones. 'OK, Jones, what can you bring to the party?'

'The two furniture lorries, seemingly used on the job, have been located in a service station on the M6 at Knutsford with a dozen or so parking tickets on the screen. Inside was a pile of low density plastic sheets which I understand are used to "wrap" vehicles with logos and names rather than spraying them. One bears the logo and name of Greenfield & Sons and a fictitious address in Margate, Kent. Maybe a link to the words written by David Grant — "Greenf…" No prints or clues that forensics could establish as valid, helped, or hindered, by the transport police who opened up the trucks thinking it was just parking violations and messed up any chance of forensic evidence. We picked it up, or rather Sergeant Shaw did, from central reporting, There is no such company registered there or anywhere else. The furniture vans we think were used to hinder suspicion — they're always on the road twenty-four/seven, and who would suspect a furniture lorry at any time of day or night? The spoils were then transferred to the Transit vans or whatever. We believe we now understand how the gang could have "created" police vehicles by wrapping them in Suffolk police livery. Quite a complicated business, but easy to do with the right experience and sophisticated kit to print onto plastic. There was a programme on TV about it recently. All you need to do the wrapping is patience and a warm air gun, similar to that found in the abandoned factory unit, although even that seems to have been a blind alley.'

'I must interrupt, Detective Sergeant Jones.' Moore had looked up from his screen. 'First, we don't need an exercise in the how something has been done. And second, that's the second time in three minutes that the expressions "kit" and "sophisticated" have been used. Any connection?'

'It is possible, sir. There was some electronic kit used in the events at

Eye St Mary — not so much expensive or latest technology but unusual in this type of event. However, Lady Charlotte's brother is a person of interest, as DI Miles mentioned, and he does appear to have the skill sets or contacts that do. He is on our radar but we haven't enough to go on to implicate him and barely enough to even formally interview him, bearing in mind we would have to seek French agreement. Yet, anyway. We are still looking for a mastermind for the robberies and believe that the murder of Lord Groombridge, if it was indeed him, is connected with but not part of the burglaries.' LeFanu nodded and Moore nodded and gestured for Jones to carry on.

'We have made a connection with the two dead bodies found in the boot of a hire car under false plates in the Paris hotel car park. They were British, ex-army, and there were two distinctive pieces of jewellery found in the glove box of the hire car, both of which have been identified as belonging to residents in the village of Eye St Mary — Mrs Stephanie Davis and the MP's wife, Mrs Wellard. They, the ex-army boys, that is...' He coloured as he saw the look on Moore's face. 'Anyway, they had been in the Logistics Corps and with some others in that unit had been dishonourably discharged for theft of stores going to BAOR bases in Wiesbaden. Another in that unit was Terry Beddall. He went to army prison for the same reason, but was seen as the leader and then was dismissed and followed a life of crime. He died, poisoned by a female, we believe, who we've not been able to trace here nor abroad. An Angela Darling, or maybe it's a pseudonym — so a lady calling herself Angela Darling. He ended up...'

'Yes, yes, we all know. Continue.' Moore sounded more irascible now.

'Four others are currently in Spain. We have no evidence, so have asked the Spanish police to keep them under light surveillance. They flew in from Paris, same flight but not sitting together. And sir, the airline Iberia says that two seats were booked at the same time, but were not taken up on the day. Therefore, we believe that the goods that were stolen, and we also believe two very precious classic cars were taken to France, probably to the location at or near where Beddall's hire car blew up. The gendarmes have taken over that part of the search in Brittany and are talking to us regularly with progress and questions. One of my team is fluent in French, more than I can say for myself, as you know, so our link is DC Mike Dodd; he lived there and was married to a French woman for some time.'

'Which cars are unaccounted for, Jones? Do we know?'

'A Ferrari 275GTB and a Porsche 356. We have the serial numbers and so on from Groombridge's safe. Value? Arguably one to two point five million pound the pair — got good provenance, as they call it. Famous previous owners can count for doubling the price, depending on who, of course. There are the other three cars that used to belong to Pchelski that have just disappeared. Scrap, I suppose. That's an E-type Jaguar, a Morgan and an old MG. DVLA say that none of these cars has an export document or has been put on a Statutory Off-Road Notification. Just disappeared. Despite being bought by Groombridge, they were never re-registered after the purchase.'

'Could they have been exported as well — all five?' LeFanu asked, puzzled as he wasn't a petrol-head and just thought of a car as a means to get from A to B. 'But hold on a moment. Porsche 356?' Jones nodded. 'That's the second time I've heard of that car,' said LeFanu. 'And I know nothing much about cars. It's just registered. When I spoke to Pchelski in Warsaw, he was hunting parts for a couple of them. Are they that rare?'

Jones flipped through some papers on the desk and showed LeFanu a picture clipped from a magazine. 'Parts for a Porsche in Warsaw? Stuttgart, certainly. Yup, pretty rare cars. More in the USA than anywhere else, but still rare, and the Ferrari? Super rare.'

'To be fair, he had been in Germany and was visiting his Polish motherland, so as to speak. Anyway, there could there be a link between Pchelski's search for parts, assuming that was true, and the missing Porsche? I hate coincidences and this is certainly one of them.'

'Possibly, sir. They could be in a container on their way to Japan or wherever. Bit of money to grease the palms and...' He paused. 'However, Groombridge's collection all seemed to be minters — sorry, in A1 condition. I've got a feeling the two valuable ones went to France. We didn't check vehicles going by tunnel or ferry, other than cars and transit types. Just too many. It's just that all roads seem to go to France and there were checks at the time being made at all ports and airports. Groombridge's wife said the noble lord had a lot of dealings with the Swiss. Maybe an avenue to explore? And then we've got the ex-army bunch. Three, including Beddall, dead in France, and at most, probably four more living it up in the Barcelona area. It may be coincidence, again, and they may be innocent holidaymakers, but the departure from a French airport makes me at least half convinced that they were in it up to their necks. It's not exactly a quantum leap to guess these guys are the drivers of the vans and cars. I've asked our French colleagues for a search at the airport car parks for British registered cars, but they were somewhat unwilling, to put it mildly, to give the exercise any priority.'

'Understandable, really. So how do you get two classic, extremely valuable cars — presumably we have dimensions and weights and so on — from here to there? Car transporter, I guess, or a big truck, or perhaps a container. I assume they would attract too much attention if they were driven.'

'Fair comment, sir. Unless it was among a load of similar cars for a festival like Goodwood or Le Mans. The car ferries are like classic car exhibitions when cars are going back and forth for events like that. However, no such events in the immediate time frame of the thefts. But they could have been stored and then moved in which case the time frame is as wide as ever.'

'Can we make any assumptions, Jones? Miles, anything to add before we get into more conjecture?'

Miles raised her hand. 'One bit that grates with me, sir, is the model of the green Mercedes. To me, it looks like someone wanted to point the finger at Pchelski, to help us make the connection. And from Pchelski, perhaps, direct to Beddall and the infamous blonde Angela Darling. Two convicted criminals and maybe a fictitious named woman.'

'Good point, DI Miles. Strange how a small detail like that bloody model car assumes an out-of-all-proportion significance. Or, was that their intention?'

She continued, 'We checked all Angela Darlings in the UK and Europe. There is only one — a business consultant in the City of London, lives in Buckinghamshire and there's no correlation in descriptions and a one hundred percent secure alibi for the dates in question. So, if she doesn't exist, it must be a pseudonym for someone else. Couple that with the marked physical similarities with bloody Charlotte Groombridge and our blonde and maybe we have a link.' LeFanu smiled at the words "physical similarities", recalling Jones's admiring glances at the woman walking away at the end of their interview. Jones noticed the smile and reddened before glancing at ACC Moore, whose face was completely implacable. Samantha Miles carried on again from her notes, with a brief smile, knowing what was going through LeFanu's mind. 'I'd take that as an assumption, to use your words, sir, worth pursuing, as we have no solid reason to do more than interview Charlotte again. She is in breach of instructions from us and what looks like a false alibi, but not enough to issue a European arrest warrant.'

Chris Jones added, 'Sir, the only problem with that line of enquiry is the motive. She, Charlotte that is, seemed to be quite enamoured with George Pchelski. Even the text message we picked up from the analysis of his phone records was, I think you call it, "lovey-dovey". Why would she stitch him up? Thoughts?'

'Careful, Jones, you're on the edge of accusing her of murder and we have zero grounds for that. But it could be a complicated diversion.'

'Maybe, sir,' Miles butted in enthusiastically, 'maybe she wanted the loot from a fairly straightforward burglary, complex albeit, and things went pear-shaped. She or her cronies create the damage to make it look like burglary. Her husband turned up unexpectedly and we know from her that he worshipped his cars. If he caught her doing some damage, then she would have had few options. Doesn't sound that plausible, does it?' She looked at her colleagues, who obviously shared that last thought. 'Leaves more questions unanswered than it solves,' she added.

Moore, with signs of a growing impatience with the conversation, interjected, 'Focus, lady and gentlemen, on motive. Ask yourself: why use an improbable pseudonym like this Darling name. If it isn't the lady you've traced, then it's highly likely it's someone she knows or has upset. It is unlikely to have been a name picked at random — there is a purpose behind it, for sure. Link that with the finger-pointing about the model car and it looks like you are being led by the nose, lady and gentlemen. And from what I've been hearing, you are seeking a motive for a relatively small but bloody time-consuming and irritating set of thefts which will net the gang, whoever they are, with thousands, maybe hundreds of thousands but compared with the millions from the death of Groombridge, his estate, his cars — peanuts. Move on to that.'

'Agreed, sir.' LeFanu had little option and was pleased that the assistant chief constable had brought the two of them back to reality. 'What is strange about these cars is that she knew Lord G was a classic car dealer but has no knowledge of what was in that barn building, claiming never to have been near it. Someone irretrievably damaged several of them but two very valuable, but not the most valuable, are missing and we have seen that both were the subject of photographs sent to Beddall's phone. They could have been stolen or removed before the damage to the remainder occurred or removed at the same time or before. We really do not know, yet.'

Jones, this time, interjected, 'Unless it was an inside job and the damaged cars are meant, like the toy Mercedes, to put us off the scent. What could be that scent, or direction we had to be diverted from? Sorry, bad grammar, sir.'

Miles, seeing LeFanu's eyebrows raised, added, 'I think the motive for everything she does is money and the high life. Groombridge's will that DS Jones found in his safe, assuming it is the latest version, and it was written only three months ago, springs no surprises. She, Charlotte, is the prime beneficiary. A few minor bequests including one for one thousand pound to Frau Braun and only two hundred and fifty thousand to each of his two offspring — a fraction of what he is worth on paper, including insurance payouts and so on. So, she wins big-time, so perhaps she's the master-mind we're looking for and George P is one of the scapegoats in the equation, and Beddall another. We have asked the solicitor for Groombridge to comment about any differences between this will and any earlier manifestations of his generosity, but they are reluctant to do so without Lady Charlotte's agreement, unless we throw the formal application from the police angle. I've resisted that for the time being...'

'Let me finish, both of you.' DCI LeFanu was getting increasingly frustrated by this going over old ground in front of the assistant chief constable and couldn't establish his motive for sitting in, short of cutting back the team. He continued, 'Let's say the gang, maybe the ex-army guys, were meant to complete the thefts from the village houses, and indeed the stuff from Porten House too, whilst the mastermind had other intentions, i.e. the murder of Groombridge or the theft of the two cars unaccounted for — either or, or both motives. One item that has been played low key is the Government papers, since recovered in France in a sorry state after the explosion. I don't think they were anything more than a happenstance. Although, I would have expected a Minister of the Crown to have a more secure repository. '

ACC Moore interrupted, 'The Honourable Anthony Wellard MP, let alone his wife, may not agree with you, DCI LeFanu.' Both Jones and LeFanu were amazed to see Moore smile but recalled the grief from

Wellard's wife after the thefts had been discovered, knowing she had raised Cain with the chief constable.

'But,' concluded DCI LeFanu, 'I'm inclined to believe that the cars were the first serious objective, perhaps stolen to order, as they are apparently verging on the unique, and the other thefts the diversion, with the death of David Grant an unintentional result. That would put the blame, temporarily anyway, fairly and squarely on the back of the thieves. Right place, right time, wrong people. Then the motive becomes more logical. Groombridge's death could be a by-product of the thefts, again, wrong place, wrong time, or a coincidence, with his murderer being in on the theft plan and using it as a diversion for his, or her, real motive.'

'But then, sir…' Miles was flying. 'What if it wasn't Groombridge in the Jacuzzi? We've photographic evidence of meddling with the photographs electronically. The circumcision, whilst not evidence, does make a strange connection. If it was Gold, does that change the motive? She, Charlotte, claims that the marriage was a bit of a convenience and they both seem to play around. But could that be a bluff. We have no evidence and Mrs Braun, the housekeeper, who could have helped us there, is dead. Maybe Groombridge is alive and kicking in the USA under Gold's name, and if so, how and when did Gold arrive in the UK?'

'If your assumption is correct, then it would be logical to assume Groombridge used Gold's passport and he used that of Lord Groombridge. They look alike — that's a given. Presumably, Gold didn't know he was going to his death and possibly the murderer might have thought they were killing off Groombridge or, taking that thought process a little further, the murderer wanted to kill Gold and make it look like Groombridge, thence perfecting his escape. Too much guesswork in all of that. Wouldn't stand examination by anyone. It fits after a fashion and that's all.' He looked at his colleagues for reaction. 'Samantha, call Guy Scott and set up a meeting. We'd like to know how he came by the wedding party photos. He inferred, I seem to recall, that he had taken the pictures himself. And root around a bit to see if his classic car auction company has any comment about Groombridge's cars. There's something there that smells, but maybe that's the way they work. Not to take our eye off the ball, but there could be a meaningful connection.' Turning to Chris Jones, he added, 'Check anything that could carry old cars across the Channel. And what or how do the auction people move vehicles back and forth, probably worldwide, let alone the Channel? Guess three to five days after the robbery and all ports in Southern England from Plymouth to Felixstowe.' And to ACC Moore, 'Sir, I think this meeting has been useful to focus our attention. I will go to France and talk informally to these people who gave Lady Groombridge the alibi for the weekend of the murders and meet and talk to the gendarmes investigating the location in Brittany and the explosion in Beddall's car.' He looked for acceptance from Moore.

Gruffly, he replied, standing, as clearly the meeting was over as far as he was concerned, and smoothing down his immaculate uniform, 'Indeed, DCI LeFanu, I hope my presence here has assisted in your collective focus. I am satisfied that you will all now have a renewed energy to bring this matter to a satisfactory conclusion and parade your results. Remember, results do not equal no results plus excuses. And we have had many of the latter lately. Sometimes it is advisable to have a senior experienced official such as me to bring out the important matters from the trivia. You will, of course, keep me directly informed of progress.'

LeFanu nodded, hoping that would be the end of the inquisition. Moore hadn't finished, he continued remorsefully, 'And I'll leave you with three questions you need to explore: first, ask US Homeland Security to contact Mr Gold's parents or close relatives to establish his whereabouts. Use my name if necessary; I do have some high level contacts there. Helping us with enquiries about multiple murders should do the trick. They may not be happy, but they are supposed to be this nation's best friends. Second, whoever flew into the UK under the name Lord Groombridge must be identifiable. Accent, the demeanour, dress code whatever. If it were Gold, then he would dress differently, talk differently and so on. He is, or maybe was, quintessentially American. Airline staff know which side their bread is buttered and recognise usual run of the mill passengers from the unusual. Check it out! If you can establish the probable identity of the passenger, then it will make it easier to use Homeland Security and stop all this maybe/could be talk. And thirdly… This seems to be an issue of wigs, passports and alibis — and too many of each. And lastly, this car emporium, may be as bent as a nine bob note, but that's the job of the fraud squad, so don't get easily diverted. Don't get too hooked up with a car dealer — I've yet to meet one that's a hundred percent kosher.'

LeFanu acknowledged his comments and told ACC Moore of his sub-group being set up to look at all the reports, cross referencing the information gleaned over the interviews and reports and videotapes and would add his questions to the brief. 'And we should have the information from the cabin crew of both critical flights soon. The team are on it, sir.'

'Good. I like these youngsters to have a feeling for detective work rather than just allotted tasks. I will be pleased to see if this lady, Ford, wasn't it, is worthy of your faith, DI Miles. If there is one message, lady and gentlemen, it is stop wallowing putting dots over every "i" and crosses over every "t". Get on with solving the murders and apportioning blame on any of the many cadavers you have uncovered.' With that, he picked up his laptop, hat under his arm and left the room.

'No comments, thank you.' LeFanu addressed his two colleagues. 'Let's get to it.' He, too, left the conference room, giving the other two time and opportunity to get the pompous comments of the ACC out of their systems. 'For my part, I am going to ring my sister, Vivienne, and ask a favour.'

***

Vivienne was delighted to assist her brother after he had explained a little about the reason for his call. He wanted her to call Charlotte's brother, Philippe Foubert, and see if he could help her with a project for Paris Match. Obviously a fictitious project, which would involve the high tech solutions that Mimi Le Blanc had outlined.

Chapter 48

Within a day, Susie Ford's team had come up with a couple of inconsistencies, picking up the comments from the transcripts of the ACC Moore conversations. They traced the KLM crew on the Paris to Norwich flight when they returned to the UK at the end of their shift and met them at the airport with photos of both Groombridge and Gold from their passport documents. Two of the stewards had remembered Lord Groombridge, whom they had been instructed to treat as a VIP, even though it was a one class flight. The photos created a mixed reaction of recognition. One recalled he was casually, but smartly, dressed in a blue button-down short-sleeved shirt, and they had had to hang up his Boss leather jacket, as he disliked it being crammed into an overhead locker. Another remembered serving him with a Jack Daniels and then another, plus a request for a bag of chips. It was the word "chips" that had stuck, and it took a moment or two for the steward to realise that he had meant crisps. They had been convinced he was an American from this and his accent. And one of them remembered wishing him a happy birthday for the Saturday — presumably part of the VIP treatment with data picked up from his passport. Instead of looking pleased at the recognition, he had apparently looked confused.

The second point they raised was the referral, twice, by Pchelski to his grandfather's escape by fishing boat from northern Brittany. Recently, there had been articles in the UK newspapers about illegal immigrants using fishing boats from Brittany, and in particular the fishing port of Paimpol, to the UK beaches. It could be a possibility for illegal entry to the UK, was all they had to add, bearing in mind the question of alibis was being re-investigated.

DI Miles snapped her fingers and smiled. 'Of course, I'd forgotten that, according to Lady C, Lord Groombridge always wore formal shirts and never short sleeves or button-down collars. It's no proof, of course, but points the finger that we were right in our assumptions. Well done, you. And my apologies for not including that in the meeting notes.'

Jones smiled at Susie Ford and admitted that stories like the fishing boat people smugglers had never occurred. 'We just assume people, including the bad guys, use publicly available transport like the rest of us. If Pchelski's name was held in esteem in the French Breton fishing community, it would certainly not have been difficult for George P to have negotiated a trip across the channel. Virtually unproveable, as no self-respecting French fisherman is going to admit transporting people illegally, but it might be a way to start thinking differently. It will be borne in mind, thank you.'

Philippe LeFanu, trying to bring the conversation back to reality, added, 'She also said he only ever drank champagne or water on flights, never mentioning spirits, let alone Jack Daniels. Add to that the language issue of chips in the States being crisps here and maybe we're getting close to identifying the person carrying Lord G's passport on that flight. Sam, next interview with Lady C, we'll pose the Jack Daniels issue and revisit the shirts and jacket with her. And yes, well done. We all should have noted those discrepancies. OK, back to the drawing board.'

After Ford's team had left his office, he commented to Miles and Sergeant Jones that they had not documented the two points about drink and shirts. And that it was good to show Ford's team that they were not above criticism nor apologising.

DS Jones nodded and raised his hand.

'No need for the hand, Chris!' LeFanu smiled. 'What is it?'

'Let's get that DC Dodd to speak to the Air Canada flight cabin crew on the flight to Montreal and see what they remember. Flight AC871, I recall. Was it Jack Daniels or Veuve Cliquot; short sleeves or formal wear, accent or none...'

'Excellent. Do it. And Sam, find me a forensic accountant and get them to start the financial analysis of the car auction company. You and DS Jones are going to visit the Guy Scott empire, despite what ACC Moore said. We've delayed this for too long. But keep it low-key for the time being.'

**

The forensic accountants from New Scotland Yard, well versed in assessing companies quickly from external data, started their analysis straight away. As there was a connection with a possible high-profile murder, this investigation took precedence. Bill Smith and Georgina Smethurst, who both had experience and know-how of motor trade businesses, started to read up on the company and commenced searching Companies House records, HMRC for tax information and VAT returns, promising to deliver a preliminary opinion within days.

DI Miles and DS Jones drove to Scott's Duxford Headquarters of his classic car auction company in Jones's Ford Mondeo. Security cameras scanned the car and a disembodied voice asked their name and business before substantial electrically operated gates opened. They parked in the designated bay next to some seriously exotic vehicles with price tags displayed on the windscreen to make your eyes water, as Jones drooled. With an entrance more or less opposite the old war-time aerodrome which was part of the Imperial War Museum, with vintage aircraft all around, there was a massive range of newish buildings faced with a glass floor-to-ceiling façade housing the management offices and the accounts department, according to the signage in reception.

They entered the reception area and showed their warrant cards to the receptionist, a pretty girl of maybe twenty-five dressed in a smart uniform verging on the sexy, as DI Miles whispered into Jones's ear. She looked flustered when told what they required and grabbed the telephone to speak to the director.

In a matter of two or three minutes, Guy Scott appeared with a beaming smile. 'Welcome, Detective Inspector. Have I got the title right? I do hope so. And your colleague, Detective Sergeant Jones, we met, if you recall, but I don't expect you remember me, bearing in mind your very important investigations, of course.' He looked at the receptionist, Melanie by name, judging by the badge on her lapel, 'Coffees, please, Melanie. In the boardroom, I think.' He looked for approval from the detectives and found stony faces. Jones gave DI Miles a look that demonstrated his opinion of the shallow, greasy approach of Scott, and received a glance which showed he was right on the button.

DI Miles started the interview. 'Mr Scott, we have some questions for you. And they are important and have a direct bearing on our investigations into the death of Lord Groombridge and the theft of his cars…' She looked across at Guy Scott who, far from lounging in his obviously expensive leather reclining chair with the "hail fellow well met" attitude he had displayed in reception, had sat bolt upright, and as Melanie knocked, and without waiting, entered the room with a tray of coffee, he shouted at her

'OUT!'

Samantha continued without blinking an eyelid, although a little taken aback at the way Scott treated his staff. Jones and Miles, too, took the hint made before by their DCI. 'As is usual in cases like this, we have started a forensic examination of your company because of the involvement of Lord Groombridge and certain inconsistencies we have identified. I trust you will support our enquiries without heed or hinderance? I can apply for a search warrant if necessary, but that could be fairly intrusive and may affect your customer/supplier relationships…' She paused, letting the message sink in and watching for the reaction which always came after the search warrant statement.

'Er, yes, yes, of course. Anything we can do to help.' He recovered his composure quickly, but the florid colour had disappeared. 'I thought you wanted some information about Tony's cars…'

DS Jones asked the next question. They had planned the approach on the drive down. 'No, sir. We require information about the way this company operates, and its ownership. My colleagues will establish and audit the financials and already have started viewing returns at Companies House, HMRC and the VAT authorities. We are in the process of clarifying what could be a strong motive.'

Again, Scott looked confused. Jones continued, 'Why were you so busy when you heard of the death of Lord Groombridge? You actually said you had a wagonload of work to do. What exactly suddenly became so urgent? Yet you managed to get to the village of Eye St Mary the next day, an hour and a quarter's drive time.'

'Well, paperwork. Tony was an important part of this company and there were always transactions to be completed. Stuff he had started but not finished. Phew. Signatures and so on and suddenly we were faced with issues like probate and never being able to locate that blessed wife of his, always gallivanting around the place, doesn't help. And how did I spare the time? Well, Tony is, was, important to the company, as I've said, and a close friend of many years. I owed it to him.'

Whilst she knew that she already had a downer on Scott, his comments were close to causing her to retch. Ignoring his placatory remarks, she started in. 'So be it. Our problem, Mr Scott, is that a good few of the vehicles we have been tracking are put to auction in good faith by the owners and then withdrawn at the last minute and then sold for substantially less than the reserve price, many to Groombridge, some to your company and one or two others whose names keep re-appearing on the documents including export licenses. How do you explain that?'

'It is quite normal practice. If the vehicle doesn't match the original spec that the owner has given, we reserve the right to withdraw it from sale. In fact, we're obliged to do so. It isn't a mystery or a crime.' He sounded quite indignant, which both Miles and Jones ignored.

She followed through, keeping up the pressure, raising her eyebrows in mock disbelief. 'Really, why? We looked at several vehicles in particular and found that they tallied with the catalogue reference, exactly. Everything you put on the internet, Mr Scott, is there forever if you have the right technical expertise. And we certainly have that.' She was really flying a kite and guessing that Scott was no more of an expert than she was. Scott, flustered by the conversation as a whole, said nothing.

DS Jones carried on, 'Let's take the case of a 1969 Mercedes, the Mercedes that you saw with me in Groombridge's barn. Market value around twenty-five thousand pounds. Auction reserve price twenty thousand pounds, give or take. Finally, sold to Groombridge for seven thousand five hundred, according to the documents. Explain?'

'Of course I remember the car, who wouldn't, in the circumstances, but I can't be expected to know every damn car that goes through this place. I'd have to examine the files and get back to you.'

'No chance, Mr Scott, we require answers now. And that was just one example I thought to mention, because you and I have seen that car in its damaged state. Starts to smack of an insurance fraud to us…'

'No, no. Nothing like that. We pride ourselves on our relationship with our chosen insurance partners…' It was Scott the car salesman speaking.

Jones, increasingly frustrated by Scott's answers and attitude, responded sharply, 'Enough of this bullshit! You are not selling us a car. You use Beech Underwriting. And surprise, surprise, Groombridge was a director there and a shareholder and some not so clever business practices were going on, we understand. The subject of another investigation, I assure you.'

Sam Miles gave Jones a look to stop him losing his rag, and turning to Scott, she abruptly interjected, 'Go and find your files, sir. The files on the missing two cars at Groombridge's place; the file on the green Mercedes PKP 166G, and the file on the fake Bugatti. And any insurance claims made by your company with your "favoured insurance partners" in the last three years.' She had put on a sarcastic voice. 'To start with just three years will do. And sir, perhaps you would send in that poor girl, Melanie, with some coffee whilst you search.' Samantha Miles enjoyed her barbs and the smile of approval from Jones. Scott almost bowed to the instructions with mutterings of 'of course', and 'right away madam'.

A matter of five minutes later, Scott returned with a pile of green and red files. In the interim, Melanie, the receptionist, had returned with a tray of coffee and a big smile for Samantha and a whispered 'thank you' as she blushed.

'Now, the Porsche, we sold that to Tony. It was a difficult transaction. It didn't live up to the specification as being the last 356C built in Stuttgart in 1965. Matching numbers and that sort of thing.' He looked to Chris Jones, ignoring Samantha, probably assuming she wouldn't know about cars. She responded quickly, 'Well, did the numbers match or not? Engine and chassis numbers from the factory, or had the engine been replaced in forty-odd years?'

Guy Scott, a little taken aback, uttered an apology, 'Sorry, madam. I just assumed that this was a big boys' toys conversation. Obviously I was wrong. Well, we had an offer, post auction, after we had withdrawn the car, as this guy had disputed the numbers, and its provenance — previous ownership history, stating that he had the last 356C in his private museum in Switzerland, somewhere. We turned down his offer and he went off in high dudgeon. So we sold it to Tony.'

'Hmm. Maybe. We will check out this story from the previous owner, of course, and we'll come back to the issue of the Ferrari and the damaged vehicles when we have examined your files closely with our experts. Meanwhile, we want to talk about the photographs that you gave to our DCI.'

'Photographs? Oh, the wedding party. Yes, of course.' He looked relieved at the subject change. 'I was only trying to assist you.'

'Indeed, Mr Scott. Our question is how did you take the pictures or, if not, how did you come by them?' DS Jones tossed the copies in front of Scott for emphasis.

'Eh? No, I didn't take the pics, they were given to me afterwards. I think someone passed them to all the guests as a memento or something.' It looked like he was playing for time.

'Who exactly?' DI Miles was enjoying seeing him wriggle, obviously uncomfortable at the change in direction. He'd had five minutes to prepare when finding the files to come up with some excuses, but this was unexpected.

He offered more coffee to be stymied by Miles's answer of 'No! Answer the question.'

'I... I don't know. A lot of the time, I was with Tony in his barn. The one you and I visited after... well you know.'

'Well, it clearly wasn't Charlotte, was it? She is in all the photos.'

'No. Maybe, yes it was, Ms Cap de Ville, I think her name was. Something that translated into town captain or some such. Certainly foreign, European I mean, maybe French, anyway. A friend, or so I understand, of Lady Groombridge.'

'First name, description?'

'Crikey. Let me think... It began with a V, bit French as well. Well, it would be, with a surname like that, I suppose...'

'You are prevaricating.'

'No. A blonde lady, quite good-looking, about thirty-ish, about the same height and so on as Charlotte. Been at school together, I recall. Veronique, that's it.'

'So you know Veronica?'

'No, that's not it. Anyway, it's Veronique, not Veronica. I knew of her...'

'Thank you, sir' Samantha enjoyed using the "sir", saying it without any form of respect. 'Now, your relationship with Lady Groombridge. You did send her a text message after we first met, did you not?'

'I've known her for a few years. First as a fiancée of Tony Waller then as Mrs Waller. But only at social gatherings and corporate functions. Yes, I did text her about Tony's death, but that was just as a courtesy. She's not a friend as such, really, just the wife of a business partner.'

'And Lord Groombridge?'

'Lord Groombridge? Well, we've been business partners for about nine years. More recently, in 2010, we restructured the company and bought out the previous owner, an Andrew Paddick, by name. He'd set the business up in the 1970s. Unfortunately, he passed away a year or two back. Now, we are fifty/fifty shareholders. Tony does a lot of the work regarding obtaining new clients who want to sell here, from Europe and the USA, largely, although not exclusively. I manage the enterprise in the UK with occasional trips to the USA. I'm the accredited auctioneer.' Both Miles and Jones grimaced at the word accredited. He carried on with what sounded like a sales spiel. 'We have something like sixty vehicles for auction at any one time, with transporters coming and going, containers from all parts of the world. Three people are involved just on logistics, full time.'

Jones scribbled a note in his black note book to check these international truck movements and passed it to DI Miles. Miles excused herself, seeking the bathroom, and spoke briefly to Melanie, who was in the kitchenette adjacent. She established that Scott couldn't keep his hands to himself when it came to the female staff, including young Melanie, but there weren't many jobs around so she had to put up with it. Now aged nineteen, having been there since leaving school at sixteen, she had learned to put up with the groping, avoiding office parties on any pretext that she could think of. Samantha told her that was only a short term solution and she should look elsewhere if she was uncomfortable and keep a day-to-day record. Melanie Griffiths had smiled and told Samantha that she always kept a full diary of her time at work, and phone log too.

Chris Jones changed tack, being bored by this readily available material sounding like the sales approach of a brochure. 'Guy, I may call you that?' Scott looked surprised by this change and nodded enthusiastically, sensing the interview was close to its end. 'I'd love to own a car like the old Merc, but only if it was at a sensible price. How do I get in on the action?' Miles re-entered the room with a smile of apology. Scott stood up and gazed out of the window, taking in the sight of the dirty Ford Mondeo parked in the visitor's bay next to some of the more exotic cars. 'We always like to help our friends in the police forces. I'll keep my eyes open, DS... Er... Mr Chris Jones.' He glanced almost imperceptibly at the business card that Jones had handed in to reception earlier.

DI Miles returned, and seeing a sheepish-looking colleague, raised an eyebrow and turned to Scott. 'Just to close, for the time being, anyway. Do you know any of the other guests at that party?'

'No, madam, I hope that is the right way to address you. No. I might have met one or two of them from time to time but none I would call a friend or more than a passing acquaintance.'

'Thank you for your time and being open with us. Our people may well turn up some other questions for you. They will be looking at bank accounts for both Lord Groombridge and yourself, alongside company accounts, normal activity in a case like this. We will take those files, and of course, give you a receipt for them.' She reached across the table to gather them whilst Guy Scott had recovered his supercilious smile, more flavoured with relief than salesmanship. Scott proffered his hand to Samantha Miles but was refused; Jones readily offered his hand, however, receiving a black look from DI Miles.

In the Mondeo driving away from Duxford, Miles commented that Jones had been risky in his comment about buying a car — close to incitement — she had added that she would document that part of the conversation quite carefully, as it could come back to bite them.

Chris, taking it as a minor ticking off, bristled. 'Well, I thought there were several key points of interest. I've written them down but from memory. Firstly, they have containers and trucks going all over the place — could be the answer to our transport problem with the stolen cars. Secondly, the guy that bid for the Porsche — worth talking to to get his take on the situation; motive in there somewhere — and thirdly, the relationship between him and the ladies involved. And maybe there's a fourth point. Has he made "offers you can't refuse" to other people? Anyway, he tried the funny handshake business with me…'

'Since when was belonging to the Masons been a crime, DS Jones?' And ignoring his likely response, she continued, 'All those points I agree with. Interesting that last point, too. Who amongst our protagonists would be influenced by such a deal? Good thought.' She gazed out of the car window and related the brief chat with Melanie. 'Whilst the sexual advances and proclivities of Mr Scott are not, regrettably, our direct concern, they do paint the inevitable picture. Interesting what the other ladies in this investigation think of the lothario Scott. I get the feeling that he is a womaniser and sails very close to the wind as a businessman, but that's it. He is definitively still on the radar, as they say. The trucks and so on — is that too obvious? I don't know, but noted.'

Jones nodded, conscious that he had recovered lost ground. 'Ma'am, the man is a motor trader. Show me one that doesn't sail close to the wind. But if there is any sort of criminal connection between them, then using a transporter known to the customs people would be quite clever. The publican's wife was muttering about the transporters that roared through the village at all hours of day and night. Maybe one was the vehicle that carried the two sports cars away?'

'Indeed, DS Jones. But establishing that is not going to put us much further forward, unless we chance upon it and can get forensics in. Let's move on...'

More to pass the time on the journey than anything else, Jones wanted to know more about Samantha Miles. He asked how she had got into the Murder Room at Scotland Yard and let her ramble on about her career. Hard work, long hours and a willingness to take on exceptional work loads had been her response, puzzling whether Jones was thinking a transfer to the Metropolitan Police was an easier, more exciting ticket than his East Anglia patch. She took the time to assure him that what was going on in Eye St Mary was high profile enough for his theoretical CV.

Chapter 49

Back at the office in Ipswich, Jones opened up with an issue that had been worrying him. 'Do you remember that publican, Whitaker? He told me that Groombridge used to drive that Bentley of his around the country lanes like it was the Monaco Grand Prix. Had a couple of near misses near the village and it was always the talk of the place. You may recall that that car had accident damage and was booked into the repairers. That was after the incidents at Eye St Mary, although we had not made the connection at that stage. Anyway I got on the phone to PC Edwards, remember him?' LeFanu nodded and DI Miles shrugged, trying to keep up with the flow. 'He has walked the village access roads and found a dented thirty mph sign with recent blue paint on it. Locals say that the pole was bent only recently, although no concrete evidence of exactly when. Had a sample of the blue paint checked and it's the same, Imperial Blue — exclusive to Bentley. Maybe the Bentley brought Groombridge/Gold to the village and that explains the dent in the car and the damaged road sign and how he got to the village. If someone picked him up from Norwich airport, a matter of thirty miles to Eye St Mary, in that car, it would not be out of place — it would be seen as a local resident. But who was driving? For ages, by all accounts it sits unused in Chelsea, then is seen briefly in Eye St Mary, then disappears, then re-appears in London with dents — all those reports are hearsay really, largely from the concierge at the Chelsea apartment, but it paints a picture. Did someone want us to see it and track its movements?'

LeFanu acknowledged Jones's news and pondered whether the "accident" had been planned to create a sort of alibi. 'Could be they want us to think that Groombridge drove to his home? Good thinking. That'd be substantially on the A11 and A140. Cameras? And the airport, for that matter. We can tie down departure from the airport quite precisely and if it is what we think it is, he would not want to be hanging around. Check it out.'

Thirty minutes later, Sergeant Shaw knocked on the door of the office. 'The Bentley left the car park about thirty minutes after the flight had landed, 18.55 hours. All recorded on ANPR cameras at the exit. Next seen at the pick-up/drop off point but at a distance, so again no detail. Difficult to see anything of the driver; cameras are pointed down to pick up the numberplate. Doesn't look like any frontal damage but cameras are not designed to look at that sort of detail. It left the airport for Eye via the A10, A11 and A14. We have several sightings of the car from cameras. It arrived at the last checkpoint at 20.30 hours. But who was driving it? Patently not our KLM passenger, as it would be impossible to get off the plane and through immigration and across to the car park and exit in thirty minutes or so — more like forty-five minutes to an hour on a good day — and why go to the airport drop-off area…'

LeFanu was getting increasingly frustrated by these conversations and stopped Shaw in full flight. 'We're ahead of you, Sergeant, just get on with where the bloody car went afterwards, as it certainly wasn't/isn't at Eye St Mary now, is it?'

Sergeant Shaw coloured. 'Well, sir, we have two camera sightings the next day. Saturday early evening on the M11 southbound towards London and a couple inside the M25 heading for Chelsea, as it turns out. Again, nothing to distinguish the driver who, according to the traffic people, kept well within the speed limits.

Chapter 50

After twenty minutes of calling her mobile and leaving several messages, Chris Jones finally spoke to Lady Groombridge, who was, she said, shopping in Harrods exclusive store in Knightsbridge with a friend. She agreed to come to Ipswich the next day, although the whole idea seemed somewhat tedious to her, judging by her reaction to the request framed as it was by Jones as an instruction.

Chris set up the interview room with videotape. LeFanu, exasperated by the lack of progress, wanted a stronger approach and briefed them accordingly. 'I want it focussed on where she's sitting to study her reactions after the interview with one of you, Miles I think, to start with facing her. Jones, watch carefully through the one way glass. We may pull you in later depending on how it goes.'

Charlotte Groombridge arrived exactly on time. LeFanu had watched from his window as she had swept into the car parking area in her silver Range Rover and basically just left it half in and half out of a reserved parking bay. No doubt with the keys still in it, mused LeFanu, surprised that she even bothered to switch off the engine and close the doors... He watched as she climbed the small flight of steps into the building until she was out of line of sight. He smiled and thought of the theatre that was about to begin.

She was escorted to the fourth floor by a WPC, and on entering the room, she visibly sneered at the décor. He mused that she was thinking her cream suit would suffer from the state of the upholstery, which he had to admit had seen many, many, better days. She started, as usual he thought, with some cutting remarks about the lack of decent coffee and that she wouldn't remove her jacket as the pale colour of her silk blouse easily marked. 'Right then, Detective Chief Inspector LeFanu, what is the subject matter for today's meeting? And where are your sidekicks? I forget the man's name and dear Samantha Smiles?'

'They will be here presently, madame. My detective sergeant's name is Jones. You know DI Miles, and in the interest of making this meeting go smoothly, may I suggest that you don't use the "smiles" approach. It adds little.'

'How very French, *mon cher. Absolument*! I would like these inquiries of yours to be short and sweet. I really do have other, more important, things to do.'

'*Bien sûr*, madame. With your assistance, we will try to expedite things.'

LeFanu's colleague entered the room and politely shook hands with Charlotte. Samantha took her predetermined seat.

Miles started without any pussy-footing around. The approach quite startled Charlotte. 'Did it slip your mind that you visited Pchelski in prison last year? The deputy prison governor is in a lot of trouble because he broke the rules and did not have you logged in as a visitor. He recalls that you introduced yourself as Charlotte Bertin, a French cousin. Why?'

Quickly she responded, as if she'd been expecting this line of enquiry. 'Oh yes. I'd quite forgotten. After all, that was nearly a year ago. Much water under the bridge, as you English say. It was supposed to be a secret between me and the deputy governor, Clive. I think that's his name. I quite liked him. And I think he liked me. Really, I wanted to see what life was like on the inside of a prison. Several of my girlfriends dared me to try. I like a sexy dare, so I did. Clive liked what he saw, if you know what I mean. I used my Bertin name to lower my profile, if you know what I mean. I said George was my cousin and that I had to leave for the USA that day, so… He was amenable…' She stared directly at Samantha and winked.

She looked back with a sneer. 'Notwithstanding your need for a cheap thrill, madam, did you meet Terry's sister outside the prison at any time?'

'Who the hell is Terry's sister?'

'Madam,' Miles continued, LeFanu being content with the way the pressure on Charlotte was rising. 'We know from recordings that you asked about Mr Beddall and his sister during the visiting session.'

'Oh. I did not know you recorded those personal conversations. That's invasion of privacy or human rights or something, isn't it? Well, maybe I did ask. There were some delicious hunks in that room and he was certainly one of them. Do you know what I mean by hunks, DI Miles?'

Miles ignored the gibe. 'No, madam, I do not "know what you mean". Is that today's in-phrase? You have, after all, used it three times in less than a minute. When did you meet Terry Beddall after his release? We have recovered the data from his mobile telephone which might just serve to refresh your memory.' LeFanu felt pleased that, whilst Miles had bent the truth about the recordings and the mobile phone data, sometimes a small trick like that helped in getting at the real truth.

'Ah! So you know about that. Yes, I did meet him. Detective Inspector Miles. I do have the normal appetite for sex of anyone my age. Perhaps you will understand that?' She stared at Sam Miles, looking for a response. Again, Miles ignored the comment as she assembled the information in her mind, ready to pounce. Charlotte continued, 'We met at a country hotel, somewhere miles from London. Oxfordshire or was it Kent, I really can't recall. A bit of discretion on my part, I have to admit, and had an amazing night. That's it. My track record is for short termism with men, bit like my husband was with his bimbos.'

'Well, madam, a bit of discretion indeed. When was your fling with Mr Beddall? When was that particular meeting and what was the name of the hotel?' She put a delicious emphasis on the word "meeting" that caused LeFanu to smile. 'Presuming you paid for your night of ecstasy, a credit card reference will suffice and we will check the name and location with your card providers. And an approximate date will do for now.' She smiled at the reference of checking the credit-card information, which clearly annoyed Charlotte.

It was Charlotte's turn to ignore the gibe and she won that round by turning on her beatific smile to Miles. 'Around Christmas time, I think, before New Year certainly. Season of goodwill to all men.' She winked at LeFanu, ignoring Miles. 'No, it was earlier in December, a few weeks, I think, after he had been released from prison. Perhaps that explains his appetite for female company? He was due up north for some meeting or other afterwards. Hotel? I'd have to think about it… No! It was the Imperial, in the wildest remotest part of Kent. Sea view and all that. I do like to be discreet.'

LeFanu stopped the conversation, switched the recorder off and called for a break. He needed to discuss the outcomes with Miles and Jones, as a clearer picture was emerging and the temperature between the two women was rising fast and in danger of losing sight of the objective of the interview. They left her in the interview room with a WPC and some coffee, whether or not she wanted some.

'Of course.' LeFanu clicked his fingers. 'Of course, the clue is the phone. How did she contact him to arrange her dirty weekend, or whatever it's called, and if it was by phone, how did she know his number? Maybe she gave him her number, but that requires a meeting with him. Either/or is the answer. Pursue it and get her phone records — all the numbers she gave us. I suspect she may have destroyed the mobile if our assumptions are correct, but analysis of the others may give us a lead. People running scared or under pressure and looking over their shoulder don't always remember to tidy up and remove loose ends. And check that bloody hotel, too.'

'Just a thought, sir, perhaps this so-called Angela Darling is in cahoots with Lady C and gave her the phone number. So Charlotte's phone records will disclose some interesting links. If that were the case, then we should look at the "gang", as she calls them, and/or the others in the photos of the post-wedding party or those that you met at that memorial service bun fight.' DI Samantha Miles leaned back on the wall, still thinking after her comments.

'There's another issue here, sir.' DS Jones questioned, 'What's the motive of this lady calling herself Angela Darling? Money — possibly, but only if she gains from the thefts. Beddall wasn't in the rich league. Killing him seems only to be purposeful if it is to keep her anonymity. Hatred or anger doesn't appear to be relevant.' LeFanu didn't answer, just nodded as he was judging the comments from both of them.

'However,' Jones continued, 'Charlotte's motive is very, very strong in terms of money. Removal of her husband's debts, realisation of insurance monies and the life assurance — even allowing for any changes his will may introduce — will leave Madame Charlotte a seriously rich woman. By removing Beddall from the equation, and I don't buy Charlotte's "bit of rough" angle, she could be removing some evidence of her orchestrating the thefts let alone the murders. Maybe it was her that placed the tracking device on his car — it's simple enough to do. And then the same argument about removing evidence or witnesses could apply to the murder of Monika Braun. Perhaps she turned up at the wrong moment. Perhaps she recognised the criminals, but that argument would tend to eliminate Beddall. We know she had met Charlotte's gang, for want of an expression; she had probably met Guy Scott too. And others at the post-wedding party... But she had never met Gold, we don't think, do we?'

'You're getting carried away, Chris. Could be, maybe and perhaps are just conjecture with no grounds of proof. Find me that proof and I'll be with you on the podium to get the accolades from our superiors. But I do like the quantum leap from both of you. Angela is the link and she seems to be a blonde, although that could be cosmetic — wigs and all that. And she has to be connected somehow. My money is on her planting the bug on the car, but whether that was at the behest of Lady C is another question. Any device like a tracking bug needs some sort of receiver; even an Android phone or laptop would do with a bit of tweaking. So where is it and who is in control of it? Overall, it doesn't matter at the moment but to be borne in mind.'

He continued after a few seconds pause. 'We must return to the enigmatic Charlotte and try to tie some things down. I want to talk about her alibis and her raison d'être for coming to the UK by ferry. Miles, you carry on with needling her about the phones, and Jones, look into Mr Gold getting into the UK. We know he was traced into France and seemingly left France for Canada. If Gold has been murdered, to use the current supposition, then did Gold use Groombridge's passport to enter the UK? Certainly looking that way, but an impression by a couple of flight attendants from KLM is not worth much in a court of law. We'd be laughed at if the comment about chips and crisps emerged in public. Anyway, if our assumptions are correct, then it would not be a leap of faith to guess that Groombridge used Gold's passport to leave France. But this could be old ground, so focus. Jones ask the question about drinking on the plane and Miles go over the dress code of Lord G. Air Canada would have been all over him like a rash if they were carrying a titled client. Business class passenger too — definitely a VIP and probably memorable. If their crew come up with similar anomalies — Englishman, quintessentially so, but seemingly an American citizen we'd have more to go on. Certainly Lady C's comments about her cheap flight when we flew her in to Norwich give support to that thought. I do feel like we've been over this ground before, but maybe Susie Ford's team has been a new focus.' He looked up at both of them. 'Any answers from that lad, Dodd, in finding the Canadian crew? And on that flight from France into the UK, if it were Gold, then he would be perceived to be a peer from his passport and vice versa. Perception is the truth! And another nag I have... I think you raised it before, Chris — would a lady, like Charlotte, with or without disguise, hang about every Thursday outside a prison for several months? I think not but...'

Jones noted his comments and disappeared to establish progress with DC Dodd, but as he reached the door, added, 'The drive time from the US/

Canada border to Albany is three hours, and by bus or train closer to four. Thinking of Lady C and her life style, is it likely that Lord G would tolerate twice that time to get to somewhere like New York. Just a thought.'

Returning to the interview room, DI Miles had the bit between her teeth and started in before she had herself sat, 'Lady Groombridge, sorry for the interruption. I trust the coffee was at least palatable compared to the last time.' Charlotte grimaced at the comment and the cold coffee in the plastic cup told its own story, as DI Miles was well aware. 'Some points to continue, please. How did you get Mr Beddall's telephone number? Where is the mobile phone you used to contact him, twenty seven times, and he you some thirty times? Why did you come to the UK, via Newhaven, in a rental car? Where did you go and with whom? When did you meet up with Mr Jerry Gold? How did you meet Beddall's sister, Sharon? Where did you find your husband's doppelganger, Jerry Gold? Your alibi for the time of the murder at Porten House is in some doubt. Your movements for that period are required in some detail. I will stop there for the time being. You will be here for quite some time, madam. You will detect that we are far from satisfied by your answers to date.'

She had been building up to another of her shallow responses; LeFanu had detected before that this would be her defence mechanism to buy thinking time. 'And I thought we had got on so well together after the jeans incident, Detective Inspector. Incidentally, I have trashed them. I didn't fancy wearing them after all your people had been poring over them. My God, Detective Inspector, is this the Spanish Inquisition? I've recently lost my husband, a peer in your God forsaken bloody country and you are effectively accusing me, by your questions, of murdering him in cahoots with Jerry. He was, just like Terry, my bit of trailer trash, as it is called in the US, or my few nights of ecstasy, to coin your own phrase. I met Jerry at a party in the Hamptons — friends of my husband, late husband, I should say. He persuaded me to take golf lessons. It wasn't a hard sell; I wanted something to occupy myself whilst staying in New York. My husband thought it a grand idea. Do I need a solicitor? I feel I'd like someone to be helping me.'

LeFanu interrupted, ignoring the gibe about the jeans, 'At this stage, Lady Groombridge, you are helping us with our enquiries. It is up to you if you wish a solicitor present. It can be arranged but it tends to be more usual if we feel we have grounds to detain you.'

She brightened at the last comment. 'I thought you were about to arrest me, dear Chief Inspector.'

'No. It is simply to remove you from our enquiries. So many of the people in this complex scenario have died, we have to assume that one of the remaining characters is responsible, so we have to ask many more questions in-depth. There is another angle, of course, that you could be a victim too — so for your own safety, we need to track everyone. We look at motive, opportunity and means. And to be blunt, we see you having motive and means and we are questioning the opportunity. That broadly means you must assist us, for your own benefit, in identifying without a shadow of a doubt, your whereabouts at the relevant times.' LeFanu stopped for effect to allow this to sink in before adding 'We are asking the same questions about the lady we mentioned before, Angela Darling. Any help you can gives us there would be welcomed.' He knew that her reaction to this statement would be vital and watched her like a hawk.

'So, as to your half a dozen questions, Mrs Miles…'

Miles interrupted, 'Seven actually. So far, unanswered.'

'As I was about to say, they are easy to answer. Where would you like to start?'

LeFanu interjected, 'Let's stick to Ms Darling to start with.'

'I've said before that I've never heard of her and I don't know any blonde woman, Angela, with the stupid name. I think it must be her that was making all those telephone calls and sending messages, whatever. Certainly not me. I can't remember which phone I used to call him to arrange our sexy night out. Sometimes I borrowed my husband's phone, sometimes my brother's, whichever comes to hand. Can't you check his phone? I will absolutely swear on any Bible or oath that I did not kill my husband nor have ever attempted to. Is that enough for you?'

LeFanu excused himself from the meeting, suspending the tape recordings, to talk with DS Jones, who was party to the interview via an audio link in the adjacent viewing room. 'Jones, I have a hunch. Call the real Angela Darling and find out if she knew, or knew of, Charlotte under any of the names we have for her, but avoid mentioning the Groombridge name. We said before, ages ago it seems, that it was an odd name and Charlotte's comments just now brought it to my mind. Whoever chose that name did it to divert attention that they knew was going to be high profile. Just a hunch, so go easy and interrupt if there's anything to it.' LeFanu returned to the interview and Miles re-activated the recording equipment.

'Right, madam. Sorry for the interruption. Another question which is prompted by what you said earlier. Where is your husband's phone?'

'I don't fucking know. Perhaps in the house? Perhaps the murderer of my poor husband took it, or he lost it, or perhaps your search team weren't looking hard enough? Didn't I give you his number when we spoke a while ago? In case you've forgotten, it is 07866 444111. Try ringing it.' She smirked. They were interrupted by WPC Judy Bell entering with a note for LeFanu. Again, he excused himself to speak to Jones.

'Sir, you really are a genius. The real Angela Darling is quite posh and was at finishing school, whatever that is, in Basle, Switzerland, between 1998 and 2003 with Charlotte Foubert. She remembers Charlotte because she managed to perfect her English without a scintilla, her word, I had to look it up, sir, of a French accent and all the vernacular English words that a lady might know but should never utter, but she did and frequently. And she was a bitch, again her word. Apparently she used to take the piss, my word this time, about Angela's name. It was a game to her.' Here, Jones smiled. 'And she poured green dye over her hair whilst she was asleep. Got a suspension for a term for that caper. Does conjure up an image of cat fighting. She, Charlotte, that is, was asked to leave after a sexual encounter with one of the male staff whom she falsely accused of rape. I asked as well about the names Pchelski and Waller. No recognition there at all. I didn't mention Beddall, as it is too current on the news and so on and it would appear unlikely due to his past. That's it. Oh, and she is a brunette, never a blonde, nearly forgot that. I was subtle asking about hair colour, honestly. Genius, sir.'

'Thank you, Jones, excellent. Useful information. Get one of the guys to check out that number of Lord Groombridge's phone, 07866 444111. It's probably dead by now.' He returned to the interview.

In reply to persistent questions from DI Miles, Charlotte told them more of the first meeting with Jerry Gold at a party in The Hamptons on Long Island hosted by a business associate of her husband. Everyone had commented about how Jerry and Tony could have been brothers. 'I couldn't see it myself,' she had added, commenting on the casual nature of Americans. Jerry drank like a fish and Tony only drank the champagne offered by the uniformed waiter. It had been chalk and cheese.

On querying the detail, LeFanu asked if her husband had known Jerry

Gold before the party.

She replied after shrugging her shoulders, 'I presumed that Tony had met him for the first time too. No reason to think otherwise. We had a fling but it is not the sort of subject you ask a lover, now, is it? "I say, when did you first meet my husband?" Does one ask the question before or after orgasm?'

DI Miles ignored the blatant base humour, although she had to suppress a smile herself as she thought of the vignette Charlotte had created. 'And the name of this socialite business man?'

'I forget. One meets so many in the US. Van der something or other. You could ask my husband. Oh, of course you can't...' She smiled at her audience. 'Or, of course, ask Jerry. He'll be somewhere in the USA now, I suspect. There's what? Two hundred and fifty million of them over there. Shouldn't be too difficult to find him.' She smirked.

DI Miles, smiled. 'Why do you say "now", Lady Groombridge?' LeFanu and she had decided to keep the questions moving, although some may not have been answered satisfactorily, but they did serve to throw the interviewee into confusion, not knowing where the next logical question would come from.

'No reason. Just an expression, I suppose. Most Americans stay in the US of bloody A, don't they? What sort of grilling is this? How the hell should I know where the bloody man is?'

Miles seized the opportunity to raise the issue of dress sense, as instructed, and to keep the subjects of the questions moving hopefully to get some casual responses, rather than thought-through structured answers from Charlotte. Charlotte had replied that her husband was a typical Britisher with formal attire even when socialising.

'Bit like that idiot Prime Minister Brown of yours who played tennis in a suit and tie.' Tony always wore a suit and never a leather jacket, jeans or chinos and open necked shirts. He always wanted to create an image, particularly with the Yanks, she had added. Jerry was typical of the casual American — kind of nice for a change, she had added with a wistful smile. Eureka! thought Miles.

Jerry Gold had started an affair with Charlotte, which had amused her due to his physical resemblance to her husband, but there the similarities ended. Throughout the affair, which had gone on for some months, unbeknown to her husband, he'd been attentive and caring, she maintained.

This tended to stack up with the transcript of the DCI's phone conversations with Pchelski, Miles thought. Gold's financial status had been confirmed by the readily available credit rating agencies in the USA, as "comfortable", so money could still be a motive for disposing of Groombridge. Charlotte, strangely, was at pains to be pleasant and courteous to DI Miles throughout this part of the conversation, almost as if she realised the goading by Miles was making her react without thinking. Samantha was suspicious, as she saw this as a diversion probably hiding some road down which Charlotte did not want to go. But which road? DCI LeFanu was not being helpful with his usual interjections and steering the conversation. She saw the tell-tale signs of puzzlement as he constantly scratched his right ear. It was one of the first things she's been told to look for when put forward for secondment to his unit.

After five minutes or more, he interjected, 'Madam, why did you say Ms Darling was a blonde? We have never said that.'

'Fucking hell, Inspector, how do I know? Someone, maybe Georgie or Terry, told me. Maybe it was on the news…'

'But you do know an Angela Darling from your finishing school days in Switzerland. It may interest you to know that she is the only Angela Darling in the UK. Lots of coincidences, I think you'd agree.'

'That fucking cow. I'd completely forgotten about her until now. Not my finest moment that school, although it did help with some things.'

'Yes, so I understand! We were told that you managed to acquire your English language skills without accent, a star pupil apparently, and the use of vernacular English you have adequately demonstrated in these interviews, thank you.'

'Well, maybe I was making an association with that bitch; she was blonde, I think. Wow, was it her?'

'Now you're muddying the waters. You know she was, indeed is, a brunette. We have already interviewed her and she is not the Angela Darling we are seeking. However, the Angela Darling we are seeking is a pseudonym. You, and one of your so called friends, poured green hair dye over the real Angela's head at one point. Certainly a memorable experience, I would have thought, and sufficient to remember the colour of her hair before your childish activity. So, back to the question. How did you know this character Angela, we'll call her that to save confusion for the tape recording, and how did you know she was blonde?'

'I really don't know. A slip of the tongue maybe…'

'Not good enough. Think again. And whilst you're about it, remind me, how did you first contact Terry Beddall?'

'Oh, now I remember! I bumped into him in the street. In Regent Street, I was shopping in Fenwicks. Pure coincidence, I assure you. He smiled at me and knew my name. He said he remembered me when he was with Georgie. Good-looking guy. I can recall Georgie telling me about him at the prison. He gave me his number then. God, he was almost drooling; I bet he was having an erection. Ah, of course, you can't prove that one way or the other can you?' She smiled and licked her lips provocatively at DI Miles.

'Crudity will not solve your problems, madam.'

'Problems? What problems do you mean? How dare you…' As quickly as she had started shouting, she calmed down and continued in a normal voice, complete with a much richer French accent. 'Nevertheless, Detective Inspector Miles, I did not call him, he called me. I did not call him twenty or thirty times, as you suggest. That must have been this bloody woman, Angela, or whatever her name really is, certainly not me. My track record is not chasing men, as you may be able to guess.' She accentuated her cleavage to make the point. 'And I have never met his pathetic sister. I saw her once at a distance in the interview room at the prison. If she is saying otherwise, she is lying. Why did I come to the UK by ferry? I wanted to, simple as that. Because I can, I suppose. I don't have to ask for permission or time off like most employees. I visited a friend who lives in Sussex, quite near Gatwick, actually, and she had been looking after some stuff from the Suffolk house for me and it was easier to throw it in a car to take it back to Montargis than pack for air travel.'

'We need a name, madam. '

'Fiona, Fiona Wallace, DI Miles. I have her phone number here somewhere. She will vouchsafe my visiting.' She riffled through her handbag and produced a number. Miles passed a slip of paper to the WPC and asked her to get acting DC Ford to verify the information.

'You had a passenger with you. Who was it, Lady Charlotte?'

'No, no passenger. It was me alone. Pretty boring ferry and only redeeming feature is it only takes four hours. I did give a lift to a nice-looking hitch-hiker for the last thirty kilometres to Dieppe, but who and where he was going is a mystery. No crime in that, is there?'

DI Miles was taken aback. All her questions that she had thought were so important had been quashed. She realised that she had given Charlotte time to conjure up some reasonable answers rather than continuing the pressure applied earlier. She knew now, without a doubt, that Charlotte would have constructed the alibi with her friend well before today.

'Incidentally, madam, were you aware about Monika Braun?' Miles watched for a reaction.

'Dear Monika. I'd quite forgotten about her in the furore. I suppose she'll be redundant now. Maybe she'll remain in Germany. What about her?'

'Bluntly, there's no other way to say it… She's been murdered too. In her cottage in a particularly brutal way.'

'*Mon Dieu*! Who, when, how…? No, don't tell me the how!'

'We believe it is someone she knew. We did wonder whether it was you, madam.' She shook her head. 'Or, perhaps the same someone who killed your husband. And at approximately the same time, we believe. Think on it. If you know or suspect anyone tell us. We are not exaggerating the fact that you could be at risk. You may go now, madam. Do not, under any circumstances, leave the country nor London. We will have more questions for you.'

'*Quelle surprise*! I can't wait. My God, poor Monika. She wouldn't hurt a fly and the soul of discretion — had to be, with bloody Tony cavorting with his bimbos all over the place.'

At least she didn't shrug, thought LeFanu. Maybe we have given her something to be frightened of.

'One last thing, madam. How did your late husband usually get to Courchevel? Driving, flying or the train?'

'Usually? With Tony there was never a usually.' She used her fingers to put the word in quotation marks. 'He didn't like leaving expensive cars in airport car parks, particularly over the holiday season. Sometimes he had a driver to the airport; sometimes I drove him to Gatwick or Heathrow or wherever. If we were both in town, that was an easy option. This last time…' She stopped and looked seriously distressed. 'Yes, last time I took him to Norwich airport. Bloody awful place to get to from London — should have told him to get the train. Anyway, I went on to Bicester Village, bitch of a journey across country, as you probably know, in the Range Rover for some Christmas shopping. Waste of time, as it happens. Full of rude Chinese buying up every designer label in existence.' As she talked, it seemed that her distress was short-lived.

'Strange that you should say that. As I recall, you told DCI LeFanu you had a dreadful hangover on the morning of the 21st December…' She let that sink in.

Charlotte looked a little flustered but recovered quickly. 'That, Mr LeFanu, DI Miles, was probably just exaggeration on my part. I can't remember every detail.'

'Also strange that the Bentley was parked in Norwich Airport car parking at the time.' Samantha Miles looked straight at LeFanu and was on the point of speaking when he put his hand up to stop her. He had decided to leave the point, knowing only that this could be another example of the half-truths, and nodded to DI Miles. 'Thank you, madam. We will be in touch again.' Miles put the emphasis on the word "will".

After she had gone, LeFanu asked Miles, 'What did we achieve this time, Sam?'

She replied that she thought Charlotte was startled by the news about Monika Braun and that, despite her bravado, she was worried. The stuff about Jerry Gold she felt was unremarkable. Checking was possible, but it would not move them forward at this stage. The question they debated was about the identification of her husband at the mortuary. Whether she could possibly have glanced at the bloated face and ticked the box, expecting it to be her husband, or whether it was Gold and she was just a good liar. Jones interjected that if she had known it was Gold, she would have been prepared at some time for that question. LeFanu and DI Miles agreed.

Chapter 51

Mike Dodd arrived at the meeting slightly flummoxed. He was not used to being called into high-level meetings and had not been able to nip home to change into his one and only suit. A tall man in his late twenties, he was in a T-shirt with AC/DC emblazoned on the front and fairly bedraggled jeans which looked like they'd fall down at any moment. DI Miles looked on in exasperation. DC Dodd had been lucky in calling Montreal at seven a.m. their time and speaking to the crew controller. The team from the Paris to Montreal flight AC871 had been available before their next departure for France. It helped that Dodd spoke fluent French, which set him apart from the average Englishman, getting him an amenable conversation with the two Quebecois cabin staff, whose first language was French, albeit an antiquated version of that used in France. They recalled the irritating Mr Gold, who had insisted on champagne by a particular brand, although they couldn't remember which and had asked for his suit jacket to be hung properly and inspected the wardrobe space reserved for business class passengers. It was always, they had said, the little things that identified a potential problem passenger.

They had both commented that business class passengers were usually pretty good but upstarts in Premium Economy, like Gold, had ideas above their station. Definitely a typical Brit — they had been in total accord.

All three detectives were pleased with the result of Dodd's conversations, combined with Susie Ford's team with the KLM people, and enthused accordingly. They concluded that they were right that Gold was the most probable Jacuzzi victim, but either way, Lord G was alive and kicking! They decided to keep the knowledge rather than pounce on Charlotte with the question as to why she had identified her husband's cadaver when it wasn't him.

'Now, of course, we can reasonably ask Homeland Security for help. We have more than just a suspicion to ask for some ID from Gold's family.' LeFanu was patently pleased with the results from Dodd.

He called ACC Moore to keep him updated and thanked him profusely, rather tongue in cheek, for his input at the previous meeting. He was greeted by a positive comment and what amounted to a stay of execution in terms of reducing his team, although there was a "for the time being" caveat and another question from his boss. 'Have you established why Gold came to Europe?'

'Not precisely, sir. We have a couple of options and we're not getting direct answers to our questions. First, maybe he came to see Charlotte to pick up where his relationship with her finished. Second, he came here to kill Groombridge or get involved in the crimes. Either way, we need Charlotte to tell the truth and that isn't happening. My money is on the sex angle to start with and then getting involved by being persuaded. '

'It always is money or sex,' said the ACC. 'Here, maybe an upmarket call-girl set-up, with finishing schools providing the fodder. Disgusting. My own daughters are grown up and settled after a normal education, thank God. But umm, he certainly didn't come here to get murdered. Probably money involved, somehow, and maybe others' plans were not the same as Gold thought. He is/was comfortably off, but not rich. Could he just be a tourist? No, that is a coincidence too far.'

Two minutes after putting down the phone, LeFanu, still with a smile on his face, looked up as Dodd knocked on the door frame of his office. 'Sorry sir. Two other things that occur to us. I'm just the spokesperson here… First, if Lord G's passport is inside a safe and no one else knows the safe code, then only him or someone he told would be able to place it inside. He used it, or someone did on that KLM flight. And sir, it must have been placed inside the safe before the burglary, unless it was the burglars themselves. We favour the former issue. And if Lord G was short of money regarding the gambling etc., then, taking your idea of Lord G doing a Lord Lucan, he would have taken the money with him when he went to France in December. So maybe the thieves got no money, just the other stuff.'

'I'm with you, eh, Mike, isn't it?' Dodd nodded and coloured up. 'What was Gold wearing on the flight? You guys did tell me. Where are they? Not in the house, that's for sure, so back to the blonde in the blue car, maybe? Your point about the money in the safe is well taken, thank you. But where is the money? Lady C said that there was always loads of it in that safe. Unfortunately, money is largely unidentifiable. Either the thieves are dining out on it or the murderer took it, or Lord G took it before he went away. Any of those statements doesn't do more than put us on notice to look for a stash, I think you call it, of money. Thanks, Mike, good work.'

Chapter 52

DI Samantha Miles and the newly appointed Acting Detective Constable Susie Ford met the business consultant, Angela Darling, by appointment at her offices of AVD Consulting Limited in Leadenhall Street in the City of London. DI Miles, not quite knowing what to expect, had dressed very smartly in a two-piece navy suit with a crisp white blouse and a gold necklace as the only obvious jewellery, remembering the time meeting Lady Charlotte and feeling too casual. The black high heeled court shoes completed her ensemble, without the need to admit she had changed from her normal flat comfortable shoes in her car. Susie Ford, who Miles admitted to herself would look bloody good in a black plastic bin-liner, had also dressed up for the part. Power dressing was her description. Power dressing to demonstrate a position of power as the training course had told her.

The real Angela Darling, as Susie Ford called her before the meeting, was a brunette aged about thirty-two or so, a pretty, slightly built lady with no resemblance to the hazy CCTV pictures of Angela in the French Railway station. She was dressed in a smart, well-fitted trouser suit in black, obviously expensive judging by the admiring look from Susie Ford, with black patent high heels which gave her an imposing height.

Ms Darling had started the conversation, after shaking hands, in a brusque fashion with DI Miles, who had introduced herself and Susie Ford by given names, keeping the detective and ranking a bit low key, trying to smooth over the obvious anxiety. A few comments about the nice offices, the air of discreet confidence that the reception staff conveyed and questions about how her consultancy business worked, Samantha Miles asked what she knew about Charlotte Bertin and any of her friends. Not being allowed to say the reason for the enquiry, she just relied on the "helping to remove some queries in the enquiry concerning a major crime".

'You will understand my attitude when you were announced, Samantha, if I may call you that. And please call me Angela. To have the police call at my offices is bound to create a rumour or two. It is a small world and small companies like mine are very vulnerable to such stories.' Samantha and Susie both nodded acceptance before Angela continued. 'One particular friend of Charlotte I remember very well…' She put the word in quotation marks by the use of her hands. 'A friend, Veronica, or Veronique as she liked to be called, was really the one with the nasty streak. She dreamt up their nasty activities and they were legion. I know, I've first-hand knowledge. She and Charlotte and another girl, I can't recall her name right now, held me down on my bed and dyed my hair bright green. I woke up the whole school with my screaming whilst the three of them looked on and laughed. They wrote on my mirror "not much of a darling now". Gosh, one's hair in those days was the most important thing, I guess you can understand. It took weeks to get it back to my natural colour and the headmistress was furious, let alone it ruining all the bed-clothes. Both Veronica and Charlotte and this other girl were disciplined by the school — suspension and a bit of community service in the school catchment, no great hardship. Their parents, I think, paid the school some damages and I had a series of hair appointments courtesy of them — that's a funny expression to use really — at an expensive hair salon in Basle and another girl just left the school suddenly. But that wasn't the first or the last incident with the self-styled Ronnie's Rebels. It was childish but hurtful, even to this day.'

Angela, with tears welling in her eyes, talked of an incident when a Clare Benfield, a plain, somewhat plump, freckled girl committed suicide after being terrified by Ronnie's gang. The girl suffered from ornithophobia — a fear of birds — and they put a bird in her room and she screamed the place down, as you can probably imagine. They had had a special delivery of a birthday present delivered at bed-time — to be delivered to her room at a specific time. 'It was a budgerigar, I think. Anyway, a little yellowish bird. And that had sent her over the top. There was no proof, of course, but all knew it was those cows who had done it. Clare's parents wouldn't allow her to change schools — best in the country and all that. So, she had taken the only route she had been able to consider, or that was how it was seen, and took an overdose. The school hushed it all up of course.' She went on describing other events; dead rats in the beds, lurid doctored photos, often sexual poses, put on her phone and Facebook, all sorts, until DI Miles, recognising that she was unloading all her frustrations of years, moved the conversation on.

'Describe her, this Veronica character, to me, Ms Darling. What was her surname?'

'Veronica van Outen was her maiden name, like the chocolate but no connection, I understand. Anyway, and I can do better than describe her — somewhere at home I have a year book and she'll have her photo in there, and maybe this other girl. I'll scan it tonight and send it on to you. But blonde, busty, tall-ish, quite well-proportioned, slim face. That much I do recall. Oh, and she used make-up and clothes and wigs to trap every male in a hundred miles.' She smiled and added, 'I do hope she gets her comeuppance, that would be poetic justice.'

'This investigation is not to accord blame, Angela. It is to sort out some anomalies and get to the bottom of the truth. Anyway, comeuppance does infer revenge and that is not on any agenda, Ms Darling.'

Angela accepted the comment and nodded, and added there were other examples, equally horrid and distressing.

'And anything about Charlotte that you can recall?' DI Miles kept trying to get the conversation back on course. Ms Darling talked for a few minutes but it was clear that there was nothing new to add. Comments about Charlotte seeking petty revenge for a slight or whatever and being a ready and willing participant in anything Veronica conjured up.

DC Susie Ford, trying to change the subject from the obvious hatred for Ronnie, asked her about the purpose of the finishing school. Angela, more in her comfort zone, used words like power dressing, deportment, dress sense, make-up, accent — all, really, creating a female to compete in the man-hunting race and success in business. 'There are some other benefits like networking, preparing for interviews, reading profit and loss accounts and so on. It has been very useful in my business, although I didn't recognise that at the time.'

'What about the cat-walk?' Susie was determined to get some answers from this lady to the multiple questions that had been raised in the squad room back at base.

'You mean modelling work? That's not really the kind of work you'd expect after going to an expensive finishing school, I'm afraid, Miss Ford.'

'Susie, please... No, sorry, I didn't mean that. It's just the walk, you know, the strut or sashay, I think it's called. I know a couple of people who have had your style of education and they all seem to walk the same. Hard to distinguish them from the back, and my colleague, Chris Jones, has a thing about the "walk", if you know what I mean...' She gave a knowing look.

'Yes, you're right. Sorry, I misinterpreted your question. Yes, we are taught to walk in a specific way. All part of gaining the advantage and attracting attention. It becomes natural after a while.' She stood and walked across her office with a simple comment of, 'Like this.' Again, Susie Ford nodded.

They asked after the other person whose name they had established, Fiona. Angela couldn't recall her for any particular reason, although her name did ring a bell. There was talk about her, she was there, but it went right over her head, Angela had exclaimed. 'I wasn't part of the "in-crowd" so much of what was said and discussed and sniggered over wasn't relevant to me. I'd had my run-in about the green hair and that was enough of that gang.' She smiled, adding, 'It is easy to laugh about it now and I have dined out on that story more than once, especially as it seems so trendy these days for young girls to dye their hair extraordinary colours. But I wanted to get a good education and the niceties of life... And so did my parents, who were footing the not-inconsiderable expense of my being there.'

Samantha enquired what the V in the company name stood for and was told it was her middle name, Victoria, and that it had helped stop people commenting on the A Darling thing — she admitted, this time with a genuine smile, that she had had to put up with that most of her life. 'At least my parents had the wit to realise that plain A Darling would give me grief in later life,' she had added with a rueful look. The meeting finished quickly as Angela kept glancing at the office clock and the detectives could see the impatience. It finished with promises to send on the pictures and anything else that occurred to Ms Darling.

Outside on the pavement, DI Miles congratulated Susie Ford. 'Inspired that bit about the walk,' she said, 'and DS Jones will be most disappointed to think that there are dozens of women out there especially trained to attract men like him.'

Ford chuckled. 'Inspired of you, ma'am, to ask about the Victoria name. I guess you were wondering whether it was Veronica?'

DI Miles smiled and nodded. 'It seems like they went to school to learn how to offer themselves to the highest bidder. Sounds like Ms Darling had an element of good sense when she was at school. Time will tell whether she's telling the whole unvarnished truth. Gosh, being the daughter of a stockbroker seems pretty tame. A few exotic trips, and corporate hospitality events at posh venues and that was excitement.'

Relating the conversations to LeFanu and Jones back at their HQ, the two detectives assessed the possibilities that Charlotte was clearly a person who wanted and sought notoriety on the back of others' plans. Apparently they took dares amongst the gang, and the more outlandish or risky the better and couldn't give a damn if they hurt anyone en route.

Next morning, on seeing the school yearbook photograph from 2002, with the full complement of that year and some notes appended by Angela Darling, it was clear that Veronica and Charlotte and the other girl, called Fiona Rampling — now Fiona Wallace, they understood from the funeral attendees listing — were similar in height and build, with Veronica being blonde and the other two brunettes. Easy to see as they stood next to each other.

LeFanu pointed at the photo and at Veronica van Outen. 'This is the first blonde we've come across that has a connection. We must find out more about her, quickly and subtly. She sounds a nasty bit of work but that could well have changed as she grew up, but clutching at straws or not, I want to know more. Let's profile this Fiona woman as well.'

***

Fiona Wallace, nee Rampling, proved easier to profile than Veronica. They had her contact details from Charlotte as she related her strange return to the UK for her possessions from the Suffolk house and then back to France by car and ferry. DI Miles, with the newly appointed DC Ford, visited Fiona with a view to building a background under the pretext of the murder investigation of Charlotte's husband and the wedding party in Suffolk, at the same time as gleaning information about Veronica.

Their first question was to seek the timing and purpose of Charlotte's visit. It had apparently been for a morning and then she had disappeared to see someone else she had known and then returned next day, packed the car with some things Fiona had been storing for her and gone back to France. 'I took her to Gatwick Airport to get a train to London and she left her French hire car on the drive here.'

The house was a recent middle-of-the-road 4 bedroom detached house in a small village development at Staplefield, about 8 miles south of Gatwick. Not at all what Miles was expecting after the high-life that, seemingly, all the other participants in the investigation seemed to have, bar Beddall's sister. Fiona's husband, Paul Wallace, was an official at the airport — involved with air traffic control — a good job, she said, but not highly paid. Fiona was above average height, just, with deep brown long hair arranged into a French pleat, dressed in a fetching trouser suit — not sexy at all, but quite nice, as Susie Ford had commented after the interview. Aged in her twenties, she had a young child, judging by the endless plastic toys around the house, and on asking, Samantha Miles established it was an eight-year-old boy called Felix who was out playing with a friend's child — appropriate, Fiona had commented, as the police were coming to talk. DC Ford had nodded accordingly and commented on it being an unusual but nice boy's name. Fiona had responded that it was good to be different and it was impossible to shorten it, as her own name was far too often.

Miss Rampling had left the school in Switzerland after a complaint had been made to her parents who were not, by any means, as tolerant of their daughter's behaviour as others. Sent to another school, where discipline went hand in glove with the finer points of "finishing", she had "grown up". She had admitted that, whilst the dare culture and riskiness had been exciting, the other pupil's suicide had drawn a cloud over it. Now married and with a child, she had become a more normal member of society with a middle management husband and all the accoutrements of reasonable good living. Her relationship with Charlotte, she said, was distanced, with only a couple of the "ladies who lunch" meetings in the last two years and the attendance at Groombridge's memorial service in Chelsea, all for old times' sake. She had reluctantly, attended the wedding party in Suffolk whilst still a regular member of the gang before settling down. And on a query from DC Ford, replied that she never attended reunions; they were dangerous and usually unrewarding, a remark which gained a note of approval from DI Miles.

Regarding Veronica, she had answered questions quickly and without hedging. DI Miles asked how they could trace this Veronica lady. Fiona remembered that she had married a French guy, lovely man, she had said when she had met him at a function — Gilles Cap de Ville, a restaurateur with a chain of restaurants. But Ronnie, now known by the pretentious Veronique, had announced at the wedding party that she had divorced the idiot Frenchman and re-married and that marriage wasn't going too well either. Fiona commented that she had been bored by Veronica at that point and not pursued the ins and outs of it, nor what her new surname was, and on enquiry from Susie Ford, no she was definitely not on her Christmas card list.

She didn't have any contact details, but expanded a little about Veronica the woman. 'She was the leader of our group. In hindsight, the natural leader. A lot of what we did was silly, I know that now. And hurtful too, but she had that ability to make it all seem so exciting and necessary. She had a mean streak too, capitalising on people's weaknesses, including mine, I'm sad to say, nowadays anyway.'

DI Miles, sensitive to the nature of the disclosures and not wishing to make it seem that the enquiry was any more than a background, probed for more information.

'Well, it was just that we always played a silly girly game we called "shag, marry, kill".'

Both detectives looked flabbergasted. Sam Miles managed to control her expression and murmured, 'Go on.'

'Well, you choose a person, I mean think of a person, and have to ask one of the others whether they would prefer to shag, marry or kill them. I admitted that I would like to shag, excuse the expression, Inspector Miles, the guy who taught us economics. Ronnie, a day or two later set it up, unbeknown to me, and I found myself in bed with him, John Kinsey. She had set up a video surveillance and it went viral, that's today's expression anyway. That got me a warning and John was sacked. A bit later, maybe a month, she did the same thing again. I should have learned my lesson and that time it was the head gardener and it was a threesome with Ronnie. Yes I liked sex, still do, but I was beyond my comfort zone.' This prompted a definite raised eyebrow. 'She promised that there would be no funny business and I fell for it. That's when my parents said "enough was enough" and they moved me to another finishing school — more like a nunnery. I was lucky that my husband took it all in his stride, in fact sparked up our sex life when he found out.' She tried hard not to look coy, but it didn't work for either Samantha or Susie from the look on their faces. 'It was so public that it could have ruined my reputation.'

'Sounds to me like it ruined one or two other people's reputations anyway.' DC Ford couldn't resist the acid interruption, despite a stern look from her boss.

'You are right, of course, Miss Ford. Basically, she was, is, a cow. I hate to think who else she has hurt. And I'm ashamed that I fell so easily into it. Anyway, you should ask Charlotte, Charlie, she is still as thick as thieves with Ronnie. Of all of them, Charlotte still is a sort of friend, hence looking after some stuff for her.' Fiona looked ashamed.

DI Miles started to close the interview by showing Mrs Wallace a photo which had been digitally mastered, of the blonde woman in the café in Paris. She nodded, shrugged and said it could be Ronnie, but then it could be any of a million others.

'None of this will get back to my husband, will it?'

'I can't promise anything, Mrs Wallace. You would be well advised to tell your husband, just in case it comes out in any court case later.' Fiona looked crest-fallen.

'Where is your husband, Mrs Wallace?' Susie Ford, gazing around the room, alighted on a photo in a silver frame, presumably of her husband, Paul.

'At work. He's up at Gatwick, hence the reason for living here. He'll be home at nine p.m. or thereabouts. It's shift work. Pays better, if you know what I mean. Money's always tight when you have a mortgage and a child.'

DI Miles, noting the comment and wanting to "shake the tree" to get information, pounced; she had learned a lot from LeFanu about selecting the right moment and changing the subject by a hundred and eighty degrees often achieved results. 'Any stealing or violence by any of you? At the school, that is…'

Far from looking shocked at the verbal attack, it looked as if she had been half-expecting it. 'Well, yes, we often stole from shops — designer label stuff. Ronnie would select the right stuff and we would divert attention. She, Ronnie that is, had a handle on the security technology and had obtained a small gadget that would negate the alarms on the clothes and enable those funny electronic button things to be removed without damage to the clothes. She got it in Hong Kong, I seem to remember. It was a buzz. We were, I suppose, privileged kids. She always said they make too much profit, so why not defraud them. They used to use each other's credit cards and the like and then tell the banks that they had been stolen.' She smiled triumphantly, but again it just gained a look of pity tinged with disdain.

'And drugs, madam?' interrupted Susie Ford.

'No. Well we all had a go at smoking a spliff, but that was all — just like many teenagers with a little spare money at the clubs. We spent the money on vodka — seemed to have the same sort of effect and a lot less after-effects and angst in school.'

'And violence, Mrs Wallace?'

'Not me, never. I can't stand that sort of thing.'

'If "not me", as you put, it does infer something else…'

Fiona burst into tears. 'Once she, Ronnie, that is, had an argument with a common girl covered in tattoos, in the ladies' loo at a club. Hit her over the head with a full vodka bottle, didn't even break the bottle. Knocked her cold. All three of us ran and never heard any more. Now we're speaking of it, we don't know what happened to her, either. That's pretty awful really. But Veronica did threaten people quite often, and so did Charlie, sorry, Charlotte. In fact, Charlotte had a very short fuse. If she took against anyone then she would go out of her way to teach them a lesson, no matter how trivial the slight. One of the girls got herself pregnant by some Swiss guy. Don't remember the how or why or the who either. Ronnie decided we should damage his car — set fire to it. There was an almighty hoo-ha about it but it was never connected to us. A posh car too, antique sort of thing. I think the girl left the school more or less straight away. It was a nine-day wonder. Does this sound dreadful? It does from where I'm sitting. She, they, were friends, I suppose, and I'm feeling I'm betraying them.'

'Madam, we're not passing judgement, we're here to try to establish movements of all parties to the Waller/Groombridge family to resolve the little matter of his murder. Where were you between Christmas and the 11th January this year?'

'Me? Why me?' She looked really surprised. 'Let me look at my phone diary.' She opened the facility and enlarged the screen and passed the phone to DC Ford. 'I know that's no proof, but I don't think that you can back date entries. I can probably get someone at those appointments to speak to you. Honestly, I was just going through the post new year madhouse.'

'We need to find Veronica, madam. It's a matter of urgency and her safety. We may have to get back to you with other questions. I'm sure you understand with a matter as grave as murder.'

Fiona blanched and stammered a, 'Yes'.

'One more question, if I may.' Susie Ford looked at her colleague for approval and received a brief nod. 'Passports. Did you ever use each other's like the credit cards?'

'Well, I certainly didn't. Although, I did lose mine once and it turned up a few days later. Can't remember how or why or even where. The others? Maybe. They did look very alike, whereas I didn't, I suppose.'

'Who were the others, Mrs Wallace?' Susie Ford asked. 'Apart from Charlotte and Veronica and yourself, of course?'

'There was an older girl, Sarah, I can't recall. Foreign, Swiss I think; quite glamourous and she might have been the ring leader. She did get involved, particularly with older men. And a load of them too, mostly Swiss business men. Uggh! I can't bear to think on it. We were all a bit jealous in a way, but I was too young to understand. Anyway, she left before that incident I told you about.'

'Thank you for your frankness, Mrs Wallace. If you do recall anything else, please contact my colleague here, DC Susie Ford.' Looking at Susie, she motioned for her to give Mrs Wallace her official card and contact telephone numbers.

Later, in the car returning to Ipswich, DC Ford commented, 'Ma'am, I think she was telling the truth. What do you think?'

Miles replied, 'Not sure. She confirmed the meeting with Charlotte and handing over the clothes and things but she could have been forewarned and spun us that story. I'll take a raincheck on the credibility thing. Check up on when she got married. Just a hunch. Why is she so concerned about her husband if she has already told him the smutty part of her life? She sounded contrite up to a point, but that may just be guarding a comfortable marriage. The framed wedding photos looked too recent, fashion and the wedding car looked too new, not fitting with the parents of an eight-year-old. Not necessarily an issue these days. And we need some investigation regarding this Veronica character, and not just because she's the only blonde in the piece. And Susie, check that Swiss finishing school for records about this car damage. Sounds like the local police would have been involved.'

***

'DC Dodd has identified another anomaly, we think,' Susie Ford spoke as soon as she had entered the room where Jones and DI Miles were sat.

'Pchelski did rent the French house on the 1st September, last year, on a three-year lease. Doddie got the paper work from the French council offices in Vannes, Morbihan. The lessor is a Mr Alan G Turner of Halstead in Essex. All seems above board. Turner used a notary as the contract signature — quite in order in France, as I'm sure you know, ma'am, sir.'

She paused and shuffled in her seat, knowing that any results they established from checking in their little room on the fifth floor could be taken as criticism of senior officers, despite what DI Miles had told them. With a smile of encouragement from her audience, she continued.

'The interesting bit is from the interview records. You said that Pchelski said that renting property in France, holiday home stuff, had been difficult for landlords due to the financial crisis of 2008 still going on with a vengeance over there. He, Turner that is, had advertised in Private Eye magazine, to which advert Pchelski responded. Strange, we thought that Turner only ran one advert, according to the publishers. Yes, he could have been advertising for months in other publications and just got lucky with Private Eye. Nothing apparent on the internet, though. We would have expected a series if it was that difficult. So we tried to contact him — no reply. No land-line. In the end, got the local boys in blue to visit his home but nothing, no sign of life. Post on the door mat, visible through a side window. Nothing particularly unusual, according to the locals, but plenty of pictures of fancy old cars, the PC, Jonathan Davey's words, visible from the windows around the back of the main property. Also, several locked, secure, outbuildings. Lastly, ridiculous as it sounds on these observations, we checked on passport movement, driving licence and so on. Couple of trips to France over the last few months — nothing out of the ordinary. Dates don't match with anything we're interested in. Passport photos blurry, inevitably as is the driver's licence, but there is we think a sort of similarity to the prison photo in Pchelski's file — take away the beard and change the hairstyle. No real conclusion, just a suspicion, but maybe we need a forensic look at his lifestyle, finances, tax and so on. Need warrants for that and we don't have much more than suspicions.'

'Just a hunch then. Fine. Don't start looking for convenient solutions when the simple one may suffice, but, and it's a big but, connections like this are worth considering. Look for passport movements by Border Security. That would give us a clue, maybe, and it is relatively easy and quick to source. Maybe check DVLA regarding licence penalties and any vehicle registrations past and present. And well done. Keep it up, all of you. And keep looking.'

Susie Ford added another comment, 'One of the team has found out that the car that was torched in Switzerland all those years ago was a Bugatti. Owned by a local big-wig called Monsieur Andervert. I may have pronounced that wrongly, but I think I've got the spelling right. I've put it into the report. The girl who was pregnant? They're not aware of any of their pupils who were pregnant whilst at the school. It may be political as an answer, but we couldn't find grounds to break their confidence.'

DI Miles nodded a thank you and made a note to explore the issue further.

Chapter 53

George Pchelski arrived in the UK at London Luton with Wizzair and had called Chief Inspector LeFanu's office from the Warsaw airport, giving his ETA and hoping that he would be as good as his word and send a car for him.

After a two hours thirty minute flight and an hour and a half in a squad car, they met in LeFanu's tiny office. He sat in his jeans and a windbreaker, shivering whilst DCI LeFanu was, as usual, in a smart suit and tie, seemingly oblivious to the low temperatures outside. No coffee, no sandwiches, nothing, George realised that this was going to be formal with no relaxation of terms of engagement.

LeFanu, armed with the thoughts from DC Dodd, changed his line of questioning and offered George a coffee in the ubiquitous polystyrene cup poured from a dubious vintage thermos jug.

With a disarming smile, 'How did you meet Charlotte, George?' George bought himself some time by sipping at his coffee and then launched into his bit of history, smiling as he reflected on his first meeting in the chocolatiers, admitting that the first encounter had led to many others, each more demanding of time and money than the last — and hence his downfall. He glossed over the details, as he was sure LeFanu and his colleagues had read every word of his file, court transcripts and prison history.

LeFanu interrupted when he mentioned the Mercedes. 'Why a car like that?'

George shrugged. 'Why not?' he responded, looking up at the detective.

'Why not a BMW or Porsche — you look like a Porsche would have suited better.' LeFanu studied George's face for a reaction.

'Basically a love of old cars and their characters. Modern stuff is so similar sometimes it is hard to distinguish between them, so it is nicer to be a little different. And Charlie, sorry Charlotte, certainly needed that stand out in a crowd way of life. Anyway, classic Porsche cars are seriously expensive to buy, let alone restore. You know that, Mr LeFanu, I told you all that sort of stuff over the phone from Poland. So why drag me here?'

'Mr Pchelski, I ask the questions… Go back over the parting of the ways…'

George sighed theatrically. 'In hindsight, I should have seen it coming — gradual distancing, excuses, meeting the old gang from school and then nothing. Not long afterwards my arrest. Anyway, the rest is history.'

'Not quite, George. Not quite. You met at the prison, in somewhat odd circumstances. We have the records.'

'Yeah, well. Charlotte always was a devious minx. She got a buzz from doing anything daring and persuading the Deputy Governor to break the rules would be par for the course, however she achieved it. But you know that better than me, I suspect. I only got the screws' version, elaborately exaggerated, as you'd expect. Got a bit of notoriety from it, though.' He smiled.

'Yes, George, but why? What was the purpose of the visit?'

'Probably so I could be coffee table talk. I can just see her now, "I visited an old lag in prison" sort of thing. I knew a bloke who was a magistrate once who dined out on stories like that — meeting the seriously bad guy in prison rather than the minor criminals he saw in court. She told me about that old bastard, Tony Waller, whatever he's called these days. He had her beaten up in the States, or at least that's what she said, along with a friend, her word, boyfriend, paramour, whatever, breaking his arm or leg or something. Anyway, she wanted revenge and thought she could drag me in. She said that it was Waller who persuaded the board to prosecute — maybe true, maybe not. What I did learn about Charlotte is that if she didn't get her way, then she sought out petty revenge — shops, restaurants, anywhere. I said no to her scheme, point blank, DCI LeFanu; I've done my time and it wasn't pleasant. My mistakes were largely due to decisions made below my waist line, if you get my drift.'

'Why share her plan with you, George?'

'That bastard acquired my little collection of classic cars, apparently. I knew they'd have to be sold — that judge said so — no profit from a crime and so on. So I'd lost them, but he, Waller/Groombridge whatever, pulled a fast one. I don't know for a fact, but that's what she told me — his company in Cambridgeshire somewhere orchestrated it all. She seemed to think it was jealousy. Jealous of what, I'm buggered to know. I'm inside and he's living a life of Riley, what with his posh title and money.'

'Seems to me that she might just have achieved her objective — he's dead, as you know, and the cars he had collected by whatever means are mainly damaged beyond redemption. So who did it, George? You do have a motive of sorts.' They had all decided to keep up the theory that Lord Groombridge had been murdered to see if it tripped any asides from the interviewees.

'Maybe in your eyes, but in the real world, I did the time for the crime — can't regret collateral damage like losing my assets and hobbies. That's me — move on, as they say. I honestly don't know more, Chief Inspector. But how were the cars damaged? Sort of stuff he would have bought would be irreplaceable, I would guess.'

'Let's start with a Bugatti Gangloff-Stelvio.' LeFanu referred to his notes. 'D'you know about them?' He passed a magazine picture to George

'Gangloffs — oh my word! That is serious stuff; only eighty or so made in the 1930s and around sixty survive. Bit out of my league. Sort of thing you see at shows or in the magazines. Mine were a Morgan, thirty years old or so, an E-type desperately needing some TLC and my Mercedes, which really was in tip-top condition, when I went inside, anyway. Oh, and a lovely little late 1940s MGTC.'

'Several cars were damaged — brake fluid on the paint, engines started with sugar in the tank, hammers on the glass etc. etc. — need I go on? Experts tell me that most of the damage is fatal. We believe that a Porsche 356 and a Ferrari were stolen and the word "fake" written in brake fluid on the cellulose paint on the Bugatti. So, it had to be someone with a love of cars or a decent knowledge of what is and what isn't genuine.'

'Again, sir, not me, guv.' He put his hands up in mock surrender. 'I hate it when they race those old cars at Goodwood and the like and they end up severely damaged and that's not intentional. I've only ever seen one Gangloff and that was in the museum in Mulhouse, years ago at the Schlumpf Obsession, as it was called. I've got a book on it somewhere. Crikey, Ralph Lauren has one, often seen in the magazines, worth forty million dollars, so they say. Definitely out of my league and most of the rest of the world, too.'

'But you were looking for parts for a Porsche 356 when I called you. Coincidence or what? And I hate coincidences, so you can understand why I raise the question.'

'Absolutely, sir. I was on a commission. That's what I do these days and I still haven't finished the job. I think it was a guy, ultimately in Switzerland and an agent in West Sussex, quite near my sister's place and a specialist repair shop in Manchester — but I'd have to check. British restoration shops are the best in the world, which is why a Swiss guy would get things done here. And then I went to Warsaw. They're pretty clued up on restoration over there too. My family are from there, as you would have surmised from my convoluted surname. And I'm sure I've told you this before, but perhaps that's the way you work to ensure what's been said is true the second time round.' He looked closely at LeFanu's face for a reaction. 'My old grandfather escaped before the Nazis got a hold — fortunately — and walked to the UK via Vienna and Marseilles to Brittany and then a boat. Being French, I don't expect you want to know that sort of stuff, but I am quite a bit proud of his achievements, and before you say it, I know full well he would have frowned on mine!'

LeFanu frowned at the reference to France and its war efforts. 'OK, OK! Yes, you have told me that before. And you are right to be proud of his achievement. Have you been to see those guys who helped him, or presumably their families, allowing for the passage of time? Sounds like they deserve it.'

George liked to talk of his grandpa's achievements. 'Not for years. We used to visit when we were on holiday, but Grandpa P is a bit old and infirm now, so the Christmas cards that he used to send are now sent by my sister and the sons and even grandsons of those wonderful guys have spread to the four winds.'

'Where were you between the 5th and 11th January, George?'

George sat quiet for a moment or two before responding. 'In France — and before you ask, no real alibi. I went there for Christmas — it was either there or with my sister and her husband. Lovely sister, but her husband does go on a bit too much about my straying off the straight and narrow. I did call her at New Year, I'm sure she'll vouch for that.'

'Going back to that hackneyed expression about coincidences, George. So much seems to be connected with France in this investigation. Terry Beddall was murdered there by a blonde woman we believe called Angela, Charlotte comes from there, her husband was on holiday in Courchevel…'

He shrugged. 'The French connection? Don't have a clue. It's a big country — six times bigger than the UK. Angela? Terry's bit of stuff. They were a serious item.'

LeFanu decided to ignore the location issue and poured another coffee, no longer piping hot but a distraction nevertheless. 'I know, but we have an identification; not a hundred percent, but a grainy image on CCTV. Did you meet her?'

'No, I saw her photo on his phone, well, there were dozens of them, with and without clothes. Bit embarrassing, really. You know what it's like when people show you their holiday photos. You look at the first one or two and comment and then acute boredom sets in. So, no! I wouldn't recognise her if I met her in the street. Blonde, smart, big boobs and that's about it. Always seemed to have a big hat, even when she was buck naked, I do recall that, now I think of it.' He smiled at the vignette he had put forward.

'George, you did tell me before that you had never seen photos of her. Tell me, and it is not being smutty, was she a natural blonde?'

'Wouldn't know. I just assumed that the hair on her head was natural. Smutty or not, the photos were pretty stunning and you would not know whether she was a natural blonde or not from them, if you get my drift.'

'Quite so, quite so! But you'll understand my persistence, as everyone in this mess seems to have selective memory until prodded or pushed or tripped up and then I get the "oops, I'd forgotten" routine. Try harder, George, or it will be the worse for you.' LeFanu prided himself in having a good retentive memory and almost instant recall of previous conversations.

He paced up and down his diminutive office, gazing out of the window as he sought to muster his thoughts. He watched, almost absentmindedly, the cars toing and froing around the busy car park entrance. A green-ish, old-ish car went round twice, before abandoning all hope of getting a place, and scooted off onto the ring road. All this in a matter of half a minute or so. He returned to talking to George. 'Remind me. What was your favourite car again?'

'A Mercedes 500SL 1969 Pagoda top. I loved that car. Did a full bare metal, nut and bolt restoration with my Grandpa P. He'd done one years before and knew all the wrinkles, and there were plenty of them with the suspension, believe me. It was the last car we worked on together, so you'll understand my feelings.'

'What colour?'

'Green. Typical 1970 and 80s colour; Moss Green metallic with green leather upholstery. Why do you ask?'

'That was similar to one that was in Lord Groombridge's garage. Registration number ALG111. Had some damage but largely unscathed, restorable I'm told by the experts. Needs an engine overhaul due to a kilo or so of best sugar in the tank and a re-spray.' George grimaced. 'In fact, I know it was the one you owned; DVLA confirmed it from the chassis number.'

'She told me he cherished that one, PKP 166G; that was its number when I had it. Course, he probably changed it — personalised plates and so on. The sort of man to go for vanity plates. No depth to the man, lying cunning bastard, but a business man, what d'you expect. He conned the company several times but we were told to go with the flow because he was a serious shareholder. Part owner of the syndicate. But Detective Chief Inspector, we've been over this ground before and a lot of your questions just now I've answered until I'm blue in the face.'

'Just checking; it's my style, as you pointed out earlier. You'll just have to put up with it, George. Now, why cherish? Strange word from someone who seemingly wanted to get revenge.'

'Well, cherish is my word, but that's what it sounded like. I can't remember every bloody word she said. I think that's the jealousy bit. Charlotte was not slow in coming forward in terms of relationships with other men and although ours was well and truly over, that's all I can think of. Irrational maybe — I expect the psychobabble people would have a word for it.'

'You knew him well, by the sound of your reactions?'

'No, not really, just the work stuff. He was the pompous director and often, no sometimes, came into the offices looking for a favour or two, bending the rules on insurance claims for a pal or whoever. We all had to get sanction from the boss, Sir Charles Beech, and Waller usually got his way. We all knew it was lies and a con but...'

'Hate him?'

'No, despised him would be a better word. Wouldn't wish him dead but maybe love to see him in the bankruptcy courts or in clink. I told you losing my cars was my own fault. What they fetched at auction or however they were sold is academic. I lost. It could have been a thousand pound or a hundred thousand, not my problem. One day, if the Gods shine on me, I'll start collecting again. Meanwhile, I drive an old Rover in the UK and a beat up Renault Clio, ex-French Post Office actually, in France. Of course, I drive other people's pride and joy anywhere else when they let me.'

'Where were you in France, all over Christmas and New Year time?'

'Yes, yes! At the house I told you about before.' George was showing signs of impatience but knew to restrain an outburst.

'Why the west of France — surely that's a nuisance for you in your job. Must need to go to Germany, and Italy most of the time.'

'No, the internet helps with sourcing parts and it is easier not having to cross the channel every time I want to get something. And there are airports — three of them about sixty miles each, let alone the TGV to Paris and then wherever. Schenegen agreement — free unhindered travel in the eurozone helps me a lot. I have got a small flat in London as well, but the expense is killing me — so that'll have to go when the lease is up.'

Changing subjects rapidly was a belief LeFanu had to throw his interviewees off balance. 'So, her plan for revenge. You turned her down? And never heard from her again?'

George reacted well, recognising LeFanu's approach. 'Well, we did meet for a drink after I'd been released and then she elaborated the pretty pathetic plan, although I'm no expert on plans like that.'

'Really?' He smiled and paused, letting the disbelief sink in. 'What sort of pathetic plan?'

'She wanted a burglary of his house, taking money and some of his cars and then destroying the others and telling the insurance company beforehand that the policies were to be cancelled immediately so it would be impossible to make a claim. I told her that she had no idea how quickly her husband would resolve that little dilemma with barely a flutter. I do remember telling her that I would enjoy his suffering, even a little discomfort, but it would be so short-lived it wouldn't be worth getting out of bed for.'

'Sounds like you would have been right; it does sound pathetic.' He put the emphasis on the word "sound" which was sufficient for George to raise an eyebrow. 'But there are some marked similarities with what actually happened, if you ignore the murders. So, George, are you denying any involvement?'

'Lord, yes. I told you I was out of the country. Can't Border Security tell you that? A plan like hers was woolly, so many holes in it that it looked like a colander, to mix my metaphors. My reward was to be the recovery of my Mercedes, a bit of nookie, and I would guess several years inside again. No way! Couldn't we have another coffee or something, Mr LeFanu? I'm parched. And anyway, I was brought up in business, where the mantra was a good plan is only a good plan if it is flexible enough to deal with something that goes wrong, even sometimes very wrong. And that was something she didn't even have on her agenda.'

LeFanu signalled to a WPC outside his glass panelled door who entered and took the order for a flat-white and a cake of some sort and his own double espresso. 'OK? Right, what did she know about the Merc? She seems to be a lady that likes modern powerful cars, not character vehicles like yours.'

'Funny, now you mention it. She did ask quite specifically about the car — colour, age, type, model. Odd thinking about it that way. Perhaps she was checking if it was the one Waller owned. Apparently he used to polish it every week — seemingly worshipping it. Or so she said! It sounds like you think she was the mastermind behind it. Ah, now I think I'm getting the direction of this conversation... You think she got hold of Terry and he did the deed.'

'Possible?'

'Lovely man, but not much on the detail. Sort of person who is good as a sergeant but wouldn't hold a captain's rank, if you get my drift. I'm sure you got that from his records. I owe him a great deal, but it would be foolhardy to choose him to do complicated things without a blow by blow list.'

'Directed by another person?'

'I guess so but... Depends on the complexity. He's no murderer. Strong as an ox, but actually quite calm; even when riled, he came down to earth pretty quickly. Plenty of need for that sort of person in prison, I can tell you. But I wouldn't have put Charlotte in the murderess category either. She always wants to get her own way, prima donna, devious minx, but I never saw any sign of violence, just the petty revenge stuff. She complained that her husband was violent when drunk and she took the backlash for it, literally.'

'She's a nasty piece of work, George. You might not think so but you got off lightly. It appears that she always got her own way.'

'Now you put it like that, you're probably right.' The coffees arrived and Philippe took the opportunity to walk round the office again, scratching his ear yet again. He liked silence and the pause was deliberate, as it usually meant that the interviewee started talking, unable to cope with that silence. And from experience, it worked with George Pchelski.

'Sir, it sounds like she, or someone, took this half-arsed idea and found someone to execute, sorry bad word, carry out the plan for a wagonload of money. Maybe not even her original idea — perhaps she overheard it and embellished it. How the hell would I know? How the deaths fit in I have no idea except, I suppose, to stop any recognition afterwards — surprised on the job, maybe. If Groombridge turned up unexpectedly whilst his cars were being vandalised, he would be more than angry — I would be, certainly, and he's, sorry was, more of a collector than I could ever dream of. Mind you, maybe that was the intention all along. Fits with the word devious?'

'Ummm! Who else other than Charlotte, George? We have sufficient reason to believe that she could not be in two places at once!'

'Don't know. I just don't know enough of the stuff you have established already and even then it'd be guesswork for me.'

Then LeFanu tried his ploy that had been nagging in the back of his mind ever since George came into his office, but how to introduce it? Now seemed to be the perfect time. 'You seem to be a perfect fit for a so-called Mr Big, George. Knowledge, motive, connection. Persuade me not to arrest you.'

George was dumbfounded. He spluttered, 'Me?'

'You, Mr Stanislav George Pchelski. We have reason to believe that your alibi has more holes in it than a tea strainer. We believe you entered the UK from France by avoiding Border Security and returned under a false passport. You told us you cannot stand fake classic cars and here is one severely damaged. You owned the Mercedes; a model of that car has turned up in a compromising place. You have a reduced life style where money could be important. Revenge is a distinct possibility and opportunity is only hindered by using traditional means of entering or leaving the UK. You had better be good at telling me why I'm wrong.'

'Phew. How, for fuck's sake, am I supposed to do that? I couldn't afford a private plane.' He looked genuinely puzzled.

LeFanu just said one word, 'Fishing boat.'

He smiled, realising that LeFanu was fishing, and the thought of the pun brought the smile to his face, disturbing LeFanu. 'Why smile, George?'

'Sir, it was the thought of you fishing for information and the fishermen you mention — nothing sinister.'

The DCI responded firmly by telling George Pchelski that humour was not required.

George, still smiling inwardly about his multiple identities, pretended to suddenly make the connection. 'What? Ah, I get it. Like my Grandpa P. Hence the interest in my story. That makes sense. That, sir, was a different era; different circumstances. Not nowadays. No doubt someone somewhere is moving illegals into the country — certainly if the media is to be believed — and charging a small fortune to do so. But who and where and… It beggars belief that you would think that. I've been as straight as I can be with you. Alibis are for the innocent. I ate out at a local restaurant or two over the festive season, I shopped locally and in the supermarket, Super-U, in the next town and made a few calls on my mobile. No, I didn't meet with anyone. I don't use a credit card much, certainly not for small stuff like food. I do get paid a lot in cash, sir — I admit that much, as an income tax thing, but it seems that'll work against me…'

'Write it down, George. Every movement and phone call. Right the way from when you arrived in France in December to the 11th January. We will check everything. We have a team visiting every northern Brittany port as we speak.' Whilst the latter statement was blatantly untrue, and were it possible, unlikely to evince any truths from the fishermen, it was worth a try to shake George Pchelski. 'I'll leave you to it for ten minutes or so.' He rose and left the office.

Returning much later, he found George Pchelski pacing up and down and gazing through the windows, clutching a piece of paper. He took the sheet of paper and arranged for George to be driven back to London, his preferred choice, with instructions not to leave the UK without seeking permission or face instant arrest at any UK point of departure. And that they would talk that evening.

He passed the sheet of paper to Sam Miles for the team to analyse.

Chapter 54

DS Jones related the conversation to DI Miles that he'd had with DC Dodd and his group, commenting in passing that the group led by DC Susie Ford were analysing all the input from interviews — and doing a great job. Sam Miles acknowledged the comment with a smile.

'Oh, and something else that's just come through... The only person who directly refers to Lord Groombridge as a womaniser is Lady G. Everyone else, it seems, gives out second-hand information, which might well have come from repeating the stuff that Lady G says - similar language and all that. We know she was fairly free and easy with it from others — friends, and of course, George P. And there were no condoms in Porten House, not that that proves anything per se.'

'Thanks, Chris. Mark it up but I think that it might...'

'And Homeland Security were not very helpful. "Out of order to track one of our citizens" routine. We made up a plausible story why and they relaxed a bit. But no chance of fingerprints or DNA. And zero feedback from the bus company, Greyhound. So we looked at the hire car possibility at the US/Canadian Border. Sorry for interrupting...' Miles put up both her hands as a mock surrender. 'Anyway, there is only a limited service at Champlain, full opening etc. only from April 1st. We spread our net to Plattsburgh, about twenty-five miles away, and checked the hire car companies at their airport. Hertz, Budget and Enterprise and a few others. We struck lucky on the Hertz — our third try. A Jerry Gold rented an Audi Q7 for a week using his credit card. Apparently his first card was maxed out so he used another Mastercard. They remembered that — bit of embarrassment for the punter but nothing truly remarkable. Bloke had an English accent. It is not possible to rent using cash and if a debit card is used, the client has to have a valid return flight ticket. Gold used a valid US driver's licence. It appears that he took a taxi or bus from Champlain to this Plattsburgh place, a matter of thirty minutes' travel, give or take, to the airport terminal. There is no relevant CCTV in the vicinity. We have the registered number of the car as JAD0502, but it is of little use as it has already been handed back to their depot in Concord airport and prepped for the next renter. What we need is fingerprints, ma'am.'

***

'Notwithstanding that we had put a light surveillance team on Lady Charlotte and decided that there was little or no flight risk, or justification in thinking that way, we have just blown it. The bird has flown the nest.' Sergeant Shaw brought the bad news to LeFanu's office where DI Miles and DS Jones were meeting to discuss next moves.

'What? What do you mean by flown the nest?'

'Simply this, sir. The PC on duty in line of sight of the entrance to Rosetti Gardens had his attention diverted. A blonde lady apparently emerged from the building and asked him if he knew the number of a taxi firm. He opened up an app on his phone and sorted it for her. Destination the West End. Why a PC should be in the business of calling cabs, I don't know. Anyway, that he did and the blonde, after a couple of minutes of chit-chat, his words, disappeared in the cab. She had no luggage, just a handbag which he held for her whilst she fiddled around with something or other. He maintains he was just being helpful and it wasn't our bird. A few minutes later, he said he could see a brunette who he thought was Lady Charlotte, our bird, in the front window of her apartment, prancing around like she was dancing, and believe it or not, our brunette was in her underwear.'

'Oh, for God's sake. Men! That's just about the oldest trick in the book.' DI Miles was angry. 'Make sure he is disciplined, Sergeant Shaw.'

'Yes, ma'am, he will be. To try to redeem himself, he'd contacted the concierge and found out that a truck had taken away some stuff from her flat, for storage they said.'

'Name, location?'

'Don't know right this minute. He's making more enquiries of this concierge fellow, who is not being terribly helpful. "Got to look after my residents' privacy" sort of stuff. I've told him to say hindering the police is an offence. So we have to wait a bit. Meanwhile, I have put out an all-points bulletin on Lady Charlotte, aka Charlotte Bertin, aka Charlotte Foubert. Every combination we've noted to date. The naked lady dancer has disappeared from view, inevitably.'

'Hmm. There's a surprise. France would seem to be too obvious. Where else? USA, maybe, if our guess of Lord Groombridge, as Jerry Gold, went there. Or, was it Lady C or another or her look-alikes?'

'Could be just a shopping trip, ma'am?' She pulled a face which told him that he was way off beam. His mobile phone rang and he excused himself from the conversation with DI Miles.

'Sorry, update. They have entered the flat with the concierge bloke and it has been stripped of personal stuff. The half-naked dancer was gone too. Still pictures on the walls etc. but clothes, jewellery all gone — like she's gone on a long holiday, is what the PC Wiggins just told me. And a blonde woman neighbour, apparently, told him just that.'

LeFanu, exasperated, looked up. 'I'll give him a good wigging if I catch him. Thanks for the information, Sergeant Shaw. I realise you are only the messenger in this instance. Please interrupt if anything fresh turns up. Sounds like Charlotte has done a runner and Veronica, if my gut feeling is right, has just spoken to the PC and disappeared too. Clever stuff — not!' He took a second to pull back the current screen on his laptop before continuing with Miles and Jones.

'Sorry, ma'am, sir, one last thing from the concierge. After we got over the privacy issue, he couldn't stop talking. There is a strong rumour that the flat will be repossessed shortly. Valuers and bailiffs all over the place like a rash, he had said. And a couple of odd callers with Yank accents. Couple of hoods, he reckoned and they were "packing", he reckons.'

'Packing? What the blazes is that, Sergeant?'

'Carrying a gun, sir. I told him he'd been watching too many Yank crime thrillers like our DS here.'

'Saints preserve us from the English language from across the pond. I hear what you say and presumably there are some on-going investigations as to the veracity of his comment?'

Sergeant Shaw nodded and threw in a comment that bad guys like that could be the murderers at Eye St Mary.

'Possible. Write it up, Sergeant. Thank you.' Shaw withdrew and once more LeFanu concentrated on the screen in front of him.

'Parking for the moment that thought from our articulate sergeant, there are some questions that keep irritating me. Firstly, why did Charlotte end up at that particular school? My sister says that it is more normal for the Swiss to take the first place in the pecking order of finishing schools.

Maybe there is more than just a selection process by her parents — worth a little digging?' DI Miles nodded and scribbled a note. 'I'll pick up that one — should be no more than a phone call to dismiss it or to open up an enquiry.'

'Secondly,' LeFanu continued, 'Porten House. It was empty of personal things. OK, so Frau Braun may have been a very efficient woman, but there are always things and possessions around — just remember when we visited Lady C's bloody flat in Chelsea. Someone knew Porten House well enough to empty the dishwasher, put glasses where they belonged, remove all signs of any visitors such as girlfriends, maybe even have to stay in the house whilst a washing machine and dishwasher finished their wash cycles — that's a tall order. So Monika Braun may have, probably did knowing the place was to be empty for a good few weeks, strip the beds and similarly the fridge and so on, but no papers, no mail, no photos, and if we are to believe Lady C about her husband's profligate nature, no condoms, as you pointed out, Jones. Has to be someone who knows the house. Comments?'

'Pure conjecture, sir.' Jones piped up. 'Wife or pissed-off girlfriend. Even a friend of Charlotte, if we call the blonde Angela that, wouldn't know where everything was kept. Although, we know several of her friends have been visitors to Porten House over the years. When Lady C took all her personal stuff after the funeral events, she had said that it was odd, and to use my words, someone had cleaned up like a new broom. That made me think that either it was a huge bluff on her part, or someone who knew the property well had done the job, and not that Frau Braun had done her usual job.'

'Agreed, Jones.' DI Miles also nodded her agreement.

'So both, who? And if we knew who it was, would we be any further forward? Person or persons unknown, a male or a female? And we must not ignore Mr Guy Scott and his cronies; they've certainly been to the house, although how many times I know not. See if he has a credible alibi. Sam, pick up that inquiry with young Susie Ford, I think. A phone call or two should keep him on edge. From what we've seen of him, a pretty female might get some better answers than me. But don't trust his answers completely.' He looked up and saw agreement. 'The blonde in the blue car? The blonde pal of Beddall's sister, the same blonde, we think, in Paris and now in London, maybe as a friend of Charlotte. So, one thought is look at the gang at the school. No other friends of Charlotte or Lord Groombridge have popped up. Back to the school, Sam, I think?' Again, she nodded.

'Sir, one point that comes back to me is the missing wedding ring of the lady called Angela Darling, if you recall the interview with Beddall's sister…'

'Yes, of course. Good point. We assumed, at the time, that her excuse of wearing a ring to keep the bees off the honeypot, literally and metaphorically, made sense, as Beddall's sister told us. But maybe it was a detail she overlooked and removed it afterwards to avoid the inquiry as to married status. So, if married — to whom? DS Jones — your question to resolve, I think. Let's have a status report on all the members of her group/gang, whatever you want to call it. The trouble is, as we all know, we have few people left that can verify anything the others say.'

Jones nodded agreement, and at a glance from LeFanu, both Miles and he left the room.

Chapter 55

DI Miles was the first to report back. She had been right; a simple phone call to the principal's office at the Oxford School had generated a lot of information about Charlotte Foubert. She had been at the Institute Finesse school in Basle and had been asked to leave due to "disruptive behaviour", as the letter from the Swiss had said. The PA to the principal in Oxford, a Miss Elizabeth Hope, was a little less discrete and referred to a raft of petty crimes, culminating in setting fire to a car, an expensive Bugatti apparently belonging to a local businessman and arranging, she believed, an abortion for one of the girls at the school, aged fifteen, across the border in Belfort, France.

DI Miles, quite shocked by the second revelation, had asked Miss Hope, 'Is any of this provable? On paper maybe? Would the Swiss Police have any records?'

Her reply related to a conversation she had had on the same subject with her Swiss counterpart, a Mademoiselle Francoise Glain. The Swiss police apparently had not been able to establish guilt, just complicity. 'Balderdash,' she had finished by saying to Sam Miles, 'Those rich bitches have contacts and influence everywhere, or their parents do,' which had brought a smile to Sam's face whilst on the phone. The official version, for the record, so as to speak, was that she needed to finish her education in an English-speaking environment, rather than the somewhat European answer of the stilted Swiss approach. Often the way that the rich French, German and Italian thought, she had added. It had prompted Sam to ask what the un-official version was. Miss Hope was conspiratorial in her response. She often talked to her equivalents in the other schools in Europe, which were fewer in number nowadays. And as there were frequent changes of establishment and staff between them, networking conversations and exchange of information was rife. She, Charlotte, had apparently been cautioned by the Swiss police, but only because there had been a lack of proof and a seemingly reasonable alibi existed, none of which did much for the reputation of the Basle school. So it had been easier for them to suggest, forcibly they had said, that Charlotte and a couple of her peer group were sent to other schools or they would be forced to prosecute for the sake of their reputation. Miss Hope, who obviously had liked to talk and didn't use words like allegedly or possibly, had intimated that the fees that all of them who joined the Oxford School were to pay, or rather their parents were to pay, had been increased by fifty percent to reflect the risk, and all records of the Swiss experience would then be redacted from their records.

Another interesting observation by the PA encouraged a question or two from DI Miles. Charlotte Foubert had joined at the same time as a friend from Amsterdam, a Veronica van Outen, the daughter of a Dutch banker currently living in Hong Kong, and another girl who had turned up some six or so months earlier called Fiona Rampling. She had confided that she thought, but wasn't sure, that Fiona was the subject of the underage pregnancy and all that implied. Pushing her luck a little, DI Miles asked about the dismissals and Miss Hope clammed up, claiming that it was, after all, all rumour and second-hand information.

DI Miles gave her direct phone number and contact details in case the garrulous Miss Hope recalled any other information and established the telephone number of the lady in Basle and rang off, feeling that she had achieved her objective although not sure if, or how, it progressed their enquiry much further. She smiled to herself, thinking that Miss or Ms Hope, as she expected it was, was really in the wrong job and the Oxford School obviously couldn't afford to be too choosy about its pupils.

She tracked the father of Veronica, Baron Jakob van Outen, to a bank in Hong Kong, where he was the COO, but with the time difference of eight hours ahead, she had to wait to be able to talk.

She called DC Susie Ford to tell her of the possibility of Fiona Wallace lying about the incident in Switzerland. Susie, losing her temper, just replied, 'Fucking bitch.' It made Samantha smile — thinking she's joining the ranks of detectives, complete with their frustrations.

DS Jones returned to the group in LeFanu's office half an hour later with his information, but listened patiently to DI Miles's digest of her conversations. He had spoken afresh to Sharon Beddall about the wedding ring incident. She hadn't been able to throw any more light on the Angela Darling married or not scenario. He had shown her an enlarged version of the wedding party photo and asked if any of the females showed any resemblance to her memory of Angela. Interestingly, he'd thought, she had offered a comment that they all looked remarkably similar, if the hair colour was changed — same style, same sort of figure and dress sense. Yes, she had said, it could have been the blonde woman in the picture, but nothing certain. Jones decided to have the picture further enhanced to pick up on an oblique angle of the rings on her left hand, the sort of thing a female would remember, and promised to contact Sharon again if it were possible.

Shaw entered the inner sanctum, bursting with enthusiasm. 'Sir we tracked the firm that took away the stuff from the Groombridge flat. Southampton based, Richman & Daughter. They told us it was to go by sea to New York, but not leaving until Tuesday next. I've told them not to move it until we give clearance. OK?'

'Fine, Sergeant Shaw. I'm not sure whether it will help us any. It will probably be better to let it go and monitor where it ends up and who collects it. Use Homeland Security in New York to put an alert out for our little madam, as she certainly now appears to be. If she is heading for the USA. Do it. DI Miles has a contact there.'

'Wilco. The other thing, sir, I have no reports of the lady leaving the country. Sorry. Maybe she is just shopping in London?'

'I doubt it, Sergeant, but you never know. Keep on it and thanks.' Shaw beamed as he turned, knowing that it could have been a roasting from the boss.

'I have nothing to add at this stage. DC Ford is to talk to Scott tomorrow at nine a.m. I have briefed her and she will take Sergeant Shaw with her for support. I have another telecon booked tonight, well, this evening actually, with George Pchelski. I think we might establish what role Beddall would have been capable of. No one knows him better than his cell-mate, leastways there's no one else that we know of.'

'Sir, I feel we are wandering a bit. Sorry and all that. There could be many ways for Lady C to get out of the UK. Many ways that Lord G could have come back here from Courchevel and then returned to France for his flight for the USA, possibly with Gold's passport. All those twists and turns are interesting but not conclusive. As you said, sir, everyone who can vouchsafe or confirm movements is dead or missing. I'm convinced that we know, or know of, all the participants. It's a bit like the TV detective stories and I know you'll laugh. But if you see a film or story, after a while you know the most likely members of the cast. That's what I feel like. So I reckon, Charlotte for the murder of Gold, in cahoots with her husband.

Angela, who is, or could easily be one of the so-called gang that DI Miles seems to have found. Lady C for the death of the German woman because she saw something. Beddall's death by Angela's hand, aided by Lady C, The two deaths in the car park in Paris by Beddall because they mucked him about somehow or other. The thefts orchestrated by Lady C and helped by Angela to make some money — her Swiss school record tells you something about her attitude to other people's property. That's me done, sir. Sorry again.'

'It does sound like one of your TV detective heroes. Sounds plausible but I'm not convinced it can be wrapped up in one episode like the TV, Jones. But thanks for bringing us back on track.' He looked at Samantha Miles and noted her agreement. 'What we need is Charlotte or Lord G, aka Jerry Gold, to be tracked down and… well, I think that much of what you have said will then fall into place, or there will be different roles for the protagonists to play. Talk again tomorrow after I've spoken to Pchelski and Sam Miles has made her call to Hong Kong.'

***

LeFanu called George Pchelski later in the evening, from home using the recording facility on his mobile. He had several questions to ask, albeit he resigned himself to the fact there would be questions with no definitive answers, but as George seemed to be the only one with no axe to grind, and seemingly one of the only connected people who had survived, he was the best bet.

'George, a question for you. The green paint for your old Mercedes, would it be a special order or off the shelf?'

'Good evening to you too, Detective Chief Inspector! In case you are worrying, I am indeed in London, as promised, and thank you for the nice car journey through our green and pleasant land.'

'Don't take the mickey, George, as you funny Brits like to call it.'

His admonishment brought George back on track. 'Sorry, sir. I was trying to dispose of the lease on my expensive and uncomfortable flat. Strange question to ask. Couldn't your staff establish that kind of thing, or is this one of your ploys to get me talking about other things?' He paused, waiting for a reaction from LeFanu but there was none, just a silence. 'OK! I guess a silence is enough for me to have to answer. Yes, it's a special order because it is a cellulose finish and that's old and inflammable paint. They can mix it in a good paint shop but that's expensive and time-consuming and you would have to buy a large quantity. I had some made up and sealed for future use not long before I lost control of the bloody car, so I suppose there was some in the side well of the boot when it changed hands. Does that answer your question?'

'Indeed it does, George, indeed. I'll tell you why I ask. And this is one thing that is not common knowledge, so it is not to be made public. Do I make myself clear?' George acknowledged the question, trying to make a connection before the DCI explained. LeFanu continued, 'Underneath the body at Porten House we found a model car, a Mercedes, the same model as yours, and it had been painted green, the right green and badly painted to boot…'

'Bloody hell. That explains a lot about these persistent phone calls from you. The constant questioning and going over the same old ground time and time again. A model car — that is bizarre. A murder? Nothing to do with me, I promise. It's almost poetic, in a black humour way of thinking. Lord G dies on top of a model car. That's really, well, weird. I think someone, maybe that bloody cow Charlotte, is trying to make a link to me but it is clumsy and muddying the waters. Why? If I had been involved in any murder, would I be stupid enough to point the finger at myself? I don't think so.'

'Mmm… Sometimes, George, it can be a case of double-bluff.'

'Not this time, guv. Tried all that stuff before and look where I ended up.'

'That, my friend, is why I am talking to you and not arresting you. For all the other mischief you have been involved in, or are involved in, I don't think you are involved in this murder or series of murders, but you might well be the key to information because you know, or knew, or knew of, some of the participants and there aren't many of you left alive.'

'Just ask. If I can help, I will.'

'OK! How many expensive Bugattis have been destroyed by arson in the last ten years? Probably in France, Germany, Italy or Switzerland.' Again, LeFanu was listening carefully for any change or inflexion in George's answer.

'If they are Bugattis, they are expensive; they're pretty rare and things like you allude to are usually well-reported. I don't recall any is the simple

335

answer, but I was not exactly able to read all the trade papers on classic cars for a few years, now was I?' LeFanu was satisfied but refused to let the subject drop.

'O-Kay. I hear what you say. Do people, notably people who own cars like that, report crimes and if so, to whom? Do they replace or move on to other things?'

'Either/or is the answer. Greatest respect, sir, it's a daft question. Some of the collectors of these cars, or these types of car, are filthy rich and like to be a hundred percent private, so something like a car being torched is just another annoying little incident. Maybe their money is not kosher, or the car or whatever isn't legitimate — just think of the Nazi art thefts of the 1940s, so they don't want investigations near them. Others resort to insurance when they're a bit strapped for cash and arson is a regular "excuse" for making a claim. I told you about Tony Waller and his cronies and the case of Lord Brockett destroying a Ferrari is public domain. Who buys Bugattis? Ask Waller's bloody auction house or Christies or any other of the famous names. Ask the ABI, the insurance companies' trade body. They purport to represent the insurance industry — based in the City.'

'George, whenever I've spoken to Charlotte about cars, she always claims that power and luxury are the be all and end all. Would she know how to set fire to a car, or fix a bug to a car?'

'Doubt it. She'd get her fingers dirty. She ran out of petrol once and called the dealer who had sold them the car — and he turned out with some fuel, even though it was fifty miles or so away. Must have had the hots for her — and I know about that! Mind you, from what I now know that could be for a few reasons or it could be another of her tall stories. Fixing a tracking device on a car? Well, it is not difficult. They're normally magnetic. Of course, a lot of car panels and bumpers nowadays are plastic, aluminium or carbon fibre, but can you see her getting down on her knees at the back end of a car? I can't. My advice? Look for someone else. Look at her bloody gang at school; they're as thick as thieves, or another of her sycophants who will do anything she asks — and that coming from me is a joke, isn't it? And no, I didn't bug Tel's car.'

'Right. Look at it from my point of view, George. No one relevant to this enquiry knew Terry Beddall apart from you and Charlotte, and I suppose, his sister. Suddenly there's a new girlfriend and a friend, equally new, for his sister Sharon — all this starting at the prison. This new friend, we'll call AD, refers falsely to a relative or friend inside the prison called Tony. Mr Beddall gets involved, to some extent or other, in a large robbery ending in severe violence. Beddall's car, a long-term rental vehicle, is bugged probably not long after he left prison, late November — we know that from a recovery and analysis of the satnav destinations in the car. The GPS destinations included Porten House, where the murder occurred, and several other relevant locations, including some in Brittany and even your French residence, remember? And the hotel in Paris where two bodies of ex-colleagues of his from the army were recovered. Coincidence or what?' He listened again for a change of tone in George's reply.

'Crikey! That's mega coincidence. I worked on insurance claims for years, so I'm cynical, but that takes the biscuit. Maybe an accomplice. I don't believe she would wait outside a prison every Thursday, as I've said before. If necessary, she'd find some other mutt to do that. And maybe that mutt would place the tracker and maybe that same mutt would know how to poison Terry and get away with it. I don't see why I'm trying to do your job, sir.' LeFanu detected a raise in the tenor of his voice.

'Simply this, George. You are a suspect. I don't have many left alive, which points the finger at you more and more. But I don't believe you condone violence, otherwise we would not be talking now. Damaging cars may be another thing but… Think on the questions I have posed. Help me and I might help you. We will doubtless talk again. And don't forget the explosive device, either. Some skill set, eh?'

George countered, 'It strikes me that the only reason you're talking to me is that once, I repeat once, I had some cars and they ended up in bloody Groombridge's hands and someone planted a model car to direct you to find me. Yes, I am an old lag, but those two things are not, repeat not, connected. I will help with what expertise I have, but I am not involved in these crimes you speak of. OK?'

LeFanu muttered, 'I hear you.' He had decided in advance to finish on such a note, to leave George thinking of what else the police knew. They rang off after some pseudo pleasantries.

Chapter 56

'What now, Sergeant Shaw?' DCI LeFanu, DI Miles, DS Jones and DC Ford were gathered around the diminutive table in his office with four laptops and dozens of empty coffee cups and biscuit packets. Shaw had knocked on the door frame and entered.

'Sir, ma'am, an important response from the US. There's been a shooting and one of the victims is our Lady Charlotte. Dead as a dodo, as is the other victim…'

'What? When, how and where?'

'Preliminary report only so far. Gunshot to the head in the street in Concord, a biggish city in New England, they tell me. Identity established from two passports and other personal stuff — mobile phone, credit cards etc. and with him, just the one passport and wallet and a hotel key for the Holiday Inn — bit downmarket for the Groombridges, I'd have thought but…' He saw the looks of impatience and continued quickly. 'Anyway, connected to us due to our enquiry to Homeland Security of the Groombridge/Waller family. It seems pretty definite, sir.'

'And the other victim?' DI Miles looked up from her screen. She had always thought that Groombridge had been involved in the murder of Gold at Porten House and hoped that her thoughts would be justified.

'Ma'am, we're being told it is a Mr Jerry Gold from Albany, New York, again, ID from his passport and possessions. Gold crucifix around his neck and a signet ring bearing the initials AW in a pocket. Interesting? They're checking ID with next of kin — his mother. The weird thing is that both victims killed by single gunshot to the head and they say it looks like a professional at work. In Gold's mouth, sir, a gambling chip. Weird or what? That's all we have at the moment. Anything for me to do?'

'No. Thanks for the interruption. Keep us in the picture. And Sergeant Shaw, try to keep a lid on this. I don't want to read about it in tomorrow's newspaper or podcast or whatever. Capiche?' He turned to his colleagues as Shaw left the room. 'I don't believe it — more deaths. Why would an American be carrying his passport in the middle of downtown Concord?

Sam, maybe this will be the confirmation, at last, of all our conjecture about who was killed in the Jacuzzi. A ring with the initials AW? Game set and match, perhaps. Still circumstantial until we get positive ID or a negative one from the mitochondrial DNA. Shaw says she was carrying more than one passport — how come? I thought we had bottomed that one out.' Before any of the team could comment, he added, 'Just a thought… when can we be sure it is actually Lady Charlotte? Seems like changing identities comes to that bunch as frequently as we change our… Rhetorical question, really, and pretty much irrelevant, at least until we hear more. Another question for you, DS Jones: did you talk to your Crockfords fellow about Lord G?'

'Yes, sir. I told them only that we were investigating Lord G's gambling habits in conjunction with his bankers here and in the USA. They promised to use their network to see if there was any fresh information in the US or France. Haven't heard any updates on the score. They do not know of any details of our investigations, well, not from me, anyway.' He looked pointedly at the door.

'Of course not, Chris. Never crossed my mind. But we have known for a long time that we may have a leaky ship. Just a rumour of investigations may have opened a question in someone's mind, over in the US, perhaps, and then they start looking and now we know what they found. Worth thinking about, that's all. Now, where were we before that interruption?'

All three looked up, puzzled about the word "interruption", to be greeted by a broad smile from LeFanu.

'Obviously, sir, the debate as to the whereabouts of our globe-trotting Lady C looks like it is now academic, but we were focussing on who was left that could have executed the other crimes — notably the so-called Angela Darling and the role of this gang of Charlotte's friends. You've sort of met them, haven't you, sir?' Chris Jones, always trying to tie down detail, was frustrated by the idea that there was a third party who was unknown.

'Back to the crime thriller thing that all the characters must be known, eh? What would your famous TV detective have done in the circumstances?' DI Miles interjected. 'Let's look instead in detail at this gang. Who is this van Outen woman, and where is she today? We need to talk to her. I'm due to speak to her father in Hong Kong at ten a.m. UK time. What do we want to ask?'

'Good point, Sam. The where and what name she is living under, alongside contact information, would be my first thoughts. DC Ford, you've been quiet; any thoughts? Off the wall stuff is just as welcome at these meetings; it is why you're here.'

'Thank you, sir. I agree with your points, but would like to know if she is a natural blonde, why she left the Basle School, and if she is or was married and to whom. Remember the comment from Sharon Beddall about the wedding ring? Hobbies, maybe.' Seeing the look of doubt on DS Jones's face, she went onto explain. 'Well, I know a bit about cars and mechanics because I had to. Cheap cars and no money forces a different attitude. But I know nothing about bombs, tracking devices, or poisons, for example. If she had been, or is, a motor racing fan, or married to one, then maybe that would come more naturally than, say, Charlotte, who has never dirtied her hands in her life, by the sound of it. Similarly, if she had chemical engineering background or military… So, what did she do for fun and what did she do for a living, if anything. That'd be the tenor of my conversation.'

'Good thinking, Susie. You should sit in with me when we get hold of her father at ten. We'll postpone the Scott interview in the light of this news.' LeFanu looked across at Samantha Miles as she said it and gave a thumbs-up.

'Now you, Chris. Anything to add?'

'Well, you guys have covered most of it. I'm assuming that she is Angela in everything I'm about to say. So, I'd like to know where she was living in relation to the prison at the time in January — has to be somewhere accessible, probably by road, if she was there every Thursday, certainly not abroad, anyway. Where was she at Christmas and New Year? Pchelski told us that Beddall had been all over Angela Darling like a rash and then it had all stopped. Why? That does assume that AD and van Outen are one and the same, but as you pointed out, sir, we're running out of associates and I do not fancy the idea of it being a random person, and equally, I don't think that Fiona is a sensible contender, but she may well be in it up to her neck.'

'True. I think you have your agenda. Report back ASAP, Sam. And have another go at Fiona bloody Wallace. And no more lies or half-truths from her. The trouble as always is that the cleverest lies are those that we are already conditioned to believe. Be cynical about all her answers. We want to know more about her murky past. Use her fear of her husband's reaction if necessary, cruel though it might be, but we're dealing with murders etc. etc., OK? One other thing, Sam, perhaps you would contact the US people and find out about personal effects in the hotel in Concord.

No one goes there without luggage. Maybe there'll be a lead? Me, I'm back to talking to Pchelski. He's coming to the top of the pile, if for no other reason than he's nearly the only one left alive. Meet again late afternoon?' Sam nodded and reached for her phone. They all agreed that they should have some answers by then.

***

The call to Jakob van Outen went through smoothly and he was helpful in answering questions. Susie Ford commented afterwards that he didn't sound too surprised that the police were seeking information about his daughter and didn't sound too enamoured about her choice of friends.

She had been married to a Frenchman, Gilles Cap de Ville, a restaurateur with a chain of middle of the road restaurants in tourist locations around the French coast. The marriage hadn't lasted long and had ended in an acrimonious divorce, with Veronica picking up a handsome settlement. He had not liked Gilles, but had a changed opinion when the divorce was finalised. Gilles had said, 'Thank God,' cheap at twice the price. An amazing use of English vernacular language for a Frenchman. Jakob had chuckled when making the point. He knew she was in Europe, but that was all. She mixed with that girl, Charlotte Foubert, or whatever she's called these days, and some others and gave them all sorts of grief. She had stayed with Charlotte in France every year for years, not being bothered to fly out to Bahrein and later Hong Kong. He had finished by commenting that even as a daughter, he would never have been surprised if a call like this one was to say she had been arrested. 'I've bailed her out too many times to believe it won't happen again.' He gave her some details of petty crimes and violence in the half dozen countries whose police forces he had had to placate. She had attended Grenoble University for a while, majoring in theatre studies, but had been suspended after several arrests for theft. Her father scoffed at the very idea of a degree in theatre, but it had the promise of keeping her out of mischief — and even that had failed. A disillusioned father, Susie concluded.

DC Ford, explaining that they were merely trying to trace her, asked her set of questions quite cleverly. Yes, she was a natural blonde. Her divorce settlement and a trust-fund he now regretted setting up when she was a child made her independent; it is, or had been, at HSBC. He'd added;

interests — motor racing, probably, he had commented, because of the macho image at the trackside and fashion; and yes, she had left both Basle and the Oxford schools under a cloud. A miasma of stories and rumours and very little fact, was how he put it. And lastly, closing the conversation because of work commitments, he had said, quite bitterly, according to Susie Ford, that he had no idea where she was living. Last he had heard had been on his birthday in November, when she had sent a text message indicating that she had met a "nice new man" and "you'd like him, Daddy", which inferred, he hoped, that she was single and so was he.

'Phew,' Samantha Miles said. 'We have something to go on, but not enough to track her down immediately. A real dysfunctional family. He said she used to bank with HSBC, and Gilles was a real fan at Le Mans every year without fail and was always seen around the paddock at Spa in Belgium with her and her little group of friends. Cars were a real thing for her. But he had no direct knowledge of the "friends" he mentioned.

***

LeFanu called George Pchelski again and asked, more like told, him to attend again at Ipswich. 'Life is getting more complicated,' he had explained. 'There are things we need to bottom out.' LeFanu wanted to stay at the HQ, awaiting more information from the American Authorities and the British and French Embassies. George had claimed he was busy and wouldn't it wait? LeFanu gave him two options, expressing his annoyance at the same time. 'George, either you turn up here today or I'll send someone to arrest you on the grounds that… well, on any grounds I can think of and you'll end up here in handcuffs. Up to you.'

'OK, OK. I get the message but I hope it's not going over old ground yet again. I'll get a train from London later, this afternoon anyway, and will be in Ipswich by five p.m. or thereabouts. Will that do? And I trust you'll pick up the train fare.' He sounded petulant.

'Yes and no to your second thought. Don't push your luck. Much better response and do not try my patience too far. Call me when you know the ETA of the train and I'll send a car.' He rang off.

***

George arrived punctually and was escorted to LeFanu's tiny office. He had arranged coffee and sandwiches as a courtesy, although it went against the grain. They passed the usual pleasantries — the weather and the trains and so on before LeFanu started in about Charlotte. He was looking for a reaction to the latest news from New Hampshire but first made the mistake of asking an innocuous question in the past tense about her.

'But you are talking in the past tense about her. Why?'

Despite the mistake, he launched quickly into the news. 'She's dead, George. Sorry, but there's no nice way to tell you. She was shot in the street in Concord, New Hampshire, in the USA, alongside a man whom we believe to be her husband, Lord Groombridge.'

LeFanu watched and listened for a reaction. George sounded shocked when he responded. 'But Tony Waller was murdered in his house in Suffolk in January, wasn't he?'

'No, George, that was another man, an American, we believe he was the "friend" of Charlotte that we talked about earlier. A Mr Jerry Gold or Goldstein. Did you know him, or ever heard his name mentioned? He did have an uncanny resemblance to Lord Groombridge. It fooled us for a long time.'

'I've told you all this before. Charlotte did mention a golf or tennis pro, I can't remember which, called Jerry. No, it was golf, now I come to think about it. Presumably that was the guy that Waller had beaten up. Legs broken sort of thing. But Charlotte... What happened?'

'The pair of them were shot dead in the street by what looks like a Mafia or organised crime style killing, possibly because he owed a lot of money from gambling. A gambling chip was placed in his mouth. We understand from the American authorities that that is a signature. Macabre.'

'As you say, macabre. Sorry to ask, but how did he get to the States? They're a real pain in the arse, these days, about Homeland Security. I have to have an ESTA and still they want my fingerprints — all ten of them — when I go to the US of bloody A.' George sighed theatrically, and watching LeFanu's face, added, 'That's beside the point, I guess you are about to say. Anyway, I suppose it was money talking, as usual. She would have inherited quite a bit from that lousy bastard, I guess... No, wait a minute... If he wasn't dead...'

'No, George, we have been a mite suspicious for a long time, so we froze the insurance payouts for life assurance and the thefts. They're still on ice. Your ex-employers have been very helpful. It seems that Lord Groombridge, whilst influential, was not a popular colleague. Back to the cars. Tell me about your clients, please.'

'No can do, Chief Inspector. And it's not the blasted Data Protection Act, believe me. These guys are seriously rich and don't take kindly for their names to be released. It would be the end of my working for any of them, even if they would talk to you. You have to understand that, here in Europe and more so in the USA, serious collectors of very valuable cars, more often than not, keep them very, very private. One guy I know has a huge underground facility, aircon, security, the works. He just wants to look at them. Occasionally he sells one or two and similarly buys one or two. That Porsche, that you keep on about, could be worth upwards of two hundred thousand pounds depending on its age, condition, provenance and so on; the Bugatti — well, one sold a year or so back for around five million.'

'O-kay!' He deliberately made the word into two long syllables as he assembled his thoughts. 'So, no replicas or fakes?' George looked up from his chipped coffee mug, scornfully. 'Fine, we'll come back to that. And if you want to work again outside a prison workshop, you will at least try to co-operate. Now, you're the expert. How would someone dispose of two very valuable cars and where?'

'Probably export them. You would have to have an export licence from DVLA if doing it legitimately, but nowadays there's thousands of containers leaving the UK for all points on the globe. I don't know, but would guess it would be easy to get a part load of cars covered, or hidden, by anything — farm machinery or whatever. In that kind of game, money would talk. Japan is a rising market for that sort of thing and they drive on the same side as we do!'

'Learn any of that in prison, George?' It was a startling reminder for George of the role he was playing in the discussion. George gulped, he got the message.

'Look, Mr LeFanu. This sounds like guilty until proven innocent. I haven't got these cars and I don't know where they are. I can make some enquiries for you, but that's about all. I was in France at the time, as I've told you. I don't have the wherewithal to set up elaborate crimes, let alone murders; nor the inclination. That much I did learn inside.'

'Right. Answer me straight. Could she have orchestrated the thefts and the murder?'

'She? Oh, Charlotte. Not without a great deal of help. She always claimed to me, and if I remember rightly, told you, that cars were to get from A to B, with hotel car-jockeys opening doors and doing boring parking and cleaning jobs. I can't believe that she would know what we're talking about with value, disposal, damage and so on. My guess is that you need to look for an expert with motive — i.e. money and the means of disposal internationally. Sounds just like Tony Waller to me, now you tell me he was alive at the time. Or maybe, from what I hear, that useless piece of shit, aka Guy Scott. Anyway, well, who killed this other chap?'

'Why so? Groombridge/Waller, I mean.'

'Sounds like he needed the money. Charlie always talked of his gambling, but you probably know that. Don't know myself about gambling but I guess most of them eventually lose. He bought my cars cheap, certainly dirt cheap, and maybe needed to sell them at top dollar and make an insurance claim. Look into that phoney auction house of his. Talk to Beech Underwriting again; talk to Sir Charles Beech, even though he's retired, he is straight. Funny that, coming from me, I suppose. Bit elaborate killing another guy, though. Lord Brockett got caught with a fraudulent insurance claim by destroying a first class Ferrari, nearly got away with it had it not been the vigilance of an insurance claims guy somewhere or other.'

'It's possible that he was the murderer, George, but equally possible that it was someone else. It could also be that all of the incidents were the plan of a third party — someone like you, perhaps... '

'I know you are clever, Mr Chief Detective, but that's a quantum leap. I could take offence but...'

'OK. Did Terry Beddall know Charlotte?'

'Don't think so. He saw her at the prison that time, that I do know, but he never asked for her number or surname or anything. Well, not from me, anyway. It was just a bloke's thing. You know, beautiful girl, legs up to her armpits and so on. Why do you ask?'

'She did meet up with him, George, and without putting a finer point on it, they did the obvious. So how did she meet him or vice versa?'

'So why are you asking me if they knew each other? Another of your fancy traps, I suppose?'

LeFanu ignored the gibe. 'Bear with me. Charlotte's gang — was she the leader or the follower? Any ideas? We need to trace them — names, locations, descriptions, photos?'

'Follower, I think, but an active participant in anything high-profile but risk free. Loves the limelight, bit narcissistic. I've no knowledge about the gang, as she called it, couple of upper class forenames but I can't remember any of them — it was years ago. She disappeared off regularly to see the gang, as she put it. Could be true, or knowing her now, could be an excuse for almost anything. At one time, I thought she was having it off with someone else. Every Christmas, she went back to France. That much I do know. Many the Christmases I had to share with my sister's family. And she, Charlotte, I mean, always talked of parties and so on. But if they were a school gang, surely someone there would have an inkling. I can't help at all.'

'OK. I hear what you say. She is, or was, a brunette. Did you ever see her in a blonde wig or with dyed hair blonde?'

'No, always brunette — slight hint of auburn, but that's it. And,' he looked at LeFanu with a smile, 'I can vouch that she was naturally a brunette.' LeFanu shook his head at the levity. George continued, 'Oh, I get it, it's the Angela character you're trying to trace. We're into disguises now? Wigs and things? Can't help you there.'

'Just so. On another subject, George, tell me about Porsche 356.'

George looked startled, even though he had expected the subject to come up. 'I sourced some parts for an original 356 for a client. It is to be restored here in England, serious gearbox issues. Ironic, isn't it, that we can rebuild them better than the Germans…'

'Diversion, George, diversion.'

'Yeah, right. The owner is a Swiss. The guy I mentioned before with the underground facility. Nothing is allowed in there unless it's perfect. He takes one out for a spin every now and then, showing off, I guess; they all do. And there's dozens of exotic things, I've seen it once — one of the privileged few. I wouldn't mind betting that some of the collectors have cars that are not entirely kosher. I saw a programme about art theft years ago, and the proportion of stuff that was bought on the black market was huge, so why not expensive cars? If the Nazis could steal art and artefacts then you can bet on it that a few pre-war Mercs and BMWs, even Bugattis, disappeared into private collections too. But really, these sort of people don't do fakes or replicas. If they can't find the real thing, they move on.'

'No history lessons, thank you. Does open a question about Lord Groombridge's fake Bugatti…'

'He's in a different league. More of a buying and selling to anyone and making a few, sorry, lot of bucks.'

LeFanu nodded, parking the information. 'Now, Porsches. Let's concentrate on them.'

George accepted the comment with a shrug. 'There's a few of them about, mainly in the US, and worth a pretty penny if they have provenance and particularly if previous owners are A-list celebs. So, who were the owners before Waller?'

Philippe ignored the question, tempted to use the usual answer of "I ask the questions here", but made a note, nevertheless. 'Could the Bugatti that was torched be owned by the same man, George?'

'He had a good few priceless cars when I was there, but that was before I went into prison. I used to dabble even then. But then there are probably more Bugattis in that neck of the woods than anywhere. They were made up the road from Basle, so as to speak. I told you, I think, there's the biggest collection in the world at Mulhouse. Might have been him, but equally one of a hundred others if you look at Switzerland, Germany, France, Italy. There's a lot of money around. Can't help you with specifics.'

Philippe LeFanu could see that the conversation was going around in circles and he was not learning much of use, so he changed his tactics. 'Right. I'll be open with you. Schoolgirl of fifteen raped and made pregnant by a Swiss "rich businessman". His car, a Bugatti, is torched by the friends of the unfortunate girl as some sort of retribution. Nasty abortion for her, we understand. We believe there may be a connection to the events we are investigating. Now, any comments?'

'Ah-ha! Yuk! You think that Charlotte and the dreaded gang at school in Switzerland, which is news to me, pissed off the Swiss guy and he might be taking his revenge. Right, who sold him the Bugatti? If it were the Duxford Auction people, and they're quite big in the market alongside Coys and Sotheby's, then you would have a connection. And a direct link to Charlotte and Waller. And a motive for topping the bastard, although he wasn't topped, was he? Not in the UK, anyway. Christ, I could be a detective.' He smiled and leaned back in his chair, reaching for the now luke-warm cup of strong black coffee.

'For sure, George, just as soon as I have established that your character is clean as a whistle.' They both laughed.

'So using your storyline, George, someone topped who they thought was Waller and it turned out to be Jerry Gold. Simple? Not! Why was an American friend of Charlotte in Suffolk, on his own, apparently, and in Waller's Jacuzzi? Someone enticed him there. So I don't think it was your Swiss man…'

'My Swiss man? No, I've never said that it could be him, just anyone with a grudge.' He put stress on the word "my". 'He's filthy rich, pillar of the community sort of thing.'

'How did you meet this celebrity Swiss? Not the sort of person you start chatting with in a coffee shop.'

'I was introduced to him at a function. Come to think of it, it was Charlotte or one of her cronies. I gave him a bit of advice and we met after that… Maybe seven years or so ago. Lost touch for obvious reasons, but picked up again after last March when I was released.'

'Uh huh. We've traced a private charter plane that flew in and out from Meucon aerodrome on the 15th January. Our friends in the gendarmerie have been particularly vigilant since the car bomb, looking for unusual patterns of activity. Checking the small provincial and private airports like Pleurtuit and Meucon. The plane flew in from an airfield near the Swiss border at Mulhouse. Funny how that place has come up twice in the last few minutes. And the pilot confirms that his passenger arrived with a brief case and left without it. The passenger's name was a Felix Andervert. The Swiss authorities are interviewing him. How does that grab you? If we, or they, make a connection to you, you're in it up to your armpits, George. Better to tell me all, now.'

'Shit! Look, he is, was I suppose now, a client and I was seeking parts for his bloody Porsche, but it is one I've had on my books for months, nothing new. Difficult part in the synchromesh box. I've done a few jobs for him — sourcing parts I mean here, in the USA, all sorts over the last nine months or so. There were only seventeen thousand or so of the Porsche 356C made in the 1960s, so it is bloody difficult and his was one of the last, maybe the last, off the production line in 1965, making it doubly hard. They were always making small changes, especially when a new model was in the offing. He's straight, or has always been with me, and pays his bills good as gold. What he was doing getting off a plane in Brittany is his business. Maybe buying a car? And as far as Meucon is concerned, a small place about thirty miles from me. Of course I know of it. I know it but only because of a restaurant in the forest nearby — Auberge du Petit Berger. Nice one too.'

'So be it, George. The pilot says two guys in a Ford Focus picked him up and brought him back to the plane a couple of hours later. Were you one of those "guys"?'

'Mine's an old Clio, Sir. Sounds more like Terry and one of his mates, if you ask me.'

'What mates, George? First I've heard of them.'

'I don't know, sir. I just know he couldn't have done that job without assistance. I don't own a Ford. I've got this beat up Renault in France, that's only a spit from the scrap heap. Fortunately, there isn't an annual MOT like there is here or I'd be looking for a replacement. Local shopping and that's it.'

'George, I know you are up to something that's not legal. I don't know what, but I'm not a fool. I can't prove anything yet, but I have the memory of an elephant. One step out of line and I'll have you. Just remember that. At the moment, I have bigger fish to fry. I realise that's a lot of mixed metaphors but you get the drift?'

'Yes. But I think you're being very unfair. I've told you all I know. I abhor violence and would never knowingly have anything to do with it. Go speak to that Scott character and play hard ball with him instead. That would be my advice. Now, I trust you'll get someone to take me to the railway station. You know how to get hold of me but I've got a small business to run and sitting here chewing the cud with you doesn't pay my bills. I'm selling up in the UK and moving to France permanently.'

'I have no doubts that we will speak soon. Stay in the UK, George. For the time being at least. Voluntarily or remember, I'll put a block on your passport.' He called a car to return Pchelski to the railway station.

A transcript of the conversation was passed to the teams of detectives, as had now become the norm.

The first response came from DC Ford. 'Felix? Sir, That is twice in a few hours that the name Felix has come up, and there aren't many people called Felix around. It's a nice boys' name and…' Getting an impatient clucking sound through the phone, she came back to her point. 'Fiona may have been the victim of the underage pregnancy, we're not sure, but she has an eight-year-old boy called Felix. I checked the births, deaths and marriages register for accurate information and her marriage was a full two years after the boy's birth, to a Mr Wallace. Child's father's name is Smith — or so the certificate says — and born in France, Belfort, wherever that is. That doesn't prove anything and Mrs Wallace's parents are dead. We will confront her, as I'm now more than half convinced that she's lying. It starts to make a potential connection, sir.'

LeFanu simply commented that a coincidence, suspicious as it may seem, is not fact, telling her to re-interview Mrs Wallace at the first opportunity.

***

Philippe LeFanu stopped by the small office space of DS Jones and DI Miles to ask something that had been bugging him. He squatted on the side of a desk and paused, mustering his thoughts. He had the sort of mind that retained small pieces of information and sub-consciously made connections.

'OK, the both of you, cast your minds back to the interview with that Scott fellow. He said something about the Porsche car that they sold to Groombridge. Try to recall it, to save me going through pages and pages of notes.'

Jones scratched his head, thought for a moment, and told the DCI that it was a dispute with some Swiss guy about its provenance. They, the auction house, had reckoned it was the last one off the production line and this buyer disputed it but made a bid, post auction, and it was turned down, and it looks like it was subsequently flogged to Tony Groombridge for a pittance. 'Apparently, allegedly I should say, this bloke got pretty angry.'

DI Miles agreed with the summary, but added that Scott had said that this had been the reason to remove the car from the auction, which, he had said, was commonplace in auctions. LeFanu scratched his earlobe.

'Funny thing is this is the second time I've heard about a Porsche that is the last one made. Pchelski told me of a Swiss who allegedly, your word, Chris, has the last one for which he, Pchelski, is sourcing some specialist parts. Maybe, just maybe, that's where the stolen one has gone. A Mr Felix Andervert is George Pchelski's client with the Porsche that is being rebuilt. Coincidence or what? Could be a motive too. Needs checking out.'

***

Sergeant Shaw leaned on the doorpost of LeFanu's small office, already occupied by the team of Miles, Jones and the DCI. 'Latest info from the USA, sir. She, the victim, Lady C as they're calling her, had flown in from London Heathrow under the Bertin name. She still had the airline ticket stuff in her Gucci handbag. He had a sheet of computer print-out for a hotel booking in Reno, wherever that is, in the name of Gold. The Yank police say that Gold's mother has stated that the dead man is not her son. They've done DNA testing — the mitochondrial check they use from the maternal side. Negative. She knew he wasn't her son from the photographs — should have had a small birthmark on the inside of his left arm, above the elbow, apparently. But then they have to double check. I checked with Dr Renata and she didn't make a note of any birthmark, but she says it rings a vague bell. She re-read her file and nothing new on that score, apart from American dental work, but she had been informed that the man, Groombridge, spent a lot of time in the USA, so nothing to remark upon. She did find reference to female pubic hairs in the filter analysis of the Jacuzzi, but as female visitors were apparently frequent and everything had been sewn up and the body released for cremation, that information was discarded.' Shaw stood waiting for an acknowledgement before continuing. He knew he had their undivided attention. 'Oh, and the US police have confirmed that a search of the hotel room in Concord has been done. Luggage? Designer label stuff with initials CG — and a lot of it. Large amounts of bundled cash — close to a hundred thousand in dollars alone. They'll send us a full inventory including two wigs — brunette. Maybe we've found our mysterious blonde? Sir, ma'am?'

'Deliver the information, Sergeant. No need for your theatricals. And check out this Reno issue. I seem to remember that it was a place for quicky divorces or marriages — most of which only seemed to last five minutes.'

'Sorry, sir. Just nice to be ahead of the game for a while. That's all.' He could see that LeFanu was at boiling point, so continued without waiting for another admonishment. 'And after the fuss we made earlier, they made a quantum leap and got Groombridge's son Richard out from New York to check, by helicopter to the morgue at Concord, would you believe. Yup, it's Groombridge all right. It's him definitely. He was wearing a gold chain with a cross, which made them think about the identity not being a white

Jewish-origin male, per the passport, more likely a WASP.'

DI Miles and Detective Sergeant Jones looked up, simultaneously. 'A what? WASP?'

'WASP, ma'am, Sergeant. It stands for White Anglo-Saxon Protestant. I only found that out by asking the American police guy. Sorry.' And looking directly at the DCI, he continued, 'And your name is mud, sir. I paraphrase what the US police lieutenant said, if you get my meaning, and the son thinks you are a heap of... well, you can guess. Apparently he got all emotional about his father and the trauma of the funeral in the UK.'

LeFanu took it in his stride. There were times, plenty of them, to be caustic with Shaw, but there were more important things to do, now. 'The son, eh? Quite unlike the image he portrayed before to us at the funeral and anyone who would listen. More likely he would be embarrassed about having to admit to all and sundry, and the media here and in the US, that it was an almighty cock-up. And his father was still alive and kicking. And now to go through the whole process again. I can see the Sun newspaper headline, already paraphrasing the James Bond movie title. You'll like this, Chris, "You only die twice". I need to talk to the ACC. This is going to get messy and soon.'

'Before that sir, ma'am... The important news is that the son says it's not the "bitch" Charlotte. His words, sir. Now that could make life complicated.' Shaw's smirk continued.

Samantha looked up at the remark, 'Holy... no matter. Well, my money's on it being Veronica... And I suppose it is not really a surprise.' She smiled.

'Well, Samantha, there aren't many other contenders that we know about.' To a chorus of 'me too', Philippe LeFanu added, 'All we know is who it isn't! Whoever it is, and doubtless we'll find out soon, where is bloody Lady C? Now, any clues as to the killer's identity?' He stared at Shaw and demonstrated by his look that the cockiness from Shaw was unacceptable.

Shaw saw that he had over-stepped the mark and changed his tone. 'No, sir. They were 19mm parabellum rounds, probably from a Glock. Normal stuff with organised crime killings like this. The gambling chip is universal and untraceable. They're assuming that it is a contract killing, maybe organised by the Mafia. That's all we have.' LeFanu nodded and returned to his desk. As Shaw moved to leave the tiny space, LeFanu again issued the warning that this information was not for the media, and for Sergeant Shaw to demonstrate his rank by telling all the team the same message.

***

DCI LeFanu bought himself a little time by arranging an appointment to see his boss. That time he spent going over old ground. Moore was aware of the possibility of a mis-identification, but he had no doubt that there would be a blame culture spreading. ACC Moore was livid when he received the news, requesting urgent clarification of the identification of the woman's body before addressing the issue of the mistake with the chief constable, and indeed, the newly appointed crime commissioner.

'Heads will roll on this one', he said, a little ruefully, LeFanu reflected. 'She, Lady Charlotte, identified the body from the Jacuzzi? The pathologist has a document to that effect alongside the report of the autopsy? All procedures followed to the letter?' After these questions, more rhetorical than genuine questions, DCI LeFanu decided that answers were not really being sought. He had analysed with Miles, Jones and Dr Renata Howe that everything had been executed in the correct fashion. LeFanu could see, let alone hear, that there was a state of mild panic in ACC Moore. 'Who actually gave permission for the early release of the body? That's where the blame will lie. That's where the media will focus. We need to decide whether to let the media find out or whether to admit that there has been a mistake, albeit not of our making. I think we'll let the chief constable decide.' LeFanu struggled to stop his reaction showing. The royal "we", he noticed, was only used when scapegoats were sought.

LeFanu could only answer, 'Indeed, sir,' smiling inwardly at the way his boss started to use the "we" and "us" and "our" words. Time will tell, he thought. Meanwhile, he had a certain Lady C to trace and a definite ID on a female body in the American morgue to establish. Let the future sort itself out.

Chapter 57

They called Mrs Wallace to arrange a further interview and suggested that it would be best for her son to be looked after off-site, again. DI Miles took the opportunity to travel directly from her home and met Susie Ford at a motorway service area on the A23 south of Crawley, West Sussex, to compare notes and strategy for what might be a difficult meeting. They decided to start the meeting by asking Fiona why she had lied at the last meeting.

Fiona had reacted quickly and burst into tears, stating that she knew the past would catch up with her. She spilled her coffee mug as she shook with emotion. Yes, she had said, she was the girl who was pregnant, and she was fifteen years of age — underage here, and in Switzerland, but not so in France. A couple of months after she had conceived, she was taken by her parents to Belfort in France to a nursing home, because it is not a crime, the underage thing, there and Felix, the father, she meant, had promised to support her and the child. She had her parent's consent to keep the baby. The school was told she had had an abortion and would not be returning to their school.

'You must understand that I didn't want to lie but he, my child, needs the stability of a family and I couldn't afford to have it made public.'

Susie Ford, who was still angry about the lying, particularly on her first detective investigation, commented, bitterly, 'Lying to the police, Mrs Wallace, is a criminal offence.' She let that sink in before adding, 'Are you sure it is not your nice comfy existence you are trying to protect?'

Fiona again burst into tears. 'She threatened me if I didn't help. She was going to make it public to my husband.' DI Miles took over the questioning as a little sympathy seemed most likely to get the truth.

'She? Who is "she"?'

'Ronnie. Veronica. And Charlie, Charlotte.'

'We'll come back to that! So Felix Andervert is the father of your son, Felix? His birth certificate says John Smith — not really very original, is it?'

'Yes, yes. That was one of the conditions from him, agreed with my parents, as I was underage and he could be prosecuted. He would pay and would continue to do so in a trust fund if his name was kept out of it. Please don't let that information out, as it will spoil my son's future. More than that, I really don't know. I don't know, honestly.' She was racked with uncontrollable tears.

'OK, OK. That makes sense, Mrs Wallace. Now, who threatened you and when?'

She wiped her eyes with a screwed up tissue. 'Charlotte, when she was here a little while ago — when she came to get her things. She said things were getting a little hot so I mustn't say anything about the past — like the car thing and the baby or it would blow my marriage out of the water. Then the day before yesterday, I got a call from Veronica on her mobile saying more or less the same thing, but adding that Felix would be very upset if I broke the promise to keep his name out of it and the trust fund for little Felix would be null and void, and we need that money. What was I supposed to do? Both my parents died, nearly three years ago in a coach accident in Corfu, so I had no one else to turn to.'

'I understand, Mrs Wallace, Fiona; take us through everything you know. You did tell us before that Charlotte was your only friend in that group. Strange for a good friend to threaten you, don't you think?' She paused, letting it sink in. 'It does sound like an idle threat to me, but to you, obviously, it is very real. Tell us the whole truth and nothing but the truth.' The sympathy from Miles helped as she wiped her eyes again, murmuring her agreement.

'Veronica can be a real bitch. She was the one who set things up with Felix. I think she had an affair with him before. Before I knew it, I was pregnant. Veronica even got me a pregnancy testing kit from the pharmacy in Basle to confirm it. She tried to get me to have an abortion, saying that Felix would pay and it'd be discreet, but I had a little bit of sense to talk to my mother about it. You know just talking to your mother can enable her to spot that something's wrong and then it all came out.' Sam Miles kept up the soothing by sitting next to Fiona and putting her arm around her shoulders.

'Tell us more, please. What about this car set on fire?' She looked at Susie and motioned about a cup of tea being sensible.

'Veronica was connected through a Guy Scott. Maybe you know him?'

Miles nodded. 'She had been having an affair with him, on and off, since she was eighteen or so, after she first came to the UK. Whilst the bastard was still married — surprise, surprise. I think Tony Waller had introduced them at some function or other. She and Charlie used to go to these events as eye-candy sort of thing and to see if they could "score". There was another girl there, older by a year or two, called, now let me think, Sarah or Sally. She used to be at the school and rather fancied herself as a man-magnet, I think it is called these days. I'm sure I've told you all this before. Anyway, she may have been part of it. I really don't know. But she was often around. I was a bit too young for all that. Anyway, sometime later, after the relationship had developed, Guy Scott gave Ronnie information about people he had as clients or wanted as clients and Felix was one of them. She'd seduce them or arrange private orgies, I suppose you'd call them, with Charlie and some of the others, often the young ones, as I was, and then blackmail them. You know, photographs and video footage.' Sam raised her eyebrows, almost in disbelief. She continued in between sobs, 'Then Mr Scott would put together deals to buy their cars or sell them others using a bit of pressure, and that's all I know. When Felix became a bit funny about the pregnancy because Veronica decided a bit of blackmail on the side wouldn't go amiss, or maybe it was Guy who arranged it... Oh, I don't know. We, or rather Veronica, set fire to this precious car whilst we watched, as revenge for him refusing to agree to the threats. And I was only fifteen. It is scary. He, Mr Scott, had hands everywhere and it was fun to start with. Well, different than the spotty boys we knew. Exciting to start with but...' She looked genuinely sad as she repeated herself.

    Miles tried to get the conversation back to reality. 'Mrs Wallace, where is Veronica now? Fiona, we need to talk to her — and quickly.' A welcome interlude when Susie brought in the tea tray. 'And some sad news, Mrs Wallace. We believe, or rather we have been told by the US authorities, that Charlotte is dead. Shot in the USA by some bad guys, organized crime, alongside her husband.' They decided not to tell of their suspicion that it was not Charlotte. 'That's why we need to talk to Veronica quickly. It seems a lot of people connected with this investigation are at risk, and that could include you. It is important that you tell your husband everything to remove any other threats. And then we can ensure your collective safety.'

    'OMG! Dead? No, no, it can't be true. She's...' She started sobbing uncontrollably, again.

'She's what, Mrs Wallace?'

'Well she's been staying with me, us I mean, for a couple of days now. This morning, when she knew you were coming, she dived off somewhere. Her stuff's upstairs, right now. How could she have got to America? She can't be dead, simply can't be.' She looked at both detectives for some acknowledgement.

'I did say "believe", Fiona. It is what the Americans have told us. We have had some doubts and really think it could be someone else but she, the victim, had Charlotte's papers. So until we know otherwise, we have to make some assumptions. What you have said is valuable information, thank you.' Samantha Miles explained more or less what they knew, and to keep up the pressure, did not mince her words.

'I can't believe it. Am I in danger, and little Felix? OMG!' She shook her head in disbelief, and looking at DI Miles, realised it was the truth. 'Veronica, well she's with Guy Scott, or was when she phoned, or that's what she said. I don't know what to believe now. In Cambridge area, Newmarket, I think, or somewhere up that way. He's the reason two of her marriages failed — or at least one of many reasons.' She gave a wan smile and then raised a finger as an idea occurred to her, reaching for her mobile. 'Here's her number.' She flicked through the screens. Susie Ford reached for the phone and copied down the number and then started looking through the recent contacts and SMS messages.

'OK, Fiona. Drink your tea whilst I make a couple of calls. And the moment you see Charlotte again, you call DC Ford, here. No more shilly-shallying around, or you could well find yourself and your family in serious danger.' DI Miles winked at Susie Ford and went to her car to call the DCI.

'Charlotte is, or was, at Fiona's house. Stupid cow. Meanwhile, try this phone number, sir. It could well be still in service and you might get an American policeman answer if our ideas are on the ball.' She had related the amazing results of the conversations with Fiona Wallace, which introduced another angle and another possible motive or set of motives and people of interest.

LeFanu agreed and asked for Sergeant Shaw to set up a formal interview with full recording with Scott at HQ, and for contact with the Swiss police to be established. 'This Porsche business leads us straight to this Andervert fellow.' Miles agreed and added that she had constructed a new take on a Venn diagram which showed where all the people and places intersected and that it was, maybe, interesting that Groombridge held directorships in Switzerland. LeFanu requested that Dodd or Ford looked for any links in the names.

Miles returned to the house to be greeted with a more sanguine Fiona Wallace. Susie Ford had established that Charlotte had come from London by train to Three Bridges, the nearest station to Fiona's home, and called ahead to be picked up. Charlie had sounded scared, she admitted, but she had not connected the "dots", assuming it was the two unwelcome visitors that Charlotte had described that had created the fear. So, she had said, a bit of sympathy, despite all that had gone on before, had seemed in order. DC Ford had looked in on the room upstairs and there were clearly suitcases missing and a tumble of other things on every horizontal surface; the duvet still showing an indentation of what could have been a heavy suitcase. A hasty retreat, Susie had mused. She took a minute to pass on this information to her boss, DI Miles.

'There will be a discreet guard on this house, Mrs Wallace. It would be better for you to explain to your husband before he asks the obvious questions of you. You will not leave this area without telling us, DC Ford specifically, and you will notify us or the policeman outside immediately if Charlotte contacts you. Do you understand?' Fiona looked straight at DI Miles and nodded, looking seriously worried.

***

LeFanu called the number that Samantha had given him. It had been answered in the Police HQ in Concord, New Hampshire, by a detective second grade, Harry Grammar. He had explained the reason for the call. DCI Philippe LeFanu had to explain who he was and why he was calling; their version of the Data Protection Act no doubt, he mused whilst Detective Grammar was checking his credentials. It seemed that, whilst not definite, the phone of the female victim was this one.

LeFanu related the outcome to Sergeant Shaw, 'It had rung in his office, can you believe? Now, she could have lost it or lent it to Charlotte. But on balance, I think we know it was Veronica whatever her surname is. We have to suspect the identity papers and must try to help the American police so, as we have the school photograph from the real Angela Darling, get a copy to the American authorities — I've written down Detective second grade, whatever that means, Grammar's contact details — and identify Veronica as a likely ID, alongside the biography we have to date — names, addresses, next of kin etc. If it is her, then they'll need to contact the father, amongst others. Oh, send a copy of Charlotte's fingerprints; that might convince them. Then let's get some thoughts — all the team — as to the likely whereabouts of Charlotte. Who is she with; who could be sheltering her? We have George Pchelski, in France, or will be shortly, with my agreement before you ask. Fiona Wallace in Sussex, although that is an unlikely location now, and the family home in Montargis. Anywhere or anyone else?'

Jones, who had joined his boss, interrupted, 'If the person killed in the USA had two of Charlotte's passports, and we still have one here, then she, Charlotte, that is, could well be, or should be, still in the UK, unless she is using someone else's documents. Maybe they just swapped passports. And detective second grade is a senior role thing, according to the Michael Connelly books I've read.' LeFanu nodded.

'Agreed. Although, with this lot, nothing would surprise me. The bad news is that Lady C could already be a victim, or certainly could be in the future. You, Sergeant Shaw, call Fiona Wallace and make sure she tells us if any contact is made. Reinforce the message given to her. It won't do any harm to keep her on her toes and nervous. And make sure we've a reliable uniformed copper on duty outside her home, and not that blithering idiot from Chelsea, and maybe a drive-by regular check for the next forty-eight hours, reviewable. I'll call George Pchelski on the same basis. And we need another "chat" with Mr Guy Scott now. This time, formal and here. Sort it out with Sergeant Shaw between you. He can send a car to get him — no excuses. Get him at his house. He lives near Foxton, not a million miles from his business. That'll shake him a mite. Mr Shaw, wait inside the guy's house and look around for any identifiers of this woman, photographs or whatever, quietly. Anything else?'

Samantha Miles nodded. 'Had I better call the father?'

'No, not yet. With Groombridge's alleged habit of womanising, this victim could be any one of dozens. We need more information. In a way, we do not care who the female victim is. We have to focus on Charlotte right now. If it works out that it is someone else who is of interest to us, then it may close other loopholes. Let the Americans do the analysis. I don't want to start telling anyone else of our guesswork until we have some tangible evidence.'

Chapter 58

When the notes were passed to the team, it was only five minutes later when DC Dodd approached LeFanu with an idea. 'Excuse me, sir. What if Scott was blackmailing the gang of girls too? We've said all along that the experts on classic cars are few and far between — and he's one of them.'

'Interesting thought. If the man is as devious as we think, then it could be possible. Certainly this Fiona woman has been the subject of a bit of blackmail, so why not... Tell DI Miles and DS Jones, please. And well done.'

***

Guy Scott was brought into the tired, tatty interview room by Sergeant Shaw and introduced formally as, 'Here is Mr Scott, ma'am, as ordered.' It was a deliberate ploy to show the roles that were to be played out. He'd regained his composure from the last meeting and seemed to have shelved some of his shiny car salesman habits.

Miles offered coffee in a plastic beaker, and whilst pouring it, asked after the receptionist and Scott asked why she wanted to know about her. Miles said she had seemed genuinely upset by Scott's attitude. And he replied, 'Melanie — oh yes, the girl on reception, little slut. She's gone. I gave her a week's money and out the door. She's a bit uppity, I found, and when I offered her a dinner and a nice evening out on the town with me to apologise for the other day, she burst into tears and called me a fucking middle-aged Casanova... Excuse the language, I ask you. She had to go.'

DI Miles smiled a genuine knowing smile, confident that Melanie had taken her advice, word for word, and then some. She introduced DC Ford, who sat beside her, facing Scott. Again, it was deliberate, to put a young pretty face in front of him.

Susie Ford, as part of a practised routine, started, 'Could you explain about Ronnie...' She paused, patiently, having learned from the DCI that silence often prompted comments, as no one liked deafening silence.

'What about her? She's a friend. Known her for five years or thereabouts. In fact, to be honest, she's a bit more than a friend, in the personal sense. I'm a single man, paying off two ex-wives, I have to admit, but I still have those natural urges, Ms Ford. I'm sure you'll understand.' He leered at Susie, giving her the "once over".

She ignored the obvious. 'Aka Veronica, we understand.'

'Yes, sometimes.'

'Veronica Cap de Ville, to give her current married name, sometimes, for effect we think, Veronique and Veronica van Outen as her maiden name?'

'Yes, yes. So what?'

'You told my colleagues at the meeting in your offices that you couldn't recall her. Yet you are, or have been, living together for some time.'

'Did I? Did I say that? Probably my mind was on other things. You were giving me a hard time, I recall. I never call her anything but Ronnie, never have. I live on my own these days, and OK, Ronnie is my girlfriend. She comes and goes as she pleases and has a key. That's no crime.' He squirmed in his seat.

'We believe you knew her many years before that, alongside Charlotte Foubert, as she then was, and Fiona Rampling.'

Over a series of questions, Scott was obviously feeling the heat and becoming more nervous. DC Ford was handling the situation well, with deliberate distractions of crossing her legs in her above-the-knee skirt and licking her cherry red lips.

'We have to tell you that we have been notified, yesterday, by the American Homeland people that two people have been shot dead in the street and one is Lord Groombridge...' she paused.

'What? Oh shit! Already dead. You told me. How can that be? Who did it? It must be a mistake. Who the fuck died in that bloody Jacuzzi, then?' He was obviously shaken by the news, not sure whether to believe it or not.

DI Miles took the cue. 'No mistake, Mr Scott. Perhaps you now understand the seriousness of our investigations and will stop telling us misleading lies. We know, for example, that you withdrew some eight hundred thousand pounds from various accounts both here and abroad in December 2014. Our forensic accountants are very, very good and very, very thorough. Why?'

'I meant to tell you last time, DI Miles, but it slipped my mind when you were quizzing me.' He smiled as he faced her. His recovery from the shocking news was seemingly complete. 'I have to admit that I agreed to buy Tony's share of the business for eight hundred thousand on the 4th January. That's what was taking the time and there is, was, still more paperwork to do, especially as there is now probate to consider. Well, we thought there was and now, I suppose, that is now irrelevant. I still can't believe it. A right bloody mess. The change of ownership is, before your gannets tell you, yet to be recorded at Companies House. Sorry but events overtook us…'

'Cash deal or…'

'Indeed, cash. US dollar equivalent, actually, from a bank account of mine, eventually, in New Hampshire, after a load of amortisations of other accounts — sounds like your people already did the tracking. And then it was to be transferred to an account of his — it was agreed before Christmas. That was the deal. We have always spent a lot of time and done a lot of business in the US, so my share has been accruing over there for years. I suppose the wonderful Charlotte will now be arguing the toss about her entitlement to pick up the cash. But she ain't having it and that's final.'

'Why did he want to sell?'

'He wanted to get involved in a new business venture in the States — a secret, he had said.' It was as if Scott was relaxing, knowing now that nothing he said could be contradicted by Tony Waller.

'No doubt you will inform the IRS and our HMRC.'

Philippe LeFanu, sitting in the room behind the one-way mirror, smiled and said into the microphone connected to Samantha Miles, 'We've already informed them. Now tell him about the search warrant for his house.'

DI Miles nodded. 'Sir, I have to inform you that we have executed a search warrant for your house here in the UK, which is being entered as we speak, as are your business premises, and your other property in the USA will, simultaneously, be searched by the Homeland Security people.'

Scott was stunned. 'Er… Fine, I've nothing to hide. Hope they leave things tidy. I do like to keep things organised. Bit like Tony, verging on the OCD.'

DCI LeFanu sent another message through the microphone to DI Miles' earpiece, telling her to mention that they knew that the articles of association of the company mean that he automatically inherits Waller's share if he dies (and vice versa), so he has a motive… The money has not been wired to the US account.

Scott was confused by the questioning. He admitted holding back the payment when he had been told of the death of Waller/Groombridge at Porten House. He explained that the company was struggling a little in the light of the financial crisis, so he had not transferred the money before Christmas as had been agreed, assuring the detective inspector that it had been agreed with Tony Groombridge around New Year.

'By phone, Mr Scott?'

'Of course. How else? He was in Courchevel; I was here.'

'We have yet to recover his phone, Mr Scott. Please leave your phone here so we may identify those calls.'

'Oh! Well, it may have been another mobile. I'll have to think.'

'I'm sure our search teams will find it, Mr Scott — either at your home near Foxton, or place of business. The warrant, as I said, covers both premises. So you're now the exclusive owner of the business and you have some eight hundred thousand pounds floating around which will have to return to the business.'

'Yes, yes, but give me time; this is all so sudden.' He was sweating profusely despite the chill of winter that pervaded the old building.

'Interview paused.' DI Miles reached across and switched off the recording device.

***

The search team had been asked specifically to gather anything that might bear Veronica's fingerprints or hair samples, such as a brush, alongside any photographs, documents and incriminating evidence. Shaw had noticed an expensive handbag on a side table and drawn the search team's attention to it. One area LeFanu hadn't understood was that if it were Veronica using Charlotte's passport, how did the fingerprint check operate? Homeland Security had said that if there had been no entry on that passport to the USA in the last five years, then they took a set and that became the comparator for the future. They needed something that was definitively Veronica's for a comparison.

***

There was a fifteen-minute break where Scott was left alone, apart from a PC on duty. A bit of silence and Scott was squirming; LeFanu watched through the one-way mirrored glass whilst drinking his coffee. DI Miles and DC Ford re-entered the room and switched on the tape machine again and repeated those in attendance and the time and date.

'Right, Mr Scott. Where is Ronnie now?'

'I don't know. She said she was going away for a few days with Charlotte. That was as of two days ago. That's the way it is with her. Just a scribbled note and sometimes not even that. And eventually she'll be back.'

'Have you called her on her mobile?'

'No, no. You don't understand. She's a free spirit. She'll come back; she always does. We don't do calls like that.'

'Fine. Let us know the moment she contacts you. That we insist on.'

Scott nodded, relieved that it seemed she was being relatively pleasant.

'OK, so who is Felix Andervert?'

'Shit, he's the bastard Swiss guy about the Porsche 356. How do you know about him?'

'We know a lot about him, Mr Scott. And a fair bit about his past relationship with you and Lord Groombridge. Care to enlighten us?'

It seemed that everyone Scott mentioned was bad news and he was the only good guy, and Andervert was no exception. Guy Scott denied the accusations of manipulation of accounts, bribery, blackmail and extortion, as was expected. Despite the forensic accountants, there was still analysis to be done before any tangible proof existed, made even more difficult by the knowledge that a used car, even exotica like the Bugatti, was very difficult to value precisely, and Scott knew that better than they did.

The interview finished with LeFanu telling Scott not to leave the area without notifying Ipswich Police. LeFanu admitted to DS Jones afterwards that the interview was far from satisfactory. They had riled him, no doubt, but no proof and that Scott, no doubt, would come tooled up with lawyers if and when they had occasion to interview him again.

***

'What the hell's going on, Chief Inspector?'

LeFanu recognised the caller's number from his screen. 'What are you going on about?'

'One minute, sir, you tell me that Tony Waller, or Groombridge whatever, is dead and then he's not and then he is. Fine, I don't really give a shit about him. But then you tell me that Charlotte is dead. Then, not ten minutes ago, she calls me. What is going on? You don't seem to know your arse from your elbow, sir.' He had a sarcastic edge to his voice.

'Mr Pchelski, I am not, repeat not, accountable to you. And if you, Charlotte, Fiona, Guy Scott, to name but a few in this sorry mess, had been honest from day one instead of confusing the issue with lies and half-truths mixed in with the occasional bit of theatrically failed memory, we would not be counting as many bodies as is currently the case. I appreciate that Charlotte is frightened. We need to talk to her immediately, so where is she?' LeFanu had pressed the intercom button and mimed to the WPC who opened his door for her to fetch DS Jones.

'She says that she will tell everything she knows, which is obviously more than you know. And she will need protection. She's seriously frightened.' George had calmed down after his initial outburst, not wishing to be interrogated about any involvement. He'd thought that LeFanu had dismissed him from the enquiries but was now a little nervous.

'Agreed, George. We want to sort this out as soon as... Where is she now? I'll send a car right now, unless, of course, you care to come in?'

'She will be with me at a safe house in about an hour or so. And no, I will not tell you where it is. She was staying in an hotel in Knightsbridge, but as I said, she's seriously scared. I've never seen or heard her like this. And whilst she has been the original pain in the backside, she is still someone to care about.'

'Be careful, George. A leopard doesn't change its spots. Take care, she's still got you by the proverbial short and curlies, as you English say. She'll sell you down the river given half a chance, to mix my metaphors. Remember, your words, "devious minx" you called her. Now, stop this nonsense of the knight in shining armour — where is she? This isn't a re-run of some B-movie spy chase.'

'She'll be safe, soon...'

LeFanu took a flier, just something Miles had mentioned. 'Is the safe house a certain farm in Essex?' He listened carefully for any change in tone. Jones had joined him and gave him a thumbs up sign.

'Er, Essex? No, why? Don't know what you mean. Er, wrong side of

London. I'll call you back.' George rang off; he'd lost his cockiness in that one answer. Jones again gave his boss the thumbs up, as he heard the answer on the speaker. LeFanu scribbled a note to him to try to get a search warrant sworn for the property in Essex seemingly owned, in innocence, by a certain Alan Turner, although he had some doubts that a magistrate would sign it off without evidence of involvement. Jones acknowledged the instruction and replied saying he would visit the site himself if no warrant was available and notify the US authorities about the identification of Charlotte as the victim being officially an error.

Two minutes or so later, his phone rang again. 'OK, George, now some answers.'

'She'll be at the Premier Inn on the Bath Road, Heathrow, by morning. Say eight thirty a.m.? I'll be with her. It's big enough to feel safe. Send your car, but not the flashing blue lights job, eh? There's lots of tourists around.'

'Fine. You and I are due another of our lengthy chats, George. Stay in the UK and available. I've not done with you yet.' Jones and the DCI compared notes, both being convinced that George Pchelski was not the innocent ex-con that he'd like everyone to believe. 'Me thinks he protesteth too much' LeFanu commented, using a famous mis-quote that he often used in investigations. Then he dialled the number for his counterparts in the Quai d'Orsay to arrange for a bilateral search of Pchelski's French property.

***

The meeting was established after a couple of telephone calls back and forth to Pchelski. They were to be picked up for the drive to Ipswich Police HQ in unmarked police vehicles. LeFanu had decided to keep the two of them separate on the journey, much to the annoyance of Pchelski.

The DCI arrived at the office early, needing some planning time for the heavy interview he was expecting with Charlotte, Lady Groombridge. The title was actually right this time. Samantha Miles was already at her desk and waved as he went past. She didn't look up straight away, as he paused, scribbling away on a pad and looking at the screen on her laptop. He took a moment to study her. Her face was paler than before, the shadows deeper under her eyes. A person who suffered sleepless nights by taking the job too seriously twenty-four/seven, probably aided and abetted by being away from home Monday to Friday. She stopped what she was doing, expecting something from the boss. He just smiled and said, 'I think we're nearly there.'

She responded by saying thirty minutes in the powder room and she'd be fine! 'Can't let that bitch, Charlotte, upstage me again.' He smiled and carried on to his office.

Charlotte was a different woman when she was brought into the CID offices. Still smartly turned out in a dark suit, albeit with a substantial split up the right hand side, but less sexy, hair immaculate as ever, Miles thought and make-up looking like she had been given at least two days' notice of the arrival of LeFanu's people in the police car. A second car, following, had collected a reluctant George Pchelski, who had been kept separate on arrival by placing him in Interview Room B with a uniformed PC standing inside, by the door.

The interview room they had selected for her was intended to intimidate. No windows, no china cups, just plastic beakers and rudimentary furnishings, plain walls, and inevitably, one mirrored wall. DS Jones took the chair by the door, behind Lady Groombridge. LeFanu looked to DI Miles, who turned on the video and audio recording and made a point of telling her that everything was for the record and could well be used in the future.

Charlotte obviously hated this sort of interrogation. It reminded her of several events at school where there had been a reluctance to involve the police or authorities, so the headmistress took over and it had been no holds barred, she recalled. She would have to be very sharp and quick thinking in her responses and to keep the barbs, for which she was renowned by this group of detectives, out of her answers. It was obvious to her, and from her body language, that this interview was going to be difficult.

'Madam, things have moved on since we last spoke, necessitating this interview. You do have the right to a solicitor of your choosing or one we will provide. You are not under arrest, but we must caution you, nevertheless. Do you understand?'

'Yes.' She had decided to keep gibes and asides to a minimum if she could — a completely foreign approach for her.

LeFanu, irritated by her attitude, decided not to be subtle. 'Your husband was not murdered in the Jacuzzi at his home, as we believe you have known all along. He was shot in Concord, New Hampshire, by persons unknown, but believed to be a major crime syndicate in the USA. Alongside him, also shot dead, was a blonde woman, wearing a dark brown wig, a similar hair colour to yours.'

'I fail to see what that has to do with me, Mr LeFanu. Some trollop or other, as I think it is called in English, that he picked up on a street corner, I expect, is being shagged by my husband. Thousands of women have a similar hair colour and certainly hundreds knew, intimately, my husband.' She couldn't resist rising to the bait of LeFanu's carefully worded statement, without realising that was their game plan.

'The point here is that you identified a cadaver as that of your husband in the morgue near here, as witnessed by DC Ford, WPC Ford as she was then. You must have had a reason. What was it?'

'I was under a great deal of stress at the time, as you will recall from your recordings of the meeting. I'd been told by Guy Scott, my husband's partner in business, that he was dead and then by yourselves without mincing your words at the time, much as now. Yes, I was taken to the place and cast a quick glance. The mortuary assistant was very sympathetic. I recall he held his hand under my elbow in case I were to faint, I suppose, and said the identification was just a formality. I glanced and it looked like Tony, horrible, all bloated and red, so I said it was. I told you at the time that I can't cope with stuff like that. Yes, I knew, afterwards that it wasn't Tony. He called me that evening, and that was a big shock, like something from the movies. He said that I had to say it was him or I would get nothing, so I went along with it. I had to call his friend in the Government Office or some department to get things speeded, sorry sped, up. By the time I had realised it was foolish, it was too late and the cremation of whoever it was, was done and dusted...' She blushed at her unintentional pun as it registered with the detectives. 'I can do no more than apologise.' She folded her arms to indicate that, as far as she was concerned, the matter was closed.

Frustrated, LeFanu signalled to Miles to play back a recording of that first interview. 'As you can hear, you shrieked with laughter at the point we told you of the body in the Jacuzzi, Lady Groombridge. Hardly the stress you mention.'

Again, she couldn't resist and commented that everyone handles stress differently. 'But not with blatant lies, madam,' chipped in DS Jones from behind her. 'So why did Tony Groombridge ask you to lie?' he continued.

'I don't know. Probably because he had some problem with someone he'd upset — plenty of those around. Perhaps you'd better ask him — of course, you can't, can you?' She smiled, pushed back the uncomfortable chair and swivelled to face him and crossed her legs provocatively, showing Chris Jones a substantial amount of nylon-encased thigh, much to his embarrassment. Miles, seeing the ploy, moved in with her questions.

'Less of the levity, please, madam. Let us move on. The female with him died with two of your passports in her handbag and certain items of your ID, credit cards and the documents supporting her single trip plane ticket from London Heathrow. How did she get those documents? Why did you not notice that they were missing?'

She shrugged. '*Mon Dieu*. I don't carry my handbag over my shoulder all day and night; maybe you do, Detective Inspector Miles. Perhaps she stole them when I was in the toilet, or distracted by a handsome man.' Again, she stared at Jones, who had moved to be in line of sight.

Miles carried on with her string of questions. 'Why did Mr Jerry Gold come to Europe in December?'

'I don't know. Perhaps he came for the art exhibition in the Louvre; perhaps to get some culture — God knows the Yanks could do with some.' LeFanu smiled, not at her answer, which was predictable, but more that she was reverting to type, which was exactly what he wanted. The adage of leopards and spots sprung to mind again. Charlotte took it, wrongly, as a lightening of the atmosphere.

'And how did Mr Gold get hold of your husband's passport and vice versa?'

'Again, sirs, madam, how the hell would I know? Tony was in Courchevel as far as I was aware. Jerry, you say, was floating around Europe. Perhaps they met off-piste or when pissed; your guess is probably better than mine.' She looked at her audience to see if there was even a glimmer of a smile and found none — just stony faces. 'This inquisition of yours seems to be seeking information that I can't possibly know.' She stood up and turned to face the door. 'I'm out of here.'

DCI LeFanu raised an eyebrow. 'Sit down, now!' he barked, quite shaking her with the suddenness of his outburst. 'We are seeking answers, madam, and you are not being helpful. If you refuse to assist us in our enquiries, then I will have no option but to arrest you for perverting the course of justice, being an accessory before and/or after the fact, parking on a yellow line; anything I choose.'

DI Miles took on the role of "good cop". 'C'mon, Charlotte, we've been struggling to piece together what actually happened. Most of the people who would have helped are unfortunately dead. That makes you a target too, you understand.' Charlotte looked at her with disdain.

'I'd prefer you to call me madam or Lady Charlotte or Lady Groombridge if you must, thank you.' Miles was amazed at the change from being the scared female in threat for her life, as George had described, to the confident, full of bluster vixen.

'So be it, madam, but I will reiterate that you are potentially a target. Please don't forget that! When did the relationship between your best friend Veronica start with your husband?'

'What? Ronnie and Tony? You must be joking. Tony always liked her big tits and she wasn't into hiding those assets or averse to flashing for that matter, but… Well, Ronnie always called him a bastard and that I should divorce him and take a load of money. I never thought that she had anything else in mind than helping me.' She looked directly at LeFanu and realised he was not making up the story. 'Cow!'

'Perhaps you didn't know that the woman's name found shot dead alongside your husband was your friend, Veronica van Outen, to use her maiden name — a natural blonde whom we also believe assumed an alias of Angela Darling for the perpetration of several very serious crimes — including at least two murders. Maybe you didn't know. Convince me, us.'

'*Merde*. The stuff on the news said it was a woman, that was all. So she's the Angela Darling you've been going on about, not the stupid girl I remember. Christ, I thought I knew Ronnie. Bitch! What a fucking bitch.' She stood up so quickly, obviously shaken by the news, that the chair fell on to its back. 'Fucking cow!'

Jones was amazed at the change in reaction, how fast she had reacted to her best friend's role and death and seeking to calm her. 'Enough of this language, thank you. Madam, you may be right, but just remember you would have been the victim of the shooting had things worked out differently. Let's take a break and get you some coffee, maybe a sandwich?' After a few minutes, where Charlotte had calmed down after uttering every obscenity her education and language allowed, they carried on with the questioning.

LeFanu jumped in with a role change to being the good-cop. 'We realise, or perhaps believe is a better word at this point, that you have only committed small misdemeanours — let's call them that for the time being.

It would allow us to arrest you with reasonable grounds, accessory before, during and after for that matter, but let us see how you can help us and help yourself too.' She nodded, looking, at least, contrite.

'Where, madam, was the Bentley after the 1st January until it was taken to be repaired?'

'I haven't a clue. We have a garage round the corner from the apartment. I don't look in there, you might understand. You know I was in France for Saint Sylvestre, so how would I know? I assumed Tony had used it and bashed something and called them. Oh, maybe it was at some airport or other. I simply got a text message from the garage people, as they couldn't get hold of Tony. They know me because of the Range Rover, I suppose. I just said get on with it and leave another car in case he needs it whilst you do the repairs.'

'OK thank you, that fills a gap in our knowledge. I'd have to check our files from previous interviews with you, Lady Groombridge, but I seem to recall that you took your husband to the airport and then went to Bicester Village shopping…' DS Jones interjected, flipping over the pages in his note book.

Charlotte shrugged and simply replied, 'Maybe, I don't recall. So maybe the Bentley was in London after all. Who cares?'

LeFanu, raising his voice, 'I do, madam, I do! It does make me wonder how the Bentley got from East Anglia, be it Porten House, Norwich airport or wherever to Chelsea, bearing in mind that Lord Groombridge was thought to be dead at the time.' She shrugged again, not offering any answer.

Jones ignored the earlier statement, as it had evinced the answer they wanted. 'Now let's talk about Veronica again. Did she take your passport and other ID?'

Charlotte, glancing at the DCI, responded to Jones's question, giving the impression of being a little subdued after her outburst and resignedly said, 'Yes. We'd done that sort of thing before because we look alike, apart from she has bigger boobs than me and the hair colour, of course, but that is easily remedied with a wig. She told me her passport had run out and she'd forgotten to renew it. She wanted to go to Mexico — Cancun — with her boyfriend and hadn't got time to go to the passport office. No big deal — we did it all the time at school. Well, it wasn't a big deal the way she put it at the time. I thought her boyfriend was Guy, Guy Scott, you know the car auction fellow. Can't stand him myself. Greasy shiny car salesman, that's what Tony called him, although he did seem good at this job, making piles of money, by all accounts. She was, as you know from your amateur surveillance operation, staying with me in Chelsea. I was going to stay with a friend — you met her I think, Fiona?' It was her turn to smile.

Samantha recognising that a little levity was getting more answers, smiled herself and just nodded and added, 'Indeed! Anyway, how did Veronica, aka Angela Darling, get hold of the strychnine poison to kill Terry Beddall?'

'Any fool who has lived in mainland Europe knows about rat poison unless you are British, and then you find all sorts of tree-huggers to ban such things. Why she would want to kill him is just another thing I don't understand about her. He was infatuated with her, she told me. Wound him around her little finger or thumb or whatever. She just liked a good bit of rough. He was quite sweet and a bloody good shag — that much I do know.'

Here we go again, thought LeFanu. 'Did you introduce Veronica to Terry Beddall?'

'Might well have done. If we met in the street, my dear chief inspector, I would not be so rude as to ignore someone. Surely in this country that is a norm? Yes, I think I did, now you come to mention it. In Bond Street. She was coming out of Fenwick's store. She pinched his backside. I should have guessed, randy cow. How she got into bed with him after that, I don't know. I wasn't there, you understand!'

'That doesn't stack up, Lady Charlotte. Unless you were the person who waited outside the prison every Thursday for several months.'

'Me? No! I don't do waiting. Maybe I was a little loose lipped and told her about this guy in prison who looked like he'd be fun in bed and she figured she'd have some too. I'd never had an ex-con and neither had she, I think. I don't expect you've experienced it either, Detective Inspector Miles.' Sam Miles gave her a filthy look but controlled her potential outburst after a look from her boss. Charlotte Groombridge continued with a smirk at the obvious discomfort of DI Miles. 'I did meet up with him, as I told you before, I think. We had a couple of nights and that was fine. He was my Christmas treat, if you know what I mean. She must have been at him before that.'

'Did you purchase and fix an electronic tracking device to the underneath of his car?'

'What the hell is that? Monsieur, just take a look at my nails. I pay a fortune to a lovely lady to keep them just so. Would I fiddle around with dirty cars on my knees? I don't think so. I drive them and other people park them, clean them and otherwise look after them.' She was starting to get aggressive again.

'OK, OK. Thinking aloud, madam. How do you think the gunmen in the States knew where Lord Groombridge was?'

'OMG! We had two nasty guys come to the apartment in Chelsea whilst your man was watching after me — not! They threatened me and Ronnie. And it wasn't the first time. I was scared, as was Ronnie, ask her… oh you can't, can you?' She smirked. 'Anyway, this time I told them Tony had gone to the USA. Maybe they can track flights. How the hell should I know? They must have followed him, I suppose. Ronnie scarpered and that was the last time I saw her. I stripped off in the window to deflect attention — always works and your man nearly had a fit, or something. Yes, I knew he was going away and now he really is dead. That wasn't the plan. Sorry, wasn't his version of the plan.'

'What plan?'

'He was in debt up to his armpits. I suppose "up to our armpits" would be closer to reality. Everything was mortgaged to the hilt. The flat, the house, a couple of other small properties he bought and even the place in Courchevel are all in foreclosure. His plan, to avoid the consequences, was to go to the USA and disappear off the radar. No more gambling, he promised. No more girls. Just him and me. He was to get the money from selling his cars and the selling of his part of the auction house and I was to stay behind to get the insurance money from the thefts.'

LeFanu interrupted her. 'And life assurance policies?' He looked straight at her for a reaction and benefitted from seeing a shrug. 'But if he were really dead, then the business reverts to the surviving partner — it is written in the original contract.'

'Shit, I didn't know that. I think he had a plan with that dreadful Scott man to get the money from the business and then disappear, but he didn't really explain that.'

'But the plan changed?'

'Well, after the drowning there was the life assurance. After his drowning in the Jacuzzi was confirmed, the life assurance policy would pay up and then I'd join him, but that wasn't part of any plan I knew about, but that was his instructions. No mention of killing anyone, I promise. It was a money thing, that's all. But obviously someone did kill someone. And that threw me, I can tell you. But that so-called friend of mine changes all that, doesn't it? And I never guessed. Are you sure it is her?' Charlotte's attitude had changed significantly, again.

LeFanu ignored the question. It would have been tempting to do the "I do the questions" routine, but pointless with this lady. 'So you are saying that the death of your friend Jerry was not on the, or should I say, "your" agenda? I'd like you to swear by whatever you hold holy that you were not involved in the death of Jerry Gold. Well?' He looked straight at her with an enquiring look.

'No, emphatically NO. I did not know he was even in the country, Mr LeFanu. The plan we agreed was simply a disappearing act — Tony had another passport and ID in the USA, or least that's what he told me, although I never saw any documents. And as far as Jerry goes, bless him, my thing with him was over ages ago in the States. I haven't seen or heard from him for at least a year or two. Tony was fascinated that he had a double but that was just party talk — or so I thought. He'd invite him to things in the States and get him to dress in a similar suit and tie or whatever. So he must have kept in touch with Jerry, I suppose. *Merde*, he was a nice man. How did they do it? Who did it?'

'That, madam, is for us to establish. But it is odd, is it not, that you identified this "nice man" as your husband without any thought of the implications, nor of his family or friends. And that, madam, is another reason for you to tell us everything you know. Your house in Suffolk; your ex-boyfriend is murdered in the Jacuzzi; your husband is somehow involved and does a runner. Your housekeeper is also murdered. Your property is stolen. It really doesn't look good for you. Did you tell anyone, and I mean anyone, of your version of the plan?'

Strangely, LeFanu thought, it hadn't registered with her that she was number one in the frame for all the issues. He added, anxious to keep up the momentum, 'Who was supposed to be the dead person in the hot tub? There has to be someone, or there is a seven year wait before death can be assumed. And I can't see either of you having that sort of patience. A bit like Lord Lucan.'

'Who?' She looked puzzled.

'Never mind. That is history. Just answer the question.'

'I don't know, just someone. Maybe someone who was already dead. Best not to ask at the time, I suppose.'

LeFanu was close to losing his temper at this casual response. 'I can't believe, madam, that a clear plan to substitute a body, alive and kill him or dead already, was not precisely what was planned. There was too much riding on successfully providing a cadaver and moving on to the second part of the plan. And you are smart enough to know your version of the "plan" didn't hold water.'

Charlotte laughed in a falsetto. 'Good pun, Mr LeFanu, good pun.'

Philippe LeFanu looked at her quizzically before dismissing the irrelevancy. 'I repeat, madam, who else knew any part of the so-called plan?'

'No, yes. Now I come to think of it, I did mention a version of it to Georgie because I needed someone to set up the burglaries… and I probably confided in Veronica to test out how it could work, but no one else. Maybe they concocted a revised plan after that. How the hell would I know?'

'Before moving on. Perhaps you didn't know, but on the death of your husband his shares in the auction house revert automatically to Guy Scott — and were it the case, vice versa.'

'So you said. You mean that Tony wouldn't get the million dollars or so he was promised from that bastard Scott? Maybe he's the murderer you are looking for, Monsieur LeFanu. With Tony dead, he's a million or so better off, if what you are telling me is true.' She smiled and shrugged. 'Serves him right for making everything so complex…' She stopped almost in mid-sentence. Then after a second or so, she continued, 'I think you English call that irony. If he had not got involved with Jerry and Ronnie we'd be living in the USA with a small fortune in our pockets. *Mon Dieu*, what am I going to do now?'

'Just so. And all the insurance payments have been frozen too. So, *rien*, zero, zilch, nothing…' LeFanu achieved his objective of catalysing the "falling out of thieves", as the expression so well summed up. Charlotte was now more likely to spill the beans. He deliberately let this issue fester and continued, 'Do you know Monieur Andervert?'

She reacted slowly. The past few sentences had stunned her. 'Oh… Don't think so. Who is he?'

'A man, a Swiss, who made that friend of yours Fiona, pregnant about eight or nine years ago and you, we understand, took some revenge by destroying his valuable car. Remember now?'

'*Merde*! Shit! Yes. I'd forgotten his surname. He was just Felix to us all. Now you put it into context, I do remember. He did make Fiona pregnant. Lovely girl, but a mite naïve, even for a fifteen-year-old.'

DI Miles's patience was running out. She thumped the table and screeched, 'Naïve? She was fifteen years of age. What would you expect? You are not the little innocent you try so hard to portray in amongst your foul language. And we know you have been in touch with this little naïve girl on a regular basis, so don't play the vague memory card, thank you.'

'Enough, DI Miles.' LeFanu, who had been surprised by the outburst, took control of the questioning and frowned at Samantha. 'What else do you know about him, please.'

'He was connected to that little shit Guy Scott somehow. We were given quite a lot of money and some drugs, not hard stuff, though, if we could get him, Felix, that is, in a compromising situation. And some other rich guys the same. It was part of an exciting game.'

DS Jones jumped in with a question, all part of the pre-planning. 'Up to a few minutes ago, madam, we had not mentioned his given name. Interesting that you were aware…' Again, she shrugged and Jones carried on as planned. 'So, again, it would seem we have to ask you when was the last occasion you saw your husband alive?'

'Well. It was for his birthday, on the 3rd January. He came up from Courchevel by train, I think. Or I assumed it was by train. And I met him at the Hotel Bristol in Paris, Rue du Faubourg Saint-Honore. We stayed the night. It was good, if you know what I mean, which is why I doubted Ronnie's involvement just now. He left the next day — presumably to go back to Courchevel or Porten House or somewhere. Sorry, I should have told you that before.'

'Indeed, madam. It might have saved some lives and a considerable amount of our wasted time and effort. He actually left Courchevel on the 1st January. Any ideas why?'

'No. I've told you, he was a law unto himself. Maybe a New Year treat at the Folies Bergère? I'm sorry, gentlemen, lady, but I find it hard to be serious when it comes to Tony's love life. I really don't understand what has happened. A simple plan to get Tony off the hook of the money lenders has gone badly wrong, but nothing to do with me.'

She looked suitably contrite, although all three detectives viewed her responses with a large degree of scepticism. Jones continued, but couldn't resist a raised eye-brows look and a cutting remark 'Nothing? Oh, really? And that lovely lady, by all accounts, Monika, could still be here to enjoy her life.' He produced the wedding party picture and placed it on the table in front of Charlotte, asking her to identify the people.

'I don't understand. That's not Tony. It's close, but it isn't him. OMG! That's Jerry. Of course. How come you have this photograph showing a different version of Tony? I have that exact photo, but it is not the same — looking at it closely for the first time in six years or so, I can tell the difference between Tony and Jerry.'

'Certainly I'd expect you to be able to identify your husband, even though it was difficult, you say, at the morgue. You tell us, Lady Groombridge. Mr Scott gave us the picture. Which is Veronica?' She pointed at the blonde woman in the foreground, without comment. DS Jones then showed the slightly blurred CCTV photographs from Paris and posed the same question. Again, she nodded.

'OK, it looks like the photographs may have been photoshopped. Let's talk about a model car. A model of a Mercedes, painted green.' To remove any doubt, Jones showed her a photo on a blank white background of the miniature Mercedes convertible.

'Looks like the one I bought in a toy shop. Well, I bought one for Georgie and was going to give it to him when we met in Sussex, but my husband found it in my underwear drawer — what he was doing in there I cannot guess, it's been a long time... We had a blazing row about the bloody thing.'

'What colour?'

'My underwear? Really! What a strange question.' She pouted her lips.

'The model car, madam. Please stop these meaningless time wasting and utterly frivolous comments.'

She raised her hands in mock surrender. 'Oh, silver — it's the German colour, like blue is Scotland for some God-forsaken reason and British racing green is England. But the one you're talking about is green?' She looked puzzled. 'Maybe Tony painted it? He was so hooked on that particular car. I think he knew it had been George's and he knew we had had a lengthy affair. So possibly jealousy. Don't see the relevance, sorry.' She paused. 'Ah, now I understand, that's why your inspector here was so keen about the green paint on my jeans. I did wonder about your thinking process.'

LeFanu ignored the comment. 'It, the model car, had been placed under the body of Jerry Gold in the Jacuzzi. We believe to focus our attention on Mr Pchelski.' He turned to Chris Jones and asked him to send someone to the building where the cars had been stored at Porten House to search for a discarded paint brush with any semblance of green on its hairs, because they knew there had been some of the right colour green paint in the boot of the car, according to George Pchelski, which he'd had specially mixed for repairs and renovation and maybe was used to repaint the model car.

'So?' She still looked puzzled.

DI Miles took over the questioning, as had been pre-planned. 'So, who else knew about George Pchelski, Lady Groombridge? Knew enough to know it might be an issue for the police to make the connection.'

'Ah, I see what you mean. Well it wasn't me and it wouldn't be George himself, now would it? It could have been Tony gassing on about his bloody cars. Could have been Guy Scott. He got the cars for his auction company thing from the courts, or it could have been anyone who came into contact with any of them. So I suppose, from what you've told me, it could have been Ronnie.' She shrugged, sat back and folded her arms, almost as if it was game, set and match.

Sam Miles wasn't going to let it go. 'Let's go back to the Bentley whilst we're into cars, shall we?' Again, Charlotte shrugged. Her confidence was returning and she seemed to have dismissed the issue of being arrested or even being threatened by a Mafia style gang.

Sam continued 'You drove it to Norwich airport, yet left it in the long term car park. You didn't go to Bicester Village. You returned by train to Liverpool Street Station in London. Tell me I'm wrong.'

'You are wrong, actually, DI Miles. I didn't take the car to Norwich. He drove himself. I can't remember why, now. I may have said differently at the time, but there it is. Surely, Ms Miles, that's not an offence?'

'It's not an offence, no. But there are so many inconsistencies in what you've told us over the last few interviews that we have come to assume that there are always alternative answers to any question that we pose, depending on your mood.'

'That's offensive, DI Miles — tantamount to calling me a liar. And your grammar is awry; it should be "that which" not "what". I simply have other more important things on my mind than recalling that which was a traumatic time in my life.' She was playing for time, that was clear and it called for DCI LeFanu to intervene.

'Behave or I will simply arrest you and you will be cooling your heels in a cold dark cell for forty-eight hours whilst I ponder my next moves. I would remind you that you were feeling threatened; you came here of your own free will and you are a suspect, like it or not. Do you understand?' He barked the last sentence and noticed a widening of her eyes as the message sank in. He turned and asked Jones, deliberately being theatrical, and faced Charlotte throughout the conversation, to get a thorough forensic check on the Bentley. Fingerprints, seats out, carpets, door panels, everything, he said. She looked back, wide-eyed.

'Well, madam. We'll soon know who was last to drive that vehicle and who was the passenger or passengers. Even a thorough clean will not remove minute traces. Anything to add?'

'I did drive it, Mr LeFanu, although I can't recall when. And I dropped a lipstick down between the front seat and the centre console thing. I'd like it back, if possible, too. It was Tony's favourite colour.' Chris Jones looked at her and shook his head. Evidence was what was needed to put her answers into perspective with the truth.

'You will remain here whilst I consult with my colleagues. And to remind you, you will at least be safe here!' He beckoned to Jones and Miles and posted a WPC in the room.

In his office, the three reviewed the odd conversation and Charlotte's mood swings. Jones started, 'Ummm. Everything fits, unfortunately, with Veronica being the likely organiser. I've a feeling that the money motive is true and she unwittingly played a minor role, being manipulated by Groombridge and this Ronnie character and maybe Scott too. It would fit if it were Veronica what's her name trying to connect Pchelski with Charlotte and therefore pointing a finger, but there is still a miasma of fact in amongst fiction from everyone concerned. Although, regarding Scott, it seems more and more probable that he was womanising and defrauding all and sundry. Let the Inland Revenue and Customs people and the fraud squad deal with that side of things — at least for the time being.' The others nodded in agreement.

DI Miles added, 'It doesn't explain the identification of Gold's body. That worries me. The attendant at the morgue and Susie Ford both told me that she was visibly shaken. Afterwards, she says that Groombridge told her what to do. Maybe the stress and panic are whatever is close to the truth, but it is still a pretty good bit of acting to carry that off.'

LeFanu nodded again. 'That's what she and all the other actors in this piece are bloody good at. We need to tie down the German lady's untimely death, too. I can only assume it was one of the protagonists, or survivors would be a better term, who is responsible. And I'm convinced Pchelski is involved, not in the murders, I suspect, although there is not an atom of proof. We need George Pchelski's spin on some of the events without giving away what, sorry, "that which" we've just learned.' This deliberate mis-use of the English language created a burst of laughter.

Chris Jones had a thought. 'Assuming we let her go, do you think we should remind her to get a new passport from the French, sir? They're blocked worldwide now.'

'Now, Jones.' He smiled. 'Do we have to wet nurse everyone? No, let her suffer at border control, wherever she is. That's poetic justice.' DI Miles laughed.

To DI Miles and DS Jones, LeFanu commented, 'Now for the enigmatic George Pchelski.' The three of them entered Interview Room B, where George was sitting uncomfortably and looking really bored. He had removed his suit jacket and placed it on the back of one of the chairs. DCI LeFanu noticed the label inside the jacket and raised an eyebrow. 'See you are doing a bit better than when we last spoke, George. Armani, eh? And not just Armani Exchange — the real McCoy. Thought you were hard up — the old Rover and Clio. Real sob story after your life before prison. There's more to you than meets the eye; more than you're admitting to.'

'Had to dress up for Charlotte, sir. No way was I going to let the side down.'

'Bullshit, sir' interrupted Jones, giving the same inflexion on the word "sir" as Pchelski.

LeFanu told George why he was required for this interview. 'Because, George Pchelski, we've come to the end of a cul-de-sac. Lies, rotten alibis but admittedly difficult to shake — a cacophony of noise from the lot of you. Time's up!' LeFanu decided to add to the pressure. 'Everyone around you, Mr Pchelski, seems to be dying violently. That makes you a person of interest to us as a survivor and should, ought to, make you very, very nervous.'

George looked puzzled at the vehemence of the comments. 'Then there must be others that you have missed in your investigations, sir. I take your point that there are fingers pointed at me. Why? I have no idea, apart from the model car issue — someone wanted to direct attention to me. Gawd knows why.'

'My advice to you, George, is "move on"; find yourself a proper girlfriend and don't dwell on the past. You've been lucky in one sense. You've been shafted because of your record and possibly because others have seen a way of diverting attention. But unlike others, you are still alive. I think you are up to your armpits in things that are not kosher, but I admit resources don't allow for me to identify anything more. Cross the line at any time and I'll have you. We have amazingly long memories. Go now and be careful.'

After he had left the office, LeFanu muttered that he was not convinced that George Pchelski was the little innocent "I learned my lesson in prison" character that he likes to portray and asked Jones to check out Pchelski's HMRC tax returns and the French equivalent, bank accounts and so on.

***

'At last, the autopsy for Frau Braun is in. She died, Dr Renata believes, on that Saturday or early Sunday morning.' DS Jones related the details to his boss. 'Apparently, she had been asphyxiated in her bed at the cottage she owned, but there had been small pieces of gravel in her heel and the skin was scraped, indicating that she was incapacitated elsewhere. The gravel has been identified as similar to that in the drive near the back door of Porten House, roughly around the area where the Jacuzzi is. It looks like she was dragged to a car or vehicle nearby whilst unconscious. Opens the question as to who knew exactly where she lived? And dumping a body, or rather they suggest, an inert body that is unconscious, from a car in that little hamlet would be open to gaze from many of the neighbours. But that time of year, there aren't many people around, I suppose. And it would only be her removal from the car into her little cottage, and she could well have been 'walking wounded' rather than a dead weight. She was a diminu… oh, smallish person and just about possible for a fit young adult male or female to move as a dead weight, and as we understand that Gold was killed and died in the Jacuzzi, it could still be the same person, or indeed persons, that we seek.'

'It has taken forever for that result. We could have done with that information a while back.'

'Yes, sir. Dr Renata apologised to us but said after the fiasco of the Groombridge/Gold autopsy and early release of the cadaver and the complications of the German Embassy involvement, it has taken longer. And although she is not saying it in so many words, she is still miffed by our senior hierarchy.'

'Yes, yes. I understand and hope you made it clear that it wasn't our doing. We need her on-side in the future. Anyway, maybe Frau Braun had partly recovered and if the person seeming to help her was known, or even the car was known, then it would pass by as a nothing. Mrs Braun's bicycle, with a basket on the handlebars but nothing in it, was found around the rear of the Porten House barn. She was a diminutive person, judging by the position of the saddle etc., so it was checked as it was of German manufacture. German bike, typical Teutonic efficiency, serial number etc. confirmed ownership by calling the manufacturers.' DI Miles commented, adding that the lads and lasses had already sourced that information.

'My money is on one person. It sounds like she was incapacitated, somehow at Porten House, and then taken to her cottage. That would explain why her bicycle was still at Porten House, albeit parked discretely. Careless to leave it, but maybe it wouldn't fit in a car, or be too unusual to remain unnoticed to any witness. We'll probably never know. There is no point in expecting honest answers to questions when all the people of interest to us know that there is no one around to vouchsafe the answer. Indeed, we will need to find her murderer, but at this stage, it is not going to help with the main source of our enquiries. These things are definitely connected and I suspect that the answers will all come together sooner or later.' Both nodded.

'Forensics will go over the Bentley with a fine-tooth comb. If Mr Gold has been in that car, then they'll find something. They've got the mitochondrial DNA specification from the US people.' Jones had the bit between his teeth. He was suspicious of Scott and wanted, almost needed, to find something to link Scott to the deaths but recognised that, apart from his shady dealings, there was little or no link to the current events under investigation. He continued, addressing LeFanu and DI Miles. 'The Bentley was left in Norwich airport car park at the end of December, 21st to be precise, and there is a return booking to Norwich in the name of Lord

Groombridge from Paris. We now know that Jerry Gold took that return flight under Groombridge's name. We are presuming, now, after the revelations from Lady C, that Tony Groombridge drove to the airport but someone else, probably, possibly Lady C, took him, or whoever it was, to Eye St Mary on Friday 2nd of January. I think she probably met her husband, Groombridge, in Paris on the 3rd or 4th January to sort out the details of their so-called plan. Or to establish an alibi? But that opens another question about when, where and how did he, she, or both enter the UK?'

'Yes, yes, Chris. Tell us something we didn't know or were guessing at.'

'Bear with me, please. Gold died on that Friday or Saturday. The Bentley was returned to London on the Sunday via Duxford, picked up on a raft of cameras right through to Chelsea. According to the publican, it was driven by a man when it left Groombridge's village. We have the CCTV footage at Junction 10 of the M11 at Duxford, north of the expected route from the airport or Eye at Junction 9. The Bentley was left there overnight on Saturday from around four p.m. No crime in that apart from, perhaps, an unproveable collusion. We have picked up a blue hatchback leaving the Duxford auctions location, from cameras opposite the premises at the Imperial War Museum's site, on the Sunday morning at seven forty-five a.m. — of course, it could be any of thousands of blue hatchbacks, but they are not open for business on Sundays. We checked and certainly not that early in the morning. Before you ask, sir, the car auction cameras on the gates were defunct — I checked. But the car was captured on camera later, at Thetford on the Sunday, travelling east under red trade plates somewhat amateurishly obscured by mud and not genuine, but not seen on the return journey. Maybe they took the trade plates off and we have no knowledge of the normal registration number, at the moment. So, impossible to track.'

'Yes, yes, Chris. Nothing new. I don't believe in coincidence in events like these. Blue car seen at the scene of the crimes and blue car at Duxford and Thetford. This could be the blonde cleaning up after the murder: the one that the neighbour saw? So where is Scott? Or, all totally innocent. And when was the Bentley picked up? And by whom? Too many questions without concrete answers and certainly not enough to accuse Scott or any of the other protagonists.'

'That's the point, sir. It could be Scott driving it from his compound, about four p.m. on Sunday. Country roads, no CCTV and we have no idea where he, or it, went, and I accept it could be perfectly innocent, but odd behaviour nevertheless. Then, however, the blue hatchback, on trade plates again, returned around four forty-five p.m., driven, we believe but can't be certain, by Scott. We took a guess and the Bentley was seen in the village of Foxton, just off the A10, adjacent to the main line rail station to and from London. Even though there are a couple of posh car dealerships in the vicinity — Porsche, Aston Martin — a Bentley still stands out and a couple of locals remember it, or a car like it. The personalised number plate is relatively memorable.'

'Possibly, possibly, but until you know more about that car, we have nothing but conjecture. Park that for the moment...' He looked up at the sound of a snigger. As he replayed in his mind what he had just said, he smiled, waved his arm and continued, 'However, you have got me thinking we've missed a trick here. That buxom woman at the pub — I can't recall her name — said that the Bentley went through the village at ten thirty or so on Friday evening. There are a few sightings en route from Norwich to Eye St Mary but nothing remarkable. What about the timing? They left Norwich about seven p.m. — you've got the exact time they left the carpark. It doesn't take three and a half hours to get there from Norwich, so where were they? Guess?'

'Eating, maybe? Why?' DI Miles replied. Jones nodded in agreement. 'Let's just think; he might have died on Friday night or even Saturday — when did he eat this salmon and whatever? More to the point, where did he eat the salmon, and again, was anyone with him? The chauffeur, maybe and who was that? Was he in a restaurant, or was the food prepared and everything cleaned up afterwards at Porten House? Worth exploring, because it could be the difference between premeditated murder and...' She paused. 'Listen, if you were planning a murder, would you make it simple or make more work for yourself and the likelihood that you were leaving more clues? Like where did you buy the salmon — was it Frau Braun shopping for you or...'

Jones nodded. 'And ma'am, those cheap flights don't do decent food, so by eight p.m. he'd probably be quite hungry anyway — so it's logical, too. And I believe Americans tend to eat early anyway.'

LeFanu, scratching his ear as usual, sighed. 'Just so, just so, lady and gentleman. My guess is we need to trace a restaurant. Put the lads and lasses onto it. Local knowledge will be useful.' Jones took the instruction and called the team to start investigating.

LeFanu, almost thinking aloud, muttered, 'So it was just the champagne in the Jacuzzi and then washing the glasses? And a bit of tidying up.'

DI Miles, equally musing, 'Or simply removing things, evidence or whatever, from the premises in a blue car over the weekend, sir. But who was the driver back to Duxford on Saturday afternoon? Charlotte or the blonde or Scott or A. N. Other, as they say?'

'Well, Mr Scott should be able to shed some light on that, unless they leave the cars unlocked and that impressive security gate open. Unlikely, I reckon.' Jones joined in.

It seemed too easy to establish the driver as Veronica, although LeFanu thought it a bit glib as an answer to the question. If you knew someone is dead and can't disprove an answer, any such answer will suffice. But they puzzled over the "why" of the Bentley arriving at Duxford and then the blue car returning to Eye St Mary. Miles gave a potentially sound answer to the enigma. Veronica drives from Norwich with the unfortunate Jerry, kills him and returns the car to Duxford next day with stuff incriminating or valuable or both in the boot. Anyone seeing the blue super car assumes it is the Lord of the Manor — just like the publican's wife by all accounts. But it is dark, so no ID is possible. It's just association — blue Bentley, owner is a village resident, therefore it is that person. Next day — cold light of day if you like — blue car turns up with the "not regular" visitor — maybe Charlotte. Nothing strange if she were seen. After sorting a few things out she puts on a blonde wig gets in the blue car full of trash and drives off. She has taken the trade plates off, so it's just another blue hatchback if she is seen.

LeFanu nodded and added a doom laden, 'All fits but it is still conjecture. And just to use an Americanism, here's a curveball…What if a woman driver is a man with a wig or the opposite — woman dressed as a man. The director of public prosecutions would laugh us out of court.'

Chapter 59

After a telephone call to the assistant chief constable's office to arrange a meeting to update him, LeFanu was greeted by a rather irascible visitor. ACC Moore strode in to LeFanu's tiny office and glanced around him with obvious distaste at the décor, declining the offer of a seat, preferring leaning against the windowsill.

He opened with, 'Seems like all the potential perpetrators are gone. I, we, think it is time to close this enquiry down and move on. DI Miles is required back in London and we have plenty of other investigations on hand or held in abeyance.'

'We are considering arresting Lady Groombridge — if not for direct involvement in the murders and the burglaries but certainly for being an accessory before, during and after the fact, with a fair assumption that fraud is involved too....'

'Ah, you've found her then? Are you sure you will get the DPP to support that contention? She is a French citizen, despite everything, and well connected too, and we will have to get their co-operation.'

'Not sure, but convinced that we can break her alibis and find our way through her forest of lies. It may be the threat of arrest will be sufficient for her to spill the beans. She was, is, visibly perturbed by the killings in the USA, but believes that the threats from organised crime will stop with her husband's death. We are not so sure.'

'Not good enough. What else, convince me.'

'We cannot afford, sir, for another killing or attempted killing of a titled lady on our territory. She is currently restricted to the UK, having surrendered her remaining passport. We have Mr Guy Scott helping us with our enquiries, linked in with collusion and conspiracy charges relating to the deaths — bribery, and blackmail to boot. But with only forty-eight hours to make it stick, we had little option than to let him go. He's got very good lawyers too. Bail would be a probability rather than a possibility, anyway. And the Swiss authorities are now involved with the actions of a certain Felix Andervert, a Swiss citizen, involved in sexual activity with a minor and fraud and accessory to theft. The sexual activity will be difficult to prove in court, as the "victim" is being financially supported by him and...'

Moore was noticeably angry. 'My God, DCI LeFanu, this is tortuous and getting more so. Can we not let the Swiss deal with their miscreants themselves? Take me though your arguments, if you must...'

LeFanu, giving a few seconds pause before resuming patiently, 'Charlotte and Groombridge had a plan to gain money from, or by, insurance fraud and to dismiss admittedly unenforceable gambling debts. That plan meant faking his death and taking over another's identity who bore a close resemblance to him. Whilst we cannot prove their direct involvement into the murder of Jerry Gold, there is, or was, no other fit. Although we accept that having a plan and executing that plan — excuse the pun, sir — is hardly a case for a European Arrest Warrant...' He looked up for a reaction and got none.

'Then enter Veronica,' he continued. 'She was in cahoots with Charlotte and masquerading as Charlotte, and vice versa, and we believe she is actually the murderer of Gold and Frau Braun, and Terry Beddall for that matter. And as you so rightly point out, she is dead too. We believe that Charlotte aided and abetted the deaths, maybe unknowingly, but with the thefts she was up to her armpits, thinking that her plan with her husband was working. Then the worm turned. It appears that Tony Groombridge's ultimate, alternative agenda was for Veronica to scoot with him and leave Charlotte high and dry in the USA after she had delivered the insurance monies and proceeds of the thefts to him in the USA. New bank accounts had been established over there and even an appointment in Reno for a marriage ceremony with Groombridge, as a certain Jerry Gold, bachelor, and Veronica as a one-time divorcee. The details registered with the authorities in Las Vegas support that — the woman was logged as Veronica van Outen. So, alongside Lady C's passports, she must have had her own passport, although we haven't been told of its discovery in the USA.'

Moore was, for once, silent, assessing the information. LeFanu carried on, scanning his notes on screen to make sure he had covered everything. 'This is where we think that Scott gets involved in serious stuff rather than just the fraud and coercion he's been up to for years. LG was to sell his part of the auction house to GS, but GS says he was unaware of the "so-called" death of Groombridge. His articles of association state clearly that the early demise of one of the partners, Groombridge or Scott, means that the other automatically gains one hundred percent control, by right and without reward or payment to the other inheritors. A motive there, no doubt.' Again, he paused, and at a wave of the hand, Moore wanted him to continue.

'Charlotte, being unaware of this alternate plan, went along with the arrangements, thinking that her friend Veronica was helping bringing the matter to a conclusion. Scott would cough up for his share of the business as if he were buying his partner out, i.e. prior to the ghosted death of Lord Groombridge. Naïve, perhaps, but maybe she didn't know the ramifications of the partnership agreement, let alone that Scott was not a man to be trusted in any way, shape or form.'

'Fine, DCI LeFanu, prove the connection when your witnesses are dead! Unless you're dammed sure, I want this closed down. Let the Swiss authorities do what they want with Monsieur Andervert, or whatever his name is. Sounds like receiving stolen goods is the measure of his problems and the child abuse issue will be difficult to prove unless that young woman will testify, DNA and so on — and that all seems unlikely. So don't waste your time, help them by all means, but no European Arrest Warrants, thank you. And if you are so worried about another attempt on Lady Charlotte's life in the UK, then return her dammed passport and ship her back to France. Then it's their problem and we can get on with some real policing. Unless, of course, you have grounds to arrest her, rather than the guesswork I'm hearing today. Regarding Scott, well, show me a car dealer who is as straight as a die and I'll eat my hat. If you must, leave that enquiry to the HMRC or fraud squad and get on with your proper job. And that, DCI LeFanu, is an order from above.'

Philippe LeFanu sighed inwardly. He hated leaving things incomplete, convinced that they were now only a stone's throw from resolving all the complex issues and bringing a couple of people, the survivors, to book. He muttered an, 'Understood, sir,' as Moore retreated from his position by the window and brushed an imperceptible speck of dust from his immaculate uniform.

'And LeFanu, get someone to call the bloody dead woman's next of kin. A father in Hong Kong or wherever he is. In fact, get the Yanks to do it. They're good at that sort of thing, and after all, she died on their territory.' LeFanu muttered an agreement and Moore left the office.

DI Miles, as surprised at the assistant chief constable's comments as her DCI, quoted vehemently Edmund Burke's comments on for evil to succeed, it is only necessary for good men to do nothing. LeFanu looked up in surprise at the outburst and nodded sagely.

Chapter 60

DS Jones's team spent time at the airport car parks, seeking information and CCTV footage of the Bentley. 'We can link the Groombridge's Bentley with Guy Scott; one minute it's at the airport parking and we pick it up again at the auction house. I know ACC Moore told us to ignore the car dealership side but…'

LeFanu interjected 'Repeatedly told us, DS Jones, but…?

'The car was parked at the airport using valet parking — can't have the idle rich using a courtesy bus, now, can we? The parking people remember the car, understandably, and a tasty brunette (their words, DI Miles) driving it in because an equally tasty blonde woman picked it up. If you were trying to hide something, why go in a bright blue Bentley? Weird?'

'We must be careful that we are not making assumptions about something that could well be innocent — or is that what we're supposed to think?'

'We contacted the girl at the car auction house that DI Miles met and she, Melanie something or other, found out the contact details of the two guys they use for valeting and cleaning up cars for sale; they're lads from the same village. They recalled the Bentley — a special job, the boss had told them. They threw some stuff into the skip as instructed, but the skip removal people have been and gone, so virtually irretrievable. Black bin bags with household stuff, that's all, and you can bet your bottom dollar that they went through it with a fine-tooth comb. Couple that with the blue hatchback on the classic car auction house's trade plates and we have a possible link. But they said they have no knowledge of a blue hatchback courtesy car, and referring to the luxury vehicles in the compound, they found it laughable that the boss would have an insignificant hatchback on his books. So we're checking, but it's a minefield. Could be privately owned, false plates, anything. And the contents could be anywhere from John O'Groats to Land's End by now.' Both nodded.

LeFanu said, 'I'd certainly bet a month's wages that they took a good look and removed anything re-saleable or usable. And there'll be nothing on their records about the trade plates being used.'

DS Jones, eyebrows raised at the thought of his DCI earning "wages", responded, 'I'm on to it. I think these guys are being straight with us, so I have discarded the idea of a search warrant of their homes.' LeFanu and Miles nodded in agreement. Jones punched in some numbers into his mobile.

After a brief conversation, he turned to LeFanu. 'And there is news regarding the restaurant, sir.' LeFanu looked up. 'You were right. Friday night in down-town Diss. El Diablo restaurant. Two people stopped in a big blue fancy car; parked on the double yellow lines outside — nothing like trying to draw attention to yourself, is there? At about eight thirty. Turned out to be the last customers of the day, because it was the day after New Year, I guess. They had salmon and whatever. Description a bit hazy. He sounded like an American, apparently and they get a lot of them up there because of Mildenhall and Lakenheath airbases, so I guess they'd know. Casual dress, not jeans. Didn't have the steak or the hamburger, though, went for more sophisticated grub. No alcohol, fizzy water only. She was blonde but dressed quite mannish, the waitress had said — trousers, boots, shirt and tie stuff, but definitely an English accent. Trouble is, we don't know whether Veronica has any European accent or whether, like Charlotte, it is almost indistinguishable.' LeFanu nodded.

Jones's phone rang again and after a couple of minutes, he added, 'Incidentally, the two car cleaning guys — one took a posh hold-all to a second-hand shop and some other stuff, suits and the like to an Oxfam charity shop in Cambridge. Got the initials JG on the front of the leather case. Nice job too. We've recovered it. They got fifty quid for it, or so the charity worker says. We have had to promise to return it or give them the money in due course. And eureka, they confessed to "acquiring" two fine dressing gowns bearing the Jacuzzi logo. Unfortunately, both been through a washing machine cycle by their wives. They admitted they'd been in black plastic bin liners in the boot of the blue Bentley. They were told to dump all the contents — so it was, is, a case of finders keepers.'

'Good thinking. Your guys did a good job; I wouldn't have thought of second-hand shops. Keep digging.'

Jones nodded. 'To interrupt your train of thought, sir, one thing that does occur to me is the small blue car and the bin liners that were seen. We think the blue hatchback was used for cleaning up after the murder of Gold and probably that of Monika Braun. What happened to all the stuff they put in bin bags which were seen by the neighbour? Where are they?

LeFanu nodded. 'Any thoughts about it being an official courtesy car of the auction house seems to be unlikely, from what you said about the prestige cars he buys and sells. I would have thought he'd be offering fancy cars in those instances, and of course, Porsche, Ferrari or whatever would require servicing by franchised dealers. However, get someone to look into it.'

'Our forensic people have found a few small shards of cut crystal glass in the boot of the Bentley. Inconclusive, apparently. No traces of alcohol or fingerprints — clean as a new pin, so as to speak. Could have been there forever, but could be the missing champagne flutes from Porten House. But fingerprints even on the car's steering wheel — none — everything wiped clean — valeting pretty good. Little progress, I'm afraid.'

'Jones, I'm fed up with having to agree with you about nothing. We need progress. It seems that I have to come up with ideas for progress and your guys follow through. Original thinking is needed. I don't often lose my temper, but with this one I'm close. Be warned!' It was Jones's turn to nod — better than words, he thought, thinking immediately to forewarn the others that the boss was on the warpath.

***

Jones said, 'The search of Scott's house has come up with something very interesting. A champagne bottle, Veuve Cliquot, with minute traces of blood, which match the grouping for the Jacuzzi victim, Jerry Gold, as we now know it to be. It has been confirmed as the murder weapon by Dr. Renata. And more to the point, sir, it has a thumb and forefinger print clear as daylight around the neck of the bottle. Best guess, so far, is it is a male right hand, as most of the time champagne bottles are opened by males. Bit of a quantum leap but… Several others that are smudged, as if someone was wearing gloves.' LeFanu looked up from his screen with a big smile. 'Find the end of the thread and it all starts to unravel, eh, Chris?'

'Indeed, sir. But it's a fucking great tangle. Excuse the language, sir. The bottle was found by our guys inside a black bin liner, secreted in what we believe to be Veronica's underwear drawer in a tall boy chest thingy in a bedroom on the first floor. I don't think it can be anyone else hiding the thing, as Charlotte had never been to Scott's house to the best of our knowledge. In looking at all the males involved in this farce, it's not Pchelski, not Groombridge — we had the prints sent over from the USA — and it isn't Beddall — criminal record and all that. Obviously, we don't have Gold's prints. So it could be him or a random person, or could it be Scott?'

'Wow, that is a new one,' responded LeFanu. 'I thought he was just in it for the main chance to make some money. But it could be — and it would explain one or two things, like his unwillingness to identify the Jacuzzi victim as Groombridge if he knew it couldn't be him. And if bloody Veronica was involved, then maybe she secreted the bottle in her room as insurance. Mmmm. We cautioned him and he is out on police bail — smart lawyer. So now we will need to bring him back and print him, even if it is just for the fraud and earlier blackmail then we can check. Prints will include or exclude him — either way, we move forward a little. And the more I think of it, he has a motive — the money he would have to pay Groombridge, if still alive, to buy him out of the partnership. But why kill a third party unless he is the main driver of the conspiracy? A thought, though, Jones — we have never asked Scott for a strong alibi, have we? And despite instructions au contraire from our Mr Moore, I need to keep our boss in the picture. And that's going to be a difficult conversation.'

'Sir, another thing. The search revealed a cinema in the basement with a pile of dirty movies, some exotic bedrooms on the second floor. Really kinky stuff, the search team leader said. And drawers full of bondage stuff — whips, handcuffs and that sort of thing.'

'What sort of thing is that, DS Jones? Handcuffs, I understand but... Beyond my knowledge base.' He laughed at Jones's obvious embarrassment. With a red face, he continued trying to regain the flow of the conversation. 'There is nothing wrong with exotic sexual tastes, within the law of course.'

'Sir, DI Miles sort of befriended the receptionist, Melanie something or other, at the auction house in Duxford. She was fired, so maybe worth talking to her about Scott's movements. I'll call DI Miles, as she'll be the best person to get any results from the girl.'

LeFanu nodded, scratching his ear and staring at the ceiling. 'Another thing, Jones — *Sacre Dieu*, Christ, it is starting to fit together — it would explain why he was here so bloody fast, as if he knew there was something going on at Porten House. You said, Chris, when he showed you the classic cars, it was as if he needed the cars to be discovered.'

Jones added, 'Miss Melanie Griffiths was easy to trace. The lads did some searching. She lived in Foxton with her parents, about five miles away from the Duxford car showrooms and about eight miles from Cambridge itself. And that's twice an insignificant village in Cambridgeshire has appeared.'

LeFanu nodded in approval and commented that the team needed to know that they were breaching the instructions from above, so to keep everything low profile.

He continued after nodding, 'Anyway, she had kept a diary and had added key points on her phone calendar and fortunately had a good memory. Yes, there had been a beautiful sexy blonde, her words before you comment, sir, visiting Mr Scott on a few occasions, and whilst it had been behind closed doors, she had overheard raised voices a few times when delivering coffee and drinks. Regarding the blue hatch-back, she is one of those ladies for whom a car is a car; she thought there might have been a small car she used on errands once or twice, but the turnover of vehicles is quite large, so no specific help there. She did feel that there were some discrepancies in invoicing and auction book entries but only because she had been told to redact some figures from the books from time to time without any explanation.'

LeFanu, exasperated, commented that all the information was not creating any situation where the DPP would agree to proceed. All very well, he had said to his team, but ACC Moore had been right. Concrete evidence or park the inquiry.

LeFanu addressed Jones whilst staring into space, 'For my own satisfaction and peace of mind, I need to have the story firm in my head, albeit we will have the devil's own job to prove anything and in that regard I have to agree, ACC Moore is right.' He looked left and right and carried on with his random thoughts whilst trying to organise them into a cogent argument.

'Correct me if you will, Chris. Whilst we will never really know, it would be a safe assumption that the two of them, Groombridge and Veronica, were in cahoots. So, if she knew she was meeting TB in Paris on a certain day and she knew his car was bugged, and maybe she placed the thing herself; she would probably know exactly where his car was and therefore where he was and probably the exact time too. Groombridge, or whoever, can then find the car and install his explosive device whilst she is "entertaining" Beddall.' He raised his fingers as a sign of quotation marks to emphasise the word. 'It doesn't help, it merely explains where Groombridge was, if indeed he was the bomber. If he knew where Beddall was, he could have gone to Brittany at any time prior to the meeting in Paris. He wouldn't have known if Beddall was coming by train or car, up to that point nor the time. But if she was meeting Beddall, no doubt he would have told her and fixed the venue at a railway station — assumption, yes, but a fair one, I think.'

Jones nodded and added, 'The bug, we're told, can fix a location pretty accurately much as satnav does. Beddall's car is bugged so they know he's left the UK and on the road to Paris. And I am having difficulty in thinking it can be the wonderful Lady C grovelling on her knees fitting that device — just look at her fingernails!' He smiled and LeFanu shared the black humour.

'Trouble is, Chris, it all fits but there isn't an ounce of proof. I'm to face ACC Moore soon and probably will get my wrist slapped.'

***

ACC Moore was not happy about LeFanu disobeying his instructions.

'Whatever the name of this second-hand car dealer is, I forget his name, what have you got? Possibly a champagne bottle as a murder weapon by person's unknown and in the personal effects of a dead woman. This man apparently was oblivious to its presence in his property. Even if you could prove its provenance, it won't cut much ice with the DPP. He might have touched it whilst tidying up or even when opening the bloody thing to have a drink. That's what the DPP and his lawyers, if they're worth their salt, will say. Leave the bloody man alone. And that's not the first time I've told you. And another thing…'

LeFanu acknowledged, not for the first time, the instruction, trying to look contrite, and waited patiently for the next the tirade.

ACC Moore looked like he was going to have a heart attack, red-faced and veins starting out on his neck above the smart white collared shirt. 'Headlines in the red top newspapers; "wigs, lies and alibis". We've got a leak in the team and a plethora of journalists sitting on my doorstep to prove it. Find that leak, DCI LeFanu. They'll all be looking to find out more, a new angle on the story. We've got the Swiss up in arms about child abuse, the Germans anxious about the untimely demise of one of their citizens, the Dutch concerned about a prominent businessman's daughter murdered in the US, the French concerned about deaths on their patch and bombs and one of their people under suspicion, the bloody US of A worried about major crime and one of their citizens dead under very strange circumstances and the British seen to be sitting on their thumbs. I want this traitor in our ranks to be quietly hung out to dry. Emphasis on quietly, Chief Inspector! Contrary to our earlier discussions, DCI LeFanu, I, we, want to see a suspect or two in the dock at the Old Bailey under the gaze of the nastiest judge the director of public prosecutions can find, and soon, or we will simply draw a line under it, simply to close the file and allow the bloody media to find another salacious story. In which circumstances, I think, disbanding the team and extended annual leave for you is called for. Up to you. You have two weeks.'

LeFanu spluttered, 'But...'

'No buts, Detective Chief Inspector. Your team have come up with many interesting but unproveable theories, but they don't cut the mustard. We will not make anything of the mis-identification and early cremation of the wrong cadaver, as that will embarrass the chief constable.' He continued with LeFanu smiling inwardly as the words unfolded, thinking that for chief constable read ACC Moore too.

'There's little or no point going after Pchelski — it looks like, from what you've told me, he's involved in theft but the media are baying for blood for the murders. Warn him but leave it at that — devil's own job to prove him being at the centre of things, as you yourself admit. As for the auction house guy, whatever his name is, fraud, bribery and blackmail, probably true but all difficult to prove and time-consuming, too. There'll be a few dodgy log-books and receipts and probably a few funny insurance certificates, if you are really lucky. So what? You are an expensive and experienced commodity in this force, as are your team, and we all have better things to do. Ignore him, I have told you that before. Dish out a heavy warning, a caution, perhaps, if you must, and let the matter rest. And I, we, do not want copious lawyers from Europe, let alone the USA sitting on our people with extradition warrants and the like. Understand?'

'All others are dead and buried. So, it's just some excuses, sir?'

'Maybe so, maybe but none of us, including you, DCI LeFanu, want to be tarred with the same brush. I don't want any more headlines.'

'So, Lady C gets off with a caution and told in no uncertain terms to leave these shores and not return or else, Fiona gets off with wasting police time etc., and Guy Scott gets fraud added to his list of misdemeanours and told not to be a naughty boy again. End of. And of course we'll have to take the restrictions we have imposed on the insurance companies involved to release the various monies to Lady Charlotte. That'll take some explaining… Probably doing just what you don't want, sir. Airing our dirty washing about the so-called death of Groombridge in the Jacuzzi.' LeFanu paused, thinking of the Edmund Burke quote from DI Miles and how relevant that was proving to be.

ACC Moore stood, showing that the meeting was over. 'Indeed, DCI LeFanu. That's a good summary. You'll have to handle that as best you can. We certainly don't want dirty washing hung out to dry and with all bar those you mention dead and buried, literally and metaphorically, what other solution is there? As it stands, someone somewhere is feeding the enormous maw of the media with snippets anyway and we're starting to look fools.'

Philippe LeFanu nodded. He'd been figuring the possibility of a leak from his team for some time. The use of the headline of "wigs, lies and alibis" that the ACC had mentioned was almost the last straw. Miles had used it, and like many clever short, sharp Sun newspaper type of headlines, it caught on throughout the team. He'd assembled all the staff files from HR and read them all from cover to cover. 'I don't want to assume anything sir, but…'

'Out with it.'

'It is totally without foundation, but we have to start somewhere. The only connection I can find is Sergeant Shaw, sir. His wife is a free-lance journalist, local stuff mainly. Jane Forbes is her by-line, I think they call it. But I haven't seen a story by her in all these rags, so maybe if it is her she just sells it on — dammed difficult to prove. We'll never be able to ascertain whether that's the source of the leak, but husband to wife is often the route — inexcusable in theory but it happens, even in Government, as we see regularly.'

'Maybe, maybe. He's due for retirement soon, isn't he? Been around a long time. Ring fence him. No new information — put him into paperwork for the while.'

'He won't like it. He's an irascible type. Had to tick him off several times. I think that's a good solution, but better to take him off the case and put him somewhere out of the media scrutiny. Transfer to traffic division?'

'Do it!'

DCI LeFanu was understandably angry at the exchange, but he reasoned with himself, that's what hierarchical structures were all about — everyone had a "boss" in the end and sometimes, often, indeed, instructions were not always palatable. He mulled over resignation but parked the idea for the present to get on with the tasks and try to help his team as they spread to the four winds.

Chapter 61

LeFanu was unhappy about the disbanding of his team, not the least of his problems was pushing Sergeant Shaw into a traffic role, seen widely as the kiss of death to a career, and the closure of the files. Media interest in the story, naturally, had died, as was common in all newsworthy stories. Sometimes they raised their ugly head again — coroner's inquests and the like. His superiors had absorbed a little flak and internationally it was as if nothing had happened. The Swiss were intrinsically private; the Americans had more convoluted murders to solve and the French, as he knew only too well, were still overprotective of their aristocracy. Philippe was stuck in his office with some minor crime solving between him and Detective Sergeant Jones — side-lined was the expression that kept floating in his head. With some time on his hands, he kept all the files at home contrary to rules, refusing to close them for archiving. When Jones was seconded to vice following a series of crimes in and around the dock area of Ipswich, he decided to follow the party line and take some time off.

***

DI Miles, back in the Scotland Yard environment, couldn't let the Eye St Mary issues out of her mind. The results of the DNA check on the cigar smoking middle-eastern Shaida came up with a result. Her real name was Janeth Abaylan, a Eurasian Philippina, resident in the UK for some twenty-five years, and whilst she seemed to have vanished off the face of the earth, history showed she had worked for a vehicle repair outfit and left them under a cloud a few years before and served a short sentence at Holloway prison for fraud — hence her DNA and personal data was available. The company secretary of the repair company had been there for thirty years or more and recalled her. Janeth, he said, had had a couple of run-ins with the police during her employment — one with an insurance company where she had been involved with a bent loss adjuster and a claims official to create false accident repairs accounts for payment. It was good reason, at the time, to update their processes to avoid any chance of repetition, he had forcibly made the point. The insurance company, long gone in the rampant mergers and acquisitions of such companies in the noughties — more so than in previous decades — had not pressed charges, as the claims clerk, when confronted, had explained how the scam had operated and that had enabled the insurance company to improve its systems and white-wash the financial implications. When pressed, the company secretary examined his archives and established it had been the Empress Insurance Company based in King William Street in the City of London, but as a result of activities of the Location of Offices Bureau, in common with so many companies of the day, had moved its administration functions to Billericay. All this started ringing bells for Sam Miles and she called DCI LeFanu to explain.

When Sam Miles called him on his mobile, he was lounging at home staring at columns of figures and files. LeFanu was pleasantly surprised that Sam Miles still had the bit between her teeth, so as to speak, much as he had himself, and armed with the name and contact details of the repair company's company secretary, he called him. The company secretary, Ron Wright, recalled the name of the bank manager at the National Westminster Bank, long retired but still available after LeFanu explained the purpose of his call. Ron Wright did recall the incident and the name of the clerk who, stupidly, he thought, had banked with NatWest, as had the insurance company. His name was Ian Stead and his long term girlfriend had been the girl at the repair shop, Janeth. Neither were prosecuted but both fired and that's where his memory stopped. It was only the location that made LeFanu think twice, much as Sam Miles had done. Pchelski had been working in Billericay, Essex, he remembered that from studying his file at the time. And there was the guy that Ramsbottom had met called Ian. It was thin, but coincidences are like that, he thought.

His next call was to George Pchelski. 'Good Lord! Long time no speak, Mr LeFanu. To what do I owe this call?'

'George, tell me about Ian Stead…' He paused. There was a stony silence from Pchelski. 'George, are you still there?'

'Yes. Funny, I was only thinking about him the other day. I haven't heard from him for years. He contacted me last after I'd been put away for Her Majesty's Pleasure, as they say — old times' sake stuff.' LeFanu was convinced he was buying time. 'Before you ask, I guess that you are thinking of him regarding the fiasco at Eye St Mary. I wouldn't know. He moved away from Essex after a little disagreement with our then-employers. What the connection is with you, I haven't a clue.'

'Oh, I think you have, George. Think again and remember that promise I made. If you were ever to step off the straight and narrow I would have you back inside in a blink of the eye.'

Ignoring the gibe, he paused for a few seconds. 'But why ask me about Issy? That's what I know him as. What's the connection? '

'Janeth Abaylan.'

'Who?'

'C'mon, George. Don't play with me. You were buddies with Ian Stead so you would know his girlfriend of the day.'

'Right. Sorry, I heard you as Janet — without the 'h'. I liked her. Lass from the Philippines. Gawd knows what became of her or Ian for that matter. Did they get married?'

'Perhaps the name Faruk, Shaida Faruk, would mean something, then.'

'Faruk? No. Why? Listen, Mr LeFanu, am I to be interviewed every time you come up with a suspect or two, another name or two out of the blue or another little gem. It's been a long time. OK, I'll tell you now, to save you time. On my mother's side, one of the family was done for cheque fraud, apart from me that is, of course. Trouble was it was in 1850 and he was exported to Australia and there was another ancestor who was done for counterfeiting in 1893 — he got six months hard labour for his troubles. Family history at its best, eh?'

'Don't be frivolous with me,'

'Look here. I was guilty as charged and admit it. Nowadays, I have to be straight as a die and that's how I want it to be, too. My clients can't accept anything that is not as it should be and I need those clients, despite you fucking up my relationship with Andervert. Look elsewhere for your excitement; there are enough bent car deals going on under your nose if you know where to look. I'm fed up with these baseless enquiries of yours.'

LeFanu closed the call that was going nowhere and sat back, musing over George's outburst. After ten minutes or so, he called Sam Miles. 'Sam? What was the result of the forensic analysis of the auction house books? Did we miss a trick?'

'Nearly all the clients that they researched were one hundred percent legit. The prices charged and those cars bought in had a large amount of discrepancies from what we know about market prices, but that's the motor trade, they told me. Bit like Arthur Daley, the infamous car dealer in *Minder*, as Chris Jones would no doubt tell you.' LeFanu chuckled. 'Worth casting your eye over the analysis, but little to surprise anyone. Right hand side, you'll find sets of initials, probably code and/or initials, of purchasers. A good few entries under LAG, which confused us, until we twigged that it was Lord Anthony Groombridge.' She continued, closing the call and promising to meet up at some time in the future.

Philippe searched the files on his laptop where all the documents, interview transcripts and notes had been scanned, before he took his sabbatical, as it was euphemistically called. He focussed on the file on the analysis, a file he had largely ignored due to the likelihood of it being typical of motor traders the world over. Staring at him from the file were the initials AQM. Could mean anything, he thought, but... Sitting there, clutching a glass of Burgundy, his mind was racing connecting the dots as he called it.

His next call in the early evening was to Chris Jones. After the usual pleasantries and listening to Jones moaning about his secondment, he launched into his theory explaining its source.

'Chris, if AQM were to stand for who we know has those initials, it does paint a different picture about the instructions to leave the auction house out of the running.'

'Another "if", sir?'

'But this is the man who couldn't remember the auction house owner's name? If he was in cahoots with Scott, then he has pushed us away from resolving all sorts of issues. What we need are some concrete facts. Just think on it, please. We know the registration details of the vehicles with those initials against them, and even if he has changed them for vanity plates, DVLA can track back.'

'Agreed, sir. And I know I shouldn't say it, but it pisses me off not being able to bring that shit-head Scott to justice. You know the ACC's address? I know he lived a way away from HQ. But be careful.'

'Will do, Chris. Keep your thoughts to yourself though. This isn't a re-run of *The Sweeney* from TV. Careful, then, on the gung-ho approach — it could back-fire on all of us. If there is something that smells, we'll find it, but if it is a cul-de-sac, then best to keep mum. There's some mixed metaphors for you. I've only seen him in a private car once or twice and it has been what we would call a fancy car, but nothing crowd stopping.'

'Cheers, sir. You really are an Englishman, with language like that! Remember, sir, what Mr Scott said to me about a "special deal for me" were I interested. Smiles told me off for that. Perhaps he does that for others. "Helping our friends in the Police" was more or less his comment at the time. It could stack up. And he is a Mason. Recall that handshake when Smiles was introduced to us, and Scott had a masonic decorated ashtray on his desk at Duxford, albeit filled with paperclips.'

LeFanu nodded at the thought. 'Good thought. Masonry, Jones, is not a crime, but I get the drift. Leave it with me. I'll be in touch and leave you to your vice enquiries!'

'And thanks for reminding me of tomorrow, sir.'

Chapter 62

That Friday, LeFanu took a trip out into the country. Taking an unmarked car from the police pound, he cruised around the north west of Chelmsford to a village, a hamlet really, called Goodeaster, some forty-eight miles from HQ, more or less down the A12 trunk road. This is where ACC Moore lived, well off the beaten track. He parked just out of line of sight of the substantial house, set back from the road by a hundred metres or so, grabbed his Thermos flask and sandwiches and settled down to wait, knowing it could be a fool's errand or, at best, a long wait. He knew the car Moore used when without his police driver, but was looking for something else prompted by Jones to see if his thoughts had any foundation. Nothing happened for several hours, but as dusk fell, headlights caught his attention. An Aston Martin appeared, to Philippe vaguely similar to the James Bond car, although he knew little enough about specialist cars. The registration number made him smile as he peered over his windscreen, trying to remain unseen — AM2340. It roared down the gravel drive, scattering gravel as it joined the road opposite. But he could not identify the driver, knowing that he would probably have to wait for it to return, if indeed it was his assistant chief constable's vehicle, and thinking that the driver would have to slow to take the right angled bend into the house. He relaxed, drank more coffee and switched on the radio.

Browsing through the list of vehicles that had the initials AQM on Scott's list that DS Jones had given him, there was one that appeared similar — he needed to check the registration number which did not match AM2340. No chance until he returned to his office. He needed to be careful, as all requests for ANPR verification from the DVLA in Swansea were checked for approval after a swathe of such requests had been made by staff for personal reasons.

A little over two hours later, the headlights of a car attracted his attention and he slid down in his seat as the vehicle approached. The indicators blinked, causing LeFanu to smile — police driving instructors always laboured the issue of using indicators, even on remote roads.

403

Chances are that it is him, he thought. A security light came on as the car approached the entrance and as it slowed, he saw his boss in profile. No proof, but a good start. He knew that he would need more evidence before he could do anything, but like so much policing, this provided the first clue to try to pursue.

Next morning, he called DI Miles in London, seeking a favour. He asked her if she could orchestrate a DVLA check on an Aston Martin registration number AM2340 and told her to keep it low profile. His next call was to Chris Jones, seeking another favour. He asked him to mirror his interminable wait in the vicinity of ACC Moore's home. Being a Saturday, it seemed probable that Moore would be using a car. Jones accepted with alacrity, commenting that the task sounded more exciting than his surveillance of street walkers in downtown Ipswich in his role as a vice cop, promising to keep in contact should anything interesting arise.

LeFanu had a week of leave to take, more or less on instruction from ACC Moore after his last fraught interview, and decided to leave straight away. His sister was delighted to hear from him so soon after his last visit and suggested he might like to be an ex-patriot Englishman who was really French. And she promised not to ask for too much information about his investigations. He laughed about her journalistic skills.

Chapter 63

He had several reasons for going to France. Another visit to his sister, always a pleasant time, a need to see the scene of the crimes in Brittany, to visit George Pchelski and to go to Montargis for some unfinished business.

After a couple of days with Vivienne in Paris, Philippe borrowed his sister's car, a zippy little Renault Clio with a loud exhaust, and set out for Brittany. In keeping with his favourite and most productive interviewing technique, he liked sudden face-to-face meetings. Body language could tell him more than the words themselves.

Overnight in the Mercure hotel in Vannes and a good bottle of Merlot over an excellent steak, he considered the line of approach with George Pchelski. Before leaving the town for the Morbihan Presqu'ile next morning, he called the local gendarmerie in Sarzeau, the chief town on the peninsula, to see if there was any information held about Monsieur Pchelski. Reluctant to answer questions to start with, they soon recognised his French heritage. One speeding ticket with a sixty euro fine six months previously, driving a BMW M5 with UK plates was all they had. The local gendarme knew of him and practised his English with Monsieur George in the local bar in the market square near the ancient Abbey — nothing untoward.

Arriving in St Gildas de Rhuys, he knocked on the door of the small detached dwelling. No answer. He calmly walked around the rear of the house, acknowledging as he did an inquisitive neighbour in fluent French. He's around somewhere, she had replied in a Breton accent, sometimes difficult to understand. A barn-like building at the end of the garden took his attention after a polite acknowledgement. 'That's where he keeps his cars,' she added.

A quick '*merci*' sufficed and he moved on. No windows and a seriously heavy duty padlock thwarted any covert investigation. Returning to the village centre to pick up his sister's car, he decided to wait a while — another coffee.

An hour later, he returned to the house to see lights burning in the front room through the tiny front window. He knocked.

Pchelski was obviously surprised but immediately covered the startled look on his face. 'Good day, George, How's France? Nothing formal today. On holiday, as it happens. Let's go for a stroll along the cliffs.'

A few hundred yards from the cottage led them to the coastal path with a refreshing wind coming in from the Atlantic across the Baie de Quiberon. 'Thought I'd look you up. This is off the record, George, hence the idea of chatting whilst we walk. Maybe a coffee or beer in the Bar Centrale afterwards?'

George shrugged and added a, 'Whatever.'

LeFanu continued, 'Hope you're keeping well and out of mischief. I was watching the preview of a film on Netflix the other day and it brought you to the forefront of my mind.'

'Mr LeFanu, France is fine. Welcome to *la belle France*, as they say. Film star I'm not.' He chuckled at the thought. 'Wouldn't mind, though. I like LA and it's a lot warmer than it is here. Anyway, a while back you gave me a lot of grief and you suddenly call on me to talk about the movies?'

Undeterred by the frivolous reply, which was quite expected, 'Well, you may recall that my sergeant, Chris Jones, is a bit of a TV and film buff. Crime films, that sort of thing. He was always looking for parallels with the Eye St Mary job, and to be fair, was often right on the button. One day, a week or so ago, a rainy unpleasant day it was, I switched on the television onto something called Netflix. My sister gave me access to her subscription as a guest or something like that. I expect you are familiar with it.'

He paused and after a few seconds, George acknowledged his comment with a, 'What of it?' response.

LeFanu continued. 'Anyway, the film preview I saw was a Spanish concoction with dubbing into English and gratuitous violence and bad language. However, and bear with me…' He felt the impatience in George's face and body language. Exactly the circumstances he liked in interviewing… 'The next day, my brain started working on the parallels, just like Jones. It was about a heist, to use the American word, masterminded by a clever guy who handled everything remotely whilst his team conducted the theft. Despite the violence that you get in these films, the core is the organisation and logistics. Then I make the connection with Mr Stead, Mrs Shaida Faruk, aka Janeth, Beddall and the use of technology…'

'Technology, Mr LeFanu? That's beyond me, unless it's figuring out the use of an Android phone. And basic Word on my laptop computer for invoices and the like.'

'Not necessarily you, as the film clearly demonstrated, Mr Pchelski. Plenty of whizz kids out there for a fee.'

'Look. I told you many times I don't condone violence and aggression…'

'I'm not talking about the murders. I know how that was orchestrated and by whom, although I admit it is proving difficult to prove, especially as most of the protagonists are dead. I'm talking about the thefts. I know you are not involved in the wholesale slaughter, as my boss calls it, I'm talking about fraud and deception culminating in theft. You're it, as they say.'

'Sorry, Chief Inspector, I don't follow.'

'George you are a clever man — no denying it. Someone, we'll call him George just for the moment, recruits whomsoever he needs for his plan — maybe he even read the book of the film, so as to speak.' And smiling, he added, 'Like the books, George, you took out from the prison library during your stay at Her Majesty's pleasure. But no matter. He organises the thefts and distributes the proceeds, but whilst he almost trusted his lieutenants to obey his rules and etiquette and maybe even trusted the judgement of those that they recruited, there was always a niggling doubt and then the deaths occurred throwing his plan into disarray. Maybe it was one or two of the team, or maybe an outsider, and coincidence is the answer…'

'Enough of this fantasy, sir. What are you trying to tell me?'

'Beddall, nice guy though he may have been, was probably trying to get inside Charlotte's pants… Probably encouraged by Charlotte herself and possibly by boasting about his "skills" a little. You said that she liked the idea of associating with the "bad guys" for coffee table talk.' He paused. Experience had taught him that a pause often drives the antagonist to make a comment. He continued, watching for reactions carefully. 'We have tracked Stead to Australia and can easily scotch his future there with the authorities by getting his visa cancelled. One phone call will suffice and he'll be on the next flight back here. Shame for his family there but…'

'Don't do that, Mr LeFanu. He's a good guy.'

'Look here, George. I don't give a damn about the winners and losers in this scam. The papers for the thefts are filed. Better things to do. Yes, I'd like to close down the murders and the statute of limitations rules don't apply, but I'll probably find it impossible to do more than satisfy my, and my colleagues', mind. This is what I think. You are, or were, Mr Big. I think that you didn't appreciate that your friend Mr Beddall broadly knew enough and spilled the beans to either Lady Charlotte or her friend Veronica, aka Angela, or indeed both. It is amazing what a man will talk about if there is a promise of something exciting... And they assembled their plan, half of which you probably knew from the ramblings of Charlotte you told me about, and tied in their dates with your dates to throw us off the scent...'

'Pure fantasy, sir. Would I be living in this fairly mediocre fashion if I was your Mr Big? I know very little of the criminal world. I was "inside" for fraud, financial fraud at that.'

LeFanu ignored the outburst and continued with his summary. 'Where Lord Groombridge and others fit, I can only guess. But I also think you thought tying the details of the thefts in with Lady C's half-baked plan would divert attention. Maybe a bit too clever, bearing in mind the outcome from violence and deaths, of which I do appreciate you wanted no part — who would? Indeed, you said about the model of the Mercedes car pointing the finger at you, and that has puzzled me throughout. It looks like they were playing the same game — divert attention, by which time they would have disappeared and dear old Georgie is holding the baby. How does that fit, eh?'

'You should change career, my dear Mr LeFanu. Try writing crime fiction, or any fiction by the sound of it. I think they, the management gurus of this world, call your idea a fit-the-facts hypothesis. So, firmly, I deny your allegations. Try to prove it. And I'm finding it hard to take your comments seriously when you arrive dressed in shorts and a T-shirt.' He smiled and added, 'Well, at least from the logo they're Hugo Boss.'

'Indeed, George, a bit of humour helps, but I'm not seeking confessions and so I would expect a clever denial or obfuscation. And what is said here goes no further. So there appear to be several overlapping plots and maybe, just maybe, all the participants are unaware of other activities on the same theme. Bearing in mind the time-line; bearing in mind that most, if not all, the participants knew each other or knew of each other; bearing in mind each had a different objective or motive if you like — what price then coincidence?'

'Forgetting the thefts then, Mr LeFanu, it's patently obvious, to me anyway, that money was an objective of the Groombridges, knowing about the gambling debts, as I do, and I believe you do too…' Philippe LeFanu nodded. 'Charlotte's half-arsed plan that she outlined to me must have been in collusion with her husband, that devious bastard, but it sounds like he had a variation on her version of the plan that involved killing — not nice nor acceptable. My guess, and it is a guess, I would emphasise, is that she thought it was a disappearing act, change of name and a bit, a large chunk actually, of insurance money, probably from the Syndicate, again and a pay-off from that other devious bastard, Mr Scott. I reckon he thought it was a winner — nobody loses, apart from insurance companies, casinos, creditors of all descriptions — so what? And then things went pear shaped. Naïve, but I think she was led by the nose by this Veronica woman — never met her myself, or someone else — perhaps a Mr or Mrs Big, to use your terminology. Veronica? Well, some friend dropping her in it like she did, eh? Good riddance to the pair of them. Groombridge and his fancy bit, I mean. And I am deeply sad about the other victims along the road.'

'I agree totally, providing we ignore the thefts, as you so succinctly said it. Beddall's untimely demise seems to be wrong place, wrong time and wrong girlfriend, but if he was involved in the thefts, which is the best guess, then Mr David Grant's death is down to him, alongside his two "colleagues" in Paris. Again, coincidence — no.'

George shrugged his shoulders. 'Don't know anything about the death of the guys in France apart from the newspapers.' He shrugged, again. 'To me, all this is speculation or, as we used to call it, "a fit-the-facts hypothesis". If I could be bothered, I would probably come up with an alternative or two.'

'Enough. I'm just trying to paint a picture. If I could nail one or two bastards, as you call them, I'd be a happy person. Now, what do you keep in that barn-like building at the back of this property, George?'

'I could say have you got a warrant that applies here in France? No, I thought not. But take a look, no problem, when we get back to my home.' Later, after stopping in the village square for a beer and returning to the cottage, he took the keys from a rack in the kitchen.

Two minutes later, LeFanu whistled. 'Phew, expensive cars, George. Nice little BMW M5 and a Venturi sports car — not quite the beat up Renault Clio or whatever it was we talked about before.'

'Indeed, to use your favourite word. Worth around twenty K, if I'm lucky, less than your daily car in the UK, I expect. And everyone of them acquired years ago, as the documentation will show, if you care to look. No Ferraris, no Porsche 356, if that is what you expected to find. Just some nice cars that are my assets.'

'Hmm! Pre-dating your run-in with the law, I suppose?' They re-entered the small cottage and George disappeared into the tiny kitchen to prepare some English tea. Philippe walked around the main room, looking at the photographs of cars, old and new, that dominated the walls. 'Nice pictures. I've always fancied a Porsche 911 in white — looks good in that photo. Nice smell in here, too; local girl, is she?

'Cars? I'll willingly talk the hind legs off a donkey; personal stuff it is a case of mind your own business. Enjoy your tea. The French can't make a decent cup of tea to save their lives — mind you, neither could your Ipswich police HQ. Anyway, back to the subject we were talking about. Some of those cars out there were acquired before my run-in with Lady Law and other matters were resolved by the nice judge at the time, and as I keep saying, I've done my time. So what happens now, sir?'

'As far as you are concerned, George, nothing. There will be several court cases to follow and you may be called as a witness, material witness at that. But keep your nose clean. I do have a long memory and the Law is even more sensitive about closed files. And George, I'll keep away from your friend in Australia, providing I find out exactly how and where a few Ford cars used as police cars in this escapade came from. A favour in return. You've got contacts, I don't doubt. I need to know about illegally changing car registration numbers and how that works. I'll leave that thought with you.'

LeFanu left, formulating his next move. A call on his mobile not ten minutes later caused him to pull over, conscious of the rules about using mobile phones whilst driving, even though half the drivers overtaking him seemed to ignore the laws. Vivienne's car, whilst fairly new, did not have the Bluetooth type of connection anyway. The memory of the perfume smell in George's house lingered in his mind. He just couldn't place it. He had even gone to the bathroom ostensibly to use the facilities but rooted around for signs of female occupation but found no clues.

It was DI Miles on the phone. 'The Aston Martin was a car from Scott's list, previously with a different registration number and owned by several people over the years — last owner, prior to ACC Moore of course, was a

Lady Eloise McKay — landed gentry from Perth in Scotland. It is a 1964 model worth, so I am reliably informed, somewhere north of a hundred and fifty thousand pound, depending on condition etc. etc. Similar to the famous James Bond 1963 model, but no machine guns and rocket launchers. She sold it to Scott's car auctions company and took a Bentley off their hands in some sort of part exchange. She told me that she was disappointed at the price she received but... well, that's the landed gentry for you.' LeFanu surprised himself by his reaction — it was almost a whoop for joy which attracted a giggle from Sam Miles. 'Sorry, sir, not a reaction I expected. But before you go and grab a bottle of champagne, Chris Jones has another one... An Austin Healey 3000, blue and silver, driven by the same person on Saturday afternoon and more or less the same route, with the top down due to the sunny weather, thank the Lord. And yet another, a Jaguar E-type Roadster, now there's a surprise, a convertible I think that means, on Sunday last. All are with a similar story to the Aston Martin — early sixties supercars. Ownerships transferred to Mr Moore over the last eighteen months. DS Jones is putting together a private handwritten report for your eyes only.' She giggled again.

'Wow! Jones was right, by the sound of it, and I don't mean the references to 007. Where would ACC Moore get that kind of money? It's OK, that was a rhetorical question.'

'Trouble is that it could all be construed as legit. Maybe he inherited some money; or his wife did or...'

'Indeed. That's the next issue. We can suspect, but can we prove anything? And would anyone be prepared to open that conversation with the commissioner — we'd be out on our backsides faster than you could say knife. Appreciate your help, and I do hope that you have covered yourself.'

'You mean covered my back-side, sir!'

He laughed and rang off after the usual pleasantries and immediately called DS Jones, leaving a message for a conversation later that evening.

En route for Paris, he decided to visit the locations that had been identified by the local gendarmerie — St Brieuc railway station and the dismal little town of Baud. No real reason than he always felt it necessary to get a feel for the issues from the locations. He was disappointed in both places. A few words with the locals added nothing to his knowledge base. The railway station car park explosion was remembered by the station master but only as a piece of excitement.

Later, back with his sister in Paris after a gruelling journey through the traffic, he called Chris Jones, who told him of his conversations with the local post office owner, a village shop with those facilities really. His comment about seeing something similar on a TV crime show brought a chuckle from LeFanu. He had continued, 'Our man is known as a guy with lots of fancy cars and his wife drives some of them too. He has a six-car garage with electric ramps to a first floor, so a local builder told the lady in the shop. They don't seem to know much about him, or her for that matter. Didn't know what he did for a living or anything. There's a local lass that does the cleaning and stuff, name of...' There was a pause and the sound of riffling paper. '...Yes, here it is, Sharon Bowyer. They only buy the odd essentials locally. However, the price of those three cars we've seen amounts to serious money. The Jaguar possibly seventy K, the Healey around sixty K to a hundred K and the Aston anything north of a hundred K. And there is obviously more, but we can't do a name search with DVLA. It'd show up straight away. All those values depend on condition, provenance etc., according to my pal in London who deals in this sort of stuff. But compare those retail prices with the bills of sale from our friend Scott, and allowing for a profit margin for him, those previous owners were diddled, big time! Not illegal, I suppose, but a bit specious.'

'Good work. Now keep this to ourselves, including Sam Miles, of course. We need evidence, but we can't just wade in there, yet. Wife's maiden name, or name before her marriage to Moore; background, location, family money etc. He, they, could have won the lottery for all we know. But tread carefully, and as you are on secondment, no papers, documents, phone calls in the office, I'm afraid. We'll meet end of the week when I get back. And take care. This is a career-finishing activity if I, we, get this wrong. Capiche?'

'Capiche, boss!'

Talking to Vivienne that evening over a bottle, or two as it turned out, of an excellent Saumur Champigny deliciously chilled, the conversation inevitably turned to the background of the paedophile English Canon Baker and his early dramatic demise. The story had died quickly, as those sort of salacious subjects do in the media. He asked his sister whether anything had turned up about Philippe Foubert, Charlotte's brother and again, apart from his flouting the rules with Nicolas Sarkozy, it was a success story, with all sorts of hi-tech expressions which went straight over LeFanu's head. Another dead end, he had mused.

'Nevertheless, Vivienne, I am going to Montargis tomorrow, by train I thought, to talk to Lady Charlotte and her family. We were given alibis which are dubious. They just don't fit. Maybe one of the family or entourage will let something slip. Your countrymen gendarmes are, shall we say, *laissez faire* about it.'

She smiled. 'What would you expect, dear brother, you are investigating one of their own.' It was his turn to smile and nod. 'Try to go on your own — you are a Frenchman, so talk to the staff as a Frenchman. The gardeners, the guy who will be cleaning the cars, the junior staff — how do you call it in your funny language?'

'Flunkies.' It was her turn to laugh, repeating the word several times.

Chapter 64

Protocol demanded he talked to the Chef de Police about his presence in Montargis. After a fairly short phone call, he declined the offer of an escort for his visit by down-playing the reason for going to Montargis, welcomed by the boss of the local police station where resources were tight but reminding him that no pressure should be applied as the rich and well-respected families were prone to make a fuss about harassment. He called the Foubert number and made an appointment simply to iron out some details and was asked to attend that afternoon. Reluctantly, he accepted the "instruction", not being used to the idle rich, as Jones called them, dictating terms and conditions.

On the TGV from Paris Montparnasse to Montargis, taking a little over ninety minutes, Philippe LeFanu planned his questions. Interrupted by a phone call from DS Jones, he listened attentively.

'Guess what, sir. Maiden name Lefevre, Swiss origins — interesting, eh? Mrs Sarah Moore has been married twice before, but no kids from either marriage. Googling around the births, deaths and marriage registers. First marriage... No, let me start with the second one. Second husband, a Mr Fitzroy Springfield, an American from California, lasted two years and three months. Nothing interesting, apart from him being a petrolhead in car racing terms and buying and selling classy automobiles. However, her first marriage was to a Mr Douglas Scott, who died in an industrial accident in Edinburgh and had a brother called Guy!' There was a silence from LeFanu. 'You there, sir?'

'Yes, yes. Just thinking. Wow! Is there anything that proves this Douglas is our Guy Scott's brother?'

'There sure is, sir. No problemo. Like you always say, start the intuitive thought and it can get quite easy to follow through, but you have to start somewhere. I won't bore you with the "how", but it is totally safe. Used my current girlfriend — she works in a library. She was a bit pissed off at using her for work, so maybe "current" is the right word, eh?'

'Get on with it. This guy Springfield in California. Not another coincidence, or am I getting paranoid?'

'Maybe, sir... I'm sending you a photograph of Moore and his wife, Sarah, at a Police conference function in Blackpool in 2010. Thought it might be useful in talking to the wonderful Charlotte.'

'Too bloody true. Thanks be that there are no kids in these precarious marriages to worry about. Anyway, proves all sorts of things straight away. Ask your car mate in London to do a car ownership search in all those names for Sarah. Got to go, have arrived in Montargis. Wish me luck.'

Stopping at the Old Post Office, now an IBIS hotel and bar, in the centre of Montargis, surrounded by beautiful little canals filled with old row boats full of flowers, he took his first coffee and examined the photograph. Instantly, he felt it would be crucial.

The grey haired waiter, Jules by name according to his badge, knew of the Foubert family, describing the young brother as an arrogant bastard and Charlotte as a woman with a reputation. Philippe asked if he knew of any of the estate employees and was rewarded with two names — one a Boris, a young gardener, one of Jules's relatives and a second, Rene, who was effectively an odd-job man. He had been employed there by old man Georges Foubert some thirty years earlier and knew everything about the family and had recently been told by the new generation of Fouberts that his services were no longer required — effectively on notice for three months in deference to his length of service. LeFanu had concocted a brief reason for his questions and was stopped by Jules. 'Whatever your reasons, monsieur, there is no love lost between us and the current generation of the Foubert family.'

A substantial tip was certainly warranted and Philippe LeFanu just needed to get at these two employees without the family being present. 'Just come here tomorrow night, monsieur, about eight p.m. and we could have some drinks, perhaps?'

LeFanu went to reception and booked a room for the night, feeling pleased with his progress. The receptionist helped him print the photograph from his mobile phone and lent him a pair of scissors to cut away the part relating to ACC Moore in uniform. He then used his phone camera to take a shot of the anonymous lady remaining in the picture.

He took a taxi to the chateau to attend on Madame Foubert, Charlotte and Philippe's matriarchal mother. As demanded, he arrived exactly on time. Being in plain clothes, albeit to Philippe's mind smartly dressed, he was greeted by a maid answering the main door bell, with a look of disdain and a whispered comment, looking him up and down, that Madam would not like it. After being kept waiting for ten minutes or so in the salon, whilst being a Frenchman by birth, he failed to understand this arrogance of the French aristocracy and smiled at the thought of the revolution and Madame la Guillotine and their erstwhile solution to such rudeness.

She swept into the salon, dressed in a high necked dress with a little lace collar — a little old-fashioned, in LeFanu's mind. LeFanu opened the conversation without waiting for pompous introductions and explanations by offering to conduct the conversation in French.

'Monsieur LeFanu, it is unnecessary to be impertinent in my house. Many French families, including this one, are perfectly bilingual, benefitting from good and expensive educations, as you probably know from talking to my daughter.' She looked directly at him, seeing that he seemed totally disinterested in her tirade. She continued, looking him up and down, 'And I would add, know how to dress when meeting aristocracy…'

'Enough, madame. I am an accredited police officer and I request officially and formally to see your daughter Charlotte and then her brother Philippe Foubert. Or, I can obtain an official French warrant to speak to them at the nearest gendarmerie. That is up to them, madame, not you. They are adults. I can call for a police car now, if you wish. And incidentally, may I suggest that you take more care about the so-called good schools you select — just ask your daughter what I mean after I have finished with her.' She was clearly reluctant, but recognising the tone used, called for the maid to fetch Charlotte.

When she arrived, looking more demure than normal, he thought, he asked to be left alone with her and met with an hearty refusal.

'*Bien sûr*, madame. We will proceed. Please understand that this conversation is not on the record, but there is a real chance that we will commence an extradition process with arrest and imprisonment being a very real consequence. There is no need for an advocate to be present at this stage, but that is your prerogative.' This stunned the matriarch into silence, with Charlotte suggesting that a one-on-one conversation with the nice detective chief inspector might be a better solution.

Left alone, LeFanu showed the photograph on his mobile phone and asked Charlotte if she knew the lady.

'*Naturellement*, monsieur. That is Sarah Scott, the sister, or sister-in-law, I should say, of that cretin, Guy. It is not a good picture and taken a few years ago, but I will not forget that woman. Mind you, Mr LeFanu, she has aged well — probably Botox and cosmetic surgery has helped. Now, that was bitchy, don't you think?' She looked at LeFanu for a reaction but saw only a stony face. Anyway, she continued, unflustered by the lack of reaction, 'She introduced us, Veronique and myself, back at the school. Ronnie had been there a term or two before me. She was, I think, Swiss, but I can't recall her family name. She was a couple of years ahead of us. She'd been at Grenoble Uni and had a degree in IT. Clever bitch and managed to hack the car registration people in France. A nasty "bit of work", as you English say. Maybe why she clicked with Guy Scott; after all that's where he made his money. She had met Scott before we knew him and was involved with some of his clients in France, Italy and Switzerland. Part of that story you now know.'

He smiled. The old Charlotte is back, LeFanu thought, at the image of being an Englishman. 'Was she at your wedding party — we were shown some photos with a few of your and your husband's friends, but couldn't identify some of them.'

'It must have been not long before she was "finished" at the school and was returning to the UK. Mr Scott told us a few months later, may have been a year or so, now I think on it, that she had married an American. That's where it all started. With the involvement of our gang and that Swiss man and others too. Scott paid for us, including Sarah, to come to the UK for an extended holiday to meet some important clients of his and the rest is history, as you know it. Maybe that's where she met Scott's brother. I don't know. I would prefer not to go into further details here, thank you.'

'Fine for the moment, Charlotte. Let us move on. I have to tell you that the block on pursuing you from criminal prosecution may well be removed. You broke the law in several ways and it will be up to our director of public prosecutions to decide on action to be taken. So please be careful what you say.' He felt exhilarated at the revelation about Sarah and was anxious to move on.

Not quite the Lady Charlotte Groombridge that he had seen many times in the UK, Charlotte looked as if she had had the stuffing taken out of her. Maybe the location of the conversation or the threat from the American Mafia with Groombridge's debts to which George Pchelski had alluded, or the pressure from her family — who knows he thought. 'Let us talk about the wonderful half-thought through plan that you outlined to George. Whose idea?' He put the word "wonderful" in quotation marks by raising his hands.

'Tony's idea, and all about money, as usual with him. Maybe I didn't communicate it well to Georgie, and I now know there was a hidden agenda. I promise you I knew nothing of any violence; it was just money and I don't have much left of that now.' Tears were forming but LeFanu had seen that act before.

'Your various alibis, madame. Let's talk about them. I have some evidence that many, if not all, were false, accompanied by a handful, or maybe a tissue of lies is a better expression. You can help with the truth or I can bring some witnesses to the table if you wish.' He knew that this was mis-representing truth, but was pretty sure those conversations that evening in the local bar would bring forth some real answers.

'*Bien sûr*, monsieur. Knowing that I, we, had no part to play in Tony's plan, it seemed easier at the time to remove ourselves from your investigation by providing the alibis to which you refer. Maman insisted. My brother helped, as any family member would. We have a reputation to maintain...'

'Reputation? How dare you. Lives have been put at risk; others have lost their lives because of your deliberate attempt to deny important information to our police, and to a lesser extent, involving your own gendarmerie in compounding those lies. Maybe they'll have something to add regarding your family reputation.'

'Sorry, Mr LeFanu. Our mother, as head of the family, required my being, well, low-key, I think would be the easiest translation. You know, you have met her. Yes, you are right about the alibis, but not to hurt anyone but simply the family standing. A weak excuse, of course.'

'Madam, talking to you on several occasions, you have avoided the issues presented and always found someone else to blame. Others would say you have lied. You have made false statements and created false alibis. Today is no exception. I am out of my legal jurisdiction, so can do little apart from reporting my findings to your own judiciary. I suspect, in those circumstances, your family's reputation will sink somewhat.' He knew that there was little that the French authorities would do as he was, as the Latin scholars would say, acting '*ultra vires*'. They would shrug their shoulders and castigate him for not seeking permission to act in their country. He continued, 'I will not at this time require to speak to your brother, even though he falsely confirmed to the gendarmes about your movements that Christmas/New Year time, but if any of this comes to court he, and indeed you, may find yourselves in deep trouble with your own law enforcement people. Perjury is a criminal offence here in France, as well as the UK. Do you understand?'

She nodded with tears welling up in her eyes. 'I will speak to Maman and my brother, Philippe. Again, sorry is the best I can offer.'

'Really?' He felt that he had achieved his objective in making the pieces fit together in the giant jig-saw using a little creative non-official, non-standard techniques. 'Madam, I will let you know what I intend to do with the French authorities in due course. I suggest you tell your mother and brother of my thoughts.'

That evening in the Old Post Office hotel bar, he established that his gamble on there being witnesses to the movements of the Foubert family and some guests over the festive season was close to the real truth. The two employees were united in their comments about the Foubert family as a whole as being typical aristocracy, treating their staff as invisible, ignoring the dissension that, to Philippe, was evident.

He was anxious to return to the office to pick the threads of the areas over which he did have jurisdiction. He messaged Chris Jones, asking him to do a full background search, including social media on all the three names associated with Sarah and to get someone to show, subtly of course, the photograph of Sarah Moore to Mrs Fiona Wallace for confirmation. Three or so hours later, he received confirmation on his phone that Sarah Moore was their erstwhile colleague at the Swiss finishing school.

Chapter 65

At Chris Jones's suggestion, LeFanu and he met in a pub, The Fat Cat in town.

'Thought it best, sir, for a casual conversation, as I've found some interesting connections about our case…'

'Well, start by forgetting the "sir" bit. Even pubs like this have listening ears.'

'Thought it was a good place to come to…' He grinned. 'Especially as Fat Cats are what we're looking at.'

Lefanu smiled and passed two twenty pound notes to Chris Jones to order some bar food and drinks. Minutes later, he gestured to Jones to give him a brief on the findings.

'My friend checked the information from DVLA — easy for a bona-fide motor trader to get ownership details these days, safer than starting a whole load of questions if we had done it internally, at this stage, leastways. Sarah Moore, nee Lefevre, and ex-wife of an American named Springfield and one-time wife of a Douglas Scott, had a range of vehicles registered to her name over the previous five years or so. These tallied with the documents in our files emanating from Scott's empire under the initials SJS and SJM, with various registered addresses that coincided with knowledge of Moore's locations in his ascendency in the Police force. It's OK, sir, I checked Scott's files myself. A further search by my friend under Moore's name was blocked by the authorities under an umbrella security tag. Understandable, in a way, for a senior Police official, I suppose.' He looked at LeFanu who nodded in agreement.

'Trouble is, Chris, valuable information that this is, it could be argued… Correction, it will be argued, that he committed no crime in buying cars at a knock-down price from an accredited dealer who is part of his family, so as to speak, and probably no crime committed by his wife too, especially as she is sort of related to the seller. Perfectly normal activity. Whether he bought the cars at knock-down prices is more an issue for Scott and his company in terms of defrauding the previous owner. We need more to make a connection with Guy Scott that is breaking the law and the protocols of Police work. ACC Moore lied about knowing Scott, but that is not a dismissible offence — bad memory and all that sort of stuff would possibly mean a suspension or early retirement option for the powers that be. Not wishing to wash their dirty linen in public. I'm thinking…'

'But aren't we forgetting that Scott said he couldn't identify anyone else in the wedding photos he showed us, yet one of them is his ex-sister-in law? And another thing… remember that Fiona lady's interview with Smiles.' His boss looked at him quizzically. 'Well, she said another member of the so-called gang at the school in Switzerland was called Sal, Sally or Sara.'

'Yes?'

'That's typically English, sir. They are one and the same name — sort of abbreviations or short forms of Sarah or Sara. Biblical origins, I think.'

'Hmmm. The English language continues to be an anathema for me despite living here for decades. So, now we have to guess whether our Mr Moore indulged himself, with or without Scott's help, in dalliances with young girls. It might not stack up with the DPP, but could be useful and make us think outside the proverbial box.' He gazed into thin air as he was trying to compute the issues. After a few seconds, he continued, 'But maybe you have a point, Chris. Here's the clever lawyer's response… Mr Scott was under considerable strain at the time/had a bad cold/flu or whatever and he did admit that the photos were not of good quality. That, Chris, is enough to get us laughed out of court. And none of that mess sticks to Mrs Moore. But still, it puts us on the right track to keep digging.'

'One more thing, sir. After her degree and the school, Sarah L worked for a European software house with an off-shoot in the US. It was called Swiss Cheese Intelligent Solutions… Yes, I know it's an odd name but these days…? Anyway, it specialised in IT solutions for automotive industry all over. The police use it, or something similar nowadays, in various countries around Europe, including the UK, to sort of track and trace traffic, licensing and insurance issues, as well as the likes of DVLA throughout Europe… The search picked up her two other names but not the Moore one. They had Government contracts all over. She was really hot stuff, leading the product development arm of the company, according to Google and Facebook and LinkedIn. Want us to dig further?'

'No, not at the moment, anyway. Good job, thanks. That maybe explains a lot about Guy Scott and Groombridge's empire, but probably outside our brief.' He mused about coincidence, and he hated coincidences, — the second time he had come across Swiss nationals and software connected to the car industry

'Sir. You remember the issues about an internal leak we had where ACC Moore insisted that we get rid of Sergeant Shaw?'

'Yes. Three months in Traffic Division and he accepted an early retirement package, and who could blame him? We had no proof positive of leaking information to that wife of his, and journalists always do the "I cannot disclose my sources" routine. What's your point?'

'Currently, he's fart arseing about as a security guard for a logistics company down at the docks and not very happy about it at all, according to a source. Hates ACC Moore with a vengeance. They've told him down at the local, the Woolpack, to quit his moaning or be banned. What if a journalist "found" some information, most of which is in the public domain?' Chris put the word in quotation marks by using his hands.

'Whoa! Let me think on it. And Chris, not a word. That sounds like a dismissible offence in anyone's book. And don't tell me that you've seen that on the TV in *Morse* or *Midsomer Murders* or whatever.'

'Well now you mention it…'

'Enough, Chris. Be very, very careful who you even mention this subject to. Sorry, bad grammar and all that, but you know what I mean.' He looked up at Jones, who nodded.

Chapter 66

An interesting story hit the red-tops three days later. Inevitably, the popular press had a field day identifying an alleged conspiracy involving a senior, known to be arrogant, police official. The newly appointed police and crime commissioner for Suffolk, Mrs Sheila Hodgkinson, as one of her roles, had little option than to investigate under the terms of the Independent Office for Police Conduct. Reluctant to make just placatory comments, she took the easy route and immediately temporarily suspended Assistant Chief Constable Moore pending investigations, offering immediate steps being taken to improve control mechanisms to prevent such potential breaches of trust taking place in the future. Philippe LeFanu skimmed the article that Chris Jones placed in front of him on that Tuesday morning with a smirk on his face.

'Well, Jones, I have no idea how that story reached the papers and before you comment, be careful what you say. IOPC will be turning over every stone to see where it came from and who leaked information. They, quite rightly, take a dim view of police officers talking to the media.'

'Impossible to tell, sir. We did have a leak before — ACC Moore himself commented on it, if you recall.'

'Indeed.' He had taken to scratching his ear again, Jones noticed. A sign of his rooting around in his brain for the answers to difficult problems. Moments later, he added '…We have to leave that to the powers that be to try to track the leak — not our domain of authority. It won't take long for them to add two and two together. All we can do, and should do, is to present the facts as we know them, and at this stage restrict ourselves to the issues that they will question — cheap cars, as George Pchelski told us and the records appear to show. We have no link relating to ACC Moore, or his wife, to the other parts of this long running saga, yet anyway.'

Jones nodded. 'The way I see it, sir, is we need to look at the bits and pieces of Guy Scott's involvement to see where he has, or may have, crossed the red line.'

'Indeed, we do. And with precious little to go on, too. It is a shame that the team has been disbanded — hardly surprising in the circumstances. We need some lateral thinking.'

'And I think I know how we could achieve that, sir.' LeFanu looked at him quizzically. 'Well, I'm still in touch with the bright sparks we had — maybe an evening at the pub or…' He looked at his boss before continuing, 'They're all keen to get a result from this saga, as you call it. We do meet and chat from time to time. It must be off-site, that's what I think.'

'Yes, yes. I've been thinking about that too. Now, how about an informal BBQ or something at my place. It's not big, but big enough.'

Jones gave his boss the thumbs up sign with a big grin and added, 'We had some success when we used that team to find the oddball bits in reports and interviews — why not try it again? I'll ask around a bit, and if they're interested, pass on the information we've gathered.'

'Do it!'

Chapter 67

Philippe LeFanu had spent the previous evening assembling chairs, tables and cutlery, glasses and so on and a quick trip to the local supermarket had stocked up on bottled beers, wine and orange squash. Tidying up his house took more time than he had planned, and he was pleased when the doorbell rang and Chris Jones and Susie Ford were standing there under a golf umbrella.

'Bit of help will be welcome,' he said after ushering them into his conservatory at the rear. He left them and changed into his smart casual wear, Armani jeans and black loafers and a crisp, white buttoned-down collared shirt.

It was a miserable, wet evening; in fact, it promised to remain so all weekend. The team came together from the various parts of the police jurisdiction, some happier with their lot than others. DC Susie Ford was beaming at being involved again, having been allocated a desk job after the team had been disbanded by order from ACC Moore. DC Dodd, the French speaker, after successfully passing his sergeant's exams waiting for an opportunity to be promoted, was sitting on a team involving smuggling and theft from the ships, largely from mainland Europe coming into the docks; PC Jamie Steadman was on Traffic, particularly trucks coming and going to the docks, and was frustrated by that role. And WPC Judy Bell, since promoted to DC, who had helped in the initial investigation and had shown promise, was now in CID in Norwich with a new sergeant from Birmingham and little opportunity for brain work, as she described it to her erstwhile colleagues.

Philippe LeFanu, having made sure they had all grabbed a drink, started by laying the ground rules.

'Sorry about the weather. Pizzas will be arriving anon — BBQ not a good idea today.' He received a snigger. 'First of all, two things. We're all on first name terms; we're off duty. No sirs and ma'am terms. Secondly, as you know, I have been told to drop everything connected with this incident in January. That instruction obviously trickled down the pile to you, which is why you have been given alternative roles, some of which will suit and others maybe not. My advice is tolerate for the time being. What we say today must be kept *entre-nous*. If you are not happy with that, then leave or agree to keep things to yourselves.' He looked around the group seeking assent. Clearly from the reaction, there was universal agreement. The doorbell rang and LeFanu went to answer it. 'Early for the pizza delivery man…' he commented, but it was DI Sam Miles standing there in the pouring rain. Despite being wet through in the short journey from her car to the front door, she looked stunning. LeFanu thought that Chris Jones would be drooling, as usual.

After five minutes of hellos and catch up chat, Philippe decided to bring things to a constructive start. 'Stating the obvious, ACC Moore has got what was coming to him. The temporary suspension we all read about has been made into an early retirement package with onerous conditions. Saves everyone in the Force embarrassment. Goes against the grain, but we simply haven't enough actual proof to do otherwise and I don't believe it is worth pursuing further. Moore has lost his not insubstantial pension and his career was over, according to a statement issued by the Home Office. And there have been the inevitable mutterings of age and stress being the excuses offered.' He paused. 'I think he lied and covered up for reasons of greed and maybe status and being involved with the wrong people at the wrong time. He lied and imposed controls on us to avoid exposure in favour of his career and ego, not to have a hand in murder or theft — wrong, yes, but Scott is the right target for our thinking. OK? Maybe there will be fallout from investigations that will bring him back into the field of play. Be that's as it may. But he will be feeling vulnerable at the moment, no doubt about it, probably seeking vengeance, so take very great care. He is, or was, very well-connected in the force. That brings me to the real purpose of tonight. I think DS, sorry, Chris, has outlined my feelings already or you wouldn't be here.' Again, there were obvious signs of agreement.

LeFanu had bought a large white A1 pad, the sort used for meetings and conferences, alongside a heap of marker pens from Ryman's stationers in town, and fixed it in a Heath Robinson way in the large kitchen-diner in his modest but comfortable three-bedroom house. A few drinks and they started. He suggested that they try the same process as that day in the Nissen hut in the village of Eye St Mary, emphasising that they had been going round in circles and that he didn't believe for a moment that all the bad guys in the plot had killed each other off — which is what did appear to be the case. So, it needed new thinking, he said, bearing in mind that to all intents and purposes ACC Moore and the hierarchy had closed the case down, adding that Moore had stymied the investigation for his own reasons.

'Any problems, you blame it on me as your superior officer. Got it?' They nodded. He continued, 'You guys are good at looking at the loopholes we've missed, and so it is timely to re-visit. You have all the info we've gleaned.'

DC Susie Ford, the star at the village hall who had spotted the possibility of the hall being bugged, sat thoughtfully for a while, slurping noisily from a can of San Miguel beer. Suddenly, she started, 'What about the blue car spotted at the scene?'

They all looked at her, questioning the statement. 'Well, if it was a courtesy car, then other people must have used it. Maybe a member of staff remembers. What about that girl secretary — I forget her name. Let's ask her. She wasn't too enamoured with her boss, so maybe…'

'Good thinking; Chris, get onto that tomorrow.' He marked it in red as an action point.

'Sorry, sir, oops, Philippe, but that's a matter for a woman. Susie will get more out of her than a senior member. No disrespect.' Sam Miles nodded approval. 'She kept meticulous records and a personal diary, I remember. Melanie something or other, that's her name. And she kind of related to DI Miles more than me.'

Philippe LeFanu nodded and pointed to DC Susie Ford. 'Over to you?'

She nodded and grinned. 'However,' she added, 'we don't even know the registration number of that car and it could be, probably is, run under trade-plates.'

'Yes, but what if we did know? Does it still exist or has it been destroyed?'

'Good point, Chris. It was reasonably newish, by all accounts, albeit evidence more like an opinion, but let's take that as a probable.'

Chris Jones continued, looking around the small group for a reaction. 'If it is still around, maybe we can trace it and give it to our forensic people to toothcomb it. Who knows. Just an idea.'

DC Mike Dodd interjected. 'I think we should look again at the Porsche 356C. Maybe talk to that Swiss Guy. They're not going to prosecute him in Switzerland, but perhaps we can do some heavy talking to him.'

'But on a good day, what could we find out?' Philippe interjected. He was interested in neither of these approaches, feeling they were due to go around in circles yet again. His focus was on the group of people that were directly involved in the plot as it had become known.

Trying not to be frustrated in the interest of getting the team to be constructive and thinking out of the box, he allowed the conversation to continue, wanting to give them time to get up to speed. As he gazed around, his mind was analysing a million different factors, or that was what it felt like, knowing that only one or two would prove productive and he needed one of them to create the spark.

'Ask that Pchelski fellow?'

LeFanu, feeling that he was stating the obvious, commented, 'Listen. We have only three people surviving these crimes. George P — whom we think was involved but not an ounce of proof; Lady Charlotte who lies though her teeth to suit herself, and again, a few minor breaches but… Guy Scott, up to his neck in it, but fraud is all we've got so far.'

As he said it, Sam Miles looked up from her drink, asking, 'Incidentally, was there an inventory of the contents of Scott's house and offices?' Jones nodded and produced from an inside pocket a thin file. 'Just that I don't recall seeing it after they identified the champagne bottle; maybe we got carried away with that.' LeFanu nodded agreement.

LeFanu carried on, 'And there's that young woman Fiona who would do anything for an easy life, and not much else. Unless anyone has a better thought. She told us some lies to help her friend, but has little to add to the conundrum we're facing. My vote is let her be — I think we have shaken her up to keep her on the straight and narrow. Now, what about that inventory?'

Chris Jones smoothed out the pages of the report, prefacing it with a comment that he had borrowed the file from a pal. So, no names no pack drill… 'Well, we found what we think is the champagne bottle in Veronica's knicker draw…' That bought a chorus of laughter from the group.

Sam held up her hand. 'Shhh, let him finish.'

He continued, 'Page five had the summary of the inventory, with the champagne bottle listed under the heading "Room Two Bedroom".'

Mike Dodd, looking over Chris' shoulder, pointed at an item found in a store room adjacent to Scott's office listing a collection of new car number plates found in a filing cabinet. Each plate had a sticky label with what looked like codes, numbers and letters, on each. 'Is this normal?' he asked the group.

Susie Ford, proving her worth to the group again, questioned, 'Odd that they're still covered individually in a plastic film, according to the listing, and one of the PCs has listed the registration numbers. Certainly not classic car stuff, which is usually early years and formats for cars, say pre-1990. So what are they for? Here's a twelve plate, that's 2012, and here's another fourteen plate. Relatively recent and there's plenty of others. OK, could be for a posh car or an import, I suppose, but why are they there? Oh, and some have the Scott's classic car company name and logo and some are plain, just the number and letters. Our guess is those bearing the company name are genuine and those without not so.'

'How did we miss that one? No blame. We should have studied this list more carefully after the uniformed people sent in the report. Ah well...' LeFanu was visibly frustrated, but it had moved his focus to a new field of thought.

PC Jamie Steadman put up his hand. Philippe smiled. 'No need for formality, Jamie, just pitch in if you have a point.'

Jamie smiled self-consciously. 'Well, in Traffic, it is easy to get references from DVLA, so I'm happy to pick up that one. Got to know a few people down there over the last few months.'

Philippe nodded. 'Do it, but keep it under wraps. Any enquiry, as you well know, leaves a flag on the record down in Swansea. And we don't know where this will lead.'

'Good thinking. I'll get a DVLA check ASAP and verify each one. We've been finding a load of cloned number plates lately. You should see the letters we get after sending out summonses and the phone calls — swearing, shouting and a few "not me, guvs" and "never been there". Messy. Not the nicest job in Traffic.'

There was a pause, as if all were seeking some inspiration, broken by the pizza delivery, followed, inevitably, by chatting. LeFanu let it flow.

After fifteen minutes or so as everyone was replenishing their glasses and grabbing bottles, Philippe tried to pull everyone back to the reality.

'My plan to map everyone's movements failed miserably — sorry to those of you who had to man-handle the information. But it does make me think "why". The only answer I can construct is that there are three or four independent plots running here, and we're spending too much time — correction — were spending too much time on trying to link things together that were never together in the first place. Thoughts?'

Sam Miles started, 'What you are saying does make sense…' A titter of laughter made her colour up. She continued, 'Sorry, that sounded rude. What I mean is that let's say Mr A organises a theft primarily directed at Groombridge but making it look more like organised crime. Objective? A mixture of greed and revenge on Groombridge, who always seemed to be underhand and never seemed to be liked. Second, someone wants to dispose of this objectionable fellow and orchestrated the death of a person they assumed was Groombridge. Motive? Money or jealousy or whatever. Complicated, and relies on that person not knowing Lord Groombridge or being in the know and that points the finger at Veronica with her paramour status. Thirdly, who told the bad guys in the USA that Groombridge was in their country and still a major debtor, and importantly, not dead after all? In my opinion, all the other deaths are, in quotes, incidental to the other plots. What remains is: who knew about the burglaries to create a smoke screen for the major plot — that of killing Groombridge? If we conclude that those people are now victims themselves, then we have reached a dead end — pardon the pun. Sorry, that was long winded.'

Philippe was pleased with the results. He beamed. 'Exactly what I was thinking. Well done. So, we're left with Lady C and Guy Scott. Let's focus on them and make some assumptions that each was, or is, up to their necks in it. Ignore Pchelski, at least for the time being. But and it's a big but… The finger, in my mind, points at Groombridge orchestrating or actually doing the Jacuzzi murder — his motive plays out when he arrives in the USA with Veronica following. However, that is not helping.'

Susie Ford nodded agreement and pitched in, 'If we assume that this number plate business is a scam, in anticipation of Jamie establishing some facts, then why would Scott be involved in a scam like that? Surely it can only be pocket money compared with the trading in super cars and the like. But only answer I can think of is money, so maybe there is either a lot of money in scams like this, or his real business is down the toilet in money terms. Chris, what were the results of the forensic accountancy investigation?'

Chris looked up. 'I seem to remember that they just reported that he was sailing very close to the wind but had a clever accountant. I'll check it out more thoroughly, but we had just discounted Scott as a bit of a chancer, typical motor trader, so moved on at the time and the assistant chief constable stopped us doing a thorough check. Guess we now know why.'

Mike Dodd interrupted him with a question. 'Who took the cash from Groombridge's safe — assuming there was a stash there, of course? We assumed it was the burglars, but maybe it wasn't. Lady C denies knowledge of the safe combination, but why should we believe her? And for that matter, where was Scott going to find the enormous pay-off to Groombridge that was mentioned? Something about money in the USA, I seem to recall. So what about the American money — perhaps it doesn't exist. Motive?'

'Good points, all good points, and some actions there too.' He listed the action points and cautioned everyone to be careful, as they were acting beyond their brief to suspend investigations, imposed by ACC Moore but never countermanded. 'Remember I pushed you into this if anyone queries your activities and that, as your superior officer. How about meeting again soon, but call me if anything interesting comes up and/or you have any additional thoughts. We haven't mentioned the ubiquitous Lady C, for example. I'll leave Chris to orchestrate another get-together.' Chris nodded.

Chapter 68

PC Jamie Steadman was as good as his word and first thing on the Monday morning, he found time to call DS Jones. 'Mornin', DS Jones. We found some of the plates were cloned. A Mr & Mrs Hanks of Hangleton, Hove, have a blue Vauxhall Corsa bought new from an Eastbourne Vauxhall dealer in 2013, but have never been north of the Thames in it, yet Scott has these plates. Mr Hanks, a JP down in that neck of the woods, called Central Traffic Command and raised a stink. It's his wife's car and she had received a demand for non-payment of a parking fine in a Tesco supermarket in Cambridge. The summons from the private parking people identified the car as being blue. And there are others... Odd, though, they all seem to be insignificant cars — nicest one was a Land Rover Discovery, 2013 plate, Scarborough this time, but a similar story. Coincidence or not, a burnt out Discovery was recovered two days later near Whitby with a scaffolding pole construction — looked like it had been involved in a ram-raid but no proof and obviously no number plates, but the VIN number survived and identified it as a stolen/not recovered vehicle. And a lot more where there hasn't been any recourse.' He agreed to send the papers by private email to Chris Jones. 'This guy is cloning car numbers, but why and how? I've talked to others in Traffic around the country and it is prevalent in the north regarding cloned cars from the south and vice-versa. Bit of a generalisation, but you get the gist.'

DS Jones asked a question to which Jamie had no answer. 'Where's the money then? Always follow the money. Presumably the cloned vehicles are identical — colour, badging etc., and presumably nicked. OK, so no road tax; speeding tickets and parking fines, and of course, no insurance, and if the cars are old enough, no MOT test but that's peanuts... Difficult to sell, except for luxury vehicles when they're off to the Middle East in a container or being cannibalised for spare parts, I'd have thought. Can't see it myself.'

'Well, guv, just a thought... what about supply to the bad guys? Nearly every crime needs a getaway vehicle of two — who supplies them as kosher rather than just nicking them off the street?'

DS Jones smiled. 'Jamie, brilliant thought! Who supplied the vehicles for the heist here? Police cars, all of which were clones, I'll bet. Thanks again, I'll pass it on to the DCI. But there is one thought that occurs to me straight away. Is there wriggle room for Scott? Can he disclaim ownership of this little escapade? We need to have proof that he is up to his neck in this cloning business. Think about it. Ask your colleagues for ideas. Yes?'

Jones called his boss and DI Miles to keep them in the picture of potential developments.

Sam Miles asked, 'Ask your DVLA chums if they know who is their software supplier. If it is connected with her, it certainly has a memorable company name! Just a hunch, but maybe Sarah Scott's, under one of her many names, IT company has or had, been involved and that would give a clue to identifying specific vehicles.'

LeFanu, impressed with the thinking, told Chris Jones that he was going to call George Pchelski, because he is an ex-con maybe with contacts and there is a bit of a hold over him at the moment. DS Jones agreed and promised to pass on the information.

***

His mobile phone call was answered, *'Bonjour, c'est George.'* LeFanu repeated his comments made in Pchelski's French house that he required information, making it sound more formal than simply a request.

George Pchelski stopped Philippe in his tracks. 'Listen, sir. I have no knowledge of the police car thing, but would hazard a guess at cloning. I would expect, if you know what I mean, that the cars you mentioned were genuine hire-cars with false plates. Where they came from, I know not. I will ask around, if you know what I mean.' He rang off abruptly.

Early the next morning, LeFanu's phone buzzed, showing a missed call from George P. Later, after a meeting, he received a further call from Pchelski. 'DCI LeFanu, if that is still the correct title, I have a bit of information for you. No names, no pack drill, as they say. The way that cloning, because that's what it's called, works for the criminal classes, not me, you understand…' There was a chuckle from LeFanu. 'Yes, where was I… Right, a bad guy calls a number, a burner phone inevitably, and specifies a vehicle type, year and colour — probably a car they've nicked or even rented legitimately. All about traceability, I suppose. Which, incidentally, maybe what you were talking about with Police vehicles. Anyway, the person on the other end of the mobile will locate a number that is pretty safe to use and hey presto, you have a cloned vehicle with only a small risk that the real owner of the registration number might be in the same vicinity as the cloned vehicle. No guarantee, of course, but what in life is guaranteed? Then there is a fee and arrangements, of course. Can't help you there, but it is somewhere in the Midlands that the packages are despatched. Got a name too. Jane, for what it's worth. Best I can do, sir.'

'That fits, George. I'm not sure what you mean by "no names no pack drill" but don't bother to explain and yes, as we speak, I am still a DCI. Thank you for the information. I will not trouble you further, at least on this matter and tell your friend to continue to enjoy his trip to the other side of the world.'

'Thanks, appreciated. Useful being inside at Her Majesty's pleasure for information like this. It is quite common. The so-called "get-away" drivers know the routine and probably have the contacts too. That's up to you. Cheers.' He rang off, leaving Philippe hurriedly making notes with his brain, making two and two equal five.

After calling from his open door for DS Jones, who arrived after only a few moments, clutching two coffees in plastic cups, causing LeFanu to sigh at the lack of china mugs, he was still staring at the ceiling for a few seconds and started relating the calls with Pchelski, holding up his hand as Jones started to question.

'Don't ask what hold we have on him, just think. Follow the money, Chris. Do your checking about the cloning thing on the assumption that we're close. No need at this stage to find ourselves with a grass who will direct us — that's possible for later. And talk to DI Miles. She's got the contact with major crime in London. We've got a provisional name and location from George P, but that could be a cul-de-sac. They're better at tracking a Jane something or other than we are. Then, if we have some evidence, we will play Mrs bloody Moore off against Guy Scott. One, or both, of them is making a shedload of money from this caper, which has led to involvement in these murders. I'd bet my pension on it.'

'Hope it's a sure thing then, sir. My guv'nor in vice said I could spend a few days on this caper, but only a few days. Can you square it with him?' LeFanu nodded. Jones had been thinking all the time LeFanu had been talking and was obviously anxious to ask a question, 'Maybe the car involved when those fires were set the night of the events at Eye St Mary was similarly cloned, recalling that we had the majority of the registration number from one of the farmers, and maybe a search of the system at the Duxford auction house might list the number. Some people are anal about lists, sir. And it is not an easy task to wipe some stuff from the hard drive of a computer,' was his final comment. LeFanu acknowledged the thought and was brought back to reality a few seconds later by Chris Jones talking again. 'I'll get it over to the tech boys to sweep the hard drives.'

'Do it, Jones. Do it.'

'Just a random thought, sir. George P talked about a bird called Jane. Turned out it was a pseudonym for the Middle Eastern woman, Shaida, if I recall.'

'Good thought. Could be a coincidence. Tell DI Miles that, too. She wasn't involved at that stage of the investigation.'

***

The next call he took was from Susie Ford. 'Hello, guv. I want to play you a recording of a conversation with that lass Melanie…'

"Conversation with Melanie…"

"I remember it now, a blue Vauxhall Corsa. Don't remember the registration number. Think it was 2013 or thereabouts — that means a 13 plate or 53 number.

"Most of the time it was under his trade plates but then it had one number and then another or it could have been a different car. He often had a couple of run-abouts, often the same type of car. I think he had a deal with a local Vauxhall dealership as he called them and then flogged them after a while. He let me borrow it once or twice if he was in a good mood. I'd forgotten about that when you asked me before. The staff often used it for errands and the like."

"That's useful, Melanie, but can you remember the number plate or some of it? It is important."

"Hang on a minute, where's my phone? I think we, my boyfriend and I, took a picture one time when we went to the beach at Frinton in it on a Sunday. About ninety minutes away."

There were noises and grunts on the recording, with Susie commenting

"Gosh, Melanie, you have hundreds of photos by the look of it."

Evidently, she was flipping through a seemingly endless series of photos, and at last with an expression of "Phew I knew I was right", said to her, "See, look at that."

Susie Ford, almost like a movie voice-over for the benefit of the recording, added, "The registration number shows clearly. When was that?"

Melanie had checked the phone screen again and showed DC Ford the time and date and location of the photo.

'There's a chance, DS Jones,' she said over the phone, 'that the blue car was driven out under trade plates, but we couldn't track its return journey to Scott's depot — it seemed to have disappeared. Maybe, just maybe, it came back under its real number. Worth a try with the CCTV and ANPR cameras on that road we checked before.'

'Go for it. Well done.'

DCI LeFanu was pleased with the feedback, commenting that once again using, as he called it, "bright young things", the strategy had proved its worth. However, and it was a big "however", he maintained, what next was the real issue.

***

'Hoo bloody ray! Here it is, and there's a close-up of the driver blown up to three hundred percent at the camera 4678, positioned at Junction 9 Stumps Cross on the M11/A11. It's Mr Scott — no doubt about it. So now we have a time and place to break his alibi. Get the interview files with the infamous Mr Guy Scott.' The registration number, GU14ANC, supplied by Melanie Griffiths, proved to be two things. Number one: it was a clone of a blue Vauxhall Corsa, 2014 registered, legally owned by a retired couple in Gillingham, Kent, a Mr & Mrs Charles Costen, who had never been north of the River Thames in it. Local journeys only, they said, and they had a nice Mercedes they used on longer journeys, holidays and so on. No reason to doubt their word, reported the local traffic inspector on enquiry from Ipswich. Secondly: it had been spotted several times on CCTV in and around Cambridgeshire and its environs in the past year. Not a regular identification, which in itself was strange, but as DS Jones pointed out, the registration number could be cloned several times to avoid identification and blue was a pretty common colour for Corsas manufactured in 2012 to the present date.

LeFanu was cock-a-hoop at the news and started to think more widely about the implications whilst DS Jones and DC Ford were checking and marking up copious maps of the region with sightings.

LeFanu contacted DI Miles in London to ask her advice about the criminal implications that had been put forward by DC Jamie Steadman and DS Jones.

She responded almost immediately with the question "where's the proof?". 'Yes, it's probable that Scott is instrumental, but the DPP won't want to run with that only to be drummed out of court by a clever lawyer. The other matter my colleagues in the Met here have had a feeling about, is that there is a central pool for the gangs to get vehicles, as car security has improved so much over the past few years, with tracker systems and Stage 2 alarms. Could be very helpful. Interesting, so I'll get back to you.'

LeFanu spoke to Jones, asking him to check thoroughly about the number plates. Jamie Steadman had been busy, knowing from his job even over a few months, that the law insisted that number plate manufacture is controlled via licensed outlets. So, he had pointed out, where Scott or his cronies were getting them made was still a mystery.

Twenty minutes later, he called Jones again, having checked the inventory of the Duxford Auction search. 'Bet you don't know what a thermal image printer is, guv?'

'No. Fancy kit for printing like a laserjet?'

'No, not really. Bit more advanced than that. Just special technology for transfer of images. Google is a mine of information — invented about thirty years ago by Texas Instruments, but nowadays pretty compact and cheap. Use a computer program to put in the number you want and insert a special plastic sheet and almost "hey presto", you have the required number plate. On the inventory and in a small side office. We missed it. Logged as an office printer, but the PC making the list had the presence of mind to comment that it looked unusual and quite old, unlike most of the technology in that place, and gave the model number and manufacturer. Quick bit of Googling and now we know how he had the plates made, ad hoc.'

'Find the software, Jamie. Find the computer and chances are we'll find all the plates that have been made on that machine. And get someone to try to find when the kit was purchased. Well done.'

'Funny you should say that, sir. It's the second time we've talked of software. And don't we have someone in mind who can write code for software systems? DVLA, incidentally, wouldn't tell me who wrote their systems — sort of trade secret, I suppose. Need someone to make an official request and didn't think we should at this stage.'

'Umm. Interesting. Does Mrs Sarah Moore still work? Rhetorical question at this stage. HMRC would know, but we should not make those enquiries yet. Perhaps we should make a quantum leap and assume we know and act accordingly. I'll think on it.'

Jamie called Susie Ford and asked her to call Melanie Griffiths again and suggest that the three of them went for a drink in the Chequers at Fowlmere, close to Foxton, and that Susie would pick her up by car, plain clothes car of course, at whatever time suited. The agenda was to be office procedures at the car auction place.

***

That evening, still smarting at her peremptory dismissal, Melanie was more than willing to help and drove herself in her parent's car to the pub to meet the two police colleagues.

The next day, Jamie Steadman gave DS Jones a potted version of the conversation. Apparently, Melanie had been employed as a trainee secretary cum factotum, or dogsbody, as she had described it. In her early days there, she had been trained to operate the obvious office machines. After a while, she was shown how to operate a machine to make number plates but always, as she had put it, under close supervision of Mr Scott. It was a fiddly job and each plate number had to be entered on a laptop to connect to the fancy printer to produce the film, which then was put through another machine, like a roller press, and then Mr Scott marked up a see-through plastic sleeve for each plate with a series of numbers and letters and locked them away with the HP laptop and a memory stick on his keyring. She said that this always took place in the tiny office off his main room and the filing cabinet was locked with his own key. All this whilst Melanie suffered what is now called sexual abuse, which she called serious groping. When Susie asked why she hadn't slapped him down and walked out, she repeated more or less what she had told DI Miles before, that jobs were hard to come by outside Cambridge. One additional piece of information that worried the girl was the she had had to sign a legally binding form about non-disclosure of information. Both the police colleagues, on asking to see her copy of the form, were surprised to find she had never been given a copy. They had logged the information about the NDA and assured her that she was safe from any action by Scott, but she could well be required as a witness and she should pass all her diaries that she had assembled at work to DS Ford and would be given a receipt and a guarantee that they would not be released to any other party.

Despite the news from this quarter, DCI LeFanu was still sceptical that the DPP would accept this "evidence" as sufficient for a potential conviction. They had to look elsewhere.

'It's high time we pulled that bastard Scott in for a chat. He's got a lot of explaining to do and we need to look for causation rather than…'

LeFanu read the brief report with rising anger. Scott was not responding to phone calls and the premises of the Paddick Classic Car Auctions company in Duxford seemed to be closed for refurbishment, as the sign outside suggested. A car had been sent to his home, but again shutters were apparently down and no sign of life.

'Keep trying,' was all LeFanu could think of, as it was not strong enough evidence to put out an all ports holding call, suggesting that giving him until morning and then the rules could change with concern about Scott's well-being being a sufficiency of an argument.

DC Susie Ford quickly found the two car cleaners from the company having a drink in the Queen's Head, Harston, not really surprising as she knew it was the closest pub to their home village. They confirmed that the company was closed, temporarily they thought, and they had been sent home alongside the other employees. They had thought that the boss was on holiday or something.

Next morning, LeFanu's office telephone rang and a cheerful voice asked him what the hell he wanted leaving messages every hour on the hour from the previous day. LeFanu was taken aback and surprised.

'Mr Scott, we need to talk to you urgently. And I'm not prepared to do so over the phone. I'll send a car for you or you can come here straight away. Your call.'

'OK, OK, Detective Chief Inspector. I hear you. I thought you were done with me after the search at my home and the offices and I was told that I was in the clear. I have heard from the Inland Revenue people, thanks a bundle for that, so I thought that was that as far as the police were concerned. And before you ask where I was yesterday and overnight, I was concluding a business deal in London and my phone was on the blink. OK? Oh, and do I need a lawyer this time? OK, OK, I'll be there in an hour or two.'

LeFanu, joined by DS Jones, raised his eyebrows as the phone was on loudspeaker. 'That, Mr Scott, is your decision. But be here by two p.m.'

After the call, Jones immediately commented that "phone's on the blink" was always a convenient excuse.

LeFanu responded with his normal, 'Just so, just so,' comment and reminded his colleague that they wanted Scott to be at ease and unprepared and in a mood to help them, rather than antagonism and shrieking for a solicitor.

***

Mr Scott, who nevertheless now looked less cheerful than he had sounded on the telephone, arrived precisely on two p.m., shaking hands, whilst going against the grain for LeFanu. 'You know my colleague, Detective Sergeant Jones?'

Scott nodded. 'Are you on the square?' He smiled at the two police officers.

'No, Mr Scott. I'm French and a Catholic which, I believe, precludes me from joining a Masonic Lodge. Mr Jones must answer for himself, of course.' DS Jones shook his head.

Scott took the seat opposite and nodded as Jones offered coffee in the nicest, friendliest voice he could muster. This introduction was exactly what LeFanu wanted and Scott responded with the salesman's supercilious smile despite a glance at the surroundings. The DCI had deliberately chosen the tattiest interview room on the fourth floor overlooking the rear of the building.

'First, sorry about the surroundings, but needs must in this cash strapped society we live in…'

'Yes, indeed, I understand, gentlemen. My own company is undergoing restructuring and refurbishment at the moment — we do need, of course, to be ahead of the game in presentation. And it is a slack time for us, so temporary closure seemed to be the obvious choice.' He gazed around the sparsely furnished and very tatty room with a supercilious smile.

'Just the formalities that we are obliged by rules to go through with you. Mr Scott, we will be recording this interview, and of course, you will be entitled to a copy of the tape, if you so wish. If you should change your mind about having your solicitor present, that remains your right. Do you understand?'

'Indeed, DCI LeFanu. I do know your Chief Constable, Mr James Gilmour, rather well through my connections at the Lodge, as you may know, and indeed a fair few of your colleagues here and elsewhere in the police force. Hence my question. Anyway, what is this all about? I have told you all that I know and your invasion of my privacy at home and the office was borne by me with patience and understanding to help you in your enquiries, as you put it, although I fail to understand why.'

Jones raised his eyebrows just out of line of sight of Scott. LeFanu, aided by Jones, outlined the direction of the interview, theatrically putting a bulky file on the desk between them.

'We need to know about Mrs Sarah Moore, the wife, as you may know, of our erstwhile assistant chief constable. Tell us more about her relationship with you and your company.'

'Sarah? Well, yes of course I know Andrew. Before she married him, she was married to my brother and when he died I tried to help her make ends meet. After all, what are families all about?' He looked at the DCI with a disarming smile. Seeing that the comment was not enough, he continued after a few seconds silence. 'She helped with developing some software for us to track ownership of classic cars. In fact, she's a one man IT department well above my understanding. Give her a problem and she's off sorting it. Just give her endless coffee and hey presto.' Again, the shallow grin looking from policeman to policeman for a reaction and being greeted by equally shallow smiles in accordance with their strategic approach. He continued, 'Our speciality, as I think your sergeant here knows, is to identify potential buyers rather than just advertising. Then we seek to buy selectively. I gave her a couple of cars over the years, stuff that was less likely to affect our profit margins, and after that, you probably know more from your Mr Moore.' He stopped and looked up, seeking a question or response.

DS Jones interrupted his flow, feigning puzzlement 'So why do you have low value cars that you give away if you only buy selectively? Sorry, just interested…'

'Well, Sergeant, as I recall suggesting to you when you turned up with your very attractive colleague… I forget her name. Anyway, sometimes we do end up with a Mondeo like yours and endeavour to sell it on pdq. Fortunately, it is not that often. The majority of nice cars tend to go to people with nice cars.'

Jones nodded. 'And Mr Moore?'

'Well, obviously he became friends with me because of Sarah. Incidentally, it did surprise me that he had taken early retirement on health grounds, or so I heard. My pal, your chief constable, won't tell me more.'

DS Jones countered to get things back on their agenda. 'Sorry, you'll just have to speculate or ask Mr Moore yourself. It is not our policy to discuss private matters concerning our people.'

Scott shrugged. 'It is of little consequence. Anyway, we had occasional dinners, drinks and the like. I don't expect our paths would have crossed had it not been for my ex-sister-in-law. Mr Moore bought some cars from us, at trade prices inevitably. He is a bit of a petrolhead, and without the expense of kids, cars became his passion, I suppose.'

LeFanu interjected with a puzzled look, rather than being aggressive, 'You suppose, Mr Scott?' LeFanu, against the grain, was determined to keep Scott amenable. 'We have your records. The cars you sold to him and to his wife are worth a considerable amount of money and the trade prices you talk about are substantially less than their trade value. We have checked with experts.'

'I told you before that it is difficult to assess the value of cars as it always depends, obviously, on condition but materially on provenance and the timing of the sale. I can give you an example. Convertibles sell badly in winter.'

'Just so. Let us move on. You have been seen driving a blue Vauxhall. For the recording, I am showing Mr Scott a photograph from a roadside camera which clearly identifies him in the driving seat. It is timed and dated on the day after the murders, the 6th of January, of Jerry Scott and Mrs Monika Braun at Eye St Mary. Please explain.'

'6th January? My word! 6th of January? I really can't recall a month ago, let alone January. Maybe I was getting petrol, maybe a sandwich. God knows. I wouldn't even have put an entry in a diary for a trip like that. Easiest car to get out of the compound; could have been an Aston Martin or a pick-up truck. I'm not a car snob, Mr LeFanu.'

DS Jones could hardly supress a laugh, managing to control his facial expression after a severe glance from his boss.

'I would like you to detail your movements on that day, Mr Scott. Perhaps you could check with your PA or employees when you return to your business premises.'

Scott shrugged and nodded. 'PA? That'll be the day. Had to get rid of that meddling little girl and haven't got around to replacing her.'

LeFanu felt that Scott was relaxed enough, judging by his responses and body language, and ready now for the real questions 'Now, please explain the number of cloned number plates in your premises.'

Scott sat bolt upright. 'What?'

'Sir, we uncovered in our search of your business premises a large number of car number plates for fairly ordinary vehicles — certainly not your usual range of exotica — many, if not all, of which were registered to people who, not to put too fine a point on it, had never even heard of you or your company. We call that cloning and your computer system has more information about those self-same vehicles. This concerns us and our colleagues in serious crime in Scotland Yard.'

'Wow. That's all news to me, sir. Let me think on it.' He paused, gulped and shook his head. 'It must be that cow, Sarah. No one else has access to the computer that operates that bloody machine that makes the plates. Can't be that stupid girl Melanie that I sacked, she hasn't the brains. She just made the plates — shoving the blanks into the machine. Why? That's the question. Cloning? Of course I know what it is. We're careful that cars we buy here, and abroad for that matter, have kosher ownership and VIN numbers and so on. Not me, guv.'

'Right, maybe we now need to talk to Mrs Sarah Moore, but as the owner of the business, you and your company will be involved in the investigation, Mr Scott. Unavoidable.'

'But Mr LeFanu, Sergeant Jones, this will kill my business. That deal I was trying to conclude in London is about selling the business. Anything like this will kill that deal stone dead. Since Tony died, I've been struggling. I make no bones about it.'

'Well, Mr Scott, you help us and we'll try to help you.'

'Shit! Yes, yes, of course. She's got contacts at DVLA. Always on the phone to a guy there. Name, name. Bear with me. Peter Monday, that's it. No, Mundy. Had to give him a nice Range Rover, red it was. 2012 plate. And at a knock down price about a year ago. Sarah told me it was essential to give us an edge over the competition. He was, is, a nasty bit of work. A real tosser.'

DS Jones excused himself from the interview and announced for the benefit of the tape that he was leaving the room in order to check the name of Mundy on the car company's records and at DVLA.

'Whilst we are waiting for DS Jones to return, please explain the next issue. The champagne bottle in the bedroom. You described that room before as that of Veronica van Outen or whichever name she chose to use.'

'She, Sally bloody Moore that is, introduced Ronnie a few years back. She knew her in Switzerland, apparently. She brought a few of them over here to help the business — sort of thing that used to happen at the Motor Show at Earl's Court — pretty young girls draped over the bonnet in next to nothing. Certainly worked, and they didn't stop just with sales, if you know what I mean.' He winked at Jones, who had just returned to the interview room.

'That, Mr Scott, sounds very much like you were, and maybe still are, involved in grooming young, vulnerable girls. We have a witness statement that blackmail was being used to encourage business. What is your answer to that?'

'Grooming. No way! They were all up for it. Few quid to strip off and have a shag. Reckon that's what they teach at finishing school. Few photos and videos and some cars bought and sold and a few perks for the rest of us, including your chief constable and Mr Andrew Moore, for that matter.' He laughed. 'Grooming. No chance. They taught us all a thing or two.'

'Language, Mr Scott, please. What happened to the photos and video footage?'

'Ask Sarah Moore. I don't know. She kept a lot of it on a memory stick, if that's the right word for it. On a keyring, I think. And I expect the video stuff is on a computer somewhere. Ask her. We all had a laugh and a few beers in my cinema watching a few of the videos, but she held onto the stuff. Oh, and there are one or two where Andrew watched his wife having it off with one or two others — good stuff when the lads are round with a couple of beers. She rationed films out for a fee or an exchange of favours, if you know what I mean.'

'No, I don't know what you mean, but let us move on to the empty bottle of champagne. A bottle that has your DNA and a fingerprint on its neck that we believe is yours.'

'In her underwear drawer in my house? OK, OK. I used to get my rocks off going through her undies, pretty sexy stuff, if you know what I mean, so I may have touched it. Funny place to keep an empty bottle, but who knows why. She's dead now so we'll never know, will we?'

'We never said it was in her underwear drawer, Mr Scott. Nevertheless, that bottle was used in the murder of Mr Jerry Gold so you become, de facto, a person of interest to the investigation…'

'I think I need a solicitor now'

'I, we, think you do. Interview terminated. You will be held here under caution for forty-eight hours whilst we consider whether to formally charge you.' LeFanu reached across and switched off the recording, then pointed to DS Jones and told him to arrange for Scott to contact his solicitor and to place a PC on duty in the room while he waited.

***

Afterwards, in the so called comfort of Philippe LeFanu's office, they compared notes. Peter Mundy was at DVLA in Swansea and was involved in the software development as the senior manager. Jones had contacted DI Sam Miles in London who was to arrange an interview with him in Wales alongside an in-depth search of his finances. This slotted in with the current, albeit stalled, investigation by Scotland Yard of vehicle cloning issues.

LeFanu made an appointment to meet with Mrs Hodgkinson, the Suffolk police and crime commissioner, as he needed to formally interview Mrs Moore. But as her husband was still the subject of investigation and James Gilmour, the chief constable, had been mentioned in the Scott interview, he had to go one higher due to the sensitive nature of the combination of internal people being involved and the earlier overruling of investigations into Scott's empire by ACC Moore and the chief constable.

'Chris, we will need to return to the purpose of Scott driving the blue Vauxhall car on the 6th January last. That is our primary purpose. The murders. Cloning we will leave to the Yard and DI Miles, who has got the bit between her teeth on this one, and similarly the blackmail and sexual… what shall we call them, "adventures", must take a back seat.'

Jones sniggered. 'Probably was the back seat, sir!'

LeFanu looked at his sergeant, mystified, before it dawned on him at the misplaced humour.

***

The meeting with Sheila Hodgkinson was to be held in a luxurious suite of rooms on the first floor of the Police headquarters building, but removed sufficiently from the operating part of the police force, thankfully, mused LeFanu.

In seeking advice from her office, Philippe LeFanu realised that the role of commissioner prohibited interference in the day to day running of a local constabulary, but had supervisory responsibility to ensure strict adherence to the rules of governance which he hoped would be enough.

She seemed a sensible person to DCI LeFanu. Around late thirties, he guessed, a certificate on the wall from Durham, a red brick university; a framed OBE from 2010 and generally unpretentious decorations. She was smartly dressed without being ostentatious.

She had listened attentively and told LeFanu that he was treading on dangerous ground unless he had hard evidence of malfeasance. She had added that if any action failed, his career would probably come to an abrupt end, which he accepted with a brief nod. She had in front of her his file showing his history with the police force, not only in Suffolk but throughout his career, and wanted to talk through the incident that had curtailed his promotional aspirations in the Met, all of which LeFanu had expected, as he had realised that putting his bosses on the line would make others in the Suffolk police and still others further afield wary of his presence — innocent or guilty.

She listened to the tape of Guy Scott's interview and asked for an hour or two to go through the files assembled since the murders. LeFanu quietly left the building, not wishing to fuel any speculation that anyone seeing him leaving her offices would be certain to happen.

Two hours later, Mrs Hodgkinson smiled as he was ushered back into her office by her confidential secretary. 'You certainly have reason to doubt the efficacy of your hierarchy — maybe, maybe not, for the crimes you are investigating but certainly for impropriety. Moore has been dealt with relatively discretely and I don't wish to retrace our steps unnecessarily. Chief Constable Gilmour is another matter which requires careful consideration, so take care what you say and do, and importantly, write down, and that applies to your colleagues too. To date, it appears that your

Mr Scott is blackening the name of his "friend", maybe to divert attention and the powers that be, including me, would not take that as a sufficiency of reason. As of now, you should proceed with your investigations ignoring any bars that have been applied. I require you to verbally report to me at least weekly. Is that understood? And please call Mrs Moore in for interview under caution as soon as you can. I want the murderer or murderers caught. I suggest you hold Scott for forty-eight hours, which will preclude him from talking to the chief constable, and indeed, Mrs Moore. But try to get the evidence to make things stick.'

LeFanu thanked her and rose to leave. She approached the door and added quietly, 'Off the record, DCI LeFanu, I admire your courage. Take care with that woman, I hesitate to call her a lady, She has ideas above her station — Swiss nobility, she told me. That is as, maybe, but she has been in and out of this office many times pleading for that precious husband of hers, more concerned about her reputation than even his, I suspect. I would offer a suggestion, off the record. Mr Moore is due for a long meeting shortly with his solicitor; my PA will give you the details. Perhaps interview Mrs Moore at the same time. Take care and do advise her to have a solicitor present on the recording, as I am sure you know. Good luck!'

'Ma'am, thank you for your counselling. From the information we have, if it is to be believed, it is ironic to talk about her reputation.' The commissioner smiled and raised her eyebrows.

Chapter 69

DS Jones rushed in with latest news, waving a print-out. 'DI Miles sent this report in, sir. That Peter Mundy guy has been arrested. When DI Miles confronted him with a verbal "witness report", without telling him who, where or why, he broke down and confessed it all. It had started when he was caught with his trousers down with two young, very young (his words) girls and photos to prove it. I am paraphrasing. Next thing, he had heard was from Sally insisting on some "help", as he put it, in exchange for some thought-provoking photos apparently sitting in an envelope or two addressed to his wife and employer just waiting for a postage stamp. The Sally later we know is Mrs Sarah Moore. DI Miles says well done, sir, to you and all the team. And she would like to sit in on any interviews, as she has an inside track on the developments by Organised Crime Unit in London.'

Philippe LeFanu was beaming. 'Now, DS Jones, we need to know the how of it all and let DI Miles find how it works and who are/were Mrs Moore's clients. Maybe this explains that she's the brains behind this and her husband, ACC Moore's involvement is liking girls from what Scott said, and association with Scott regarding cheap luxury supercars. Pass it on to the team and let them think about it. Back to the murders, eh? But to repeat the crime commissioner's comment, be careful, all of you, and record every damn thing.'

DI Miles told Chris Jones that the search for a Jane in the Midlands was proving difficult. Janeth Abaylan was easier. She had married a William Hand and was living in Cheltenham, Gloucestershire — still with a current Philippine passport and no further criminal record. There was a triangulation report on a lot of mobile phone activity from a disposable untraceable phone in the area, but nothing accurate enough to take further action. But the information was useful enough to suggest maintaining monitoring activity.

She suggested that, with the interest from Scotland Yard, she should be at the forthcoming interview, which was a suggestion that LeFanu had hoped for.

Chapter 70

Mrs Moore was collected from her home in an unmarked police car after a telephone call suggesting it might be a better idea than her arriving to the police HQ in a super car.

Again, they chose a poorly furnished and shabby interview room quite deliberately. DS Jones and DI Miles sat at the side of the room whilst the plan was for Mrs Moore to be sitting directly opposite DCI LeFanu, next to her solicitor, with the tape machine running to the side of the table.

She was dressed immaculately in a pin-striped, straight skirted business suit with a serious diamond cluster brooch on the lapel, which gained a look of approval from DI Miles. Again, as expected, perfect make-up and her blonde hair held in a French pleat. A good looking lady, fairly vain, by the looks of her, was Philippe's thought, had it not been for the background that they already had of this woman.

Mrs Moore was to be interviewed under caution in accordance with the instructions from the police and crime commissioner. She approached the interview with a frosty attitude, repeatedly saying that her husband was an assistant chief constable and this whole affair was unnecessary and totally without authority.

'For God's sake, Inspector LeFanu, this place looks like a public convenience, and I suspect the same colour too. I would have thought, out of respect for your superiors, that you could have found a more pleasant office for my interview. My husband is at an important meeting right now, otherwise I would tell him to do something about it.'

LeFanu insisted that she have a solicitor present, but she refused point blank, stating that that would be tantamount to admitting guilt.

He introduced his colleagues and offered her coffee, which she promptly declined. 'My husband told me about your office coffee, thank you.'

He smiled, acknowledging the reply with a shrug. DI Miles, according to their plan of playing to Sarah's vanity, sweetly complimented her on her beautiful brooch, and received a theatrical smile in response, informing her that it was part of an inheritance from her Swiss family and was, of course, the real thing.

LeFanu picked up the reins again. 'We wish to talk to you about several matters, madam.' And then he fell silent, knowing that silence in a formal interview was a powerful tool, as most people can't stand silence so they start talking.

'What matters are they, Mr LeFanu? I suppose you want to talk about my relationship with bloody Guy Scott. Well, let me tell you, he means nothing to me. A job in the past; a bit of sex and some fun, but that is all in the past...' She was trying hard to put a lot of emphasis on the word "past".

LeFanu and DI Miles just stared at her. He just shrugged and waited.

'You want me to go on? OK. My husband and I went to a few parties at the Scott house. A few girls and some champagne. Nothing to feel guilty about. We led a pretty free life as far as that is concerned. It might sound a little blasé, but we do have an open marriage, as it is often called. Anyway, DCI LeFanu that is my, our, business and not for public consumption.'

LeFanu pursed his lips, clasped his hands together under his chin as in prayer and stared.

'What are you staring at DCI, LeFanu?'

After a minute or so of complete silence, he launched his questioning. 'Why, madam, are you harbouring this idea of guilt you mentioned a minute ago, if you don't feel there is anything to worry about?'

'Just a figure of speech. Andrew always said that, of all his employees, you had the most difficult sense of humour. Anyway, I thought this meeting is about my husband's position with the Suffolk Constabulary. God knows you've had enough of your people crawling all over my house. What next!'

LeFanu decided to ignore the gibes. 'Mrs Moore, for the tape, please confirm your name and maiden name and your current address, and of course, date of birth. This is standard procedure, as your husband has probably told you. This meeting does concern you personally and is in connection with a range of enquiries we are making. That was made clear to you this morning when we called for you, in case you have forgotten.'

She sighed theatrically. 'OK. My name is Sarah Moore, nee Lefevre. I am a Swiss national with some influence. I fail to see why I should disclose my date of birth, and you certainly have my current address on your records.' She sat back and folded her arms.

'Yes, I did know about your citizenship. Indeed, I understand that you went to a finishing school there, near Basle, I believe.' He looked at her.

She frowned. 'I suppose asking me about my schooling, university or maybe even the Montessori nursery school I think I attended, but I was very young at the time to remember the GPS co-ordinates for you, is also standard procedure.'

Philippe LeFanu nodded, thinking it was pointless to react to the sarcasm. DS Jones interjected, all part of the plan, 'Yes, Mrs Moore, we are aware of your Swiss background. Something about a Swiss chap, what was his name? Now, let me think... yes, began with an F, wasn't it...?' He let the words sink in.

She blanched. 'That shit, Andervert, I'll bet. I could tell you quite a few things about him. What has he said about me? He's so wrapped up in making money I don't expect he'd give a damn anyway.'

LeFanu was secretly pleased. No lies had been told, yet she was unnerved by DS Jones's comment. He chose to ignore the question she had raised.

'Ah yes, Felix, wasn't it? Felix Andervert?' He looked straight at her for a reaction and she nodded, about to make some sort of comment

'OK. University, madam? Grenoble, I seem to remember from your file?' He tapped the thick buff file on the table in front of him. A theatrical prop he had used many times in interviewing to make the suspect think that more was known about them than actually was. It was plain that the point of the file was not wasted by her body language. She nodded. 'An IT qualification, we understand,' he continued. Again, she nodded, trying to look amused by the interrogation. 'Then you went to the USA, or have I got things in the wrong order? And please, a verbal response for the tape.'

'No. I came to the UK first to improve my English and to use my education in IT. I married far too young and he died in an industrial accident in Scotland — some sort of machine collapsed. Poor mutt. From there, I went to work in Silicon Valley, California. It is where I met my second husband, Fitzroy Springfield, a real petrolhead, but fast cars and booze didn't mix. He died after a couple of years in a head on collision with a school bus. I don't expect you have that information, do you? I probably have the marriage certificates somewhere. And death certificates too. Yes, both died.' Her sarcasm was wasted.

'Your IT consultancy, if that's the right word for it, was involved with our DVLA?

'Was, and still is, alongside many of Europe's and US organisations. I take a back seat nowadays, just checking in, so as to speak.'

'Mrs Moore. May I ask a question?' DI Miles looked and sounded sweetness and light, but not waiting for an answer, continued, 'As you'd expect, we have contacts at Swansea. What police force doesn't? There is a chap there who is under investigation as we speak. I wonder if you ever came across him? Peter Mundy is his name.'

Sarah Moore was caught off guard. Should she deny it or dismiss him as an also ran? Her face told the police colleagues that was exactly what she was thinking. Lying obviously came easily after a few seconds. 'Yes, I think so. Some sort of systems analyst, I think, one of many. Just a junior, I think. Of course, I met a lot of them as they were integrating our work with theirs. On a Government protocol project. Dare I ask what has he done?' She smiled at Sam Miles.

'No, madam, I can't tell you. Our protocol, you understand. It was just curiosity. Time will tell what he has to say, no doubt, and about whom.'

'OK, let's move on.' LeFanu was anxious to keep up the pressure. 'Talk to us about creating number plates for your ex-brother in law. That would be your first husband's brother, I think.' She nodded. 'We have been talking to him, as I expect you know. He doesn't seem to be up to speed, sorry about the pun, with technology.' He smiled.

'We developed some software to link with DVLA to prepare number plates on a piece of kit invented in the USA. First in the world, I believe.' She beamed at LeFanu. 'This is how it works. Scott sells a car; the owner wants a personalised plate; we prepare it and stick it on the car. Simple. Things like that are simple if you use the right people, like my group. And it goes wider, picking up the authorities concerned in many different countries. Good little earner, as they say. Guy is hopeless with technology but there is, or was, a bright young girl there who fed the machine and the computer does all the rest. Enough? Or shall I bore you with detail?'

LeFanu put his hands up to show that enough was enough. 'Now let's go back a bit. Switzerland and the girls and the blackmail both there and back in the UK.'

She was not so shocked as they had expected. Perhaps the earlier revelations had sharpened her thinking. 'My, you have been busy, Detective Chief Inspector LeFanu. But you shouldn't believe all you hear. Guy always did suffer from what the English call selective memory.'

'Far from it, madam. We have the evidence and the statements from other witnesses too. And like it or not; deny it or not, your name is in the frame. Mr Scott was quite elaborate, as were others.'

'Lying bastard. I suggest you check his books, carefully. He's no fool and neither is his accountant. And not just that set for the auction house but the three other businesses here and in the USA. He was blackmailing me, not the other way round. And that bitch Veronica is involved, too, and she is, or was, vicious.' She sneered as she said it.

LeFanu, again ignoring her flow of invective went on, 'So, madam, a lot of stories about undervaluing of cars is today's version of blackmail?'

'But of course. How do you think that lying bastard, Guy, made his money? And that other man, Lord Waller or whatever-his-name is, sorry was, was in it up to his armpits. And mostly cash too. So screw him and look for money laundering big time.'

'Well, thank you, madam. I presume you are just a hard-working innocent when it comes to all this?' He nodded to DS Jones who excused himself from the meeting and informed the tape recording accordingly, to seek information about the other businesses she had referred to. Continuing, Philippe LeFanu asked, 'May we assume then that our investigations will not involve you, or, for that matter, through you to your husband?'

'Your sarcasm is wasted on me, Mr LeFanu. I have, I admit, not been whiter than white all my life, but nothing to rank with that unholy duo, let alone Andervert in Switzerland.'

'Let us return to the issue of the girls.' Looking at DI Miles, he asked the question, 'What was it now? Eye candy with extras.' Sam Miles nodded. 'We understand, Mrs Moore, that you provided the "escorts". Shall we call them that? And many times, your husband and various clients participated in those romps.'

'Chief Inspector LeFanu, I'm sure you are a man of the world. My marriage to Andrew is an open one. He likes girls; I like men. So what? If sex sells, sell it, as some nobody in an insurance company years ago told me.'

'Madam, it is called grooming and procurement and it is a crime in this country and probably elsewhere too. But you are not denying it.'

'Harmless fun by consenting adults, that's all. It started at that bloody school in Basle. Charlotte, of course you know her, jumped up old French aristocracy that she is with no money, Veronique, as she called herself then, and I needed some spending money and we all enjoyed sex. OK, later there was a bit of pin money involved when Guy realised it was a way of making money from selling and buying fancy cars from clients who were vulnerable. Just a few photos and videos did the trick. I don't think that the law would be bothered with my part in all of this.'

DI Miles, frustrated by the blasé way that Mrs Moore reacted, had to interrupt. 'Harmless! Consenting adults! Sex with a minor is illegal and immoral. And procuring for such a purpose puts you into the frame for an arrest and the DPP to seek a court hearing.' She paused for effect. 'And your husband could well be facing charges in the same genre.'

'Listen! Guy was often asked why he had never married. He said "I was once, but I always get the girls I want so why tie myself down again?" He started in on me not long after I arrived in the UK, that's where I met his good-for-nothing brother and later stupidly married him. Poor mutt, as I said earlier. Guy liked young girls — the younger the better. And several at the same time. So I was a willing partner. I can fuck anyone I choose. So what? You are going after the wrong person.'

'We shall see, we shall see. I think that you were pulling Scott's strings, like a puppet and he danced to any tune you played.' LeFanu was anxious to increase the pressure, as he felt that she was relaxing a little too much and her participating in sex was missing the point. 'Madam, arranging the procurement and blackmail is a different matter — for a considerable later investigation, no doubt. Right now, cloning of cars for criminal pursuits and manipulating the software of, probably amongst others, the DVLA, is our next subject.' And turning to DS Jones and DI Miles, he asked if they had anything further to add.

DI Miles started, 'Madam, you mentioned photos and videos. Where are they? And where were all these goings-on going on?'

'I thought you would have searched Scott's home. Two bedrooms on the second floor were specially kitted out with video equipment, mirrored ceilings and other equipment. And then there's the private cinema in the basement.' She smiled at Jones, 'You know the sort of thing, surely you've seen it.'

'No, madam. DI Miles asked you the question, not me.'

'Well, maybe they aren't there now. How would I know?' And looking at DI Miles, she added, 'I expect Scott has the tapes and photos, or had them anyway.'

'OK, thank you. A further question then… If Mr Mundy is to be believed, then you threatened to expose him, excuse the pun,' she smiled at Sarah Moore, 'with photos which could be sent to his employers and family.'

'His word is that credible? I might have mentioned to him about his little visit to Guy's pleasure palace. That's what he called it. Andrew says nearly everyone is dead in this fiasco, so you are trying to pin it on anyone left, including him and now me, despite him ordering you to close the investigation, if you can call this farce today an investigation, and for you to move on to more important things.' She folded her arms. Moments later, she leaned forward, having regained her composure and continued, 'I think I want a solicitor now. I thought this was just an interview to help Andrew's cause, but now it's all about me. You should have told me.'

Pointless to argue, LeFanu arranged for a telephone for Mrs Moore and suggested a ten-minute break, leaving a WPC on duty in the room and closing the tape recording.

***

'Chris, naughty but nice the way you introduced some chap called Felix and let her run with it. Not that we can do much about the Swiss end, but it ties a lot of loose ends together. We know that Scott and Moore were driving this, but it doesn't get us closer to the murders and that is our prime purpose. Sam here will pick up the threads of the cloning. Cloning for us today is just the money as a motive. How do we tie Scott and others into the Jacuzzi murder and that of the unfortunate Ms Braun?'

Samantha Miles added, 'I think she, Mrs Moore, is the key. She provides the money. God knows how much she makes from her little enterprise, but it will be considerable. Scott's business is not healthy and we know that he was unable to pay Lord G the amount he promised to close the partnership. So, sir, follow the money is usually the way, as you often say. My colleagues in London estimate there are several thousand crimes associated with get-away driver requirements and even insignificant burglaries need a car. ANPR is forcing the bad guys to think differently — and here is a solution for them. And that's just the UK. It's neat. She, or whoever, answers the phone, looks for a car on DVLA that matches the specification, produces a self-adhesive number plate that matches, ships it out; the bad guys steal, or even hire, the original car and stick the plate on it. She collects a cash fee. Simple. And big money attracts violence.'

A timely breakthrough from the IT team at the Moore's house was communicated to LeFanu. They had broken the code for the password and were searching the hard drive of Mrs Moore's laptop, but it would take time.

***

They were told that a solicitor had arrived, so returned to the interview room. Mrs Moore was obviously annoyed, having found out that the solicitor she had expected was in a meeting with her husband at the same time some miles away, so the firm had sent a junior.

LeFanu smiled, knowing that what was playing out had been precisely what the police and crime commissioner had outlined. 'Madam, I think you are involved, if not actually orchestrating the cloning. You are also involved in the procurement and grooming of girls and were involved or knew of the murder of the person thought to be Lord Groombridge.' He paused expecting a response from the solicitor.

He told his client, Mrs Moore, that she didn't have to answer, as what DCI LeFanu had said was pure speculation. Sarah Moore told him to shut up.

'DCI LeFanu, that is rubbish. I did my job at the car place and did it well. Scott and Groombridge's empire would have collapsed without my help. You people always talk about motive, or they do on the TV. What's my motive. Eh? No money for me, a nice lifestyle, yes. A bit of sex on the side, absolutely. That's it? Kill people? Not my style. I suggest you arrest me or I leave with this legal eagle here right now.'

'One more question before we make that decision. Your system is cleverly encrypted. No criticism intended. Whilst you have been here, and indeed your husband, I understand, is in a meeting regarding his past and future performance, we have executed a further search warrant on your private house. We had, already, done similarly on the properties of Guy Scott, business and private, as you may know.'

'Yes, yes. So what? Get to the point, I am in a hurry.'

'Yes, ma'am, I'm sure you are. Bear with me. We had tried to break your encryption after the search of the software at the Duxford auction company, but as I said before, it was clever. A few minutes ago, in the break whilst we awaited your solicitor, our analysts found the key, so as to speak...'

She visibly blanched.

'However, not quite so clever, madam. Often, I am told, vanity and lifestyle have a direct bearing on the choice of passwords. True to form, the personalised plate on your Aston Martin, combined with the number sixty-nine and an exclamation mark, allowed our experts in. Not so clever after all, eh? And we found a memory stick on a key ring, looking like an Aston Martin key fob, which our technicians are opening as we speak.' She blanched but said nothing. 'Oh, and we are opening up several mobile phones that were found in a biscuit tin.'

'So what?'

'I can't tell you yet, but we will find out everything about you and your movements. No one else has accessed your computer records. So you have recorded on the hard drive, series of car and commercial vehicle number plates which are cloned with innocent, so as to speak, vehicles, including, I suspect, one Porsche 356C. So, to answer your earlier question, we are going to arrest you on the grounds of fraud and blackmail. In due course, that process may well be extended as a result of investigations relating to our earlier conversation which, as you know, has been recorded. You will be held here meanwhile.' And glancing at Jones and pointing to the tape machine, 'DS Jones, please do the necessary.'

Sarah Moore, red faced with anger, looked at LeFanu. 'Fuck you. The sixty-nine is for a certain type of sex that you won't have enjoyed, you French shit.'

The solicitor, patiently until then making copious notes, said to Mrs Moore, 'Say nothing,' so she turned on him with a sneer.

'You are worse than useless. Get out of here.' And turning her face to LeFanu, she commented, 'I'll be out of here. Your investigations are pathetic. I know someone else has manipulated my records. Maybe that Melanie girl, she's brighter than she appears. In cahoots with that bastard, Guy. And look at that Charlotte woman, too, she has an axe to grind and Ronnie... oh no, you can't, can you? And the, what do you call him, the DPP, will dismiss this and I'll be in my Aston Martin laughing at your pathetic attempts whilst you are put on traffic duties.'

'Maybe so, maybe so, but for now, you are under arrest.'

'My husband will hear of this so-called interview.'

'So be it, madam. Please remember that marriage to a high ranking official in this country does not, and never did, protect anyone from the law.'

'He's a useless lump of shit. A fool with most of his decisions made by his cock. I will leave him as soon as I'm out of here.' LeFanu shrugged. There was little left to add.

As he stood preparing to leave she, in a pleading voice, said, 'I could help you with lots of things if it were made worth my while.'

LeFanu, sitting again, gestured for her to sit. 'DI Miles here has vast experience in dealing with complex crimes, including murder, of which there has been a plethora in this, what was it you called it, farce.'

DI Miles picked up the thread. 'Madam, in our experience, murderers in particular think they are super clever and we, as "wooden tops", are struggling to keep up. The truth is that in most instances, the perpetrators of these crimes are so full of their own importance and ego that they always, and I mean always, make mistakes. Today, alone, you have given us just cause to investigate further. We will talk again, but not about deals.' She stood but added for the benefit of the solicitor and Mrs Moore, 'That part of the conversation is not recorded, but we are all witnesses to the offer of information in exchange for favours by Mrs Sarah Moore.' The solicitor nodded and scribbled some notes on his legal pad.

LeFanu and DI Miles left the room. Miles immediately asked, 'How on earth did they twig to the "sixty-nine" in the password?'

He answered, almost shrugging, that apparently all around the house there were artefacts that had sexual connotations, including what seemed like a shield featuring a stylised sixty-nine. Apparently, he added, that vanity plates on cars were often used in passwords, combined with some other number of letters. His body language showed he was as surprised as the rest of them.

'But,' he added before she could interrupt him, as she clearly wanted to, 'I had to take a flier that the hard drive would give us the information we needed. If she had scoffed at my comments, then I was, as they say in this country, up the creek without a paddle.'

'Exactly what I was going to ask, sir.'

'The real issue is we have forty-eight hours to come up with something concrete. I want those phones opened up and the computer stuff. We need our young team to start the analysis right now. DS Jones will set that up.

For the time being, DI Miles, we will leave the pornography and the blackmail. We now need to talk again to Mr bloody Scott. Our forty-eight hours has not got long to run for us to formally charge him, but we now know more. And I suppose I will have to notify ACC Moore of his wife's arrest.'

DCI LeFanu arranged an appointment with the police commissioner to update her, as they both knew that these revelations would cause a furore.

Chapter 71

Detective Constable Susie Ford had an inspiration after DS Jones had filled her in with the detail of the interviews. She had mused that what if the blonde they'd been seeking on the morning after the murder at Eye St Mary in the blue car was not Charlotte or Veronica, aka Angela, but another blonde. Or, as she put it, 'What if our blonde driving the blue hatchback Vauxhall was the woman you are describing in somewhat lascivious terms, DS Chris Jones?'

He had started to protest, but as the thought germinated, he grudgingly ignored the gibe but thanked her. He suggested she look at the phone logs from Mrs Moore's bunch of mobiles and to check the CCTV on the M11 going northbound towards Duxford from her home in Goodeaster, Essex, on the night before the murder and the day after for any of the cars in the Moore stable.

Two hours later, DC Ford confirmed her earlier suspicions. The Aston Martin AM2340 had been clocked on the M11 several times on the thirty-three mile journey. Twice exceeding ninety-five miles per hour, it had left the M11 at the Duxford slip road at ten past eight a.m. on the 6th January. At eight twenty-five a.m., a blue Vauxhall, GU14 ANC, had crossed the M11 at Junction 9, heading east, with a female driver, maybe a passenger but no details, but it had been picked up before the motorway on the cameras facing the auction house premises from the Imperial War Museum's premises. Camera records at the two locations were being digitally enhanced to attempt to identify the female driver, but it would take time. DS Jones nodded in appreciation at Susie Ford's intuition.

His view was to question and review the movements of Charlotte and Veronica, a much more difficult process. DS Jones observed that it had always made him think that the logistics of the movements they had discovered almost from day one were very complex, let alone whether the driver was a blonde or brunette; let alone the alibis given. Addressing Susie, he commented, 'We need to break the alibis or get Mrs Moore to admit to her movements after arriving at the auction house that morning.' Again, she nodded, flattered that she was asked to contribute.

Jones continued, 'So Charlotte or Veronica did the elaborate pick up of the American, Jerry Gold, at Norwich airport and drove him back via the restaurant to the family home, Porten House, at Eye St Mary. Then, the Bentley was returned to Duxford and later the blue car went from Duxford to Eye St Mary. And after a thorough cleaning/valeting, the Bentley is driven back to Chelsea and the blue Vauxhall puts on its trade plates and shortly thereafter is disposed of or sold or whatever. The Aston is driven back to Goodeaster on the Wednesday, according to the CCTV, southbound on the M11. It fits! But I am finding it hard to believe that Charlotte had a direct hand in the death of Jerry Gold — ancillary maybe, quite likely indeed, but actually murdering him and then pretending, at the morgue, well that takes some acting prowess, and I don't believe that she has that skill set — too temperamental. My money is on Veronica! I feel Charlotte should be detained on the grounds of wasting police time; aiding and abetting before, during and after the fact; insurance fraud — probably, but difficult to prove — blackmail, soliciting etc. etc. Should be enough to hold her under caution. I'll check our findings with the boss.'

***

Philippe LeFanu listened attentively to DS Jones. 'Mmmm,' he pondered. 'I have been thinking that I, we, maybe, convinced ourselves that all the bad guys were dead so the guilty party or parties, could be counted amongst those that remained that we knew of. And now we find a new participant. Are there any more? Was there a random killer with an axe to grind?'

Samantha Miles interrupted. 'I've been thinking about this during the interview with Mrs Moore. My considered opinion is that we were not sidetracked. We were given a clue about Sally/Sarah, whatever she calls herself, but she appeared to be just a friend of Charlotte. One of many, by the sounds of it. Granted that we didn't make the connection between a Swiss national and the ex-wife of Scott's brother. No reason why we should. There are plenty of females with that forename. Now we find she's connected to Scott and the others and seems to have a motive...'

DS Jones interjected. 'Thinking of Mr Scott's first visit to the barn at Porten House with me, we did think afterwards that it was strange that he got to us so quickly. But what I'd forgotten until now is his actions in the barn. He was all over those cars, each one, like a rash. He touched everyone of them, quite sickening in hindsight, bearing in mind we were dealing with a dead body of someone he thought of as a friend and business partner.'

DI Miles, thinking quickly about his comments, added, 'Good point, Chris. Maybe to stop us wondering why his prints were all over those pristine cars that were, by his own admission, untouched and cleaned lovingly by Lord G. Relevance, I'm not so sure.'

DS Jones glanced at his phone, having been alerted by the annoying ping. 'Excuse me, sir, ma'am. This is relevant.' A few seconds elapsed before Jones looked up at his boss and gave a thumbs up signal. Puzzled, LeFanu waved his hand in exasperation. 'Sorry, sir. DC Ford and the team have been watching for hours CCTV footage from all the cameras in the region, a huge job. But traffic cameras west of Newmarket on the A14 showed, as luck would have it, road works in line of sight of the cameras. And lo and behold, the Vauxhall Corsa was first in line at the road works stop light. And there she is, apparently, complete with the much admired brooch, visible without much digital enhancement. Gotcha comes to mind. A passenger in the front seat, a male, but indistinguishable, unfortunately, but certainly her driving.'

LeFanu, scratching his ear yet again, said, 'Maybe it was Mrs Moore at Porten House in the blue car. Maybe she's the one driving the Bentley. Maybe she would say that she was at the auction house for work reasons unless we can prove otherwise. Maybe we'll take a flier to see whether she reacts. Interesting. Well done to all.'

Sam Miles smiled. 'Gotcha seems appropriate, I think.'

***

With both hands, LeFanu did a fingers crossed gesture. 'DS Jones, arrange to bring Mrs Moore back from the detention area and then we'll deal with Mr Scott. And you lead the opening with her.'

Minutes later, she was brought into the interview room. A smile on her face puzzled LeFanu. 'I suppose you have come to your senses, Mr LeFanu. I will call you that in preparation to your return to civilian life after this farce you call an investigation.'

Philippe LeFanu did no more than raise his eyebrows. He waved to DS Jones to start the proceedings with the inevitable caveat about recording the conversation.

'Madam, in the light of our recent investigations, we are arresting you for complicity in the murders of Mr Jerry Gold and Ms Monika Braun.'

She blanched. Her mouth dropped, the smile disappearing instantly. 'No! No! It wasn't me. I did not kill anyone and never could. I didn't know what they were up to. Look at Guy bloody Scott and that Veronica woman, they're in it up to their armpits. Yes, I helped clear up and taking away stuff from the house as a favour to that lazy bitch Charlotte. But that was concerned with Charlotte's plan to get someone to break in to the house and claim on their insurance; nothing to do with hurting anyone. So, yes, I'd plead guilty to that, but murder — no.'

'Where were you going in the blue Vauxhall Corsa with a passenger on the 6th of January? We have you on film.'

'Going, no, coming from Eye St Mary with some black bin liners, with Guy Scott helping. I had dropped him off in the village and parked out of sight in a field behind the barns and then picked him up at the other end of the village near some old cottages. I never went near the house itself. Then we drove back a long way round to the Duxford base and then I drove home in my car.'

'Doesn't quite stack up, now does it?' commented DI Miles 'Firstly, the car you were driving was facing east not west. But I do accept that you returned to Duxford. Secondly, on your own admission, you were to help, or actually do, the clearance of the house which, inevitably, means you entered the premises. A witness places you around three p.m. that day alone in the car, passing a bus stop on the main road. What were you doing? And thirdly, somewhat damning we feel, is taking Ms Braun to her cottage some way away. Had to be done with a vehicle. Explain that.'

'I drove round the village onto the main road and then came back in by the east side to pick up Guy. He walked down to the village hall. That's where I picked him up. And yes, yes, OK, I did go into the house, through the back door, which was wide open near the Jacuzzi, but only to clear up. Charlotte told me that they were going to close up the house and sell it and would I help clear things up. Nothing more to it than doing a friend a favour. Emptying the dishwasher, taking away some towels and things and removing stuff like post and some photos. I wore gloves the whole time, so you won't find my fingerprints or whatever you look for. But I never saw this Mrs Braun. I've never met her. Charlotte told me about her, but she was in Germany, or so she said. I wouldn't know her if I bumped into her in the street. I swear. Guy Scott will back up my story. Some of the stuff had been put into the Bentley, and the personal things in the little blue car, and the rest in a skip near the auction house.'

'You are not off the hook, madam. We require a statement from you about the instructions you were given and by whom and when, added to which your admission that you were involved in the pursuance of these crimes, even though you may, and I stress "may", have been involved on the periphery. The issues we discussed earlier regarding procurement, fraud and cloning are still being investigated. Therefore, for the time being, you are still under arrest. Should your statement assist us, then we may, and again I stress "may", release you on bail with the surrender of your passport, but that will be up to the director of public prosecutions. I will leave you with this WPC, who will assist you.'

All three of the detectives left the room and the tape was suspended, having briefed the WPC.

Chapter 72

'Wow! That was a turn up. But now we have to break the alibis and excuses of Guy Scott. Play one off against the other. A change of interview room, I think. Get him up to Room 7, Chris.' With that, LeFanu sighed. 'We may be getting to the hub of this at last.'

Minutes later, an irate Guy Scott was wheeled in under escort, looking much scruffier than usual, having had to sleep in his clothes in a cell. 'Well, Mr Scott, we seem to be going around in circles. On the 6th January last — yes, yes, I know you can't remember dates... However, on the 6th of January, you were driving the blue Vauxhall Corsa — or should I say 'a blue Vauxhall Corsa' as you seem to change number plates regularly. You are on camera to that effect. Mrs Moore was also seen on that day, driving the same car. Now we don't care who was driving to, and later from, Eye St Mary. What we need to know is why you were going to the Porten House crime scene the day after the murders with Mrs Moore. She describes her movements and leaves you at one end of the village. We have her full version of events, now yours, please, and go easy on the bullshit. You told us on the day you went to the barn full of cars with DS Jones here that this was all news to you — patently, it wasn't.'

'Well, I don't recall that part of the conversation, it was a pretty stressful time. I was asked by Sal to help her clear some things out of Porten House. She said that Charlotte had asked her, as her marriage was breaking up. No real surprise to me, as Charlotte had high expectations and Tony had his mind on other things. Ignore Charlotte at your peril, sort of thing. He was an inveterate gambler, as you may know. Why she dropped me off at the end of the village, I couldn't tell you — ask her.'

'And Mrs Braun?'

'I know of her, of course. I've visited Porten House several times and she's always been there, making coffee and lunch and other things around the house. Really nice lady, but apart from courtesy greetings, nothing.'

'You see, Mr Scott, there are a few things that puzzle us. She was injured at Porten House on the 4th or 5th of January and then moved, by car, we believe, to her cottage a couple of miles away. A diminutive lady, but nevertheless heavy. And that included dragging her a few metres. Unconscious, we think. Not a one man, or should I say, woman job. Her bicycle was left at Porten House and had been moved out of sight. We have a crime scene photograph showing where it was normally left. Tyre marks that match the bike and some scrapes on the wall against which it had rested many, many times. And we found it outside the main lounge window. Funny place to park it, don't you think? In full view of the owner and any guests he may have had. Silly mistake by someone. Don't you think?' LeFanu put a real emphasis on the "you" and stared at Guy Scott.

Scott shrugged and LeFanu continued after a pause. 'Then she was murdered — suffocated in her bed and the heating turned up to maximum to, we suspect, defeat the best efforts of our forensic team. Another mistake by someone, don't you think? Perhaps, like my sergeant, that person or persons have been watching too many TV police dramas. Now, two persons only were at the house on the day in question. You and Mrs Moore. You are it, as they say.'

'Not me, not me. Yes, yes, I helped move the lady to help her and Sally promised to call the ambulance people straightway. I didn't want to get involved — my business, you know. I was concerned for my business. I don't know how she was knocked out — perhaps she fell.'

'One more thing, Mr Scott. You left your finger prints on the bicycle. Just two fingers on the main frame near the saddle. Explain?'

'I tore my vinyl glove, I remember now. So, yes, I just moved the bike out of the way; nothing sinister about that.'

LeFanu shook his head. 'Sinister? And this is a, to use your own words, "a nice lady". You conspired to kill her and cover up the evidence. I, we, do not believe that she fell. She suffered severe bruising in several areas of her body, conforming, we are told by the pathologist, with serious restraining. You, sir, are guilty before, during and after the fact of the assault and subsequent murder. Your involvement will be assessed in court and the penalties appropriately dispensed. Frankly, you disgust me, sir. Consider yourself under arrest with other matters such as the criminal cloning of vehicles and the earlier murder of Mr Jerry Gold, still under investigation.' Collecting his papers and signalling to Sergeant Jones to formalise the arrest, he left the room.

Chapter 73

To his colleague, LeFanu smiled. 'Maybe, at last. Now we must revisit Mrs Moore with Mr Scott's testimony and see if she breaks'.

Sally Moore was less indignant than her co-conspirator when she was wheeled in to the same interview room as before. She turned her nose up at the dis-array on the table of the earlier meeting's coffee cups and scraps of paper.

'The same rules apply as before, Mrs Moore. The interview will be recorded again. Do you wish for your solicitor to be recalled?' True to form, her aggression surfaced, with a sneer and a shake of her head.

'For the record, Mrs Sarah Moore has declined the attendance of a legal representative.' LeFanu checked for a reaction and was greeted with another shrug, so he continued. 'Mrs Sarah Moore, I am arresting you for the murder of Ms Monika Braun on the 5th of January last. You do not have to say anything, but anything you do say will be taken down and may be used in evidence against you. Do you understand?'

In a very subdued voice, she acknowledged the question. 'We know that you, with your accomplice, took the unconscious Ms Braun in the Vauxhall car commented on in the earlier interview and suffocated her in her own bed at her cottage.'

'With that rat, Guy Scott. It was his idea, I just helped to move her. I think she had banged her head. He promised to get medical help. And wanted me to pick him up later so he could make an anonymous phone call to the hospital. He said he needed to think of his business reputation. If you ask me, the little shit doesn't have a reputation to worry about.'

LeFanu looked across at his colleagues in exasperation. 'I cannot detect an ounce of remorse, madam.' He shook his head and continued, 'And the pillow over her face, Mrs Moore? Enough of this pile of excuses and palming off the blame for a horrendous crime to another. This was all part of a plan to aid and abet the crimes of murder, theft and fraud and the aftermath of knowingly clearing up the evidence for others, many of whom are now deceased, for a motive of self-protection and greed. Couple that with the violent death of the unfortunate Ms Braun who, being in the wrong place at the wrong time, paid the ultimate price for your actions.' LeFanu stood, exhausted by the concentration and frustration of not being able to tell her, and Scott earlier, exactly what he felt because of the recording machine.

After a few seconds, he resumed. 'The courts will decide which of you were the instigator and your other admissions will be involved in those decisions, no doubt. The director of public prosecutions is already exploring the facts submitted earlier. You will be incarcerated immediately. Frankly, Mrs Moore, you disgust me. Perhaps you will think of the implications of your actions on your lifestyle and that will wipe the smile from your face. Detective Sergeant Jones, do the necessary.'

***

An hour or so later, the whole team convened in the conference room to tie up all the loose ends. LeFanu knew he had to seek advice from the police and crimes commissioner who, doubtless, would have to escalate some of the issues to the Home Office, but before doing so, he needed to create the defining report and further actions that were necessary.

'DI Miles, DS Jones, all of you, we have some further investigations and questions to answer, not the least of which is the role of Lady Charlotte. This is, without a doubt, the most bizarre case, probably in history, with virtually all the proponents in the direct issues deceased. Nevertheless, what started off as a cleverly organised series of thefts with, possibly, motives beyond just money, degenerated into what I think was the murder of an innocent, David Grant, the suicide of a paedophile member of the cloth, and almost in parallel, the killing of an American citizen. And then things got complicated.' He smiled as he looked from face to face.

DS Jones had been scribbling notes and glanced up, waving his pencil. 'Sir, we started off months ago trying to separate the two issues. Thefts and the death of the American. In my mind now, without a doubt, the two main issues are definitely linked. Thefts created a money motive; the death of Gold, almost in lieu of Lord Groombridge, created an identity theft and therefore potentially a new life for Charlotte and her husband. Then there was a big fall-out between what had been friends. Money was still the big issue.' He looked at his colleagues. 'But why did Beddall have to die?'

Sam Miles saw that Chris Jones was reacting to the stress of the interviewing. 'Listen, Chris. He could have been the fall guy, but probably knew too much. Maybe even witnessed the murder of Gold. After all, he was on the scene and if his car had been bugged, they, whoever they are, knew exactly where he had been. We'll never know who set the bomb or whether it was Veronica who was the Angela who administered the poison. But one of them did and they are no more, so another dead end.' That drew a brief laugh from the team.

After a few seconds, Philippe LeFanu added, 'We're not here to analyse what we did nor what we didn't do; nor what we thought then compared with now. There are too many people out there — in the force, in the media, everywhere in the world, who try to analyse things with the benefit of hindsight.' Nods of agreement all round pleased LeFanu, who hoped he had released some of the tension.

Jones added, 'That's why in all the police thrillers the team always ends up celebrating down the pub. Always thought it a bit macabre after sorting out a murder or whatever but now I understand.'

'Just so, just so. Now we must prove things beyond a shadow of doubt and not provide defence lawyers with red herrings we have given them on a plate. My advice is we stick to the areas that are therefore provable. Mrs Moore and Mr Scott are involved in the murder of poor Ms Braun. Lady Charlotte is involved in misleading the investigation, but it's difficult to pin anything about the actual murder of Mr Gold on her. Even her asking for Scott and Moore to help in cleaning up is dubious. Fiona Wallace is a by-product in wasting police time and a caution will suffice there, alongside her possibly appearing as a witness, which will probably shake her up. We should stick to prosecuting Moore and Scott and allow DI Miles's people to pursue the cloning operation and the sex trafficking and grooming issues, let alone the fraud. Vice, fraud squad, major crime — they will all be involved and that must not take our eyes off the ball. But all that is secondary to the blatant killing achieved by those two. Put them inside and then let the DPP proceed. Regarding Mr Moore and the chief constable, their careers are over. There may well be a cover-up of their activities for the dubious reasons of politics — be that as it may. However, be warned there may be repercussions for all of us. Investigations, call it whistle blowing or whatever, of our own tend to be very, very, unpopular. I will seek advice from the commissioner, but doubtless there will be some moves or career paths looming, including my own, I suspect.'

'And what of Pchelski?' Sam Miles asked.

'Nothing to interest the DPP. He could be Mr Teflon. Nothing sticks. I'm convinced that he was, or is, involved, but where is the evidence; who is going to be the witness, and a reliable witness at that? Charlotte? No, she is like a sieve in terms of truth. Andervert? Again, unlikely, as he seems to be part of the closed shop of Swiss business, like the Gnomes of Zurich. Everyone else seems to be squeaky clean or dead. I will go and see him again in France, now that the hue and cry has died down, but that is more to satisfy my curiosity.'

Chapter 74

Both Sarah Moore, nee Lefevre, and Guy Scott were found guilty after a few weeks of tying in all the loose ends of evidence before the actual hearings. Scott received a twenty-year term and Sarah Moore similarly so. Andrew Moore's career ended that same day as the convictions were handed down, and the chief constable was encouraged to retire on the grounds of stress. He and Moore had been given an option by the police and crime commissioner: dismissal and a potential ten-year prison sentence for misconduct in public office, or resign. The DPP decided not to pursue the sex trafficking and grooming evidence, as it would serve little useful purpose due to Mrs Moore and Scott being incarcerated, Fiona Wallace being reluctant to expose herself to publicity, and others being largely unnamed.

The data found about cloning cars, coupled with a thorough investigation into complaints from the public about unfounded traffic and parking offences added to the information derived from the Moore/Scott computers, was useful in compiling evidence to close down that aspect.

DCI LeFanu had decided to take an early retirement package on the advice of the police and crime commissioner, as she had already indicated his role would be difficult after being the main protagonist in the investigation of colleagues, as life did become uncomfortable in the Suffolk Constabulary, and almost by definition, other constabularies in the country. Philippe LeFanu was not happy about the sweeping under the carpet of the activities of both the ACC and the chief constable, and hence took her advice to retire on a full pension.

Chapter 75

He decided that there were some loose ends needing clarity for his peace of mind. Having some outstanding paid holiday allowance to use, laughingly called gardening leave, he went to see a certain George Pchelski in Brittany, preferring face-to-face than a telephone call.

He called Pchelski and arranged to have dinner with him at the Le Roof Hotel in Conleau on the outskirts of Vannes in Brittany, explaining to him that he just wanted to chat and that he was now officially retired from the police force and taking a long, long earned break before considering a new career.

After a bottle of wine and some pleasantries about the weather and the location, he struggled to convince the cynic in George that he was curious rather than inquiring. 'You know my car, George. Well, it has to go back. I have it for the rest of the month — they call it gardening leave... Anyway, I need a nice car and you are the only one I know who is honest enough about cars. So, as proof, if you like, that I am genuine and this is really off the record, as I couldn't be seen as having a business relationship with a person of interest in a current investigation, can you find me one, toute suite? Maybe a Porsche 911, doesn't matter whether it is left hand drive. About twenty-five thousand pounds. What do you think?'

'Can do. Give me a few days and I'll call you. And I do trust you to be discreet about any information I tell you, but only for my own safety. If you learn anything, use it to beat those bastards, but let me know first, eh?'

Over a strong coffee, the best he had had in a long time, LeFanu commented, 'George, there are plenty of unanswered questions to satisfy my curiosity, so I'll tell you what I know, off the record all the way, ninety percent of which is in the public domain anyway.' Ten minutes was all it took, during which George's face showed what Philippe considered to be surprise

'Sir...'

Philippe interrupted and added, 'No need for the "sir" stuff, I'm just a curious private individual, and unless you agree specifically, I will not pass on any information to my ex-colleagues. So, just Philippe will do nicely.'

George told him, very much off the record, that he had heard tell of a network to source vehicles for crimes. LeFanu raised his eyebrows at the comment "heard tell", but listened intently. Trucks and other commercial vehicles were wrapped in vinyl to display plausible logos and details often very close to the real vehicle, cars similarly so.

Philippe asked if police cars could be replicated under a cloned number plate with the wrapping process.

George replied with a shrug and a, 'I suppose so', but added that it sounded like it would be very complicated.

After a few moments, almost as if he was weighing up the relationship issues with LeFanu, he added, 'You might find a woman called Jane, that's not her real name, I understand. She lives in an expensive gated development in Cheltenham. She's married to a guy called Hand, so she shouldn't be too difficult to trace. Anyway he is a journalist, big time on national media, so that's how they afford to live where they do. I don't know how they get their customers for cloning, but word of mouth is a strong suit in that game. Anyway, that's not of much interest to you now, is it?

'So how come you know this sort of stuff, George? Tried it out, have you?' He smiled.

'I told you before, Philippe. You learn a lot in prison and you learn not to use names unless you want trouble — and I don't.'

'But you knew of Charlotte's plan and you seem to know the sources, so does two and two make four?'

'Charlotte's plan was half-baked. Whether she thought it up herself or whether it was fed to her by others is a moot point. I think she thought of the idea more out of spite than anything. She always had a track record for petty vengeance, as she called it. Now if someone else — friend, husband or whoever — knew of that character trait, they could individually or together capitalise on it.' He could see Philippe nodding.

He countered George's hypothesis. 'Manipulation? Umm. It is possible. So you think person or persons unknown, but probably dead...' George chuckled. 'Those people,' he continued, "plant the blame on her whilst escaping the strong arm of the law by going to the USA or wherever with bundles of cash and new identities. Could be... could well be.'

'And Philippe, remember the green model Mercedes trying to point a finger and your resources at me.'

'Indeed, George. That always seemed an odd move, unless, of course, you were involved in some way.'

'Listen, personally, I love the lady, always did, but never attributed to her the kind of analysis needed for a foolproof plan. Let's face it, Philippe, I'm not the best person to comment, otherwise I wouldn't be a convicted criminal. Anyway, I think she was played like a real patsy by that bastard husband of hers and her best friend, Veronica. I believe that if it had all gone wrong, from their point of view of course, then she would be held to blame. And let's face it, from what I knew and what you have said, it did go badly wrong and people paid for it with their lives, including the two that started it all. I liked the idea of shafting her husband, but killing, no way. I would have wanted to see her husband's face after she had achieved her objective. That would have been real satisfaction. And I'd have liked to see the man's face that tried to set me up with the model Mercedes car, just after the judge had passed sentence — a long sentence.'

'You are being very careful with your words, George. I agree she should pay for her involvement, but it is clouded, between you and me, by the behaviour of the hierarchy at Ipswich, and for all I know, beyond. They don't want to wash their dirty linen in public, so let us hope she has learned her lesson.'

'She has, Philippe, she has. Last time I saw her, contrite is not a strong enough word. She had been shocked and her petty vengeance was probably no more than a catalyst to a terrible nexus of events. She is a changed woman. Maybe just growing up and facing reality.'

'I hope so, George. I sincerely hope so.' They paused over another coffee and a large Armagnac, strolling around the gardens of the hotel.

George broke the silence after a few minutes. 'I knew that Scott bloke was bad news, but his sister-in-law. Wow, that is a turn up for the books. Makes Andervert fit in with it all. But as there is only one person left, using your own words of a few years back, Philippe, you must have been seeking to nail Charlotte for all the blame. And whilst I am still a trifle biased in that quarter, I don't think she had any motive for violence, just the money. I believe that she was manipulated by that bastard husband of hers and the thought of having plenty of money and living the life that she was, is, I should say, well used to. Excuse my grammar.'

'I agree, George. Accessory before, during and after the fact is her responsibility. My sergeant, Chris Jones, now an inspector, incidentally, had an irritating habit of relating each and every case he worked on, sorry for my bad grammar there, relating each to a crime story he had read or seen on the TV, but there was one that actually stopped me in my tracks.' He paused. George looked at him, puzzled. 'I think I may have mentioned this hobby horse of his before, but no matter. The film/book/whatever majored on what is now known to be a distract technique; the Americans call it misdirection. In simple terms, it means set up an elaborate crime to focus attention away from the real issue.' He looked again at George in the half-light, noticing a brief nod of agreement. 'Anyway, although I haven't seen it, there is a film starring Sean Connery called *The Anderson Tapes,* where an ex-con seeks to steal something really valuable from an apartment in New York or somewhere, so he sets out to rob all the apartments in the block by pretending to be a painter or interior designer or something like that. And by so doing, diverts attention or distracts the police. Now, we know that as Ockham's Razor, which basically says that the simplest explanation is often, maybe usually, the right one. Unless some bright spark criminal has read the same book or seen the right film and second guesses the police enquiry by creating distraction.'

'Yes, yes, I get it, Philippe.'

'Well, George, forgive me for the digression, but it was interesting in searching the records at both Ford Open Prison and Upper Heywood, in their libraries, to find out who had borrowed the book or seen that particular film. Need I say more?'

'Damn. I had thought I'd wiped the memory on their silly computer system. OK, OK, yes I've seen the film and it was at Ford. And I've watched *The Great Train Robbery* film but I haven't robbed a train. And I enjoyed all these films. Enough said?'

'Thank you, George. I've made my point. Now back to Lady C. Undoubtedly, she knew about the violence after it had occurred. And the proposed ripping off of the insurance companies. She showed little remorse and aided and abetted her spouse to escape apprehension, not knowing, I suspect, that the organised crime bad guys in the USA wouldn't let it go. She is back in France, as far as we know, and living a relatively quiet life, I expect not knowing whether the threat to her life from the USA still prevails.'

'So she gets off scot free, so as to speak and pardon the pun. She paid off the debts, Chief Inspector. The insurance monies came through after you removed the block on the payments. It sounds like you had no option on that score. I'm sure she'd thank you personally for that, if she could.'

'Maybe so, George. Maybe.'

'Well, she sought to get some peace of mind by buying off the debts Groombridge had incurred. That much I do know; she told me that, but wouldn't tell me anything about the matters that interest you.'

'Sorry, and I know you are a little biased on that score, but the reason we didn't pursue her, because she did break the law, like it or not, is that we were told not to pursue it and that instruction is now being investigated by others in the force. Maybe a few heads will roll, but best not to go into that.'

'Enough, I think. Thank you for the dinner and conversation. I must get on with my life. Good night, sir — I mean, Philippe.'

'Incidentally, did you ever find the parts for that Porsche 356?'

'Yes, and made Andervert pay dearly for them. Judging by what you told me about his using underage girls in Switzerland, and other places too, I expect, he deserves to suffer, but that's Switzerland…'

'Drive carefully, George, I wouldn't want the gendarmes to arrest you.' He smiled and shook George's hand.

'No chance. I have someone picking me up. I'll call you about the car.'

Philippe glanced out of the reception area window to see a white Porsche 911 arrive, and he could have sworn it was a brunette looking like Charlotte driving the car, and then the memory of that particular perfume came back. Of course…